Applause enveloped him, deafened him, shook him like a dog shakes an old rug. Dazed, he froze as the audience stood, beating palms together as if it mattered to him that they'd enjoyed it, as if he'd skated for *them*! House-lights up, he turned slowly to the celebrity seats, the freebs, still warm from the important behinds of officials, judges, time-keepers, referees, toadies, hangers-on, patron saints . . .

For, in the safe middle of skating's aging aristocracy, one young face looked out. Who else but the other love of Grant's life. Slender, elegant, lightly tanned by some exotic sun, Deirdre stood wrapped in jewels and furs and the total invulnerability which only total security bestows.

Across the headers and the barrier Grant stared into her eyes, locked into them with a bitter fury he would not let her evade. Her chin softened and quivered as she tried to turn away – but she was pinned, trapped by a mechanical show-biz smile sparkling with betrayal, ambition, and the unmistakable promise of debts to be collected.

Also by Margaret P. Kirk and published by Futura

ALWAYS A STRANGER
A LONG ROAD WINDING

WINTER'S GOLD

MARGARET P. KIRK

for Lee Kirk from
Margaret P. Kirk.
My best for your fiction
efforts. And my thanks,
MPK.

Futura

A Futura Book

First published in Great Britain in 1991 by
Macdonald & Co (Publishers) Ltd
London & Sydney

This Futura edition published in 1992

Copyright © Margaret Prasniewski 1991

The right of Margaret Prasniewski to be identified
as author of this work has been asserted by her
in accordance with the Copyright, Designs and Patents
Act 1988.

Printed and bound in Great Britain by
BPCC Hazell Books
Aylesbury, Bucks, England
Member of BPCC Ltd.

ISBN 0 7088 5250 5

Futura Publications
A Division of
Macdonald & Co (Publishers) Ltd
165 Great Dover Street
London SE1 4YA

A member of Maxwell Macmillan Publishing Corporation

ACKNOWLEDGEMENTS

Relationships formed over two decades at ice skating's international centres have made this novel possible. I am indebted to the entire fraternity, a host of nationalities united by an overwhelming passion, the grace and tyranny inherent in the sport itself:

Judges whose integrity sustains them through countless hours lost to home and family; whose knowledge gives them courage to weigh the perfect against the sublime. The difference, often subjective, is forever arguable — but judges alone must find it and score it. Within seconds.

Coaches who nurture talent, shape it, steer it through adolescence to bring it to confident maturity. Like their skaters, they rise before dawn to face the chilly medium of the sport. Alongside mind-bending schedules of travel and teaching, they encourage, they discipline, they care.

Special kindnesses in rinks around the world inspired this book, as did friends of a lifetime — JoJo Starbuck, Ken Shelley, Dianne de Leeuw, Almut Lehmann, Herbert Wiesinger . . . Their performances linger in the heart long after they have faded from the retina — magic moments preceded by a dozen years of sacrifice, disappointment, and sweet, fleeting triumphs.

Is there a living soul who can hear Ravel's 'Bolero' without falling once again under the spell of Torvill and Dean? Who among us can forget the fabulous B & B's . . . the delicacy of Peggy Fleming, Ekaterina Gordeeva, Janet Lynn . . . the drama of Curry and Cousins and Cranston . . . the effervescence of Dorothy Hamill and, later, Liz Manley . . . the spirit of tiny Irina Rodnina . . . most recently the artistry of Katerina Witt and Brian Boitano, talents which may never be equalled — except the nature of the sport tells us otherwise.

My gratitude also to many judges who, to preserve their privacy, would I'm sure prefer to remain anonymous. Under the pressure of major competitions they nevertheless answered my questions thoughtfully, with good humour and integrity. To coaches Tamara Moskwina, John Nicks, Barbara Roles, Frank Carroll, Jutta Müller, Christy Kjarsgaard, Barbara Kossowska, Linda Leaver . . . over the years I have watched you all and a hundred more, marvelled at your skill. The list should be as endless as my admiration. Special thanks also to Pat Terry and her Welsh friend.

Any errors in competition procedure or skating technique are my own.

For Deborah Byrne Prasniewski and Jan Prasniewski, with my love

Gold! Gold! Gold! Gold!
Bright and yellow, hard and cold.

Thomas Hood

On the upper reaches of Mount Olympus the thin sheet of ice creaks with tension. At this elevation, charity is thinner yet, brittle with envy, malice, intrigue and heartbreak. Who will take home the Gold, worth millions in contracts and endorsements — and a tidal wave of worship from a grateful nation?

A fraction of a point may separate Gold from Silver and Bronze, but they are struck from baser metals for lesser mortals, scarcely worth the ribbons they hang from. Of the fleeting residents of Olympic Village, who can match the glamour of the Ladies' Figure Skating contenders? Hounded by reporters, adored by the mob, hated by rivals, they are presumed to float serenely over their chilly medium and the myriad trials encountered thereon. Public presence is all. A dazzling costume hides supportive bandages as effectively as practised smiles conceal love, hate, and crushing disappointment.

In pursuit of immortality every fragile goddess denies the flesh and flays the spirit. Her retinue surrounds, protects, and encourages; parents battle ambition and anxiety; lovers are kept under wraps — our idol's mystique is anchored in her presumed innocence; psychological adviser, make-up artist, ballet mistress, hairdresser, physiotherapist, all insulate her from reality and a demanding public.

The coach is paramount. He cracks every whip, bends every rule to ensure the events of her skating life spin as smoothly as a well-centred cross-foot.

But when the moment comes, when she stands at centre-ice waiting for that first note of music, the skater stands alone.

PROLOGUE

London, 1975

Messages from friends, enemies, and hangers-on framed his dressing-room mirror in lukewarm sentiments and blatant lies — barely a hint of the astringent malice so typical of the sport.

All love on your Wembley opening . . . Up and at 'em . . . Bravo! . . . Thank God and Grant Rivers . . . Delighted, just delighted, pal!

And why not? Grant Rivers' signature on a professional contract had forever lifted him out of amateur contention, leaving a vacancy very high up on the competitive tree. Not high enough, as he well knew, yet already the also-rans bickered for his empty perch, straining for their own glimpse of Olympus.

A draft from the open door rustled the telegrams — dead leaves of his old life sweeping the stage clean for the new — which he had not sought and did not want. Show business was only the last desperate avenue in a race against time, an avenue which could at any moment close into a cul-de-sac, leaving him trapped and alone.

Behind him, hands wringing, mouth working, Grant's ex-coach edged through the door and into the mirror. 'Scared you've done the wrong thing?'

Grant clenched his teeth. They both knew he had, but it was the only thing, thanks to timing, circumstance, Mum's health, the Swansea climate — and Deirdre. 'I'm dressing,' he said, pointedly glancing at the open door.

Coach, his moon-face apologetic in the glare of dressing-room lights, looked away. The boy, over-young for irrevocable decisions, had been forced into this one. Coach knew himself to blame. Not that Grant had blamed him — he didn't have to. They both knew the rules: an amateur athlete dare not solicit financial aid for himself. That was a coach's job, but he'd been too humble — or maybe too proud — to try; even for Grant, the most promising skater he'd ever coached, he hadn't been able to rattle the tin cup louder than a whisper. Now he sighed. 'A rich man's sport, always has been . . .'

Grant shrugged. 'Don't worry. I'm professional now. I'll manage fine. It's too bloody late to change anything anyway.'

Coach recoiled from the mild obscenity; back in Swansea he led the chapel choir and believed in every word of every hymn. 'Language helps nothing, Grant. 'Tis early days, you're a young 'un, plenty of time to make your mark in the world, haven't you just?'

His Welsh inflection, always rising, lifted every statement into a question. Grant, no longer a student, could answer any way he pleased. He chose silence, and through the mirror held the other man's gaze. Coach flushed, adjusted his tatty rink balaclava, and backed out of the room.

Grant watched the door shut. Make his mark? What else did skaters do, dammit? For upwards of sixteen years they traced figures-of-eight on the ice, and when the 'eights and jumps and spins got good enough they aimed for the only other mark they wanted, that giant step up to an Olympic podium, a band blaring an anthem, a flag fluttering on a pole — not that they cared much for flags, skating being a singular effort, a singular triumph — but a medal would have paid back all Mum's pinch-penny years and more: 'My son won that.' Support at the right time would have given him a shot at one proud thing to warm her wheezing, asthmatic days. Now he'd earn money instead, paid performers being unfit to contend for the Olympic ideal. With a stroke of the pen he'd signed off an adolescence of taped ankles, of bruised thighs forever marbled in yellow and blue, of chilblained fingers and ice-chapped lips. And now Dad, wherever the handsome swine might be, would never glance at the telly and see his son staring back at him from an Olympic podium, never feel that wounding stab of guilt for deserting a wife and baby to chase after a livelier bit of skirt.

Coach didn't know about Dad. None of them did. They

2

believed what had been hinted, that Mum was a widow. Skating was for pink-and-white children of upwardly mobile parents who worked hard at respectability, that sure path to a genteel English heaven unruffled by the likes of Grant Rivers. Grant had a suspiciously even tan and his mother — too pale for her own good — staffed a day-desk at the town hall and worked the rink box-office at night. That's what it took, two full-time jobs to buy ice-time, boots, blades, lessons, hotel beds, and train tickets to the next competition. For one skater. And it was never enough.

He'd thought Deirdre had understood, but he'd been wrong. Not even a telegram; no acknowledgement that if she'd kept her promise . . . He told himself he'd expected nothing and tried to fend off memories of the scented silk of her, the soft welcome of her arms, but tonight a word from her could have changed desolation to triumph, or at least acceptance. In the small world of skating, Deirdre and her sports-empire husband reigned as current patron saints; she must know tonight was Grant's professional début. And *he* knew better than to be disappointed. A year ago he'd realized he'd never hear from her again, so why expect miracles every time a door opened — as his was opening now, letting in the stage manager, new to skating shows, to deliver his traditional good wish. Break a leg. Jesus, what if he did? How to pay the Harley Street wizard then? Grant towelled his palms, wishing the man would go; but no, he must go through the motions.

'So, how does it feel, working for a living?'

Working? What did people think training was, an eff-ing vacation? From now on he'd perform fifteen minutes a night, max, and work out just enough each day to stay sharp. The real work, every slogging year since his first pair of skates at six, was over. Already he missed the grind, the dawn world of practice ice, its quiet concentration on school figures which he'd loved and which were reputed to be on their way out. A bracket so perfect you couldn't bear anybody to skate over it; the triumph of landing a new jump clean — you might fall on it the rest of the session but what your body had done once it could do again. God, he wanted it back, all of it.

'Fine,' he said. 'Working for a living is just fine.'

'A grand turn-out of skating big-wigs out front. Nice that, the amateur officials showing up to support their own.'

Grant's fists tightened under the table. Nice? Support? 'You're missing the point. I'm not "their own" now, am I? I'm professional, and you doled out complimentary front row seats, I'm sure, and there'll be a champagne buffet later, right?'

Stung, the stage manager said, 'They requested a seat for your mother, right in there!'

Very democratic of them.

'She *is* coming? Your mother?'

Grant swallowed the sudden knot in his throat. 'Sure.' Anything to get rid of this well-meaning fool who, if he knew Mum wasn't coming and why, would sympathize. It worked. He left. Grant didn't want sympathy, just a pay-packet; tomorrow he'd give it to the London consultant who was already primed to spring Mum from the spitting, hacking ward of the public infirmary and whisk her off to a private sanitarium quicker than you could say 'cash'. He hoped to God it wasn't too late. He'd planned instead to get her a sheepskin coat for winter to replace the threadbare green thing familiar at every rink in the country. So much for good intentions.

He slipped her telegram behind the tissue box, wondering how she'd managed to send it from the medieval hell-hole they rushed her to after she coughed blood all over the town hall desk. Oldest hospital in the city, the NHS said with pride. It smelled like it — a pervasive alliance of formaldehyde, Mansion Polish, and the ubiquitous slop to which they were ashamed to put any other name than 'brown soup'; it sometimes smelled of mutton, sometimes beef-fat, but its bland, smooth brown never varied.

Her words on the yellow paper came at him as if she were reading them over his shoulder, whispery, economical, a cough just around the corner. Parsimony had by now seeped into her nature along with her Vick's Vapour Rub and her bronchitis: '*I'm proud, son. Good luck.*'

Not that she believed in luck or much of anything beyond Grant, his ambition, and the Royal Family. That he was born the same hour as Prince Andrew she took as a sign that God had chosen Grant for glory.

4

Coach edged back into the mirror, pointing at his watch. 'Relax, sport, you'll do fine. Don't forget the hairspray.'

'I *am* fine, I *am* relaxed!' He aimed the aerosol and shut his eyes against Coach and the tension he generated. Willing himself to loosen up so he could skate easy, he escaped back into the tempting territory of the summer before last, when Mum had been only a little bit sick, and he'd had Deirdre in her exquisite room in her rich house and his weekends — No! His life! — stretched before him in a bright prospect of Gold, his nerves aquiver with Deirdre, his porcelain goddess, his ivory angel, who hovered miles above him, but who he'd expected to marry when she shed her present husband — which showed how naïve he'd been.

'When I'm through competing, say in seven years, I'll join a show, we'll get married — or I'll coach and —'

'Grant, listen.'

'Don't you want to?' But she *must*! She let him sleep with her, let him do . . . anything! 'Is it my dad, me being half-Spanish, not quite white —'

She laughed softly, ran a fingertip across his thigh. 'You're the perfect shade of tan for me, and that's *not* the reason, Mr *Rivera*. No, don't worry, I shan't tell anybody, but why did you change it to Rivers?'

'Mum thought . . . hell, you know skating judges, doddery old sods with their little bit of power, they'd call me a foreigner and mark me down.'

She shook her head. 'No. You're so beautiful it wouldn't have mattered. Look at those glossy black curls, the kind mothers hate to cut because they never grow back. You'll have yours all your life. And such shoulders,' she said, stroking his burning skin with cool, tapering hands. 'My husband doesn't have any. A chap in Bond Street tailors them in for him.'

'It's him, your husband. That's why you won't marry me.' He thought of Lloyd Sterling, his grey hair and silky grey suits, and a shifty, clouded shadow in his grey English eyes. They reminded Grant of a barracuda.

'Let's not talk about him,' she said. 'He's evil. If people knew why he's such a benefactor to skating, always hoping, the access it gives him to —'

'Then divorce him and marry me.'

5

She twisted her rings. A massive solitaire shot daggers of brilliance across the quiet, understated room. 'When you're older you'll understand,' she said gently, a wisp of pale hair trailing across his chest.

'Give me a reason,' he demanded.

'There are several. I'm entering my thirties, you're still in your teens. When you're thirty-five I'll be middle-aged. The next will sound selfish and shallow and probably is: money. Once one's had it, it becomes a necessity —'

'In five years if I win the Olympics I'll make lots of money.'

She sighed. 'Darling, you can't imagine what my life-style costs. This town house, the Haslemere place, the villa on the Costa Brava. By now luxury's grown around me like moss. I'd be naked without it.'

She was naked anyway, soft and warm as her tongue licked his chest, his navel, his throbbing penis, which must surely drop off if they did it one more time, but they would and of course it wouldn't. Something else she'd taught him. The resilient texture of her nipples, which stood to attention like hard, pink little soldiers when he sucked on them. They made him feel older, yet infinitely younger too. 'Sometimes you make me feel like a baby,' he murmured.

She smiled, guiding his mouth back to them. 'I'd love a baby. Maybe that's why I love you. You're young enough, God knows. If I'd married the right man at the right time I could almost have — oh yes! Yes! My God yes!' as his teeth teased the hot, tight buds. 'I'm sorry, I can't wait, I —'

She mounted him, impaled herself on him. Inside her he felt enclosed, protected as she reached behind her to brace against the saddle of his rock-hard skater's thighs. He gasped as she gripped him with finger and thumb as if measuring him for a bizarre engagement ring. 'Keep still,' she whispered, rocking gently. 'I have to be sure, stay there, right there, the perfect place, just let it happen, oh my God, let it happen —', sobbing at his involuntary thrust, her answering contractions drawing him again and again into her deepest, hottest core.

Later, side by side in the darkening room, he wondered how many men she'd had. They both knew how many women he'd had. One: her. His rite of passage, she called herself, but she was more than that. He couldn't imagine ever wanting anyone else.

'It could be like this all the time,' he said, returning to the future. 'Mum and me are poor but we manage, we're happy, more or less.'

'No. I grew up in genteel poverty. The thought of returning to it . . .' She shuddered. 'Daddy was a clergyman, a widower, a bit of a boozer, and we connived, I guess, without really intending to, to marry me off to the highest bidder. I had a certain innocence and my husband was in the market for it. He likes to buy it, you know, then play with it until it's worn out.' There was an apologetic note in her voice and Grant wanted to tell her not to apologize, that he understood. But he didn't, not then. To fill the silence he said, 'Mum works two jobs for my skating.'

'She won't have to much longer. When you're old enough I'll have my husband put you on the payroll — no actual work, you'd be free to train. He's helped others like that. You're dangerously beautiful, but I'll protect you. I can rattle some scary skeletons at him if I have to.'

He still didn't know what she meant, and he didn't want Lloyd Sterling's money — but even as he said it a treacherous demon in him knew that he'd take it because he'd need it.

He may have slept a little then, her scent covering him like a mist. When he woke twilight had seeped into the corners of the room, lending a brief radiance to cream roses on the dresser and the tender curve of Deirdre's neck. In the shadows her skin had the same satiny texture as the roses, and he felt himself stir, then; 'God, I've ice-time. Coach expects —'

'Wait.' She closed her eyes and read his features like Braille, tracing chin and mouth and nose and eyelids with careful, lingering fingertips.

'What are you doing?'

'*Remembering.*' The word was wistful, deeply sad, incomprehensible.

'When will I see you again?'

She sighed and turned away. 'I'll try to phone within a few weeks, but darling, do be patient . . .'

She didn't phone within a few weeks. Since then, he'd seen her only in the society pages. He'd tried notes and calls, but maids always intercepted. Madame was entertaining. Out. Indisposed. When he'd refused to be pushed aside, she picked up the phone. 'Please,' she begged. She was run-down, leaving for Antigua with her husband, and Grant really *must* not call again, *ever*. Did he understand? She sounded as if she'd already left.

A year later, desperate for sponsorship to ease the load on Mum, he asked Coach's help, who appealed, naturally, to Mrs Sterling '— because she seemed so partial to you last summer, remember?' She didn't answer Coach either. 'Busy with the new baby, I expect. Only natural, boyo.'

Thus Grant learned the truth of an old cliché: his heart was heavy. For the first time he was conscious of the weight of it in his chest, and also a stabbing replay: 'I'd love a baby.' And now that she had her husband's there was no further need for a teenage surrogate.

More news arrived that day. The offer, duly made through Coach to protect Grant's amateur status, of a contract with the show. 'Take it. The writing's on the wall, the timing's all off for you. The big-shots send their best, but offer nowt. Don't need you. There's Curry in place for the Games, Cousins warming up in the wings for the next. Wonderful boys, the pair of 'em. And when they're done training in America with the Italian chap and his like they'll be better yet. If not them, there's Tickner, Hoffman — Cranston if the old school lets him in. All kinds of talent out there and never enough glory to go around. Soon you're eighteen. How many years can you wait?'

'I have time,' he said, knowing he didn't.

'And potential. But you need backing. I'm no supercoach, not in their league, but I'm all you can afford, see? Look you, join the show. When your knees go, then coach. Like me.' So Grant had signed.

But he wouldn't be like his coach, nothing like him, too humble to lead anything but a church choir. When Grant coached he'd make damned sure he got up there with the best of 'em — the Fassis and Nicks and Roles and Carrolls, the Zhuks and Moskwinas. So, okay, from tonight he was pro, one step closer to the greats, the wizards who sculpted Gold Medallists from raw clay.

Still waiting, Grant reached for white powder to set his

make-up against beads of sweat already oozing through a Panstick mask. He checked his watch. A half-hour to intermission, the clutter of skates in the tunnel, then his big clear-ice number set like a jewel in the show's second half. He wondered who was out front. Friends, enemies, maybe talent scouts from the States, maybe even that anonymous Mr Rivera who he'd never known and who didn't know him? No way, not good old Dad who, even if he knew of Grant's existence, of Mum's illness, wouldn't be caught dead anywhere near his responsibilities. He hadn't known how to be a husband, Mum said, much less a father. 'Come to think,' she'd whispered against the ever-hovering cough, 'maybe he didn't know how to be a man.'

Damn, he'd show them. He *would* skate well, like the year Deirdre loved him. He'd done 'Mancha' that season, pouring into it all his yearning for her because she *was* his impossible dream, her image shimmering just out of reach, leading him on tantalizing wisps through the ammoniac smell of ice, of leather, and of wool which never quite dried — a smell peculiar to skaters because eventually they absorbed it — skin, clothes, car, home — wherever their skates lived. It had even impregnated Deirdre's pink-and-cream room, her long hands caressing his boots, a pearly fingernail drawn across a stainless blade. 'Steel wings,' she'd said, 'dangerously macho. Not like *him*.'

Grant, younger then, had known only skating and bewildering, sudden erections. He had known nothing about vice. Now, like everyone else, he understood the rumours, and realized she'd almost never said her husband's name. Mum never said Dad's either. Odd that the only women who meant anything to him, complete opposites, should have one corrosive thing in common: each hated her husband.

At intermission he suffered the make-up woman to add finishing touches to the paint-job for his all-important solo, 'Send in the Clowns', in which he could make an impression if he skated a mood. If should be easy, considering the melody, the lyrics, the moody, brooding lights and his own sense of futility. Silver bodysuit, stylized white face, elongated black tear-drops and spider-spiked lashes. The lashes were sods to skate in, but the production manager sat out front with his effing clipboard. After one warning for wearing incomplete costume they'd dock his pay.

He heard the Zam trundle off and the chorus clatter into the tunnel, where they'd stand tall, show teeth, and skate out to open the second half. They made so much din Grant almost missed the tap at his door.

The stage manager ushered in a faceless nobody Grant vaguely recognized, a man with something in his eyes — embarrassment? Pity? An overwhelming desire to be someplace else? Then Grant saw the uniform beneath the everyman face and placed him. A neighbour from Swansea, an ambulance man if memory served. But why here? Now?

He shut his eyes. He knew. Oh yes, he knew. For a blinding moment it seemed he'd always known this day would come. He stood there in his silver glitter and spiky eyes, and under the white face-paint felt his blood drain into his boots. He looked down, expecting to see crimson staining his silver boot-covers, but no, they were bright, new. Under the covers the custom boots she insisted on instead of the warm clothes she needed, the clothes he'd begged her to get. Wintertime in Swansea the winds swept in off Carmarthen Bay sharper than the blades on his feet.

'You'll not remember me,' the man said. 'I have the flat above yours. It *is* Grant, isn't it? She often mentioned you. Really proud, she was . . .'

Was.

He nodded, acutely aware how ridiculous he looked, a man with whitewash on his face and black rhinestone tears stuck to his cheeks. For a second all sound cut out but he already knew the script, had learned it deep in his subconscious on a thousand rink mornings, Mum blue-lipped at the door, a wad of tissue at her lips as she waited to drop him off at school, anxious to get to her desk at the town hall because if she showed up late she'd get the sack and then how to buy boots, ice, lessons . . .

'You'd better sit down,' the stage manager said.

'No.'

The neighbour stammered out his story. The pneumonia had taken a bad turn. True to Grant's orders, and over her protests ('No, save the lad's money!') they'd called in the man from Harley Street, but too late —

'We thought you'd want to hear from somebody who knew her, like —'

That's what they thought, huh? Who in hell would want to hear a thing like that from anybody?

'Thanks,' he said. 'Now if you don't mind, my number's coming up —' The treachery of words! When Mum's number really *was* up.

'Grant, wait.' The stage manager was clearly wondering how to fill a hole which, even as he spoke, now gaped in the second half. Gala opening. Shit. 'We wouldn't ask you, honestly. I'll announce a "due to circs" . . .' But he clearly hoped Grant would do the right, the British thing, and skate. Chin up old chap; don't let the side down. 'Naturally we don't expect —'

Liar. Grant heard himself say, 'No trouble. The officials came to be entertained. Let's get on with it. But after, when they're sitting on their self-satisfied old arses guzzling champagne, make sure they know Mrs Rivers — no, Rivera! — is dead, and that skating killed her. That she worked harder for their sport than that whole boiling pot of do-gooders lumped together. That she — oh, sod it, let me out, that's my cue.'

He never knew if he hit it through sheer luck or if the orchestra leader saw him and gave the signal.

The music — magnet for lights, ice, and skater — took him into its heart and he gave himself up with a desperate, anguished passion. Mum loved this number. Empty twilight ice, swirling mist, a single white spotlight seeking, stalking, at last pinning its quarry. Bathing in silver, the pursued, the hunted, who flew from his captor on a high, slow axel, wide open, an elegant move which seemed to hover at the top of the arc, then whisper to a perfect landing on a clean running edge — a risky edge because he jumped from light to dark and landed blind, at speed, on a burst of applause for the dramatic, unexpected opener. As planned, the light caught him again and held. He heard himself breathe as he raised his arms (look, Ma, no hands!) and closed his eyes to the glare, a pre-arranged signal for the lighting engineer to go to soft.

Isn't it rich . . . my fault I fear . . .

11

Yeah. For the moment he was the star and therefore rich. And it was his fault — not just for now but forever. If he'd never wanted to skate — no chance now to make it up to her, to send her some place folks didn't cough their guts out, where rooms were warm, walls dry. Where a middle-aged woman didn't have to work one job, never mind two. Where maybe they had holidays in Antigua like pampered little Deirdre, whose fault it truly was, who was to blame for every rotten thing, always would be, who he'd never forgive for her cruel lie, which trapped him in his premature professional spotlight, which sent Mum to hospital, and would next week seal her in the earth, and — oh, God, Swansea earth was so damned cold, so show 'em what you could have been if they'd given her a ha'porth of help and himself half a chance.

Wembley disappeared as his blades cut through a world of loss and guilt and wild, vengeful schemes of what he would do when, and how he would do it — but what scheme would let her button-up her old rink coat, bring back the perpetually apologetic smile?

Slowly the melody unwound, a thread lasting minutes, or was it a lifetime, and did it matter anyway, all the careful choreography forgotten as he skated through emotional thickets too dense to ever let him go.

His performance matched the song: yearning, wistful, pensive; dim blue headers painted the ice with cool, fading light, his blades whispered over familiar terrain, home ground as the Swansea flat had never been home, tracing curves and sweeps and figures-of-eight. Just Grant Rivers and his Sheffield steel Gold Seals, blade of champions; Mum never skimped on equipment. A cheap blade breaks under you and what then? The same with boots. God knew where she found the money for custom-builts from California, but she did. ' 'Tis a terrible fine line between broken in and broken down. Your feet need all the support they can get.' But what it came down to was all his support came from her, not a lick from the coven of geriatric power-brokers dispensing grants-in-aid, young careers at the mercy of their clouded vision. Now they were happy, these old ones, anticipating smoked salmon and cucumber and a mutual ego massage when it was all done . . .

It ended on a last plaintive line . . . *maybe next year* . . .

Except for Mrs Rivera, who wouldn't be having one.

Applause enveloped him, deafened him, shook him like a dog shakes an old rug. He reached up to touch his white face, spiked lashes, black glittery tears wet now and possibly clouded by the real thing. Company memo to Grant Rivers: salt-water damage to one set of rhinestone tears priced at — my God, the price! One nice, well-meaning woman dead after years of wasted sacrifice. One orphaned, angry, grieving son hell-bent for success, now staring at an empty future with nobody to succeed *for*.

Dazed, he froze as the audience stood, beating palms together as if it mattered to him that they'd enjoyed it, as if he'd skated for *them*! House-lights up, he turned slowly to the celebrity seats, the freebs, still warm from the important behinds of officials, judges, time-keepers, referees, toadies, hangers-on, patron saints . . .

For, in the safe middle of skating's aging aristocracy, one young face looked out. Who else but the other love of Grant's life.

Slender, elegant, lightly tanned by some exotic sun, Deirdre stood wrapped in jewels and furs and the total invulnerability which only total security bestows. By her side the Honourable Lloyd Sterling, who was not honourable at all. Deirdre did not look happy.

Across the headers and the barrier Grant stared into her eyes, locked into them with a bitter fury he would not let her evade. Her chin softened and quivered as she tried to turn away — but she was pinned, trapped by a mechanical show-biz smile sparkling with betrayal, ambition, and the unmistakable promise of debts to be collected.

PART ONE

The Foothills

CHAPTER ONE

Los Angeles, California

This morning he watched them from the shadowed office; yesterday it had been the darkened coaches' room behind the music booth. It paid to keep them guessing.

They knew he was in the rink some place, checking on them — but he never let them be sure where. That way, they worked. The minute they sensed his attention drift, they'd slouch to the rail in whispering little cliques, vital practice-time melting away in gossip.

The Games loomed too close for that.

They were working well this morning, especially the five who mattered. Five. *Five students of his own*, all qualified for the Olympics. Two had outside chances of a medal. Another was odds-on favourite to bring home the biggest prize of all. Roxanne Braun Kramer, current US Champion, who he'd tended as lovingly as a prize orchid through her last four years of training, was primed to bloom in time to win the Gold. Her club, her home state of California, her entire country willed her towards the winner's stand. Only Grant himself, who'd nurtured her talents so carefully that he'd come to love the girl behind them, entertained doubts, saw hair-line cracks appear daily in the glossy surface of her confidence. He knew her too well. If she failed in what they'd both come to regard as a joint effort, she'd feel she'd failed Grant himself. And then wander forever in a minefield of guilt expertly seeded by her own mother? Roxanne had always been dependent, first on Noni, then on Grant — but until now she'd been dependable.

Skating champions were made, not born. Grant had sculpted his Olympic front-runner from talent perilously

17

flawed by a fragile ego. Most of the time it had been a labour of love, but still he'd earned this Gold. He wanted it as much now as he wanted Roxanne herself — perhaps more. One Olympic Gold Medalist guaranteed a permanent niche in skating's hall of fame. He shook his head but doubts remained, the culmination of years rushing in, clouding his judgement. God alone knew what it was doing to hers.

He snapped on the light. Work. The answer to everything. His skaters, startled, instantly alert, pretended not to notice him in the yellow square of lighted window — but they skated twice as fast, twice as controlled, twice as *well*. Excellent.

He zipped up parka and moon-boots and strode to his customary spot at the hub, his mood as unyielding as the morning ice of which he was emperor. A ringmaster whose whip, silently wielded, hissed with the ultimate threat: do as I say or find a new coach. And there was the rub: who better than Grant Rivers? This was his year. He was in vogue, had clout where it counted, with knowledgeable judges, and charisma with that all-important breed, the skaters' mothers. How many top coaches were young, darkly handsome — and known to be single but tantalizingly unavailable?

So what if rumour mills from here to Helsinki circulated tales of his live-in affair with his star student? At twenty-two Roxanne was of age, more than willing, and proximity kept her firmly under his control, well away from her mother. The arrangement suited everybody but Noni. But like all who knew her, Grant had written off Roxanne's mother long since. Like any wounded feline she bore watching, but Grant knew he'd drawn Noni's fangs the day Roxanne left home and moved in with him. Free from the emotional roller-coaster ride of Life with Mother, the girl had steadily improved. Until now.

Until the Games, distant as the moon a year ago, suddenly cast their impending shadow over them all. Where had time gone? This was Roxanne's only shot at Olympus; already at twenty-two there were murmurs that she was over the hill, past her prime. Lately, in waking nightmares, Roxanne sound asleep beside him, he re-ran mental videos of her competitors, often reaching out a protective arm as if to shield her from their confidence, their youth, and above all their greater strength. But with the daylight his own confidence took over — he had enough for them both. If Grant was celebrated for one quality above all it was implacable purpose. Their affair would help her win the Gold and polish his own reputation to a higher, deeper shine. If, in the nights, he remembered another woman, another room, cream roses and ivory satin — then he waited for the California sun to rise, willed it to chase away old memories, shine its dazzling light on his career prospects instead — dispel old fascinations to the shadows where they belonged. *This* element was his. Renowned coach, king of the rink, his loyal subjects all about him, their awed parents grouped in the bleachers. He held the skating world in his palm.

He raised a gloved finger and someone's anonymous mama trotted to the barrier with coffee. Parents, eager for a sign, took his acceptance as proof positive that he saw unimaginable talent in their offspring, allowing them to spin beautiful dreams of a future world champion — theirs.

Grant smiled upon this morning's honoree, who blushed and scurried to her seat, humbly proud to have served.

The twenty skaters formed groups as rigidly defined as the social system he remembered in the Britain he'd long ago abandoned — where he could not have prospered and to which he had not returned. The difference, as he saw it, was that here the kids grouped themselves naturally, according to ability. On American ice, social standing was nothing unless buttressed by talent and drive.

The smaller kids, not yet warmed up, bulky in sweaters and mitts and striped scarves, buzzed at the ice's edge like worker-bees sluggish in the freezing dawn. Afraid, as yet, to venture into that whirling inner circle where it was every skater for himself, and no mercy for the faint-hearted. This close to major competition, Grant gave the juniors scant attention. Their turn would come. Maybe. Indistinguishable under layers of wool and fear, huddled potential champions and certain losers, but at this stage only God knew the difference. Mr Rivers didn't have time to look. Right now they were also-rans who knew their place — and it was nowhere near centre-ice.

The *crème*, the five, did minimum on-ice warm-ups. They'd already worked their stint in the ballet room. Now they circled him with long whispering strokes, the hallmark of the superior skater. These he would take to Montegreco in seven short weeks. No time at all. Even this early, in ratty practice outfits and reeking of linament, the five looked superb. Thoroughbreds at their morning exercise. Opaque latex tights covered Ace bandages remarkably well; aspirin on empty stomachs blasted pain clear into San Diego County; Rolaids buffered Anacin; last night they would have swallowed Ex-Lax. After work-out and weigh-in, most would rush to Pete's Pantry and devour double eggs benedict as if they hadn't eaten in days. Some hadn't. Some thought he didn't know.

A distinctive crunch broke the rink quiet. He sighed. 'Beejay, we don't eat on the ice. What is it this time?'

The little redhead, sixteen, took the last bite. 'Dill pickle.'

Jesus. At six in the morning. 'You deserve a bellyache.'

'Thank you, Mr Rivers.' She curtsied without breaking stroke.

If he talked that way to Roxanne she'd be in tears. She cried a lot lately, but was skating well, despite that air of frailty which seemed to intensify a little each day. She had her period, maybe that was it. Or maybe she was playing the cosmetic game again, wanting sympathy. It wouldn't be a first; at twenty-two her pretences were childishly obvious. Perhaps it was the black dress. This close to Montegreco the last thing they needed were rumours of poor health. Vital not to upset judges' preconceived placements. Time to go to work, to show she was fine.

'Start with the triple-loop combo. Roxanne first.'

The combo that gave her the most trouble, and he was forcing her hand. Unfair. Her eyes, a desperate pleading blue this morning, signalled alarm, but she said nothing. She knew better than to bring their relationship into the rink — but later there would be tears. Too bad. She had to conquer fear. If she couldn't control it on home ice, what would she do in Montegreco?

She missed. He made her repeat. This time she hung in, barely. In the bleachers parental tongues wagged, just as they'd wag across phone lines when they all reached home. Damn.

The Carlsens, his Swedish Pair, didn't try it. Pairs didn't need it. Jeff Dunsmuir, competing for England, did — but he missed too, and something in Grant was obscurely, shamefully gratified. He'd been reluctant to accept Jeff just three months before the Games for what the Brits quaintly called a buffing-up, but the temptation to make them crawl to him, to show what he could do with a talented, undisciplined skater, was too much. And *that* was unfair too. It wasn't Jeff's fault the Brits dumped Grant Rivers all those years ago. It wasn't even *their* fault. They could only support so many. No, it was still Deirdre Sterling, treacherous composition of scented curves and deceit. Dammit, concentrate! No time now to probe old wounds, which had in any case healed over.

He signalled Beejay to make her pass at the combo. Naturally she nailed it. An innate performer, Beejay loved nothing better than an audience, even if it was just parents in the bleachers. Not waiting to be asked, she compounded her triumph by rocketing round and knocking off the same thing again, higher than before. Someday, when this little whiz-bang found elegance, she'd grab an Olympic medal, no sweat. But it wouldn't be yet, thank God. This year was Roxanne's turn. And his.

'Fine. Show me spins. Clean, controlled, and fast.'

To restore Roxanne's spirits, if nothing else. Her spins were legend, still the world's best; they didn't travel, and she could hold the momentum almost forever. Beejay's were sloppy and travelled, her arms all over the place. He told them both exactly that. Roxanne beamed.

'Watch Roxi, Beejay — maybe you'll learn something.'

'Yes, Mr Rivers,' Beejay said, mild as milk. She knew exactly what he was up to and why. She'd make a good coach someday.

He saw Beejay's mother's lip twitch. Some partnership between those two. Beejay and Emma Crisp. As a breed, skating judges leaned towards grey hair and the far side of fifty, but Emma, a widow, couldn't be much above thirty-eight. A fair judge who cared for the sport enough to put principles before friendship, politics, even before country.

'Dammit to hell!' Beejay said, missing a landing, bouncing

back off her neat little tush to roar round the rink for yet another shot at her own nemesis, a triple-lutz she was determined to have ready for the Games. Some chance. Already her thighs had more colours than Picasso's palette.

His flock diligently at work, he again scanned the bleachers to make sure Roxanne's mother was not present. He'd seldom banned a parent from the rink, but Noni . . .

God, there she sat, huddled in the darkest corner of the rink, her eyes hooked into Roxanne like she was a prize salmon. If Roxanne spotted her —

'Shit!' Beejay shouted, as once again her blade shot out from under.

My sentiments exactly, Grant thought, sending a discreet signal to Roxanne's mother to quit the premises. For a moment she stared him down, but they both knew he meant it, held all the cards, that they'd come much too far for much too long, and were now too close to the Games, the grand prize, to disturb the *status quo*.

So Noni Braun Kramer, divorced ex-skater and quint-essential stage mother, an aging blonde, still pretty in a raddled, intense way, moved stiffly to the exit, flashing Grant a murderous glare before slamming the door behind her.

God, how Roxanne wished her mother would stay away. Just the door closing behind her gave the United States Champion and hands-down Olympic favourite the necessary energy to get through her programme. Just once. But near-perfect except a triple which she 'elected not to do' as the sports commentators loved to say. Elect, hell. If you didn't do it it meant you *couldn't*, not right then. That you were off-beat, off-balance, or just plain off. A split second to decide to go for it or not, to figure out if this was or was not one of your better days.

Beejay flashed past her, cocky, full of bounce and ginger — but she was a kid still, no pressure, no *demands*. Sometimes Roxanne actually felt *physical* pressure, decades of ice-chapped Braun hands bearing down on her shoulders. If she could just feel good all the time, instead of now and then, if her weight wouldn't yo-yo, if Mom would disappear

22

until Roxanne won the Gold for Grant Rivers and could wear him around her neck forever-after-in-holy-matrimony, amen, if . . . if . . . if — then she'd toss her skates in the nearest trash, sleep late when she wanted, eat Saturday pizza without a pang of guilt, have Mom over now and then — but above all cherish Grant Rivers so he'd never want another woman ever again. But Mom couldn't disappear any more than Roxanne could.

Letters arrived daily from Germany in Gran's crabbed old hand, imploring, instructing, above all expecting. The Braun's, among Germany's oldest skating families, corner-stones almost since the day somebody strapped runners on boots to cross a frozen lake, lived in a glorious ghost-ridden past in which Brauns won, won, won. Grampa still taught from a wheelchair. Gran supervised group classes, but even they knew their methods were hopelessly outdated.

Which left it to Roxanne to gather up the family honour and do for the United States what her mother had so wantonly failed to do for Germany. Noni had almost done it, but at the crucial moment had eloped with Dad, a US skier at some way-back Games, which Noni had been touted to win. Instead of a medal and added lustre to the Braun name, Mom came out of it with her parents' undying shame, a baby in her belly, and eventually a divorce.

'Roxanne!'

She finished drying her blades and looked up. Grant with the rink scale and the list. Saturday-damned-weigh-in.

God, but he looked tired. For a dreamy, wishful moment she imagined she walked out with him into the California sun, drove to Malibu in his Porsche, soaked up the heat of hot sand, held him no matter who saw them. *How* she hated this hole-and-corner skulking about, driving back to the apartment in separate cars, calling him Grant at home and Mr Rivers, *always* Mr Rivers, at the rink — as if it fooled anybody! But he had this theory: insist people use your formal name and you created distance. It seemed to work, kept the kids' parents off his back, and guaranteed the respect of the kids. So she went along. She went along with whatever pleased him. But when, dear God, would he want to please *her*?

Like an echo, she heard the answer. When you, Roxanne

23

Braun Kramer, win the Olympic Gold and set the seal on Mr Rivers' reputation, that's when he'll love you, when they'll all love you, when Mom would talk to her about something else besides skating, when the old ones in Bonn would dimple up at her again, and Grossmutti bake her favourite strudel, ice-chapped old knuckles coaxing the dough into a wider and wider circle, sprinkling it with raisins and cinnamon, and Jesus *Christ,* quit thinking about food! Fat skaters won no medals. Braun Law, handed down like a family heirloom.

Predictably, Beejay hit her target weight of 102 pounds, all wire and crackle and unburned energy, the type who never gained dot. Jeff Dunsmuir, having discovered pralines-'n-ice-ceam, was five over par, earning Grant's frown but no real concern. Guys were naturally skinnier anyway. Maybe there'd be a note to his Brit sponsor — which Roxanne would type; what he did for a secretary before she lived with him, God only knew.

Dag Carlsen, half the Swedish pair, was okay. His sister Lise, Princess Pain of the Rink, was not. Neither was Grant after he read the scale. 'Seven blasted pounds in a week? Damn it, Lise, Doug has to hoist it all overhead fifty times a day! What d'you think he is, Superman?'

Lise gave him her most kittenish smile. 'No, Mr Rivers. My brother's much too pretty for Superman.'

Grant's lips tightened and Dag flushed to the roots of his flaxen hair. Dag *was* gorgeous, that was his problem. Both the Carlsens were, but on her it didn't matter, except she played her looks like a concert grand.

'Have your father call me tonight, okay?' Grant said. A mulish silence from Lise. 'Did you hear me, Lise?' Grant persisted.

Roxanne turned away. There went her quiet evening at home with Grant. Ben Carlsen could harangue all night, always in Lise's favour. The family had left Sweden when the twins were babies; as skaters they were so-so, Dag the worker, Lise the graceful indolent. As a Pair they were not good enough for the US team. Then Ben Carlsen remembered where his kids had been born. Dual citizenship was an umbrella under which many a skater had sheltered, bringing deserved fame to some. Why not Ben's kids? So twins Lise and Dag Carlsen would skate the Olympics, a Swedish rock star reputedly picking up their tuition bills.

'Your turn, Roxanne.' At home he called her Roxi. She stepped on the scale, striving to add to it the weight of hundreds of Braun hands pressing her down, down. As she stepped off, Grant quietly told her to stick around.

The session over, he shooed everybody out the door before turning to her. 'Now we'll take it without sweaters, coat and shoes, and purse. And don't cry, darling, please don't cry.'

She swallowed the lump in her throat. They read the scale, accurate to a fraction of an ounce. At 5'6" she weighed 104 pounds. Breaking his own rule, he cupped her face in his hands and gazed down into her eyes as if through them he could pour into her brain his own monumental purpose.

'And muscle weighs much more than fat. Look, you've worked sixteen years for this. The Gold is yours. Now for Pete's sake go to Pete's Diner, eat steak and eggs, then come home to me. Okay?'

Panic washed over her. Eat. Steak and eggs! 'Mom'll be at your place.'

'I'll handle Noni Braun Kramer. Is there a law saying you have to be the *skinniest* medalist in the Games?'

Easy to say, hard to keep the food down. Sitting at the big table Pete reserved for 'Mr Rivers' Olympic Squad' she watched, revolted, as the Carlsen twins and Jeff Dunsmuir downed bacon, eggs, sausage, ham, hash-browns and muffins, all smothered in ketchup and blueberry syrup. Beejay, thank God, wasn't there to see Roxanne trail a sliver of toast through egg-yolk and dash for the bathroom. Back at the table she pushed the plate out of sight and ordered dry toast and black coffee. It stayed down. She had consumed. Now she could go home.

At the sidewalk she turned back to see Pete punch numbers into the phone. Reporting in. To Grant.

Noni yelled at her when she ate; Grant scowled when she didn't. Monitored at every turn. How important she must be, this celebrated Roxanne Braun Kramer, whose head, after the morning cocktail of zinc from Germany, kelp from Finland, beef tea from England, mega vitamins from

Healtha, felt light, filled with air, something to which she could have tied a string, floated it over Lakewood Center.

Sudden weak tears blinded her to a cyclist at the intersection. Brakes shrieked. The cyclist picked himself up, shook his fist at her through the windshield, then gave her a goofy grin. A cop pulled her over, and he too recognized her, waved her on with a smile. 'The USA's pulling for you, Roxi! Don't let us down!'

She gave him the public smile, smudged around the edges. 'Thanks. Thanks a lot.'

Noni brewed coffee and kicked her shoes across Grant's ultramodern, upmarket living room and stared out at the sea view. It was no accident she'd arrived a full hour before Grant and Roxanne. An hour to check the fridge, trash, freezer, then to Grant's desk, his accounts, investments. Christ, his credit balance alone shot her temper clear into the ether.

Great. She subsisted in a one-bedroom hovel. Her daughter lived in this . . . this bachelor pad. Well. Noni still had her keys from when they'd been halfway friendly, and they'd never-never-never get them back. Roxanne was *her* daughter, her discovery, she'd given her her start, that girl, that Gold, done things Roxanne couldn't even imagine (much less condone), all to advance Roxanne's career one step at a time up the skating ladder. Fifteen years of it! She'd be damned if she'd let them push her out just when it counted. Damned if she'd let that Englishman, Welshman or whatever the hell he called himself tell *her* what to do, where she could go —

No. Hold tight, Noni. Hold your temper. You still need *him*. Roxanne needed judges in her corner and there were some, *one*, who wouldn't give her so much as a dose of the clap if she knew exactly what Noni had done to keep one judge sweet. And maybe she did know, that Emma. Mrs Crisp was no fool. So keep your head. *Use* this time, *use* him, call Germany on fucking Mr Rivers' phone. A little chat with Bonn, all the sweeter for being free.

Like fireflies her green-lacquered nails flew over the phone buttons. *Ja*, Mutti was home, Papa at the rink. And how did our sweetheart skate today? Jesus, but the old woman sounded . . . old, old.

'She's a dream, Mama. You'll be proud, a triple-axel high as a seagull, loops such as you never saw —' She recited a glowing catalogue of jumps Roxanne had landed that morning, and many she had missed.

'Tch! These days is all jump jump! Are our skaters kangaroos —'

'Mutti, I have to go, I call next week, *ja*?'

She set down the receiver as Grant's key clicked in the lock. When he came in she was seated on the black leather couch, slender ankle swinging, patiently waiting. He looked angry. Good. He also looked worried. Bad.

'I told you to stay out of the rink.'

'Grant, a mother must to see her daughter, no?' she wheedled.

'You saw. So what's the expert Braun opinion?'

'So Roxanne has a bad morning, what's to worry?'

'Worry? The pills you get her from that bloody quack. And the dieting. You've got her to where she thinks eating is a sin!'

'How many fat skaters do you see win the Olympics?'

'How many skeletons?'

Noni turned arch. 'Is it possible my daughter is pregnant?'

Grant flushed a deep brick-red. 'You think I'd be that stupid?'

No. He'd wanted a champion, as she did. A signal to Bonn, Noni's home-rink, that Roxanne Braun Kramer would make up for every expectation Noni had failed to fulfil. Oh, but this olive-skinned bastard knew how to manipulate, to squeeze every last drop of juice . . . But she could squeeze too. 'I can force the management to let me in. I still have my credentials.'

'And four years' of bills for my professional services, Noni. My other students pay me. Lessons don't come cheap. We had a deal.'

She smiled a thin, bitter smile. 'You get your money's worth, yes?'

'Roxanne's of age. Our relationship is personal. I'm the coach, know exactly what I'm doing — and that's her car now, so watch your mouth.'

'I only ask my daughter where is her strength? Is it too much?'

'Yes. Right this minute it is too bloody much.'

Now Roxi was in the room, looking from one to the other, her face, her whole posture tightening like the knot in a piece of string. Noni wanted to rock her, stroke her, take her away from this man, but instead gave her a quick peck on the cheek. 'Darling, I call to Dr Reiker. We go to see him Monday, yes?'

'We'll see. But Mom, I gotta lie down now, okay?'

'Yes. Don't worry. Dr Reiker will make my Roxi skate like a champion.'

'She already does, Noni. Goodbye.' Icicles hung on Grant's words.

Roxanne watched by the window until Mom's battered old Buick shot into the Pacific Coast highway and out of sight. Then she let the tears come, slow and hot, trickling down her cheeks like transparent lava. 'I'm sorry, Grant, I'm just so sorry . . .'

He reached for her. 'For what, darling?'

'For skating lousy. For Mom showing up. For — oh, everything.'

'Forget it. And forget her pills and her Dr Reiker. Get your things off, take a hot bath, and we'll order from room service.'

'But I just ate!'

He said nothing. Of course. He knew. 'Not with me, you didn't.'

He peeled off her sweaters, skating dress, leotards, all the way down to where she was a bundle of bone and muscle with two little black bands, bra and bikini pants. He kissed the hollow, deep as a teacup, in her collarbone. Whimpering, she wrapped her arms around his neck to pull him to the bedroom, to persuade him to make love to her, to maybe make him *admit* he loved her. He never had.

He refused to be drawn. Instead his chin set like a clenched brown fist as he led her to the mirror. 'Pretty soon you won't have a curve left.' He handed her the menu from the downstairs grill. 'Order 2000 calories at least.'

She tried to read but everywhere she looked she saw fat. Dialling fast, she told them to hurry — if they were quick she could throw hers in the disposal and tell Grant she had eaten it while he was in the shower. Which ran and ran under Grant's fine Welsh tenor, deliberately raised in song: *Guardian angels watch beside you, all through the night* . . . She squeezed her eyes closed. Night. Seven more weeks of night.

Palos Verdes, Los Angeles County

The chrome-and-white Carlsen dining-room looked out on to an aquamarine pool banked with pink-and-white oleander. Mrs Carlsen, a shadowy figure in a gown of soft rose, drifted from dining-room to kitchen and back again. Just your average family helping Mom with dinner, more or less. Saturday, the one evening they broke bread together. Dad's directive.

And if Lise broke just one more bread roll with her teeth as she shuttled from serving hatch to table, Dag swore to himself he'd staple her lips together.

Mom spoke. 'Lise, tell your father dinner's ready, please?' Her low, patient voice failed to mute the tension in the light, bright rooms.

'He's finishing his drink in the den. He'll be out when he's done with Mr Rivers on the phone.' Lise helped herself to salad and buttered a roll.

'Hey, go easy,' Dag said. 'That's your third.'

Lise gave him a dead pan stare and took another pat of butter. 'I am *not* fat, brother dear. Ask your friends — the ones who prefer *me*, I mean.'

'You gained *again*, dammit! The Games are only seven weeks off —'

Lise speared a cherry tomato into her beautifully curved mouth. 'You ruin every meal I eat.' A tomato seed shot across the table.

'Obviously not,' Dag shot back.

'Oh, children . . .' Mom's soft exclamation didn't stand a chance.

'I'm 119 pounds, and not an ounce more!'

'That's nine too many.'

Lise smirked, preparing an ace. 'Discuss it with Dad.'

'Dad doesn't whirl you over his head like a damned lasso every day.'

'Nobody's twisting your arm. Anytime it gets too much.'

'*Lise, if you want to quit skating why don't you say so?*'

'I've *been* saying so for years. Nobody listens.'

Knots of muscle stood out on Dag's perfectly sculpted jaw. 'You agreed to switch to Pairs *four years* ago! Now is *not* the time to quit.'

Lise fluttered her lashes. '*You agreed to switch.*' She mimicked Dag almost too well, but gave his voice a subtle effeminacy it did not have. '*Then* I agreed, yes! I'd just been screwed out of a Bronze in Singles.'

'You skated lousy. You got beat out of it fair and square.'

'*Did not.*'

'*Did so.*'

'If Emma Crisp just gave me one fucking tenth of a point more —'

Mom's lips quivered. 'Lise, please don't talk like that at the table? If we could get through one meal without skating, skating, skating —' Abruptly she drained her burgundy and refilled the glass to the brim.

Lise pursed her lips. 'Dad says Emma Crisp robbed me blind because I'm better looking than her Beejay, that's why.'

'Aw, come on!' her brother said. 'If you told Dad you were the Angel Gabriel he'd run buy you a gold-plated harp.'

The door crashed open. Silence, broken only by the chatter of crystal set down on polished wood, fell like an extra cloth over the dinner table. Rocking on his heels in the doorway stood Ben Carlsen. His face, all bones and hollows, reflected a virulent, unslaked fury.

Downey, Los Angeles County

The Crisps' home lacked a dining-room. Emma and Beejay ate off lap-trays in the worn kitchen–family room, which mirrored their diet and income — but never their aspirations.

On the sink two pairs of white freshly polished skates

stood drying, black lacquer sealing their soles against ice-rot, their reek of paint and polish an added spice to virtually every meal in a haphazard cuisine. In the living area beyond, a decade of Harlick boot-boxes served as files overflowing with bills, receipts, memos for Emma to judge here, Beejay to skate an exhibition there — all *gratis*, natch — lending a semblance of order to a cluttered corner desk.

Few things in the world scared Emma Crisp, but she brooded long over the papers in the 'pending' box, shuffled them like cards, scrunched them and cursed them. Bills for blades, leotards, dressmakers, and ballet classes — she shifted their order in what had become a daily review. Who to pay, who to put on hold?

The skating-connected bills posed the worst threat, not because they were due but because nobody pressed for payment. The mailman delivered no final notices on these. Beejay had made the team. Creditors were at pains to show consideration, even pride that she used their products. An ominous sign. God knew she didn't begrudge Beejay this chance, but lessons and ice-time added up to big bills. The Committee picked up some, the Club some more and Grant billed her for the balance. But he didn't press either. Already the numbers were too big to meet, but as a judge how could she take charity from a coach? She must be whiter than white, or every time she judged a Grant Rivers' student her integrity would be in doubt. Right now she was so clean she squeaked; her husband had been liked and held in high regard on the judging circuit too. In Montegreco, Beejay would need all Emma's honesty and her late father's popularity behind her, just to counter the gossip.

Already some pointed the finger, said Beejay was lucky to make the team, luckier that Mommy was a judge. They were wrong. An older girl's injury opened up a spot; Beejay saw the hole and aimed her skates at it. She deserved her place. Emma figured she'd be unbeatable in two years, but Emma was partial and knew it — which was why they never let you judge your own kid. This year Emma would be assigned to Pairs or Men. Beejay would be judged by Emma's friends or enemies. Friends would bend over backwards to show impartiality. Enemies, and Emma had some, would seek out and punish every flaw they saw, or thought they saw, in

Beejay. Between her mother's principles and skating's politics, Beejay hadn't a prayer this time out of the shoot, poor dab. Maybe she should warn her.

Emma watched her chew fiercely on hot dogs and beans as her small fists oiled and polished old blades. She'd skated the tempered edges right off them, but some beginner would snap them up. Around such economies their lives revolved. Having neither funds nor inclination for much else, skating was their life. They wanted no other.

'The Games will be rough, sport,' Emma began, knowing she might as well shout against Niagara's roar. 'Don't set your hopes too high, huh?'

'I don't.' Beejay wiped her hands on cut-off jeans, leaving a smudge of lacquer to match the triple-lutz bruise on her thigh. 'But hell, I'm going. I hope they'll remember I've been.'

'Beejay — and watch your mouth, okay? Suppose they talk to you on TV and every other word comes out "hell"? So listen. This is your first crack at big thunder. Except for St Ivel and Skate Canada —'

'Where I did okay, right?' Her sherry-coloured glance swept to the shrine, a feature of every competitor's home, showplace for the medals and trophies and silver plate, framed news clips and her first pair of blades, all of six inches long — even then she'd nicked and gouged them from one end to the other. A soft skater Beejay was not. That was Roxanne's forté. 'I landed the lutz clean this afternoon. Three in a row, all clean. In *a row!*'

Emma supressed a surge of triumph. That was a skating mother's reaction. 'Good. Maybe your bruises'll fade. I remember you when your behind was pink.'

'Roxi chickened out of hers. Doubled every one.'

'She's the favourite. That's big pressure. You all get bad days.'

'She gets a lot. You want I should warm up your plate?'

'Uh-huh.' Emma was resigned but tired. She knew better than to expect the microwave. Beejay squirted Tabasco on baked beans and handed it back. 'Look Beejay, I won't have you tracking gossip in here, okay?'

'About Roxi? It's not gossip, it's the honest-to-God gospel —'

'You know what I mean.'

32

'Okay. Okay! But she really did screw up.'

'Again, watch your mouth.'

Nobody could look more indignant than Beejay when she put her mind to it. 'What have I said now?'

'Screw.'

'So?'

'So don't say it. It's eight o'clock. If you want to make first Sunday freestyle . . .' Jeez, what a life for a kid! Up before dawn seven days a week, Christmas and Easter excepted — maybe.

'Yep.' Beejay shrugged, hiked her skate-bag on her shoulder and headed for her room. Her chant followed her down the hall: '*Montegreco, here I come*.' At the end of the hall she turned to wave, ' 'Night, Em.'

' 'Night, Beejay.' Emma would have given anything to hug her daughter goodnight, but Beejay had never been much for kisses and the like. Sometimes, when she'd mastered a difficult move or won a competition, she'd give Emma's hand a fierce squeeze and whisper, 'Thanks, Em.' That was about it, but it made every sacrifice worth while.

Suppose she did well at the Games, though? Where could she go from there, at her age? Sixteen was too young for a show — but what a relief to be out from under this snowstorm of bills. Lord, the temptation! Not that she had a chance. The competition stiffened up every year. Grant thought all Roxanne had to do was skate her best to take Gold. He was wrong. If he had a failing it was in underestimating the competition, not studying their tapes, their strengths and weaknesses. Emma did. She'd seen them all, knew who coached who, had judged most of them one time or another. Roxanne Kramer could skate a perfect programme and still come home from the Games with nothing but beads round her neck. Emma hoped not. She'd tried, ever since it happened, to keep Noni and Roxanne apart in her mind, not let bitterness against the mother splash over into her genuine liking for the daughter. What would Noni do, she wondered, if all her conniving schemes came to nothing but a wistful write-up in *Skating*? Look back on every rotten thing she'd done for that damned Gold, the lives she'd wrecked? Not Noni. She'd be crushed, finished — but unrepentant to the end. And Roxi *could* lose. Lose bad.

There was the Tokyo girl, Mieko somebody or other. A plain little thing with a smile big enough to fill a stadium and pull every heart inside it. The right conditions and Plain Jane could be dynamite. Maybe somebody *had* given her the right conditions — unlikely though; there were no secrets. International skating was a goddamn village. Sneeze in Bremen, they heard it in Montreal, Leningrad, Denver, LA, every training centre panning for Gold. The top German could turn the heat up on a good day, too, damned near as pretty as Witt — and looks did count no matter what they said. Then there was the sleeper, trained some place near London, who had just placed at Europeans. Grant likely had not seen *her*. Where the Brit skating world was concerned he had a blind spot a mile wide. She could guess why — too many good skaters died on the competitive vine for want of a sponsor. Likely he'd been one. Whatever, she covered the spot for Beejay's sake. With judging pals all over the globe, a video of Europeans was one phone call. The tape was an eye-opener.

The English girl was eighteen, seemed to have been protected from virtually all international competition until now, but Holy Mother of God, that girl *fell* prettier than most girls jumped — and she hardly seemed to jump at all. She *floated*, no other word for it. A decade of dance discipline skated under those blades, and did it ever show! What was her name again? Black curly hair and blue eyes, hovered over her mother like she was her nurse or something. A mental scroll unwound, but there'd been so many names — Russian names alone drove her up the wall. Mo? A connection with Jeff Dunsmuir's sponsor? She shrugged. Skaters switched sponsors every five minutes these days.

Emma gave herself a shake. What she *should* do was her own homework, study Pairs and Mens form books for skating's brightest prize. Who won what when. It paid to know which skeletons rattled in whose closet. But, oh Lord, let them assign her to Mens. Not Pairs. No way did she want to judge the Carlsens. Lise was bone idle, Dag a time-bomb ticking away, and Ben Carlsen reeking of bitterness. One day that family would explode, and no way did she want to be around for the big bang.

CHAPTER TWO

London, England

Maureen Sterling reached across and tucked her mother's hands under the chinchilla lap-robe. No matter how high the chauffeur turned up the heat, Mother's long hands, so pale as to be almost transparent, felt cold to the touch, almost too frail to bear the weight of the massive emerald in its antique setting — not her style at all, but Daddy insisted she wear it. He liked his assets on display. 'You're sure you want to go right home, Mother? We could stop for coffee at the Hurtswood, break up the trip a little.'

Deirdre Sterling's blue eyes flew open. So she *had* been napping again. 'No, we'll soon be home; the Latin chap will be waiting. How you juggle all these tutors I can't imagine.'

'It's German today, and my schedule's fine. I'm the only skater I know who's driven from ice to ballet to townhouse, then home for the weekends, a tutor on hand to suit my schedule, not his. Not to mention a friend for constant company.' She rubbed her knuckles lightly over her mother's cool, delicate cheek. No sarcasm had entered Maureen's voice; she intended none.

Deirdre held her daughter's hand in hers as if seeking more warmth than could be found within the furs. 'You're quite sure you've *wanted* to skate all these years, darling? I mean, it's not been just to please me.'

Maureen turned to the window and saw the countryside between Ascot and Windsor sweeping by in a Christmas-card scene of snow-laden boughs and rosy children. She sighed. Of course she wanted to skate — she'd do anything to please Mother, to whom she owed far more than mere kinship could repay. But if Deirdre ever lost interest in the ice, Maureen could give it up without a qualm.

She knew just why her mother accompanied her everywhere, slept in the next room at home, the adjoining door unlocked, never left her for a moment if it could be avoided, especially at home. If Mother was within call, Daddy couldn't touch Maureen. Perhaps Mother thought Maureen had been too young to remember, but she remembered all too well the brandy-breath on her neck, the almost-silent rustle of a hand approaching under her nursery blanket, then her scream of outrage. She shuddered now, twisting the memory away as she had once twisted her six-year-old body away.

After the first time she didn't have to scream. Mother's constant presence made screaming unnecessary. Mother had been her saviour. Now, subtly and slowly, their roles were reversing. No matter how Maureen tried to shake the idea, the feeling persisted that Deirdre must be guarded, a creature too fragile to be left long alone, as if some dark sorrow waited to move in, crush her elegant wisp of a mother between unimaginable tortures. Perhaps in Spain after the Games she'd feel better, more . . . alive. Mother had always loved the Palamos villa, its sun, its peace.

'Of course I want to skate,' she protested. 'Who in their right mind would pass up the Games?' After twelve years of the training grind, she was no longer sure if she spoke the truth or not.

'What worries me, darling,' Deirdre said, her voice suddenly stronger, 'is that I perhaps drew you into it because of some need in *me*. Oh, what *do* they call it, those chaps in Harley Street, I can't seem to remember. You don't suppose I have Alz — whatever they call it, on top of the other thing? I can't even keep up with the jargon.' Her voice faded again, weakened by its brief effort.

The other thing. Some kind of anti-anxiety therapy administered for an hour a day, while Maureen was safe in ballet class and could be left to *plié* and perspire, surrounded by a score of other bodies.

'You don't have Alzheimer's. It's the medicine that makes you forget. Once they stop it . . .' She opened the panel and whispered to the driver to get a move on. 'Mother, the word you meant is "sublimation". They use it about those stage-mother-types, of which you are *not* one, could never *be* one. *You* didn't push me into skating. *I* did! I loved it the first time you took me.'

She remembered a Christmas party when she was six, balloons, a puppeteer, a clown on skates who fell and fell and never cried. A dozen or so children from Mrs Pringle's Primary in the village, who'd barely filled a tenth of the privately hired ice, which was so gloriously crisp and clean, surprisingly friendly to her new skates — and what a lucky little girl to get such a splendid present. And how quickly indulgence became self-induced tyranny, above all lone-liness, for soon everything, even friends, were sacrificed on the altar of the blades, leaving only other skaters to fill the void. Which reminded her.

'I called Jeff yesterday. He loves the California weather, thanks you and Daddy for sponsoring him, and says he really feels he has a chance now. Roxi Kramer's sweet; she's got a touch of 'flu or something, but they all expect her to win. The redhead, Beejay Crisp, Jeff says she's a talent, an odd little bod, still a bit rough around the edges — you said so, remember, after St Ivel? Jeff says I'd have beaten her if I'd been entered.'

Deirdre roused herself under the fur. 'Did Jeff mention his coach?'

Maureen laughed. 'Oh yes! The man's a slave-driver. Jeff also says . . .' She looked sideways at Deirdre. Mother thought she was far less worldly than she was. True, she didn't get out much, but she did read and watch the box. 'Jeff swears Roxanne actually *lives* with Grant Rivers! He says her mother's an interfering bitch who Mr Rivers will not allow into the rink! He sounds frightfully overbearing. I don't think I'd like him at all.'

Mother's pale skin flushed to an endearing, delicate rose. 'Don't even think that! He had appalling luck as an amateur, all talent, no support — well, some was offered, but the wrong kind, quite wrong for him!'

Maureen looked up, surprised. Dierdre, emphatic? 'I didn't know you even *knew* him!'

'Well, not now, but when he was competing . . . Daddy and I were more involved then . . . it was before business took him away so much . . . and then you arrived . . . and I guess I sort of let everything slide but you . . .'

God, Mother had done it again! That voice, stiff with barriers. Vague. And somehow sad . . . and why the devil not? Daddy the way he was, Deirdre trying desperately to keep the closet door locked. Maureen chose diversion. 'Remember the Russian boy who won Mens at Europeans?' she said. 'Wanted our phone and the Spanish address?'

'Intense, thin? Alexei Finsky? Moscow?'

'Yes. See, your memory's fine. Well, we haven't heard. I'd write, but could it get him in trouble, d'you think? He was so keen to keep in touch with us, yet some of the others still write, no problem.'

'Then write to him.' No caution now, only weariness. Diversion successful. 'We'll see everyone at the Games, anyway.'

The Games. Maureen felt her calves tighten and automatically shook them loose as she'd been trained to do. If they could programme her to do that, why couldn't they programme Mother not to be anxious? She resolved, again, to talk to the doctor, ask point-blank what was wrong.

'Do you really want me there? At the Games?' Deirdre said. 'Suppose I make you nervous — not that you *have* to win a medal or anything —'

'Of course not — and of course you'll go!' Maureen said sharply. Deirdre must go, to remind herself why *she* was there, who it was she skated for.

Haslemere loomed out of the early winter's dusk. In seconds the car swept them through the avenue of chestnut trees, their limbs stark, groping at snow-laden clouds. She sighed. England in winter. Even the rink was warmer. No wonder Deirdre was sick. They'd both be glad to see the Costa Brava after Montegreco.

She gave her skate-bag to the housekeeper for the evening ritual of dry-and-polish, simultaneously hurrying Mother into the warmth of the study. As the tutor, patient soul, waited, Maureen tucked her mother into the day-bed by the study fire and rang for tea. Mother was asleep even before it arrived.

Alone, Deirdre woke to the sound of coals settling in the grate. More or less rested but still sleepy — the damned drugs! — she stared into the glowing fire as into her past, her dead father momentarily alive and well, rocking slowly in the firelight, swirling the golden depths of a fine sherry, proclaiming to her the facts of life. His and hers. 'Trust me, Deirdre gel, I guarantee you'll not be poor. I have commanded, nay, demanded it!'

Somewhere, sherry had slopped to the shabby Persian rug as Daddy sat heavily, and not quite accurately, into the rocker. Brave, boozy talk, she'd thought then. But who or what did he command? She'd looked around her at worn cretonne and threadbare Axminster, the mantel with the boys' pictures taken at a long-ago cricket match. Her brothers, whose education took every shilling, with nothing left for Deirdre, who'd seemed destined to pour tea for the Friday Ladies Guild forever. Then one day her older brother smashed up himself and the vicarage car. Soon after, the surviving brother got into a spot of bother at prep school and was sent down. Expelled really. (At the vicarage they didn't only talk euphemisms, they lived them.) To the vicar, his son's expulsion meant they'd all been tried and found guilty.

'Caught him up to something unsavoury, gel, know what I mean?'

'Yes,' she lied. Such was her innocence, then, that 'savoury' covered only one topic. Food. She nodded anyway; it was easier to agree with Daddy, who went on to hint that Deirdre should maybe set her cap at Lloyd Sterling, who'd just bought and was renovating The Hall at great expense. New money, a little vulgar, but genuine, know what I mean?

Married to him, she soon learned. Lloyd was a genuine swine. New money purchased debaucheries undreamed of by the Friday Ladies. By then she also knew about 'not quite savoury' and sighed with relief when her disgraced brother took himself off to Australia and out of their lives forever. Lloyd, by donating stained-glass and hymn books, and marrying the vicar's daughter, had redeemed his new money and rendered himself respectable. And so, more or less, he had remained, having learned, with the caution of increasing wealth, to seek his pleasures away from home.

It no longer mattered. She'd almost finished what she had set out to do. Like everything, it had it's down-side; to guard

Maureen from Lloyd's excesses she'd also had to shelter her from life, fill the child's days so full of skating there'd been no room in them for Lloyd. And she'd done it, kept a lecher's soiled hands off something sweet and pure. A pity about Jeff though. Lloyd had long hands; she couldn't keep them off all the goodies. Heaven knew when Lloyd would cash in on that particular investment. If she were not around, then Jeff would have to look out for Jeff. She'd done all she could — and just in time.

Two years ago the family doctor had called her in for tests. 'But I'm not sick,' she told him.

'Neither is Lloyd,' the doctor said. 'But I ran his blood through a few extra hoops this time. They came up positive. He's a carrier.'

No. Oh *no*.

She'd seen the papers, of course, the latest scourge already touted as mankind's deadliest epidemic. And she knew Lloyd, in which particular sink-hole of the world he could be found at any given time, but this —

So she'd let the doctor run his tests. The next week he called her in for more. Then again, this time to the big easy-chair in his office, where a soothing glass of wine awaited her. That's when she knew. He spread his hands. 'Positive and active. I'm sorry, Deirdre.' The words dropped like tombstones, every fragile dream but one crushed under their weight.

Pretending to test for glandular fever, they ran Maureen's blood through the same hoops as those of Lloyd and Deirdre. Negative. Pure. Clear. So maybe there was a God after all.

Ironic that Lloyd, too, was healthy and might remain so all his life. How long did *she* have? The doctor didn't know, but lately they'd begun week-day chemotherapy. The results were not promising. Each day she tired easier; each week waited more eagerly for its recuperative end.

But she'd have the Olympics, Maureen skating for the world — surely she'd have that. She'd earned it, her gold star for good behaviour. If there was a God he would give her the star, would not punish her for that small, lovely sin so many years ago. If. For despite typing her father's hearty sermons since she'd learned to two-finger on the prim old upright, she'd never believed in Daddy's God, alternately punishing, forgiving, loving, much too well rounded to be true.

Only when she'd looked into her baby's face had she felt the slightest stirrings of faith. In the first year Maureen's hair, a neutral, ambivalent fuzz, thickened to curls so glossy, so black, that total strangers were moved to hover over her with outstretched hands as if in benediction; to touch the satiny tan cheek with its undertone of rose; to gaze into the wide, startlingly blue eyes — Maureen's one resemblance to Deirdre. Even in gawky adolescence heads had turned in envy at Maureen's natural beauty, untouched by eye-paint, lip-paint, cheek-paint, even, God help the country, hair-paint, which daily appeared in multi-coloured crests and spikes, first in the mean streets, but now Windsor, Ascot, even Haslemere.

In the Sterling's social set, the young females, discreetly segregated from the pack, came in two basic flavours: horsy, reeking of the riding-club and closely resembling their mounts: well fed, well brushed, heavy in the flank, and a tendency to whinny when amused, stomp when angry; or the 'Tatty Exclusive' — vague, doe-eyed waifs covered in layers of depressingly similar garments, fringed, laced, frantically antiqued, and surely retrieved from granny's loft until one glimpsed the trendy Bond Street labels.

In this company Maureen Sterling bloomed, unique and alone, a cross-bred exotic aloof among the dandelions, daisies and hedge-roses of the local gentry.

Watching her mature, treasuring each small distinction from the norm, Deirdre's suspicion grew that God did perhaps exist, had created Maureen Sterling and given her to Deirdre — consolation prize for innocence lost or too cheaply bartered; a treasure to nurture against a world hostile to what it could not corrupt — and at the right moment to exhibit that treasure. Could the right moment be a short month away? On a medal platform in Montegreco? Deirdre smiled. If Roxanne, favourite, had 'flu or something equally weakening, perhaps it was a hint from God? An unsporting hint, perhaps, but where was it written that God was a good sport? Besides, Roxanne already had Grant Rivers. How greedy, to expect a medal too.

*

The doctor gazed down from his heavily draped window into the sleeted traffic of midday Harley Street. 'Maureen, I know you've been sheltered, but you certainly understand the doctor-patient relationship is privileged. You're asking me to breach a confidence.'

'I am not! You're the *family* GP. Mother told me she was seeing a shrink! For anxiety or something, and instead —'

'I've steered her towards other physicians, too. She *is* anxious.'

'Sick people are,' Maureen said steadily. 'So am I. She's weaker every day and none of you seem to be doing much. I have a right to know.'

'It's a question of professional ethics. You're young —'

'And preparing for the Olympics, right? She told you not to upset me, right? Maureen Sterling, England's bright candle in the dark, right?'

The doctor examined his hands. 'She didn't have to. You're all over the media. Perhaps you're worrying about nothing.'

'If I am, I trust you to tell me so. You're our doctor.'

He turned away. 'Perhaps if you discussed it with your father . . .'

'*Him*?' Pouring the scorn of a lifetime into a single word, she picked up her skate-bag and ran down to the waiting taxi. Hard enough getting away from Mother as it was, and now this opportunity, a pretend manicure, wasted. She knew no more than when she'd arrived.

The doctor, watching from the window, was reminded of some delicate bird, a heron perhaps, and was deeply glad that Maureen Sterling was not his daughter, would not have to face what Maureen soon must. He'd wondered, once, how Lloyd Sterling had managed to produce anything so breathtakingly lovely as that child, but then there were the blood tests, which had answered everything.

From the rink Maureen called Sterling Enterprises and asked her father's personal secretary — elderly, discreet, who'd known Maureen all her life — where Lloyd could be reached. 'He was in Macao, dear, hot on the trail of some investment. It could be Florida by now. How's the ice?'

'Cold. Give me the numbers, will you?' She tried the suite in Macao first. A young man answered in a silky Oriental accent. Houseboy? She gave him the benefit of the doubt.

'Sorry, missy, Mr Sterling in Palm Beach —'

Uncharacteristically, she didn't even thank him, just hung up and called Florida. Lloyd was at his desk.

'Look,' she began, 'I know you don't give a damn about her — or me for that matter — but Mother is ill and seeing doctors all over London. They'll tell me nothing so's not to worry me before the damned Games, but you're her husband, they *have* to tell you! Just call the old family faithful.' She babbled on and on, couldn't seem to stop until finally he did it for her.

'How's the skating? And what d'you hear from Jeff?'

'Didn't you hear me? I'm telling you Mother is ill, maybe very ill!'

'And I'm asking about you and my protégé in a civilized manner.'

She pictured him, grey on grey on grey, variations on a theme of barracuda. 'I am skating fine and from all accounts so is Jeff. Now. What are you going to do about Mother?'

Across the wide Atlantic she almost heard his smile. 'Deirdre is in her fifties,' he said smoothly. 'Old enough to take care of herself.'

'You are the *coldest* —'

'Young lady —' He flicked the word with the lightest weight of disdain as he paused to select his harpoon. 'You must be aware that any time I choose I can pull those fine Persian rugs out from under. Yes, I know her state of health. I provide the resources. What more do you expect?'

'Nothing. I should have known that. She always has.'

'Careful. You're deeply indebted to me already.'

'Oh, we all know you pass out credit slips like after-dinner mints, but we're your family, not protégés like Jeff.'

'Maureen!' Harpoon turned to whip and she felt herself flinch. 'That ice of yours on which I have melted a small fortune is not the only treacherous surface in your life. If I were you . . .'

'You're not, thank God.' Something hard and cold settled

43

in her chest. She was about to hang up when an unbidden thought turned verbal, jumped out of her mouth before she could stop it. 'But if I should *win* the Olympics, Daddy, it will be through *her* resources, not yours. Remember that!'

If I should win the Olympics. *Win? Win?* Light as a breeze, the memory of her mother's touch, soft but constant, at her shoulder: *Why not, Maureen darling, why not?*

CHAPTER THREE

Los Angeles

At 6.50 AM on a Wednesday morning, three-and-a-half weeks before the Olympics, Roxanne Braun Kramer, in a shell-pink practice dress that added a faint glow to her delicate, cameo-like colour, skated her original short programme without a flaw. Immediately thereafter, to build stamina and confidence before the session ended, Grant Rivers signalled her to remain at centre-ice and slotted the cassette for her long programme into the tape player. She sighed, nodded, and took up her opening stance.

It happened less than thirty seconds into the sprightly, playful opening of 'Jewels of the Madonna'.

Grant, adjusting volume, had his back to the ice; the juniors were already off, swarming around the hot-chocolate machine, missing not a moment's action on the ice as they blew and sipped, sipped and blew. Which, among the intensively training Olympians, was hitting or missing what? Who looked in trouble? What fragment of gossip could be savoured over algebra, embroidered in Spanish I, rehearsed in English Comp? All for dramatic delivery at ice-ballet class this afternoon? In the engineer's annex the Polar Bear machine rumbled over the snow-pit, ready to smooth out gouges, frost piles and crevasses, to iron the ice to a flawless sheet of glass — but the operator knew the sport; these athletes, like race-horses, needed their gallops. What was five minutes? Besides, Kramer in action was a feast to be savoured. He let the great machine purr, envying Grant Rivers his rumoured privileges.

On the top row of the bleachers Emma Crisp juggled next week's judging assignments, deciding to duck a few; the car's clutch was sticking, and no way could she afford repairs this month.

Ben Carlsen stood behind her, eyes glued to his daughter Lise at the top of an overhead lift that teetered one way then another. Dag should steady her better than that!

Noni Kramer, in the dim recesses of the lost-and-found closet, well out of sight of Grant, sorted through treasures left behind by the 'publics' the night before, wasteful nobodies who skated the evening public sessions, notoriously careless with expensive sweaters. 'Publics' didn't even bother to enquire after them; the janitor tossed them in the closet and carted them off to the charity shop twice a week. A disgrace. Skaters' mothers scrimped, and all the time cashmere and lamb's wool sweaters lay around for the taking. This morning Noni found two: a fine-stitch black alpaca, and a bulky Aran knit, off-white, practically new. After a moment's reflection she tossed the Aran back. White added size. Roxanne must look slender.

Five skaters remained on ice.

Beejay, in cherry red, set her teeth and hurtled down the west end of the rink like a fire-cracker for another shot at a triple-toe, the timing of which had for the moment deserted her. 'Jesus Christ,' she muttered, picking herself up and going for it again.

Jeff Dunsmuir worked complex footwork at the top-end under the pipe organ, last remaining link with an era when couples swayed and lilted like figures on a music box. The organ was now a museum piece among hi-tech video gear and the rattle of mega vitamins from every skate bag. Lise Carlsen, down from her lift, was where she liked to be, close to the ice in the comparative safety of a death spiral. The most she could fall now was three inches. If she could get her head *all* the way down, where it was supposed to be (but got her hair wet), she'd have no distance to fall at all! Dag clenched his teeth, wishing she'd put *something* into it so it wouldn't be like dragging a sack of potatoes round his ankles.

With 'Jewels of the Madonna' filling the rink, nobody really watched Roxanne closely. She wasn't into the jumps yet, and everyone knew the lyrically choreographed opening almost as well as she did.

The music swelled towards the first jump, a double-axel. Grant and Emma looked up; Beejay, Jeff, and the Carlsen twins all moved to the rail. Noni, in lost-and-found, peered around the slightly open door. They saw Roxanne gather necessary speed through the corner, turn to a firm forward edge and prepare to throw the right leg up, up, up — high enough to lift and rotate her two-and-a-half times and bring her safely, gracefully, triumphantly down in what was always her finest jump. Which this morning would not lift.

The slender leg thrust up and out, but the rest of her seemed undecided about following it — until the leg dropped again, too weak to pull the load.

She did not fall. Instead she skidded to an awkward stop and looked back, puzzled, as if searching for lost impetus, strength, which should have been there when she asked for it. Then her colour ebbed, a tide which started at her forehead and washed slowing down until her face turned to chalk under the harsh white lights. Dreamily, a surprised smile on her face, she sank down to the ice until she was lying on her side. She could have been taking a nap.

Everyone, bound by the doctrine that skaters aren't *helped* up until it's obvious they can't *get* up, waited at least half-a-minute as 'Jewels of the Madonna' drifted ghostly and light-footed on the empty ice. Then Grant, snapping the tape deck mute, vaulted the rail, picked her up, and carried her to the bench. Setting her down, he beckoned Emma.

'Fainted,' he muttered, raking the bystanders with a glance. 'Find her a drink, okay? I'll bring my car to the back, get her the hell out of here.'

'*Nein! Oh, nein!*' Noni shrieked, darting out of lost-and-found, still clutching the black sweater. 'I take her to *my* doctor!'

Grant waved her aside, a field surgeon swatting a gnat. 'Off! Give her one more bloody pill and I'll have you arrested for practising without a license. Now get out before I have the cops chuck you out. A sensational headline that would make for Montegreco, huh? "Olympic Champion's Mother Banned from the Rink"!'

Roxanne stirred. Colour crept back into her face. 'Grant —'

Every ear in the rink stretched in their direction. 'Shhhh.

47

You hit your head, knocked you dizzy, it's nothing. I'll drive you home, secure the door, then come back here to finish up. I'll send my own doctor over to see you. And don't let your mother in — she doesn't have the new key.' Across several feet of ice he looked straight into Noni's face, a bitter, harder, version of her daughter's. Their glances clashed like cold steel, then shifted to softer targets. Noni stroked Roxanne's forehead and muttered endearments in German.

'Emma,' Grant said quietly. 'you and Beejay hang around awhile, okay?'

Emma, thoughtful, tapped her teeth with her pencil. 'Sure,' she said. 'Sure.'

The rest couldn't get out of the rink fast enough.

Jeff Dunsmuir called London, waking Dierdre Sterling from her afternoon rest.

'She just . . . *fainted*?' Deirdre said, her voice fuzzy with sleep.

'Yep. Skinny as hell. Thought you ought to know.'

'But how sick, I mean we barely *know* her! Do we send flowers or something? Goodness, she's not out of competition, is she?'

'Heck no, I just thought you might be pleased, that's all.'

Deirdre caught her breath. 'Oh Jeff, how unsporting! You've always said Roxanne was sweet to you. Of *course* we're not pleased! And don't dare tell anyone we are, or even that you called us! It's despicable!'

She hung up, turned the electric blanket to high, and pulled the comforter tight around her shoulders. Drifting back into sleep, she smiled. Jeff wasn't half the innocent she'd thought; he'd be able to handle himself with Lloyd quite well after all.

As for Maureen, well . . . Deirdre relaxed. Her daughter's chances had never looked better. Maybe God was on their side at last. 'Thank you very much, God,' she whispered into the empty room. Fleetingly, she thought of poor Roxanne, who'd seemed quite a nice girl — but she still had Grant for consolation and no one could, or should, have everything.

Lise Carlsen called a Japanese skier who trained in Hokkaido. 'Know Mieko Nakashima, your Lady champ? Trains in Tokyo?'

The friend laughed. 'Who doesn't? Her grandfather could *buy* it! Didn't know you were friends.'

'We met at last year's Worlds is all.' Friends? Lise shuddered. The Nakashima girl was shy, unremarkable — but Mieko's cousin, competitor in the 70-metre hill, glowed as darkly in her memory as an Oriental god. And yes, the family was indeed rich. The girl would surely welcome today's little morsel. She knew *she* would! And if she, Lise, scratched one Nakashima back, maybe another Nakashima would later scratch hers. Worth a try. Never let a rich boy languish, that was her motto. 'Tell Mieko to tell her mom that Roxanne Kramer's not feeling so hot, huh?'

'Oh-ho!'

'Yeah. Like passing out and stuff. See you, huh? If my brother doesn't drop me before Montegreco.'

Noni, throwing caution clear across the Pacific, called Frau Braun in Bonn. 'Mutti, our girl is weak, weak. That idiot Grant Rivers is pushing too hard. He's obsessed with making her eat. My doctor says let her stomach rest, purge her of toxins, she'd be fine within the week!'

'Now listen.' A hint of asperity crept into Frau Braun's voice. Doubts as to Noni's stability crackled across the ocean loud and clear. 'Leave her alone. Have them take out some jumps, add more spins —'

'God, she's doing all of them *now*.'

'Oh no, she is not. You forget *my* spin, the Braun spin!'

'That antique?'

'I too am an antique, but my name is on that move and I am still alive. Who will perform it if not my granddaughter?'

'Nobody, Mutti, believe me. Nobody!'

Frau Braun stared at the dead receiver and hung up. Another coach, privy to the Bonn end of the exchange, called *her* friend at the Garmisch Partenkirchen rink, where the German Lady champion trained. After the briefest chat the friend laughed heartily, said she'd believe it when she saw it, but would pass the word anyway. The Braun Spin, indeed!

*

After tucking Roxanne into bed and scrambling up three eggs in cream, Grant stood over her until she ate the lot, followed by a plump peach. Then he kissed her and phoned the doctor for an appointment before hurrying back to the rink, where Emma and Beejay waited. Thank God for Emma and Beejay.

Waiting at a red light, his mind a sudden blank, Grant felt a forgotten voice touch the back of his memory. He winced, trying to dismiss it, but it clung, and carried the accents of Swansea and his old Coach. *Play fair, dai bach, it's only a sport.*

A conscience, after four intense years at the coaching game. But a mistake to listen if you wanted to win. Roxanne, ever anxious to please, was still vulnerable. Noni's fault. When Grant took over, Roxi had been at anorexia's half way house — binge today, starve tomorrow. Now it seemed she was set on a return trip. Competition nerves, and maybe Noni, must be getting to her. But much as he loved her he could not be her guardian angel, not if he wanted a career too. Roxanne was no child. This morning shed an ominous new light on Montegreco. If she had to withdraw, or simply turned sour and skated like hell, then he had to write a fall-back script now, while there was time. Time.

Emma still worked her sheets, efficient, matter-of-fact. Next to Roxi, who this morning had looked like a wax taper in an old Spanish church, Emma Crisp was a sea-breeze right off Malibu.

He sent Beejay to warm up, blinking against the clash of ginger hair and that darting cherry-red dress, before drawing Emma into the musty quiet of the organ loft for a very private chat. Which surprised Emma some, but not much. She'd figured out what was coming. Nobody could say Rivers was not resourceful, which was why she'd picked him for Beejay's coach in the first place.

'Normally I'd figure it was too soon,' he was saying in his English voice with that odd lilt on the end of it, 'Beejay's young, and needs a lot of polish — and there's Roxanne in her path. But you saw what happened this morning. If Roxi blows it the country loses Gold. I don't think the Japanese can get it — all jumps and no technique. Her landings scratch like hell and the judges are close enough to hear, right? Which leaves an opening pretty high up for Beejay, if —'

Emma held up her hand. 'You keep ignoring the Germans and that other. Silver or somebody, she's a new breed, believe you me.'

Maybe it was the gloom of the unlit loft, maybe old skating ghosts haunting this room for Emma — her husband had played the organ for the Club dance sessions before the new sound system appeared — but for a moment she saw something shift in Grant Rivers' face. Hard, soft, then hard. A coach, then a sixteen-year-old curly-topped competitor tense as a young animal seeing its image in a mirror, the next moment back to the hard-driving trainer in his thirties, hungry for glory. And suddenly angry.

'If she's that good, where was she before Europeans? There are no dark horses. If they're great we've seen 'em. Besides, I'm going to beat her. If not with Roxanne, then with Beejay. Sterling will *not* win, leave it to me.'

Emma's eyebrows shot up. Sterling! *That* was the name. And *Grant knew it and was going to beat her!* As if he personally would skate against her! Interesting. 'I thought you didn't know her,' she said mildly.

He kept every feature even, smooth, but the effort showed. 'I know the family. What I started to say is, *if* Roxanne blows it, we need strength at the team's front-end. Beejay's got the jumps but she needs ballet from now down to the wire. We've got three weeks to make a fireball into a swan.'

Damn if he wasn't the kid again, pleading for an extra ride on the roller coaster. But something stiffened in her own spine. 'I'll go along with extra ballet, smooth her some, but otherwise she's fine the way she is. If she comes across like a fireball, that's Beejay. I want her that way, not cloned into a Kramer or a Sterling. It wouldn't take, anyway. She's immune. And I won't have her used as ammo in some war I know nothing about.'

He turned a deep brick-red. 'Meaning?'

Good. She'd struck a nerve. 'Whatever you think I mean.'

He worked with Beejay on two hours of empty ice, at the end

of which there was little difference. She was a brilliant technician on the fast stuff, but she needed a set of brakes more than she needed a coach.

'Dammit, Beejay, *listen* to the music. It's romantic, Romeo and Juliet. Try to look like you're in love!' She rolled her eyes and missed the next combo. 'Look,' he pleaded. 'At your age there must be *some* kid you'd like to date, huh? Think about him. Skate for him.' Blank silence. Clearly there was nobody. 'Who *do* you skate for?' he insisted.

She popped her gum and wrinkled her freckles. 'God, I never thought about it. Me, I guess. I just like to skate.'

While this baffling kid unlaced her boots, Grant edged over to Emma at the rail. 'She's single-minded, an absolute innocent.'

'Uh-huh. And I want her kept that way.'

All the way home he thought about that, remembering when he'd been innocent, when he'd loved to skate for skating's sake, before Deirdre, before Mum died, before he knew there was a future on the ice, something beyond the sheer challenge of doing impossible things on a knife-edge and making it look easy, inevitable. He wondered if Roxanne had ever known that. No. Noni's ambition ruled them both.

He expected Roxanne to be in bed resting, perhaps waiting for him to make love to her. Instead she was working out to an aerobic video, her red leotard black with sweat. Christ! And for this sick girl he'd called the doctor to come out as a personal favour! Snapping the video off, he hurled the tape into the trash and pulled a panting Roxanne to her feet. 'Just what in hell are you doing?'

Her eyes were wide, scared. 'Working out, what else?'

Her thin shoulder-blades cupped in his palms, he felt control slip away as he began to shake her until her teeth rattled like castanets and beads of her sweat sprayed over him. 'You weren't working out! You were working off three eggs and a peach, weren't you? Weren't you? *Weren't you?*'

Her lips quivered. 'Don't yell,' she whimpered. 'Please don't yell at me, don't hit me, I won't do it ag —'

Hit her? He felt like *he'd* been mauled. 'I've never hit you. I never would. Why do you even *say* that?'

She swallowed, dried her eyes, and slowly the confession came sobbing out. 'When I was little and missed a jump Mom used to take me to the girl's room and . . . and pull my pants down in front of everybody and hit me with my skate guards . . . and they knew, all the girls knew I'd skated bad, and I couldn't ever skate bad because I was a Braun and had to be best . . .'

He drew in a long, shuddering breath and brushed tangled wet hair out of her eyes, his own knees suddenly weak. 'I'm sorry, I won't yell at you any more, that's a promise. But the doctor will be here in an hour and you're not a little girl now. You have to tell him the truth.'

'But I'm still a Braun.'

'The best of them. Noni wasn't, but that's her problem. There's only one person can hurt you now, and that's you.'

She shook her head. 'There's you. If I win the Games maybe you'll love me, maybe. And if I lose —' Her pale-blue eyes, wide open, vulnerable, locked into his, pleading for an answer.

Slowly he nodded. What choice did he have? 'I'll love you anyway.'

'You're just saying that.'

'No,' he said steadily. 'I mean it.'

But all the time he was stripping her, showering her, drying her tenderly with a soft, fluffy towel, all the time his lips travelled over her bones, her fragrant, transluscent flesh, her freshly washed hair, he knew himself for a fraud. When the time came to enter her, to prove to them both that he did indeed love this frail vessel, he closed his eyes and mouthed a name silently into the pillow, drew on a picture from the far distant past. A memory of a room very different from this, all pink and cream, Oriental rugs flowering on the parquet, the bed an oasis, the creature in it a mature woman, an Eve whose pearly fingernail drawn across a stainless skate blade was the most sensuous image he could remember, the resilient thrust of her nipples to his tongue the only texture in his world, the place inside her a warm, pulsing haven to his new, driving passion.

Drifting towards sleep, he wondered when Roxanne would cross that emotional barrier from girlhood to womanhood? Make decisions for herself without benefit of direction? Or had Noni's ministrations, far from tender, forever trapped her inside a childhood she should have long since outgrown?

CHAPTER FOUR

Moscow, USSR

The matched visiting cards of Deirdre and Maureen Sterling could have been hot coals the way Alexei Finsky handled them, each by its well-thumbed corner.

Sterling House, Haslemere, Surrey, England
and
Casa Plata, Palamos, Costa Brava, Spain

The second a Spanish holiday villa, one more Sterling cliff-top roost, nothing more — but enough, surely it would be enough.

When, at the European Championships, they'd casually invited him to drop in for a day or so after the Games, did they know his heart leapt in his chest, that he'd rushed to the atlas to confirm that, yes! Yes! Palamos was little more than a hundred kilometres from Montegreco, that the very idea flung open doors to the dream of his life, that even through the writhing, precipitous roads of the Pyrenees a fast car could surely make Montegreco to Palamos in under two hours?

With planning, nerve, and considerable sacrifice, Alexei Finsky, Solo Mens Champion of all the Russias and the world, and strongly favoured to take Mens Olympic Gold, could flee the system. Two hours to freedom if the Spanish authorities were sympathetic. If not, then the French were just across the border . . . If not them, any one of the embassies. The Sterling name carried influence, could move the Pyrenees if necessary, and if it suited the Sterling whim.

Through all the weeks since Europeans, every midnight

he had checked his wallet, afraid the precious cards would be gone. No. Always the cards lay safe, tight between his ID and that other ticket to ride, a 'Merited Master of Sport' certificate, passport to endless perks the average Russian dare not dream of. But the Sterling cards promised all that and more.

The havoc they'd wrought, those elegant cards, in him and those around him. Their embossed letters rich to his fingertips, smooth, tormenting, unbearably inviting to the touch . . .

But smoother than Galina's soft breast? More inviting than her smile, her endless faith in him? More tormenting than the weight of betrayal, which, once committed, could never be retracted?

He frowned, slipping the cards in his pocket when a light footfall sounded in the great foyer of the Sports Centre. It was Galina, of course, colleague since childhood, from whom he had few secrets. In their teens they'd shared triumphs and tragedies, and on occasion the comfort of each other's arms — defeat was a colder bedmate than the ice itself. Of late he'd been undefeated, in small need of comfort, but still they shared an apartment and much of their lives.

She refused to marry until after the Olympics. The unspoken question hovered between them, a stumbling block mightier than the Urals, of greater moment than the Olympics themselves.

She spoke quietly now, with caution. 'So write to the Sterlings if you must. Nobody will shout "Stop!" Such friends could be useful to you, yes?' Useful. So she did know. Soon he must ask her.

She fell silent as a coach slammed through the door, cursing. 'Skaters!' he shouted. 'Do they think medals drop like plums off the tree? In my day —' And disappeared through another door.

'I'm giving the juniors a Stretch session,' she murmured. 'Want to come? Show them some *real* flexibility?'

Was that a feline innuendo at the heart of the compliment? No. He grew paranoid. But she was offering more than a stretch class. To walk to the gym — there could be no listeners out of doors — presented a chance to confide;

if he could trust anyone with what pounded daily upon the walls of his mind it was Galina, who it would most affect. But Stretch? He almost laughed. He was racked already, his nerves tighter than fiddle strings pulled between love and ambition. An ambition aglow with riches, fame, and, above all, freedom. But without Galina, where did freedom live? He shook his head. 'I need to sleep a little.' And think. 'Later we're due at the club for orientation.' Meaning pep-talk, propaganda.

'Then we stop by my family?' she said. 'I promised. They are so proud.' As always her voice softened at the thought of her family and the fact that Alexei had none.

A year ago his mother had died in circumstances that, had she known, would have squeezed at her heart more painfully than the attack that brought death itself. She hadn't known. Neither had he. He'd been winning a world title for the USSR. They saved the bad news for the plane trip home, characteristically attacking before they could be attacked. '*Of course* we gave her a fine cremation, with full honours due the mother of our champion! How *could* we tell you, you were about to take the ice at the major turning-point of your career. Would we be so insensitive? And if you'd known, what could you have done? You have our deepest sympathy.'

Of course. But cremation? For his fervently Orthodox mother? *Dear God.*

Later, going through her things, he found her old Bible in its place behind the panelling. Riffling the pages he read aloud the words his parents had read to the small Alexei. The wrinkled, well-used pages, their measured cadences, brought her back, showed him at last what she had been and what she had given up to buy his medals.

Secrets, his life a pack of lies which mattered to nobody now. But lies corroded; they'd eaten into her conscience until she was a bitter shell who prayed to the God of Moses and Abraham secretly in her room, who kept to herself, obeyed the dietary rules, yet shunned her own people; to associate openly would, she said, have shadowed Alexei's career. Perhaps she'd been right.

When, in Kalinin, the six-year-old Alexei had announced he would become a skater, she'd laughed. 'Sports?' she said.

'My son, sports are for empty people who must fill empty days. Real life is medicine, music, commerce, law. Ice skating indeed! Our people are not athletes!' But a skater he had become, which made the move to Moscow necessary, and forever after changed their lives. He was accepted into a training school and allowed home once a month. Her hold on him began to slip until she could no longer grasp the simplest facet of his disciplined life on the ice.

Now, walking with Galina down the corridor, the need to pour out his heart almost overwhelmed him. But this was not the place, filled as it was with more holes than a beggar's coat. The sports complex crawled with athletes, coaches, and nameless, faceless officials bristling with authority, notebooks, and large ears.

Recent years had brought advances, minor freedoms, but this was not the West. Freedom and the means to travel abroad came to pitifully few. He was lucky — but his luck could disappear at the drop of an ill-chosen word.

At the apartment he unpacked and set aside the latest perk, a team cap of the finest Pushkino sable designed to impress the world at the opening ceremonies. In the bitter Moscow winters Galina's father needed it more than he, who had a dozen such caps and only one head, which was seldom outdoors long enough to require a cover. He read the label on the package. 'Alexei Finsky, Merited Master of Sport'. The highest honour a skater could achieve — but the perks gave the title weight. How eagerly bureaucrats heaped rewards on the successful in this patently unsuccessful regime. Car, apartment, a *dacha* in the country. All bounty from a grateful nation, prizes which could melt faster than the ice itself if ever he chose to switch to a less strenuous line of work.

But who in his right mind would pass up travel outside the Block — for which any Russian would give his last ruble? Of course he would go to the Games. With only three more weeks to countdown, the machinery gathered momentum every day, his schedule crammed with ice-time, massages, dance classes, refreshers in Spanish and French, even a crash course in conversational Catalan. And the inevitable, inescapable invitation to take coffee with the Director:

What a superb opportunity he had to win, yes? Alexei

would do his best. (They admired modesty.) How honoured he must be that the State, from its teeming millions, had selected him on whom to lavish a lifetime of training, and then reward him when that training, all free, paid off? But of course. Gratitude overwhelmed him.

Yes, indeed. Alexei Finsky (aka Alexei Feinstein, if only to himself) was so inflated with gratitude he could have floated to the top of the nearest onion dome and shaken his fist at the city, run pell-mell through the show-place halls of the underground and punched out the nearest armed guard with bare knuckles, his head, and his over-educated feet, twin assets which made him at once a prince and a prisoner. The temptation, oh, God, the temptation to get *out*!

But where? His only marketable skill was to move across a sheet of ice with athleticism and consummate grace. The UK? The USA? And could Galina be persuaded to go with him? — a trick infinitely more complex than the quadruple-axel, which, if he missed it, would cost him the Gold. He did not intend to miss.

Galina's parents drew him into the apartment, two middle-aged peasants eager to touch, to worship at the shrine of their famous daughter's even more famous fiancé, who they'd seen just that moment on television winning the world title last year. In the run-up to the Games, Alexei's image was on some screen somewhere in the USSR every moment of the day.

Galina's mother poured tea over lemon slices, releasing a sharp citron scent into the tiny kitchen. There was butter and black bread, and a small piece of ham sausage, for which she'd queued two hours that morning. 'Maybe this time Galina will also win a medal,' she said wistfully.

Galina shook her head. 'Not now they've dropped school figures, Mama. Between Kramer, Sterling, Nakashima, Crisp, and maybe the German, I don't have a chance. There are more good skaters than mushrooms in the forest.'

'Don't be too sure about Kramer,' Alexei said. 'I forgot to tell you. Igor called. Somebody on the Olympic Committee in LA says Kramer's sick, fainted or something. It could give you a better placement.' But he doubted it. As usual, the

USSR was strong in every event but Ladies. Galina would be about eighth depending on who judged and how Kramer skated. Galina made the team because she was the best available. Good but not great. Still, her parents smiled with love and pride upon their daughter's milk-maid complexion. Alexei saw her squeeze her mother's hand, softening the shattered hope. 'Watch for me anyway. That long spiral you like, the coach says it's too easy? I'll put it in just for you.'

For which the coach would give her much heat. Dear, foolish Galina.

Her father frowned. 'Will it get you in trouble?' Ten years in a labour camp had ravaged his courage more deeply than his body. His reaction to the mildest proposal never varied: could it get them in trouble?

'No, Papa,' Galina lied, looking at the clock and giving them each a fierce, spontaneous hug. 'We're busy from now to the Games, then we come for a big dinner, okay? But now we have gifts from Europeans. Perfume for Mama from Paris, tobacco from Italy for Papa. And also for Papa, but *after* the Games, a hat. *Such* a hat! Alexei, "Merited Master of Sport" and soon your son-in-law, will present you with the hat of the Official Olympic Gold Medal Winner.' She smoothed the lines between his eyes. 'Don't worry, Papa. After the Games he will be permitted to give it to you. Imagine! A Pushkino sable!'

Over her father's head, Alexei felt her glance touch him, question him. Gold Medal Winner. And the other. Son-in-law.

Lately, every dream she wove had the same codicil: after the Games.

Next session, when his music swelled through the arena, other skaters willingly cleared the ice as usual for the World and Soviet Champion.

Jump here, spin here, smile here, drop the arms, close the eyes, lift the head, three-turn here, give the camera a profile, turn again, blaze the eyes into TV lenses, drench the audience in drama, the judges in admiration. Breathe with the music, ache with the composer, orchestrate every emotion, just as he'd been taught.

He was done, his performance the joint effort of many talents. Ballet master, drama coach, skating coach, programme director, dietician, costumier. In the process, Alexei struggled to hold an emotional centre constantly swamped by the impassioned input of a multitude.

Today he'd skated well, the landings nailed solid, smooth, no visible effort. The applause of his peers ringing over the ice, he stroked slowly around the edges, wondering vaguely what kept Galina. This close to the Games she could not miss a session.

'*Alexei!*'

She was there, waiting for him at the rail, still in street clothes, no skates on her feet, no skate-bag on the bench. An injury?

'No.' Tears glittered in her eyes. And Galina was no weeper.

'Darling, what —'

'Later, under Pozharsky in the Square.'

God, what had happened? An accident to her parents? Trouble with the aunt in Leningrad? Still an hour before he could leave, always the postmortem with the coach after a session; morning; afternoon; evening. Damn.

In Red Square she was pacing the pavement around the statue of Prince Pozharsky, oblivious to the disciplined lines at Lenin's tomb and a few intrepid tourists wiping frost from camera lenses.

'Let's walk.' Alexei took her arm, leading her quickly through anonymous alleyways towards the melting Moskva, ice-floes clotting its shallow, remorseless flow.

On the riverbank, if they walked and talked fast enough, they could not be overheard. 'Tell me,' he said quickly, pulling her with him, catching the spring violet scent of her hair and a powerful impression of fear and need. The way he'd felt when they told him about Mother.

'I've been dropped from the team,' she said quietly.

He stopped mid-stride, panic scrabbling between his ears. This changed everything. *Galina wasn't going, wasn't going . . .*

'They can't drop you!' he shouted. 'Three weeks from the Games they'd never —'

'Shhh! They have. The Director called me this morning.'

'They can't,' he repeated flatly.

Her next breath was a ragged sob. 'My replacement has her parade uniform already. A perfect fit. Amazing, no?'

He stopped her on a bleak, deserted corner. 'Why? Did they say?' The unexplained was dangerous, as Galina's father knew all too well. Galina's replacement, at fourteen, had no foreign experience, could no more control competition nerves than Alexei could stop the Moskva in its flow. There was doubt even about her talent. 'What reason did they give?'

'None.'

'And what do *you* think?' He knew, but he had to ask.

The lines of her face seemed to melt, settle. Already she accepted. 'Two reasons. I have a better chance of a medal than she does, so we discount that. Which leaves . . . you. Alexei Finsky. You have no family. I am *all* you have. You're almost certain to win Gold — which outside the Bloc is worth a fortune. Surely it is obvious? With me trapped here in Moscow you will be more likely to return. That's what they think.'

'Bastards!'

'But you *do* consider defecting, no? You hoped I would leave with you?'

Oh, God, he'd wanted to wait until Montegreco, after the medal, the prospect of a future cushioned in luxury, a lucrative show contract to sway her, a contract for them both. He'd rehearsed all his arguments. 'We could meet your parents some place else, at least once a year. Yugoslavia perhaps — maybe we could even get them out of Russia.'

She turned on him, her eyes a blaze of blue. 'Who says they *want* to go? How can you fool yourself? My father's afraid to go to the Baltic for a summer holiday, he's afraid his own shadow will get him in trouble.'

'All that's changed now. Everything's eased up.'

'Convince him. Besides, you have not asked me. I don't *want* to go to the West. I am not a political animal. This is my home. I am Russian.'

'Yes but —'

'And so, Alexei, are you. Your parents, grandparents, great-grandparents were all Russian. This is your homeland!'

He stared into the face of a stranger. 'Look, when we first

met I told you the truth, remember? I'm a Jew. A *Jew*.'

She nodded from many miles away. How did she get so far so fast? 'A *Russian* Jew, Alexei. Which you'll always be no matter how you skate or how you hide. The State spent years training you to be what you are.'

'With a little help from me?'

Fresh tears sprang to her eyes, but now they were bright with anger. At him. 'Don't be sarcastic! It takes fifteen years to build a World Class champion — and if you shatter a knee before you're ripe? No, Alexei, your career was a gamble the State took because *they believed in you*.'

'But *I* don't believe in *them! You apparently do*!' he shouted.

Instinctively they each looked behind them. 'See?' he said. 'We're not even free to have an argument. The apartment is bugged —'

'We can't be sure of that.'

'In New York we could have a fistfight in Rockerfeller Plaza and be sure nobody gave a damn.'

'That is such a privilege? To abuse and nobody to care? If they're so open why do they need a CIA?'

'Come *on*, Galina! You're being deliberately naïve!'

'But I am not disloyal.'

'You are to *me*! We're engaged.'

'I thought so, too.'

Her lip quivered and he thought then she might break, but her mouth was set firm and she stepped well away.

'I didn't know you were a thief then. When you sell the medal for a fat contract in the West, strike a good bargain, Alexei. We all invested very much more than we could afford.'

'We?'

'Myself, yes. My family. And the State. The medal will belong to all of us who gave you our hearts, who took pride in your talent. When you sell your talent and the medal for a show contract you will sell stolen property. You will be nothing more than a fence.'

She squared her slender mink-coated shoulders, tilted her head Bolshoi fashion and marched gracefully away. When she bumped into a parked pram he realised she was weeping and took the first step to run after her, stop her, promise to come back to her no matter what.

But she'd reached the top of the bank, the Kremlin walls a grim backdrop to her hurrying, loyal figure. Loyal not to him, now, but to the State.

He stood dead still and cupped his hands over his mouth. '*Galina*!' he shouted, his voice bouncing off stone walls and cobblestones. '*How does it feel to be a hostage of the State*?'

CHAPTER FIVE

LA County, California

Roxanne looked on Dr Jasinski, father of Grant's racquetball partner, with growing suspicion. Grant said he was a great guy, but . . .

Stooped, bespectacled, he'd spoken to her briefly at the apartment, then directed her to his clinic to 'talk to her with a nurse present'. The clinic, in the poorest part of town, sat peeling in the sun; a scruffy black tot played 'jacks' on its front step, and the windows were painted over.

Now he'd kept her here too long, asked questions Mom's doctor never asked, touched where Mom's doctor never touched. She tried to signal that she was tired, wanted to leave, but for half-an-hour this man had ignored her every hint. In the waiting room outside she heard patients chatting, coughing, shuffling. Surely they needed him more than she did?

'Your last period?' he said, probing the flaccid tissue of a breast.

'I am *not* pregnant!' she cried. 'I have ballet this afternoon and you'll make me late.'

'Please do not shout. I hear well. I understand. Relax. I know you are not pregnant. I ask again. Have you missed periods.'

Oh, hell, what did it matter? 'So I'm irregular. Am I tied to a damned calendar?'

'But you still have them, that is good,' he said evenly, as if remarking on the weather. 'You know you are . . . somewhat underweight?'

'I'm an athlete. We don't run to fat.'

'Nor do corpses as a rule. You know of course that you

flirt with anorexia. This is not the first time, I think.'

God, that word! Ignore it! 'Who says? Who told you that?'

He shrugged. She made herself concentrate on his old-fashioned suit, his shirt darned at the cuff, his watch from an era other than this. Pathetic.

'I think that you know all the tricks,' he was saying. 'You eat alone when you can? Play games with food? Work-out to burn-up what you have consumed? Tell me, do you also make yourself vomit?'

Hang in, Roxi. Don't let him get to you. She stared resolutely at the ceiling, unblemished but for a T-bone shaped stain near the light fixture. 'No I don't. I just have to be slim to win the Olympics, that's all.' To keep Grant, placate Mom, please the grandparents . . .

'Young woman, you are not stupid. You are more than slim. Almost emaciated. Do you still know the difference?' For a moment he turned to the window, his hands clenched tight on the sill. Then he signalled her to dress, dismissed the nurse, and directed her to his office.

'I understand your mother is German,' he began softly, cautiously. 'I imagine she was born soon after the War. Perhaps she has told you of the Camps? Of Oswiecim, Treblinka, Maidanek . . .' He would have listed more but his voice had begun to tremble.

'She just said when she was little she saw a movie of Auschwitz.'

'That's the German name for Oswiecim. It's in Poland. I was born there. I, too, was a child when I saw Oswiecim, but not at the movies. We saw it, smelled it. When I was five I saw my first corpse, a girl in her teens, dead of starvation.' He paused, fought to keep his voice level. 'You understand this was a crime against humanity?'

'But I didn't do it, honest!' God, why was she apologizing?

'What you try to do to yourself, Miss Kramer, is also a crime.'

He turned to the window, staring out onto the crowded roofs of the inner-city, acres of parking jammed with

Toyotas, Hondas, Mazdas, and wheezing, elderly Chevys. Good. Think about cars. Years ago they would have been VW Beetles, saviours of the working girl. He shook his head. This was no good. He inhaled and tried again.

'The dead girl I spoke of, the multitude whose funeral pyres filled my childhood, they had no choice. You begin to suffer now from a fashionable illness, one for which I have little sympathy, I'm sorry. You are the idol of many young girls. If you were my daughter I would be tempted to punish you so perhaps it is good I have only sons.' He sensed rather than saw her alarm. So she had been abused also, this obedient, unhappy child. 'I could direct you to . . . other sources — but I have little faith in them either and by the time they cure you, if they can, it will be too late to achieve your goal. But Grant asked me to help so I try my best. A car with no fuel will not run. A body with no food will not work, eventually will not live. You must seek other advice or help yourself. From my experience, as a species we seem to do better if we help ourselves.'

The girl's eyes looked past him. 'Doctor, I have to be ready for the Games, that's all, and I didn't want to miss Early Ballet.'

He ignored her wailing panic and stared at her, a girl he had watched for years on television, a creature admired and emulated by the young. What he saw, dressed, was a lovely young woman stewing herself in layer on layer of clothes. To make herself sweat. To be thinner. Acceptable. Successful. Lovable. God, how to help her? How to stop his hands shaking?

The nurse brought his afternoon coffee and cookie and an extra cup. Startled, he looked up. So much time spent on one patient!

'Since you have probably missed early class, you'll take coffee, Miss Kramer? Relax, I do not offer you food. Dieting may be your vice; coffee is mine. We all have one. I seldom get to enjoy mine in the company of a famous young woman, so you will indulge me, yes?'

That seemed to be the end of his conversation as he busied himself with the coffee. She watched him add sugar and cream to his, and offered hers black. The yellow napkin with its single large cookie he kept for himself. She tried not to look, but saliva rushed to her tongue and she found herself counting each raisin as it disappeared. Eleven. Ten. Nine . . .

He ate neatly and with great concentration, taking small, identical bites until only a few crumbs were left. Then slowly, like a sacrament, he manoeuvred the remains, crumb by crumb, into the exact centre of the napkin, folded it, and hid the perfect tiny square between his saucer and the empty cup.

Looking up, he flushed a deep, guilty crimson. 'Forgive me. A habit from the past. I learned it from my family, and somehow . . .'

He stopped, perhaps waiting for her to speak, but she didn't know what to say. Sighing, he stood up, squinting as he cleaned his glasses with tissue, and turned again to the window. 'I was taught to hide my crumbs against the rats and our fellow inmates. So perhaps you see, Miss Kramer, why I cannot find more sympathy for your . . . affliction.' His head, his stooped shoulders, the back of his neck, all seemed to shrink against the sky as he muttered, perhaps to himself: 'That first corpse in Oswiecim was my sister. After her my grandparents, my parents, then at last my older brother. They all fed me, the youngest, that I might survive to freedom. To treat the sick.'

Abruptly his spine stiffened and he turned to her, eyes blazing behind the pebble-thick lenses. 'I think you must surely have another class, and I have another patient.' When she didn't, couldn't move, he added in a voice thick with anger or tears, she couldn't tell which, 'You have my permission to leave, Miss Kramer.'

She sat for a long time in the parking lot, stereo off, windows and doors locked, all the bits and pieces of her folded up inside the sanctuary of her car, shaken and shaking, thinking, then hiding from thoughts she could not seem to push away. The nondescript doctor's tale would not leave her, and she couldn't bear anger, cowered against it, wanted to huddle on the floor out of its way . . .

Perhaps he'd lied. But no, her grandparents would starve for her. Certainly Noni, with all her faults, would do anything, anything. And even Grant, who'd given her so much time, maybe even he would die for her if he had to, if she won the Gold. But she didn't want him to die, didn't want anybody to die. Just to not be angry with her, to love her, to help her.

As a species we seem to do better if we help ourselves.

She closed her eyes but he was still there with his stilted, too formal English, his mild, blinking gaze so vulnerable when he took off his glasses, and so terrifying when he turned the thick lenses on her, all the force of his outrage behind them.

Without checking her watch she knew there was time to make Second Ballet but she couldn't find the will to start the car, to leave this shabby little man in his shabby little neighbourhood. She watched patients stream in and out, stepping around the black kid who still played 'jacks' until a car stopped and he hopped in. Eventually the stream of patients dried up to a trickle, then the nurse bustled out, calling something over her shoulder. Within seconds the doctor followed, blinking against the sun, rubbing his eyes and cleaning his glasses again. The gesture seemed like a spring releasing her, a signal she'd expected and subconsciously wanted. She opened the door and followed him to his car, a bottom-of-the-line import several years old. Through the open window she could almost smell his fatigue, but his tone was polite, almost welcoming. 'Miss Kramer! But you had a class?'

'I missed it. I thought maybe we could talk some.'

He appeared to consider. 'I am a widower and hopeless in the kitchen, so I normally dine at MacDonald's. But since you are free —' A huge grin showed her his smile for the first time, open, remarkably sweet. 'You shall decide where I take my dinner.' He blinked again. 'You, of course, need not eat, but I should enjoy your company anyway.'

Roxanne took the first place they found on Sepulveda, a pasta place so modest the patio vines were real, the wine-list narrowed down to one — the house red, product of the owner's parents' vineyard in Paso Robles. The menu offered one dinner: a main course of veal scallopini and enough assorted extras to satisfy an elephant. Roxanne, inhaling the menu, a starveling who had not intended to eat, was instantly ravenous. She ordered antipasto, minestrone, veal —'

The doctor put out a wrinkled hand. 'I think it best you start with soup, then see.' Dr Jasinski smiled across a red-chequered cloth. For himself he ordered the veal and a vegetable, nothing more.

Just as she was saying, 'I need help, I know I do,' the soup arrived, a tureen of vegetables simmering in honest broth and fragrance.

He shook his head. 'All most of us need is commonsense. Take your soup slowly with a little bread. I think you will find it sufficient. Now tell me as you enjoy your meal what is it like to contemplate the Olympics, to wear your country's honour. Exciting, no?'

'Scary. I feel like everybody's depending on me to win but they all expect me to do it *their* way.'

'Perhaps if you do it your way at least one person is happy.'

'But I don't *have* a way, I'm coached.'

He helped himself to warm bread and passed the basket across. She took the smallest slice. When the waitress stopped to refill her soup plate, she shook her head.

'You have self-control,' he said. 'One stout patient of mine is very proud that she speaks five languages. She has yet to learn "no" in any of them.'

'Do you . . . you know, have patients who binge and make themselves sick?'

After a puzzled frown and her brief explanation he shook his head. 'My patients have other worries than food. And in my own country, which I visit when I can, there is never enough. People wait many hours to buy what we take for granted. We are fortunate, are we not?'

'I guess.' The thought had never occurred to her. Now, for some reason, it filled her with shame. She found herself chewing very carefully, tasting each bite. 'I thought maybe, if you've time, I could come see you again next week.'

'To the office? But my dear child, you are not sick. Yet I would be honoured if you shared my coffee-break when you wish.'

She was not sick. Not sick. Not sick.

Driving back, she didn't know what had prompted her

question, still less why the answer satisfied her even more than the meal itself.

Eager for the apartment and Grant, there was one stop she should make, the final fitting for her Olympic dress, a rich sea-green, sequined waves breaking on the shore of her bosom, the entire concept a secret. It would never do to skate out for final warmup in the same colour as the others. The idea was to stand out for the judges, not blend into the crowd.

The dressmaker worked out of her home on nothing but the elaborate dresses of top skaters. Although she farmed out much of the beading and embroidery, it was easier to crack a top CIA code than find out who would be wearing what colour on the night. Next to her artistry, her biggest asset was discretion.

Roxanne's appointment was for tomorrow and it was a little late to be dropping in, but she was passing and restless. Besides, as Olympic favourite she was by far the designer's most important client. Grant, contrary to his own rule, had been in on every decision, a chore he found boring in the extreme. Wild horses wouldn't get him here for anyone else, he said. Now, relaxed, happy in the discovery of a doctor who felt more like a friend, proud of one day's normal eating pattern, Roxanne couldn't wait to rush home and thank Grant for everything, show him how she looked in the lovely, lovely dress.

The fitting-room door was closed as usual and there were raised voices seeping under it, so Roxanne settled to wait in the hall with a magazine. Which she soon set aside. She recognized every voice through the door. Emma Crisp. Beejay. The dressmaker's soothing murmur. And the deep male rumble of Grant Rivers.

'Red,' Beejay said. 'Just red, dammit.'

'Long sleeves, high neck, one row of *diamanté* beads,' Emma added.

'Perhaps red isn't *quite* the choice for Beejay, Mrs Crisp.'

'If she wants red, red's what she gets. Very plain.'

'But Emma, this *is* the Games,' Grant put in. 'She *is* a carrot-top.'

'And she *is* sixteen.' Emma was implacable. 'We'll have no high-cut leg-holes, none of that jewelled net that looks like she's half-naked. I saw Peggy Fleming *win* the Games in a green frock no fancier than what today's kids practice in. She *looked* a Lady Champion. A *lady*, not a candidate for Miss Universe. I don't like the sport made into a peep-show.'

'Times change. They call them Women now, anyway. The question is, Emma, do we want Beejay looking like a promising newcomer or a possible medalist? She has a chance. There's really only Kramer, Nakashima, and the German.'

'Don't forget Sterling.'

'And less than a month to go. Injuries happen. Skaters get sick . . .'

Hearing him, Roxanne felt sick herself. Grant. Hedging his bets, angling Beejay into position in case the favourite, *Kramer*, got sicker. Kramer.

To call her by her last name, like she meant no more to him than Jeff or Lise! Would it have leaked a state secret if he'd said 'Roxi'? But what could she expect? The odd little doctor made her think: act like a child, be regarded as one. Grant was ambitious, intelligent; he read, he *thought*. He needed a woman, not a doll programmed to skate, to live as instructed.

At home, fixing supper for them both, it came to her that her thoughts all revolved around medals and how they affected Grant's feelings for her. Maybe, just maybe, there was more to Roxanne Kramer than a deep hunger for a Gold medal and Grant Rivers. If not, there soon would be.

When he came in she joined him in spinach and lobster, drank her milk, and went to bed. He would never know she'd been to the dressmaker. When he made love to her she didn't ask him if he loved her and she didn't tell him she loved him. Oh, she wanted to, but she forced herself to silence, just as tomorrow she would force herself to skate her best. Force herself. For herself. *As a species we seem to do better if we help ourselves.* Yes. But the world's top female contender for Olympic Gold fell asleep with her fingers carefully crossed.

72

CHAPTER SIX

Tokyo, Japan

Mieko Nakashima's preparations for the Games paralleled Maureen Sterling's in so many ways that each girl could, with minor cultural and motivational changes, have switched lives and known exactly how to function.

Weekdays, each girl lived in a modern townhouse with a doting mother and a clutch of discreet, anonymous servants. Weekends drifted by — if competitors' lives could ever be said to drift — in remote country homes staffed by what could still, even in this last decade of the century, be called retainers. The fathers of both girls travelled incessantly, remote figures who exerted little positive influence on their daughter's lives. Like Maureen, even Mieko's weekends in the country were hardly holidays. She was in training. Montegreco's small shadow engulfed Japan as it did Britain, the USSR, even the USA. But there were differences.

The Tokyo penthouse Mieko and her mother were permitted to occupy Monday through Friday looked down over the frenzied business district, the tranquillity of the suite itself a product of technology rather than location, reflecting Grandfather's taste, but mainly his wealth. This high, serene isolation, the scurrying masses in the Ginza far below, was less a state of mind than a state of the art. Subtle wall-silks concealed foot-thick insulation; swathes of velvet and triple-thick glass silenced every window; pale carpeting, its pile as dense as the district's Saturday crowds, served to eliminate footfalls and frame the priceless Chinese rugs whose shades of rose, peach and softest lapis lazuli complemented glass tables from Denmark and modernistic couches from Germany. In footage alone the women occupied more space than the largest, most affluent Tokyo families. No furnishing was scratched or soiled, no item of Nakashima electronic wizardry too advanced for this, the company townhouse, Mieko's weekday home and, much more important, the weekend showplace in which Nakashima executives pleasured their Western clients.

Mieko's mother, while hinting that the 'office parties' cemented business deals and provided the company with mysterious insurance, discouraged speculation as to what form the entertainment might take, but once, blindly slotting a tape into the company's latest VCR to study Kramer's delicate technique at a previous World Championships, Mieko saw for herself. She had chosen the wrong tape.

Instead of Roxanne's cool blonde beauty revolving at centre-ice, a snake's nest of writhing bodies, naked pink and ochre obscenely entwined, filled the screen in a room she quickly recognized to be her own, though her *futon* and carpets were gone and sheeting of contemptuous quality covered floor and furnishings.

The one clothed figure in the picture was Grandfather himself. Set apart from his guests, he watched the action, motionless in a high-backed ivory chair. Contrary to his custom when conducting business with Westerners, he wore the kimono; stranger yet its texture, coarse grey cotton such as a menial might wear to scour floors — or an aristocrat to shrive himself for shameful acts committed under his roof. Rough kimono immaculately pressed, his wide, unlined face betraying nothing, in his detached stillness Hiro Nakashima made a remote and god-like figure. Occasionally sipping tea from an ancient porcelain cup, his left hand never ceased to stroke a carved wooden monkey, a *netsuke* by Masanao of Kyoto, a family heirloom for almost two hundred years.

His guests, as they rested from their labours, guzzled cocktails from frosted glasses Mieko recognized as those normally used by the house servants. When a drunken Westerner stirred the pitcher of martinis with a penis the size and colour of a peeled cucumber and forced the hired bar-girl to lick it clean, his colleague, not to be outdone, instructed another girl to lie flat, tilt her hips and spread herself. Shaking with giggles, babbling that he'd show them how to *really* serve cocktails, he emptied the pitcher's frosted contents into the girl's vagina, followed by a swizzle-stick and an olive on a toothpick. The girl did not move.

Nor did Hiro Nakashima — except to curl his lip at the carved, wizened face of the monkey. 'Thus you see, my *saru*,' his expression suggested, 'with what primitives the house of Nakashima must conduct business . . .' The hooded, watchful eyes glittered.

When Mieko asked Oka-chan what the tape meant, it was quickly locked away. 'Better forget it, my daughter. Such debaucheries serve as business insurance between our company and Western officials. The men are Grandfather's best customers. Mementos such as the tape will keep them that way. If their wives were shown such scenes they would . . . how to say — quick make divorce. They have power over their men.' Envy flashed briefly in her eyes before loyalty, as always, took over. 'Your grandfather is a brilliant businessman. *You have not seen the tape, Mieko.* Forget it.'

Mieko forgot it — stupid men to play childish, obscene games! — but she committed every image of Grandfather to memory, and her pride in him grew. How admirable his disgust! How noble his contempt!

Although, after that, Mieko loathed the penthouse and especially her room there, her admiration for Grandfather deepened almost to worship. If he could find some small morsel of love for her, not much, just sometimes to touch her with a fraction of the tenderness he lavished on the Masanao, then she would gladly — well, perhaps not gladly, but at least willingly — have given up skating, which he despised for a Western fad, a disgrace to his ancestors who must certainly despair of their youngest descendant.

But Grandfather did not love her. After the nation saw her qualify for the Olympics on a million Nakashima TV sets he'd refused to speak to her at all, dealing instead through Oka-chan, who tried in vain to negotiate a truce. Japan had no tradition of skating, she pleaded. Mieko was a pioneer. A pioneer? One who disgraced him before the world, throwing her legs in the air, inviting his thousands of employees to whisper about this brazen girl who was Hiro Nakashima's one grandchild?

Perhaps if she'd been like the famous *geishas* of old, their bird-like laughter, tiny feet, boneless ivory hands and drifting gestures . . . but they'd worn their hair long, oiled and coiled to towering heights, hair which took experts half a day to dress — and she was an athlete, such things not merely impractical but impossible! In vain Mother assured her she looked what she was, a healthy Japanese girl of the twentieth century, and that a loving soul blazed in her eyes, thus timeless beauty must dwell in her heart. Why not out front, Mieko wondered, for the world to admire as it admired Maureen Sterling and Roxanne Kramer, both tall, elegant? As it marvelled at little Beejay Crisp's bouncy copper curls?

Friday afternoons, Mieko and her mother battled the crowds for a streetcar to the station and from there a train for Atami. In Tokyo a bitter wind pinched their noses. The bullet train, once they'd elbowed themselves aboard, was a furnace in which dark-suited businessmen arrogantly filled every seat. Had there been space to hang the women's winter coats there was in any case no room to struggle out of them. Not for the women of this family the chauffeured luxury of a leisurely drive home; no matter how wealthy, the distaff side shifted for itself if it was to shift at all.

At Atami station they were lucky. The housekeeper, laden with fresh fish for the evening's *sashimi*, waited for them, her muscular fist grimly clasping the arm of a taxi driver. Lucky for them her intimidating tactics were known and feared. She presided over the Nakashima country estate like a giant she-bear tending her cave. In her youth she had wet-nursed Grandfather, thus creating loyalty no amount of money or tradition could have bought. If he asked it of her she would without question have impaled herself on his sword — first reminding him that her unworthy peasant flesh was a grave dishonour to the ancestral steel. By extension, Mieko and her mother were as cubs in this throw-back's cave, to be roughly cared for and kept in their place when necessary. Not for a moment did she forget that Hiro Nakashima was her lord.

Directing the driver up the mountain to the Great House

— she disdained to identify it further — the old woman raged at the price of tuna and octopus. Time the fishy old widows in Usami earned themselves an honest yen, she'd a good mind to start herself, dive off the rocks with spear and gutting knife as she'd done as a child. Why not? She was only eighty!

Mieko leaned forward, always eager for the first sight of the old house perched high in the hills above the resort, *tatami* on its floors, its garden artfully terraced to hug the slope. As the taxi snaked and twisted up the mountain road the terrain fell steeply to the winter-grey sea and the massive hotels huddled like white toy blocks at its edge. To her left the bay swept to Odawara and her old Catholic school; to her right the Izu Peninsula stretched into the Pacific, its edge dotted with fishing villages like warts on a gnarled old finger.

Izu *was* old. Long before the resort sprang up there had been a peninsula and a Nakashima family to look down possessively upon its hot-springs. At least two of the hotels were Nakashima-owned but Grandfather long ago forbade Mieko to set foot in them — perhaps because in one such hotel she'd seen her first ice-show, an import featuring Western performers who worked wonders with small ice, lavish costumes, talent, and energy. Atami had been a provincial resort then, the kimono everywhere, visiting foreigners a novelty; shopkeepers pointed them out like prize *koi* in Atami's insular little pond.

In a hotel lounge for tea, tiny Mieko had reached up in wonder to stroke the long golden hair of a young woman; she even, to Mother's embarrassment, fingered the girl's strangely round eyes that were the colour of the sea in summer. Later, drawn by distant music, the child drew her mother up a flight of stairs to watch entranced as these aliens rehearsed. Spinning in a shaft of sunlight, the girl's hair whipped around her head in a circlet of living gold.

As Mieko watched, hypnotized, the skater's face faded from pink to ivory; her features blurred; her eyes took on a familiar slant and changed colour to match Mieko's own. It seemed no time at all before the circlet of hair darkened to the glossy blue-black Mother brushed lovingly every night of Mieko's life. Before her hypnotized gaze the vision revolved, infinitely beautiful to a child who knew herself to be unremarkable. Her imagination chased the image, caught it, pinned it down. If she learned to jump high enough, spin fast enough, who would care that she lacked the affectations of Japan's past generations? Even then, the logic had seemed undeniable. She confided in her mother, who, had it been in her power, would have turned Fuji on its pointed head for this loving, lovable child. From that day on they were a team following a single, glittering goal. From that day they became the single target of Grandfather's frustration.

His opening salvo was to withdraw her name from a weekly skating class in Tokyo in which Mother had enrolled her. Mother defied him, *argued* with him — 'You haven't *watched* her, she shows promise!' — and arranged private lessons with the only available coach. Grandfather, in a fit of pique, threatened to throw his daughter and granddaughter into the street. As they all knew it must, pride of family stayed his hand. Faced with their unprecedented disobedience he had little choice but to strew random pebbles in Mieko's path, but with each setback her spine hardened, her talent bloomed ever brighter, her accomplishments more difficult to ignore, and now she would carry Japan's colours to the Olympics, where, if only she had the sophisticated lustre of a Kramer, a Sterling . . . She shook her head. Thump! And she was back in Atami, the old housekeeper rapping the cabbie's knuckles with her purse. 'Stop! Don't you see?'

Indeed. They all saw. As the taxi swept up the immaculate driveway of the Great House, Grandfather's black car stood squarely in its path.

Mother gripped Mieko's hand. 'Smile. He must by now have received my last letter,' she whispered, 'asking that you train in the United States.'

Mieko gasped. How could Oka-chan have dared?

Unaware, the housekeeper leapt babbling from the cab but managed a reverent bow. 'Nakashima-sama! We are honoured. Blessed. I serve the *sashimi* now or perhaps tea if my lord wishes, a moment only —'

'— A moment only and he will be gone.' Grandfather spoke from the balcony, tapping ivory fingertips on the rail. Naturally ignoring the housekeeper, who he called his 'senile burden', he looked only at Mieko's mother. 'I will speak to you in the *chanoma*. Now.'

She touched Mieko's hand and hurried to the living-room.

Ten minutes later she was in Mieko's room, her eyes red, her mouth quivering, her arms opening for her daughter. 'I'm so sorry. I had thought perhaps . . . but look, if you want to try . . . it is unthinkable but if. . .' She took a quivering breath. 'For many months I make economies in the household accounts, from the . . . entertainments, you understand?'

Mieko nodded. Inferior drinks, cheaper bar-girls. . . The lady of the house could hold the purse-strings as loose or as tightly as she chose. It was a small freedom, but it served.

'See,' her mother went on. 'You write English. Maybe you write that woman coach you admire? With a female coach he may not be so —' The enormity of what she suggested opened like a chasm and instinctively they both took a step back. 'If you write today, perhaps she would coach you through the Games. Time is short, Mieko, you need much polish.'

She looked steadily into her daughter's eyes. They both knew her suggestion to be unthinkable — but to give up, to concede every point to a tyrannical old man — 'If she agrees, we could fly to the USA the same day, yes?'

Mieko looked back down a tunnel of hard-fought years to master this jump, that step; her instruction coming from minor coaches she'd outgrown years ago. She trained in a vacuum and knew it. She'd learned more and better by freeze-framing tapes of top skaters brought back from foreign competitions. But God, to openly defy Hiro Nakashima himself!

Oh, to fly away to a pro she'd worshipped for years! Unconventional, not serious like most, this woman bubbled with laughter, cheered when her students learned a difficult move. A past Olympic Medalist herself, she cared how success and failure felt. Her students smiled more, perhaps because she read the judges' marks through Elton John glasses. When Mieko, trembling at her first international competition, waited to skate, she looked up into the woman's blue eyes behind the enormous eyeglasses. Fear melted as this coach smiled, took off a high-heeled shoe and held it to the light to soothe the nerves of a frightened girl.

Inside the transparent heel a goldfish swam round and round, a frivolous toy for a serious moment. That night Mieko skated totally free, her anxieties routed by a stranger's warmth and the memory of foolish little fish-mouths popping bubbles in a shoe. But for all her froth and fun this woman produced superb skaters. How Mieko had dreamed of working with her. . .

'Well, Mieko? A few weeks with her could make a difference —'

'It's too late, Oka-chan,' she whispered. 'And besides —'

'This is the only Olympics you'll have. You've worked hard.'

'Yes. But if I train abroad he will never forgive me, will say I am not truly Japanese. He is proud and full of years — and he despises foreigners. I cannot do it. I am sorry.' She bowed her head.

Her mother's sturdy shoulders sagged as she slumped down to the table. As always, she made herself as small as possible. 'I too. I have spent my life sorry because of that stubborn old man. I was plain so he married me to a company robot who can't bear to come home to such a wife . . . but I had no choice, no talent. For you it is different.'

Mieko lifted her mother's chin and stroked her face. 'Remember what you told me of the best coaches? It takes talent to nurture talent? If I have a little, then you must have much.'

From far below, the housekeeper's endless adoration drifted up like a litany as she trotted behind her imperious, furious lord. A door slammed. Mieko looked down to the forecourt and the black Toyota, Hiro Nakashima's leonine head ducking behind the wheel. She raised her hand to wave goodbye, but he did not look up. She had not expected that he would.

She switched on the *kotatsu* to warm Oka-chan's feet, now tucked protectively under the table-cloth, and pretended not to notice a tear-drop fall from the short-sighted eyes and glitter in the evening sun.

Quickly, as if it were a new toy, Mieko flipped on the VCR to run Maureen Sterling's European programme. 'Why, look!' she said, as if she'd just that moment noticed. 'In some ways Sterling is as good as Kramer!' She did not add, did not even wish to wonder, how many others were now as good or better than Mieko Nakashima.

Or if those other girls had grandfathers like hers.

CHAPTER SEVEN

Bonn, Germany

Herr Otto Braun spun his wheelchair expertly on the ice to check the landing of his top student's lutz. Atrocious. They all were.

And why not? He looked around at peeling walls, pitted benches, an ice surface less than half regulation size, with, according to the skaters, more ridges than Frau Braun's Sunday wig. What skater of stature would train in a rotting ruin like this when a new facility sprang up in Germany every year? Not ten miles from here they'd just built a sports complex with a heated ice-rink and swimming pool, tennis and squash courts, and, for those with energy left over, a gym. As if that were not enough, they served gourmet meals in a three-star restaurant that looked down on everything. The sporting world had gone mad!

The student had waited long enough. 'Again, Herr Braun?'

'Why not,' he said heavily. As if again would help. He shut his eyes but could not block out the resounding thud of a jump landed on the flat of the blade. 'Try, *try* to find me an outside edge? Just once? But first ask Frau Braun for a warm cushion.'

Which wouldn't help either. After an hour on the ice, during which he must keep spinning the chair to stop the wheels freezing in, his spine shot daggers clear up to his temples. After two hours the curtain of pain blinded him. How much longer must they continue this monstrous discipline? But he knew: when Roxanne *Braun* Kramer polished up the reputation her mother had dragged through the mud. Brigitta would have it no other way. To quit now was to concede wasted lives — his, hers, their daughter's and their granddaughter's. When Roxanne won the Gold, then and only then could they lock the door on this ice-house forever. It would close in triumph or not at all.

Snuggling the cushion, still warm from the stove, behind him, his thoughts dared to touch his dream: a villa on the fringe of the Med, an orange tree in the garden, bougainvillaea rampaging down to the sea, and every morning the cry of seabirds and the sun on his face.

'*Kommen*, Otto!' Frau Braun called. '*Mittagessen!*'

'*Ja*, Gitta! *Einen Augenblick.*' Always impatient, his Brigitta. He sighed and spun his wheels towards what she called the kitchen, an old oil stove on which she prepared luncheon for themselves and such students as chose to order in advance. She seemed not to notice that none did. Just as she didn't notice that her Saturday Beginners, the feeder-pool from which private students were hooked, was now down to three pre-teen girls — far too old to cherish dreams of medals or even of chorus work in a show.

Meanwhile the cold layered itself in clouds upon the morning ice and wrapped his spine, his days, his life, his every breath in a frozen limbo from which there were only two escapes: a gold medal or a box in a hole in a cemetery. But even that must be warmer than this.

Three times Brigitta clanged the spoon on the pan lid before her husband left the ice and trundled to the counter.

Men! *Einen Augenblick* indeed! Just-a-moment, just-a-moment. He lived his life by just-a-moment. If he'd stopped that affair between Noni and the American all those years ago the family would have a world title today, something to be proud of, that the rink could advertise. But no, not Otto. It was *Einen Augenblick* then too, and look where it had got them!

The same with her. Forty-odd years ago, her period a week late, it had been 'wait till tomorrow, my darling'; a few more days, then weeks. One month followed another until her belly was so full of Noni even the blind beggar on the corner of Gartenstrasse must have known young Brigitta, surely destined to be another Henie, would never win an

Olympics. Lucky for her Germany was deep in post-War construction, too busy to listen to the spate of gossip that shook the local skating world, the only world she knew or cared about — not that she'd admit to a soul how she welcomed the need for reconstruction, no time for ice queens then! — but it kept the Braun name on ice just long enough for young Noni's talent to surface, then the endless years training until she too was groomed to receive the chalice. Being Noni, she'd dropped it — but she'd always been a butterfingers. Now it rested safely with Roxanne, a steady, diligent girl, thank God.

Over the years Brigitta had learned patience, but now it wore as thin as her hair as the Games drew close. She touched the travel agent's folder on the counter and pulled her hand away as if from the fire. The tickets to Montegreco had been there for a week, but after the first fluttery reading she tried to ignore them in case a longing too keenly felt might bring bad fortune about their heads. Always this feeling of anticipation. Or was it premonition? Or just old age? She must phone her daughter. Unstable, that Noni . . . impetuous. Such a promising child to grow into so disappointing a woman. She shook her head. The past was the past.

'I think, Otto,' she said when he wheeled himself up to the bench, 'that tonight I call Noni. Advise her.'

'Of what?' He growled through a bite of black bread dipped in bean and bacon stew, already cooling in the frigid atmosphere.

'Maybe she could bring Roxanne here for *us* to supervise? Just the final week or so? Give the rink a bit of . . . *tone*. God knows we have empty ice. Why do you look at me as if I'm insane?'

He set down his spoon. 'Gitta, after seven years my best student has yet to find an outside edge on which to land his double-lutz. Of the triple we do not even speak. What do we old ones know of today's techniques?'

'But she's with foreigners! Capable of anything, they are.'

'Roxanne *is* a foreigner, an American.' He dabbed his moustache with a red handkerchief. 'And it is our dear Noni who is capable of anything!'

She couldn't deny it. Even here in this backwater of a rink

she'd heard tales of Noni sleeping with this judge and that to ensure Roxanne's success. She'd shrugged off the rumours then as she shrugged them off now. Who decided at what point maternal ambition shifted from virtue to sin? God? Never! He rewarded winners very well, and He most certainly punished losers — this rink alone was proof of that!

'Nevertheless,' she said, 'I shall call.'

'Gitta, do not agitate Noni further. Already she loads much pressure on the girl.'

CHAPTER EIGHT

Los Angeles, California

The old Brauns phoned so seldom that Noni's immediate reaction was panic. What had happened now? Which of them was sick, this close to Roxanne's triumph, to her own absolution? When she discovered once again that there was no emergency, relief snapped back on itself, bringing exasperation and echoes of the old guilt.

Mutti played her usual game, speaking clearly, with studied calm, deliberately controlling her breath as if trying to reach rapport with a backward child. 'Everything is as it should be, Noni? All according to plan?'

Noni, who took perverse pleasure in playing her assigned role, said, 'What plan? I forget. Or is there something I don't know?'

Across the grey Atlantic and a winter continent a vast maternal sigh echoed the frustrations of motherhood. 'Our Roxanne is skating well?'

'I guess. Better anyway, except for the timing on a few jumps, not to worry, they can be moved around before Montegreco —'

'Pressure . . .' Now the old girl would be nodding her everyday wig with grey, sage understanding. '*Ja.* I was thinking, if she trained with us for the last few weeks we could, well, protect her. What do you think?'

Jesus Christ, every week a new idea. Noni pulled off a glove, the better to count off points. 'Better *you* think, Mutti! One: that igloo of ours is too small to train a chimp. Two: cobblestones are smoother. Three: which pro do you have there to coach a skater of my daughter's calibre?'

Noni almost heard Mutti grab on to her pride, temper,

86

and blood pressure, clench her strong white choppers rather than acknowledge the implied affront. 'And the Braun spin we discussed?'

The other glove came off. '*You* discussed.' The ball was on Noni's side, and begging for the smash — but not yet. 'Does Crisp do it? Nakashima? Sterling? I told you, it's old hat. I can ask the coach but —'

'Ask? You *tell*, not ask! It is Roxanne's duty to bring it back! We *insist* to the coach, Noni. We are Brauns! We have the right to demand!'

Noni paused. Demand of the coach? The way Beejay Crisp was coming on, Noni dare not breathe, much less demand. So attack, follow the familiar formula established in the crib, a ping-pong game both women knew to a hair, a game trotting out assorted guilts which would eventually relax in a mutual outpouring of griefs and regrets. 'Mutti, who is this "we"? I can demand nothing. The rink janitor is allowed more to say about Roxanne's programme than I. I told you. Officially I am not permitted in the building!'

'Tsk! This skating is cruel, cruel. Think, her own mother!'

'Maybe. But I pay no bills, therefore I can say nothing.'

Mutti let the ball bounce twice. Noni waited. It was not her nickel.

'Oh dear, I'm sorry, business is slow here, I only wish we could help. This Crisp woman, what does she think of Roxanne's chances? A top judge, she could smooth a few avenues, advise the coach of America's number one skater, the favourite —'

Yeah. And that judge's husband died purple in the face from a coronary at a cut-rate motel, and maybe this Crisp woman knows who with and why, maybe knows that 'our girl's' mother might have called for help instead of panicking and getting the hell out, maybe — but Mutti in Germany wouldn't know that. If she did, then surely Emma Crisp in Los Angeles knew. . . No. She gave herself a quick shake. A lot of water under the bridge since then and not a hint, not a murmur. She was in the clear.

'Mutti, you forget.' Now it was Noni talking to the backward child. 'Crisp's daughter also competes, is trained at the same rink by the same coach for the same event. And she is very good.'

Instantly her mother's voice dropped to a whimper. 'Not better than. . .' She couldn't bring herself to finish.

'Not yet. Raw. All flash and not much flow. But in time —' Mentally Noni dusted off her hands. Mutti's silence confirmed her defeat. Good. So consolidate it. 'And now our Roxanne begins to gain weight.'

'*Ach Mein Gott* — (Quick, Otto, pass my white pills!) — *Gains weight*?'

'Her new doctor insists. Jasinski. He can do no wrong. A time like this, he even tells her of the old Camps, as if we *starve* our Roxanne!'

'The swine! What does he know of athletes?'

'The man's an idiot, but as I said, I have no control. Now he tells me — I went to ask him — that she is getting well. As if she had been sick!'

'My poor Noni, how you stand it! Look, this is costing, do try for the spin though, huh?'

'I'll try, Mutti. You know I'll try.'

The call amicably completed, Noni dialled Roxanne.

'How about lunch with your momma after dance class, baby?'

'Sorry, Mom. I have to see the doc and the chiropodist, okay?'

'Sure.' Noni bit her lip. 'The old one called. She wants her spin, sweetheart. Talk to Grant, eh? She is an old woman, we don't ask for much.'

'*Mom*!' They didn't ask for *much*? What was the Gold for God's sake?

'Try, huh?'

That night Roxanne tried. 'It could be pretty in the programme, Grant. Kati Witt did a spin like it once, different arms and free-leg but —'

Grant frowned. She couldn't leave it alone for a day. Anything to make it easier. 'Her jumps were solid. Let's just get yours the same, okay?'

'But if it's polished and centred . . .'

'Roxi, you've already got more polish than a new gold chain, what you need is difficulty. If the old girl's spin is only pretty, I can give it to —' He ducked, just avoiding the hurled cushion — but rejoiced in her new lightness of spirit. Rivalry between the girls grew pretty intense some days. But today Roxanne had skated well.

'Give Beejay that spin and the folks will never speak to me again, Grant Rivers!'

'Beejay wouldn't take it as a gift. And neither will you.'

'Please, Grant? It *is* my programme.'

Her lips pouted daintily and he bent to kiss them. She was trying. Best not to push too hard. Jasinski had spun a miracle, true, but the result was fragile, as the doctor was first to admit. 'She eats,' Jasinski said yesterday, 'but still without appetite.' But already, to Grant's palms, her shoulderblades, under powder-blue angora, felt rounder, softer. Please, he prayed to nobody in particular, let her be okay, so I don't have to play this double game much longer, training her as if she were the only possible winner then hustling her out of the rink to train Beejay almost the same way. 'Roxi, I know that spin is your Gran's last hope, but no. Got it? No.'

'Spins are what I do best. You said so.'

'Yeah. When you win and join a show, you can spin all you want and the crowd will ooh and aah and love you to death. But next month we play Big Time, where the judges will ho-hum and knock off three-tenths of a point quicker than you can say knife. And you know why.'

Unlike the bedazzled public, even a raw judge knew that all it took to spin fast and straight was to whip in straight, pull tight, and let your eyes drift out of focus; with practice you could rotate for damned near ever. And nobody drifted out of focus better than Roxanne, who worked her spins like prayer beads. But after all the extra coaching, her jumps were still here-today-gone-tomorrow, and there'd be no raw judges at the Games. The hell with the old bird in Bonn who figured to be queen bee because way back when, she'd hoped, *hoped* to win a medal except for that naughty Herr Hitler. Hoped! As a fellow coach told her students, if all you took to competition was hope you'd as well take a bucket of horseshit. All these years patting hands and heads and whatever else needed attention, kowtowing to Noni just to *train* Roxanne for free, all he still had was a bucket of hope that could quickly turn to the other thing.

As if reading his thoughts, she said, 'You saw my long programme this afternoon, right?'

Post-mortems at home. He groaned. She was testing him because he'd been teaching Beejay at the time. Would she ever believe he missed nothing? 'Parts of it. You doubled the triple-toe, left out the salchow, pulled off a decent flip. . . Yes, I guess it was clean.'

He passed the test but she frowned. She'd been fishing for praise where none was due. 'It was my best all week and I did finish it!'

'Look, let's not talk shop at home. Why don't I fix us a drink and we'll whale-watch till dinner gets here.'

Her features sharpened till she looked like Noni. 'Okay.'

Jasinski was right. Mention food and she tightened like a trip-wire. When he brought them each a Perrier and a twist she'd snapped out of it, sitting at the fixed binoculars by the window-seat. 'Do you believe that!' As she spoke a pair of whales leaped clear out of the sunset water, sleek grey torpedoes shooting up a fountain of golden drops as their massive flukes slapped at the sea. 'From their faces you'd swear they were happy.'

'Why not? They're heading down to Baha for mating. Give you ideas, Roxi?' He rubbed the back of her neck with his nose. 'You smell of talc and lemon peel. Very nice.' For once she shrugged off the invitation, her attention firmly on the whales as room-service wheeled in dinner.

'I don't get it. That heavy, how come they jump that high?'

'For joy?'

She nodded, chewing slowly, thoughtfully, on chicken kiev until it was gone. 'Yeah,' she said. 'Tomorrow I'll land the triple-toe, no sweat.'

He refused to be drawn. Two whales jumped. Big deal. She clutched at any hopeful sign at all — but she'd eaten. When she disappeared into the shower he filled out Jasinski's log. One chicken kiev. Salad. Water.

The green phone rang just as they climbed into bed. The other was switched to 'answer' and he wouldn't touch it after eight, but only friends or important contacts had the green. Never parents. He reached for it.

'So much for mating,' Roxi murmured. 'Only when it's convenient or when you think I need a confidence-fix, right?'

'Sorry, hon. Be right with you. Yeah? Yeah! *What*?' After the first minute he tuned Roxanne out completely. He listened, nodded, and at last lay back on the pillow and let out a long, low whistle.

'Jesus Christ. The Russians just withdrew Galina.'

'So?' Roxanne frowned. 'She was no threat. Who are they sending?'

'Somebody. Nobody. A novice, no problem for you . . .'

'Well then —'

She reached out to him but he waved her aside. Had to think, think how to use this nugget, turn it to shine on Grant Rivers. Why withdraw Galina now, this close to the Games? She wasn't great but she was the best they had. So *why*?

Because she was Alexei's lover. Alexei, who couldn't lose Gold unless he tried real, real hard. That's why. To stop him defecting after he won. So what would Alexei do and how to use what Alexei did? Grant had watched him for years. A trainer's dream, Alexei was the most stubborn, determined competitor the circuit had seen in ten years. One missed jump and most skaters walked through the rest of the programme. Not Finsky. He hung in, couldn't be psyched — not even by himself. So what were his options, what would he do?

Grant knew the Russian skating machine, too. All power drive but no reverse gear. When it met the immovable object — impasse. Maybe Alexei would appear, then refuse to skate. Show the buggers. Develop a last minute 'injury'. If anybody was capable of deliberately throwing away a Gold to prove a point it would be Finsky. Or he could refuse to go to the Games at all unless Galina went too. He had the guts. But did she? A quiet girl, she faded almost to invisibility in the shadow of Finsky's talent and personality. If he had to bet, Grant figured Finsky would refuse to leave Mother Russia without her. He'd stay home. And laugh when some foreigner picked off the Russian Gold.

Which foreigner would it be? The field was wide open. Six or seven had a chance. His blood sang in his ears and in the dark he felt himself grin, almost laugh out loud. *This* was the beauty of coaching. He snapped on the light and reached again for the phone.

'Grant!' Roxanne murmured. 'It's eleven! We have to be up —'

'Sleep tight, baby. I'll be at first free-style ahead of you.'

He punched numbers for the rink night-man, issued brief orders, hung up, then punched a different set.

'Jeff? Jeff Dunsmuir, is he there?'

An irritated whine answered. 'Jeffie's napping.'

'He's supposed to be. Wake him up.'

'Well, all *right*, man!' Woman's voice or man's? Hard to tell.

Grant drummed his fingertips on the curve of Roxanne's slender haunch as he waited for the British contender for Gold. When he came on, half asleep and yawning, Grant kept it short:

'I've booked us three hours private ice starting midnight. We're going to re-do your entire programme — what? *Yes*, this midnight! Why else would I *call*? So *what* if it's late? Be there.' He heard more yawns, finally a coherent objection. 'Jeffie. I *know* private is expensive. Trust me.'

And trust Lloyd Sterling, the honourable gentleman, to pick up the tab. Grant was just following the written orders issued when he took on young Jeff, described by Lloyd as a promising jumper, a possible eventual winner: 'Spare no effort to advance the standing of Jeffrey Dunsmuir, Esq.' Grant remembered every word. Now, scrambling into his rink clothes, he gave Mr Sterling a mocking *salaam*. 'Why not, old chap? You indulged all your dreams, some at my expense. Now we get to share one. For you, an A+ for benevolence; for me, an extra shot at a medal for my coaching crown.'

He looked back at the bed. Roxanne was pretending sleep so he could tend to business without guilt. No recriminations. She knew the business, thank God. There were the Games, then the aftermath — which could be sweet or bitter, depending. But guilt rode the midnight freeway with him anyway. There'd be time for Roxanne, he'd *make* time . . . but now his hours all trailed strings behind them, ambition, guilt, need, threads of rejection, old angers, snaking about his ankles, distracting him from the goal. Which was . . . was. . .

Noni walked the night beach under Roxanne's window. She

walked almost every waking minute no matter what else she was doing, even watching television. Exercise and one tiny speed-ball burned off the caloric intake of the day. Her doctor said two, but she'd cut back, saving against a rainy day. *Are you listening, Mutti*? Your darling Noni weighs the same in her thirties (well, okay, forties) as she had at twelve, so surely after all these years she's doing *something* right. Right? All due to walking the midnight beaches (a risky locale, the cops said) and one pill each noon — oh mild, mild, but it kept her slim and vigilant, alert to events in the round tower of Camelot. Night after night, watching Roxi's window in the complex, she re-lived and cursed every mistake she ever made, and planned what to do after Roxi's Gold Medal paid up that crippling debt to the folks in Bonn.

Just before midnight she saw Grant's high-powered car streak out of its pampered berth, heard the electronic gates to the underground parking whisper shut behind it, securing the fortress against beach-bums, burglars, and a mother who had become an impediment to her daughter's career. So somebody had midnight ice and the jailer had deserted his prisoner — but the security man had his orders. No way could a commoner like Noni Braun Kramer enter Camelot.

She lit a cigarette and checked her watch. A selfish mother would phone Roxi now for a cosy mother–daughter chat and to hell with the girl's sleep schedule, but not Noni. Noni was not selfish, that was her problem, all her life lived to commandments carved in the ice by Mutti: Thou shalt not go barefoot in this good life, not even in thine own home, for did not needles wait like darts in the rug to fly at the instep of a careless Noni? Yea, verily, Mutti says unto thee. At competition thou shalt leave no skate untended lest some rival gouge thy blade with a rusty nail, thus stealing thy glory. Thy face shalt register no outrage at a low mark, for, with guile and wiles and smiles never-ending, the hostile judge of today will worship at thy shrine tomorrow. Thou shalt not consort with thine enemies: bread, butter, cakes, strawberry ice cream, and chocolate, for God pins no medals on the fat of the land. Above all waste no ice, for every idle moment is bought with endless rue, the bite of a leather strap, and another stroke in God's big black book of uncollected debts.

When she was little she pictured God with icicles in His beard, His hair, and His thick fur jacket. When He walked towards her, frowning because she'd missed a jump, the icicles shattered and tinkled in shards upon the ice and the vapour clouds of His breath smelled of brimstone and liniment but mostly of ice. Then the vapour cleared and it was only Mutti after all, dear, kind Mutti who hit her only for her own good, so she could win medals and be the best skater in the whole wide world. '*Isn't that right, Mutti, isn't that right?*' she shouted at the soft slap of a wave.

Under the pier Noni caught a gleam of naked white flesh, two men touching each other, unaware that somewhere an icicle man scribbled frantically in a big black book. Fools! Didn't they know He was always on the watch? Where was she? Oh yes. She was going to be the best skater the world had ever seen, and she would have been too but for that damned American who swept her off her blades and her winner's stand and told her she was more than a skating machine. Believing him, like a fool she'd let him put a baby into her svelte and supple body. He had then abandoned the sporting world to open a gas station, deserting everything when he discovered that even with little Roxanne in the house, the life of mother and daughter revolved around skating, skating, skating. What the hell did he expect? Do you marry a princess of the ice and expect her to pump gas? If skating was a spiritual aristocracy, as Mutti said, then Noni was at least royalty, and Roxanne destined to be the most regal queen in its world. *If* Grant Rivers didn't mess things up for her, *if* Roxi drew a good spot, *if* the programme firmed up soon, *if* she hit her peak at the right time. Meantime, the future queen's mother tended her guilts, her remorse, her stash — her lifeline against tomorrow and a shiny medal. Spit on Grant Rivers! She had her methods, would make sure that in the temples of the ice-gods Roxanne shone brighter than the North Star because Noni Braun Kramer planned for every eventuality.

'*See how well I plan for us, Mutti?*' she bawled at the Pacific, which must, some place, join the Atlantic, which must, somehow, reach Bonn. Even as she spoke the moon goddess shone her silver spike into Noni's frantic blue eyes, a promise of vows to be kept. Vows. They had less substance than this American surf, creaming and sucking back into the waters circling the earth, circling . . . Lord, but could that Roxanne spin and spin and spin. . .

Dizzily, Noni shook her fist at the surf and a strolling couple giggled as they passed her and edged away. As well they might. She was cursed, Noni Braun was cursed from the day Mutti set her on the ice. Just as she'd laid a curse on herself the day she handed Roxanne over to Grant. But what choice did she have? She wasn't learning from Noni anymore. All she did was cry every blasted day until Emma Crisp — that was a laugh — Emma Crisp took her aside and said: 'Noni, I've seen it over and over, coaching your own kid never works. Let me talk to Grant. Roxi's got a good track-record. Maybe the Committee will come up with financing.'

So they came up with half-tuition and Grant agreed to pitch in the other half. Which left Noni to find everything else, and meantime Roxanne, then eighteen, was falling head-over-tip for Grant, which did her skating the world of good for a while. Cosy, one hand washing the other. But then scratches appeared under the smooth surface of the deal. Noni wanted a jump this way, Grant that way, and Grant always won. Noni wanted one piece of music, Grant another, Grant won. Roxanne wanted to move in with him and it suited Grant's purpose so Grant won that too. He swore he could get her to the top if Noni would butt out and true enough she got her title. Twice. Roxanne had her crown and Grant's reputation was as shiny as the trophies — but they shone on *Grant's* hall-stand, not the coffee table in Noni's little one-roomer. So what in hell had she got out of it? She'd sold her daughter for what? A sliver of glory was all she asked, people to say: 'Yes, that slim woman at the rail is her mother, Noni Braun, remember her the year she could have won World's except she ran off and married a nobody? Was it too much to ask? That and a picture of Roxanne with the medal to show off in the rink in Bonn, three Braun women in the picture. A skating dynasty. Then Mutti would put an arm around her, give her that rare smile because the trial of Mutti's life had finally come through, paid off, had bred and managed an Olympian.

And now nothing was certain. Little by little Noni lost

access to her daughter. Yesterday a doctor and a chiropodist, tomorrow a dress-fitting or skate sharpening or some damn thing that Noni used to do for her. Now she wasn't even trusted to *talk* to her! If she won the Games would Noni even get a look-in? Between press, officials, coaches and promo-men, they'd try to elbow Noni out, and Roxanne would help them. After everything she'd done. She'd even delivered throw-away papers to buy extra lessons. Saturday midday for three years on California's 100° days she'd trudged residential streets stuffing ads for pineapples and corn-on-the cob into unwilling post-boxes, snarling back at hostile dogs and kicking out at the yappers, all to make a few extra bucks for blades and ballet classes.

But now Grant took care of that too. The Almighty Grant. Never mind what she'd done on the side with this judge and that. Gossip-shmossip. If nobody knew for sure, whose business was it anyway — except Emma Crisp and oh God if that woman knew what her dearest darling got up to at competition, how freely he awarded his top mark to Roxanne as long as Noni came through . . . He could never get enough of her — until the day he got too much. And Grant Rivers thought it was his training alone that got Roxi to the top! Noni believed in insurance. She'd take it out double at the Games, the hell with all of them. Roxanne was best, no question, but many a 'best' died on the vine for want of the right judge in the right pocket. And whatever other requirements were needed. She'd see to it the girl had it all. Oh, but Mutti wanted that medal. Papa too. And Roxi. But some days Noni wondered how much. No matter. Noni wanted it enough for all of them, would find a way to get when the time came. Soon, now.

She checked her watch. Three o'clock. Passing again under the pier, the same young men were still at it, pumping their white behinds like pigs. She began to mutter, softly at first then louder and louder until she reached the very edge of the water and waded in ankle deep, high-heeled pumps and all. Waving her little prescription bottle at the tide, she shouted one last message over the sea to Bonn: '*See, Mutti? See what a good mother I am? What I sacrifice for your goddamned dream?*'

The young men under the pier giggled again, and up in the

round tower Roxanne Braun Kramer dreamed of Nakashima and Sterling and Beejay Crisp, and groaned softly in her sleep.

CHAPTER NINE

London, England

Fittingly enough, the new leather case — tall, round, and monogrammed — dominated Deirdre's dressing-table. She turned away, but the inevitable mocked her wherever she looked. Travel trunks filled with garments whose fleeting vogue would outlast their wearer, and were in any case already too large. Even her rings had been taken in and in until they could be taken in no more, and had now been placed in her solicitor's safe for Maureen. God, even her shoes seemed to slip off her feet. . .

Only vanity and fatigue stopped her from sweeping the dresser clear, smashing the photograph in its silver frame, which mocked her more each day. Soft lights and heavy drapes didn't help, any more than the array of scented oils and unguents from Paris, guaranteed to give back a semblance of her youth, some fleeting connection between the girl in the picture and the woman in the mirror. As disease drained her, drop by slow drop, she knew that life gave no guarantees, that hers wound down like a worn-out clock. Even after the diagnosis she'd been able to count her future in years, then months. Now she felt it was down to weeks, days. Soon Maureen would skate for the world, and Deirdre would see Grant Rivers one more time. Then she would welcome that last tick of the clock, the painless sleep.

The picture, taken just days before her wedding to Lloyd, showed her another Dierdre, silvery blonde hair worn innocently long and in charming disarray, not sleek as the fashion of the day demanded. But what had the minister's daughter known of fashion? She'd looked unsure, that young woman, gazing into a future peopled by Lloyd's smart friends and already feeling like the country-cousin, unutterably naïve and scarcely worth their time. Suppose she embarrassed Lloyd? She, alone among his friends, was a virgin and desperately afraid they knew and ridiculed her for it. Lloyd knew, of course. She realized later that that was her main attraction. Like a fool she'd equated chic with sophistication, Lloyd's wealth with future ease and content. Now, in her quiet room, her bitter laugh was perilously close to a sob. Content! She hadn't known a contented day since her honeymoon in Buenos Aires, during which, on the third morning, she emerged from the shower to find Lloyd sampling the ultimate in room service with the maid who delivered their morning tea. Smiling broadly, he'd invited her to join them.

Of course she'd phoned her father, begging him to send her money to come home, sobbing her outrage. The reverend gentleman didn't wish to know, and was in any case low on funds. 'You think weddings come cheap, gel? You married for better or worse, and a damn fine catch I got you, too! For God's sake, don't whine. That's one thing a man can't stand.'

And she couldn't stand any more poverty, a future forever presiding over the Friday Ladies, typing Daddy's sermons with two clumsy fingers, trying to make Sunday's tiny roast last through Monday's cold beef and chutney, Tuesday's meat-and-potato-pie, boiling the naked bone with carrots and onions for Wednesday's evening soup. Her meagre training pointed to only two possibilities. Skivvy, or pampered wife.

Naturally she chose the wife and stayed with Lloyd, knowing that a stronger woman would have struck out alone, but assuming, since she had no one to compare Lloyd with, that men were all alike in the bedroom. No wonder religion equated sex with sin. To inflict pain *was* sinful, and the only kind of sex Lloyd cared about. It took eight years and one gentle, ingenuous lover to teach her she'd been wrong.

Grant Rivers. A few weeks now . . .

She'd seen him on television, those awkward moments when coach and skater wore their camera faces as they waited for marks, but it wasn't like seeing him, touching him, a man in his mid-thirties and still unbearably beautiful to her eyes. And she, who'd been so beautiful to his, what would *he* see, and how could she bear it? Would he recognize her? She thought not.

She'd had breasts then, and hips — 'You're all alabaster and cream roses, like that statue they have in the museum, except you're warm . . .' Remembering, she felt again his lips worship her shoulders, her thighs. How she cherished her memories, every moment he'd given her, re-living them endlessly until she was no longer sure where true memory left off and fantasy began. His strength, his glorious health. And hers. Then. Now her flesh hung in sallow folds. What man who had kissed her soft tapering hands in adoration could touch these peeling claws? Her pale, soft hair, pride of her youth, hung from a scalp obscenely blemished with the bald patches of chemotherapy.

Gloves and a full-length Saga mink would hide body and hands, the contents of the round box would cover her head, but her face, dear God, her face, eyes so deep in their wrinkled sockets even she could scarcely tell their colour anymore. 'Blue jewels,' he said. 'What are they called? Sapphires. Yes, the minute you step into the rink I feel them on me. It's like you've touched me. I want to kiss you and never stop, your arms, your cheekbones. . .' And now each bone was stark, distinct, grotesque. Grant Rivers would not see Deirdre Sterling at all. He'd see a death's head and recoil.

There was one bitter satisfaction. Lloyd would see the same thing and know the scourge that waited for him. He thought he was simply a carrier, had casually passed it along like a case of measles — but he'd see. One year, two — his turn would come. . . No question that he'd be in Montegreco, just as he'd been at Nationals and Europeans. To see Jeff, his protégé and potential lover. At what point, she wondered, would Lloyd claim his reward? Before or after the competition? But did it matter?

She'd stopped worrying about Jeff, or anyone but Maureen. Such a sheltered life she'd had; soon she must wander in it alone. Would she marry? She seldom dated; outsiders never understood that 6 AM patch ruled out nights on the town. When she went out it was with a dancer or skater or coach because that was her circle. Impossibly small, but what choice was there? At Europeans she'd come to know two more male skaters, one, the Russian, Alexei, but Galina was there . . . lucky, Deirdre thought. All of Maureen's eighteen years had been cushioned by wealth. How could such a girl live in Russia? The other boy, a Swede with an American accent, and so perfectly proportioned as to seem unreal, had shown interest but seemed dominated by his sister and an overbearing father.

Deirdre no longer feared for Maureen at Lloyd's hands. Somehow the girl had plumbed the murkiest depths of her father's character and despised what she found. But she needed a man in her life, a beautiful girl needed *someone*. Suppose — Deirdre barely dared touch the thought — suppose she asked Grant to watch out for Maureen?

The face in the mirror answered her. How could she let Grant see her up close, destroy whatever illusions he might have left? But maybe in a dim light and the right make-up. . . Feverishly she slathered her raddled face with creams, blushers, shadows and highlights. Stuck false eyelashes where her own had been, painted brown arches for eyebrows and defined her lips with the colour of ripe cherries. Frantic now, not even looking in the glass, she dragged the floor-length mink over her nightgown, climbed unsteadily into high heel pumps, and reached into the case on the dresser.

The wig was so beautiful it could have been the young Dierdre's own hair. They'd followed the photograph exactly — shade, style, length, even the texture achingly familiar to her fingertips. Shutting her eyes, she set the wig firmly on her head and turned back to smile at the finished product in the mirrored door of the wardrobe.

A poor painted thing with no more dignity than a rag-doll smiled back. The smile became an 'O', then an anguished howl, which filled the quiet corners of the room.

Under the storm of weeping, Maureen ran in, a new skating dress forgotten on its hanger. She took in the scene; her mother sobbing on the bed, the grotesque make-up, all-concealing fur — but mostly the wig. A maid helped her off with the coat and eased her mother into bed, replacing the cruelly young wig in its case because she dare not, yet, throw it away. Instead she gathered the wasted body into her arms. 'Don't cry, darling, please don't cry.'

'I'm not. I'm not, I was just trying on clothes for Montegreco. I thought I'd take the big coat, it will be cold. But it's heavy and I get so tired. . .'

'I know. You do too much. There's no need to come to the rink with me now. I'm a big girl, you know. I talked to the doctor and he said —'

'He had no business discussing me, worrying you at a time like this. As I say, I just get tired.'

'That's all he told me, really. And after the Games we'll go straight to Casa Plata for the sun. Bliss. But you haven't seen my dress for the main programme yet! They dropped it off at ballet this afternoon.' Anything to distract her as the maid cleaned up the dresser. 'Been rehearsing your makeup for the Games? You'll have to help with mine, Mother. I can't decide which lipstick's best. What d'you think, hmm?' 'La Mancha' had been Deirdre's music choice for the long programme, though Maureen and her coach had other plans — a surprise — but they had all agreed on a coral colour scheme months ago. It kept Deirdre part of the team. 'My hair's a problem,' Maureen said. 'I know you prefer it loose — right for "Dulcinea" — but I tried today. It nearly blinded me coming up out of a lay-back spin. If we're not careful that impossible dream could turn into a blasted nightmare.'

'Oooh . . . your hair's so glorious . . . a shame to bundle it in a net.'

'But safe.'

Maureen shook her head as the housekeeper inquired about dinner. Deirdre wouldn't be hungry. The doctor had explained about nausea and chemotherapy. She knew anyway. Amazing what you could glean if a sympathetic medical librarian showed you where to look. 'After your nap we'll have a grand rehearsal, okay? The Sterling Women Conquer the Olympics! Meantime I have to visualize.' She rolled her eyes at the training jargon, but Deirdre did not giggle. She hadn't for a long time. Perhaps she never would again.

In her room Maureen flicked on her music, forced herself to relax, and in the vivid eye of her mind skated the perfect programme, breathing to musical cues, mentally floating from move to move exactly as she'd been taught, for the moment shutting out her own uncertain future and Deirdre's suffering. It was set to play over and over until the perfection of it hypnotized her.

In the next room Deirdre drifted off to sleep on the same impossible dream, which swiftly turned to delirium. She, who had chosen the music entirely from sentiment, no longer saw her daughter skating it. Now it was Grant as he'd been the year they'd loved, when he'd skated for her and only her. How beautiful he'd been, his youth a shining gift offered to her in tribute — except now as she watched him, longed for him, another figure circled him on the ice, one too often envied on video tapes.

Roxanne Kramer skated into the picture now, also young, supremely graceful — and healthy. In sleep Deirdre called his name, but as she spoke he turned into Roxanne's embrace, and Deirdre lay alone with her empty scarecrow arms and her tears.

CHAPTER TEN

Los Angeles, California

Waiting for her newest doctor, Noni shivered in the unheated, unsterile room. Her skinny buttocks chafed against a week's worth of grit. Normally this guy never used an examination table, and from the look of the outer office she could guess why. The other patients, all women sweating in prisons of fat, waited for him to dispense over-priced diet pills, and his sing-song, obligatory warning, a chubby nurse as witness. A consultation consisted of stepping on to a scale, a bored receptionist noting the weight and holding out her hand for a cheque in advance. No one balked when asked for ID. They were too eager to count their pills. New to town, this guy already had a reputation for shorting his packs. Noni figured he flirted mighty close to arrest. She sighed. Soon she'd have to hunt up a new source.

He came in so quickly she knew he'd put her ahead of the queue. Again. The curtain hung loose but he closed it anyway. The surrounding gloom threw his white turban into dramatic effect and mercifully softened his outline as he shimmied out of white cotton trousers and tunic and hurriedly spread Noni's legs. She shut her eyes, but there was no escaping the curried miasma of his breath. Perhaps from necessity he went about it like a rabbit, in-and-out, in-and-out, done. He didn't speak during, and his labours tired her less than the insertion of her diaphragm. True, he didn't do much for her pride, but in this world you couldn't have everything.

Already dressed, he smiled his white smile and said, 'Most enjoyable.' Into her open purse he tossed a handful of samples as if they were *baksheesh*, then complicated the transaction by bowing. 'Be my guest.'

Frantic with gratitude — on the street these white babies came high — she pressed his moist brown hands in hers. 'Thank you, thank you —'

'Anytime. My wife weighs 250 pounds. For me it is a great pleasure to fuck a woman whose bone structure I can still see.'

Noni edged towards the door. Was there a socially correct form on which to end encounters such as these? 'Well, like I said, thanks a mill. . .

He bowed lower, then abruptly straightened, his small feet twinkling towards the packed waiting room. On the way he adjusted his turban, which had begun to slip.

To celebrate Roxanne's stunning, almost miraculous return to form, Grant gave her dinner at a garden restaurant perched high above Beverly Hills. Under a clear night sky filled with stars, Roxanne, in slim cream lace and a chunky jade necklace, glowed with a radiance seldom seen since she'd won her first important title. Today her skating had been sublime, a World Champion at her elegant best, and Grant had again felt the Gold Medal within his grasp — or theirs, which was the same thing. Her transformation had been so astonishing he even summoned Noni from her hiding place in lost-and-found. The whole world deserved to watch Roxanne that morning, even her mother — whose excitement gleamed through last night's mascara and her constant Mutti-inspired frown.

Across the table, Dr Jasinski beamed. He too had much to celebrate: a long-sought partner to ease his heavy patient load, leaving him free to accept an official invitation, prompted, he knew, by Grant — a place on the Olympic squad as Roxanne's personal physician. 'Which you are,' Grant pointed out.

For Grant, the long run-up to the Games was almost over, and at last filled with promise; in ten days his entire stable, near peak performance and uninjured, knock wood, would be at the Games. Most teams had two weeks at the site; Grant's skaters would have an extra week for altitude training. Insurance. You couldn't get too much of a good thing.

Watching Roxanne's lowered head as she delicately tapped

excess herb butter from an escargot, her total dedication to the job at hand, he felt a sudden rush of tenderness, of gratitude. She would do it for him, would do anything for him because she loved him. What more could he ask? Beejay, prodigiously improved and raring for glory, skated only for Beejay and her Em. Jeff Dunsmuir aimed to bask in the spotlight, to be admired, envied, ultimately to be as rich as his Sterling sponsor, if he could, if he skated his best and the other contenders did not, if Alexei Finsky failed to show up. If, if, if. Dag Carlsen skated in a futile attempt to keep peace at home, shield mother and perhaps himself from father's endless rage. Lise skated because it was the most direct route to father's American Express card.

Only Roxanne skated for Grant because she loved him, wanted to give him, them, the status of Olympic Gold Medallist. Unselfish girl, how could he not love her for it? As he watched, the waiter whisked away her empty shells to replace them with slivered tempura chicken and mange-tout. She smiled directly into Grant's eyes and bit into the chicken with apparent delight.

'Mmmm,' she murmured. 'We'll come here again.' Not, 'Please will you bring me here again, Grant?' But, 'We'll come here again.' In the evening light her glance sparkled with promise, and, for the first time, maturity. It was as if in one day she'd grown into every one of her twenty-two years. Amazing. A single morning session of glorious skating, and her confidence surged back. When the *maître d'* asked for her autograph 'for his little girl', she gave it with assurance, not a single questioning glance at Grant. When the chef announced his new dessert, *crème olympiques*, a froth of lacy meringue garnished with whipped cream and kiwi medallions to honour Roxanne's presence, she responded with gracious modesty and ate an entire portion.

Then she excused herself for just a moment and the two men were left alone. To Grant, whose social circle was the skating milieu of judges, coaches and officials, this unlikely new doctor friend constantly surprised him. Jasinski lacked any interest in gossip — coin of the realm within the sport's tight-knit community. Jasinski's interests tended to books, international politics, and world events. In Grant's set, politics meant who was judging which competition and how;

which skaters would find international approval this season, which would fall from grace. A well-thumbed official rule book was the literature of choice. World events was rink gossip on a global scale.

Jasinski, pure in heart, knew nothing of these. Sugaring his coffee and adding cream, he said thoughtfully, 'Roxanne's weight is stable? She ate well but looks thin — but vivacious, happy, of course.'

'Because she skated like a dream this morning.'

'That is all it takes?'

With Jasinski's question the picture shifted again. Why must this man question every motive, lift rocks that shouldn't be moved, not now, with Montegreco rushing in, exposing what was best kept dark?

'Look,' Grant said, aware of the impatience in his voice and his powerlessness to stop it, 'for you this may be the ultimate in trivial pursuits —'

'Not at all,' Jasinski interrupted. 'I find nothing trivial in a young woman afraid of her mother, her grandmother, her fiancé, her mirror, the very food on her plate.'

'You heard her, she's not afraid of me, she's beginning to assert herself! And you admitted she was improving, beginning to eat normally —'

Jasinski sighed as he nodded. 'Beginning, oh yes. But patterns formed over a lifetime seldom. . .' He seemed to shake his shoulders, straighten out their stoop. 'My friend, we start to quarrel. Bad for the digestion, and such a splendid meal, this celebration for Roxanne —'

Grant willed himself not to turn, to look for her, as Jasinski drew his attention to the window. Far below them a black-and-white howled its siren, flashed its lights. Jasinski pointed down to Bel Air streets lined with sumptuous homes. 'Once, when you were very young, those houses blazed like torches.' He spoke quietly, as if feeling again the heat of the fire. 'The flames drew closer and closer. A fire storm, yes? up and down the canyons. People were told to leave, that their homes could not be saved. But some of them hoped, waited for the last moment, watched their family life-style burn away in an excess of hope.'

Grant barely heard. He was checking his watch. Roxanne

was gone a hell of a long time. He could hardly follow her to the girls' room but —

'Don't worry.' Jasinski's smile had a sad edge to it. 'You said yourself, today she is happy. Beautiful young women spend much time at the mirror.'

Just then she appeared, her hair freshly brushed, face immaculate with a new make-up job, that unmistakable glow of assurance still intact. She stooped to drop a kiss on Grant's forehead and he caught the fresh, minty odour of toothpaste and mouthwash. She took hygiene seriously, this girl.

'So that's what you were up to,' Grant said, pulling out her chair. 'It was worth it. You look like you're ready to step up to the podium.'

'Oh, I will. You don't have to worry about that.'

Hallelujah! Confidence at last.

It held all the way home to the round tower, where she slowly stepped out of her cream dress and underwear and stood only in the jade necklace, brushing her long, ash blonde hair. Tantalizing. Tonight there was no plea in the gesture, no please-make-love-to-me-so-I'll-know-I'm-worth-something. Without it she was infinitely more desirable, an equal instead of a child to be comforted. He felt that anticipatory tightening in his groin as he reached out to Roxi, his lover, not Roxanne Braun Kramer, potential Olympic winner.

But God, she *was* thin. The mirror's reflection glanced off jutting scapulas, skeletons of angels' wings, despite the increased food intake prescribed by Jasinski and supervised by Grant. She ate three good meals a day now, more food than at any time since he'd known her. On Jasinski's advice he'd stopped weighing her on the grounds that she'd never take responsibility for her own body as long as they checked up on her but. . . But she was skating well, so the strength was there, had to be.

'You looked beautiful tonight, Roxi —'

'God, and I wasn't even *skating*?'

'Darling, why would you even say that?'

'Why not,' she said sweetly. 'That's when you're nicest to me. You're always nice to people who can do you some good. Beejay, Emma. . .'

Jeez, where the hell was this coming from? 'If I'm "nice" to them it's because I like them. I like Dag. I don't fancy Lise or Mr Carlsen or Dunsmuir, so I don't go out of my way to be nice . . . So what the hell does any of that have to do with us? We love each other. It's not the same thing at all.'

'We'll know after the Games, won't we?'

'I thought we knew now.' He felt he'd been kicked in the balls and made a subconscious gesture to protect himself. 'Look, let's not fight, we've had a great day —'

'Because I skated great.'

'We're talking in circles. You know that is not it.'

'I don't know anything anymore.'

'Want me to show you?'

She shook her head. 'Uh-uh. No sex until after the Games. As you keep telling me, I need to build strength.'

He drew away, intimidated by this new Roxanne. Almost new. In bed she still wanted to sleep with his arms around her, spoon-fashion. Before she dropped off she said quietly, 'I'm having lunch with Mom tomorrow.'

He held his breath. 'Fine. Enjoy.'

'And I'm putting Gran's spin in the programme.'

'There's no spot for it.'

'In place of the triple-flip.'

Which she needed. 'See much of your mom?' he asked carefully.

She shrugged, and the knife-sharp angel wings cut into his chest. 'I run into all kinds of people while you're busy teaching Beejay.'

So that was it. Still. 'You've not kissed me goodnight.'

As she turned to him briefly he caught the odour of peppermint and something less pleasant, muted but familiar. He was almost asleep before he recognized it. Oh, not again, Roxanne, not again! Jasinski had known, damn him — and said nothing! Hints, suggestions, they were Jasinski's coin. He lay back in despair. They were too close to the Games now for a solution, maybe too close to each other. Their relationship lay stretched on the rack of competition and they were fresh out of time to pad or patch it. It all came down to the Gold, rotting their relationship from within.

If she won, the Games would make them both. If she lost, the loss would be mainly hers. He would still be a top coach;

she'd be an 'also-ran' forever. The Games' fault, they'd been the trouble ever since he'd weaned a dependent girl away from an abusive mother so that she'd depend on him instead. And win for him. In the process they'd grown together like a double-yolked egg. Now Mount Olympus loomed too big on the horizon for either of them to see around it into the future. Its sharp, thin air clouded the vision, distorted judgement, its top prize so rich that everything measured against it shrank in comparison.

The honour of the Gold went on echoing down the ages, creating an instant legend with a highly saleable name, a name pregnant with fame and the promise of riches far into its owner's future. Well invested, its dividends accrued for ever and ever, amen. Silver and Bronze got you a soloist's contract for eight or nine seasons — if the bones held out, if you could stand life on the road that long, city after city, hotel after hotel, year in, year out until you forgot where you were and recognized the hotels only by their bedspreads. Every bed had its logo, but when all you did was sleep in it alone. . .

He remembered his last year with the show, the ninth. A sprained ankle that never had time to heal, a bucket of chipped-ice backstage to reduce the swelling before and after so he could lace his boot, skate his number, then whip the boot off quick while he still could. After that a taxi back to the hotel and bandages soaked in more ice so the ankle wouldn't balloon up for the next day's run-through. A sandwich and lager from room-service, then sleep. You never met a girl unless she skated the show too. Touring performers hit town and were gone too soon to meet anyone else — stay-at-home girls don't date guys who work six nights a week and fly to another town on the seventh. In the end, you lived only by the applause. Was it louder tonight than last night? Last week? Month? If yes, you were holding even or they were being kind. If not, you were slipping, slipping. Somehow you never moved up because you had no Gold to dazzle the medal-blinkered networks and viewers. For an 'also-ran', the glamour of the road lost its shine pretty damn fast.

Roxanne couldn't handle that and shouldn't have to. When she skated, just plain stroking the ice, there was a delicacy about her that tore your heart out. It had little to do with costuming, nothing at all to do with jumps. On the cool ice Roxanne's spirit seemed to flicker to life, a slender flame which lit her from within and warmed all who saw her. Her unique talent cried out to be nurtured, but so fragile . . . and slender flames died on the lightest breeze.

Vulnerable in sleep, she trapped his hand under her cheek the way a child might. For a long time he lay awake, the ridge of her hip outlined against the moonlit window. Touching his lips gently to her hair, he tasted tears in his throat for another vulnerable, remembered spirit caught in a biting winter with nothing to shield her but an old green coat.

Mum would have understood Roxi.

CHAPTER ELEVEN

Moscow, USSR

Until the past few weeks Alexei assumed he had an affable working relationship with the Director. Alexei won medals for the State. In return, the Director won special privileges for Alexei, who now sat quietly waiting for the older man to squirm, to show remorse, or at least to acknowledge that the system treated its athletes as pawns and that the Director was sorry, even embarrassed.

Not quite. The Director rubbed his hands and offered Alexei a brandy. French, of course. He smoked Cuban cigars and wore Saville Row suits of fine grey worsted, silk shirts tailored in New York, and custom-made shoes from Milan. When he chose to, the Director indulged himself in caviar from Astrakhan, champagne shipped in from Paris, and when in Vienna, a top-of-the-line call-girl. His Moscow wife shopped at Dom Modeli, his garage housed a ZIL, and once a year he found occasion to visit Geneva. God bless his Party membership card, which permitted travel outside the Bloc for those who nominally lived within it. Secure behind his symbols of power, the Director was seldom embarrassed.

'I've won three World Championships for you,' Alexei persisted. 'You owe me *some* consideration. I've put in almost sixteen years.'

'So, my boy, have we,' the Director said smoothly. 'The decision is irreversible. Galina is off the team.'

'We're engaged. Even if she's not a competitor, she can be my guest.'

The Director spread his hands. 'She tells me she doesn't wish to go. Besides, you know bureaucrats. They'd never get her visa through in time.'

'She *has* one! You issued it when she was on the team.'

'The Department cancelled it when she withdrew.'

'She didn't withdraw. She was withdrawn,' Alexei shouted. 'You twist my words.'

Alexei resisted the urge to twist his neck. 'You could have it re-issued. You have the authority. A visa for the guest of your three-time World Champion?'

The Director laughed, genuinely amused. 'If we permitted guests at the Olympics, we'd be shipping wives, husbands, lovers, parents, children and pet poodles for the entire team! We have a budget, you know.' To prove his point he stubbed out the cigar and lit a domestic cigarette, just failing to control his disgust as the harsh smoke reached his throat.

'The entire team will not win top Medals,' Alexei countered.

'Gold? Among the figure skaters we anticipate —' The man wrinkled his brow, appearing to count, but Alexei knew the number to be carved on the man's heart, along with the next exalted title to which he aspired. 'I've never kept secrets from you, Alexei. I hope for five Golds. Two for Pairs, two for Dance, and, of course, yours. Mens. You cannot miss.'

'Then why throw this last-minute bomb? What's Galina done wrong?'

The Director stood, checking the creases in his finely pressed trousers. 'Nothing. But if she does not mind, why should you? We waste each other's time, my friend. You know why she was withdrawn.'

Alexei knew he should go. Madness to fence with them. He wielded a foil, they thrust with naked steel. He drew his last puny weapon.

'And if Alexei Finsky, who can't miss, declines to compete?'

The Director flushed an angry magenta. 'There's a US prospect in Boston; the Brits have Dunsmuir; two Canadians have a chance. Can you throw away a certain Gold, for which we have all worked so hard?'

'Why not? It means nothing to me.'

'Of course it does. Your people have pride.'

Alexei felt the blood drain from his face, felt, for a moment, that he might pass out. 'My people —?'

'You thought we didn't know? Can you be so naïve, *Mr*

Feinstein? Because your mother worshipped in private does not mean —'

The tide of blood surged back and for a moment he actually saw the Director and all he represented through a smear of crimson. 'You knew she was Orthodox *and yet you cremated her*?'

The Director shrugged. 'Are we expected to know every tenet of every superstition we permit to flourish within our borders?' Briefly he examined his well-manicured fingertips. 'Who are we, mere civil servants, to expose her secret at her death? She herself turned her back on the Talmud when she changed her name to Finsky. Presumably she had reason.'

'Of course she damned well had reason — I wanted to be a skater! That was reason enough for her. She couldn't find a single Jewish name in this illustrious skating school so —'

'That is not true!'

'You know it is. So I became Finsky. The best skater you've got. Now you turn my fiancée into a pawn. While we're at it, understand this also. When I compete I skate for me — not for Almighty Mother Russia!' In the room's shocked silence he realized what he'd said, the echoing volume of his voice.

The Director looked over his shoulder — a reflex, the door was closed — and allowed his lips to form the shape of 'Ssssh.' As Alexei's chief mentor over the last ten years, his star skater's marked deviation from Leninist doctrine would hardly enhance his own chance of promotion. He laid a prudent hand on Alexei's shoulder as he opened the door. 'Good luck, my boy. We know you'll do your best for us.'

Alexei shook him off. 'I am not your boy,' he whispered, 'and when I do my best I do it for me.'

Despite growing tension there had been no open break, no admission that their affair neared its end. Galina waited for him at the apartment, mushroom soup simmering on the stove, the room filled with the clean smell of laundry warm from the iron, shirts and blouses on racks, sheets and pillow-cases in tidy heaps. On the table a bowl of tulips, each scarlet bloom wide open to its yellow and black centre, petals ready to fall on a white lace cloth set for two. By the great feather bed, the window stood open to the dusk.

Technically they lived together still; practically, now, they were farther apart than strangers. Between strangers no chasm of uncertainty gaped wider with every silence, with each carefully avoided intimacy. He'd said he had an appointment with the Director but not why. She knew anyway.

The moment she saw his face she also knew he'd failed. There would be no visa. Against everything her body told her, against her love, no, her worship of Alexei, her reaction was an overwhelming, draining relief. Now the decision to defect or remain was not hers to make, to leave her parents forever or return here and thus betray all Alexei's dreams for their future in the West. The authorities had decided for her. Her relief was a weakness, she knew, but now she could rest as she had not rested for many months, looking at Alexei and suspecting, knowing he wanted her to go with him, knowing she could not bear to leave Russia forever.

Like the others, she envied the West's abundance, but it was not home. Better a stroll down Kalinina Prospect with Alex than a shopping-spree on Fifth Avenue. Once, on an exhibition tour in LA, the team had a free day. The others piled into taxis for the nearest mall. She wandered through the Museum of Natural History. 'You're crazy,' they said, 'anybody who prefers Cro-Magnon to I.Magnin —'. Perhaps they were right. She didn't hunger for expensive clothes, rich foods. Only people, her people, and the occasional small treat. One perfect banana, queued for and slowly peeled, each tropical morsel savoured, gave her more pleasure than a whole sack of peaches bought at a street-stand in Paris. For her, abundance dulled the appetite. For food, clothes, travel, books — even love. When Alexei exhibited in Prague or Warsaw he wanted her with him. Usually she refused. Time apart sharpened her pleasure when they were together again. Maybe she was a masochist after all. Alex often said so.

'How was our dear Director,' she began. 'Greedy as ever? Counting his medals before they are struck?'

She wasn't fishing, not exactly — but he knew she was. The subject they'd skirted for weeks couldn't be avoided forever. 'He's counting on mine,' he said carefully, offering her the cue, dreading she'd take it.

She passed. 'We have soup. If you turn up the heat I'll just. . .' She gathered up the freshly ironed clothes, hung them or stacked them on shelves, her expression hidden from him by shared linens and solo intent.

'The Director said no. They won't give you a guest visa.'

The back of her head nodded. 'Of course.'

'He said you told him you didn't wish to go anyway.'

'He asked me. I told the truth.'

'He's a bastard. They all are!'

She was quiet, her fingers caressing his clean shirts as she buttoned them on to hangers, a breeze from the darkening window ruffling her hair, sending a scent of spring violets across the room to him. Oh, if he could stand behind her, whisper that win or lose, he'd come home, marry, give her children to love. He couldn't. He wasn't sure. Children would trap him here forever. If he took Gold he'd be retired from competitor to coach with full perks. If he lost, they'd retire him anyway after today's outburst; the perks would be in doubt. They seldom took risks and wouldn't now except for the Medal, the damned Medal — which, when he brought it home, would slam his only door on the West.

'What shall I do, Galina? Tell me what to do,' he said softly.

She turned, pink cheeks in a pale, frightened face. 'It's not fair to ask me.'

'If I don't skate, I give away Gold. *My* Gold. Probably to Dunsmuir. They say he's doing well with Grant Rivers, but, oh God, Galina, I'm so *tempted* to develop a cramp when my turn comes to skate. Punish the swine.'

'The choice is yours, but to chicken out is unworthy. Of you, of us.'

Chicken out. The Western expression leapt out of its surrounding Russian, buzz-words which seasoned rink conversation throughout the USSR, used first in arrogance, proof they travelled outside the Bloc, like Galina's designer jeans and his Canon camera were proof. Now they used it naturally, but each time it brought reminders of foreign skaters, locker-room anguish for planned moves not made because maybe the timing was off, the music too slow, the surface too — but, hell, if you 'chickened out' it cost you, cost you. This move, far more vital than any he would ever execute on ice, would cost him whether he made it or not. Flee to the West, he lost his Galina. Return here, he lost his freedom. And Galina would not beg. Quite the opposite, as she was now to prove.

'Today I called home. My father's not well again. Since I'm not training right now I told Mother I'd move back with them for a day or so. Take care of him while she's at work.'

'A day or so?' Alarm bells rang somewhere very close.

'I promised them a week or ten days, time to get him really well. I'll go tomorrow morning.' She reached under the bed for her suitcase and added a couple of blouses to its bulging top.

'But in a week I leave for Montegreco!'

'Yes.'

'Then this is our last night! Before the Games, I mean.'

Meeting his, her blue eyes held steady. 'You will think clearer alone.'

So she was opting-out, refusing to influence him. He should have known. She refused to fight. For him. For freedom. For anything. That's why she was a so-so competitor, he thought in sudden, vengeful anger. 'Thanks a lot.'

Calmly she ladled mushroom soup into bowls, buttering fresh black bread at the table. 'As you said, this is our last night. Let's not fight.'

They ate in silence, staring only at their plates. Midway, he got up and closed the window against the night now almost upon them, the sky a bruised indigo over a Moskva relentlessly rolling to the south, her black waters already studded with reflected stars, her shallows lapping in moonlight. Galina's city, her river, her country. Behind him the smallest sound, like the breath of a child. Galina, weeping? It came again as he turned to her. No, there were no tears. Just another red petal falling to the lace cloth.

She had finished her soup and was collecting them as they fell, running a forefinger over each scarlet splash in her palm. 'Feel them,' she murmured. 'Like the best satin, yet they're dying. . .'

'We'll get more tomorrow,' he said — then remembered she wouldn't be here tomorrow, perhaps wouldn't ever be here again.

This evening she made coffee a ceremony, with honey cakes served on china plates bought last year in London and never before used. 'They're stock pattern,' she'd said. 'Next trip we'll get cups and saucers to match.' Next trip. All for the future home of Alexei and Galina Finsky.

At bedtime, she emerged from the bathroom in a blue silk nightgown he knew she'd been saving for her trousseau. She looked grave, wistful, but the usual calm governed her every move. At the mirror she brushed out her hair and creamed her milk-maid skin, then reached in the drawer to dab a little 'Joy' in the hollows of her throat.

To lighten the moment he said, 'Go easy on that. Remember I'm in training.'

'How can I forget?' In the mirror their eyes met, hers a brave, determined blue which speared him where words could not. In the heart. They were killing each other. Or the Gold was killing them both.

'If I promise to come back this time,' he whispered, 'will you at least consider —'

She laid a finger on his lips. 'Don't make promises you're not sure you can keep.'

He pressed her cool hands against his burning face, kissed their palms, the shell-like nails, the small, efficient wrists which polished his furniture, kneaded his bread, wrung his heart. He had hoped that one day they would soothe the fevers of his children. 'In some holy book it says a wife leaves her parents and cleaves only to her husband, follows him wherever he goes.'

Her smile curved into a sad, indulgent line. 'Does it? Holy books mean nothing to me. My family means everything —'

'More than I.'

'We're fighting again. On our last night.'

'Only until I come back.'

She looked up at him, drew him with her eyes until he could see his face in their blue depths, could read her thoughts as clearly as if they were written. 'You will not come back,' her eyes said. 'You are leaving me.'

'No!' he cried. 'No, no, no. . .' burying his lips in her fragrant hair, stroking his ice-chapped hands over cool blue silk, then warm satin flesh, cupping each full breast in his palm, committing its sweet, soft weight to memory. 'Come to bed,' he whispered.

Again the strange, sad smile. 'You're in training.'

'The hell with training, with the Medal, with Mother Russia! Please. . .'

He slipped the thin straps from her shoulders and a pool of blue silk whispered at her feet. Kneeling, his lips followed it, lingering at the perfumed hollow in her throat.

'You didn't put out the light,' she said softly.

'Let me see you, tonight let me see you.' Always she wanted the light out, he never knew why. The sight of their joined bodies a secret from whatever or whoever might be watching? Perhaps her own modesty? But tonight she conceded, her lips full and moist, waiting for his mouth, sighing with pleasure at the touch of his hands.

His eyes drank her in: the compact skater's body, firm calves and thighs, pubic hair modestly shaved for the briefest of costumes, stomach muscles long and flat, a sweet curve of waist, breasts unexpectedly full, round, their nipples as hot and ripe as rose-hips on an autumn day. No need for his mouth to seek them, they were there, eagerly pressed to his lips, unbelievably responsive to his tongue. Her thighs parted, and he savoured the unique taste of her, the gathering warmth of her secret places. 'Oh, God . . .'

She pressed him to her, opened herself to his mouth. 'This is the last time,' she thought, 'the last time I will feel his hands on me, stroking, pressing, adoring. The last time his tongue will touch me there, the last time he will worship me with his lips, the last time I will press his head to my breast, the last time he will enter me, the last time my muscles will draw him in, hold him tight . . . I would hold him forever if only I could, if only I could, if only I could, if I could, if I could, could, could, faster, faster, faster — 'Alex!' she sobbed, 'Oh, Alex —' She shuddered, gasped, forced herself not to say the words, not to beg him now, in this weakest of moments, to come back to her. Don't ask, set him free, give him to the West if he wants to go, but, dear God, how could she bear it if he never came back?

How can I go away and not come back? he thought. How can I leave this loving soul who demands nothing, gives everything, who knows me better than I know myself? Whose body accepts me eagerly, warmly, avidly, who draws me to her heart again and again, whose breath is warm on my cheek, whose arms embrace but never cling, always ready to open, to let me go. . . Blood roared in his head, his heart, his groin. In the last breath-stopping moment, approaching that orgasmic peak from which he could no longer hold back, he heard an inner voice whisper, unbidden, unwanted, an echo that would remain with him tomorrow, and maybe forever. 'For you, Alex,' the voice whispered, 'perhaps Galina *is* Mother Russia.'

Later, in the quiet darkness, it seemed to him that one of them had died — but their lives, their limbs, their memories were so entangled it was impossible to know who.

She must have crept out very early next morning. She'd set the breakfast table for one. A coffee-pot, a cup, bread, and a single brown egg ready to poach.

No doubt running late, she had not cleared the tulips.

In the night the last scarlet petals had fallen, and now lay like splashes of arterial blood on the white cloth.

CHAPTER TWELVE

Los Angeles, California

With Emma Crisp as top judge and referee, a figure-test scraped to its inevitable conclusion, one small aspirant skating specific figures-of-eight required for advancement within the sport. Emma thought, not for the first time, that too often it was the parent who aspired, the child who was tested.

Today was no exception. Judges and judges-in-training loomed like canyon walls between which the trapped eight-year-old, pink bows in her hair and terror in her eyes, must demonstrate her wobbly circles. Her mother, as nervous as she, had poured last minute warnings into ears deaf with panic. If she failed or if her figures were so bad the judges elected to abandon the test, she couldn't take it again for a month, she did understand that? The child nodded, shivering. A whole month! An eternity of shame for the small one.

Up in the bleachers Grant's Olympic stars perched like a flight of hawks scanning their terrain, five pairs of gimlet eyes watching the progress of the tiny apprentice across the rink. They sensed that the ice, freshly and carefully made, which the Club hired by the hour, would soon be theirs by default. They were warmed up, skates tight, ready to swoop. Too bad if the kid's test failed but, hell, no sense wasting empty ice this close to the Games.

Below them on the rink, Emma sighed. After several spooned turns and a multitude of flats, after the kid lost her centre, found it, lost it again, Emma had no choice but to make her call, abandon the test. The little candidate's worst nightmare now a reality, she burst into tears, wet her frilly panties, and ran howling for the restroom, closely followed by her mother. The judges hobbled cautiously off and the ice lay open to the élite. Grant, who'd anticipated the result, stepped into the centre: the Carlsens, Jeff Dunsmuir, Beejay and Roxanne all followed, the small aspirant already forgotten.

On the bench Ben Carlsen's eyes never left Lise and Dag; Noni's never left Roxanne — though her fingers picked nonexistent lint off her imitation suede purse. Emma, her judging duties prematurely over, seated herself well away from Ben and Noni and settled for an Olympic preview.

Beejay was right. Roxanne was indeed skating better despite a touch of 'flu — not five minutes ago Noni had given her an aspirin. Maybe that's why she'd subtracted a few jumps and added spins, one of them unfamiliar to Emma, who thought she'd seen them all. It was different but easy — not that she'd get points for 'different' unless there was real innovation. There wasn't. It was a variation on an old faithful, but Roxanne spun well. She jumped stronger now too, but something seemed a little off. Then Grant played her music. She began her long programme and now Emma saw it. Roxanne, who usually had to chase the beat, was ahead of it. Way ahead. Grant stopped her, ordered her to start over, slow down some, thus Emma got a closer look at the current world Champion and the United States' best hope for a medal, the expression in her eyes. Jesus! Surely Grant could see it? Yeah. A muscle jumped in his jaw and his mouth was a taut, furious line as he snapped the tape off and marched over to Noni. Reading his lips, Emma could swear he was telling her to get the hell over to the apartment with Roxanne and wait for him there, that he wanted words. Words. Roxanne, looking mystified, left with her mother — who looked anything but. What she looked was guilty as hell as they disappeared through the great side door.

The Carlsens had their usual problems, only more so. Every lift teetered this way and that, the effort printed clearly on Dag's perfect features. Lise contributed zero. She could have jumped into most of the lifts; instead she held herself stiff as mutton, left all the strain to Dag. She messed up the diagonal sequence and singled three out of five doubles in the combo; their spins were out of synch and in the slow part, meant to be dreamy and romantic, Lise actually opened her healthy pink mouth and yawned. Charming.

Emma, of little faith, sent up a swift prayer that she did not draw the ticket to judge Pairs at the Games. It wasn't just that the Carlsens had no chance to medal — only three did and Lise and Dag were nowhere near the calibre — but the way Lise was skating now made everybody look bad — coach, the country she represented, but worst of all her brother, who deserved better.

Jeff Dunsmuir, next up, skated a perfect programme well within his confident new grasp. He'd always been good but now he was elegantly consistent — maybe a mite *too* elegant for Emma's taste. Daily ballet sessions had borne fruit. Too bad. The Russian, if he showed, had hair on his chest.

Now Beejay. Emma's eyes opened just that bit wider. Busy part-time at the hospital — that nursing course taken way back when had sure come in handy — helped pay for what was shaping into an expensive trip. But the job cut deep into her time with Beejay. Emma hadn't seen her daughter skate for days. Now, despite her contempt for parents who lived through their children's achievements, she wanted to stand up and cheer as Beejay zipped through 'Bugler's Holiday', the music as peppy as the skater. Grant had chosen well. Seldom had she seen such a perfect match of skater to music. But what the devil was this? A wrapped, incomplete lutz right at the end? But Beejay *had* no triple-lutz in her programme!

Grant climbed all over her. 'What d'you think you're up to?'

Beejay's lower lip came out. 'I could have it dead solid by next week.'

'You could not. I don't want to see that again until after the Games, hear me? This close, it's too bloody risky. Start over.'

Beejay glanced up at her mother, no doubt expecting support. No way, José. Emma smiled at them both, said she'd wait in the car, and walked out into the California Sunday afternoon, sane people in flowery hats and gloves pouring from the church across the street. Conspicuous in sheepskin jacket and moon-boots, she ducked quickly into her car and privacy. Not for long. Damn. She heard footsteps, knew whose they were, but refused to turn until she must.

'Emma!' Ben Carlsen rattled the handle too late. She'd locked herself in, rolling the window down just a crack. Bourbon breath wafted through it.

'So what can I do for you?'

'The Games. Look, Emma, I know we've had our differences, but are you . . . Well, will you be judging Pairs?'

'Dunno. We draw when we get there. Even if I knew I couldn't tell you.'

'I might have known you'd say that.'

'Suit yourself.'

'But if you do. What chance do you figure Lise and Dag have?' She knew he was trying to sound casual. He failed. The pores on his nose beaded up with booze, and a flush mounted his gaunt cheekbones.

'I wouldn't know.'

'Not much you wouldn't! You've never liked Lise. She's too good-looking. Women judges are jealous to death, they hold it against her, always did.'

'I don't judge beauty contests, Ben.'

'You robbed her once, in Singles.' He rattled the door handle in futile rage. 'Four years back she could have made Nationals, but no, you marked her down, killed her chances. By now she could be where Beejay is!'

'Move, Ben.' Snapping on the ignition, Emma shot her car out of the slot and roared into the quiet Sunday street.

'Just you wait,' he shouted after her. 'I don't forget, I —' She left him mouthing his frustration to empty air as she circled the block until Beejay darted into view, skate-bag in one hand, pastrami sandwich in the other.

'Get in fast, sport. Ben's smashed, he's on the prowl. Don't ever let him pump you about Dag and Lise's chances, okay? You know nothing.'

'I don't anyway. God, is she ever something else! Dag's neat, though. I'd do Pairs with him any day. I do now sometimes, just for fun. It's like having a mountain under you. Dead solid he is. Want a bite?'

'No. All I say is, watch out for Ben. When he looks at Lise he sees perfection. That's all he wants to see.'

'The lifts scare the holy shit out of her —'

'Beej, what did I say about your language?'

'— she's even scared of the death-spiral. But God, is she gorgeous! She could be a movie star any day. Oh crap, will you look at that!' A gob of mustard drizzled on to her sweater. 'Got a Kleenex?'

Ben watched them go, hating their confidence, what he presumed to be their influence. But he should watch his mouth. Suppose that bitch *did* judge his kids? Grant would know, he knew every damn thing. But it was too late to ask him. As if the thought conjured up the man, Grant's Porsche swerved round Ben on two wheels and ran a red to make it on to the freeway.

They were waiting for Grant at the apartment, Roxanne apprehensive in the rocker, Noni tapping long magenta fingernails on the window.

Grant wasted no words. 'Okay. What did you give her?'

'I don't know what you're talking about.'

A vein throbbed in his temple. '*What did you give her*?'

'I had a headache,' Roxi whimpered. 'She gave me an aspirin, that's all.'

'Sure. Want to show me the bottle, Noni?'

Noni smiled, her eyes a hard blue glitter as she reached into her pocket. 'Catch.' The bottle of aspirin just missed his head. He emptied it on to the table. Every tablet had an innocent logo. Damn.

'Where's your purse?'

'In my car. I've got a date, can't stay long —'

He plucked the keys from her pocket and tossed them to Roxi. 'Go down and get her purse.'

'*Oh no, she doesn't*.' Noni lunged for the door, but Grant had her wrists tight behind her. She could have been in handcuffs.

He nodded to Roxi. 'Get it. Now!'

'Christ, Rox, after everything I've done for you!' Noni screamed.

Grant ignored her. Even as she kicked at his shins, butted his chin with the back of her head, he fixed Roxanne with a steady gaze.

'This is decision time, baby. Level. *What did she give you*?'

'What I said. It made me feel better. I skated all right, didn't I?'

'No aspirin in the world does that. Either I find out what you took or we let the cops find out. Or you can make it easier still, go get her purse.'

She looked from mother to lover and — 'Oh, Grant . . .' she wailed.

'Or go live with Momma and find a new coach.'

Creeping out the door, she looked frail now that the drug rush had faded. No spark left, no colour, even her hair a mass of limp strands on her neck. If Noni were any kind of mother she'd tuck her into bed, feed her, then let her sleep for a week. If he were any kind of lover he'd do the same. But Noni was no kind of mother and he was — he was a coach, and the Games rushed at him, no time left to be a lover. Roxanne, his brightest hope, was less now than a flickering candle. The time he'd devoted, his vaunting hopes of Gold almost certainly squandered, he should feel cheated. Instead, an overwhelming compassion swept over him, bringing a rock to his throat that he couldn't seem to swallow down, not even to answer Noni when she muttered:

'You stupid swine! If we get her through the next few weeks she'll win! She'll be set for life!' She flailed her arms, a bird beating its wings against a hunter's net. He gripped her tighter, saying nothing, waiting for Roxanne.

Like a fugitive, she scuttled in with Noni's cheap purse. 'Empty it,' he said curtly. The damage was done. No time now to be gentle.

Lipstick, mascara, wallet, a gap-toothed comb, condoms, breath mints. And, wrapped inside an orange chiffon scarf, the rattle of pills in a bottle.

'You can't *do* this!' Noni screamed as he tossed her into a heap on the couch and unscrewed the bottle cap.

'Sue me . . .' The pills stared up from the palm of his hand, small white eyes with no logo whatever. They looked like they'd come from some backstreet lab. 'Will you tell me what they are, Noni, or do I get them analysed?'

'They're legal!' she shrieked. 'They're appetite suppressants prescribed by a licensed doctor, and they make her skate better than you ever —'

'Diet pills?'

'Like I said, they're legal.'

'They're speed.'

'Don't be dumb. As if I'd give her that poison!'

'Of course you would. You taught her to starve herself because fat wins no medals, then you had to give her speed because she got too weak to skate without it. You said it yourself. "A few more weeks and she'll be set for life." So would you. And the old folks at home might even forgive you at last.'

The thin, small-featured face sharpened to that of a cornered ferret. 'So okay, what's the goddamned harm, Mr Self-righteous Rivers?'

'Grant, Mom wouldn't give me speed . . .' Roxanne's voice trailed off. She'd seen Noni's face, the combination of fury and guilt and desperate unslaked longing.

'I'll tell you what's the goddamned harm, Noni. I've seen skaters hooked on speed — not many because they don't last long. They think they'll get that extra edge, get their heart pepped up, yeah? Except we're talking big time. Olympic competitors are tested.'

'She could quit taking 'em a few days before —'

'And where would her strength come from? Throwing up her meals, like she's been doing for months? Your schemes and lies have painted her into a corner. Now get the hell out and don't come back.' With quiet fury he poured the pills in the disposal and switched on the motor.

'No!' she howled over the rattle. 'If you knew what they'd cost!'

'I know what they could have cost. Gold. Maybe they already have.' He scraped her few belongings into her purse, zipped it and threw it at her, literally ran her to the door, thrust her out and shot the deadbolt.

Roxanne sank into a crumpled heap on the couch. Now he turned on her. 'And you. You stood obediently in the corner while she worked her paint-brush. You thought I didn't know about the vomiting? I smell it.'

'But you didn't *say* anything, you didn't yell at me.'

'Because I've yelled too much, we all have. I've tried, Jasinski's tried, but your mother's sabotaged us at every turn. Next it'll be a needle. Then you're finished. It's up to you. A grown woman, you'll have to find your own future, be responsible for yourself.' He gathered her up, all one hundred pounds of her, and cradled her on his lap. 'Look, for a while I used you. Maybe I used you badly. I wanted a winner. But I've never given you drugs. All that means is that I'm not as bad as your mom, which isn't saying much. But if we want any kind of future I've got to change and so do you. I want children, Roxi. Kids need a mother to raise them. So far you've had no chance to grow up yourself. Now you have. I'll coach you through the Games if you quit the drugs and start to *eat*. If not, I won't. I love you, but I won't live like this. So let's not make commitments we're not sure we can keep, huh?'

'But what do I do about Mom? She's got nobody else. If I shut her out altogether I don't know what she'll do. She gets real strung out sometimes.'

'I know.'

What would he have said if anybody had asked him to shut his own mother out of his life? Punched 'em in the mouth, very likely. 'Maybe you can help her, who knows. Just don't let her near you, okay? Especially with a needle. Right now you're going to pack a bag for yourself and leave.'

The words were out almost before he knew they were in his mind. Maybe he was nuts, maybe he was finally sane. It was a move he had to make but it was damned dangerous, a strategy he might bitterly regret if they draped the Gold around the wrong neck.

'You said you loved me —' she whimpered.

'I do. But you have to trust me on this. There's more at stake now than a medal. Be at the rink every day as usual, but I want you out of here until we leave for the Games. For the next three weeks I'm just your coach, you're just an athlete. I hope you stay with Jasinski. He's offered, but it's up to you. But you, your mom, me, we're all under stress. Jasinski could be the safety valve. If you stay here I'd monitor your meals, your sleep, everything. Whatever you do will be because I told you to. This close, the lines get tangled — right now I'm too involved with you *and* your skating. So is your mother. Jasinski won't meddle. He might even let you grow up.'

The row at the Carlsen house raged all through lunch and

looked set to accelerate in the afternoon as Ben's trips to the liquor cabinet became more frequent, more unsteady. Lise locked herself in her room with her stereo, her little peach phone at the ready should she get lonesome. Dag and Mrs Carlsen found refuge with iced-tea under the oleander by the pool. Ben, who burned easily, seldom ventured into the sun, and never, never swam.

To Dag's surprise Jeff Dunsmuir had just called to invite him to an LA bar that evening. 'I don't know . . . I don't like Jeff that much,' he was saying.

'You *need* a social life,' Mrs Carlsen said gently. 'Skating takes everything. We don't talk anymore. I don't even know what you plan to do after the Games. College, maybe?' She fretted her long hands in a vague, graceful, gesture, and they both laughed at skating's biggest lie. After competition they were all going to college, learning to be brain surgeons. Yeah, sure.

'No. I want to earn my own way. I won't ask Dad for another dime.'

'Don't worry about that! He swears the rock group's picking up most of the tab, so . . . well, it's nothing to do with him.' Her voice suddenly sharpened, and he realised she looked better, more focused, than she had in a long time.

'But I need my own money. Maybe I'll do a show for a year or so if Lise . . . the thing is, I feel bad about leaving you here with Dad.'

'Don't. When you come back from the Games I'll be gone. What d'you think I've been waiting for all these years?'

For a second it seemed like the world turned upside down. In this divided, divisive family Mom stood at its centre — always gentle, always *there*, his one certain ally. 'Gosh, I'd no idea, I mean, you're married a long time. It's not like you to rush into a divorce when things get rough —'

'Rush? "Things", as you call them, have been rough for twenty years, but I always believed kids deserved a full set of parents. I think now I was wrong. A bad set is worse than no set at all.'

'But what brought this on now, I mean —'

Slowly she raised the hem of her sundress. Purples, blues,

yellows, the entire spectrum of pain covered her upper thigh in a massive bruise worse than any he'd gotten from the ice. 'Homesickness. When I mention Sweden your father says I'm a poor transplant to his adopted country. Sometimes he speaks with his fists.'

Under the rage welling up in Dag, this evidence of his father's abuse, his parent's marriage blown apart, his own future uncertain, he should have been shocked . . . but in some way he knew he'd been ready for it, expected it. Lately there'd been changes in Mom, subtle but firm. 'You'll go back to Sweden?'

She nodded. 'I've never quit being homesick. This is a good country but it's never become mine. With the right woman your father might have made the transition. As it is, he's an alcoholic, and if I stick around I'll be one too. That's what unhappy people do to each other. Even Lise —'

'Oh, her!'

'— would have turned out fine if we'd had a better marriage. He made her what she is. Ben needs a weak woman to make him feel he's a strong man, and she's available — no, not that way, she's far too selfish, but I've read enough psychology. It'll kill him when she marries. And she will. When I'm gone she'll leave him for the first boy who asks her. Can you see her keeping house for an ageing drunk who has to be put to bed every night?'

'No.'

She nodded toward Allez-Oop, the white Persian cat playing statues among pink oleander petals. As they watched he leapt down and crept flat-bellied towards the hedge to stand guard at a gopher hole. 'She wanted him so badly yet she's too lazy to feed even him.' She smoothed her beach wrap over a figure still elegant, slender. 'I'll feed him. If Ben comes out, don't be drawn into an argument, okay? Stay out of his hair, and think about going out someplace with Jeff. You need to meet people on the outside.'

The darkened bar smelled less of booze than of men's cologne, expensive cologne. When his eyes adjusted to the gloom, Dag looked around, puzzled, but at first not sure of what. Yellow candles flickered on small tables for two, on carafes of wine and intimate, whispering couples. It took him a moment to register that while every customer was beautifully dressed, all were male — mostly couples but here and there men sat alone, bored, handsome as posed portraits. All had that predatory air of waiting, watching the door.

He ordered a beer, wishing he could leave now before Jeff got here, but who would he tell, who would take a message? And out of all the bars in LA why had Jeff specified this one? He had doubts about Jeff; maybe it was the way his lips shaped 'hot pink' in describing his Olympic costume that made the hair on Dag's arms stand up. But hell, his father had so often hinted that Dag was what he now realised Jeff could be. So how come Jeff invited *him*? What was it about him that made both Dad and Jeff think he belonged in this scary world of beautiful young men and sharp, hunting, old ones, hungry as wolves in winter?

He'd been dating girls since he was sixteen, had even taken Roxanne out before Grant arrived in LA. He hadn't slept with her; they were young and shy and double-dates to Disneyland were the rage that summer. There'd been beach picnics with girls from other clubs, and after a couple of glasses of jug-wine he'd tumbled a few in the dunes. Girls at school, ignorant of skating, understandably objected to being taken home at nine because Dag always had morning patch. Counting, he figured he'd had sex with three girls and come close with a couple more. Was that average for twenty-one? Hell, he *felt* normal. But how come Dad threw out these hints? Lacking time, skaters didn't date nearly as much as other kids. Some of the guys were overtly gay, but not the majority. Like dance and gymnastics, the sport attracted them, maybe produced a few; hours posing at ballet mirrors fostered narcissism, but Grant Rivers was straight enough, most of them were, so why . . .?

Eyes watched him in the gloom, saw the strong column of neck, well-muscled shoulders, the tight legs of the athlete. A whisper, who knew from where: 'Hey, catch the buns on this guy!' Then intimate, answering laughter.

He felt a hand brush casually across his thigh. Christ! He looked hastily around for Jeff and met instead the glitter of diamonds clustered on a well-manicured hand. Dag looked up into brown, knowing eyes.

'Waiting for someone?'

'A friend. He should have been here . . .'

'What's his name. I know most of the regulars.'

'Jeff Dunsmuir.'

A thought, perhaps, a sensual memory, curved the stranger's mouth into a smile. 'I know Jeff — and I think now maybe I recognize you from the box? Pair skater? Representing . . . what did you say your name was?'

Dag knew he hadn't said but floundered anyway, out of his depth in the man's liquid brown gaze. 'Dag Carlsen. I skate for Sweden with my sister.'

The man laughed — a soft, easy sound that excluded everyone else in the room. 'Jeff was here already. I think you got pre-empted. He left with a grey bozo who rolled up in a limo. Swept young Jeffie off his feet, you might say.' Again that easy, almost contemptuous chuckle. 'Jeff introduced him around as Lloyd. Lloyd spoke just like Jeff, Limey accent and all. Know him?'

Dag shook his head, his tongue frozen to the roof of his mouth.

'Know *anybody* here?'

An older man wearing eye-liner and mascara slithered by, whispering in the stranger's ear. 'Going to let me in on your new friend?'

'No. See you around, okay?' He took Dag's elbow and edged him away. 'Look, kid, all I know about your sport is what I see on the box, but I know the Games are coming up, that you're getting promo, that you'll be recognized any minute now. The guy who just came over writes for the *LA Times*; the tweedy character in the corner scouts for a TV gossip bitch. You're taking one hell of a chance in this place. We get raided, you know. For drugs, that's the excuse — a few jocks come in for *roids*. It's your first time here, right?'

Dag nodded, his mouth still too dry to speak. He'd kill that damn Jeff!

'What makes you think you belong?'

'I . . . it's just that Jeff asked me and —'

'And you were lonely?'

'I guess.' And fed up with home — but how did you tell a stranger that?

The man tossed off his drink. 'Follow me to the door. Walk normally.'

Dag made it outside amid soft knowing laughs, flutters and murmurings. He felt he'd disturbed a gathering of bats from their accustomed roost. With his new friend's prompting he claimed his car from the attendant and climbed in. Through the window the other man tapped his diamond-encrusted finger on Dag's shoulder and flipped a business card into the back seat. 'Do yourself a favour, kid. Don't come back — not that I'm not tempted.' Square white teeth flashed in a tan face. 'You're too fucking gorgeous to be true, sweetie. Now go home to mommy while you're still in one piece. But if you ever do decide you belong on our side of the street, give me a call, okay?' He pointed to the bar. 'Just don't go in there. They'll eat you alive.'

As Dag waited for a green light to let him into the boulevard, he turned to wave at his saviour, who wasn't looking. Instead he was shouting up into the neon-night sky. 'I hope to God you were listening, God! It goes in the credit column, remember?'

CHAPTER THIRTEEN

London, England

'Mother, there's really no need for this.'

Deirdre roused herself from the cream satin pillows in agitation. 'Oh, but there is, there is! Lloyd can be a vindictive man. We can't be sure of the place in London, but this house is in my name.' A gesture of bony fingers indicated the intensely feminine room, a symphony in creams and yellows and palest apricots, the window a tracery of elm branches laced with snow, glittery with icicles. 'I've taken care of what I can. All this jewellery, stocks, that kind of thing. I did well with the bit my father left too — invested it all in your name, of course. You'll have enough to live on if — if anything should happen. You will go to my lawyer, not Lloyd's, right?'

Maureen swallowed. More and more, Mother's conversations turned on a future in which she would not be present. 'Nothing's going to happen,' she said steadily. 'After the Games we'll rest up at the Palamos place then take a cruise to somewhere warm. The travel agent's touting New Zealand with a stop at Bora-Bora on the way. It sounds heavenly. What d'you think?'

'Later . . . the world's full of heavenly places . . . can't see them all. We'll make plans after the Games, maybe,' she said vaguely. 'I can't concentrate on anything else until they're over. I've waited so long, you see. And you've worked so hard.' Absently she let diamond and sapphire rings, a ruby necklace, an emerald pin, a string of pearls and a handful of unset opals drizzle through her fingers as if too heavy to hold. 'See they're put in their proper boxes . . . and do poke around for that opal from Australia, the one with coral fire in the middle. If it's not too late I thought I'd have it set into a brooch for you. It would look splendid with your Olympic dress.'

The opal, big as a robin's egg, lay smooth and cold in Maureen's palm. She, too, felt suddenly cold, shivering as she dropped it into its velvet nest. 'People say they're bad luck.'

'No. We make our own luck . . .'

Her mother's voice had grown faint, and Maureen had to lean in to hear it. Up close, she saw Deirdre's eyes close again, their lids almost transparent. But she was hardly past fifty!

'Good luck or bad,' Maureen said, 'it's too late, there's still a final fitting on the other dress for the short programme and —'

'I haven't seen you skate for ages and I do love it so . . . tomorrow I'll definitely make the effort and come down to the rink for —' Deirdre's head drooped into the pillow. She was asleep again, dropping off as she often did now, mid-sentence, or sometimes even mid-word. As Maureen straightened her on the pillow and pulled the covers up to her chin, clasped her own warm tan hands around Deirdre's cold white ones, the wide sleeves of the robe fell back with a whisper of satin. Looking down, Maureen gave a little cry and Deirdre's eyes flew instantly open, her skeletal fingers plucking at the sleeve until it once again covered a large purple patch above her wrist. 'Oh dear,' she said faintly before closing her eyes again. 'I always did bruise easily.'

Shaken, Maureen backed away and sank into the polished cotton depths of the couch with its pale print of apricot and peach roses in delicate bloom on an ivory ground. With a shock she remembered when the colours of the room had reflected the colours of her mother. But that angry purple patch was not Deirdre. Nor was it a bruise. It was a lesion. The first. She should have been ready for it.

Just as, the next morning, she should have been ready for the white froth foaming suddenly from Deirdre's shrunken lips. 'Nurse!'

The practical nurse bustled in and whisked it away with a sterile cloth which she instantly burned in the grate. It was clearly not the first time she'd performed the service.

'Thrush. It's *such* a nuisance! There,' she said, after scrubbing her hands. 'Are we ready for our breakfast now?'

Deirdre looked from her nurse to her daughter in panic. 'I don't think . . .'

'Tsk! How will you get better if you don't eat?'

Like a conjurer the woman produced poached eggs, bacon, a mountain of toast, fresh orange juice and a pot of tea. 'Now be a good Deirdre and —'

The tray flew across the room as Deirdre rushed, hand over her mouth, for the bathroom. Her legs gave way before she reached it. When she'd been cleaned up and put back to bed and her face sponged with lavender water, Maureen slipped away to the study and called the doctor at his home.

'I need to see you,' she said. 'I'll be at your consulting room in an hour.'

As she replaced the phone it rang under her hand, shocking her already ravaged nerves. It was Jeff, calling from California, with a purr in his voice. 'Mo? Howdy, as they say in these parts. You'll never guess who's right here in my apartment?'

'I've no time for twenty questions. What d'you want?'

'Oh dear! To *tell* you, silly! Or if England's skating wonder is just too, too rushed I could talk to your mom.'

'Mother's . . . otherwise engaged at the moment, too.'

'Well, la-dee-dah! Anyway, your dad buzzed in from Florida last night to see how I was coming along. He drove me to the rink this morning — in a limo, natch — and he's delighted, simply delighted with my progress. He thinks I've really improved with Grant Rivers.'

'How nice.'

'Lloyd's coming to the Games too, of course. Isn't that great?'

'Tell "Lloyd" the Palamos place will be fully occupied, all right?'

'Suppose we want it, too?' His growing American accent sharpened with the triumph of newly discovered power, the 'we' hardly accentuated at all.

'If you tell him Mother will be there I can guarantee Daddy won't be.'

'Ah, rats. Oh, by the way, Kramer's all better, skating like a goddamned angel again, and Crisp's nailing everything —

thought you'd want to know.'

'Now I do,' she said sweetly. 'Is that it?'

'So how 'bout Lloyd? He's right in the next room — wanna talk to him?'

'Thank you, no.' She replaced the receiver with a sharp click.

The doctor sat at his desk, a dab of shaving cream clinging to his ear. 'Abroad for three whole weeks? But my dear Maureen, *any* trip is out of the question for her! She should be in a sanitarium *now*, but she refuses to go. She's way beyond the care of practical nurses and a housekeeper.'

'Doctor, she is coming to the Games.' Maureen spoke quietly, evenly, but with absolute authority, each word distinct, no argument possible.

'I'm sorry.' The doctor stood up, stretched, and looked down onto the street. He always did, Maureen realized, when he had unwelcome news to impart. 'If you take her abroad now, I cannot be responsible —'

'For what? Her life? Are you saying if she spends three weeks on the Costa Brava, which she loves, she'll die. And if she stays in your ugly, sterile little hospital she'll live, that you'll restore her to health?'

'You're putting words in my mouth. I can promise nothing. All I say is, she needs blood, drip-feeding, skilled nursing, total rest and constant supervision.'

'She'll get it.'

'You'll be training at the Olympic complex. I'm afraid, I am very *much* afraid she'll insist on being there with you —'

'No one is allowed in Olympic Village except officials, athletes, coaches, and judges. Security's tight and badges are hard to come by. For the two days of actual competition she can stay in the nearest hotel and just come to the events I'm in. For the rest of the time, the villa has more room than we know what to do with.'

'Maureen, listen to me. The crowds, the cold, the excitement . . .' He lifted his hands, beaten. 'But if you insist, I can't be responsible.'

'*She* insists! She's determined to see me compete. She deserves that. She's given everything for it. It's all worked out. They're equipping a room at the villa as a fully stocked sick-room. The flight itself is short. We'll have the company Lear fitted with whatever bed you recommend, drip systems, blood, oxygen, you name it, we'll get it. We'll take round-the-clock nurses with us.'

'What kind of nurses?' he cut in.

She waited, forced him to face her, to stand self-consciously with his back to the sulkily burning fire.

'Nurses who understand whatever it is you say is wrong with her,' she said quietly. 'I hope you'll choose them, tell them all they need to know. I'll be with her every night until I have to check in at the Village. I can care for her as well or better than strangers can.'

She was suddenly aware of the doctor's knuckles gleaming white against the mahogany mantel. 'Maureen . . . When you "care for her", touch her in any way, either in Spain or at the Games or even at home, may I suggest that you, er — wear disposable gloves?' He ran all the words into a string, as if she might not notice them that way.

'She's my mother.'

'Yes. But if she should weep or sneeze . . . you can't possibly be expected to grasp the complexities, but in her condition all body fluids . . . as I say, you couldn't possible grasp . . .' His voice trailed off.

Medical discretion, what cowardice it concealed! She let him wriggle on the hook in the long silence that fell between them, broken at last by a shift in the carefully constructed pyramid of coals.

'Doctor, I'm not afraid. I know the complexities. She will see me skate.'

He chewed his lower lip, his ultra-clean doctor's hands fretting the edge of a prescription pad. 'Damn, I wish Lloyd was here,' he said. 'I should much prefer to consult with him.'

'My father,' she said coldly, 'is in California, consulting with his protégé.'

CHAPTER FOURTEEN

Moscow, USSR

In ten days the Olympic flame would light up the face of every television set in the great outside world.

In one inner cell of international skating's tight-knit world, members of the Central Army Sports Club — very few of them soldiers — rose a little earlier each morning, worked a little longer on the ice, spent extra hours with their specialists of sports medicine. No effort was spared to hone mind and muscle for expected triumphs. The day after tomorrow they would leave for the Games, and an extra week of buffing up their skills at altitudes close to that of the Olympic arena. Little, if anything, was left to chance.

Alexei Finsky's phone rang before the team transport picked him up for his morning workout. It was Galina's father calling in from the suburbs, breathless as always when using the phone. Like every benefit received since his daughter was raised up to the exalted honour of 'Master of Sport', the instrument intimidated him.

'Alex!' he called, as if pitching his voice over the Urals. 'Is that you?'

Fighting back a sigh of relief — for surely this meant Galina needed him, had changed her mind, wanted to see him before he left, would perhaps find some way of getting to him if he should decide, if he should —

'Yes, Papa?'

'Papa.' For Alex, this timid man who'd spent his youth in a labour camp for a minor infraction of a minor law, a man orphaned by a monstrous ship of State when Josef Stalin stood at the helm, was the closest thing to a father that Alex had ever known. 'Don't worry. This is Alex. Tell me what you need.'

'Oh, thanks to G— No, no, all is a jumble, where to begin? Leningrad calls. You remember my sister, her poor apartment she must share with so many?'

'Yes.' Alexei had visited her once, a hell he'd never repeated.

'Today they kick her out! A man comes from a bureau with papers, her space is needed, her neighbours have another child and my sister must go to the train station, take a ticket to Moscow, come live with us —'

'A mistake,' Alex said quickly, to stem the rise of panic humming over the wire from the suburbs. 'Such things don't happen, they haven't for years.'

'But this has! And anyway, she is welcome. Always we ask her to live with us but no, she is stubborn, we know how old women can be.'

'Papa, listen to me. It's incompetence, nothing more. They mess up paperwork all the time. It will be cleared up. They can't force her.'

'They can do anything,' whispered the expert, who believed if he spoke quietly they might not hear him. 'But don't speak of it! She arrives tomorrow night with all her things. Galina is to meet her at the station with the car. We thought two trips would be enough, but this minute our Galina goes outdoors and poof! Her car is gone! No, not *her* car, of course it belongs to the People.' Now he spoke loudly, to balance the books in case the People were listening: 'So kind they are, she doesn't have to wait in line for service, or even ask. They just take it like that for its six-month check.'

'Which wasn't due until Easter, the same as mine. I keep a log.'

'Details . . . so my wife thought — Galina said we must not bother you, that you had much on your mind — but my wife thought that she, our Galina, could drive *your* car to pick up my sister and her few things. Clothes, pots and pans, linens, her pet pigeon, her sewing machine.'

'Of course she must. I'll be airborne then, anyway, she knows that, but she has a key. Tell her to use the car as she likes. My apartment too. It's bigger than hers or yours . . . more comfortable for your sister.' And Galina knew her way round it so well.

'Oh, Alex, thank you, we thank you, what would we do without you . . .'

Exactly.

Alexei hung up with the suspicion, no, with the *knowledge* that he was being manipulated, twisted like a length of wire into a specific shape, a Gold Medal swinging from a coloured ribbon. Not by Galina's father, who could not have manipulated a hairpin; not even by Galina, who would protect her loved ones at all costs — but by a mighty machine with much skill in the art.

His doorbell rang. The training transport! — and Alexei Finsky, Champion of the USSR and of the World, was late, training time scarce. He grabbed skate-bag, extra socks, and a box of band-aids and BFI, standard remedy for blisters. The lift was open, awaiting the apartment block's only 'Merited Master of Sport', its Number One resident.

At the moment. If he missed the quad axel, if he missed Gold, priority could go to some other. But right now priority was his to use as he wished, confident a lift would wait on him. Except there was no time for wishes. The Olympics loomed too close, too intimidating, there was much last-minute work to do, and it was very late indeed before he was returned home exhausted, but massaged and relaxed, before he eased into bed, the volume on his phone adjusted down.

The next day he woke feeling like a winner, refreshed, ready to drive himself on a few last-minute errands, then rest until take-off.

He sang as he showered, pressing back doubts suddenly elbowing into his mind, his heart. Nah! Foolish. Everything was fine. They would not dare. Brushing his teeth, opening the curtains to the dawn, he turned on his battery radio — and vague unease rocketed to panic stations.

Dawn was not dawn at all. It was dusk. It should be six in the morning. It was four in the afternoon. They took off for Montegreco in two hours! He took a deep, even breath, and relaxed as he'd been taught. So. He'd slept through. No problem. Still time to dress, go down to the garage, make sure Galina had taken the car. He even smiled. Driving it was a treat for her. She was only a 'Master of Sport'. He, with major world titles to his credit, was a 'Merited Master', his apartment more spacious, his car more powerful, closer to the top of the line, with tape-deck and stereo, even burglar-proof windscreen wipers! — rubber being always at a premium behind the Curtain.

The car. Which was not in its privileged spot by the ramp. Why should it be? Galina had it. Hadn't he said she could take it? For ten seconds he lulled himself, allowed himself to believe. No paranoia for Alexei Finsky, top gun of the USSR's team — the very thought reminding him that he was even privileged to watch Western films. No paranoia. Then he saw the world-weary shrug of the parking attendant, the expression in the eyes of a man who had seen them come in triumph and depart in disgrace. Then he knew. The State had, after all, dared.

One by one the perks were vanishing. First Galina's, now his. Begin on the outer strands of the web, say an old aunt in Leningrad, and work inwards. A taste of what Galina and her family could expect if he did not return.

'Galina did not take the car?'

The attendant shook his head. 'She got here too late. They towed it away first thing this morning for —'

'Service,' Alexei finished for him.

'They left a message. You shouldn't worry, the Director himself will pick you up for the airport.' He scratched his head. 'So how did you know your car was being serviced?'

The Champion of all the Russias was suddenly very tired. 'Call it, as they say in the West, an educated guess.'

Just then the ZIL roared into the lot, the Director jumping out, grinning, pumping his hand. 'You slept late! Sure sign of a clear conscience. Yes, I heard they've taken your pride and joy for service so I came to get you —'

'Yes.' He wondered, bitterly, if Jeff Dunsmuir's car had vanished into some service-station's maw. Or the cars of the American threat from where was it, Boston? And the Canadian? No way. What they earned they owned.

'So get your things, we're running late.'

'My costume, skates —'

'On board. Trust me.'

'I have to use the phone —'

The Director checked his watch. 'Five minutes.'

The Director was safe. Alexei tried her apartment, then

her parent's apartment, which was never empty. The phone rang and rang, an operator at last coming on to say the number he was calling was not in service. So what? On any given day half the damned phones in the Eastern Bloc were not in service. *Do not let them drive you to paranoia.*

The Director was cheerful, even jovial. 'Cheer up! Don't worry about your girl or your car. Your girl will be waiting. And if you bring home the right medal your chariot may be a different model entirely, even something like mine.' He tapped its gleaming black hood. 'It's not so bad being favourite, is it? Millions would switch places with you in a moment.'

'Yes,' he said. 'I know they would.' And after sixteen years bone-bending work, the investment of their own unique talent, if any, the State may harvest a million Gold Medals.

143

CHAPTER FIFTEEN

Atami, Japan

The mother of Mieko Nakashima ironed each item of her daughter's travel wardrobe with exquisite, almost morbid attention to detail. This bra, these panties, this slip, blouse, frill, this suit carefully fashioned by the best Tokyo tailor, all must be carefully prepared and scented, exquisitely packed as if for a honeymoon — for how many times would her daughter experience an Olympics in person, much less compete in one?

As she ironed, as she listened to her daughter's skating music drifting through the paper panels of the girl's room, her fingers reached again into the sleeve of her kimono to finger the envelope with Hiro Nakashima's arrogant rooster crest heavily embossed on the seal. She frowned, still uncertain whether to wait for Meiko's return from the Olympics or to break the news now, before she left.

Good news, the wise ones said, should be savoured slowly, every sweet morsel tasted to the full; bad news was best swallowed and fast digested, all the quicker to forget it. But this news could never be forgotten. The girl would live with it forever, as she herself had done. The wise ones were no help, none at all.

One thing she knew. The letter would change Mieko's life as hers had been changed, and in exactly the same way. For the dependents of a stubborn traditional man, history did indeed repeat itself, perhaps into infinity.

So should she spoil the girl's pleasure in this, her first and last Olympics, by breaking the news now? On the other hand, if Mieko skated less than her best and returned home feeling she had dishonoured her family and her country, to

144

find this further blow lying in wait would be cruel, cruel. A woman's lot *was* cruel. Hers had been. She'd spent the better part of her own years trying to spare her daughter the same fate.

The letter said she had failed.

A peremptory thump from the kitchen told her the housekeeper prepared dinner, Mieko's last before she left for Europe. Like a prisoner waiting for the firing squad, she thought, trusting that the housekeeper had prepared Mieko's favourites. Yes. Thin, delicate soup. Small broiled trout, twisted and skewered to rear up on the plate like golden dragons in combat. Crisp vegetables from their garden. And a cake so light it must surely have been anchored to the oven lest it escape. And how strange that the ungainly, vigorous, sharp-elbowed housekeeper could produce this miracle for Mieko — to whom she would not even speak when Hiro Nakashima was in the vicinity. Not even when he was expected.

The postmark said Yokohama. He would, thank God, stay there until Mieko left. Imperative that the girl leave with joy, good wishes, smiles —

A gong deep inside the house reverberated through the thin walls, calling them to the feast, a servant and two mistresses with less power than — than a broiled fish. Three women who for once could relax — no men to please, to smile upon, to defer to. And now behind her a soft footfall, Mieko's arms slipping about her waist, her firm cheek briefly touching Oka-chan's neck, the small space between kimono and coiffure. She turned, and Mieko too was wearing traditional dress in this, the ancestral home. As the thought crossed her mind she felt the weight of the letter in her sleeve, heavier than the iron, more lasting than the hills, more brutal than the sea pounding far below them.

'Oka-chan, stop with the iron! Soon you will iron me, my hair, even my fingernails! Come. Today we celebrate not two things but three! I skated the best programme in my whole life, I made the triple-loop perfectly, almost silent, no scratches — and tomorrow I fly away to skate for Japan!'

Happiness glowed in her daughter's eyes. For a moment she was truly beautiful, and her mother could hardly bear the burden of it, to send this trusting child with her loyal heart half round the world, to try her best, her very best — then fly home unaware, straight into the trap opening for her. She sighed. Maybe after the tea and cake she would speak.

She did not have to wait. Mieko already sensed something. Before the small skewered dragons were served, she asked. 'What is it, Oka-chan?'

'I am sorry, how I am sorry. Your grandfather writes to me that when you return it will be time for you to marry . . . that he feels his years . . . that I have provided no heir. He has a promising young man at the Hokkaido plant . . .'

Mieko, silent, the light gone from her eyes, slowly crumbled bread into small, neat balls on her plate. Promising? What could a stranger promise? Respectability? Permanence? Children? Was there nothing more?

Her mother sighed. 'I expect he will be like your father, a company man. But of course he could be handsome, charming — you could even love him.'

You could even love him. The desolate hope hung between them across a string of silence as Mieko slowly twisted the last small trout on its skewer.

The housekeeper, listening from the kitchen, elbowed in with the cake, for which they were not yet ready. 'Time she is married, the master is correct.'

'Hold your tongue!' Oka-chan seldom rose to anger. Today she blazed with it, and Mieko was obscurely pleased. Bad enough Mother could not come to the Games. It was Grandfather's rule that one member of the immediate family must be in Japan at all times, and he himself may have to fly to Hong Kong. He considered them as royalty, and that, Mieko thought, was the source of his power and of her mother's misery. Now it appeared it was also to be hers. Hokkaido was many miles away from Tokyo, from Oka-chan.

'You have three glorious weeks ahead,' her mother said with forced brightness. 'May they shine in your memory all the days of your life!' She raised a rare glass of plum wine and drank to the three glorious weeks — Mieko's last chance at happiness. That's what she meant. Mother, a failure because her womb had refused to yield sons — only a stubborn daughter who was now expected to fill the void.

Her mother's hand covered hers across the table. 'No son could have pleased me as you have. I am so very proud.'

'Proud? She's in all the papers!' the housekeeper shouted from the kitchen. 'He won't like it!'

At last Oka-chan smiled. 'She is right. Every paper. Headlines, even. Hiro Nakashima's granddaughter tries for Gold. Can she beat Kramer? Sterling? Crisp?'

Mieko shook her head. 'Oka-chan, I lack so much polish.'

'Perhaps the judges look for something else.' Determined to hang on to the positive, Mother passed her the Atami paper, it's entire front page given over to Mieko in a fast scratch-spin, her hair whipping about her like a lasso, just as she had one day dreamed it would be.

'This one speculates that your grandfather *made* you learn to skate so he could sell more Nakashima television sets! Our illustrious name is on the lips of all Japan. Every news bulletin. Nakashima, Nakashima, Nakashima. Such excellent publicity he could never buy, not for all the yen in the world.' Her smile turned mischievous, almost sly, and for an instant Mieko saw the young woman she had once been, carefree, sharing a titbit of harmless malice with a friend. Oh, Oka-chan.

'Free publicity? Grandfather will not see it that way.'

Reality returned. 'No. For him, change is not possible.'

Nor for you, my mother. It is too late. Even the housekeeper, chained as she is to the past, has more freedom. More even than I. The housekeeper is old, if she dies tomorrow she is free. But I must settle for a promising man from the Hokkaido plant, a man I have not met, a company robot like my father, a man with whom I must lie, to whom I must give sons. Then perhaps Grandfather will love me as I love him. Perhaps.

She picked up the last golden dragon from the black enamel tray and carefully removed its skewer, breaking it with a snap before the first tear could fall.

CHAPTER SIXTEEN

Los Angeles, California

Last-minute crises swarmed like locusts over every skating outpost in the Olympic world — outposts now insular to the point of paranoia. In Los Angeles, Grant was daily bombarded with complaints based not on fact but on fear.

Roxanne wept that her best boots — custom-built to cushion bone-spurs and callouses, their contoured padding lovingly broken in to reach perfection for the Games — had, according to her, broken down overnight into leather-clad mush, sapping her already shaken confidence. That she was wrong didn't matter. Time was short. Excuses must not be allowed to take root.

Beejay, her blades recently sharpened to their final millimetre of tempered steel, wore off the last of their biting edge; they were fresh out of temper and so was she. Replacements had been found, attached, and adjusted. Now her feet must learn an unfamiliar code to the familiar lament of 'Oh, shit.'

Jeff's costume, which a week ago fit tight as his own skin, now required an infinitesimal adjustment, without which he just could not compete! Worse, his landlord's runny-nosed kid, to whom Jeff never even spoke, cornered him for an autograph and sneezed right in his face. *In his face*! After all these bloody years, was this any time to get sick?

He was not alone. Panic and hypochondria threatened all. Sniffles, cramps, headaches, a cough or a scratchy throat all heralded glandular fever or pneumonia or at least 'flu. Problems arose; blame must be pinned. A spot erupting on Lise Carlsen's flawless cheek was attributed to lingonberry sauce regularly shipped from Sweden by Aunt Signe and

148

served by Mom with damn near everything. Lise's timing on a double top-loop, a snap for a skater this level, disappeared due to some change in Dag's position — just what, she couldn't specify. Dag brooded through the sessions, his interest stirred only by what and how much food Lise consumed. Too late now to build muscle bulk with steroids. They'd be detected for sure. So much for integrity.

Even the familiar rink and all its advanced equipment seemed to turn on them. Music tapes tied themselves in knots and videos developed blank spots; emergency copies became more vital than life-rafts. Inadequacies and mishaps fed one off another — but all must be hidden from the press who, with two days to departure, descended en masse and instantly perceived everything on skates to be a Medal Hope. In an excess of enthusiasm they snapped the backside of an engineer kneeling on the ice as if in supplication, filling toe-gouges with shaved ice before resurfacing the entire rink. The result appeared in the papers from LA to New York under the caption 'Praying for Gold' and a bashful young man's hindquarters found brief, if embarrassing, fame. But despite their ignorant zeal, Grant welcomed the press, if only to give his competitors a taste of the hysteria waiting for them at the Games.

Media glare put normal rink life on hold. Brisk young women hefting minicams sauntered in, requiring the girls to train in full make-up and the boys to shave between every hourly session. Leg warmers, grubby sweatbands and ubiquitous layers of old wool disappeared; instead, each girl wore sleek leotards and the sheerest of tights. Instead of Vick's Vapour-Rub the skaters spun in a heady mix of Chanel and 'Grey Flannel', and even, around Lise Carlsen, an aura of 'Joy'. Paper-cups gave way to china mugs; Twinkie cakes, a morning staple, were now wolfed in the secrecy of the lost-and-found; shiny apples adorned the barrier as proof of wholesomeness and a canny instinct for promo — what better excuse to approach a rail lined with reporters, what better shots than athletes aglow with health and national pride sinking perfect white smiles into the polished flesh of Red and Golden Delicious? The apple industry was ecstatic.

Noni, who could no longer be kept away without risking

'scenes' on which the press would pounce with delight, wore a fixed grin and lacquered hair-do instead of her usual harried frown; Ben Carlsen sacrificed his goose-down hunting jacket for an overcoat, a folder of press releases, and a stack of 8 × 10 inch glossies he proudly fanned open at the hint of a request. Both parents spoke faster than usual, fingertips beating tattoos on the wooden barrier, anxious eyes turned again and again on their hopes for glory. Emma, more blasé, kept away from both, and also from the immaculate stranger in a grey suit and a grey, fur-lined cashmere coat. The man's predatory eyes, also grey, followed Jeff Dunsmuir's every move.

Amid all the hoopla and last minute nerves, Grant Rivers stood calm at centre-ice, his own yearning buried deeper by far than that of skaters, parents, or sponsors like Lloyd Sterling, who clearly wanted words with Jeff's coach and who could bloody well wait.

Grant's bitter memory had lived nineteen years in the dark, a festering wound nurtured in silence, an ache always present but never disturbed — for a touch could change its form, its content, perhaps even weaken its power, which he chose to nourish until he could retaliate in kind. The last thing he wanted was to pardon the unpardonable, bleed off the pulsing fury of his anger — for surely revenge almost two decades in the growing would be the sweetest harvest a man could know, the memorial Mum never had.

As the Olympic drum beat closer, louder, as Lloyd Sterling made his daily appearance, grey as a shadow but watchful, Grant's thoughts touched the wound a thousand times and a thousand times drew back as if scalded. Soon he'd see Sterling's wife. Time then to gauge the cost of promises broken, dreams unfulfilled, a life lost that could have been saved. Time now to drive, cajole, motivate and sharpen the weapons that would beat Deirdre to her pretty, dimpled knees. How could her precious Maureen stand up against Roxanne and Beejay, the two finest skaters he'd produced?

Meantime he was the hub of this icy circus, its performers with problems that he, the ringmaster, whose black curls Deirdre had loved, must solve.

*

Some problems were beyond his reach and even his knowledge. For Judge Emma Crisp, discretion within the sport came as naturally as breathing. You heard tales inside the judging enclaves that made your flesh crawl, but that's as far as gossip was allowed to go. Sure she heard talk of deals, they all did; sure national bias ran amok at international competitions, her own nation no less culpable than the rest; sure she did her best for her own side if they deserved it, if she fairly could. *If she fairly could*.

But when she saw perfection it didn't matter where the skater was born, which flag fluttered in his cheering section. The hair on her neck lifted, goosebumps rose on her arms, and she knew she'd witnessed living art. She'd experienced it maybe a dozen times — Curry, Rodnina, Cousins, Boitano, Torvill and Dean, Witt, Orser, and tiny, magical Gordeeva — but the hope of it happening again kept her and others like her going back endlessly for more.

It was that same tingling thrill — seeing Fleming skate in person for the first time when Emma herself had been a competitor older than Peggy — that had changed Emma's entire future. Emma saw then, and knew now, that she could have trained a hundred years and never been a Fleming; extraordinary talent was unique, bred in the bone, and manifested in countless different styles; instinctive coaches like Nicks, Fassi, Roles, Lever, Moskwina, Rivers, all could shape it, mould it, but the basic clay had to be there. But she knew too that skating was her love, her dream, that she'd hang on to some part of it for the rest of her life. There were opera-buffs, ballet-buffs, aviation-buffs — Emma was a skating-buff. Decision made, she quit skating for nursing school, and, in her spare time, Judges' School. To become a good nurse took less time than to become a good judge. She became both.

At Judges' School she met and married Dave Crisp, whose enthusiasms crackled with the same fire as his red hair, all of which he passed on to Beejay. Dave, the perfect father, was her ardent fan since the day he laced up her first tiny pair of skates. His brief, amiable affairs with skating mothers were small blemishes to which Emma turned a blind eye until Noni swept in, zeroed in on his weakness, and kicked his fire out with her pointy-toed shoes, scratched obscenities in the ashes of his reputation. Damn Noni. No. Forgive Noni. If the past was too painful, turn away. There was still Beejay, whose love for the sport was as thrilling as her talent for it.

But Dave's death turned a page. Emma began to glimpse the dark side of the dream. Each year that she judged and Beejay competed, Emma saw the negative facets the public, entranced by grace, never knew existed: not all great skaters won. Some years, talent lay so thick on the ice that ninety percent of it got slashed to ribbons by other skaters' blades. Adolescent bodies grew in unexpected ways, playing havoc with jumps and confidence. Nerves and the fear of losing defeated most skaters before they ever worked themselves out of the kindergarten leagues.

And skating mothers crippled more talent than injuries ever could. A teenager Emma had judged and liked, of immense promise, half-way up the ladder, underwent vital ankle surgery. Her orthopaedist ordered three-months off. The girl's schedule could easily afford it, but within the month Momma had her on the ice 'just to stroke, honey, keep your muscles in trim.' Minutes later, the kid half-crying, Momma pacing the rubber tiles, cajoled her into an axel to remind her body it could still jump. 'Mom, it lands on the sore ankle! I don't think . . .' But Momma had thought. She produced a $100 bill, waving it like a flag. 'Remember that cute Sheltie puppy that cried for you? This'd buy him.' The kid did her axel. One. They carried her off screaming. Emma never saw either of them again. Two years later, old enough to make her own decisions, the kid reminded her body and her mom that she could *still* jump. She took a header off an overpass, straight down into the freeway rush-hour.

For a judge, the most personal negative facet was public opinion. Armchair experts, egged on by flag-waving media, routinely second-guessed judges and were routinely wrong. TV cameras mercilessly lingered on a dissenting judge as if that judge were prime suspect in a police line-up. Well paid anchormen who'd never set foot to ice, with no more knowledge of the sport than could be gleaned from babbling their 'expertise' into a mike at major competitions, readily impugned the integrity of experienced, unpaid judges. But that, thank God, was changing fast.

Other ex-champions had at last joined that inimitable diplomat Dick Button as commentators who knew whereof they spoke. There was less talk, now, of partisan judging. Not before time, in Emma's opinion. For her, when she wore her judge's hat, pride of country took second place to pride of sport. She called 'em as she saw 'em and she missed damned little.

Thus she was surprised, the Saturday before they left for the Games, by a call from a powerful camp follower from Central Europe whose tongue slipped oh-so-deftly over his name. He was passing through. Could he perhaps offer her dinner? — murmuring the name of a trendy place at the beach. No-o-o, she thought not. It was late, and — Would she, then, take pity on a visitor and invite him for coffee? Talk over old times, when her husband was alive . . . such a *good* man, Dave Crisp. Emma cautiously agreed. The voice was vaguely familiar. 'But I'm busy as all get out, what with packing and getting Beejay squared away.' Yes, he understood perfectly, naturally he wouldn't impose *too* much.

He arrived late. Beejay was already in bed, supposedly asleep, but very likely listening from her room. There wasn't much she missed, either.

The man had scarcely aged since Emma first saw him. He'd appeared then as he did now, a well-preserved fifty wearing a little too much cologne, a little too much flesh, teeth a tad too square, accented English smoothly perfect. His pallor matched his banana-and-white seersucker suit (tailored for the tropics) and his creamy-white hair, its waves expensively barbered. His amber cat's eyes, speckled with brown, scarcely ever blinked, and took in the battered fridge, the worn rug, the cluttered desk, in one hooded glance.

In the middle of the slap-dash living-room, every chair but one piled with ironing and open suitcases, band-aids and foam pads, the stranger seemed momentarily uncertain, a cream-and-yellow parfait she wanted to stick a cherry on. That was it! Willi Vanilla, Dave had called him. Willi, representing a tiny Middle European principality, judged or officiated, depending. His grandson, who also competed, was a Willi too.

153

'Take the weight off, Willi. Coffee's warming up,' Emma said, deliberately down-home until she knew for sure what he was after.

He lowered himself into the empty chair, straightened the creases in his pants, and pressed his knees together like they had a rubber-band round them. When she handed him coffee — in an old mug from the back of the cupboard — he stuck out his plump pinky and smiled with his lips shut.

'Delightful,' he murmured, sipping coffee Beejay had made two hours ago. Even fresh, it could have wilted a six-inch nail. Best not roll out the welcome-mat until she knew what beast would be lying on it. She figured she already knew the nature of this one.

'Pity about your late husband. A *friendly* man, I always felt there was no soul in the world Dave disliked.' The barb of Noni swiftly planted, he pushed aside the coffee and showed his cards. 'I hear your daughter skates the Games this time. Such an honour, so young, delicate —'

Talented. Emma could guess the script and sure enough, here it came.

'Talented. She will not go unnoticed, I'm sure.'

She sighed. What the hell, give him an opening, let him get it over with. 'They're all in the spotlight now, aren't they? Your grandson too, I hear.'

He brightened. 'You've heard! I am proud — and humble, naturally. Since your daughter's competing, I suppose you'll be judging Mens.'

'Maybe Pairs. We draw for it.' Just like she'd told Ben Carlsen.

'You will recognize my grandson. He looks like me. A chip off the old block, as the British say. He is young and promising also . . . much like your Beejay.'

'I wish him luck, then.'

'I hope so, Emma — I may call you Emma?' He stood up, again adjusted his pants, and kissed her hand. 'Should you judge my grandson, I know you will remember our old friendship. Not that I wish to — how do you say it? — twist your arm. Ha-ha.' His laugh was as rich and creamy as his suit.

Dave had understood him, all right. 'Goodnight, Willi.'

He bowed himself out. He honest-to-God *bowed*, was still

bowing as she shut and bolted the door behind him.

Right on cue, Beejay appeared from the hall, anything but delicate in red butcher-striped pyjamas, her Orphan Annie hair standing out like copper wire. 'Jesus Christ, is he something or what! Remember his grandson? About twenty-two? No eyelashes? Looks albino? At Skate America once, or was it St Gervaise? Wraps his jumps tighter than spit-curls?'

Wraps. Once you learned to wrap it was damned near impossible to open 'em up. A good jump soared free. Wrapping made for cramped, twisty little things, safe but ugly. Poor little Willi. And knowledgeable Beejay, a living compendium of every skater's strengths and weaknesses.

'You're supposed to be in bed, not listening at keyholes.'

'I *am*. I fancied a sandwich, that's all.' Her small hand rummaged the back of the ancient fridge until she found a pack of salami. 'It'll dry up while we're gone, anyway. Christ, are we out of rye again?' She slathered salsa between two slices of salami and rolled it into a cigar.

'Gee, that Vanilla fella . . . where do they get the idea —' Emma mused.

'Hey, it's not like he's — how do you say it? — twisting your arm, right?'

Her mother laughed and peered at the midnight snack. 'A good thing you can skate, sport. You'd never make a caterer — you got salsa on your chin. Now go brush your teeth and bed. Tomorrow's a big day.'

In the familiar darkness of her room, the moon glinting off four pairs of teddy-bear eyes gazing down at her from the shelf, Beejay lay awake longer than Emma knew. Jeez, but that guy was a goddamn creep! Where did he get off, worrying Em like that — as if she didn't have enough on her plate with the blasted bills. Not that she bitched, but Beejay could count, she looked in the chequebook every now and then. They lived on Em's part-time nursing, a tiny pension from Dad's old job, and dividends from a few stocks — when they paid off. Out of that came whatever skating bills the Committee didn't pick up, and all of Beejay's correspondence-school fees; no way could she, or any of them, go to regular school, not with training schedules like they were. She hadn't much chance this year, she knew. Pushing it, she figured she'd an eyelash in hell's chance to take Roxanne, who wasn't back to form and who could be psyched. But there was Sterling who moved like a dream, and Nakashima popping off tripples like a jack-rabbit; so her jumps scratched, big deal; scratching wasn't wrapping; a decent coach could fix scratches in jig-time. Whoever didn't win this time would hang in for the next Games, improving all the time. She'd improve right along with them — if Em could keep finding the cash. Money was the pits. Then in sashays Willi Vanilla to rub it in.

Next morning, the last day, a delivery van was blocking their drive as they arrived home from morning session. A new fridge-freezer, banana-coloured and a mile wide, stood by the door.

'Name of Crisp? Show me where you want it, okay? I'm late already.'

Emma dropped her purse. 'I didn't order that! Take it back.'

'Can't. It's paid for.' He shifted his wad of tobacco to the other cheek, spat into a dusty laurel bush, and handed her a clipboard. 'Sign there. Line 23.'

'No way. Like I said, take it back!'

'Look, lady. My engine's reading *hot*, I'm on overtime, and I'm running late. Want it inside or do I dump it out here?'

In the driveway? 'Wait. I'll go phone,' she said, unlocking the door.

'Like hell I'll wait.' He trundled the fridge in after her. He had the trolley straps unbuckled before she finished dialling her contact on the Committee. Hearing her story, the harried official at the other end chuckled. This was Emma's first time to judge the Games, right?

'So? I've done Worlds lots of times, what's the difference?'

Olympic fever. Came round one year in four. She was lucky it was just a fridge. One time a judge found a new sports car in his garage. He returned it. Guess what came back?

'A 747?' she said, eyeing the fridge, which dwarfed her kitchen.

'Not quite.' Another chuckle. She hadn't signed for it,

right? Good. All she had to do was call the store to come get it.

Like she didn't have enough to do. 'We're leaving first thing tomorrow!'

That's how come she'd got it today, the voice explained patiently. She was in the clear, she'd reported it. Just get rid, pronto, okay?

The phone went dead — but behind her, Beejay had the answer in hand.

'I'm telling you it stays here,' the driver was shouting.

'And the truck? Do we get to keep that?'

Beejay dangled his massive bunch of keys just out of reach. The driver turned purple. 'Kid, you got no call messin' about in my fucking cab!'

'Better watch your language, mister. I'm a minor. Still want your keys?'

He scowled, secured the fridge back on its trolley, practically ran it out the door, slammed the tailgate, shot the bolt, and roared down the sleepy morning street. Beejay blinked at her dumbfounded mother.

'Relax, Emma. It's not like I twisted his arm.'

Emma waited for her blood pressure to settle to neutral. 'Okay. Best start in packing for tomorrow, sport. You know the drill.'

Yeah. Costumes and skate-bag went *on* the plane, the rest under it. If security argued, argue back, but never-never-never let 'em stash your skates where you couldn't keep an eye on 'em.

Noni couldn't be kept out of the rink now, but there was still no way to talk to Roxanne unless Roxanne co-operated, which she wouldn't damned-well do!

As she fixed a late breakfast of melon, black coffee, and a cigarette, she argued aloud and endlessly with herself because there was no Roxi to argue with. Not for want of trying. She'd tracked her to the doctor's small house, not too many cuts above this hole-in-the-wall Noni lived in, so you knew how good a doctor *he* must be! She left messages for Roxi at his office but her calls were never returned. She stormed and pleaded with the doctor's phone service but *they* wouldn't give her time of day either. She hissed messages into Grant's machine, many of them obscene just to get a reaction, but he, like Roxanne, never so much as looked in her direction at the rink.

It was like she wasn't there. Didn't exist. The World Champion's mother. What kind of attitude was that, after everything she'd done? Not that she was surprised. A bit of European wisdom came back to mock her: a son's a son until he takes him a wife; a daughter's a daughter all of her life — unless she's a skater, then the ice becomes her mother. Something else she'd always known. If anybody ever served Noni Kramer breakfast in bed it'd be an attendant in an old folk's home. There'd be no loving daughter waiting on *her*.

She looked around at her one-roomer, its shabby blue carpet that never came clean no matter how she scrubbed it, the furniture all oddments because there was never enough cash at one go to buy things that matched. The one thing tying it all together was the smell. Bug-spray. A weekly bomb and nightly spot raids on stragglers wandering in from next door. Until Roxanne made the team everything had gone to the ice, the greedy ice, and after that the money had gone to . . . well, other things . . . hell, she deserved *some* pleasures. If a few little pills put her on top of the world instead of the bottom of a barrel, why not? Why the hell not? They'd no business treating her like she had some disease. They'd change their tune fast enough if she opened up to the press, sold them the real scoop about Grant and Roxi living together all that time — but hell, a scandal would kill Roxi's chance this close to the Games, judges being a bunch of hypocrites, every one. And she daren't forget Emma Crisp, who had clout. If she had a certain knowledge too, and spilled it, then all the sacrifice would have been for nothing. Dave Crisp: 'Roxi *is* a lovely skater, a credit to her lovely mother,' but when it boiled right down, he did Roxi no favours either. She won Worlds because Noni had trained her to be the best, no thanks to Dave Crisp, who screwed himself into a coronary on a motel bed.

For the umpteenth time she checked her ticket. Not the Olympic plane. Hers was a cheap charter which got her there just in time for the opening ceremonies, then Mutti and Papa would pick up the hotel tab, thank God, but she'd no accreditation to get into Olympic Village. If she couldn't reach Roxi now, she couldn't get at her at all until it was over. But at least the spin was in. For the present. Mutti would be pleased about that. On impulse she called Bonn. She caught Mutti in a foul mood.

'Collect? All the time you call collect! D'you think we're made of money?'

'D'you think *I* am?'

'The generator broke again, the north end's like a swimming pool, and Otto's two best students left us. Said they weren't learning anything.'

'So let them go. When Roxanne wins the Gold they'll be kicking the door down to get back in the Braun rink. Mutti, listen, your spin is *in!*'

A long, breathless silence. 'The Braun spin? OhmyGod-ohmyGod — Otto! Otto! Roxanne will make my spin. My sweet Noni, my dearest child, how did you do it? Now listen to me, listen good. Make sure nobody sees it until the Games, *ja*? We don't want anybody should steal it.'

Noni didn't laugh. 'I'll see to it.'

'And kiss Roxanne for me, kiss her beautiful face! Tell her how I am happy! And you tell *me* how she is skating, my darling, darling Roxanne.'

'So-so. She could use a little more pep.'

'Give vitamins! Double, triple, mega-doses! They work, they do!'

Vitamins were not what Noni had in mind, and would not in any case do the trick, but with no access what was the difference?

But hadn't Mutti just provided it? Noni hung up and dialled the doctor's machine, speaking slowly and clearly at the beep. 'Tell Roxi there is word from the old ones in Bonn. It is urgent she call her mother.'

She lit another cigarette and settled down to wait.

Jasinski hollowed a valley into his mashed potatoes and flooded it with a fragrant lemon-parsley sauce. He did not allow himself to look to see if Roxanne had done the same. 'This is delicious. Who taught you?'

She laughed. 'Mom. Back before food turned into a mortal sin.'

So he could look after all, and yes, her portions were small but she was eating balanced meals. Halibut, mange-tout, carrots and potatoes. And sauce. The weight was slow coming back because she burned so much off, but she was no longer killing herself. 'But I think you miss living with Grant?'

She considered, then blushed — and looked naturally, touchingly beautiful. 'It's, well, personal, I guess, but before a big competition you don't . . . sex doesn't cross your mind that often. After, yes, but not during.'

'Energy goes to the ice?'

'How did y'know?'

'Doctors are supposed to know such things.'

Out in the hall the phone buzzed. They heard the answerer click in.

'That'll be Mom again, I'll bet. God, I wish —'

'Yes?'

'I feel lousy, ignoring her — heck, I'm leaving tomorrow. If I had a daughter do that . . . I wish Grant hadn't told me not to talk to her.'

'I think he told you to make your own decisions,' Jasinski said gently.

She bit into a crisp mange-tout and nodded, but the moment she finished her meal she darted into the hall and played back the message.

The old ones in Bonn. Not Otto, please God, not Grandpa, who'd sat her on his lap in the wheelchair and given her her first 'spin' on the ice. She'd been about three, shrieking with delight when he spun the chair so fast she couldn't see or hear anything, just bury her face in his neck and breathe in his smell of harsh soap and clean washing and absolute security. Not like Grossmutti, all bones, who never held her except to guide her first steps on the ice, never stroked her hair unless she skated an extra good figure in that crummy little rink when she and Mom took vacations in Germany. Vacations. With Grossmutter there was no such thing.

Her fingers trembling, she dialled Noni. Who wanted to see her. Naturally.

'But Grandpa? Is he okay?'

'Of course, but I have a message from your grandmother.'

Which meant Mom was up to her tricks. Roxanne sighed. 'Look, Mom. To give me speed like you did, I —'

'Diet pills. They were good for you. They made you skate better.'

'I'm not gonna argue about it, okay?'

'My daughter's leaving tomorrow. Don't I get to kiss her for good luck?'

Hell. 'Look, hang on, okay?'

She stuck her head round Jasinski's living-room door. 'Would it be okay if Mom came over for a bit? She wants to wish me luck and I don't want to go to her place.'

'Fine. Take her into my study if you like.'

Mom wore a royal blue almost-pure-silk jumpsuit, matching fingernails, and way too much make-up. Her hair needed a touch-up. Two years ago she'd looked hard but pretty. Now she just looked hard, with a wild light in her eye that disturbed Roxanne more than the smeared lipstick, the smudged mascara,

'Sit down, Mom. What can I get you? Coffee, wine?'

'Diet Coke and an ashtray.' She tapped a cigarette on her blue, glittery fingernail, looking around the book-lined room.

'I wish you wouldn't smoke so much, Mom.'

'What d'you care? Since you met *Grant* I don't exist, I'm just a nuisance.'

'Look, he wants me to make my own decisions, that's all.'

'If they match up with his. Were mine so bad?'

She should admit to Noni that once upon a time her decisions were okay. She'd never dumped Roxi with babysitters like most moms. Noni had given her lots of time — only trouble was, eventually all the time turned into ice-time.

'Not all,' she admitted. 'But the speed. I mean, I'll be blood-tested at the Games, surely you knew I couldn't *keep* taking it right down to the wire?'

'I'm not stupid. But your confidence was going, and without that . . .'

She'd justify it till the cows came home. 'So what's Grossmutti's message?'

'I told her about the spin. She's so happy you wouldn't believe.'

The spin. Whoop-de-do. 'Did you tell her it's in the programme because some of my jumps are not? Does she for God's sake understand anything?'

'So she's old. She wants a taste of glory before she dies. Do you blame her?'

'Mom. Listen. Make her understand. Every four years one woman *in the whole world* wins the Figure Skating Gold. Just one. *In the world*.'

'But *you're* the World Champion, it's your turn!'

'And I'm off form. Now I have to go to bed.' Roxanne offered her cheek.

Noni, reeking of tobacco and bitterness, kissed it. And left.

CHAPTER SEVENTEEN

Los Angeles, California

Meeting Lloyd Sterling's eyes across a sheet of ice, Grant felt as if he swam close to a barracuda in the Arctic; that everywhere he moved the grey eyes stayed on him, alert remora which missed nothing. Seldom cold in this, his own element, Grant shivered, wishing he'd worn a heavier sweater.

'So, Lloyd!' he forced himself to say. 'Pleased with your protégé?'

'Jeff is much improved, yes. But I expected it. A diamond in the rough. The talent was always there, it just needed buffing up.'

Posture, smoothness, polish, consistency, all concentrated into three months training, and Lloyd Sterling called it 'buffing up'? 'You realize there are no guarantees? Competition is stiff. Jeff could blow under pressure.'

'I doubt it,' Lloyd said, eyes still drilling their piercing grey holes.

So did Grant. Jeff was irritatingly confident. 'I have this month's bill in the office, warmer there . . . and coffee, if you can stand plastic cups.'

Lloyd frowned slightly at the bill. 'You rented a lot of private ice.'

'No choice. The music he brought over was pap, choreographed straight out of the '60s.' Grant spoke with some satisfaction. Jeff had said Mr Sterling had chosen it and helped choreograph it. 'Strong music needs professional choreography. When it seemed Finsky might not show I went all out, since your letter said *carte blanche*. The results, you'll agree, are worth it.'

163

'Is Finsky injured or something?'

'Not that I've heard, but when the Soviets pull his fiancée off the team —'

'Why would they do that?'

'— one draws the obvious conclusion.' Go fish in your murky grey mind, Lloyd old chap. If your line comes up empty, buy a primer on skating politics.

'What does the Russian boy have to do with Jeff?'

'Plenty. If Alexei doesn't compete the top spot is up for grabs. Jeff has a shot at it. Slim, but . . .' He spread his hands. 'Hence a new programme, private ice, extra lessons. Top competitors don't leap out of boxes of Crackerjack.'

Lloyd Sterling bared his teeth in what could have been a smile. A tremor in his finely manicured hands was the only sign of irritation as he reached for his chequebook. 'I'm aware of the costs. You forget, I have a girl at home who may well give your Crisp and Kramer a run for their money.'

Crisp and Kramer. Not Kramer and Crisp. An ominous distinction.

'Your daughter, Britain's newest hope? I've not had the pleasure of seeing her skate. Maureen, isn't it?'

'Yes. Her mother, you recall, is . . . *Deirdre*?' The emphasis was slight.

Grant glanced at him quickly, but the steel grey rivets held firm, seemed to linger on Grant's dark hair, tanned face — hell, they seemed to bore holes into his brain! 'I've been away from Ye Olde a long time now, Lloyd. One loses touch. So how *is* Deirdre?'

'Oh, off and on. You know how women are.' He gave Grant a conspirator's smile, deprecating and urbane, and handed over the cheque. He then produced a silver hip-flask, unscrewed its double cap, and poured them each a shot of brandy. 'Melt the ice a little, huh?'

Grant lifted his silver cup, suddenly impelled to be 'teddibly' Brit. 'To the women — or ladies, God bless them. What would we do without them? Now. A lift to your hotel? All part of the service. No? But of course, you've a limo outside, if the locals haven't lifted the hub-caps.'

Lloyd looked momentarily uneasy. 'Jeff will be at the penthouse by now — I promised him a slap-up lunch. A reward for all his hard work.'

164

'Not *too* slap-up, please. He *is* still in training.'

As Lloyd departed, Grant, amused, patted *his* reward, the hefty cheque, and replayed a private vision of Finsky as he'd skated for the World title last year. Jeff Dunsmuir would need a hell of a lot more than a buffing-up to match that. They all would. He found himself hoping that Finsky would tune out the Soviets' emotional blackmail and compete after all. Sure it would lose Grant, and half-a-dozen other hopeful coaches, a shot at Medal fame in the Mens' division, but it would also black Lloyd's fishy eye, a prospect of infinite delight. Besides, he'd met Finsky and liked him. He knew Dunsmuir and didn't. Jeff was bright but calculating. Perhaps Sterling had met his match.

Lunch was exquisite, Lloyd's selection. *Escargot*, veal, *mange-tout*, a lime sorbet, Bosc pears in a delicate cherry sauce, all served in the hushed splendour of one of the finest suites the Beverly Wilshire had to offer. Plum-coloured carpet, crushed-velvet drapes the precise shade of raspberry sorbet, and in the middle of the starched pink table-cloth a bowl of anemones — magenta, purple, and lavender, their black stamens a dramatic accent to the setting Lloyd had so carefully ordered.

'I really am delighted, Jeff. I had confidence in you, of course, otherwise. . .' He set the bill conspicuously on the cleared space between demitasse cups and the hovering waiter. Lloyd nodded his dismissal to the menial and turned to his protégé, waving a languid hand to indicate the private suite, its lush appointments, its privacy, and the mammoth bill. For just one month's training. 'As you see, dear boy, this kind of investment doesn't come . . . cheap.' He let his hand rest, ever so briefly, on the boy's wrist.

Which the boy instantly withdrew. 'You've been very good to me. I appreciate it, Mr Sterling, I really do.'

'Lloyd. Call me Lloyd.'

'Yes, Lloyd.'

The grey eyes warmed, darkened, as he reached for Jeff's hand, and then chafed the boy's ice-chapped fingertips between his own softly creamed palms. 'The ice . . . so cruel to our tender English skin, isn't it?'

'It never seems to bother Maureen's,' Jeff said smoothly.

Lloyd darted a glance at his face, but the boy's eyes were wide and guileless, a clear English blue. 'Maureen has fortunate pigmentation. But let's talk about us. What do you think of our chances, eh?'

Jeff blinked, innocent still. 'It would help to have Emma Crisp in our corner, chat her up a bit. She'll be judging Mens or Pairs.'

'So I gather. I'll make a point of seeing her at the Games, but I meant *our* chances, Jeff. Yours and mine.' Jeff's hand was now imprisoned, trapped between Lloyd's elderly, tightening palms. 'As I mentioned, this training you're in, which has prepared you for a splendid future, doesn't come cheap.'

Deftly, slowly, as though after much practice, Jeff extracted his hand from the trap and stood. Quite deliberately, using his youth, confidence, and extra height, he loomed over his benefactor. 'As you said,' he drawled, 'I'm in training, Lloyd. Which, as you also keep saying, doesn't come cheap.'

'Which means?' Lloyd Sterling seemed to turn pale, but since his skin was already grey, Jeff couldn't be sure.

'Which means *I* don't come at all until after the Games.'

He gave the implication a moment to register, a moment in which Lloyd felt he was being swallowed by a great white shark. Then, without so much as a flicker, Jeff gazed down, long and deep, into the glistening fish-eyes turned up to his — a young teacher lecturing the oldest, slowest kid in class. 'It's this way. The sports psychologist says we've all got just this much creative force. In a training run-up, like for the Games, all this power, artistic, physical, sexual, our fantasy life, our imagination, everything — all this energy pours into a single storage tank, building and building like heat in a volcano.'

Lloyd moistened his lips. 'Yes?' he said, his smooth voice suddenly hoarse.

'So: I'm at centre-ice, poised, waiting to be announced. "Representing Great Britain, *Mr Jeff Dunsmuir*!" BAM! My music starts, builds, slow, throbbing, faster and faster, all that energy, all that boiling, stored-up lava just explodes! It's firework time, four-and-a-half incredible minutes of sheer ecstasy — for audience and judges, naturally. Me, I'm concentrated, using all that training for which you've so generously coughed up. A businessman like yourself wouldn't screw up an investment for the sake of a few weeks, right?' He took a deep breath and strolled away, powerful muscles of his backside rippling him to the door. 'Too bad I have to go back to my hovel now. There's packing, then the masseur, a final session with the sports psychologist, and after that a hair appointment and —'

'Wait!' Lloyd Sterling spluttered at the centre of his beautiful stage, all set for a performance which had been inexplicably cancelled. 'At the Games we'll have no time together at all!'

Jeff turned his youthful blue gaze directly into that of the ageing barracuda. 'After the Games there'll be all the time in the world.'

Jeff waved himself out of the suite and took the high-speed elevator, whistling as he stepped out at the corner of Wilshire and Rodeo Drive.

After the Games? Daft old fart. If he won the Gold he sure as hell wouldn't need any 'time together' with Lloyd Sterling. Even with Silver or Bronze there was younger, hotter talent, just as rich and generous, any place in the world.

The evening before they left, Ben Carlsen took Lise to a good-luck dinner with every intention of dropping in on Emma Crisp after Grant's final briefing at the rink. To his credit he went through the motions of inviting his wife and son to dinner. Both declined, Mrs Carlsen for reasons of her own and Dag because he could no longer watch the efficient delivery system of Lise's fork.

Dag, mindful his mother would not be here after the Games, sought her out. She was in her room with its white-painted Scandinavian furniture, all clean lines and that sense of casual efficiency Mom had too. Surely Dad had it once, but drink and some deep inner lack had consumed it. Now all he had was a failing business and Lise's skating. His marriage, for which he perhaps cared nothing, would soon evaporate.

Spare but elegant, no longer vague, Mom leafed through Aunt Signe's Swedish magazines, flipping their pages not so much to read, Dag felt, as to touch base with the past and project herself into the future. She had a new short haircut, a straight, shining beige cap which showed off the shape of her head and framed a face unmistakably stamped with intelligence. Neither Ben nor Lise had remarked on the change in her — well, they wouldn't — but the glow hung about her like a new love affair. For a moment Dag wondered, then dismissed the suspicion. It would take her a long time to recover from Dad; years before she'd want to look at another man, if ever. She was in love with Sweden, the prospect of freedom from Ben.

'When are you leaving, Mom?'

'The day after you. Neighbours are feeding Allez-Oop while you're gone.'

'You still won't come to the Games?'

'No. I haven't been asked and couldn't bear to be there. I shall watch for you on television, be wishing you well, but I can't, won't pretend I care about the outcome of the Games.'

'Mom, it's a great sport and I'm good at it —'

'Yes. On your own you'd have done well, but with Lise . . . Until lately I blamed skating for ruining my marriage and my daughter, and there were times I've worried terribly about you, all unfounded, but that's skating for you. I see now that *we* ruined the marriage, Ben and I, we didn't care enough, wanted different things. Still do. I've packed your underwear, a few personal things. I'll be with Aunt Signe. If you want to live with us, or visit, we'd adore to have you. I've packed emergency cash in the toes of your socks. I doubt you'll get anything from Ben.'

'What about you? What will you live on?'

She laughed, truly laughed, a sound not heard in the house since Dag was small. 'It seems impossible we've all forgotten, but we have. I illustrated children's books before I married. If I can regain that child-like perspective I expect I can do it again.'

In the back of Dag's mind a memory rose up, hazy, Lise and him on a blanket on the lawn, building a red-and-white castle from blocks, Dad sorting fishing lures in the garage, a younger, sweeter Mom under the great elm tree, a pad in her lap, charcoal stick sketching two angelic children building a red-and-white castle.

Then Lise's demand, 'Mom, stop it, stop it! You're making them 'xactly the same as us!'

And Mom laughing. 'Why not, darling?'

And Lise answering: '*I'm* Lise! Lise don't *want* anuvver Lise!' Then the real Lise weeping, beating the castle to rubble with plump, dimpled fists.

Now Mom's smile was etched with sadness. 'You're not to worry about me. My family is comfortable — perhaps that's why Ben married me. You'll look after Lise if you can? I've lost her. I know she won't stay in touch. It's a terrible thing to love your daughter yet dislike what she's become. She doesn't like me either, but I wish she could be happy. I think she won't be. She'll do what I did, marry for the wrong reasons and live to regret them.'

'If she wouldn't eat so goddamned much.'

Mom shook her head. 'Don't worry about it. The Games will soon be over. Her appetite is the symptom, not the disease. Rubens would have loved her.'

'But what's the rock group going to think? They've spent so much!'

'No. Dad's business foots most of the bills. The group has spent little and can afford much. Remember that, okay? *You* owe them nothing. Nothing!'

Her voice, usually soft, had suddenly turned emphatic. It startled him. 'A moment ago you said that for a while you worried about me. Why?'

She seemed to study the page of her magazine very carefully. Then she looked up, her blue eyes dark, full of clouds. 'You have no friends. Yes, I know that's due to skating, but, well, I was afraid you were going to be gay.'

They were both still, a breeze rattling dry leaves outside her window.

'But you urged me to go out with Jeff!'

'Yes. I knew you had to decide, that you couldn't stay in limbo. Did you? Decide, I mean?'

'I don't know, but I don't think . . . I mean, I like girls, it's just there's never —'

'Time to meet them,' she finished for him. 'After the

169

Games there will be. Maybe you'll meet another skater, make another Pair team . . . but if you decide you do like men better, be what you are, don't pretend. I hope it won't be that way for you. Young gays seem happy, but there are few things sadder than a lonely old homosexual shopping for young love. Youth can be so cruel.'

Dag fidgeted in the chair. 'Mom, we've never . . . we haven't talked about sex before, it's just that Dad always acts like I'm such a nothing, and —'

Her blue eyes suddenly impaled him, startled him. 'Don't let him do it to you. His inadequacy doesn't have to be yours. And remember what I said about the rock group. Watch the leader. There's something . . .'

'You think he'll make a play for Lise, is that it?'

'I don't know if it's Lise . . .' For a moment her old vagueness was back. Her eyes lost their focus, her voice fluttery, uncertain. 'I don't know. He disturbs me, that's all, there's something . . .' She shivered and reached for the thin wrap on the back of her chair. 'You'll remember what I said, yes? *You* owe no one anything! Now why don't you take a swim, your last for three weeks?'

Dag felt, somehow, he should say his goodbye to her now, not wait for the airport and all the hoopla of leaving, but she'd turned back to her magazine, and it was only when, restless, he arched into the pool, that he realized how swiftly she'd dismissed him, how she'd turned her face away, how the light glittered on a single drop of moisture sliding down her cheek.

He knew then that no matter what the outcome of the Games, that it was Ben Carlsen's house to which he was saying goodbye. Not Mom. She'd always be in his life no matter where he went, what he became.

Grant had called them all to the bleak rink conference room somewhat late for their final briefing. Maybe that way they'd remember it. The aim was to focus them on the Games, only on the Games. Personalities, for the moment, must take a back seat — though he couldn't help noting that Roxanne's colour was good, that she looked eager. Thank God for Jasinski.

They'd all showed up. Almost. Beejay with Emma; Jasinski with Roxanne, Noni drifting about like a ghost in the background; Ben with Lise and Dag. Jeff, to Grant's surprise, was alone, looking too cocky for his own good.

'I'll make it short,' he began. 'The Games are important, something to tell your children and your children's children about. Between you, you represent three good nations. Represent them well. I know you won't let yourselves or them down. Or me. You're all ambassadors, though right this minute a few of you look anything but.' He smiled.

Beejay wore cut-offs and a multi-stripe tank-top. Dag was in jeans and a sweatshirt, hair still damp like dark honey. Noni floated in white chiffon and red pumps, as for a party. Emma, already in judging mood, wore sensible shoes, a dark suit, and white shirt — and still looked more woman than Noni. Lise was stunning in pink silk, hair freshly done; she could have been a model and no doubt wished she were; few models had to worry about overhead lifts. Jeff was immaculate, colour co-ordinated, and expensive. As usual.

'Okay. You all know the rules. Behaviour: judges will be everywhere. You may not see them but they'll see you, especially if you're loud, obnoxious, or rude. I don't say it could drop your placement, but why plant a negative image before you take the ice? In competition, stay calm. Don't panic if something's off. If your marks are less than you think you deserve, smile even if it kills you. At practice sessions I shall not remind you of ice manners. I have my pride. Judges will be there. In theory they don't prejudge but they sure don't show up at six every morning out of insomnia. They're watching you. So watch yourselves. No kicking ice. No chewing gum. No bad language.'

He saw Emma's dark-suited elbow dig firmly into Beejay's ribs, and smiled at them both.

'I'll see you all at the airport. So will the press. Say little, be positive, and smile, smile, smile. You can afford it. You are all very good. You are also privileged. So am I. For having taught you. Good luck.'

He watched them file out, each a little taller than when they filed in. He felt an unexpected surge of pride in them — and in himself for producing them. In the frenzy of the Games no doubt his pride might get mislaid, but for this moment, he had it. Somewhere in that five was an Olympic medal.

Something else too, a shadow tugging at the corner of memory, smiling, anxious, whispering against an expected cough. What had her telegram from the hospital said? *I'm proud, son. Good luck.*

Into the empty room he answered her: 'If we get a medalist out of these Games we've made it, Mum. It will be as much our medal as if our names were engraved on it. We can *be* proud then, me and thee. The sardines and potted meat will have paid off.'

But suddenly there was doubt, a thumb light and delicately manicured forever on the scale, forever threatening, forever keeping Mum in the red, robbing her sacrifice of its due. But if he should prise that thumb off the scale, beat Maureen and thus Deirdre, the sacrifices would surely be vindicated.

He smiled into the cold room and the bitter, echoing past.

CHAPTER EIGHTEEN

Eight days to the lighting of the flame. Days. Years of training had telescoped to months, to weeks — and now to days. In the ice palaces of the foothills, the sport's élite were poised for the final ascent. Close up, Olympus loomed steep, unimaginably vast, its summit wreathed in mystery, a storehouse of impossible dreams. Now the last assault was at hand, reducing each pathetic strategy to scale. Wasted moments over the years accused them; pride in past victories mocked them; an avalanche of their images, touched and retouched and splashed on screens and newspapers the world over, intimidated and exhausted them. How to justify such trust? How to fulfill such high-flown hopes? These were not gods but humans, young in the arts of battle, creatures of flesh and blood, of frailties beyond number. They loved and hated, rejoiced and wept, enjoyed no powers beyond those of mortals. Where had the legend begun? What cruel deity devised it?

In Moscow, Alexei Finsky stood for a moment at the top of the Ilyushin's ramp and looked down. Flash-bulbs blazed, an army of fans, friends, and foes waved, a nation's television cameras rolled, but nowhere a Galina, nowhere her parents — who had never failed to see him off, to wish him well. Behind him the Director smiled. 'I hear the highways are jammed. So many to cheer our gallant team to glory.'

Alexei turned to look down at him, snug in his Western-tailored coat. 'The highways would not affect Galina. Like me, she is without a car.'

At the very last second before the plane's doors sealed him in, still debating if he should disappear into its belly or descend its steps back to Moscow, to interrogation and obscurity, he compromised. Catching the eager eye of a live camera, he whipped off his glorious team cap of Pushkino sable and waved it until it flew from his hands as if on wings, directly at the eye of the camera. Behind him the Director sympathized. 'Such enthusiasm! Don't worry. For a "Merited Master of Sport" we carry a spare.'

In the suburbs a plain man obedient beyond the norm smiled into the window of his television set and then into the eyes of his wife and daughter. 'Only think,' he said humbly. 'Our Alexei remembered me.'

Japanese skiers checked their bulky equipment before boarding. They were many, Japan fielded full teams for Nordic and Alpine; a cheering section showed up for the intrepid fliers of the 70- and 90-metre hills and for the downhill racers, heroic Rising Sons even before they departed the soil of Japan. Speed skaters next, amid the staccato rattle of officials and trainers.

Figure skaters followed, darlings of the cameras — one in particular, Mieko Nakashima of the famous Nakashimas. An enviable child, born to both talent and wealth! From her window-seat she was seen to wave a doll-like hand to Oka-chan, a distant figure weeping at the barrier. Through the army weaving and scurrying between them, their eyes locked and held, a plain woman and her child, only their shared dream private, breathtaking in its beauty. Friends from Atami waved flowers and perhaps, hidden behind a pillar to inspect the merchandise in person, a promising young man from Hokkaido.

In vain the media hunted the crowd for a glimpse of Hiro Nakashima. Mieko did not. She saw the great Nakashima television camera roll in for a close-up. As the engines roared for take-off she gave its lens a graceful nodding bow, presenting the tender nape of her neck as if to Grandfather's sharpest Samurai sword.

The main UK team flew from Heathrow in the usual clatter of departure.

The Sterlings — mother, daughter, nurses and equipment

—boarded the company twin-jet at a lonely airstrip in Surrey. The weather was appalling, but Deirdre, whose newest battery of treatments offered promise of better days to come (though no one spoke of a cure), wore her full-length fur, her beautiful wig, and a chic little hat with a compassionate veil. Through a driving snowstorm and at a distance of, oh, fifty feet, she looked much as she had nineteen years before, when Grant Rivers' heart skipped a beat at her every sweet smile.

'You not cold, darling?' Maureen asked, relieving her of the heavy coat and tucking her into the small airborne cot. 'The pilot says there'll be turbulence until he can climb over it. Would a warm brandy settle you?'

Deirdre shook her head. 'Just hold my hand.' She closed her eyes as the small plane raced down the runway and lifted. 'Do you know,' she murmured, 'how many years I've waited for this? Since the moment you were born, when they put you in my arms and I saw your beautiful face, touched your warm skin. Then you looked at me and it was all so lovely. . .'

Maureen sighed and listened. She'd heard it so many, many times.

The departure from Los Angeles could not have been more different. Grant, Jasinski, Emma and Ben boarded first, before film began to roll and while sanity still prevailed. Emma refused to speak to Ben, who scowled and bided his time, waiting for the kids and the drinks trolley.

At some point before correspondence school, when Roxanne and Beejay were beginners, they attended the same grade school, different grades. School spirit, hurriedly rekindled, honoured them with a marching band send-off. All shared the excess of publicity, happily roping in Jeff and the Carlsens.

Which was fortunate: it kept the cameras off two lonely women who watched from the departure lounge.

Noni Braun Kramer chewed at her lip and wished Roxanne had landed her triple-toe yesterday, last chance before judges began their spying. Roxanne had promised to phone her. Noni had promised to phone Mutti. If they could.

The wife of Ben Carlsen, soon to be an ex, watched her son board the plane with pride and regret. For Lise, who turned and gave her photogenic smile to the world before ducking into the plane, her mother had only tears.

Grant Rivers, fastening his belt, knew he was in for the ride of a lifetime.

CHAPTER NINETEEN

Getting There

A week and a day before the lighting of the Olympic flame, at roughly the same hour, a diverse international fleet lifted off from Olympic foothills around the world to make the pilgrimage to glory. On engines throbbing with power and hope, they soared into the atmosphere.

To earthbound well-wishers waving goodbye, the planes and the dreams they carried appeared indestructible to the limits of their earthbound vision and far, far beyond it. But inside the streamlined shells, their human cargoes knew a swift panic for which no amount of visualizing or hypnotherapy had prepared them.

They were on their way to the Games. Committed. The expectation of anonymous fans, the faceless mass, for years heavy on young shoulders, now had less substance than confetti drawn into a vortex. In the next weeks, under the merciless gaze of world cameras, they must justify years of effort made by them and for them. They could not all expect to win but they must not lose badly, must not shame themselves, parents, coach or country. They must not allow themselves to think the unthinkable: *not last place . . . no . . . no . . . not last place, never the ignominious last place*.

But even as fear sent out a quivering tendril, self-hypnosis clicked back in as it had been designed to do, faint but comforting; they could hold on for three more weeks or until they failed to qualify, whichever came first. But failure did not compute. They were programmed for everything but that.

*

Inside the airborne Ilyushin, privilege reigned everywhere, immutable as the roles in a pre-revolutionary fable.

The posted seating plan left little doubt. Alexei the loner was cast as Crown Prince, the certain Gold Medalist of whom they could not be certain, therefore to be watched and courted until he reflected glory upon the *apparat*. The aircraft's finest appointments were at his disposal: priority access to a compact gym with physiotherapist and masseur on hand to ease any kink or strain in the Finsky skating machine. On boarding, they ushered him into a club-sized chair he could tilt to 'total recline' should sleep overtake him; a gardenia (cut that morning from the botanical gardens near the Kremlin) floated in crystal on his tray of salad and wafer-thin roast beef; then an obsequious visit from the team dietitian, who begged to know if anything further was required.

Alexei almost said, 'Yes, my passport,' but that would instantly cancel every perk and possibly turn the Ilyushin back to Moscow to throw the Crown Prince to the dragons now guarding the fair maid Galina in her dungeon. But passports stayed in the cockpit with the pilot — and Alexei was trapped into a window seat beside the Director, an unlikely squire who normally sat in isolated splendour.

So. This trip Alexei was to have access to power and a preview of wealth undreamed of by the peons in the tail section, some of whom wouldn't even be relied on to bring home a Bronze.

'We cherish our national treasures, Alexei. You've seen Irena's *dacha* on the Baltic? Given to her after the last Olympics. Better than mine, I can tell you! My wife wasn't too thrilled, but as I reminded her, "Who has brought us more honour than Irena, my dear?" So what could she say?'

What indeed. As the Director mentioned his wife he whipped out a Cross pencil, black with gold trim, and prepared to list purchases he simply must make for her. 'Wives, Alexei. You either have to drag them along or return to them bearing gifts. In the long run, gifts cost less. I know how women think,' he murmured, just under the efficient surge of the Ilyushin's engines.

He confided that if he didn't make a list before landing, the excitement of the competition caught him by the throat and — phftt! — these little mementos slipped clean out of his mind. Alexei did of course remember that Galina liked 'White Linen' — Estée Lauder, yes? — *parfum* not cologne — and Yardley's lavender for her lingerie drawer? And she favoured a 'Spring Violet' shampoo, the Director thought Givenchy, but he'd check. And if Alexei had forgotten her size in underwear, ha-ha, the wardrobe mistress had her measurements. And doubtless he'd want more 'Grey Flannel' aftershave for himself? — his bottle was almost empty. . .

He hardly noticed the Director slide another Cross pen identical to his own on to Alexei's table. By the time he read the inscription — his monogram fashioned inside a miniature Gold Medal — it hardly seemed to matter.

Was there a single intimate thing these magpies did not know about the Crown Prince and the fair maid? What they ate for breakfast? The words they whispered to each other in the night? How often and in what positions they made love? He felt as though he and Galina had been thrust naked into the spotlight at the Central Army Sports Club rink. He shivered and drew a blanket across his so-valuable legs, touching off another burst of advice. The Director patted his shoulder: 'And pick up blankets for her hope chest! Germans make an excellent quality, light but warm. And maybe a cashmere shawl from the Scottish Highlands for Galina personally — they sell them at all the EEC tourist traps. Front Office hasn't allocated us enough currency, they never do, but I have connections, leave it to me. Galina would prefer red, you think, and perhaps a touch of black for drama?'

For a moment the memory of scarlet tulips blinded him, the satin texture of black and orange centres, the whisper of death as petals scattered the table and their last meeting with portent. Red for drama. Black for mourning. The *apparat* had not missed a trick. Alexei closed his eyes and ears against the picture, Galina's eyes steadfast beyond the petal-drift separating them, and forced himself to concentrate, sure there must be a point to the Director's monologue, that soon it would be reached.

The man's cigar sickened him, but there was no escape yet. 'Take my advice, son,' his mentor whispered at last.

'Prudence pays. Gifts ensure our future . . . our happiness, shall we say?'

Yes, let's. Under the blanket Alexei spread his fingers until the knuckles cracked. The speech was over. An insurance policy against Galina's future. Available for the price of a bottle of scent, a Gold Medal, and most particularly the return of their big investment, the Crown Prince himself, to Russian soil — failing which Galina, unskilled in everything but skating, sure to be denied her except as recreation, would be consigned to serfdom. She would have no apartment, no car, no future beyond serving behind a counter or teaching calisthenics to kindergarten chubbies. At night she would return to a tiny apartment crowded with a mother, a father, and now an old aunt with a pet pigeon. Without his success to ensure the perks of power, Galina would wait in line for bread, shoes, a scrub-brush, an umbrella, and perhaps in the summer a single peach.

Oh, how the powerful hung you out to dry on the spikes of their little luxuries. The Director had not been subtle. It was not his function. And if this Director died of excitement next week his successor would not be subtle either. Beyond a certain point diplomacy gathered no points. Only time and power won them apartments, titles, villas, cars. Power pushed them step by step up the ladder — power and a skewed, highly developed vision, allowing them to guard against traps ahead and knives in the back at the same time.

A vision he must acquire himself when he returned bearing appropriate gifts and, of course, a Gold Medal. To return empty-handed would be . . . imprudent. Assuming he returned at all.

The Japanese team engulfed the JAL plane. A host of uniforms crowded the aisles, the wearers proud to have been chosen, confident of their place in the hearts of their families, their nation.

Mieko's second cousin, the Rising Son of the 70-metre hill, unquestionably the team's bronze god and a daring athlete, possessed great personal charm. Too bad he was related to Grandfather through an aunt's line, and did not bask in the Nakashima name. Had he been so blessed, Grandfather would have been at the airport to wish him well; he might even have made time to journey to Montegreco — always assuming the business appointments could wait.

Mieko sat apart with her coach, who would read a paperback all through the long, long flight and leave Mieko free to play her music tape, to sleep, to think, to avoid the other competitors, speed skaters, cross-country skiers, hockey players, the flashy stars of the down-hill, soaring ski-jumpers . . . most from circumstances humble indeed compared to those of a Nakashima. But to her eyes they moved in a universe infinitely more hospitable than hers. Japan's golden youth. Who were still free. In time they would grow older, slower, fatter; time would bind them to desks instead of skis and skates — but for the moment and for the world they shone like armour in the sun.

Against this, what was a great name? A house commanding a bay? Scrolled records of thousands of samurai who had once owed allegiance to some long-dead Nakashima? And now the computer network, its employees no less loyal, no less beholden, than the retainers of old. Was she, heiress to the present fiefdom, any less so? And Oka-chan, who had failed to produce sons and gave him, instead, a granddaughter whose only talent drew unwonted attention to a family in which high aspiration was the singular province of the male? This must be how he saw them, burdens superior to the housekeeper only in that Mieko herself might one day produce an heir. If she too were to fail, forcing him to rely on playboy nephews who now flew the white mountains, then Oka-chan must bear an added shame. Poor Mother, whose soul already bore the welts of so many lashes as the head of the clan cast about him, ever more desperate to find a suitable husband for a granddaughter who daily cost him face by indulging in this unseemly sport, her one inexplicable rebellion and an added hazard. If she did well he would scoff at her achievement; if she did poorly she brought dishonour upon Grandfather and, by extension, Japan.

Was Roxanne Kramer so hampered, she wondered?

Roxanne chose her seat companion with care. It was to be a

long trip. She must gather herself. Last-chance time — vital that she isolate herself and her emotions, her will to win. But the plane was overbooked as usual, and her face was known, oh boy was it known! She'd seen at least five versions of it on tabloid covers and weekly news magazines as the team hung about the airport waiting to board. So John Public as a travel companion was definitely out — he/she would blab on about the Games clear to Montegreco.

Beejay was also out. Better to ignore competitors as the Games closed in. They could psych you without even trying, and Beejay talked nothing but jump, jump, jump; she should have been a damned kangaroo. Worse, she was enjoying the trip! A year ago Roxanne wouldn't have considered her any threat at all, but God, she'd improved!

If only people expected less, perhaps she could give more. Being favourite was the pits. Always on view, in shops, elevators, restaurants, taxi-stands. How Kati Witt stood it and kept her cool for so long, God only knew.

Emma was out, too. Gossip being what it was, you didn't want to look like you were kissing up a judge. Not that Emma could judge her this time, but anything you said could be repeated in the Judges' Lounge and rear up later to bite you. Besides, Emma was the wrong generation. Beejay's *mother* for heaven's sakes! Thirty-six if she was a day. Roxanne tried not to remember that Grant was mid-thirties too, and that he and Emma got along exceptionally well. But a coach had to be friendly with judges.

She didn't want anybody around who'd be counting calories either, which eliminated both Dr Jasinski and Grant, who she didn't want to be close to anyway at the moment. When they looked at each other now they looked across four years of desert, the atmosphere between them so laden with their coach–student past that she'd need a compass to find the Grant who'd held her with tenderness. She loved him, maybe always would, but the medal swung between them, a gold barrier neither could ignore. He wanted a winner and she wanted to win *for* him, but there had to be more to marriage than that. She'd learned more from Dr Jasinski than Grant would ever know.

Something else she'd figured out too at the doctor's place, answering his back door to the penniless, who were too ashamed to come to the office but who knew where to find free samples if they needed antibiotics or a salve; then the street-kids who maybe needed a knife-wound stitched and daren't go to the clinic because cops asked questions. Roxanne had never wanted money before, only a wedding-ring and 'Mrs Grant Rivers' embossed on her stationery. Now she wanted money of her own, a cushion to lean on, to give her a decent place to live so she wasn't dependent on Grant. The Gold would give her that. Yes, she had more than a wedding-band riding on this Olympics now. No wonder Mom was bitter. Achievement *deserved* money. Noni had wound up with zero, so who could fault her for wanting to see Roxanne get something? Somehow it was easier to see Noni's point of view when they were not together; maybe mothers and daughters just naturally liked each other more when they were apart.

So in the end she sat with Lise Carlsen, who she couldn't stand. Since Lise didn't like her either, it made for a peaceful journey. The pairing worked well for both. Roxanne took the vitamins Dr Jasinski gave her, drank eight ounces of fresh squeezed juice, special order, and ate a fair meal, but she was damned if she'd pig-out *now* — and Lise was only too happy to eat her own and Roxanne's créme caramel desserts, first dousing them with fudge sauce and chocolate cream liquor.

Lise, despising Roxanne for not getting all she could when she could, nodded off to sleep with the texture of cream and chocolate on her tongue, the latest rock band sweetly raucous in her earphones, and behind her blue eyes a vision of the matching blue skating dress hanging in her garment bag. If only she was in a show where all you had to do was look beautiful. If only Grant wouldn't make her do the damned overheads. If Dag lifted her like he was supposed to, like Atlas, like Superman, but no . . . Softened by wine and liquor, she renewed her sporadic entreaties to a god she was not sure she believed in except at truly desperate times, like when her period was late or a spot erupted on her chin. 'Please,' she begged Him now. 'Don't let Dag drop me out of the triple-twist, and I promise to feed the cat forever and ever, Amen; I'll clean his litter-box; I won't charge on Dad's cards — well, not much; I'll stay out of Mom's purse; I'll give up french-fries and onion rings, I'll —' Her pink mouth slightly open, drooling gently at the pictured delights she contemplated giving up, the Nordic Queen nodded off, her snores so faint and melodious they could have been set to music.

So thought her brother, who sat immediately behind her and had a fair idea of what ran through Lise's mind most, if not all, of the time. Thank God she never knew what ran through his. It probably never occurred to her that other people thought at all. What Dag thought now was what in the world would he do when the Games were over? In future there'd be no Mom at home in California. And no way would he live with Lise and Dad, who both thought him a wimp. Maybe Mom was right. Get a new Pair partner who really wanted to skate. No problem. Not a week went by that he wasn't approached, subtly, by hopeful mommas. But where to train? Live? Which flag to skate for? Those were the questions. He'd always loved Sweden, the people and the country. Logical, tolerant — but his friends were all California-based skaters. But with Mom going to live in Sweden . . . if the Games were just over, if he never again had to lift Lise. . .

In front of him Lise thumped her pillow with a dimpled fist, and far down the aisle Beejay Crisp yelped with triumph as she won another round of cards. Dag envied her. To be that carefree! Of all the competitors, Beejay seemed happiest. Maybe because her Mom was Emma, camly reading a book. Emma could be judging them next week. Too bad they had no chance.

Jeff Dunsmuir had an aisle seat but he too kept a surreptitious eye on Emma. The minute the chap next to her toddled off to the loo, Jeff hopped into the empty seat. He didn't like Emma. Her tongue could grind you to dust if you caught her on her wrong side, and she never really showed which side was wrong, which right, until you'd stepped over the line. But a judge was a judge, and there was a fifty–fifty chance she'd be his. He'd helped with her suitcase, eased her out of her coat when she boarded, and even considered a split of champagne with his compliments — it would be a long flight — then decided it might look crass, something Lloyd would do. But where was the harm in oiling the wheels of judgement with a little flattery?

'You must be so proud of Beejay, Mrs Crisp,' he began. 'She looks better every day, no nerves at all. I was *thrilled* for her this morning. She did a fantastic programme, absolutely perfect!'

'I was there,' she said, each word distinct, a rap across the knuckles.

'Ah! You saw Roxanne too, then.' He shook his head. 'Too bad.'

Emma turned back to her book.

'Too bad,' he repeated. 'Must be tough being favourite, people wanting miracles, but she really should try harder right now.'

He winced as Emma slammed her book shut, as her eyes met his with a slam no less violent for its silence. 'Jeff, why don't you do what *she's* doing right now? Like keep your mouth shut? And you're in somebody's seat.'

She watched him blink, his pupils skittering like trapped ants as he hurried off, the back of his neck stiff and flushed. She brushed her palms together and turned to check on Beejay, still playing game after noisy game in the aisle with the US Men's Champion from Boston, a brash kid who, if he was on, had enough in him to swipe the Gold from everyone but Finsky. She hoped the American kid *would* be on, that he'd beat the pants off Jeffie Dunsmuir. Nationality had nothing to do with it. The Dunsmuir kid made the hair on the back of her neck stand up.

With Jasinski asleep on his left, Grant was trying to avoid Ben Carlsen, who hovered between the drinks trolley and Grant. His kids' first major competition, maybe the guy just wanted reassurance? Lise and Dag were too beautiful to be true. The press would eat them alive and there'd be no shortage of show offers. Too bad Lise couldn't skate, but in a show who'd notice? At the Games everyone would. If Ben wanted an assessment of their chances. . . To protect himself he encouraged the coach on his right, another transplanted Brit, to shop-talk. Internationally known as Yum-Num (he said 'yum' for yes and 'num' for no) he had trained countless champions in the last two decades and was again headed for Mecca.

'Yum, you've done well with Kramer,' he allowed. 'With

Noni she had figures like a damned compass, but not a jump worth looking at. When the Committee dumped school figures we all wrote her off — too soon, obviously.'

'Wrote her off?' Grant said, unexpectedly nettled that this pip-squeak had had the gall to speak of Roxanne as if she'd been the sport's bad debt. 'The potential was always there.'

The other man laughed, short and sharp. 'Yum, and no place like the bedroom to realize it, right? I'd have done the same. Have, in point of fact. Sometimes it's the only way to pry talent from possessive momma's little fist. Your first Olympics, right?'

'Uh-huh.' As if this veteran didn't know. 'I imagine it'll be much the same as Worlds.'

Again the laugh, a yap like a miniature terrier. Grant wondered if he hailed from Yorkshire. 'The same as Worlds? Oh, num! You can't mean that, old chap! Num, num, num! Have you thought of the Village problem?'

Grant heard himself adopt a crisper accent, an older, graver expression. 'I hear the facilities are excellent. Dorms, cafeterias, gyms, infirmaries . . . Has to be better than Worlds, I should think.'

'Ha! Ha-ha! All you've seen is a hundred or so skaters, mums and dads and trainers, and they all know each other. Annual old home week. In the Village you have thousands of athletes penned up together, fresh blood, the fittest human machines in the world, honed, toned, trained to a whisker, with one aim and only one. To be strong enough, to abstain from sex long enough, to get that blasted medal they hope some old geezer hangs on them at the end.' He smirked like he was telling a smutty joke. 'Meantime, down in the dark that old devil libido's thumping like a tom-tom, fizzing up the hormones, champagne bubbles with no place to pop, nowhere to spend 'em but on skis, skates, and sleds. They've focused on nothing but this all their lives — so okay, maybe they've caught the odd quickie, but no heavy-duty screwing, no sweat-and-come-again stuff. Then it's over, they've won or lost, and bubbles explode like crazy. They hear a noise they've not heard for years. It's like the Indy 500. A thousand sex drives all revving up at once. That's when they really go for the Gold, chum. They've waited so long they go fucking ape, and believe me *that* is the adjective of choice.'

Grant tried not to remember that it was his own edict —
no personal contact — which had exposed fragile Roxanne
to this risk, one he had not even considered. 'But they
segregate men and women. A no-man's-land between the
compounds. Guards to check badges!' He spoke to reassure
himself.

'Guards? They're in the sack, mate, first come first served!
It'd take eunuchs with Uzi's to stop it! No messing about
with "What's-your-name?" "Come-here-often?" "Care-for-
a-drink?" Nobody talks at all. They get down to business,
make up for lost time, and do they have stamina, old chap!
By the time they douse that torch, no-man's-land is
every-man's land. And woman's. Guards, nurses, bus-boys,
athletes — being there is all it takes.'

Grant felt a tap on his shoulder. He was almost glad to see
Ben Carlsen frown over him. So he'd picked up on the
conversation. 'Come over for a drink, Grant, okay? Few
things I gotta get straight.'

The first thing Ben got straight was a large scotch tossed
off in one gulp while his other hand beckoned for a refill.
'And the same for my daughter's coach here.' Ben gave the
attendant an unsteady leer which sat ill on his craggy face. It
was as if Mount Rushmore had burped.

Grant shook his head. 'Club soda, please. I'm working
tomorrow.'

'Your loss.' Ben shrugged, running every word into the
next. 'I heard what that little old Limey —'

'— And you believe him?'

'Hell, he's been around the track enough times, I
mean —'

'Please yourself. So what can I do for you?'

'I'm comin' to that, but first . . . you've got a coach's
badge gets you in that Village. I don't. I'm only her father!
So look out for my girl or. . .'

Or what? 'Ben. I'll be busy all day, every day, and Lise is
of age. If you'd wanted her chaperoned you should have sent
her mother. Now what else did you want to know?'

Ben stared down upon a sea of puffy white clouds for
several minutes, then, 'Yeah. Okay, we're in the air now, no
point being cagey, right? Riiiight.' He leaned closer, spilling
booze between his knees, whispering in Grant's ear, nearly

felling him with a blast of Chivas. 'Is Emma judging Pairs or isn't she? I'm telling you straight — and if you want to tell her, feel free — if Emma Crisp louses things up for Lise one more time . . . she's always been jealous, you know that. Women are. It's Lise's looks, see?' With the gravity of the truly soused he frowned and tried to focus his eyes. 'Men are fair — well, they would be, know wha' I mean? — but that bitch Crisp . . . hell, she couldn't even keep her husband in her own bed, know wha' I mean? Poor ole Dave . . . and that Noni's pretty hot stuff . . . no love lost there, 'tween Noni and Em, know wha' I mean?'

His elbow tried to dig Grant in the ribs and missed. 'Wha' I wanna know's sis: is Crisp on my kids' panel or not? Yeah or no. If she is, what's their chances, know wha' I mean?' Hope touched him briefly with innocence, even a semblance of youth as he strove to control his wayward tongue. 'I'm talking medal-wise, Grant.'

Medal-wise? Grant did not laugh. Despite their incredible good looks there was no way in the world they could make top five. Lise had eaten them right out of contention. But it didn't pay to be frank with a father this desperate, this close to competition. He recalled the last bill he'd presented, and Ben's resigned acceptance as he wrote the cheque.

This damn Olympics was damn near breakin' the back of his contracting business. Damn rock group to pick up the tab? Don't make him laugh. Their flea-bite was a drop in the dyke. Not that he grudged Lise her finery, but the Pair outfits alone set him back over four thou, remember?

Grant remembered. Their costumes *were* elaborate, Lise opting for silk chiffon; no tacky polyester for the Nordic Queen. And her dress had to be let out twice before the dressmaker got it beaded. So Grant must tread softly.

'Ben, nobody knows what they're judging. It's announced later. Lise and Dag's chances? Let's be realistic. It's the lifts, you see, and Lise's weight. She gets too nervous up there. If she'd jump for them, help Dag get her up. . .'

'Oh yes, it's always *her* fault accordin' to you! It's that damn Dag who's bone idle. Between you and me,' He leaned closer again, and whispered into Grant's ear. If a whisper could mutter, Ben's did. 'You know what *he* needs?'

Grant knew exactly. A new partner.

'Trip to the woodshed. A bite of leather. Hate to say it, my own son and all, but I reckon he's headed s-s-straight for fairyland. Whoa! Whoa there! *You didn't hear that*, I never s-s-said it and don't you go s-s-saying I did —' He sagged into his seat, his jaw relaxed; maybe he'd dropped off, forgetting what he'd said. But no. His eyes flew open, darkly, menacingly alive inside that bony skull. 'Or I'll get you. One way or another I'll shoot your Limey lights out. Nobody says that about my kid, hear me? Hear me?'

At that moment the movie abruptly ended, and into the hole of silence Beejay's shout rang clear. 'Gotcha!' She'd just won another round of cards.

Ben's head turned to peer down what must have seemed like a river of blue and gold carpet, shooting her a look that could have levelled the Alps. 'It's *her* fault as much as anybody's. Emma wouldn't knock Lise if that brat wasn't in the Games. Crisp better watch her goddamn ass. Dag better. Everybody! I've had all I'm gonna take!'

So had Grant. He settled back beside Jasinski, closed his eyes, and gave himself up to a luxury he seldom indulged in. The memory of Deirdre Sterling as he remembered her, and the way he imagined she must look now. In her fifties, but beautiful, well preserved, delicate. Deirdre had always known how to take care of Deirdre.

London to Barcelona, winter clouds layered and shrouded land and sea; only the pilot's expertise and the Lear's superb engineering held them steady. Deirdre slept, her little army of nurses for the moment idle. Maureen, loathing the hospital smell they carried on their skin, in their clothes, their hair, flew jump-seat with the pilot. Unlike the nurses, he didn't attempt conversation.

Empty sky slipped by her, empty time. She'd be damned if she'd play her visualization tape again. Hear Maureen Sterling's music; see Maureen sail effortlessly, faultlessly, through her programme. See Maureen receiving the plaudits of the crowd — all leading inevitably to: see Maureen step up to the top platform, bow the Sterling neck as a nice old gentleman drapes a ribbon on it. Feel the weight of the Medal. A Gold Medal, Maureen. See the Union Jack ascend the flagpole. See Maureen victorious, see a tear shine on Maureen's cheek.

Childish! Idiotic! Most competitors played the same game, which had somehow entered the respectable embrace of sports medicine but was nothing more than self-hypnosis, supposed to work like a charm. If it did, how come they wouldn't all get the medal? For herself, she'd be glad when it was over and she could concentrate her time on Mother, on shielding her from the worst of Daddy's scandals. Before she got sick he'd at least co-operated slightly, aware Deirdre could apply social pressure. Not anymore. These last weeks it had all fallen to Maureen, who had to demand every facility they'd once taken for granted. Like the Lear and the villa. When she called Daddy about it in Los Angeles he had the gall to say they'd have to fly commercial, and if Deirdre insisted on going despite the doctors' advice then she could damned well go to a Montegreco hotel.

'Take a suite! Set her nurses up there! I've got my own plans for the villa.'

'Yes, Daddy, and I'm sure they're unwise. People aren't stupid, you know. The team officials would never put up with an overt show of —'

'That will do, you . . . you . . .' he blustered. 'Why shouldn't I have the villa? I have entertaining to do . . . business plans . . . all sorts of people. . .'

His voice began to fade and she knew the words 'team officials' had penetrated. Good. She had stumbled on a lever to control him a little longer, make him behave until the Games were over. Many Committee members were respectable businessmen whose goodwill Sterling Enterprises could ill afford to lose. He must often have been an embarrassment to them, God knew, one they could tolerate when their suspicions were just that. But now the spotlight shone on the British Mens and Ladies Champions. Suspicions would have to be examined closely. It offered her a modicum of power.

'Daddy,' she murmured, 'we don't want Mother exposed to the press sooner than necessary, surely?' She reminded him that Deirdre had not been seen in the papers for years and that she looked nothing like her glamorous old self. There might well be insinuations and the tabloids could be so aggressive. When they saw the nurses they'd wonder, question them, perhaps even offer to buy their story, and he knew how susceptible hired help could be to a bribe. A secret, any secret, would be almost impossible to keep. 'It really would be better for her at the villa, Lloyd.'

Lloyd. She'd never called him Lloyd before. The shift was subtle, and perhaps in his agitation he didn't notice it, but she did, and knew she'd never be afraid of him again. It was as if she'd cut him out of their family, that he was no longer her father, that she was free to despise him without guilt. 'You won't forget Jeff's also a front-runner, Lloyd? The press will be watching all of us.'

'Meaning?'

Dizzy with power over this man who had overshadowed Deirdre's life and her own, she gave him a moment to draw his own conclusions before she asked, as casually as she could: 'When people ask what's wrong with Mother, what will you tell them?'

She heard his quick intake of breath over seven thousand miles. 'They wouldn't be so vulgar!'

'You know they will.' She set the phone into its cradle with quiet but definite authority.

PART TWO

The Ascent

CHAPTER TWENTY

The Games

The four craft sailed remote and beautiful in the blue and white skies of Montegreco, the host principality. The smallest, a private Lear, its shadow running darkly graceful across snowfields below, circled the terrain before veering off towards the coast, flashing once, twice, in the sun before winking through the mountain's saddle to rendezvous with an ambulance in Barcelona. Its personnel, crisp in hospital whites, stood ready to cushion the transfer of Deirdre Sterling to her villa on the Costa Brava. The others, an Ilyushin and two Boeings, landed at Montegreco's new airport, built specially for the Games, but planned with a view to year-round tourism far into the twenty-first century.

Here limousines sped travellers to the official hotel, the newly built Palacio de Estrellas, its name reflecting not merely function but size: fifteen hundred rooms, two hundred suites and penthouses, their potential as yet unrealized. But now the athletes, source of invaluable free publicity, swept into the lobby on flurries of snow, stomping boots, a Babel of tongues, forests of skis and the pervasive reek of polish, damp wool, and ski wax — and, as always among the well-travelled young, topnotes of French perfume and Gucci leather. Special procedures had whisked them through Customs but, given the occasion, bedlam would prevail in the lobby until the Village gathered them within its confines next week.

'I *know* you had my passport, you must have left it in the limo —'

'My skates! A green bag, under my seat all the way, where the hell —'

'I don't care what they say, I'm *not* rooming with *her* —'

'For the nineteenth time, yes, I packed your music —'

'Sign-in's supposed to be in the lobby, not up in the damned rafters —'

'I *know* that's my garment bag, it's got my outfit, practice stuff, spare tapes. D'you think I don't recognize my own — oops, sorry —'

Olympic frenzy. With hundreds more competitors still to arrive, excitement already bubbled and foamed like ale in a keg.

Officially hosted by the principality, the Olympiad was largely financed by a Swiss consortium whose cautious research into the financial future had preceded the outlay of every Montegreco *litera*. The hotel included ballrooms, intimate bars tucked into every conceivable corner, a casino, conference halls, restaurants, an arcade of boutiques and beauty shops, a subterranean pool and grotto, gyms and steam-rooms, and a small, well-equipped hospital with a house doctor and a resident orthopedist, whose second speciality was a reassuring smile. Equally vital, Montegreco's first TV station hummed with state-of-the-art equipment, ready to transmit a barrage of interviews into the darkest, farthest corners of the globe.

Within the facility's two regulation-size rinks, on the slopes, and around the speed oval, the consortium controlled every cablecar, warmhouse, and snackbar in the valley. Olympic Village, built on utilitarian lines, crouched behind a stand of pines, and would later serve as staff quarters for the playground of the wealthy this valley was destined to become. With the Palacio as the official hotel, management had seized every opportunity to hike prices into the stratosphere.

Soundproof rooms set the tone. In Emma's, antiqued Olympic rings studded each padded, leather-covered door. The same motif in a muted beige-on-beige was woven into bedspreads and ankle-deep carpets, etched into bronze-tone shower doors and mirrors, and even, Emma was amused to note, deeply embossed into the bathroom tissue. 'Not exactly home sweet home, thank God,' she said.

Even Beejay, who'd chatted nonstop throughout the trip, uttered a hushed, 'Wow!' before testing her mattress for bounce.

'Quarters at the Village won't be this plush, Beej,' Emma warned. Kicking off her shoes, she took one look at the room-service menu and tossed the velvet-covered folder into a drawer.

Beejay, ravenous after the long trip, retrieved it. 'Hey, it sounds neat! *Haricot verts vinaigrette!*'

'Green beans, oil, and vinegar,' Emma said.

'Yuck! What's *oeufs en gelée?*'

'Cold poached eggs in aspic — and that's jelly made out of pigs' trotters. Boiled long enough, the water wobbles. Prices are out of sight, sport. Back home I'd get a whole loin of pork for that.' Not that she did. But Emma dreamed of someday filling her shopping cart without predicating every item on how many lessons it would buy. Meatloaf could make do for steak, canned tuna for halibut, but time with a coach like Grant had no substitute.

'I thought the Committee picked up the tab for all this!'

'They do, and a lot of donations come from folks who can't afford it.' Not many, true. Most came from companies who wrote it off, but Emma couldn't abide waste, welfare, food stamps, or anything that came 'free'. No strings, they said. My eye, she said. You made your own strings, tied yourself in parasitic knots with 'em. You could deck your kids out like King Tut and drink coffee from fine china, but if you hadn't earned it you drank the sweat of strangers. No matter what they called the programme, everybody knew its real name: charity — which clung like tatters to the soul, skulked behind the eyes where nobody was supposed to see. But folks did see. She'd be damned if she'd condemn Beejay to that.

'Mom, there's not a thing on here under fifteen bucks! No burgers, fries, nachos, chili, ham-on-rye. No *food!*'

Emma yawned. 'That's *haute cuisine* for you. Eat in the Competitor's Café and be glad of it. Grant Rivers says it's good.'

'How come he knows?'

'He checked. I met him in the elevator on his way to the Building.'

Beejay bounced off her bed, rummaged under it for her skate-bag, and emerged crackling a pack of sunflower seeds. 'How come he calls it "the Building"? Same with the rink at home. See you at the "Building".'

'A holdover from the shows. On tour, rinks are called the Building. Less to remember, I guess.'

'How come he checks it first thing? Ice is ice. It's not going any place.'

'If you ever want to coach, figure it out for yourself. And that's the last "how come" I'm answering for a week. I have to unpack, take a nap. . .'

'When's my first practice time?'

Emma ignored her, checking the red competition dress at the back of the closet, admiring again its simplicity. For a wonder, it had travelled without crease or stain.

'So okay. Where's the competitor's trough?'

Emma sighed. Raising an independent teen got harder every year. 'Beej, you are way too old for Mommy to hold your hand. At check-in they gave you guide books, umpteen maps, ice schedules, what practice group you're in, when you skate, where you eat . . .'

'Okay-okay-okay! Roxanne and Lise get all that stuff highlighted in day-glo! How come he doesn't for me?'

'I told him not to. Grant Rivers is a coach, not a nursemaid.'

Beejay paused at the door. 'If I'm not back soon send a St Bernard.'

As the door closed behind her the phone hummed, as if cushioned in the same velvet as the menu. Grant. Could Emma come to his room?

'We need words, Emma.'

His view drew you into the valley, a vista of jump hills, speed oval, bob-sled and downhill courses. In the centre of the picture the ornate façade of the main rink shone like the spun-sugar turrets of a winter castle.

He pointed it out as he poured her a glass of wine, and a sudden new snow fell like a blessing on the arena. 'The ice is great, a texture like silk except for a wash-boardy bit where Beejay puts her lutz. The engineers are fixing it, but in case . . . And the judges line up on the east side. It would be an idea to turn her whole programme round so she finishes facing them. Would it throw her, d'you think? We'll re-do it first practice tomorrow, so she gets used to a new direction straight away, okay?' He kept his tone light. This close to countdown, changes scared everyone. If he altered so much as a step for Roxanne she'd panic, but —

'It won't bother Beejay,' Emma said. 'She's fine. No shakes.'

Grant wondered for how long. She was a kid still. But when you were on your last shot, like Roxanne, and expected to win, nerves took over.

Emma paused, her glass half-way to her lips. 'Will Roxanne show up, her first day?' Usually the favourite made her appearance later.

'Oh yes. No time off for anybody. She'll tense up at first anyway, might as well get it over.'

'Think she'll stand up?' Emma's tone was cautious.

He turned away. 'Why not? She's paid her dues. If she doesn't fall all over they'll give the Gold on a plate . . . if she doesn't chicken out.' But if she did, after all these years. . . As snow tried to seal the window against the view, Swiss technology beat it back. Silently the heated glass wept, but in a moment, clean and dry, it opened the view of the rink again, amphitheatre of his own personal conflict. 'I expect her to hit top form just in time.'

But so much doubt hung on his words even he heard it.

Of the American team Roxanne stood the best chance of a medal. The Russians had the cream of Dance and Pairs this time out and the undoubted top gun among the Men — for Alexei Finsky had indeed arrived. Grant spoke with him not ten minutes ago as they each dug an investigative fingernail into the rink surface. Finsky appeared calm, but set apart from the rest of the Soviets as usual, handling himself more like an individual than a team member. When Grant asked after Galina, Alexei shrugged, said she was fine, and changed the subject. Grant pressed no further. A moment later a reporter did. Alexei gave him a cool smile and left. So yes, the Russians would almost certainly take Mens. Which left Ladies for the USA, and Roxi the country's best shot. Emma might well look concerned. So did every official on the team. During the entire trip Roxanne had barely spoken. She played tapes, read, and sometimes appeared to sleep. Appearances deceived.

Emma stirred. 'Hell, we always take home *some* medals. If the Games had been last year she'd have won for sure.'

'Yes.'

Watching Emma chew her lower lip, Grant figured that if skaters' parents competed for fairness, Emma would take Gold. How many mothers, their own kid competing, would worry about the team's overall showing? 'Roxanne's looking better, Beejay's a cracker, and the Boston kid's terrific on a good day. Relax. Drink up.'

She chuckled. 'Trying to get the judge drunk?'

'No.'

The window's unforgiving snow brightness lit her face but Grant still saw a handsome woman, her features small but strongly formed. Emma had already become what she was going to be, her uncompromising stance, the glint in her eye as firm as her character. Unlike Roxanne, he thought, whose face was all softness blurred by youth, as if she hadn't yet *become* anything at all — after years in the spotlight as world champion, followed constantly by the media, her performances televised around the globe. Perhaps, he thought, she'd always be insecure, incomplete. At twenty-two it was surely time some clue surfaced as to the woman she'd be at thirty, forty?

'Last year she was under control,' Emma said. 'What happened?'

'Gold fever. She's never had real confidence, then Beejay came on strong, and Nakashima. And others.' Again he turned away. 'And Noni's over-anxious, and there's the old Grandma in Bonn . . . this close to the wire they get crazy, want to call the shots. They can't see Roxanne now, just a skating machine that's never good enough or thin enough for them.'

'Anorexic?' Despite her smile Emma seemed hesitant, as if nerving herself to broach a subject far more damaging than an eating disorder.

He shrugged. 'Roxi likes being thin, and Noni's forgotten the changes since her own day, no warm rinks then —' He heard himself run on, make words, but dare not stop. 'No warm-ups, just hose and wool dresses. It gave them legs like porkers.' And it gave some of the mothers tuberculosis — but don't for God's sake think of that now. 'Roxanne'll come through.'

'Grant, I hear rumours, I see things. If a can of worms opens up on us, the team officials have a right to know beforehand. Her fainting spells, her strength, here one day, gone the next. Is she on something? Or not?'

Deep in Grant's chest a hand seemed to squeeze. All the years, the work, Roxanne's and his. If Emma suspected drugs, others might. Even a doubt, widely held, could tip the scale. One-tenth of a point would do it; judges knew to a hair how to dump a skater without making waves. Roxanne's chances would be no better than that of a snowflake hitting this window. He could say, and did, a firm: 'She's clean.' But how could he be sure every second what Noni slipped her in the guise of vitamins or pain pills? Noni, who desperately wanted her to win and whose mental state was ever uncertain. But who, thank God, would arrive after Roxi was in the Village, to which mothers had no access. She'd show up at the rink but he'd be there, watching. There'd be no problem. 'She's clean,' he said again.

Emma must have read his face. 'Nobody would blame you, you know. As I'm sure you've heard, Noni's antics are known from sea to shining sea.'

Her voice had a bitter edge and Grant remembered an old rumour about Dave Crisp and how Emma came to be widowed so young. He also recalled a hopped-up, fast-talking Noni shouting, '*I* trained her, *me*! You don't know what I've done to get that girl where she is — at the top, where she belongs!'

'Are you making a report to the Committee, or what?'

'I hope not. I'd hate the sport mucked up with gossip — and I want to shove Beejay out its way, I don't want her splattered.'

Grant made himself laugh. 'Oh, Emma! Ice is built on gossip! Didn't I hear about a mammoth beige fridge rolling through your front door —'

'The shade card said "vanilla". And it backed out pretty damned quick!'

'That too. But Noni's out of the way, Roxanne's eating with the others right now. She'll be fine. She knows the circuit, the rules, that she'll be first to be tested. She's no fool. We go with what we have today, not last year. A gifted young woman who's scared she'll blow seventeen years of work sky high. The last time out they're all scared. Can you blame 'em?'

'But Grant, just between us, what do *you* think?'

He thought, no, he *knew* he wanted an Olympic winner for Mum's apologetic old bones in a cold churchyard in Wales. For himself he could no longer be sure. He missed Roxanne's closeness, he wanted the woman he thought she could be, medal or no medal, but his hunger for the prize so distorted the picture that he could no longer read the simplest emotional signals.

'I think I should take a judge to dinner. I think she might fancy *sushi*. I think there's great Japanese in the basement. What *d'you* think?'

She laughed. 'Plain or fancy, it sounds great.'

Lavish elsewhere in the hotel, the consortium had stayed its hand in the Competitors' Dining Room. Knowing their athletic guests to be transitory, unlikely to return, the décor was spartan, the food plain and wholesome. The designers could hang their sumptuous velvet swags later, fuss over imported orchids from the tropics, conjure up ingenious ice sculptures — but not until the competitors had ambled their casual manners and dress to the Village. For them a simple mountain of russet pears and golden apples was enough to grace a buffet surrounded by small, tightly-packed tables, plain white linen, stoneware, and stainless cutlery.

Lise Carlsen poked at a tuna salad. This was Europe? Where was the *escargot* swimming in garlic butter, the cherries jubilée? Not a single wine waiter hovering in the background, not even a damned menu! She'd had enough of this slop, thank you, but Dag was watching her so she helped herself to rice pudding, which was at least sweet. Also watching her was a Soviet Pair, the girl a mere eighteen, cute if you liked the little-girl type. Lise gave the boy a full-bodied smile and licked her spoon sensuously.

Keep at it, sister mine, Dag thought, eat us out of the Games — which she'd done anyway. If he just had a partner like the little Russian, so light you could toss her around like a snowflake and know she'd land on her feet, smiling. But for the run of the Games he was stuck with Lise, too full of herself to see the Russians' sympathetic glances at Dag. She fluttered her lashes at the boy, who murmured to his partner and two other Soviets nearby, one of them Alexei Finsky.

Who, Jeff Dunsmuir thought, looked altogether too confident, the sod. Everywhere Jeff competed he tripped over him. Europeans, Worlds, hell, it didn't seem fair. After all that extra work when it looked like Finsky might not come to the Games, new music, programme, costume. Mind you, that hot pink just s-c-reamed sex-appeal, sure to pull down a show contract if he won any medal at all. With Finsky here they could kiss the Gold goodbye, and you couldn't hang in till kingdom come, not with youngsters like the Boston kid coming up. Competition got boring. Same old faces. Sure, Lloyd would take care of training expenses for as long as Jeff wanted to compete, the question was, did Jeff want to take care of creepy old Lloyd? No way. He hoped Lloyd wouldn't be in the bleachers for practice tomorrow, the first day was always a nerve-ender. Now if it was Dag Carlsen after him, the guy was gorgeous, nothing less, but if he wasn't available — somehow you always knew — then others just as sensational panted in the wings. Poor Dag, you had to pity the guy, a sister like that. You wouldn't tempt Jeff with Pairs. Though it was the quickest way to the top, one try-out showed him the flip-side. A fifteen-year-old Single wasted half a day plaiting her hair to a whip, peeling off gloves, twisting off rings, working rosin into her palms before reluctantly condescending to skate next to him. Jeff knew right then it was all her Mama's idea. The girl had *known* she could make it on her own — and today rang up groceries at Sainsbury's. Jeff's heart bled, bled!

A murmur of Russian reached him. The Soviet Men's second banana chatting up Finsky. Too bad Jeff didn't know Russian, but who did, and who in hell cared? Tonight was the one night off; Jeffie meant to enjoy it.

Alexei liked his companion well enough to let him talk, but he was the Director's son-in-law, too close to power to be trusted. Three years on the run he'd skated badly, he'd grown a paunch, surely he must be worried about his own future, so why trouble himself with Alexei's — as he seemed determined to do?

'Called Galina yet?' he prodded.

They'd know *that* anyway. ' "All circuits are busy to the country you have dialled," ' he mimicked. 'You know how it is.'

'Yes. The Director reached his wife via the consul in Madrid.'

'I'm asking no favours.'

'The swine wouldn't grant any — but he's running scared right now.'

Alexei smiled. 'Scared I won't come up with his Gold?'

'Yes. I said he'd made a mistake pulling Galina off the team. He said not. Sure, we'll win Pair and Dance, but he can't take credit for them — they were in place under the last Director. And you, you're "Merited Master of Sport" for life. You'll always get top treatment, and they'd make a place for Galina, you can bet money on it. But the Director? You're his nest-egg. Two World titles, an Olympic Gold expected. You are all he can show in return for a plush office, car, and *dacha*. If you lost he'd be deep in the bog.'

Alexei couldn't resist it. 'And you with him.'

The other man laughed. 'Hell, I'm through, I don't have it, I never did. D'you know the humiliation, taking titles you haven't won? If his daughter hadn't fancied me I'd be coaching juniors now in Chelyabinsk where I grew up, where I'll end up, and that's fine with me.'

Alexei desperately needed to confide, but who to trust? Not this one. Too risky. If he decided to defect he must plan ahead, talk to the Sterlings. Carefully. They wouldn't give him away but secrets leaked. And if he did defect, there was infinite, certain loss. Galina. Since meeting her he'd felt not the slightest interest in other women; he doubted if he ever would. So what to do with the rest of his life?

He was ready to leave when a Pair coach, an old friend, stopped by to pass time and rumour, which Alexei preferred to avoid — but abroad it paid to listen, sift the grain from the chaff. Alexei had seen the curves on the Carlsen girl? She'd give the brother a hernia one day. The tight little isle had sent its ageing Pair, thank God — androgynous hangers-on never sure where they belonged except near the top if they could ever land jumps like they landed sponsors, ha-ha. Speaking of sponsors, Jeffie boychick was skating like a winner on Lloyd's chequebook. A Hungarian judge caught his number in LA — a word to the wise, not that Alexei should worry . . . Of course he remembered the Brit girl from Europeans, right? Her mother sick now, met by nurses at Barcelona, so how Maureen would perform was a toss-up. Oh, and the Czech man had added a solid quad since Europeans, Alexei shouldn't sell him short. The Japanese were coming on fast too, they spelled trouble for the future. On and on. Truth mixed in with the chaff.

Deliberately Alexei yawned. If he showed concern about rivals — but the titbit on Deirdre Sterling saddened him. Ach, it was the usual gossip!

Mieko Nakashima prodded a lamb chop. This one free day she longed for *sashimi* in the basement restaurant but dare not be seen eating alone in an expensive restaurant. Instead she chewed at this distasteful animal and stole discreet glances at Dag Carlsen. So beautiful a man, an angel, golden and somehow tragic, his mouth sad as if he would be somewhere else, as if his bitterness ran deep as the lake at Hakone where Oka-chan had taken her when she was small. If she were here now, if Mieko could share such thoughts! If. *If* there could be such a young man in Hokkaido as the Swede, how happy she'd be! And if Grandfather knew she even *thought* of Western men, their eyes like the sea in summer. Nakashima women did not stare at men. Safer to admire her competitors. The small Beejay, her incredible hair like flames . . . Roxanne, elegant even with the barbaric fork between her fingers . . . No sign of Maureen, perhaps she could not come, but surely her coach had mentioned a villa the Sterlings owned, somewhere close, maybe Spain? Where Maureen and her mother could be together? Oh, how she yearned already for her own Oka-chan, whom she already missed.

Stiff from the vigil of the flight, Maureen escaped at last towards the welcoming surf of the Med. Palamos in winter, its gentle, uncrowded shores — but many times she'd regretted persuading the doctor to let Deirdre travel, the skies over the Channel hanging in tattered shrouds that clung all across France. For Mother every bank and turn of the powerful little jet, normally a joy, triggered a new agony; of the nurses, two clung to seatbelts, the other bustling up and down the aisle as if she had three patients instead of one.

The moving-in complete, dinner ordered, her coaches alerted by phone that she'd arrived, Deirdre drugged to the roots of her thin hair — Maureen escasped through the terraced garden. Unlatching a gate hidden in a thicket of bougainvillaea, she started alone down the zig-zag path to the beach.

Beside her, flashing crimson among coarse grasses which had once stood taller than Maureen herself, patches of geranium tumbled in sheltered hollows, bringing back all the summers of childhood. Deirdre walking this same track with her, edging daintily past a blue-bellied lizard to delight in wild lupine, coast poppy, tangles of pink and purple vetch, pausing to point out the flotilla of yachts rocking gently below them, expensive toys on a blue bay . . . And always her long white fingers crushing a sprig of lemon-mint from the kitchen garden for Maureen to catch the sharp fragrance on their joined hands. Which would never be joined again in the same way. This path was for the healthy. This trip to the Games would be Mother's last. Of all the places they'd lived, Palamos was their warmest dream in the winter chills of England, the place that called them back season after season, any time the routine of the rink offered a break.

Maureen shivered in the soft breeze. Why, without Deirdre, did the path seem steeper, the beach below her a harbour she must navigate alone? In the distance a man threw sticks for a stocky black dog; closer, a blond child tugged at a kite-string as his father tossed pebbles moodily into the sea — but nowhere a slender woman in floating pastels and a wide straw hat who peered into tide pools and called to her daughter, 'The *loveliest* shell!' Or starfish. Or frond of seaweed bleached to white lace by sun and salt. Once a speckled bird's egg fallen from the cliff above, which Deirdre had replaced in the tide pool as if tenderness alone could heal its cracked shell.

'It's useless, Mother,' Maureen remembered saying impatiently. 'The yolk's broken.'

'It doesn't matter,' Deirdre said, 'the sea wastes nothing.'

But time wasted Deirdre minute by agonizing minute. Years ago at Palamos they'd been mother and daughter alone in a perfect world — but it seemed now that Maureen plotted every course and Deirdre followed. And when it was over, what then? She knew she would not compete when she was alone. What for, with the reason gone? And was anything more frivolous than posturing for the crowd when women like Deirdre suffered and men like Lloyd prospered?

Lloyd . . . Jeff would be at Montegreco. She'd worried about him when they were growing up — two dedicated rink-rats among a hundred others. They'd been friends then, but under Lloyd's sponsorship and spell Jeff had changed; now he'd be changed again, having been taught by Grant Rivers. Every coach subtly transformed an athlete into a different person. All of hers had. Presumably the two she had now would be her last, ice and ballet, both waiting for her at Montegreco. Tomorrow she'd drive down for first practice. Ring up the curtain on the last act.

CHAPTER TWENTY-ONE

Hotel Palacio de Estrella

For her first public appearance in the lobby, Roxanne Braun Kramer dressed as carefully as for a network camera. Nothing flashy. Her muted make-up, her ash-blonde hair swinging in a smooth, polished skein; a peach angora sweater adding softness and bulk above a flared taupe skirt, its suede folds rippling expensively about elegantly long legs as she moved to meet the Canadian team, newly arrived and containing friends — vital she be seen in motion, not standing at loose ends in a corner someplace. Keep moving, that was the trick. It fended off groupies and showed you were welcome and gracious. In her wake drifted a whisper of 'Tea Rose' perfume, and a less discreet chorus of 'Mama, it's her, it's *Kramer*!' 'She looks fab!' 'Who in hell said she was 'rexic?'

She spotted the Nakashima girl buried in a deep plush chair. Alone — a mistake. Roxanne aimed a smile in her general direction before floating towards her friends. As reigning World Champion she'd had two years to rehearse this role; she played it well. The admiration she read in Mieko's eyes stroked her ego, but then the girl's legs — sturdy and power-packed in yellow warm-ups — reminded Roxanne just what those legs could do that her own never would, not even if she trained for a hundred years.

She made herself wave gaily at a German skater, her glance touching but not lingering on a bandaged ankle rumoured to protect shin splints — but still the replay of the Japanese girl's big triple clung, ominous in its clarity. Symmetrical as Fuji, it spanned the width of the rink and invariably brought a standing ovation. Honesty demanded it deserved nothing less — but the Games loomed too close for honesty. Don't think about it. Nerves attacked all. Mieko could miss and her landings grated anyway. Kramer touched down on a smooth running edge. Kramer spun like a perfectly balanced top.

Thinking of herself in the third-person helped. Through impersonal eyes Kramer looked infinitely better than she did to herself. She'd seen the swift appraisal of rivals in the lobby; they knew about her fluctuating weight, the fainting spells — there were no secrets. But Roxanne, steering expertly around the roadblocks of her own thoughts, tuned into her programming. Within its comforting approval she congratulated herself on halting the slide, on distancing herself. Even outside the shield of Grant's embrace she was in control, could cope. She knew that her walk, smooth and serene, emanated confidence, as if she had already won the crown and now strolled graciously among her court. Some courtiers were missing, true. Sterling hadn't arrived and Beejay was out someplace, but word carried. If Roxanne felt like a winner, behaved like a winner, she'd *be* a winner. Confidence showed. The hypnotherapist guaranteed it. Even Grant said . . . but where *was* he? Keeping a distance was fine when *she* kept it, but she hadn't seen him in hours. Panic gnawed once again at the fringes of her equilibrium. What to say when friends asked if she and Grant still . . . well . . . *saw* one another?

Just then she glimpsed the top of his thick black curls as the escalator transported him up from the *sushi* bar. With Emma! Emma-damn-Crisp! As Roxanne watched, pride and insecurity nailing her taupe high-heels firmly into thick Olympic-ringed carpet, Emma murmured something as Grant, laughing, led her by the elbow to a shadowy bar in the lobby. But in mid-stride they stopped dead, Grant's tan paler, Emma's smile creased with worry. Roxanne thought for a moment that they'd seen her, but no, they were staring beyond her into the back of the bar. When she turned to look, her own blood drained from her face.

At a corner table a couple sat silent, an impossible, preposterous couple. Ben Carlsen gazing morosely into a glass and opposite him . . . Roxanne blinked and shook her head to clear it, but the dim light did indeed finger Ben's companion; blonde hair, dark at the roots; a tight red trap of a mouth; thin, gold-tipped hands reaching for Ben's lighter, shaking a cigarette from a familiar pack. The flame etched Noni's taut profile against dark panelling. *Ben Carlsen and Noni Braun Kramer.*

'*Mom!*' Roxanne darted forward but Grant reached them first, setting her firmly behind him as he loomed over Noni.

'What in hell are you up to? You're not due till next week.'

Noni smiled up at him, eyes monkey-bright with triumph. 'My plane just got in. You know me. Always the early-bird, first on the job.'

'Job?' Grant's question splintered Noni's smile, but she hung on to it.

'Special correspondent, *Parkrose Review*.' Rummaging into a gold plastic purse she whipped out a press card. 'They pick up my fare, hotel, meals, and an all-events ticket to the skating. I come up with rink news and views and a few in-depth chats with front-runners like Roxanne.'

'The *Review*'s no newspsaper,' Grant said. 'And you're no reporter.'

'I am now. For the run of the Games.' Noni's high, brittle laugh turned heads. 'I *was* a world competitor, I *am* a coach. I *am* qualified, remember?'

A spasm of nausea clutched at Roxanne's stomach. She knew, no doubt whatever, how Mom had earned that press card. On her back. The *Review* was a throw-away, a bird-cage liner, used-car ads and restaurant 'reviews' nobody read — the hobby of a local eccentric with more money than sense.

For a second they all froze, waiting for someone to make the next move. It was Grant. He thrust Roxanne and Emma into empty chairs, told them not to move, and disappeared. In moments he was back, a colder, angrier man. Ignoring Ben and Noni, he grasped Emma and Roxanne by the wrists, thrust them towards an elevator, and punched the express button for the tenth floor, on which the US team was housed. Bewildered, they followed him into Roxanne's room. He held up two keys, their number-tags a matched set.

'Until we move the athletes to the Village, *this* is what

passes for hotel security! "Return Keys To Reception When Vacating Your Room." Right?'

They nodded. Emma said, 'Sure, just like always. I reminded Beejay. If your roomie's got both keys, you're due someplace and can't get in your room to change, you got yourself a real problem —'

'No problem,' he said bitterly. 'I asked one clerk for Roxanne's room number, another for her key, and another for the second key. Certainly, sir. Yes, sir. Right away, sir. Nobody looked at my face. Meaning Noni — or anyone — can go anywhere any time. So *we* turn no keys into reception. Period. They either make up the rooms while we're in them or we make up our own. The team leader has to be told, Emma.' He gave Roxanne a key and thrust the other into his pocket. 'If they ask, you haven't seen it. Keep your safety-chain on. If Noni comes around, call me. Don't let her in, okay?'

She took a breath, tried to stop her hands trembling. *Oh, Mom!*

Emma left, and Roxanne was alone with Grant for the first time in weeks. He looked confused, exhausted, and apologetic — all uncharacteristic.

'I was sure you'd be better rooming alone,' he said, 'Jasinski agreed, then . . . *she* shows up again!' He lay his cheek against hers. 'I don't know how to help you, baby.' If she turned to him now their self-denial would be over, she knew, but doubt, rare in Grant Rivers, gave her strength; Jasinski's voice came back to her: *As a species we do better when we help ourselves.* She let her lips brush Grant's lightly before moving away.

'I'm fine,' she said. 'In a way it's kind of nice Noni could come early. God knows she's not perfect, but she's worked hard for this.'

Her rejection seemed to puzzle and anger him. 'So have we.'

'Not for a lifetime. She has. When I take that empty ice it's not just me, it's her too, trying to make it all up to Gran. That's how she sees it. If I fail, she fails. Again. Skating's been her whole life. This is her last chance at it.'

'She's living through you, using you.'

'We all use somebody. If she got what she wanted just

211

once, if I could make her happy, maybe she'd change, be different.' Go, she wanted to beg, just leave. 'Grant, I want us to be happy too, but we have ice tomorrow. . .'

He nodded, reminding her to shoot the deadbolt after him. He knew if he'd applied the least pressure they'd have spent the night . . . but then he'd be no better than Noni. In his own way, for his own reasons, he too wanted Roxanne to win more for him than for herself.

In the room next to Grant's, Jasinski was reading, his door ajar. 'Night-cap?' he offered. 'There's brandy . . . Didn't I see you with Roxanne earlier? I assumed you'd be gone for the night — not that it's my business.'

'It's not. But she turned me down, anyway.'

'Ah! The lady develops a mind of her own!'

'Thanks a lot, partner. Would you believe she wants to please me *and* her mother now?'

'A normal desire, surely?'

'Noni is a normal mother?'

Jasinski shrugged. 'The need to please parents is universal. It was my father's dream that I become a doctor, and I did.'

And Grant Rivers became a coach to win his mother a medal — through the capricious talents of an exploitable young woman.

His phone rang just as he was settling down for what was left of the night. The temptation to ignore it almost overpowered him. This had been his one day off. Tomorrow the hullabaloo started, the intense run-up, pressure and panic, every move examined, every falter noted, no let-up for any of them then until it was all over. From tomorrow, each day would blur into the next, a coiled spring of tighter and tighter circles as the world closed in — reporters, judges, parents, lies, truths, evasions, smiles broad and unashamed when your rival blew a training session. For the US girls the practice order, drawn by lot, could not have been worse. They shared ice with the Japanese and Canadians, their strongest competitors except for Sterling and the German girls, who practised right after them, every day until the finals. So day after day they would all watch each other skate, every hour a contest of nerve.

Was it too much to ask then, this one day of peace and

quiet before the screw began to turn? Yes. He picked up the phone on the tenth ring. It was Emma Crisp. She sounded shaken. Emma?

She spoke from the housekeeper's phone in their hall. Somebody had been up to something. Could he come down right now and keep it quiet, not wake Beejay or Roxanne? He reached for his robe. Surely Noni wasn't up to her tricks already?

Waiting by the elevator for Grant, Emma clenched her fists to stop the trembling. She tried not to look at the zippered garment-bag draped over her arm. One glance at the contents had already paralysed her for a full five minutes. Now she knew what had been done and that she must undo it, make it right. But how, when there was neither time nor money? When —

'What's the problem?' Grant said, his hair tousled from bed.

Her fingers shook as she drew out what had been Beejay's competition dress, now a red, brilliant heap of fresh-cut ribbons joined only by the zip. Efficiently slashed with scissors or razor, no possibility of repair.

'Bloody hell.'

'Yeah.'

'Maybe on the plane?'

She shook her head. 'I checked it before we went for *sushi*. It was fine. I locked the room and left both keys with reception.'

'And we know how efficient *they* are. Beejay seen it yet?'

'Not till I've figured out how to . . .' But there *was* no figuring! She'd been so set on not over-protecting Beejay, on raising her so she could look real life in the eye, but there were limits, there damned well were. Must the eye *always* be evil? A sixteen-year-old like Beej, what had she ever done to anybody? Who could hate, or fear, this much?

Grant touched her shoulder. 'Emma, it's you they're after. We were gone a long time, so was Beejay — building that snowman with the Aussies. First snow any of 'em have seen this year.'

'Yeah, it seemed a shame to waste it. Like a fool I let her go.'

'Don't blame yourself.'

'Then who? I'm her mom. Who else will look out for her if I don't?'

'Why not figure out who did it and blame them?'

She sighed. 'Noni has it in for me, I know that. Folks think it should be the other way around maybe, but I quit holding a grudge long since.' Grant didn't ask what grudge. Well, he wouldn't, even if he'd heard.

'Have you considered Ben?' he said carefully. 'He's concerned you'll judge Pairs. Damn, he already blames you for taking Lise out of Singles —'

'Uh-uh. This feels more like a woman's trick. And Grant, if I worried about every father whose kid I've had to mark-down . . . I'd quit. Judging takes a big bite out of my life and lord *knows* we don't get paid. Hell, it ends up costing! So maybe there's a crooked arrow or two in the ranks, judges are human — but we judge because we love the sport, we want to see it better and better! Some win, some lose, so you make enemies. But I don't see a man's hand in this. Just malice.' She turned away, reluctant to face him while she said what was on her mind. 'You said Roxanne was worried about Beejay —'

'— Roxanne is not malicious.' He spoke fast, a man defending his mate. Or his ambition.

'Somebody is.'

He let ribbons of chiffon drizzle thoughtfully through his fingers in a crimson cascade. 'It's early days. Nobody's seen the skaters work out yet, but Emma, you've not been offered a deal?'

Her spine stiffened. 'Everybody knows I don't *deal*!' Deals, when offered, came via a third party, hints and ever so subtle innuendos designed to be unprovable, but could be picked up or ignored at will, slimy little grubs sucking at the life-blood of a clean sport. Rare grubs, thank God.

'Sorry, Emma, but this *is* the Games. Beejay *is* in them. No foreign judge offering to "do his best" for her, should you deliver a decent mark for their own hot-shot? That mutual back-scratching the media always hints at?'

'*This* is back-scratching?' She touched red chiffon and drew back as if scorched.

'A threat to reinforce an offer? Maybe the fridge.'

'That was skating. This is hating. Different sports.' But even as she spoke, Beejay's bright dress of demure but impeccable cut, her *Olympic* dress, drew her inner eye like a bleeding wound. Maybe they weren't such different sports these days. At every Olympics the stakes rose a little higher. Maybe she lived in fantasy-land — a doubt she could not examine and would not share. 'You're positive it's not Roxanne? Her room *is* close.'

Grant sighed and rubbed his eyes. 'As I said, *malice is not her thing*. Let's concentrate on getting Beejay another outfit.'

'I can't afford one.' Competition dresses were not bits of froth run up overnight on the old kitchen treadle. They were *constructed*. Beejay skated for the USA, not some swamp on the Lower Zambezi, its leader dolled up in a beach-towel as he swished about him with the ceremonial fly-swatter.

'The seamstress has her size, everything. I'll call her right now, have her make a duplicate, top priority, ship it out by overnight courier. Six days max, no problem.' He wadded the tatters into his robe pocket.

'You're not listening. I can't afford a duplicate. *That's* the problem.'

'We file claim. The hotel's insured. Their negligence caused this.'

'God, it makes the sport *look* bad, bitchy. The scandal, headlines. . .'

'May not happen. And if it leaked it wouldn't hurt Beejay. If anything, judges would sympathize. But team officials have to know, all costumes stashed someplace secure. What's happened once can happen again.'

To Roxanne in her new-grown shell, which could not take much, which could crack. She read the anguish in his eyes as clear as if it were in bold print. It made her feel better, some, that a coach might care more for a student's feelings than for the medal he hoped she'd pin on his record.

Back in her room, she figured she needed something to feel good about. Over the years her faith had been tested, and sometimes almost lost. Parents (and who could blame them?) used the sport as a golden cage to protect kids from the street, from drugs, from casual sex and its anything but casual results. It worked; packed schedules left no time for outside adventures. Nobody spoke of the downside — teens growing up with no value system beyond the next test, the next competition. How, when they knew you could barely scrape up the mortgage cheque but then saw you blow $2,000 on a dress? A competitor needed several a year; they must appear ethereal — but work like armour-plate; let a jewelled sleeve snag a skirt at the wrong time and you'd zapped a landing, maybe a year's work, maybe a career. So you kept on paying until the kid quit, won a big one, or joined a show, whichever came first. They saw you shell out this kind of dough, how to teach values? Was it any wonder Noni's were all corkscrewed up, with a background like hers? That she'd try every wile in the book to get Roxanne to the top, to make it all up to Mutti in Bonn? That she'd shred Beejay's dress if there was any possible way it would help Roxanne? Would a monkey steal nuts?

Emma looked at Beejay in her yellow flannel pyjamas. In this slumbering starburst of energy only the eyelids were vulnerable, a tracery of thin blue rivers on the transluscent skin of the redhead. Above them, copper curls springy to the touch; below them, thick crescents of auburn lashes. Even now, in deep sleep, she clenched jaws and fists as if gearing up for a jump. Picturing again the dress in which she'd chosen to compete, Emma gave in to a rush of tenderness, of regret, brushing her fingertips lightly across Beejay's cheek, chapped from ten years of ice and now a biting alpine wind.

To touch this daughter was to touch life, vibrant, crackling, intense. But, dear God, what kind of life was she putting her through? Nearly seventeen and the kid had just now built her first snowman? Like her team-mates, Beejay had never been to a dance or a ball-game. Summer camp was skating camp — another rink, another town, but the terrain was always ice. On the other hand, this fusion of bone and muscle could count a circle of friends around the globe, an élite international club, dues payable in that rarest of all currencies, talent. A minus and a plus equals what?

A vibration under her fingertips and Beejay's eyes flew open, sherry-coloured and instantly aware. Nothing vulnerable there. And thank God for it, in a world crawling with Nonis, Bens, Willis, and Jeffies.

216

In one swift move she sat straight up, legs crossed. 'What's up?'

'Nothing's up. Can't I look at you sometimes?'

'Hell, Em! You think I can't tell? So give, spill it!'

'You've got early ice. Get back to sleep.'

She rolled her eyes. 'I could sleep with this fantastical worry pressing on my brain, my old Mom looking like she's about to bawl?'

'I'm not old and I was not about to bawl!'

'Yeah. So tell, then I'll go to sleep.'

Emma shut out the flippant words and read instead the anything but flippant look in her eyes. After, she would know that this was the moment in which the balance of their relationship shifted, in which Beejay began to emerge as a young woman, not the perpetual teen. She'd have to tell. She'd preached honesty for sixteen years, how could she go back on it now?

'Beej . . . not everybody in this world is your pal, understand?'

Her eyes widened to Orphan Annie's. 'No kidding.' The flip remark gave notice that she was not about to help out. At such frustrated moments Emma knew a swift urge to pop her one, but she never had and wasn't about to start now. Independence was too rare to punish.

'While we were out. . .'

'Yeah?'

'Somebody trashed your new dress.' No need to say which. Even for the Games, only one new dress could be managed. The red had been it.

Beejay blinked, a slow deliberate move which seemed to absorb the outrage, examine it, and look beyond it. 'So I'll wear the pink. It's a comp dress, and it fits.' No word about who could have done it or why, yet questions must be spinning around in her mind.

The pink. Four competitions old, tight in the bust, a mite pulled in the underarms. This time out, its last, it would do, just, for the short Original Programme to be skated the last afternoon but one. Unheard of to wear the same outfit again for Finals the night after. The whole world watched the ladylike clash of the long Free, the programme loaded with points to be won or lost. 'Beejay, the pink's been seen and seen, damned near worn out.'

And me, she thought suddenly, sinking on to her bed, face to the wall, the values of a life time in question all at once. Skating had cost her financial security; the demands of judging rendered a private life virtually impossible; last and worst, it had killed the husband she'd loved and who'd loved her — no use blaming Noni, if it hadn't been her it would have been another skating mother. Dave couldn't pass up a bit of skirt, that was his weakness, one she'd accepted as relatively harmless until it killed him. One by one she'd accepted every minus, built her days around them the way she hammered a new roof and property taxes into the budget. But must Beejay accept them, too?

Beejay, who said now: 'So what if it's not new? It's comfy.'

'How many athletes dream of the Games, Beej? And how many get here? You're skating for your country, you can't dress like . . . like you don't care, like the USA and the Games are nothing.'

'I thought it was me skating, not the dress.'

Trust her to have the answer. Which didn't help. 'Anyway, Grant's sending for a duplicate, the hotel's expense. If that doesn't work the Committee'll pick up . . . pick up — look . . . it'll *be* here, don't worry —'

'Why are you crying, then?'

Because she had to make an impossible choice. Her girl wearing a ratty old dress or shiny new charity for all the world to see, just when she'd need every dab of pride she could scrape up. It wasn't fair!

There was movement behind her, scents of talc and toothpaste as yellow flannel sleeves wrapped around her. 'Em?' The name caught itself up in a sob, quickly swallowed by a fierce, breath-stopping hug. Her voice turned husky, ageing her at least twenty years. 'What the hell, Em, it's only a damn outfit. I don't care what I wear, honest. Just knock off the crying, huh?'

Emma tried to respond but the words never made it past the boulder in her throat. God knew she wasn't a crier, but the Games, the enormity of them! If they did this to *her*, who'd seen it all before and whose daughter was too young to make her splash, what in hell were they doing to Noni and the old Brauns, who expected one gold medal to turn their failed lives around? And how could Roxanne live under the weight of that expectation? And what would Noni do as the finals closed in? Inventive, twisted Noni, who brushed off scruples like bits of lint? What would Noni do? *Oh Jesus!* She turned inside her daughter's embrace and pressed her palms against rosy, chapped cheeks.

'Look, sport, you know I trust you round the world and back, right?'

'Yep.'

'We've never talked about this, but if anybody but the team doc ever offers you anything, *anything*, aspirin or whatever, don't take it, okay?'

Beejay, reverting to teens again, looked at her with bemused pity. 'Mom! What d'you think I am, a stupe?'

'You don't know the *names* of half the stuff out there!'

Beejay slipped back into bed and let Emma tuck her in, a concession seldom granted. She reached up and knuckled Emma's forehead with a warm fist meant to iron out fear. 'I know the rules. One drop of mouthwash in your pee and you're out. Then it's "goodbye skating" forever and ever, amen.' She yawned. 'Early day tomorrow. Coming to watch?'

Emma sighed. 'Want me to?'

'You've a long coupla weeks coming up, judge. Hell, sleep in.'

'Thank you, boss. You're very kind, but if you don't need me, I'll start work. Check out Pairs and Mens at the other rink. Just remember that your language is foul and from tomorrow the rinks will be stiff with judges — and they can lip-read. Don't mouth 'em any juicy titbits to bring back to the Judges' Room, okay? We pass them around like low-cal candy.'

The corners of Beejay's mouth, innocent in half-sleep, twitched. 'Golly, Momma dearest, how you do fuss.'

CHAPTER TWENTY-TWO

Management scarcely needed to advertise the breakfast buffet. Smells of bacon, oven-fresh croissants, roasted coffee beans, and oranges from Seville wafted under every door, through the corridors, even seeping into the elevators. Grant, obeying the aroma, suspected they piped it through the air-ducts. Not that he had time, with that vital first practice due, to linger, to give himself up to the sensuous pleasures of good food impeccably served. Coffee would have to do; even that would go down bitter with Ben's frown across the table, but what choice was there? Ben must have known that with two rinks in the complex, this situation would come up sometimes, but Grant had hoped it wouldn't come first day of practice. It had. But, as he was trying to explain, Olympic training schedules were as unbending as the ice they governed, no choice but to accept them.

'If you'd just watch, Ben, make them do *all* the programme? It'll look bad if Lise chickens-out, and there's no reason she should. For the run of the training they're on with the Russians and Canadians, all experienced, all careful. There'll be no trouble.'

'Don't trust commies farther than I can throw 'em, they'll go out of their way to get in Lise's way, if you catch my drift? If *you* stood at the rail they'd mind their manners. Me, I'm just a father, you're the coach. Her first Olympic session, how's she going to feel, you not there?'

Grant knew exactly. Relieved was how Lise would feel. But what could he do but spread his hands, paste on a smile, and refer to a world-renowned coach who Grant did not personally like? 'I know it's disappointing, but things could be worse. Poor Emilio has three girls, all national champions of different countries, plus two American boys and two pairs

— their schedules all round the clock. We all play it by ear. I can't be there all the time for all my skaters, it goes with the territory. It might even happen again.' He'd studied the posted schedules. It *would* happen again. Often.

'My kids don't count, not like your World Champ and the judge's kid and John Bull Jeffie.' Ben stirred his coffee furiously, splashing one sugar lump after another into the centre of the whirlpool. 'Mine don't count, right?'

For once Ben was right. No way he'd neglect three skaters certain to make the top ten in favour of Lise and Dag, who'd done poorly at Europeans. Here, with Canadians, Americans, and Japanese added, they could only do worse, a prognosis Ben could have figured out for himself. 'Ben, when I took them on I pointed out that schedules might clash.'

Ben continued to stir the brew. 'But you took 'em.'

Grant checked his watch. Five minutes left. He'd taken on the Carlsens unwillingly. Because of Lise's weight and fears, they lacked potential, but they *were* National Champions and as such competed at all the majors, thus cutting Grant's travel expense for all the others into a fifth each instead of a third. He figured Lloyd Sterling owed him and always would; you could roll the private ice-mat out at will, and Grant had, but no way would he cheat on lessons. Which didn't help Ben, who right now was mad as hell, justifiably so. The hollows in his cheeks deepened to craters. Time to puff them out with a little flattery. 'You'll stand buffer between Lise and the press? No interviews yet, okay? We don't want her over-exposed.'

Ben scooped out a smile. 'One guy already asked what colour she'll be in on the night so he can "set his camera for a calendar shot" — can you beat that? I'm telling 'em nothing, what colour or where I have their outfits stashed, either. Doesn't pay. You can't be too careful, not after the bucks they set me back.'

Grant shot him a quick glance. No guilt that he could see, but Ben's face was a pale version of the Grand Canyon — which so far as Grant knew didn't register guilt either.

In the main arena of waiting ice, tiers of burgundy plush gave way to crimson wool moquette, then a cheap navy rep, at last to serviceable grey denim, each fabric reflecting the cost of the seat and its distance from the action. Steam heat and fresh paint combined, its smell rising with the seats until Noni, alone, in hot pink fake fur, muttered that she finally knew what TV meant when it yammered on about the greenhouse effect. From here, calculating that Roxanne would look small, she focused so the binoculars could catch her expression before panning around the thousands of empty seats, then the cluster of engineers scuttering at the fringe of the ice watching a Polar Bear shave its cool creases in a final remake before the girls took over. Officials hurried everywhere, trying to look important. She ignored them, panning higher, almost as high as she, to the truly important, the scattering of judges scrunched deep in their seats, anonymous from choice and far from the ice as they waited for the skaters to appear.

The binoculars picked up one of the Russians first. Who could miss her, a pre-glasnost suet-pudding with black-currant eyes; not a dab of make-up; short, straight hair limp with grease; the whole unappetizing dish served up in a ubiquitous navy suit Noni figured they issued pre-dandruffed at Sheremetyevo airport. Never idle, this woman or a clone showed up at every competition, stop-watch and pencil in one hand, tape-recorder in the other, diligently timing the routines of the favourites as she whispered into the recorder what they comprised. Noni laughed out loud. They'd got Dance, Pairs and Mens to a tee, but couldn't groom a contender for Ladies or even understand why. Noni knew. Did a bulldozer know from silk stockings? The suet puddings were on their way out, they just didn't know it. Diet pills, a few more years of Raisa, a shampoo, and a man might help. . .

At the other side of the arena a Finn — young for a judge, pale shining hair, a bright silk scarf, the perfect lipstick picking up the reds, a wide belt around an actual waist, slim legs (shaved!), and high-heels.

In the last row, burgundy section, distant and anonymous, a chubby American (male) and a beanpole Brit (female) shared a joke, but they too had notebooks ready. The good ones — and these two were seldom off by much — did their homework, hit every session, often racing from rink to rink to catch the leaders. The judges who waited until the finals to pick the stars out of the pack never reached Olympic level; their results couldn't ever come close to the norm; until they did, the big Games were out. Better to use the wrong fork at the banquet or tip your wine over the ISU president than be caught more than two placements off the final count. They bore watching, those two. What they said when Roxi skated. Their faces. Not that they'd give much away, especially this Olympics. Usually the USA and UK voted close, but this time out Sterling could be the spoiler. The Brit would pull for her. The American was in Roxanne's corner, no problem unless Beejay came on full fucking throttle, Emma Crisp being a member of the goddamned club and Chubby's pal, and Noni being on the outside, far, far on the outside. Oh, well, she wouldn't be on the outside for long.

At ice level, the PA system invited Ladies from the USA, Japan, and Canada to take the ice. After a ten minute warm-up their music would be played in the order posted. Roxanne looked around before stepping out, saw the far seats, judges sparsely scattered, goggles appearing like magic, a dozen pairs of round over-sized eyes, black eyes that picked up every bead of sweat. Her heart lurched and raced. Not fair! First practice, strange ice, and they show up in force to prejudge the field. And, oh hell, what *was* the posted skating order, she couldn't remember. How long did she have before they called her name and played her music? What *was* her name, Roxanne, Roxanne Braun Kramer — Beside her, Nakashima set her skate-guards on the rail, took a breath and stroked out, followed by Crisp, who didn't so much stroke as dart. Show off! Roxanne looked for Grant. Yes, there he was at ice-level, nodding that she should take the ice, smiling encouragement at her and surely that was Jasinski next to him? The Canadians were on now, then the other Japanese. She'd be last on! So what? The World Champion didn't *need* to chase every second of ice time like a greyhound after a hare.

She lifted her chin and began the smooth, exquisite stroking that, with her spins, was her trademark. Passing Nakashima, she refused to see her, firing the competitor's unmistakable shot of disdain across her bows. 'I don't see you so you're not important, you don't exist — but if you did you'd learn something. Do you hear my blades? No, but I hear yours, thought they were tire-chains.' Oh no! those damn Oriental legs, not warmed up yet and she'd just popped a double-axel like it was nothing, five feet up if it was an inch! Roxanne hadn't even started singles yet, which Grant said she mustn't do here, they were babyish, but she needed to work up through single, double, triple, she couldn't just — oh no, don't, *don't* turn around, that whoosh in the corner sounded like Beejay's triple-flip take-off to the life — and that *is* her damn landing and she's going for another.

Now the Canadians were at it. They swarmed all over her, the lot of them, leaping over her like frogs — be calm, steady, find Grant's eyes, find the focus, narrow it down to the next thing, one movement at a time the way she'd been taught, don't panic, smooth yourself out, smo-o-oth, smo-o-other, she was World Champion, she would do a perfect jump, and there! She had. So what if it was a single? And there's the double, see it, everybody? See it, perfect again, pure silk landing. Satisfied? So trap that in your chopsticks and choke on it, Nakashima.

Now Roxanne shifts into gear, coming up for her triple, why not? She is strong, she's been eating well, scrambled eggs and cereal for breakfast yet, and here's the jump, wait for it, don't rush, wait, wait, so what if it's only a toe-loop, it's still a triple and Noni says half the judges can't tell one jump from another anyway and what in hell's that flash, that flame way up in the top seats — a cigarette lighter dammit, couldn't people read, didn't she know she couldn't smoke in here, that stupid Noni in her hot-pink fake fur, that Noni would know, no fooling Mother Nature, she'd *know* Roxanne ate breakfast and her focus was slipping, slipping, but too late now to abort the launch so up you go, baby, but not straight up, off by a hair, a misfire, and, oh shit, now the edge was shooting out, lost, no way to save it, and splat! And here she is, World Champion yet, the first skater to land ass-first on a brand new rink! The world's best can't be first to fall, she can't! Scrambling up she switched to stroking mode, back straight, head up, glassy smile in place. Somewhere somebody called her name over the PA and somewhere else she decided they could all go to hell, the

announcer and that man at the rail, Grant, who was
beckoning her, no way she'd go to him right now for a
chewing out, no way she wanted any 'Jewels of the
Madonna' this minute. She'd stick right here in the middle
where he couldn't get at her. Thank God coaches and
mothers weren't allowed on Olympic ice, only skaters, and
she was the best there was, she could spin like a top and if
she spun long enough and fast enough she'd disappear into a
blur until maybe they couldn't even see her, that's what
she'd do, all her spins in turn until the ref blew the whistle on
the session. But who is this circling me, this copper-nob,
hell, it's Beejay whispering, pretending like we're kidding
around, waiting for —

'Roxi, Grant says to pick up your programme from the
next cut as if you'd planned it that way, forget the triples and
project, okay? *Project!*'

Yeah. She shook her head to clear it, refocus. Christ, her
music was a third over, the next cut coming up! She forced
herself to giggle with Beejay, but humiliation burned under
it. Grant had sent this . . . this *snip* to give her orders! But
be reasonable, what choice did he have, so move, dammit,
move! This is it, the big one's starting, don't blow it first day
out. She caught her music. The others retired to the rail
from courtesy and curiosity, a gesture given only to the
hot-shots and only on the early sessions. Soon it would be
everyone for herself, but their respect, and the respite from
triples, picked up her confidence. She finished brilliantly and
skated over to her coach, as always, when it was over. Grant
smiled, but a muscle pulsed in his neck.

'You had me sweating there for a minute, babe.
Everything all right?'

Be casual. 'Sure. I picked the wrong time to spot Mom in
the bleachers. Shook me up for a second. I'd forgotten she
was here, can you beat that?'

He sighed. 'She'll be here everyday now. Stroke for a
minute or so, cool down, then get off. Beejay's next to skate,
so stay out of her way, okay?'

Nobody cleared the ice for Beejay. Naturally not. She was
an unknown, had to steer around everybody's jumps, spins,
and falls. Roxanne thought she'd give up everything, title,
fame — and yes, even Grant — to be in Beejay's boots right

now. But even Beejay made a mistake, trying for a triple-lutz when Grant had expressly told her to leave it on home-ice until next year, and Roxanne watched his anger shift from her to Beejay, who over-shot her landing and carommed off the boards, a pool-ball that had missed its pocket.

Then it was Nakashima, and Roxanne had to stand there and watch as once again the others cleared the ice. Why clear for an 'also-ran'? Curiosity, that's why. But with no one else moving they'd hear her landings. Roxanne, herself again, free of programmed focus, blushed with shame at her flash of pleasure, but it was honest pleasure she'd come to via a steep and rocky path. Not sporting, perhaps, but normal. She said the word aloud. Normal.

Mieko frowned, puzzled. Why had they granted her clear ice? Beside the World Champion, who so graciously smiled upon her and inclined her head, Mieko lacked stature and accomplishment. Even the small Beejay darted like the humming-birds she'd seen at Grandfather's guest house on Molokai when she was tiny, before they told him he'd have no more grandchildren. How could she compare, the others polished jewels, each with her own glow, her presence? All Mieko had were steps and spins and jumps, which she must do perfectly, no errors, for already she'd glimpsed a camera following her, 'Nakashima Electronics' emblazoned in its side, the same name on the cameraman's huge ski jacket, as if he too would be in the cold, nothing at all without the family name to cover him. So Japan must plan to show this, if not now, live, then later. Oka-chan would see her. Oka-chan! She lifted her chin, smiled into the lens and her mother's eyes as she swayed to her music, a Western melody from a popular show orchestrated just for her, the unexpected echo of a samisen in the after-sound. For Grandfather, for her Oka-chan, she *must* do the big axel, a triple she loved and did not miss, ever — but Roxanne had jumped tentatively today and on the rail she also watched, might be hurt . . . Mieko hesitated, but family, country, and her own wistful ambitions won. She soared into this competition's first triple axel by a woman. From today on she was to be the sensation of the Games.

Grant saw Roxanne's hand tighten on the rail. Me too, he

thought. This Mieko was effing marvellous, nothing to touch her. Easy to argue that one incredible jump did not make a winner, but once you'd seen it, exulted in it, you knew that it could, it most certainly could.

'Courage, sweetheart. She's super on the jumps, yes, but it takes more and you *have* more! You're World calibre.' Behind her he saw Jasinski's frown, and quickly added: 'More to the point, you're *my* calibre, Rivers-trained, Rivers-nurtured. In a minute you'll take a nap in your *locked* room! — for me, it's politics time.' Jasinski nodded, and Grant felt like a puppet. For so many years he'd pulled students' strings, why now did he permit his doctor, his own man, to pull his? Because he'd invited him to. Help me with Roxanne, he'd said. And Jasinski had helped, hadn't he?

No time to wonder, time now to do his job, mend fences Roxanne had kicked down, casually stop by each judge who would be comparing her stuff with Nakashima's. Time to casually talk up Roxanne, to damn all others with tentative praise. The Crisp girl? Oh, thank you, yes, very gratifying, unlimited potential there, but next time, he felt. The young Canadian? She still wrapped a little, more so under pressure, an easy habit to acquire, hard to lose. Made jumps easier, of course, but did it really look well? The Japanese girl? Which one? Ah, Nakashima! He allowed himself to smile with amusement. Yes, some kangaroo, ha-ha, but technically there were rough edges compared to Kramer . . . Kramer off form? Kramer? Quite the reverse! Peaking too fast, that was *her* problem, it was all he could do to slow her down. As usual they invited the favourite to skate every benefit on the circuit and she couldn't say no. Show Roxanne a good cause and she'd be there. Health? Lord, she *exuded* it, a dynamo, he wished all skaters . . .

When he'd made the rounds he caught Jeff's practice, so-so, mended fences again, and headed for the bar. Early, but he needed to wash his mouth out with Dewar's. God, he hated the politics, but if a skater was to succeed. . . Lloyd's efforts in that area had kept Grant off the international lottery board and he'd never forgive him, never. Would the kids he'd just back-stabbed, if only mildly, forgive him if they knew? But they didn't. By the time they knew how the game was played they would be coaching, playing it themselves. Scotch did not swill away the bitterness, nor did Dag, who appeared down-in-the-mouth and looking for a shoulder. Where else would he find one? Skating was a small world, Dag an Adonis trapped inside it.

'Lise!' he began. 'She wouldn't do one lift! The place crawling with judges and not a lift! The Russians toss partners up like pancakes, *great* overheads, *great* throws, *great* side-by-side triples — and my sister spends the session auditioning a sound man. She said he was a "lollipop".'

Well, she would. Grant drained his glass. He would have given anything to get this talented young man a partner with drive to match his own, but there was Ben . . . 'I'll be there tomorrow, Dag, sort her out. Excuse me, okay? Gotta call California while time zones more or less mesh.'

Dag turned scarlet, looking like he wanted to discuss other things too, but Grant hurried off. Damn. Every major competition the same. You looked forward to seeing old show buddies, hours of nostalgic 'remember when', then suddenly it was over, you were all packed, yelling goodbyes in the lobby, and nobody had talked to anybody. No time.

The dressmaker answered on the first ring. Of *course* she was up, a big sea all night roared its head off, who could sleep and how were her dresses? 'I can't wait for TV to see if they "move" well, you know what I mean —'

He cut in, rapidly explaining what had happened. She sighed, wasting no time lamenting her ruined creation; she scarcely needed telling what she must do about it. This was not the first time, it would not be the last. She'd sewn for many skaters. Competition fever ran high, none higher than the Olympics. Everything had its dark side, jealousy twisted people to wicked shapes, even in the genteel sport she'd made her own. How many years she'd recorded her dresses on the VCR, basking in the dazzle of TV's spotlight! Endless hours of pleasure, making up in part for her fruitless womb. Her dresses filled the void, a lifetime of media stars she'd designed herself.

'. . . ice a darker blue than usual.' Grant was saying, answering her only question. 'Do your best. I know you can't turn a lightning bug into a luna moth overnight. And for God's sake don't outshine Roxanne, huh? Keep it modest the way Emma likes it, but *not* red. If Emma asks, you couldn't find it in a hurry, okay?'

She chuckled. 'I hear you. Leave it to me.'

As she hung up, the day's first pale light touched a copper vase on the windowsill. Until California's gaudy sun took over she studied the exact colour of that early light, saw it bleach the copper almost to gold, subdue and enhance at the same time. She saw the same light transform a glass of milk to almost the exact shade of Beejay's remarkable skin. That light. . .

Her mind made up, she sipped a last cup of coffee and aimed the car at her customary fabric house — on the seedier side of Hollywood, but heavily patronized by studio designers. Ben and Mort had known her for years, didn't mind if she climbed ladders, rummaged in the stacks and delved elbow-deep in scrap boxes for oddments of lace, bugle beads, sequins and *diamanté* ribbons. She knew the colours and trim she wanted and didn't leave until she found them. Her fingers itched, actually itched, as she tromped on the gas pedal and headed for home. She could hardly wait. By the time Emma and Beejay received this little number it would be way too late to change it. As she drove she pictured the blue ice darker than usual, a quick-silver girl, a surprising dress, TV cameras turning, herself at home taping the action.

Morose, anxious to avoid the sympathy in other skaters' eyes, Dag hunched into his parka and took the cable car to the warmhouse atop the slalom course. He should have taken up skiing. You didn't need a partner for that. He seldom drank, but this afternoon he ordered coffee with a side of Aquavit, the strongest liquor he could think of, and took it to a window seat by the fire and overlooking the mountains. The bar was quiet, empty, and warm from a grate blazing with logs. After the drink his fists began to uncurl, relax, the pulse behind his eyes throbbed to a calmer beat, and well-tuned thigh muscles lengthened and softened as he stretched them towards the flames. The bite of the icy liquor shocked his palate but the frosted glass cooled his palms where his fingernails had dug half-moons into the flesh, stigmata of the Games but mainly of his sister. What was wrong with his family? Other families cared for and protected each other, but with the Carlsens it was always Ben and Lise versus Mom and Dag. He screwed up his eyes as tight as they'd go, opened them again and looked straight down from the mountains into what, for the next two weeks, would be Golden Town. Then, except for vacations, it would sleep again, more or less, a small, exclusive resort. But the mountains would not change, they'd be here, timeless and impassive, unimpressed by the sweaty strivings of mere humans. They could afford to laugh, these giants, at the dramas played out in the valley. Land was secure, dependable, didn't shift like the underpinnings of a marriage. It settled perspectives. Mom had the right idea. A place of one's own. Sweden was hers and she'd returned to it.

Last night she'd called him, sounding younger, more confident than he'd known she could. Already she'd negotiated a contract on a children's book, and another in the offing. Almost in passing she mentioned that agencies were calling, wanting to represent her, but she enjoyed the challenge of doing it for herself. It was fun, she said. Stunned by her new-found ambitions, Dag could only wish her luck and tell her he missed her.

'Come stay with us for a while after the Games, then,' she had urged. 'You've always liked Sweden. Your Aunt Signe wants you, I want you, there's even a rink close by, they're crying out for a coach . . .' Then her voice dropped almost to a whisper. 'Dag, it won't be . . . pleasant when you get home and Ben finds I've left. He needs to blame someone and you'll be handy. Lise won't stick around long, cooking and cleaning up after him. She'll join a show or find a man. The business is almost through, there'll be no money, and Lise needs money more than she needs Ben. He'll go to pieces, Dag.'

'Maybe he'll follow you back to Sweden?'

She laughed softly. 'Ben? He's not an international, like us. He stopped being a Swede before we landed in California. He worked hard at becoming his idea of a John Wayne. He couldn't possibly change back now.'

Dag saw now that she was right. In striving to match his cockeyed concept of the true American, Ben had burned his

emotional bridges — and he'd never been much of a
swimmer.

Idly, Dag watched the next car crawl up the cable and
bury itself snug as a bullet into its flood-lit tunnel. Its bell
clanged, and a single parka-clad figure hurried out of the
cold into the bar. A small figure, a Rising Sun emblazoned
on the back of the parka. A Japanese skier, no doubt. Then
a hesitant voice speaking English softly but too clearly,
obviously afraid of it, 'May I please to buy a Pepsi, please?'

A girl. When she turned, Dag saw it was the little skater
with the big triple. She saw him at the same moment and
promptly dropped her change. In stooping to gather it off
the carpet she dropped her mitts. As a fellow member of the
small world of skating they both inhabited, he didn't hesitate
to help. 'Here, let me!'

He heard a gasp, a stifled sob, just as the last of the
daylight lit her face. Tears were welling up in her dark eyes,
trembled perilously on her lashes before losing the battle,
spilling down her cheeks to splash on the front of the yellow
nylon parka with dark, ominous drops.

What had he said, to prompt this waterfall? 'Tell you
what,' he said lightly, 'the view's great from my table, sit
down and *I'll* carry your Pepsi over. We don't want the
barman should quit before the Games even start!'

She swallowed, nodded, mopped at her streaming face,
and did as she was told. He took just long enough picking up
her stuff, then her drink, to give her time to gather herself
together and dab powder on her nose. She bobbed her head
in a thank you, briefly and instinctively covered her
quivering mouth, and took a long drink of Pepsi. 'So sorry,
my Engrish not good yet.'

'Better than my Japanese, I'll bet. I know *hi* and
mushi-mushi — and I'm not sure about *mushi-mushi*! I'm
Dag Carlsen, Sweden via California.'

'And I Mieko Nakashima, Japan.' She did not pronounce
the final 'n'.

'All Montegreco knows who you are. Something about a
triple-axel?' He grinned, but she seemed uncertain, gazing
about her. What was she afraid of?

She looked down at her folded hands, and he thought for
a moment that he'd pushed the rain button again, but

suddenly she smiled. Instantly he felt it, a great comforting warmth, as if the sun shone on him despite these cold, pristine mountains which had no heart, only beauty and longevity.

The bartender moved deftly through the warmhouse lighting small red candles at the tables; in their light her hair gleamed like onyx. 'So how does it feel to be talk of the town?' The more he talked, the longer she'd stay.

She shook her head, bewildered. 'I feel . . . not good. Today I am lucky, I have good day, and Roxanne has not so good day. I admire her very much, for a very long time. Therefore I am sad for her.'

'You're also too altruistic. For Roxanne, from what I hear, the day could have been worse, so cheer up or sympathize with me. My day bombed too.'

She frowned. 'Bombed? Not understand. I *must* make better English.'

'Keep talking, it'll get better. What brings you up here all alone?'

'The hotel is . . . lonely for me, I am wishing my mother can be here, or my grandfather, but is not possible. . .' She spread her hands in a helpless gesture. 'And sometimes I must . . . e-e-escrape from my team.'

'Why?' But he could guess. Her remarkable talent, her name and the family's wealth splashed all over the world, the rest of the team probably envied the hell out of her.

'I am not . . . used to so many peoples around me. You understand?'

He nodded. 'My only team is my sister. I love to "escrape" from her, too — and the word is "escape". No "R".' He spoke slowly, and it seemed to help.

She bobbed her head, an apologetic but endearing gesture. 'Then it is easier. But your sister is like a movie star, so beautiful . . . handsome?'

'She's both of those things, in a way.' He thought of Lise and compared her with the young woman opposite, who wept in part because she might have spoiled the day for Roxanne, who she admired. 'I think it's time for you to learn some old sayings —'

'Like speakings?'

'More or less. Mottos. Clichés. What you call them does

not matter. But Mieko, the words do. They are true, important.' He waved to the barman for refills, waited until they arrived, then took a napkin, heavily embossed with the Olympic rings, and printed on it for several minutes before passing it across to her. 'First lesson. "Read this", ordered the professor.'

She concentrated for a long time, a child learning a recitation. Then she smiled. 'I am ready — but do not be angry at me if I read slow, okay?'

'Slowly. Read slowly. Go ahead.'

'One: "Handsome is as handsome does." Two: "Beauty is skin deep." ' She frowned. 'But I don't know what they mean.'

He laughed as he helped her on with the bulky parka, Japan's proud Rising Sun on her small shoulders. 'That is your homework for tonight. Tomorrow at breakfast I shall give you a test. By then you will know the words in your head and you will have figured out what they mean, yes?'

She beamed on him, and again he stood bathed in the warmth of her spirit. 'So I may take your English speakings with me, to room in hotelu?'

'Sayings. And it's "hotel"! And you *must* take it with you, how else can you learn by morning? Is seven too early? Pair practice is at nine.'

She folded the napkin and slipped it into her pocket, and together they rode the cable car down to the lights of the Olympic valley. He delivered her to her door, touched her hand briefly, and was gone.

In her room she pressed to her lips the words he had written, seeing again his pale hair, his eyes the colour of the Atami bay in summer, just before a storm. Then she opened the Olympic souvenir programme to his glorious picture, so blond, so vibrant, so tall — cradled it under her pillow, its fold in the hollow of her hand, and willed herself not to think of a promising young man in Hokkaido or anywhere else.

233

CHAPTER TWENTY-THREE

In the departure lounge, waiting to board for Montegreco, Brigitta and Otto Braun looked much the same as the dozen or so other elderly couples bickering as they munched on slabs of pumpernickel, bratwursts, and a thin drizzle of mustard. Brigitta wore her Sunday wig, freshly set in sharp grey corrugations, which moved not a centimetre as she squirrelled away the change left by the waiter.

'How can they ask such prices?' she demanded. 'The corner butcher sells two kilos of sausage for less than that — better sausage, too.'

'Which you never buy,' Otto pointed out, knowing she did not hear, that today she delivered observations via a reflex system which engaged her mouth via a detour which avoided her brain. Olympic-bound, one subject only engaged Brigitta Braun's brain. There was room for none other.

'You did leave word to scrape the ice every day, Otto? It must not be ankle-deep in frost when we return. The public will be kicking down the doors to skate at the Olympic Champion's home rink. It must be perfect.'

He sighed. Their granddaughter Roxanne was born in, trained in, and competed for, the USA. She *was* America. From habit he resisted comment on his wife's dream of a clamorous public beating down the rink doors for tickets. Old women attached themselves to rosy fancies. 'Don't want your sausage?' He speared the last of her bratwurst on to his plate. 'Too much cauliflower cheese at lunch. I said so, but did you listen? No.'

'*Schwein*,' she said amicably, returning to a faraway land behind her eyes where the name Braun was synonymous with Olympic Gold Medallist.

Otto munched stolidly at the sausage, spinning his

wheelchair to check the board as each flight was called. Naturally they were hours early, a life-long habit of Brigitta's. The only event for which she'd ever been late was her period. Noni was the result. He grunted over the last morsel of bratwurst. Like a worn easy-chair, their relationship had settled into the familiar creases common to all old marriages. Each partner knew the locale and exact perimeters of the danger spots; a rancorous soup-stain on the chair-arm; a spring which had creaked for forty-odd years and would continue so to do; the precise point at which the entire structure could give way to a chaos of accusations, shards of broken lives. For the Brauns, Noni was the point of strain, a subject to be avoided if possible. All others were fair game — compensation for bitter pleasures sacrificed with reluctance.

Brigitta stood. 'I shall buy a newspaper,' she announced.

'Why not a novel — there's time to finish it before take-off,' he said. 'You realize I could have driven us? But no! We must fly. Money to burn, that's us — and with no car, how are we to get around Montegreco, tell me that!'

'With useless legs, how could you *drive* around it, tell me that!'

'I still have my licence.'

'I still have my womb and *that* hasn't been used for forty years, either! Noni is renting a car. She will drive. You will pay.' Triumphant, she picked up her purse and paused by his chair. 'How would it look, the winner's family begging rides of strangers?' She kicked the door shut behind her.

Otto closed his eyes and waited. It seemed to him that he spent his life waiting. For warmth, sunshine, a release from the tyranny of the ice, its endless cold. Too much to ask? Apparently. If Roxanne won, Brigitta would never sell the rink. She'd hang the champion's photograph on every wall and he'd be condemned to worship at his granddaughter's frozen shrine for life. If Roxanne lost, they could sell and move to the sun. A sour victory for him; one final, shattering defeat for Brigitta; a disaster for their foolish Noni.

In a moment Brigitta was back with her newspaper and some of her youth, an innocence totally misplaced under the circumstances. 'See, Otto?' she shouted. 'It begins! Roxanne on the front page. See the caption! "Olympic

Favourite for Gold, Granddaughter of Brigitta and Otto Braun of Bonn." Our day is coming and it will be glorious, glorious!' She waved the newspaper at him as she laughed, spinning his chair on one wheel like a coin on its edge. He groaned, unable to look at her face, its heart-breaking certainty. She *knew* the sport, she *knew* the ice! Who should know better than they how fast certainty could melt away?

'How can I read when you make a child's toy from my chair!' Look at her now, deserting his chair to rush from one traveller to another, showing the picture. 'Our grand-daughter,' she babbled. 'We are the Brauns.'

In her demented circuit of the lounge her wig tipped sideways, her scarf trailed behind her, and as she swooped down on another unsuspecting stranger, sound asleep, Otto saw that her hem was caught up in the elastic of her heavy flannel bloomers. Later. He would tell her later.

Noni waited impatiently for their plane to land. She'd hired a car, charged it to the 'Parkrose Review', and made a copy of the bill for Papa. Years ago she learned never to turn down a possibility for money, she was not about to start now. She lit a thin brown cigarette, tapped long gold fingernails on her imitation leather purse, and switched her portable radio to an oldies station, which set her red shoes tapping to the melody. *'Dream a little dream with me . . .'* And why not? They were cheap enough. Dream that Sterling cracked a collarbone, that Beejay caught the mumps, that the German and Canadian champions collided on warm-up and knocked each other out; dream that Nakashima came down with yellow jaundice, why not? She laughed out loud. Passers-by glanced at her and turned away, smirking. The hell with them.

Checking her watch, she dug in her purse for a 'trank'. Mutti always made her nervous. Never mind, if the plane arrived on schedule she'd make Roxi's afternoon practice and give the old ones a treat at the same time. Last night she'd invested a little time and a few veiled promises in a security guard on the press entrance. He'd let Mutti and Papa through the gate on Noni's pass, no problem. Mutti would feel part of the 'in' crowd again, she would praise

Noni. The 'in' crowd. That was a laugh. She couldn't wait to see Mutti square off with Grant Rivers. Or even with Roxanne these days. Fame must have gone to the girl's head. That or Grant Rivers. The way she'd spoken to Noni in the lobby this morning! Mothers knew nothing. Oh no, they were stupid. Roxanne knew it all now, no telling her a thing. Noni had only meant to remind her, jog her memory.

'Roxi when you're on TV don't mention getting married or joining a show after the Games, okay? You're going to college, get it? College.'

Roxanne had blinked. 'To study what, Mom? Tell me again. I forget.'

'Who cares? Go for the top. Brain surgeon, why not?'

Her daughter laughed at her. 'Mom, that is such a *dumb* lie! What for?'

'It's supposed to be an amateur sport, that's what for. Winners always lie, their last year. College sounds good, pleases the public — but nobody who is anybody expects her to actually *go*. She'd have to be stupid to flush sixteen years of slavery down the toilet for a lousy degree, when she can join a show and pull down millions in endorsements! Now *that* would be *dumb*!'

Roxanne said nothing, just sighed and rubbed her eyes.

'Tired again? You never see me tired. If you'd take the vitamins I get you and quit ramming food down your gullet — '

'I do what the doctor tells me. He's helping.'

'And I'm not, I suppose.'

'Mom, what I'm really tired of is this whole script. We've played it so many times we know each other's lines, even down to the ad-libs.'

'Look, smart-ass, the *real* last line is your name on a winner's contract. You'll thank me then. That's all I ever wanted for you. Is that so bad?'

'I've not won yet, remember?'

'You have if you push for it. *If you want it.*'

Roxanne stared down at the thick beige carpet, tracing its pattern of Olympic rings with the toe of her shoe. 'Maybe I just want to be happy.'

'Winning *is* happy!'

'Mom, have you *seen* Nakashima? The tapes on Sterling at

237

Europeans? Even Beejay when she's on? I am not the only game in town.'

'You would be if you got smart. Smile nicely at a few judges. If not for yourself then for me. It's about time you paid me back for the years I've put up with rented pig-pens, roaches in the cupboards, stains in the carpets. But not you. You've had the best, your world's been clover, I saw to that!'

'No, mother, you seeded it in ice. It's hard and it's cold.'

'Poverty's one hell of a lot colder, girl. And what about the old ones? Don't you care anything about your grandparents, their hopes?'

Roxanne flashed her a look even colder than poverty. 'Grandpa wants out, he doesn't give a damn about the medal, and Grossmutti's getting her ghastly spin. If I lose, she'll have to make do with it.'

'*What d'you mean, if you lose! You're programmed to win!*'

But Roxanne had walked away, tuned her out. Noni shivered at the memory, at the ice in her daughter's voice. So much for gratitude.

Ladies practice sessions were heating up, would reach fever-pitch in a day or so. The top Canadian, nursing shin-splints, might have to withdraw, the leading German had already bowed out for the same reason, but Kramer, Nakashima, and Crisp were all on the ice now, and Sterling due next session. Grant leaned on the rail, unobtrusively instructing as he, like the coaches of the other girls, worked the room. All spoke to their charges in low tones through almost-closed mouths (lip-readers routinely touted for the networks these days); all tried to look monumentally bored, each day just another practice; all played a role, their eyes and ears tuned to the max.

'Roxi, give me a layback over by the French judge? Pick her out? Blue hat? Smile coming out of it, okay?' If the Canadian had to withdraw, maybe France would shift into Roxanne's column. 'Beejay, see the network camera on the Japanese? When she exits that spin you do a triple-loop *right there* before he can shift focus. Nail it and sell it.' It wouldn't help this time out, but no harm beating the publicity drum for next year. He checked his watch. When they were done, there'd just be time to catch Sterling's début before Pairs, then Jeff in Mens at the other rink.

Skaters, coaches, parents, hangers-on, and every judge on the Ladies panel now dotted a rink officially closed but open to anyone with the right badge and a little free time. Free time translated to don't-miss-a-thing time. Accreditation covered a multitude, and all, it seemed, were here.

Jeff and Lloyd sat first row up, Lloyd's full-length cashmere coat draped casually over his thigh and partially over Jeff's as he tried, with no success, to make contact. 'Judges are around, Mr Sterling,' Jeff pointed out.

'Forgive me, dear boy. I get carried away.'

'My practice doesn't start for three hours, I can't be distracted, sorry.'

Lloyd smiled, folded his coat, and settled patiently into his burgundy pew; mustn't interfere with the boy's concentration. Jeffie's answering smile conveyed contempt thinly glossed with regret. Silly old sod, Lloyd, playing into his hands like a starving mutt grateful for any scrap you threw it. And tomorrow, after they officially opened the Village, he'd be out of Lloyd's reach for the rest of the Games. Whoopee.

The Carlsen Pair sat a few rows behind them with Mieko's bronze-god cousin, a competitor on the 70-metre hill and Mieko's more-or-less watchdog appointed by Hiro Nakashima. Some watchdog, Dag thought, as the cousin wound a strand of Lise's flaxen hair around his finger. He couldn't keep his eyes off her long enough to glance at Mieko, just now ending her programme. She had not skated well. At the last moment, as they announced her music, she'd seen Dag, and stumbled badly on the first beat. His encouraging smile seemed to ruffle her further and he was sorry, after all, that he'd come. If there was one thing Mieko needed less of, it was humility. She had learned her English 'speakings' as diligently as she worked her practice sessions; she obviously understood the words, but still failed utterly to relate them to Mieko Nakashima.

Across the rink Ben Carlsen scanned every side, every second, dare not miss a move. Stuff happened and nobody told him zip. How the hell did Lise meet that Jap and why was she letting him play with her hair? So *what* if he had rich relations? He was yellow as a buttercup and that ruled him out, yessir! As if that wasn't bad enough his airy-fairy son sat with the Nakashima girl all through breakfast. She could have been a porcelain doll the way he gazed at her. And vital, most important of all, Ben dare not let Emma Crisp out of his sight. Ninety minutes from now he'd know if she'd be judging his kids. That's when Pairs worked out on this rink, Men on the other. Emma would have to choose who to watch, and when she did, he'd know what event she'd be judging. According to hotel gossip, they'd drawn assignments this noon.

Much closer to the roof — her tame security guard had indeed come through, even taking Papa and his chair up the freight elevator — the Brauns sat in isolated splendour, three pairs of binoculars trained on the ice. Noni would have preferred to be closer, but Grant knew Mutti had no pass; he'd have her thrown out without a qualm if he spotted her before the rink was officially open to the public; Grant Rivers would do anything to make it difficult, God alone knew what Roxanne saw in him. Looks? Huh! After the first three months who noticed a man's face? *She* never had. Beside her, Mutti breathed on her binoculars, dried them on her skirt, and said, 'Noni, I thought you said the Japanese had a chance.'

'She jumps well,' Otto said.

Brigitta sniffed. 'So do fleas, but I haven't heard they win medals.'

'The judge's daughter skates next, Mutti. One of Grant's students.'

Mutti didn't even bother bringing the glasses to her eyes. She'd come to see Roxanne and only Roxanne, who skated last, after Beejay, and who did not in any case know they were here.

Perhaps that was why she skated so well, her best in Montegreco so far. Brigitta ooh-ed and aah-ed and applauded the disputed spin — which Noni had reminded Roxanne to include and for which Grant might have killed them all later had she not skated so well — and then the elder Brauns were tired, surely time for Noni to drive them to the hotel?

'No way,' she said. 'Sterling's group is up next. I'm not

missing it, neither is Roxanne. Wait here, I'll bring her up. I hear the top German's out but they still have a couple of hot-peppers as usual. Roxi might as well know what she's up against, get her ass in gear.'

'I thought Roxanne skated well, Noni,' Otto protested, but only mildly.

'You think she's the only one, Papa? You don't keep up. Come every day. You'll see. Time to talk to some of the right people down there, but that damn coach spies on me all the time — even at the hotel I can't get near my own daughter! Mutti, you'll use your influence with the German officials when we come to the hotel. Pressure them. Go for national pride. Most are middle-aged, they'll remember me, maybe even you.'

Otto looked at her quickly but no malice showed on her face. Did it ever cross her mind she could bruise Brigitta's feelings? But no, Brigitta beamed, flattered someone thought she still had influence to use. So strange, this mother and daughter, such coldness between them. The one consistent emotion they showed for each other was contempt, with a brief armistice when life bestowed some prize for which both yearned and could equally enjoy. Roxanne's Gold would unite them. Briefly. If she won it. For their sake he hoped she would. For his own, he prayed she would not. He would have preferred a lager in the hotel, but having no choice he settled back, waiting for the arrival of the Sterling girl much as a captive bird-watcher awaited the first spring sighting of the white stork.

241

CHAPTER TWENTY-FOUR

Delayed until the last possible moment, Maureen's début into the main arena could not have electrified the faithful more. Before she appeared, Beejay had joined her mother, Roxanne had joined hers. Alexei Finsky, anxious to renew contact with the Sterling women, also waited. Even Lloyd and Jeff, still *tête-à-tête* in their burgundy seats, began to wonder. Under the great tropical plants wheeled in just hours ago to dress-up the rink for the cameras, Mieko Nakashima voiced her shy curiosity to Dag Carlsen; above them, even the great sago palms seemed to hold their breath, to mute the oasis rattle of their swaying fronds as word went out.

Maureen Sterling was in the Building but not yet on the ice. Could she be passing up another practice? Such was speculation that even those who knew her had forgotten that Maureen warmed up behind the scenes with a complete off-ice barre rather than on the cold rink.

Grant had moved as far from the ice as it was possible to get, a speck under the high-domed roof, at the top of the web of seats radiating from that blue, frozen centre. Directing his binoculars at the ice, he scarcely noticed the hollowness in his stomach, the arid dryness of his mouth, the deep ache in his chest as he waited for his first glimpse of Deirdre's daughter — perhaps even Deirdre herself sitting in the bleachers the way the other mothers sat, on the edge of their seats, trying to look casually about them, but always, in the corner of their vision, watching the ice, their child. But he could not find Deirdre and was afraid, at first, to seek Maureen.

The Polar Bear rumbled off, leaving a sheet of perfect ice. A large rink, three girls, none of them Sterling. The

Germans warmed up, Frau Müller at the rail, Katerina Witt an interested observer. Then two girls were finished, the third almost through, and still no Sterling. But as the last German girl completed her final spin, a subdued murmur rose from rink-side.

A girl had taken the ice quietly. Tall, in a white dress with flowing, pointed sleeves, her arms somehow evoked the feathers of a lone white bird on water. She stroked the edge of the ice, waiting, her only ornament an exotic blossom of a face framed in cloudy black hair. Her American and Oriental competitors, who'd seen only blurred videos of dark hair and delicate grace, were prepared for an English pink-and-white skin — certainly not this vibrant Mediterranean peach undertoned with rose, nor the startling contrast of brilliant blue eyes. Deirdre's eyes.

Today there was no Deirdre. Maureen skated for two men at the rail: one unknown to Grant, the other known to the entire world, a mega-star of ballet, long-time defector from the East, a satyr, a sardonic faun, at times a god. Even motionless he drew the crowd like a magnet. Until Maureen Sterling, a white bird on an ice-blue lake, began to move to her music.

In the lingering opening beats she seemed not so much to skate as to drift, a creature of secret dreams and fathomless yearnings. Where the music soared she followed, an egret lifting to the sky; when the melody sobbed, her dancer's arms, slow and boneless, embraced it, white wings mourning in sympathy, her dramatic dark head drooped in sorrow. The required elements of skating were there and perfect, jumps, spins, and intricate footwork, but her grace, or perhaps simply her long training in ballet, lifted every move to a higher plane, a union of grace and melody. Her arms caressed the music, sang its pleasures and wept its torments. Impossible to even consider this ethereal creature 'nailing' this or 'missing' that. Could snowy pinions 'nail' an updraft? Could a bird 'miss' the sky?

To the knowledgeable in the arena, Maureen Sterling was indeed skating's impossible dream. When she left the ice it was as if she'd broken a spell. As quietly as she'd arrived she returned to the ballet room to cool down under the satyr's direction. Word of that innovation, too, ran like whispered wild-fire round the rink, to be examined, interpreted, admired, or condemned. Certainly emulated.

Brigitta Braun sniffed. 'No wonder she only skates two hours a day. She must spend all her days at the barre. I would never permit it.'

Nevertheless, it seemed to work, Otto thought — but dare not say.

'Well!' Noni said to Roxanne, almost with pleasure. 'Now you know what you're up against.'

Roxanne didn't answer. She knew what she was up against. This was the best trained skater she'd ever seen, and from now on they would all train more in a ballet studio than in a rink.

Emma paused by Beejay before hurrying over to the other rink to study the Men, her assigned judging stint. 'What did you think, sport?'

'Holy cow,' breathed her daughter.

'Of course the tan helps,' Jeff was saying to Lloyd, his voice tipped with spite. 'If you didn't know better you might think she skates for Spain.'

'Perhaps for the whole world,' said Jasinski, sitting behind them. 'Surely such artists give universal pleasure.'

Lloyd turned his glacial stare on the doctor, who he had not met. 'I beg your pardon? She is my daughter. She represents Great Britain.'

Jasinski's glance flickered over Jeff before again meeting Lloyd's cold grey eyes. 'Then I expect she is happy that you are here.'

Lloyd shrugged. 'Her skating's her own affair. I don't interfere.'

'What is it that you don't interfere with, Lloyd?' It was Maureen herself, standing over her father, her smile offering little more warmth than the ice she'd just left.

'Well,' he said, shifting ever so slightly away from Jeff. 'Finally you come to say hello. You look well.'

'I am well. Are you going to ask about Mother?'

He raised an eyebrow. 'If you give me time. How is she?'

'She's . . . ill. The doctor says no visitors at the villa.'

Lloyd shrugged into his coat and made to follow Jeff, whose session was about to start. 'Actually, I hadn't considered visiting. Far safer she be quarantined, I'm sure.'

Grant, high in his eyrie, folded his binoculars and tried to stop his hands trembling. Don't think about it, can't think about it now, go to the other rink . . . to the ice . . . work with Jeff. . . Slowly he picked his way down the long staircase, surprised by the mist clouding his vision, not sure exactly what he'd seen through the glasses because after the first moments of Maureen Sterling he refused to focus on her face, to look at it. He took the decision subconsciously, far, far back in his mind, in a place he dare not examine. What remained was an agonizing swell of music, a memory of blue eyes, a disturbing doubt tugging at the edge of his awareness, a surge of anger that Deirdre was not here, yet she — and it could only have been she — had chosen Maureen's music. Did it have no more meaning for her than that, that she could select the one piece which had meant so much to them that unforgettable summer of his sixteenth year? That, for him at least, the impossible dream had once seemed not merely possible but probable. Bitterly, he remembered his innocent castles built on the creamy beaches of her flesh, his adolescent dreams reflected in the blue pools of her eyes. Deirdre, apparently, remembered none of it.

As Jeff warmed up Grant did his job, stood by the ice watching his student but seeing instead the figure who'd just skated, a white bird. . . No time yet to analyse her performance, what it could do to his plans — though he knew what he'd seen, and there were no superlatives to touch it. When he compared it with Roxanne's sacrifices, her vulnerability, her touching and often misplaced obedience, his chill of doubt warmed to a smouldering anger. Beside him, Lloyd Sterling's arrogance fanned the flame.

Lloyd, maddeningly confident through his contacts with members of the Committee, persisted in standing by the rail, traditionally reserved for coaches and sound-men. But no rink-guard dare challenge Lloyd Sterling.

'Jeffie's definitely improved. You've done well, Rivers.' Lloyd's every word rattled at Grant like pennies tossed into a beggar's cup.

Bastard. 'It wasn't easy. Jeff's a minor talent, you sent him to me poorly trained.' Perhaps irritation made him add, 'Unlike your daughter. That is talent, perfectly trained. Maureen? Is that her name?'

'Yes.' Lloyd spoke through teeth which, Grant suddenly noticed, had serrated edges, sharp as those of a scavenger fish. 'Tell Jeff I'll be at the hotel. We're dining out before the Village absorbs him tomorrow.'

'You will remember he has early-ice tomorrow and he can't afford to miss?' Grant nodded towards Alexei Finsky skating meditatively round, calmly waiting his turn.

'So? Jeff can give *him* a run for his money any day of the week.'

Fool. Grant smiled at Lloyd's expensively clad back as he departed the rink. Finsky had no money to run for, but it didn't diminish his chances in the least. The Lloyds, the Bens, where was their grasp on reality? The wordless anger in him flared again, its heat fanned this time by a camp follower, a skating mother whose son might be good enough to make the national team in a couple of years. If. She cornered him in the coffee shop where he sipped on machine-brewed coffee as he told himself again and again to get back to the job, to stop thinking about the girl in white, to forget the unforgettable glimpse of her face. Go check on the Swedes, he told himself — just as the skating mother came at him.

'A word in your ear, Grant,' she cooed, settling opposite him.

They'd never met, yet she called him Grant as if they were old friends. He knew now what was coming. 'I only have a minute —'

'All I need. You saw my son at Nationals?' She spoke fast, testing the waters, not sure if they'd scald. 'Want to take him on after the Games?'

He took a deep breath and made a conscious decision to string her along, punish her for what she was, what Lloyd was — and perhaps for the way Maureen Sterling had skated.

The woman wore Gucci boots, purse and watch, a Hermès scarf around her perfumed neck, and full-length chinchilla with matching hat; no threadbare green cloth coat for this one. She'd dragged her son half-way round the world, first-class, holed him up in a plush suite for the run of the Games, to give him 'a taste of the greatness of the Olympics. To whet his appetite.' She licked her lips seductively.

Grant paused. One of the wealthiest families in skating, yet it was common knowledge that they owed the kid's coach, who was a soft touch, a mint, figuring they could get away with it because the kid was a comer and would make it — if they didn't run out of coaches. 'I'm overbooked,' he said carefully, 'but if an opening should come up . . . you realise I'll have to check it out with his present coach first, of course?'

She actually looked offended. '*Him*? Why would you call him?'

She knew damned well why. 'Professional ethics?' he suggested, waiting for her next move and knowing she didn't have one. Top coaches didn't play dog-eat-dog, avoided students with a history of owing and switching. Courtesy and collective self-preservation. If they left one coach in a financial hole they'd leave the next, and the next. How long did it take a woman like this to learn? Coaching was a business. The successful ones were smart. That's why they succeeded. 'And now, if you'll excuse me. . .'

'Take my card,' she said quickly. 'You'll be needing my number.'

At the door he turned, made sure she was watching, and casually flipped her card into the trash.

Alexei Finsky caught his trainer's nod and drifted over to the rail with desultory strokes. He'd done all the elements once, no sense leaving the day's only performance on the warm-up for it. He hadn't been able to speak to Maureen privately, and dare not approach her publicly. From everywhere, now, eyes watched him. Even in the super-clean hotel, the rink, on the streets of Montegreco, the quiet corners of coffee-bars, he felt eyes crawling over him like lice.

'How long to my music?' he asked the team trainer, who he liked.

'Plenty,' the trainer said. 'I have to talk to you anyway.' He too had developed the public way of speaking, lips scarcely moving, unreadable from a distance. 'My sister phoned me this morning. She tried to contact Galina. No answer on the phone, so last night she drove over to Galina's folks' place. They're not at the old address. A neighbour said they'd been moved right after you left. Their permit to live in Moscow had expired —'

For the first time in all his years on the ice Alexei felt intense cold creep into his boots, up his legs, his torso, to settle, implacable, around his heart and in his larynx. 'That's no reason. It expires every year at the same time and every year it's been renewed.'

'Was,' the trainer said carefully. 'In the past.'

'What reason?'

'None of them works in the city now. That's all the authorities need. They moved them to the Park.'

The Park. A cluster of peeling stucco blocks, institution-beige and ugly as sin. Bilious green stains oozed like sores under every window; iron railings dripped rust from every balcony. Five miles out of Moscow, from the cosy flat where Galina's mother had plumped cushions, where her father had agonized endlessly about 'them', the authorities; where Galina had ironed the family wash, filling every room with the clean scent of sun-dried linens. It could have been five thousand miles. 'The Park. Why not Siberia while they were at it?' Alexei shifted his blades on a surface more familiar to him than pavements.

The trainer chuckled. 'The Park is closer. Less trouble to move them back when you win the Gold and go home in triumph.'

'The Director ordered you to tell me?'

'I imagine that's the whole point, right? Temporary, they say. Extra insurance. Since when did they neglect that?'

'Her family must be miserable.'

'Who wouldn't? Are your laces tight?'

Their heads bent to check. 'Your sister get the new phone number?' Alexei muttered.

'Under the tongue of your spare boots.'

'Tapped?'

'Dunno.' At a signal from the sound-man the trainer straightened, shrugged and nodded. 'Your number's up.'

Hands clasped leisurely behind him, Alexei ambled to centre-ice, stopping twice to wipe tiny accumulations of frost from his blades, then turning back to scrape at an infinitesimal something on the surface, skating ever so slowly to the rail and handing it to an engineer. A bit of thread no longer than an inch, far less hazardous than the ice itself. But it gave time to think, decide, to lock glances over the man's shoulder with the Director, who monitored Alexei's every run-through. Today their eyes clashed like sabres as Alexei flicked swiftly through his options, appalled at how few he had. He could 'walk through', move vaguely to the music but leave out every element, a studied insult to the Director but also to the judges, all of whom were now present, dotted inconspicuously about but *here*, their clipboards and eyes calculating just what this jump was worth, that spin . . . but how would the Director react? He'd assume he'd lost the battle, that Alexei had already decided to defect, and Galina would then be punished more. A national champion such as she accumulated many perks, large and small, over the years; like all luxuries, they inevitably turned into necessities that could be withdrawn one by one for maximum impact.

Alexei's other option was to skate his best, force the Director to slaver like a dog after the Gold, holding his own decision until the end as he tried to reach Galina, persuade her to leave. She *could* leave. Since Gorbachev, everything had eased up — but would she abandon her father, paranoid as he would always be? And he must, must talk to the Sterlings. . .

Didn't she, the reporter persisted, have *any* message for the British public whose hopes skated with her? Firmly, not quite slamming it down — she'd been gently reared and in any case Mother was sleeping — Maureen Sterling unplugged the phone by Deirdre's bed and signalled the nurse to leave it that way. She let herself out quietly to rest, stretch, and pack for the Village.

As the door closed behind her daughter, and eventually behind the nurse, Deirdre allowed her eyes to open. God alone knew how the press wormed phone numbers out of people — in this case probably Jeff had supplied it. She hoped they'd paid him. Knowing Jeff, they probably had, in cash or in kind, a nice little puff-piece on the front page under his prettiest smile, a new British lion set to roar from the Olympic platform. With two Brits suddenly favoured, national pride had taken a great leap upwards, and every TV set in the country would be tuned to the Olympics this time around, so they said.

National pride. Deirdre smiled her drugged smile, pushed off the covers and let her skin feel the touch of the Mediterranean afternoon sun, which it craved, would always crave. How long was always? It used to be forever, she had thought once. She used to think a lot of rubbish. Did it endure longer than national pride? She laughed softly in the quiet room. She'd even had that, once. Now, the sicker she became and the more British press hounded Maureen, a song hummed somewhere in her head . . . imagining no countries . . . perhaps it was her illness but she *could* imagine it.

Nationality was a bigger gamble by far than a shot at the Olympics. 'I'd *love* it if you won, darling,' she'd said when Maureen asked her just how much she wanted it — but a medal as compensation for Grant, who they'd lost, not a prize for the bleak little island which had nurtured not only Maureen and Grant but also Lloyd. No, Mrs Sterling had no time for countries at this stage in her life, thank you. When time ran out she'd take the same ride through the labyrinth as everyone else, black or white, and which of them knew in advance the hooded face of the boatman? What difference did one's flag make to him? She hoped for a smooth trip, but first, a little more time? Please? Not much, two, three weeks and enough strength to see Maureen skate once more, to look into the eyes of a coach and recapture for herself a time when she'd called him Grant Rivera, two small memories to pack in her skull against the fears of the labyrinth. But was there room enough . . . the skull was bursting already, every day more. Could it be time for the next injection? Time, it all came down to time — 'Nurse!' she called feebly, reaching for the little silver handbell which weighed more each time she rang it.

The hotel lobby, now *the* social scene for everything, for snacks, drinks, meetings, and chaos, buzzed with a dozen tongues. Where *have* you been . . . No, not since Sapporo . . . You caught Binky in Copenhagen? . . . Still fat I suppose? No? You're kidding! . . . But yesss, darling, she's in a show, a bit on the naughty side . . . Him? Lord, nobody's seen *him* since Sarajevo. Sauced out of his bird when it was over, remember?

Everyone talked, no one listened. One had to be seen, part of the crowd, in the swim. Tomorrow the athletes all left for the Village, and not one among them could wait. To escape the nagging parent, the vigilant eye of a coach, the evening post-mortem on mistakes made this day which must be corrected tomorrow.

In honour of the family reunion the Brauns sipped champagne — except Roxanne who, not consulted, got Diet Pepsi. When Noni and Brigitta left for a moment to 'wash up' Otto handed Roxanne his champagne.

'Drink!' he ordered. 'I don't care what they say, you're too thin.'

'Thanks, but it's not worth it.' Noni would smell it — and she didn't like it anyway. At least at the Village *nobody* could check what she did or didn't eat. With meals available all hours, who'd know if you'd eaten and what? Her weight crept back, slowly but surely. Two pounds since she left LA. But didn't Grandfather, or Grant — realize it was two more pounds to drag up into the jumps? She looked across the lobby at Beejay happily crunching bar snacks; Nakashima and Dag drinking sweet, creamy coffee; Lise Carlsen doing her Nordic Queen act for a circle of skiers, opening her luscious lips, letting them drop glacé cherries and sugar-frosted grapes into her mouth; Lloyd Sterling, his fur-lined coat slung casually across his shoulders as he steered Jeff towards the Pump Room for, he'd explained, the feast of the boy's young life. Gluttons! Except Grant. He huddled at a corner table with two judges, ordering them streams of vodka, straight, while he eked out a single scotch on the rocks. But when she left for the Village, what then? Dinner with Emma again?

Emma had her own worries. She sat alone, facing the door and the constantly arriving limos from the airport. In one of them should be Beejay's dress. If it arrived after Beej went to the Village there'd be no chance to check the fit; was it too bold, too *much*? When Ben Carlsen threw himself down beside her she barely bothered to greet him until she saw his haunted, hollow face, his obvious eagerness to talk.

'Can I get you a drink, Emma?'

She shook her head. 'Waiting for a package, then bed. I'm beat.'

251

'Me too. Tried to call the wife all morning. Nobody home, she'll be out spending my money. I took Lise round the boutiques today. My God but they're pricey! . . . She found a pin, what she's been wanting for her Finals outfit, so I let her get it. Hell, they're only young once, right?' He beckoned a waiter, taking a deep breath before turning back to Emma. 'I hear you're judging Men's, that right?'

'Yeah. See, all that fretting for nothing.'

He didn't quite look at her. 'Well, there's a lot of pressure right now.'

'Tell me about it,' Emma said thoughtfully, her face grim as she craned toward another limo rolling up, unloading passengers, baggage, and what might be a load of Federal Express parcels. Impeding her vision slightly was Lise, torn between an egg-roll or smoked salmon on a passing tray.

'Listen, Ben, if I *had* judged your Pair I wouldn't have trashed them. Some folks just naturally trash themselves.'

He followed her gaze, flushing a livid magenta as Nakashima's cousin bit into one end of the egg-roll and Lise wrapped her mouth round the other. 'What are you getting at, Emma?'

She locked into Ben's eyes and refused to let them off the hook. 'I'm waiting for Beejay's new skating dress, Ben. Somebody trashed hers.'

Ben's flush drained down into his shoes someplace, leaving behind a tide the colour of candle-wax beaded in sweat. So. It was Ben who'd done it. Emma stood. 'Well! And I was half-way ready to blame a woman. I see an old pal, Ben. Excuse, huh?'

Just in time. She felt sick to her stomach. But she'd told no lie. Climbing down from the limo was a judging buddy from Norway. When Dave was alive they'd made up many a foursome with Nils and his wife. But now Dave was dead and Nils divorced. She never would have believed it until a Finnish judge told her at last year's Worlds. She looked at him critically. Divorce agreed with him. He'd lost weight, looked forty instead of fifty, and crossed the pavement as nimbly as any of the athletes clumping down with their burdens of gear. She was about to call out to Nils when a bus driver waved a package and shouted above the uproar of arrivals: '*Package for Beejay Crisp!*' It was a toss-up whether Emma or Beejay reached him first.

'Holy shit, Em, it's my dress!'

'Upstairs, Belinda Jane. Try it on for size.'

Grant bowed the judges off to dinner, figured he'd done his stint and deserved a night-cap and a free evening. Jasinski wasn't around so he joined his yum-num coaching buddy at the darkest bar.

'Grant! Scotch? Yum, I thought so. You look worn. Students?'

'Uh-huh. I don't mind it once they start competing but —'

'What d'you mean, *start. They* start the effing minute they arrive. Animals! Thank God they lock 'em up tomorrow, then we humans can get down to some serious trading. I don't mind telling you, num-num-num, one more tantrum out of my Boston Bean and I'm on the next plane home. Who needs it, huh? Spoiled bloody brats, the lot of 'em. See the Bean today? Skated like an angel, behaved like Old Nick himself. He's up in his room this minute, "Do Not Disturb" on the door, screwing himself cross-eyed with some down-hill wench out of the Pyrenees! She's sure to have the stamina of an ox. Wait till I tell his Dad! The little sod thinks I don't know, thinks I'm stupid, yum. He'll be too bow-legged to skate tomorrow. If he were a dog I'd have him fixed.'

Grant wondered if the chap talked any other subject besides sex, but his empty room waited, filled with thoughts which company held at bay. So he let him blather on, only half-listening until, 'You caught the Sterling girl this morning, of course?'

Grant froze. 'Yes. She's . . . good, very good. D'you know her?'

'Yum. I hear Momma's holed up at the family villa. Too bad you're stuck with Jeff and lewd Lloyd. I'd let them disconnect my family jewels for a chance to coach that girl. Speaking of which, I seem to remember the mother as a looker, too. Hell, I wouldn't mind —'

Grant resisted an unwarranted urge to crumple the chap's amiable grin. Instead, he bid him a civil goodnight.

CHAPTER TWENTY-FIVE

'Oh, Em! Oh, my God! Just look at this! Will you look at this thing?'

'What *is* it? Unlock the damn door, will you?' Emma figured another disaster for sure when she heard Beejay's wail. There were tears in it, actual tears! Now, she thought, frantically rattling the knob, what else could happen? Beejay, finally reaching the age where she began to exhibit some modesty, had locked herself in the bathroom to open the dress-box and get into her new competition outfit.

The first thing Emma saw was her daughter's face in the bathroom mirror, suddenly a woman's face, wonder, disbelief, and something close to awe fighting each other as she held the dress in front of her, bright over-head lights catching every subtle gleam.

'I can't believe it . . . I can't believe it's mine, I can't . . .' Beejay whispered over and over again to the mirror, the dress, her mother and herself.

'Jesus,' Emma echoed, 'I'd never have believed it. Beej, look at the fabric, the beads, the way the colours seem to come and go.' She blinked in the soft glow of the dress and the lights. 'Sport, it's gotta cost a fortune.' She could have bit her tongue the instant the words came out but it didn't seem to matter. Beejay hadn't heard.

Yeah, just *look* at the colours. Colour — for it was only one. Not quite white, not quite *eau-de-nil*, maybe clean river water with a tree hanging over it in the sun, maybe the palest inside of an abalone shell. No, she had it! Sauterne in cut crystal caught under iridescent lights.

'Try it on, Beej.' Dear God, let it fit.

'I'm scared,' Beejay breathed. 'Suppose it gets ripped, suppose I lose a bead, wreck the zipper?'

Emma fingered one of the beads edging the small, hand-kerchief points of the skirt and knew she'd been right. The beads *were* cut crystal. Not many, a dozen or so, and small, but the genuine article. The fabric was luminous — but only just and only in a certain light. With Beejay's hair and the speed she moved she'd look like one of those pearly little tropical fish darting across a blue aquarium. Oh, God . . . 'Will you get it *on* for Chrissakes!'

But Beejay's eyes just grew bigger and bigger until Emma couldn't stand it. Deftly, with many years of practice to guide her, Emma zipped her into it, tamed the flaming hair with swift brush-strokes, and stepped back. They didn't speak for whole minutes as the vision in the mirror stared back at them. Almost white and almost gold and almost mother-of-pearl. And definitely beautiful. Lights and fabric turned her skin to pale cream, her hair to antique gold and her eyes to a dark, luminous amber. The cut of the dress was faultless. Nothing showgirl about the leg-holes under gauzy silk handkerchiefs. They ended where they should, at the top of her leg, not half-way up her behind.

'Holy moley, Em, I got boobs!'

'They didn't grow in five minutes.'

'Well, I know *that*, but they were just lumps. Now . . .'

Now she figured she was growing into a woman. Emma didn't know whether to bless Mrs Cox or to blame her. 'We have to check it with Grant.' Their eyes met in the mirror, asking the same question. Would Grant think it too pretty to go up against Roxanne? No, Emma decided. Grant was no fool. He'd have instructed Mrs Cox not to go too far this time around. 'Call him anyway, have him come down before we get Security to lock it up.'

'I can't sleep in it?'

'Get on the phone.'

Grant approved the dress with a deep, satisfied growl and spoke over Beejay's head. 'Not too shabby for a rush job, huh? Now she looks like a lady she'll have to talk like one — maybe even act like one.'

'Yeah. How's this?' She blinked at herself in the full-length mirror, postured a little, lifting her arms into a graceful curve quite atypical of Beejay Crisp. Her eyelids drooped into what might, with practice, become a pout. Very effective. 'What time is it in California?'

'Eight — maybe nine hours behind us. Why?'

'Think we should call Mrs Cox and say thanks?'

'I think this little number's going to cost quite enough as it is. I think it's time you went to bed.'

Later, packing the dress into its box as tenderly as if it was a new baby, Emma discovered matching tights, whisper-thin and shimmering softly within the layers of tissue paper. A note came with them. *'Wasn't sure you'd be able to find a match. VCR ready to roll, Mrs C.'*

Emma called Mrs Cox herself, finding it surprisingly difficult to say a business-like thank you to this talented woman who'd run up a small miracle out of a yard of lycra and forty years of lonely.

Parting from Dag in the lobby with promises to meet tomorrow at the Village, Mieko gazed up at him. Was it possible to die of happiness?

'This coffee-house near the Japanese compound, okay?' he said, inking a large blue cross on the map of the Village. 'If we miss each other, just stay put, I'll find you. Don't get lost, huh?'

'Stay put? Tell, please, what is "stay put" and how I can get lost? All the time you say my English it is better.'

'Well, but it's not great yet, and the Village is going to be a mad-house, first day,' he said. 'If we don't connect — but we will — you have my training schedule, I have yours, so we'll cross paths in the buses —'

'Cross paths?' Again she floundered, far, far out of her depth. This English made her head ache, and when Dag's Swedish friends spoke it with that unfamiliar lilt it was like a whole other language. But then he smiled at her, the most handsome man in the Games — in the world — and she knew nothing else mattered because they understood each other; for that moment she *almost* understood how so beautiful a man could look at her so often and for so long. 'Okay,' she said, 'I wait for you, I . . . what —' Her small ivory hand flew to her mouth as the hub-bub around them suddenly stilled.

Silence had fallen like a blanket over the chattering,

name-dropping mob as a blast of freezing air swept through the massive lobby doors. A group of new arrivals shouldered through them, four men and a girl all with the unmistakable panache stamping them show business celebrities, even before the athletes of the world broke into sustained, spontaneous applause. The Swedish rock group. In the party atmosphere, four of the internationally famous group acknowledged the tribute and applauded the athletes in return. It was a rare moment, all smiles and warmth and fellowship.

Only their leader stood apart, arrogant, weighted down with patent-leather coat, thick gold chains, and the plastic, immovable smile of a star. Clearly he was 'on'. Behind the ominous shine of black sunglasses he cased the lobby, allowing the light of chandeliers to linger on the diamond in his left earlobe before striking sparks off a bigger, brighter diamond embedded in an upper right incisor. From lacquered head to patent-leather shoes, he glittered. The others sorted luggage, greeted well-known faces from the skating world, instructed bell-boys, shuffled passports, plane tickets, paperback novels, lap-size chess sets, all as their leader stood, arms folded, offering nothing but his spectacular self for the admiration of the crowd.

Beside her Mieko felt Dag Carlsen stiffen as the leader spoke briefly to the bell captain, nodding in Dag's direction. The beige uniform approached Dag and bobbed in a flustered bow. 'Sir, the group asks for you attend them in their suite when they're settled. Perhaps in one hour?'

Dag went very still and Mieko knew from the set of his mouth, just moments ago smiling at her, that the summons was half-expected, but unwelcome, perhaps even dreaded. He responded smoothly but with uncharacteristic formality. 'Is my sister Lise invited?'

The bell captain shook his head. 'There was no mention of her, no, sir. The gentleman was specific.' And only the leader had issued the invitation.

'Please make our apologies. Tomorrow my sister and I have early training. Maybe some other time . . .' Dag let his voice trail off as he took Mieko's arm, deliberately turning his back on the leather-and-gold masterpiece staring at him — or maybe not — through ink-black shades.

Dag drew in a ragged breath. 'Mieko, I have to find Grant Rivers. If you see him, say I've gone to his room, okay? If he's not around I'll have to find my dad. Look, I'm sorry, I really *am* sorry . . .'

He looked so helpless that she didn't think to ask what he was sorry for. Then suddenly he'd gone, disappearing into an elevator, leaving her to watch the green light of its progress as it sped him to Mr Rivers' floor. Only when the light stopped blinking did she realize that she'd never before heard him mention his father, nor had she seen father and son speak to each other, even in passing. Perhaps everywhere it is the same, she thought. She too had not spoken with her father for over a year. She seldom knew where he was and only with great effort could she remember what he looked like. Unsmiling, always hurrying, a single spur in his voice and his walk. Ambition. Like Grandfather in all things but one. In Grandfather, ambition did not show, eclipsed as it was with pride — in tradition, in the family name. Beside her a bell-boy trundled the rock group's luggage into the freight elevator. Dragged monotonously across the grooves of its threshold, the wheels of a dozen suitcases set a locomotive beat to the music of her Grandfather's name: *Nakashima — Nakashima — Nakashima — Nakashima —*

It was the middle of the night, Japanese time, when Hiro Nakashima phoned his daughter at the house in Atami. 'You hear me?' he barked.

'*Hai! Hai! Hai! Hai!*' The call was not unexpected. Alone in the middle of the great hall, antique swords hanging all about her, from habit her head bobbed humbly with every *Hai*! Yes. Yes. Yes. And yes. Anything you say, my father, anything. Even her voice seemed to bow, fast and very low.

'You read the newspapers? Watch the television?'

'I . . .' She closed her eyes. Perhaps a sword would fall upon her neck.

'At dawn send the idiot to town for papers from Osaka, Yokohama, and Kyoto. Expect me for lunch. And pack your things. We are disgraced.'

The receiver crashed in her ear. Her knees weak, she

whimpered as she stretched out on her *futon* as if it were a cross, certain she would never sleep again. *Pack-your-things-pack-your-things-pack-your-things*, the words chased each other around her head like three mice on a wheel. Trembling for Mieko, she waited for the window to lighten.

As she waited fear gathered, every corner of the house filling up with it in concert with roiling clouds over the bay. Perhaps it would rain and he would not come, perhaps. . . but no, Hiro Nakashima would cleave the sky itself to wreak his will. He would arrive as threatened. The housekeeper seemed to know, was up and dressed before first light, so perhaps she too had not slept after the phone call. Probably listened on the extension, claiming a proprietary interest in everything connected with her lord. The possibility that her direst predictions had come to pass would prove to her yet again that only she knew the heart and will of Hiro Nakashima. The knowledge, if she had it, gave her a strident new energy as she ordered a taxi, forgetting even to haggle in advance over the fare.

All too soon she was clumping back into the hall, slapping the papers triumphantly on the table. 'As I thought, the whole town knows and is talking over our business! Satisfied?' Hiro Nakashima's performing she-bear certainly was.

'Please, please, I should like tea, I have a headache . . .'

'You'll have worse than that soon!' But she trundled off to her kitchen and Oka-chan was free now to look at the papers, each worse than she could have imagined. Fighting for calm, she picked up the phone and dialled Mieko's room at the Palacio de Estrellas. When Mieko herself answered, she knew a swift moment of relief. From the papers, it could have been a man!

'Oka-chan!' Mieko sounded warm, welcoming, and intensely happy. Hearing her happiness, her mother was not sure she could bring herself to say what must be said, but she took a quivering breath and began:

'. . .no, no, not in the family papers, he stops them printing such things, but his rivals! All Japan reads the stories, sees the pictures, repeats them on television, they say now that even Nakashima station managers pressure him to use the newsfeeds, to let them show you and the golden one, the boy from Sweden. He tells me our family is dishonoured. He says I must pack my things because you smile upon this young man . . . photos in the hotel . . . holding hands, riding the cable car! He is not pleased, he says we are shamed before our employees, our country. He will be here at noon, I think to order us gone, to say that he is done with us. Where shall we go Mieko, where, where? Who will take us in, give us shelter? How can we live? No use to call your father, even if I knew where —'

She paused to draw breath and Mieko's tear-filled voice broke in, 'Oh Mother, stop! I do nothing wrong, I meet a young man, beautiful like a god and yet he likes me, he likes *me*, speaks with me, helps my English, takes coffee with me, I know he does like me.'

'But he is not *Japanese*, Mieko. Your grandfather is so angry, never have I heard him so . . . so cold . . .'

'Don't cry, please. Be glad for me, I have a friend. I am happy.'

'Now, yes, but when we have nowhere to go —'

'Oka-chan, I have so little time here. In two weeks I must come home.'

'If we have a home to come to, child.'

Oceans howled between them as her mother wept in great gulping sobs. Mieko pictured her wide patient face blotched with tears, and she too wept for Oka-chan's pain, for the prison in which she lived, had always lived, and always would live.

'Mieko, hear me! I call you again after he comes. Now I send his idiot to town again to the machine, what do you call it? Fax. She will fax everything to you at the hotel, you will see what they say, why he is so angry.'

Mieko smiled bleakly into the dead receiver. Fax indeed. Imagine their blundering family retainer, possibly Japan's last living vassal, throw-back to feudal times, faxing pictures across the world! But what could they show, these pictures? She had told Oka-chan the truth, she had done nothing.

The pictures, obviously taken by telephoto lens, confirmed it: she and Dag laughing in the lobby, the picture shot from the mezzanine, focused on their locked fingers; another in the arena, one dark head and one gold, poring over a list of 'speakings' as they laughed together at her mistakes; a fuzzy print of them at the warmhouse door, Dag zipping up her parka against the mountain cold the first night they met. The captions shocked her back to Nakashima reality: 'New Blood for an Old Family?' 'Language of Love' 'Hot on the Slopes'.

As Grandfather had consolidated his power he had inevitably gathered enemies. Now the hyenas closed in — and who to blame but his daughter and her offspring? She remembered the video she had not been intended to see, Grandfather's contempt as he stroked the little carved monkey by Masanao as an orgy went on round him, and knew that a man who set such store by a *netsuke* because it was old, honoured, and *Japanese* would see even innocent encounters between the nations as dangers to be shunned. To build a financial empire on the backs of white consumers demonstrated racial superiority — but to associate with them socially was at best a distasteful necessity for men; unthinkable for a young woman of family. No wonder Oka-chan trembled in fear. Grandfather was correct always, but was it possible for a man to have too much honour? She willed the phone to ring, for Oka-chan to say everything was well.

She almost did. Not well . . . but acceptable.

'Yes Mieko, he is angry, humiliated, and of course he will punish you when you come home, but now he must stem the tide of innuendo — though of course he cannot admit this. Just now he made a statement on TV, our bay in the background, very impressive. His granddaughter has the honour and duty of Japan in her keeping. While she plays her part in the Olympic tradition, making friends for Japan around the world, women as well as men, his enemies at home print lies and distortions. Since they so lack honour as to accuse an innocent child of improprieties, he must dispatch her mother — sorely needed in Atami to manage the family home — to the site of the Games to chaperone his granddaughter. *This* is the new Japan? And so on.'

Mieko shrieked with joy. '*Oka-chan! He is sending you here!*'

'Wait. He showed a picture of you as a baby at the house in Molokai, and he said, "Perhaps other families have less reason to trust; they are to be pitied. The house of Nakashima is proud to send its members anywhere in the world." Then he sent the cameraman away and gave me a plane ticket and a black eye. I hope it will fade quickly.'

'Rice powder!' Mieko cried. Like the housekeeper, Oka-chan was no stranger to black eyes, and was adept at concealing them. 'Oh, I am so glad you will meet my friend.'

'Be happy while you can, my daughter. You may not be so when we come home,' her mother said quietly. 'Today he flew to Hokkaido.'

Mieko's gladness evaporated as snow clouds sailed dark and ominous over the peaks outside. Vultures sensing blood. She shivered. 'Why to Hokkaido so soon, Oka-chan?'

Mother's laugh tinkled like bits of broken glass, all the pain and pretence of their lives swept into one small heap. 'The same reason he made the broadcast. Today you have a reputation left, you are still a desirable match.'

As Mieko hung up, a joyous roar seeped under her door, her cousin leading the Japanese ski team as they cheered a new snowfall. Around her, white mountains frowned to slate and charcoal, finally to black.

When Grant reached his floor after the unveiling of Beejay's dress, Dr Jasinski was waiting in the small square hall that led off to the rooms. 'Roxanne's in her room and needs to see you later, but first the Swedish boy waits by your door. They both seem . . . troubled.'

'Who isn't? These young adults, pardon the term, haven't graduated from emotional primary school yet. Can't Dag go to his father? If his problem is his sister's weight, nothing will help but surgery. Preferably with a machete.'

'With such a father, perhaps the advice of a man. . .'

'Ben's a man.'

'As much as a foetus pickled in alcohol is a baby. Dag is worth saving.'

Grant rubbed his eyes. 'Too bad you took up doctoring. You could have made a fortune in emotional blackmail.'

'Don't forget Roxanne later. She goes to the Village —'

'Tomorrow. Yes, I know.'

Dag was sitting on the carpet in front of Grant's door like a particularly handsome golden setter waiting for its master. Grant let him in. 'Okay, let's have it.'

'The rock group's arrived.'

'So?'

'Something weird about the leader. He more or less ordered me up to his suite. I said no, what else, but I want to know where I stand.'

'On what? Spit it out, Dag. We've all got problems. Right now I've got mine, yours, your sister's, your dad's, Roxanne's, Jeff's, and Beejay's.' And the memory of Deirdre Sterling delicately elbowing in someplace as well.

'Grant, just how much help has the group forked over?'

'Half-sponsorship is what I heard, but the cheques were drawn on Ben's business account. I suspect it's feeling the pinch. Does the source matter?'

'Yeah. The leader wants to see us. Sooner or later he will. I'm not sure how grateful we're expected to be.'

'Send Lise, she's great with the rich-and-handsome.'

'From what Mom hinted, I don't think Lise could cut it with this guy.'

Oh no, not another. First Lloyd, now the rocker. 'Look, I know you and Ben are not exactly buddy-buddy, but you've a right to a straight answer. Just keep out of the star's way, okay? *You don't owe him*, hear me?'

'Uh-huh, but he looks nine feet tall and I think there's a bodyguard.'

'Yeah. See Ben first. If necessary I'll talk to the star tomorrow, but you'll be in a show one day, Dag, handling the come-ons yourself. You shouldn't have to do it at the Olympics, but. . .' But Dag was an innocent, too beautiful for his own good. 'Look, usually a straight "no thanks" works just fine.'

Ben Carlsen took a long time answering his door until Dag whispered an urgent, 'Dad, I gotta ask you something. Like right this minute!'

Right this minute Ben had half a bottle of scotch in him and designs on the other half. 'Wa'ya'wan'? Don't ask f'r no money, 'kay? I got none. . .' Still wearing his suit and shoes, he sprawled on the hotel's beige-on-beige Olympic bedspread, symbol of the family's goal for longer than Dag could remember.

'It's the rock star. How did the sponsorship deal work? Mom said —'

'*Mom! Don't mention her to me, don't even mention* —'

To Dag's horror his father's arm came up over his face, trying with no success at all to stifle a deep, gut-wrenching sob. 'She's left me, l-l-left me . . . don't you s-s-start now . . . the day I've had, I don't know what I've done, whatever I've done to deserve all of this . . . that bitch Emma pointing the finger, and I never, honest to God, I never touched the kid's lousy red frock, so damn plain it looked off a rack at the charity shop! Women! What d'they think I am, huh? I called the house and called, trying all day, nobody home . . . so I call the neighbour, what's-her-name, "Yes!" she says. "Didn't you know? Mrs Carlsen left with a cab full of suitcases . . ."' He began to laugh, the sound more frightening than his sobs. 'Know what she said, the neighbour? "Don't worry, Mr Carlsen, I'm taking good care of Allez Oop for you!" The cat! Who gives a shit about the fucking cat? The house is empty, nobody home, after all these years Mom's gone, left us flat! And not a word!'

He was shouting now. Dag moved closer to the door. 'I just wanted to know about the group, Dad, the guy seems a bit weird.'

Ben laughed again, except his face looked like it was crying. 'Weird? He should be right up your street then, shouldn't he? The wife's left me, my Lise chucks herself at a goddamned Jap, my son's a flaming fairy, my business is on the skids and I'm supposed to take it lying down!' He struggled to sit up and spilled scotch all over the bed. Dag thought of the guy in the LA bar, a flaming fairy but more a man than this one.

'I'm not gay, but I've met some I like a lot better than I like you right now. I want a simple answer, Dad. Who's been picking up the skating tab?'

Ben tried again to stand and this time succeeded, swaying between the reading lamp and a full-length mirror. 'That's another thing! I paid and paid and sent 'em the receipts like we fixed up, they were supposed to pay me half back, but they're shorting me, nar-mean? I got bills running out my ears, the company's damned near shot, but the skating's paid for, oh yes, patsy, me, I paid *my* dues, so if your goddamned rock star's here to collect on his investment he's gonna have ta pay *his* dues first.' His hollow, scooped-out face seemed to crumple like that of an ugly baby as he fell to his knees and tried to grasp Dag's ankles. 'Help me Dag, I'm finished, done for!'

Sickened, shaking with grief, pity or fury, he didn't know which, maybe all three, Dag dumped Ben on the bed, took off his shoes, and threw a blanket over him. He looked down at this man who begged for help, who could even suggest that his son sell himself on the corner so long as the buyer paid the 'dues' in advance — all to keep a sinking business afloat — and wanted desperately to smash the lamp over his father's head. Or over the rock star's head. One louse or another, what was the difference?

It was late, the hotel corridors empty. He roamed them all, neither knowing or caring what floor he was on, an unworldly young man who knew only that his adolescent insecurities had only brushed the borders of this world; that he'd now been pitched head-first into a stink of innuendo, shame, of slime that wouldn't let you breathe. The corridors were civilized, clean, carpeted, but in the wild country of his brain his father's voice sang one song over and over again: *If the star's here to collect, he's gonna have to pay his dues first.* If the rock star paid what it had cost to buy Lise the limelight, what he did later with Dag was fine with Ben. They'd been a decent family. How had Ben sunk so low, to wade into this muck?

On the floor reserved for the Japanese team, he tapped quietly on Mieko's door. He'd not been inside before and wasn't sure she'd let him in now, but she too was weeping, the bed strewn with faxes. He saw and recognized the images, and knew there was a whole lot to talk about with Mieko, too.

It was after midnight. Already she wore her sleeping kimono; her own *futon* from Atami lay unrolled and waiting for her. She'd brushed her hair, done her exercises for the muscles of her legs. It was beyond time for sleep. She *must* not invite him in; in her world every wall and door had the ears of Hiro Nakashima pressed to it. But Dag Carlsen's blue eyes were filled with clouds, and if she loved him how could she turn him away?

'You look like a little girl,' he said. 'A sad little girl. What's the trouble?'

She shook her head. 'Sad'. Another word she did not know.

'Unhappy,' he said. 'That makes two of us.' This she understood. Much of her English had been learned from American movies.

Perhaps he moved first, perhaps she, but she was in his arms, tight enough to feel his heart beating through his shirt and her thin cotton kimono as he rocked her, his fingers stroking her hair. 'Don't cry,' he whispered. 'Today — yesterday now, I guess — has been a bummer all round.'

His sympathy, his nearness, and the knowledge that in less than two weeks he wouldn't be near again, ever, brought on a fresh torrent of tears which she hid against his shirt, afraid to show him her swollen eyes. But he lifted her chin and looked into them anyway, dabbed at them with a tissue and gave her another for her nose.

'Blow, and tell me about it, huh?'

Blow. Oh, shame! Like Oka-chan used to say when she was small. But she *was* small, only up to his chest.

Controlling her shaking fingers she gave him the faxes and all the problems she faced, Grandfather's anger, his statement on TV and radio stations, the family's enormous wealth and its emotional poverty, the promising young man from Hokkaido, Oka-chan's black eye and the possibility of worse to come when they returned.

'But that's medieval, Mieko! We're almost through with the twentieth century! Nobody has to put up with that!'

'You don't understand. I am only a girl, a woman. He has no grandsons. It makes him crazy. There must be Nakashima men for the companies . . .'

He pulled her on to his lap in the large chair. 'So the rich got problems too.' He told her about his mother leaving his father to return to Sweden just this week, about Ben's drinking, the business going under, about Dad trashing Beejay's dress because it had to be Dad or how did he know so much about it? He told her about the rock star and what Dad had said, as if he, Dag, were a property to be loaned out to the top bidder just so long as Lise. . . 'See? We've all got problems.'

He tilted up her face and kissed her softly, the way an adult kisses a child, but her arms slipped around his neck and her lips pressed and opened under his. His arms tightened and he stirred beneath her and groaned.

'Mieko, listen. I want to stay, to make love to you, but you were raised —'

She nodded. 'I never have but I want . . . well . . . you know I am —'

'A virgin. If I stay here now, you won't be. The guy from Hokkaido wouldn't like that a whole lot. But maybe you won't want to go back, maybe you'll give Sweden a try.'

'*Not go back to Japan*?' Again tears welled up in disbelief. She'd heard him wrong. 'You don't know Grandfather. His pride, reputation.'

'And his problem! A company in the next century, a mind still back with the *shoguns*. If you don't go back what's the worst he can do to you?'

She closed her eyes. 'It's what he can do to my mother! But I love Japan, my Grandfather, never before I speak of him like this.' But now she loved this man too, wanted to kiss his eyes, touch his golden face, watch his smile curve under her lips. Reaching, she placed his hand slowly, experimentally, on her breast and gasped with the pleasure of his touch. Quickly she moved it away, pressed his fingers to her lips instead.

'What did I tell you,' he said quietly. 'If I stay now. . .'

She swallowed hard and pushed herself away from him. 'We have almost two weeks. We can think, you will meet my mother —'

At the door he studied her face, stroked its flat ivory planes and thought of Ben; the empty craters of his face where flesh and values used to be.

'Mieko, you look so good to me that I don't ever want to stop.'

She hid her face against his chest. 'Please not to joke me. Your sister is good-looking.'

He shook his head. 'It's not the same thing, sweetheart.'

267

CHAPTER TWENTY-SIX

Waiting, Roxanne heard Grant's private quiet signal-tap at her door. She shot the deadbolt, slid the chain off, and opened a crack just wide enough for him to squeeze through. He didn't have to remind her to re-lock it. To be certain, she switched the portable radio to soft music and set it behind the door; no way, now, could they be overheard.

Grant looked drawn and harassed, and she felt a sharp stab of guilt to be dragging him from his sleep again. Five students at the Games were at least three too many; they never had time alone now, but before the Village swallowed her up she needed reassurance, not just that he loved her but that he'd love her win or lose. *Win or lose.* She still wasn't skating like last year; she had every spin in the world, but half her big jumps were gone; she knew that if she pushed it she'd fall and fall again, but eventually she'd hit the timing on some — but Olympic ice couldn't be tumble sessions, not for the favourite. She wondered what excuses Grant trotted out to the judges as he made the rounds each day, mending her fences.

He kissed her, pulled her on his lap, and stroked back her hair. 'You're looking better. Still a bit thin. Promise you'll eat at the Village, huh?'

'As much as I can. It was dumb, shrinking my appetite on the starvation game back home, but Jasinski looks out for me.'

'Hmm. He'll check on you in the Village. So this visit means you just want the pleasure of my company? Or has Noni been at you again?'

'Both — and something else. Sure I wanted to see you before the Village, well, you know that . . . but a few things are bugging me . . . like the jumps? I'm out of condition,

268

and yes, I know it's my own fault, but look, Grant, I've *got* to work triples someplace where nobody's counting falls —'

He laid a finger over her lips. 'Say no more. I have *very* private ice lined up in two rinks, Barcelona and Perpignan. Spain and France. How's that for touring while you train? But you'll see no scenery, sorry. Both rinks are a hundred miles plus, by fast car, and since we need closed rinks, you'll jump the nights away, nobody there but thee and me. I've got team permission to spring you from the Village, hush-hush. We'll work the triples till you're black-and-blue, and some will come back. You'll have to make up your sleep any way you can. A deal?'

'A deal? I feel like you just shook a rock out of my boots!' And like he was making a last-ditch effort to land Gold. But for her? Or for him?

'Private ice was a breeze. Now for the blizzard. What's with Noni?'

She hesitated. Loyalty, guilt, and exasperation were tearing her apart. 'Mom and Grossmutti try to get me alone every day. I hear them whisper at the door and one of them turns that knob every hour I'm in here. Maybe they think I'll slip-up, forget to lock it one time.'

'Why didn't you tell me?'

'I'm twenty-two, Grant! Jasinski says anybody but a skater would be self-sufficient by now. You can't hold my hand forever. After all these years I shouldn't even need my coach at competition at all!'

'And put me out of a job? Look, Jasinski's great but he doesn't know the sport. This is the biggest of the big-time. I trained you at home. Here, I run interference and help you find a few lost triples. Did you talk to the corridor guards about Noni bothering you? Or not?'

'I tried. They no speaka da English.'

'Bull. Noni got at them.'

Roxanne's face burned at the euphemism. Noni must have given them a preview of her charms to keep their eyes shut as she passed them in the hall. 'It'll be over tomorrow, Village security's tight. They can't get in without badges and Noni wouldn't slip me pills this close to the Games anyway. She understands all about the blood and urine tests. No, the thing is, with all the Security there . . . I'll only ever see them at rink practice.'

'So? Isn't that what you want?'

She sighed, wanting to explain without sounding weak, vacillating. 'I guess, but right or wrong they worked their wholes lives to get me to the Olympics in top-spot. I feel like a louse shutting them out of the glory. To them it *is* glory, they think I can't lose, that the medal's in the bag. Reality's taken a hike for the duration. They don't realize they're drivers. They've pushed me and pushed me, and they think it's all been for my benefit.'

'Stage mothers always think that, love, and I'll tell you something. A lot of them overdo it, yes, but with no moms or pops cracking the whip there'd be damned few stars. Don't quote me, but the world's full of kids who want to be skaters, gymnasts, dancers, you name 'em, you'll find 'em; dreaming of fame until they find dreams come in one colour combo: black-and-blue. With no mothers urging 'em on, most would give up at the first bruise. It's brutal, you know that. On your own, would you have kept at it?'

'No way.'

'Yeah, so now you're grateful they pushed — but you can't afford to lower your guard just now. They shove too hard, badger you to think thin, skate pretty, forget the big jumps — but Noni and her mom are twenty years out of date. You can't afford to be. You've seen the quality here, tougher all the time. It'll be harder than we expected but I still think you can do it.'

Why did it sound so forlorn? She was still favourite, he was her coach — but even he only *thought* she could do it.

'And if I can't?' She held her breath, his light cologne coming at her like a lovely memory, as if he were already in the past, as if —

'That's skating. Right or wrong you've tried all your life to please somebody else. After the Games you can please you. Whatever Roxanne wants —'

Roxanne wants Grant Rivers, that's all! But she knew better now than to say it. Grant avoided clinging vines, jealousy, possession. 'Promises, promises,' she said as lightly as she could.

His deep-brown eyes smiled. 'Would I lie to you?'

No. He wouldn't bother. 'Sure. I figure you'll live it up the minute they lock me up in the Village. You can get in, but I can't get out.'

He shrugged. 'Socialising's part of the sport, you know that. We speak a language nobody else knows. We are all we've got and we give the sport most of it. I'm even driving one of my brats to Barcelona and Perpignan, missing my beauty sleep and everything. Some would call that dedication above and beyond. Hell, it's a rough life but somebody's got to live it. You know what they say, a coach's work is never done.'

She smiled with him but she was never sure. Why couldn't he let her be sure that they had a future together that wasn't tied to skating?

'So, Miz Kramer, that's Noni and the ice squared away. Now what could be next on the agenda? There must be something, you'd never have sloshed "Joy" all over yourself and summoned me to the presence just for business.'

He was laughing at her still, yet she knew he wanted to make love. It was just that he'd never ask, never initiate anything. The first move had to be hers, always. She nuzzled his neck and circled a shirt button.

'Didn't we agree to fast until after the Games?' he said.

Her fingers paused on the second button. Don't play cat-and-mouse, she thought, just once pursue me, make the first move — but he never would. For the first time she saw the pattern of Grant Rivers' life clearly, all its edges sharply defined: he never set himself up for rejection. He'd rather die, so he never asked; the risk must be hers. She closed her eyes, uncertain what to do with this new perception. She'd found the key but she wasn't sure which way to turn it, how to unlock him. Maybe she'd have to figure out what, or who, had locked him into the pattern to begin with, but persuading him to talk about his past was like mining gold with your bare knuckles. Even harder, she thought bleakly, than winning it.

Slowly she unbuttoned his shirt. One of them had to.

Emma woke to a sharp, crisp morning as freshly white as the three envelopes which silently and separately slid under her door during the night. She grinned as she brushed her teeth.

Two hours before the string of luxury buses purring outside the lobby would transport the athletes to the Village, where they'd be safe from the world if not from each other. But off-stage drama panted in the wings, could barely wait. The ingredients of major competition were seasoned and thickening, the political pot turned up to 'simmer'. Before the buses left, the stew would be at a rolling boil which, according to every recipe Emma had ever read, was when you stirred like crazy, and hoped to God it didn't burn.

In the shower Beejay sang Sterling's music at the top of her lungs, so wildly off key it was more 'Probable Nightmare' than 'Impossible Dream' — but not many kids sang at competitions and she was relieved Beejay still could, that she didn't chew her nails, that she slept like a top and enjoyed it all, even performances better than her own. Soon this room would be quiet for the run of the Games. She tried not to think of Beejay alone, at the mercy of experienced psych-out artists. When the rink cleared for finals, the honeyed tongues of top stars just naturally turned sharp, lethal as ice-picks — many a first-timer opened her programme with a bewildered sob: 'Lord, you should *see* the press section out there, SRO already!' . . . 'A zillion experts at the cameras, playing back every fall in slow-mo, over and over and over . . .' 'I'd hate like hell to flop tonight, the whole damn world watching.' 'Trying your big combo after all? In finals? You *brave* little thing!' Brave translated to risky, to foolish, then to inevitable disaster. The minute they called you brave your nerve snapped like a twig. With her judge's badge Emma could get behind the scenes, no sweat, but it wasn't smart to hover. Beejay had got this far without a prop; with any luck she'd go the whole route alone, emerge the other side an adult, undamaged and mature, which would be a miracle in itself. Right now she emerged from the shower. Her red hair on end from the dryer, she looked like she'd jammed her finger into a power socket.

'Guess what Alex Finsky told me,' she said, raking her fingers through the mop. 'We can eat at any compound in the Village we like. In bed last night I got it mostly worked out. About twelve dinners to go, right? Japan for *tempura*; Spain, *paella*; Germany, beer sausage; Norway and Finland do great fish, Alex said; Sweden drenches herring in sour cream'n'onions; then I thought China for sweet'n'sour; I'd planned Greece for baclava but I don't fancy grape leaves and I forgot to ask Finsky if he knows —'

'*You* forgot to ask something? *You*?'

'Can we have a main course in one country and dessert in another?'

'While you're solving the world's food surplus, will you pass the dryer? Thanks. So what did you decide, grape leaves and baclava? Or what?'

'Dunno. I fell asleep in Austria. What's all that mail?'

'Official secrets. Private.'

'Mom, you're only judging *Men's*. I could place *them* myself!'

'No kidding. Want to tell me, just so I don't make a fool of myself?'

'Sure. If they skate their best it's Finsky for Gold; Boston Bean for Silver; the Canadian for Bronze. Or the Czech or Jeffie, depending.'

Emma laughed. Beejay might not know where in the world her next meal would come from, but she'd make one hell of a judge. 'You know they can't all skate their best, they never do.'

'So? That makes it a horse race, right?' Beejay checked her watch. 'Holy cow, I should be in the lobby, we're first bus out, when will —'

'I'll see your practice, you're after Men's on the big rink, okay?'

'Gotcha.' Beejay paused at the door. 'Sure my outfit's safe in Security?'

'If it isn't you're all in trouble. Roxi, Lise, Jeff, Dag, all the costumes are locked in a vault, round the clock guards and German shepherds yet! Talk about security, the Queen of England should get so lucky.'

'Hell, what can she expect from Corgis? She should go for bigger dogs.'

'I'm sure she'd want to know that. Why don't you tell her?'

'I will if I ever run into her. See ya!'

The door slammed and Beejay was gone. Was Emma abnormal, she wondered, enjoying the company of her own kid, dreading the day when she lost her to some show, and eventually to a man? Nah! Beejay was a keeper. They could be at opposite ends of the earth and still know what the other was thinking. Emma turned her attention to the notes:

Emma Dear: Do they still 'do' dinner in California? If so, let's. Not necessarily today. I know you're busy; I'm only an alternate this competition, so I've lots of time and it's all yours — Nils.

Emma: After we get the kids off to camp, let me pick your straightforward brain, maybe even a word to the Committee? Noni and mum are laying seige to the German judges; the old girl's as subtle as a left-hook, and Noni might as well sashay through the lobby with an ad on her G-string. Some official should drop them a hint before they do any damage. You?. . . Grant.

Dear, sweet, incorruptible Emma: How naughty to return my little tribute — you'll at least let me give you luncheon? I'll call you this morning. . . Pleadingly, Willi.

Problems. Emma ripped the notes from Grant and Willi to shreds and flushed them down the toilet. No point taking chances. Noni caused more trouble than the other parents put together — and Willi Vanilla — what a pair they'd make; in tandem they'd make the Mafia look like toddlers.

Good to hear from Nils, though. On impulse she picked up the phone and called his room, arranging to meet him that night.

Grant she'd catch at the rink, but from his note this sounded like it would take an urgent meeting of team leaders. If only Noni would keep her glittery fingernails out of politics . . . you'd think she'd have learned by now that you didn't win competitions on your back; worse, it made no friends and it could sure make enemies fast. And the way Roxanne was skating, enemies were the last thing she, or the team, needed.

She tried to put Willi out of her mind for now. Tomorrow there'd be a reminder, no doubt. Like a faithful hound he'd track her until he cornered her before baring his pale yellow porcelains. It looked bad, to be seen with the Willis of this world, but you never knew when they'd come at you, grab your arm as if you were best buddies and start a yo-ho-ho chat. Once they hooked in they could give lessons to a leech. Lord, oh lord, how could she have forgotten? She was judging Mens. Willi's grandson. Wouldn't it be the pits if Willi were to judge —

She riffled through the sheaf of colour-coded hand-outs that arrived daily, listing competitors, judges, everybody but sweepers-up. Colours made your own stuff easy to spot and the others easy to chuck — she'd checked the blues for Men. She was listed as 'Judge No.5, Mrs Emma Crisp, USA'. Idle curiosity had made her leaf through green for Pairs and yellow for Dance before heaving them into the trash, so why hadn't she checked pink to see who'd be judging Ladies? Because subconsciously she did not want to know? To know was to be tempted. To be a tad more cordial than you might normally be, especially if a judge you didn't like showed up on your daughter's panel. If you did like them it was worse. Then, you daren't risk a friendly 'Hi!' in case they got the wrong message. Pink. Here they were. List of judges and damn, damn, damn, there he was. 'Judge No.3, the creep's name', aka Willi Vanilla. Poor ole Beejay, one judge lost before she even competed! Save it for Nils, she thought, he'd know how to handle Willi. But first, solve this shinola for the home team. Set Noni and her mom straight.

The Committee held the informal meeting at a table in a quiet bar, a coffee pot brought in, the radio chirping cheery morning music in the background. It looked business-like, Grant thought: himself a detached observer watching out for the interests of his student; Emma and a senior US official chatting affably to Noni; beside her, Brigitta smiling upon them, honoured to be included in what she'd taken, at first, as a strategy session for Roxanne's ascent of Olympus. But smiles fade, none faster than Brigitta's. In no time at all her wig fairly bobbed with outrage and Noni's metallic orange fingertips tapped a furious semaphore on the edge of the table.

'You forget,' Brigitta interrupted, her cheeks two round red beacons. 'We are Brauns, not new to the sport. We know how things are done.'

'That's part of the problem, Frau Braun,' the US official slipped in silkily. 'If you and Mrs Kramer were anonymous nobodies, who would care if you chatted to old friends? But you're both ex-champions. It's because you *are* so famous, *are* remembered with affection, that people notice . . . and . . . er . . . gossip when you spend time in judging circles. All old, trusted friends, of course *we* know that. With your accomplishments, you're naturally on a first name basis with everyone of stature —'

Brigitta, thin and stiff as a taper in a grey polyester suit, began to melt. To be sure she'd catch every word, the official had spoken slowly, lingering lovingly over 'famous' and 'affection' and 'accomplishments' and 'stature'.

Noni looked him over with a speculative little gleam; he was old for her, but finely tailored, groomed, wealthy — and dripping with clout.

Grant wanted to laugh. This chap was wasted on skating; he'd be a nine-day wonder in politics. His voice alone sang you to sleep.

The official had decided early that Brigitta held the reins; that for Noni the winds of change were never still. 'You *do* see our position, Frau Braun?'

'*Ja*! Buried as we are in Bonn, we forget we have a great name, responsibility. And so happy to see old friends —'

'Easy to get carried away,' the official murmured obligingly. 'An awkward sport, ours . . . subjective judging . . . not only must we be impartial but we must *appear* to be. A tightrope, Frau Braun . . . *such* a relief to deal with an intelligent woman who understands. . .'

Brigitta blushed, almost pretty in her pleasure, but he wasn't done. 'We all think highly of Roxanne, you've done a splendid job with her. It would be too tragic if anyone said something to impair —'

Noni's fingernails picked up tempo; her mode shifted from speculation to indignation. 'Then how to get the word out, tell us that? You Americans *invented* advertising, how can you sell a product you don't talk up?'

'As I said, Mrs Kramer — with all the media ballyhoo it's easy to lose sight of the ideal. Exactly what product is for sale here? None. We are at the Olympics.' His voice sank in reverence before rising sharply to disapproval. 'We're not beating the drum for Oscar night in Hollywood, you know!'

But he'd misjudged Noni. She came back fighting. 'And Maureen Sterling's father? Who will zip Lloyd Sterling's lip?'

Mr Smooth looked over his shoulder before turning the charm up a notch. Something in the gesture pulled Grant forward in his chair. 'It is suspected, Mrs Kramer, that Lloyd is not here . . . er . . . canvassing for his daughter,' the official murmured. 'In any case, we can safely leave him to the British officials.'

Next to him, Grant heard Emma's heavy sigh as she gathered up her purse and turned purposefully towards Nils, who'd just entered the bar behind Willi. 'Excuse me, an old friend.' Outflanking Willi Vanilla's sly approach, she let Nils lead her to a table for two in another corner.

'See!' Noni hissed. '*She's* a judge *and* her daughter's competing! Did you order *her* not to talk to friends? No!'

What remained of the official's smile frosted over. 'Mrs Kramer! Nils is an Alternate, unlikely to be judging — and surely *you'll* recall he was an old friend of Dave Crisp, who we *all* remember as a *good* man —' He allowed himself a slight emphasis. '— too young to have died as he did. Was it only yesterday in the judge's lounge we spoke of his death? Emma and Beejay lost a wonderful husband and father. We can't restore him to them, but we all can and must offer them the comfort and support of old friends.' He stood, bowed slightly, and left.

Neatly done, Grant thought. The reference to discussions in the Judges' Lounge had been heavy-handed and probably a lie, but soft words didn't muzzle pinschers. Only the flick of a whip caught their attention. It certainly seemed to have caught Noni's. Her lips puckered to an impotent 'O' as she drew furiously on another cigarette. Grant checked the clock over the bar. She'd be more furious when she realized she'd missed Roxanne's departure for the Village — and her last chance to get the girl alone before competion. Thank God he'd stymied her request for a chaperone's badge to get her behind the scenes and into the Village. Roxanne was twenty-two. What, he'd asked, did she need with a chaperone? They understood perfectly. She could still make the rink sessions, but with blades on Roxi's feet what was easier than ducking an embarrassing Mom whose high-heels were stuck firmly in the press section of the bleachers'?

But Roxanne knew Noni as Grant was beginning to. Because her mother's nerves balanced on edges thinner by far than Roxanne's blades, Noni could never be written off. Five students needed some attention some of the time; Noni Kramer bore watching all of the time.

CHAPTER TWENTY-SEVEN

Action in the lobby rose to fever-pitch as team buses pulled out one by one, drivers waving cards with hastily scrawled numbers and initials. A bus with GRB No.2 shook and thundered at the curb as Lloyd softly tapped in one last exhortation. 'Remember, Jeff, when it's all over we'll have the holiday of a lifetime! Anywhere you want to go, dear boy, anywhere at all.'

'Thanks Lloyd, but right now —' Jeff tore himself away, sharply aware of Maureen Sterling smiling coolly from her seat on the team bus. Lloyd hadn't told his daughter goodbye or good luck. From the bus steps, Jeff turned to wave at Lloyd. Toodley-pooh, old cock. When it was all over he'd tell Lloyd just where to shove his holiday of a lifetime.

But looking down he felt a twinge of pity for this ageing lover-boy, for his big false teeth, his liver-spots encroaching like rust through the cultivated shine of thin silvery hair. Jeff Dunsmuir shivered. He'd never let himself get that old, no way! Jeez, Lloyd must be fifty-five if he was a day!

Mieko Nakashima waited stubbornly for Oka-chan's arrival before she would allow the team leader to assign her a seat on the Japanese bus. Any second she'd be here, but until Mieko saw her with her own eyes —

'Oka-chan!' She struggled out of the couch to greet her mother for the first time on foreign soil. But Mother? *This stranger was Mother*? Her Oka-chan? Had the rice powder worked? And how to know? Oka-chan wore dark glasses, a black fur coat and boots, her hair swept back in a glossy bun skewered with a single jade and gold pin; matching earrings swung to her shoulders; as she turned, a glimpse of jade-green silk flashed at her throat. Here, in the midst of athletes laden like pack-horses with skis and skates and costumes, Hiro Nakashima's daughter stood unhampered, exotic, almost a jewel herself among the clutter of the Games.

'Oka-chan, you have lipstick on, you look. . .'

Her mother embraced her, whispering swiftly in Japanese. 'Fantastic, I know. Imagine. All my life I am plain, he tells me so, but when I go away on his business, in the light of Nakashima cameras, he sends me stylists, artists to make me . . . not lovely, that I can never be, but . . . well, interesting —'

'Elegant, Mother. You're . . . what do you mean, cameras?'

Oka-chan's laugh had a bitter ring that cut Mieko to the bone. 'He had them at the airport, I must be seen hurrying to protect his granddaughter, our name. In the eyes of our people I must make jackals of his enemies.'

For all that they noticed the hubbub around them, the two women could have been on a desert island. 'And *your* eye?' Mieko said at last.

'Still swollen.' Oka-chan shrugged. 'But without the black eye and the trip how would I know I can look mysterious?' Now she really laughed, and for the only time that Mieko remembered, her mother showed her teeth, did not cover her mouth in the customary gesture. 'I tell you, Mieko, now I know what I *can* be, it will be difficult to be humble again. He made a mistake throwing me to the pack, making me answer for him. In Japan I am now a celebrity. Me! When I call a press conference, reporters come!' With this smile she did cover her mouth — the habits of a lifetime did not blow away in the jet-stream of one overseas trip, however long.

Quickly Mieko explained that she must go, Mother must get her badge for the Village, must come today to the compound and the rink, must watch her skate, '— and meet my friend. You *must* like him, Mother!' She blushed.

'Will they let me in?' For an instant it was the old Oka-chan, fearful, of no importance to her father and of none therefore to her world.

'Of course. How can you chaperone me if you are not there? You must sleep at the hotel, but you can visit me at the Village any time, meet *all* my new friends, not just . . .

well, you know. Maureen Sterling talks to me, she is very beautiful, but unhappy I think, maybe more unhappy than us. Beejay Crisp — she has electric hair — is never unhappy. Roxanne Kramer is the star, she has much pride, but I think she might be afraid of her mother. And of course there is my *very best* new friend, Dag Carlsen, whose picture you have seen? His sister Lise looks like a movie star.'

The bus driver tapped her shoulder, which was fortunate because Mieko's face darkened as she said Lise's name, and Oka-chan knew then that the Carlsen family was no happier than their own. Or the Sterlings, obviously. Or the Kramers. She sighed, watching her daughter disappear into the bus. Did skating make unhappy families? Or perhaps it was the other way, that unhappy families came to skating to escape their misery? Turning, she caught a reflection of a mysterious woman in a mirrored panel, smiled at herself, and stood taller. Because Hiro Nakashima's daughter had been unhappy did not mean she must always be so. Nor must Mieko, oh no! Now they knew the secret. To wait. Even the powerful made mistakes.

The middle-aged watch-dog, who Father had sent along to keep her out of mischief, beckoned a bell-boy. Without a word Oka-chan swept to Registry to claim her badge. The watch-dog could not get one of these no matter how many pockets Hiro Nakashima lined with yen. Badge in hand, she snapped her fingers and handed him her key. 'You may unlock my room,' she said.

'But the bell-boy —' had already loaded four large suitcases onto a trolley.

'My father sent you half-way round the world to assist me. What do I need with a boy who cannot understand my words?'

Following her father's flunky into the lift, she saw his humble head droop and realized how swiftly power could turn to arrogance. A dangerous weapon, this power, one she must learn to use with skill.

Mieko and her mother were gone when Dag Carlsen appeared in the lobby with friends from the Finnish, Norwegian and Swedish ski teams, one golden boy among an army of them, their suntans from the Telemark and Riksgränsen mountains no less rich than Dag's from the beaches of Malibu. All smiled the enviable white smiles that came with perfect tans, matched sets of healthy good looks, living guarantees of perfect happiness. Maybe.

Dag should have blended in and strolled on by — but a pair of ink-black sunglasses and a leather coat still dressed the plush set of the lobby. The rock star had not given up, had in fact hung around for three hours. With no accreditation for the competitor venues, after this morning he must rely on the rink itself during practice sessions — an iffy proposition for a man given to certainties. He looked relaxed, easy, but behind the black glass his eyes blazed with a fierce blue anger that would have matched and beaten Ben Carlsen's any day of the week. Behind him, a giant who made no attempt to look anything but what he was, a body-guard. As the blond horde tumbled past, white and cold and carefree, the star moved.

'Carlsen,' he murmured. His hand, smothered in rings but surprisingly strong, clamped fast to Dag's wrist. 'I said to come to the suite. You didn't.'

Dag's heart pounded but he had little choice. He stopped. The blond army stopped with him. 'Talk to my dad, he's got something for you.'

The star smiled a slow invitation, well rehearsed in front of a mirror. 'Your dad's got nothing I want. You do.' The jewelled hand shifted to Dag's thigh. 'You're . . . gorgeous.'

'You're pathetic. Get lost.'

The rock star licked his lips as he squeezed Dag's thigh. 'Mm, muscles . . .'

Dag punched the hand away and then everything happened at once. The body-guard lunged forward. White smiles vanished. The blond army closed in, blocking the guard, leaving the rock star to Dag. The star backed away, eyeing the hostile army which just last night had cheered him to the rafters. Now they simply stared.

'Hey you guys, this is between Dag and me, I'm just collecting what's —'

As he spoke, Ben Carlsen's head seemed to float on the star's shoulders, saying, *He's here to collect on his investment.*

Dag had never punched a soul in his life, but when his fist came up there was no question it would connect. His hands, granite hard from years of clutching Lise on overheads, were primed. The star's jaw fell. No time to duck, protect his caps, look for a body-guard who should have been there and wasn't. Just Dag's bunched fist coming at him like a sledge-hammer. The crunch of bone on bone sickened and satisfied Dag at the same time. Perhaps he'd aimed at the star, perhaps at his father, and maybe it didn't matter because maybe there was no damned difference! Instinctively he checked his knuckles. Two bled a little, and one grated ominously as he flexed it. Not too bad. Tape, aspirin, a shot of pain-killer into the knuckle — he'd be able to hoist Lise for the Games, no sweat.

But now Lise was forgotten as behind him the skiers applauded Dag Carlsen as loudly as they had welcomed the rock group last night — but their bodies still blocked the guard as the hotel manager hurried forward with prissy little steps to help the star up from the beige carpet on which for some reason he lay sprawled among the custom-woven Olympic rings.

'Everything . . . satisfactory, gentlemen?' Glancing swiftly at the new carpet (no blood, thank God), he eased the star into a Danish lounge chair next to a table of Italian marble. 'Coffee, sir? A brandy? A doctor?'

The star massaged his chin, anxious to reassure the manager, get rid of him before the press closed in, but as he opened his mouth a chip of porcelain clinked against the marble. A shattered incisor. The diamond. Oh shit!

The golden army laughed, hoisting Dag shoulder high, flashing their undamaged smiles at the star as they tumbled into the bus with such joyful babble you'd think no Scandinavian had ever punched a soul before. Dag, remembering his gentle mother, thought it possible they had not, except for cause. For all their size they were reasonable people, not counting the rock star of course — but what was one crooked stick in a hail of golden arrows?

As the bus waited for a green light, an Oriental woman stepped out of the lobby and lifted her face to the bus and the winter sun of Montegreco. She wore plain clothes impeccably cut, and walked with short, confident steps to a taxi, ignoring an anxious-faced man who seemed uncertain if he should follow. Like the rock star, the woman wore sunglasses. Unlike him, she had dignity. Dag closed his eyes and tasted again the salt of a young girl's tears as she told of Oka-chan's black eye. So this was Mieko's mother. Then the taxi shot away in front of their bus and she was gone.

As the Scandinavian buses revved up to a trembling thunder, the Russian team, their turn next, assembled on the pavement. Their officials lined up tidily, stern-faced and determined, clipboards under right arms, umbrellas under left. The skaters were less regimented, but to Dag's eyes their Pairs looked depressingly hard and slim and disciplined; how could they lose? The ice-dancers, more exotic, were equally disciplined. Single skaters and their coaches all swarmed round a street vendor with Western magazines; in the centre of the group one scared young girl, their Lady champion's replacement, tried and failed to look as if she belonged.

Finsky, as usual, did not try. He leaned against an ornate lamp-post, eyes closed in what could have been boredom. Dag was not fooled. No one who knew Finsky would be. Behind a still face his mind never switched off. Of the entire team, Finsky alone chose not to wear the uniform. Perhaps, Dag thought, he declined to accept orders at all. In a team of awesome depth and strength, Finsky was the strongest of the strong. Dag envied him. How must it feel, to know that Olympic Gold was yours for the taking?

Her voice had come from a damp, draughty flat in the Park complex of Moscow, her distress sighing over the frozen marshes of the Pripet, across the upper reaches of the Black Forest and the silver ribbon of the Rhine to accuse Alexei — who was equally powerless to cushion her loss and the knowledge that she was a pawn in a game for which she lacked the skill and the power.

From his plush hotel room he'd wanted to give her sympathy, warmth — but he resisted, would not take the bait. Make them sweat, as he did. As Galina did. He'd reached the new number first try, which meant that somewhere between Moscow and Montegreco they had an audience. Machines listened and recorded. So he too was a pawn; temporarily he had the power and skill to play the game, but the weight of Galina's love handicapped him more surely than prison bars or a ball and chain.

'It's *not* good!' she'd answered him, close to tears. 'No meat for a week, the heater cracked. Now it's fixed but today Mother found flea-bites on her neck. She is shamed, wants to complain, make them spray, but Father . . . you know how he is.' And how *she* was, faced with a faceless bureaucracy and a father so paranoid he'd grovel at his own shadow.

'Too bad,' Alexei said, deliberately cold. 'Here all is new, very fine, the hotel a palace, ice like satin, food. . . Galina, they fly in fresh produce every morning from Spain and Israel, meat from France, Germany, fish of every kind, too much to comprehend. And the shops, well, you know the West! These are the best yet, I don't have to tell you.' Every word baiting, tempting, beckoning. Come. There is nothing to hold you. Yes, I love your parents, but leave them, your devoted mother, your foolish father who will not see that the prison doors are open, have been for years. Leave them alone to their misery. He said none of this: they were not alone, any of them, so long as the unseen audience recorded their voices. But Galina knew all the arguments too, by now.

'You're skating well?' she asked, making words because she could not say what must be said and was reluctant to break the fragile connection.

'Of course. I have trained well. How can I skate badly?' Each word slow and clear for the benefit of the 'bug'.

'Your competition?'

'USA and Canada good, a Brit boy who could be trouble on a good day, a Czech who is sound and a Japanese boy coming on strong for next time.'

'And *my* replacement?' Her voice had sharpened, so perhaps she did resent this young usurper thrown in only to hold Galina in Moscow.

'Galina, the kid's frightened. Out of her depth.'

'I know.' Now the inevitable question. 'When will you be back?'

'After the Games I must do Worlds, then the tour. Europe, America . . .' He was afraid to dwell on that. Last year they'd done the tour together, and it had been like a honeymoon, each new city building their love and their understanding of the other.

'And after?' Her voice flattened under its weight of anxiety.

After. This had been, was still, his dilemma. 'I thought a holiday . . .' He did not specify where or with whom, but in spite of himself he said 'I miss you,' because suddenly, fiercely, he did. And the possibility he might never see her again hurled him to panic stations. 'Galina! Insist you be moved out of The Park!' he shouted. 'Don't be afraid, they can do nothing —'

'I know. They *will* do nothing. They will not answer — or reinstate me . . .'

She was right. There was nothing more for 'them' to do. The next move was his. Win a medal and take it home.

'Will they let you phone me from the Village?' she said.

Of course 'they' would. They were now an audience anxious to know which way he'd jump. As Galina was anxious. As he was anxious.

And now this morning the Director had treated him with velvet gloves, offered him breakfast in the French restaurant instead of the Competitor's Room, invited him to share his limo to the Village rather than take the bus. '— with the rank and file,' he said smoothly, dismissing the rest of the team with a contemptuous flick of the wrist.

Alexei declined everything. He'd shunned the Director and the team, and taken coffee and a croissant with Maureen Sterling, who was at the hotel only to be signed in and transported to the Village and, like himself, obviously shunning the crowds. Alexei had asked about her mother.

'Not well, but we're keeping it quiet. She hopes to come down for finals, but she said to invite you when I saw you. When it's over, will there be time to visit us before you go on to Worlds and the tour?'

Didn't this girl know? But of course she must, she was too intelligent not to know how good she was. 'You'll be on the tour yourself, Maureen.'

She shook her head. 'No. Even if I won a medal and was sent to Worlds.' To be invited on the tour was an honour, the pressure of competition over, a sightseeing dream-trip in which intense friendships were formed, where you were whisked like royalty from one major city to another round the globe to skate exhibition numbers; easy, fun. The tour admitted you to an exclusive club of perhaps fifteen members — and after six weeks or so the club disbanded forever. 'I couldn't leave her,' she said simply.

'Maureen, the tour's the one part of competition that's a pleasure!'

She nodded. 'But I have to stay with Mother. I'm not even sure she'll — but no, about you now. Where is Galina? Is she really off the team?'

'Uh-huh. She loves Mother Russia too much to leave.' He spoke lightly, but without being told Maureen Sterling grasped the nuances.

'What will you do? Do you need . . . anything?' she said quietly, from behind her coffee cup; her lips could not be read, her voice could not be heard. A valuable ally, this girl, far more than a set of rich parents and a pair of highly-trained feet. He recalled seeing her father fuss around Jeff and he wondered, did it embarrass her, that Lloyd could be so obvious?

As if she read his thoughts she said: 'We're not close to Daddy. There's room for guests at the villa. *He* won't come as long as Mother is there.'

'But when she leaves. . .'

She shook her head. 'I don't think she'll leave,' she said slowly. She looked down, but not before he'd seen tears spring to those startlingly blue eyes. Odd. With that complexion, a warm Mediterranean tan, the eyes should have been brown. Something teasingly familiar lay just out of reach. He tucked it away for later, a puzzle to be solved. 'My mother's very lonely now . . . but she still has contacts, Alex, maybe she could help if you wanted . . .'

Maybe. Alexei Finsky boarded the team bus alone. He had much to think about, his head bursting with unanswered questions. If he were not careful someone would read them, perhaps answer them for him.

'Thank God they've gone,' Grant's yum-num pal said to Nils as the last bus, laden with stragglers, left for the Village well into the afternoon. 'Now we can get down to business, yum indeed. Care for a scotch, old chap?'

Nils grinned. 'I'm sitting this one out. Maybe one of the Soviet judges could use a drink? I hear the stuff's expensive there.'

Nils headed upstairs for Emma, to take her out on the town if there was a town out there. Like everyone else, he'd hardly stepped out of the hotel yet.

They found a little Scandinavian place, new, the help inexperienced but eager, not at all upset that Emma and Nils clearly had catching up to do. He knew about Dave of course, perhaps more than he was admitting, and over buttered trout and white wine she made the decision to tell him. Skating being what skating was, she'd talked to no one about it, but she had the feeling everybody knew anyway. Not that they'd tell her.

'I worry about Beejay finding out,' she concluded. 'She adored her dad. I'm not sure she'd understand.'

'From what I've seen, I think she'd understand the Dead Sea Scrolls, no problem. She's smart, Emma, and today's kids aren't the innocents we were. That kind of fidelity wouldn't matter to her nearly as much as *why* Noni offered the bait and why Dave took it. That might bother her. It does everyone, the gossip, I mean. So far it's not hurt Roxanne, she's highly regarded in Scandinavian circles, but. . . A nice girl too, bad luck if her mother's ambitions spoil it for her, she's not to blame.'

'But mud sticks, Nils. I thought I'd got over it, but when Beejay's outfit got trashed my first thought was "Noni!". And it wasn't her at all!'

'Trashed? You mean —'

'Shredded.' Nils had been in town twenty-four hours and hadn't heard? The gossip mills *were* slipping, she said, admitting the incident bothered her more than it had Beejay. 'I guess I am a skating mother after all.'

'No. It didn't scare Beejay?'

'The idea maybe, such a dirty, smeary stunt to pull, but not the dress itself. I wish she *could* scrape up some vanity, show an interest in how she looks. There was a glimmer when the replacement arrived but —' A flurry of waiters, trout bones disappearing, a vast selection of *smørbrød* taking their place. 'Heck, Nils, I thought we'd *had* main course.'

'There is no main, they keep it coming till you shout uncle.' Deftly he helped her to a roast beef sandwich, open-faced, simply garnished, and she thought how these people resembled their food. Straightforward, clean, and wholesome. 'When are you going to ask me about my divorce, Emma?'

She hadn't meant to actually ask, but hiding the truth could be one hell of a strain, as she'd discovered over Dave. 'Now, if you like. I couldn't believe it when I heard. You seemed . . . comfortable, happy.'

'Yeah. All those years, me buying, importing, she kept the shop and the books — then suddenly we were almost bankrupt. It took three years to pull back. I should have seen the problem when business started to slide, debts to climb.' He crumbled a crust of brown bread and seemed to talk to himself as much as to Emma, who remembered, now, that Nils' wife had always been extravagant. When they'd been out together Dave used to worry that maybe the Crisps couldn't keep up. Even then Nils' wife had been into fur hats and rented limos, but heck, they were on vacation, away from home, it seemed not such a big deal.

Nils nodded. 'It got big when fur hats turned to coats. Not just one coat but three. A woman needed a change, she said. Then it was diamonds and a top-of-the-line Merc — she couldn't drive her six-year-old Volvo wearing mink, right?' He shook his head, bewildered still by the speed with which everything had run down hill. She'd been poor as a kid, he knew that, he said. Fear of poverty haunted her, but he never thought it would ruin her. Or him. They'd had a good business, secure — 'But then every friend she made was richer than we were. She started cooking the books so I wouldn't see how bad. But, Emma, I *should* have seen, it was my business to see! Easy to be blind when you don't want to know. Her ego hounded her to keep it up until I think it was truly a disease, but I still loved her. Hated the ego, loved the woman. Even when the tax people clapped a lien on the house I could maybe have accepted that, my folks' old place, yet! — then a small thing — it's always one last, thin little straw . . .'

One day, off to one of her luncheons with a new friend, she wore an antique ruby pin, a collector's dream that even in their prosperous days they couldn't have touched except on consignment. She'd bought it, she said, from an old aristocrat who brought it in to hock, he was on his beam ends, she said, weren't they all? Singing his sad old song about debt collectors and the château needing a roof. Proudly she told Nils what she'd paid the old lad. 'She might as well have stolen it, Emma. Next trip through the Loire I stopped in to give the guy a cheque, what the books said we could afford. He was gone, an Arab was having the place fixed. The old man was in some genteel *pension*, a blanket over his knees. Em, when I gave him the cheque he cackled like an old hen. "Independence!" he laughed. By the time I got home the cheque had bounced. That did it. The ego had finally swallowed the woman. There was nothing left to love.'

He spoke simply, matter-of-fact, so why did she feel like crying? Because on the surface they'd been happy, like her and Dave. Easy to ignore the termites until the walls cave in. Nils reached across and touched her hand. 'Don't worry about it. As I said, I should have seen it, stopped it in time. It does take two, Emma. Sometimes three.' Clear as if he'd said it, she heard his next thought.

Don't pile *all* the blame on Noni Kramer. Dave connived. Emma looked the other way once too often. 'But it hit you for a loop, Nils?'

'No,' he said. 'By then it was a relief. I'd made one excuse after another until I couldn't face myself in the mirror. When I had to, what did I see? An average chap who'd just wanted peace and quiet at any cost. And what about you? Any new prospects on the horizon?'

She shook her head. 'No time for much besides getting Beejay through the competition tunnel.'

'Then I guess your horizon's clear, Emma Crisp.'

No. There was still that nasty business with Willi Vanilla.

Nils roared. 'Lord, is he still at it? Em, the man's a joke!'

'But that joker's judging on Beejay's panel — and I'm on his grandson's.'

Nils gestured for the bill as he looked Emma firmly in the eye. 'Then you've got two choices — and for you, one of them's unthinkable.'

Which wasn't a whole lot of help. 'Easy for you,' she said lightly. Boy, but Nils sure had great eyes. They probed right down to the bone.

CHAPTER TWENTY-EIGHT

As the drums beat faster through the days, none among the faithful dared miss a second. From one venue to the other they flew, frenzied bundles of energy, red cheeks, noses, and chins to match: skiers, skaters, sledders, ski-jumpers, coaches, parents, hangers-on and hangers-in, media hawks hunting headlines to feed the medal scoreboards on TV sets back home.

Sweden, Norway, Denmark, Holland, and Japan, heads down, elbows, calves and thighs pumping, looked to corner glory on the speed oval; sleds from Austria, France and Germany could hardly miss on the iced chutes; Scandinavian birdmen soared solid and majestic off the 90-metre hill, with Mieko's cousin promising Japan a strong shot on the 70; racers said the slalom and downhill courses had never been better, with medal hopes wide open. Hockey chances blew hot and cold, teams touted as sure things one day were eliminated the next. The preliminaries of ice dancing were over, leaving the USSR and Germany in the lead, USA and Canada closing for third. Nobody, yet, had competed in figure skating, traditionally saved until the last few days, the icing on the cake.

Seven days to figure skating finals, five if you counted the Original, a short two-and-a-half minute hell the skaters called and counted Compulsory because compulsories counted — did they ever! — a pre-set group of elements in which only the choice of music was original. All must demonstrate a mastery of specific elements which grew more difficult each year. The Original was make-or-break time. Missed one key element? Too bad. No starting over, no squeezing it in someplace else. One miss cost. Two, you were bankrupt, a fistful of points gone, any chance of a medal flushed down the spout, only a fool believed otherwise. But competitors were still at the Games and the public *were* fools so, teeth gritted, they'd go through the motions even if they knew they hadn't a snowflake in hell's chance. Not a soul admitted it, but the Original could zap the chances of a front-runner like Roxanne quicker than you could snap your fingers. One error spelled purgatory. Two, hell everlasting. Supporters expected miracles. Mess up on the SO and they'd resent you forever — do okay and they forget in a second because, hey, compulsories were just for starters, right? Sure they were.

Grant cut Roxanne's short programme to the bone, kept it conservative. As favourite, she could get by without razzle-dazzle, but could not afford missed elements. To have a prayer for Gold she *had to* win the Original, hold off the challenge of more powerful skaters in that killing four-minute Final, where stamina was vital. Nobody knew better than she how little stamina she had; the knowledge played holy hob with her nerves. Noni and the old Brauns in the bleachers, perched like crows on a wire, didn't help.

'She's exhausted,' Brigitta Braun said.

'Nervous as a cat,' Noni said. 'Calcium would calm her, niacin —'

'Do not!' Brigitta said sharply. 'No drugs. This is the Games.'

'Quit worrying, they're vitamins, Mutti. You forget, I live in LA. I've forgot more about drugs than you'll ever know! A vitamin supplement and she'd be fine, but who listens to me? It's Jasinski this, Jasinski that! I'm gonna talk to him. If he can't see the problem he needs new glasses.'

'He *is* a doctor,' Otto said. 'Perhaps if we did not come day after day . . .'

United for once, his wife and daughter turned on him. 'Not come? You must be mad! Not come to support our own skater, our Roxanne?'

'This is our support, to make her nervous?' he said, sighing with relief when they turned back to the centre-ice action, at the moment the Japanese girl soaring across the rink in that enormous triple. Poor Roxanne, to watch that every day at the rink and again in every nightmare. Such a *good* child she'd been, always did exactly as she was told —

but she'd been told so often and so much. And poor, foolish Noni, selling all her chances for a wedding ring, nothing back but ambition only her daughter could fulfil. And especially poor Brigitta, who skating had already cheated twice. He looked at her now, a fake fur hat on her head because this week the hotel beauty shop restyled her best wig per Noni's instructions. 'How will it look,' Noni had said, 'when they interview the winner's grandmother in that godawful wig? You gotta get with it, Mutti!' Noni hadn't specified with what, but Brigitta had worn the ratty fake fur two days now, and under it her own hair so sparse he could actually count the hairs per square-centimetre when she lay snoring, open-mouthed, on the beige hotel pillow.

Godawful. As a boy he'd thought of God as a stern old man meting out justice, but as the years passed He became Father Time with icicles in his beard and a vindictive ice-pick for a staff. Now Otto knew there was no justice. What kind of God turned a woman bald while her husband's hair sprang from his head as thick as the day he married her? Another year and Brigitta would be bald as a bullet. What kind of God withered a man's legs but kept him in otherwise perfect health, but gave his hard-working wife dangerously high blood pressure and angina? What God kept them spinning their wheels in a deep-freeze waiting for a miracle, instead of warming their bones under a clear blue sky with a sun in it?

The Japanese girl had finished her programme, bowing her head briefly in three directions, her mother, her coach, and a blond young man opposite.

'All that bowing and scraping!' Noni exclaimed. 'Imagine, young Dag Carlsen with a Japanese!'

'They were our Allies in the war,' Otto reminded her.

'Oh my God and hallelujah, the whole *world's* changed its mind since the war, but not Mein Papa!'

'You rent a Japanese car for us,' he pointed out, 'we buy their radios, watches, TVs, cook in their microwaves — why, even my camera is —'

'Okay, okay, okay! Pardon me for breathing!'

With each word Noni stabbed her pencil deeper into the yellow pad she imagined to be *de rigueur* for a member of the working press. Otto had yet to see her commit a word to it. The pencil's other end looked as if a rat had been at it, and two of her fingernails, today a livid blue, were gnawed to the quick. Otto tried and failed to shrug off the unease he felt when he watched his daughter for very long. Intense, hungry, always hunting, but for what? No doubt love, but Noni was not lovable. Even as a child she had railed against every perceived threat, often where none existed. With the years her fuse shortened. Yesterday the Sterling girl. Tomorrow it would be Crisp. Today it was Nakashima's strength which set the match to Noni's blue paper. Otto admitted (to himself, of course) that they all presented valid threats to Brigitta and Noni's dreams of Gold, but . . .

The Nakashima girl, who'd surely earned a rest after her strenuous programme, was still soaring easily through several triples. She lacked Roxi's grace, but that phenomenal power could tip the scale. The Crisp child had speed and daring, and in a couple of years might well have everything else. Sterling, it seemed, already had everything. Even wealth, from what Otto had heard. He sighed. Some families had all the luck. Sterling's father reeked money, from the fine worsted suit to the camel-hair overcoat lined in white fur he'd worn to the rink yesterday — quite unnecessarily. The rink was warmer than the Braun's living room in Bonn, but. . .

The Carlsen man was a different story, just looking in his eyes brought goosebumps to Otto's muscular arms. Between the pair of them, Noni and the Carlsen man packed enough anger to blow up the world. Why, he wondered plaintively, did people whip themselves into a froth over a sport that to him was nothing more than a livelihood — and a poor one at that.

Otto was mistaken. Ben Carlsen was not in a froth. He all but twitched with an escalating, shattering rage. Just wait till he got Dag home, the little shit, away from the protection of the Village goons. He'd show him who was boss then, by Christ. Look at him slavering over Madam Effing Butterfly — and look at *her*, bowing at him like a servant or something. Last night, to be sociable, he'd tried a little chat with her mama in the lobby, thinking he might at least let her know that Dag was off limits. Turned out Mama spoke not a word of American. It should be mandatory. Take him.

Within three years of landing in LA nobody knew where he'd come from, and he made damned sure he didn't volunteer information, either. The Old World was done, America was the future, he'd known that twenty years ago, couldn't wait to wedge himself into it so tight he'd feel it holding him up, and he did! he did! — once he'd even seen John Wayne at the beach and he was great! The Duke gave him a real man-to-man wave and everything.

So how come the wife pined and whined for Sweden? That's why she'd left him, no question. Nothing he'd done, a good husband and father, fine home, great provider, everything. So he'd belted her a time or two — it was a man's job to keep the family in line. That's what he liked about the USA, every man a king. So how come Dag turned out such a wimp? You'd never catch Dag making the rules in his own house. He'd do as he was told, just like he always had — except he'd always been told to look out for his sister, but did he? Did he hell! All he did was whine about her weight, as if a woman should look like Kramer, skin and bone, nothing for a man to grab on to. What Grant saw in her . . . A wonder her bones didn't slash him to ribbons when they went to bed.

For a moment he diverted himself with visions of Grant and Roxanne getting it on, but then his eye caught a flutter of white across the rink. Dag, waving to the little Japanese, and Jesus Christ if that wasn't tape on his right hand! Tape! Oh, dear God, a Pair partner with a smashed-up hand, all that stood between Lise and the ice, all these years, his business down the tubes, everything sacrificed for the effing Games and that stupid bastard fucks up his hand at the last minute!

It took maybe three seconds to leg it over the rows of seats reserved for competitors, elbowing guards all the way. Guards! Jumped-up nothings! In the States they'd never be allowed to shove paying customers around, but in a one-hoss little berg like this —

He loomed over Dag from behind, the steep slope of the arena sides adding to his sensation of power, headier still when Dag turned, surprised at the shadow, and looked up to his father's face. That sure wiped his moonstruck smile off pretty damn quick! 'Your knuckles. What you done to 'em?'

'Chipped one,' Dag said, cool as you please. 'Grant knows about it. The doctor says tape'll hold it together through the Games.'

'And who's going to hold Lise together, huh? How's she gonna feel, that white flag waving under her nose, telling her she's not safe up there —'

'She is safe, I told you. I can lift her. I just tried it.'

'*You can lift her. You just tried it*,' Ben mimicked. 'Loused up your hand in time for the Olympics. Brilliant! D'you want to tell me how you did it?'

'As a matter of fact, you did it. I had to punch out your rock star.'

'My rock star . . .' For a second a red haze washed over Ben's eyeballs, he heard nothing but a thunderous pulse drumming in his ears. No music from the rink level, no guards in their stupid burgundy monkey-suits opening and shutting their mouths and pointing to the door like he'd no business being here. Punched him out. Dag had punched out the rock star.

'*You done what*? That queenie owes me thousands, *hundreds* of thousands — not a damn thing in writing and you *punch him out*? My son the genius! How'm I gonna collect now, huh? How'm I gonna keep the business afloat? Hell, you're a big lad now Daggie, you could have gone along once, twice . . . but not you, pretty boy. Dammit, you owed me!' The little shit was turning white around the lips. Good. This kid should stew in hell. 'After all I've done for you I oughta beat the crap out of you right here and now!'

Dag's face closed up like he'd drawn a set of drapes. 'You're behind the times, Dad. I'm taller than you. I have been for years. Everybody around is listening so keep it down, huh? I won't shout and I'm only saying this once. A chipped knuckle heals. A chipped reputation . . . I'm not so sure.'

Dag nodded briefly towards Jeff, who had just entered the arena with the rock star. They swung through the doors and watched, like everyone else, the Carlsen commotion in the bleachers. The star, in triumph up to the fringe of his mauve silk scarf, smirked.

Dag said, 'Oh, and by the way Dad, I smashed your star's tooth — the one with the sparkler in it. Sorry about that.'

Dazed, Ben let the guards lead him over to the spectator seats close to where the star and Jeff were headed, buddy-buddy, laughing all the way — ignoring Lloyd Sterling, who'd also just appeared and was smiling fixedly at nothing at all. So today everybody got screwed, Ben thought. The star's right incisor not only lacked its diamond but the new cap was less than a perfect match with its mates. A rush job, obviously. He felt better somehow — until, with a sinking in his belly, he spotted Lise sashay up to the star and Jeff. God, what was she thinking about, giving the likes of them the goo-goo eyes! This is what came of protecting a girl child, raising her up innocent. She didn't know right from wrong anymore. No mother, was it any wonder? What he *should* do was get the next plane to Uppsala and beat the holy hell out of Lise's loving momma. But Sweden was a long ways off; the nearest bar just a cab ride away at the Palacio de Estrellas.

'Roxi's rattled, pooped,' Noni said, glaring at her reflection in Jasinski's Coke-bottle specs. 'She needs vitamins, man! Calcium, niacin . . . calm 'em and nuke 'em! I know all about that stuff, I'm not a fool, you know!'

No, he thought, you are a conniving bitch, but a troubled one. He felt rather than saw Grant's shadow appear behind him. He ignored it. Medicine was his province. 'Mrs Kramer, Roxanne has ample access to vitamins in wholesome food. If, when she consulted me, her strength had not been depleted by — shall we say *extraordinary measures* — no medical supervision would have been necessary. She is a healthy, tired young woman, trying her best. I suggest we back off, let her discover her own dietary needs.'

Back off. Behind his eyes rose, unbidden, the emaciated images of his sister, mother, father, uncles, who, but for extraordinary measures by the Third Reich, would be around him today; his boys would have substance, a knowledge of grandparents, of Jasinskis reaching back in Poland's past, would have heard first hand of the Holocaust — not today's single-minded thrust to focus sympathy on one segment of society. The Jews had claimed the Holocaust for their own, cornered the market on suffering, even chased the nuns from Osweciem as if they were a flock of useless geese, but what of us, what of the rest, he wanted to shout in his dreams, his nightmares, were we nothing? No, do not rage or weep before this cracked vessel. The old were gone, fury could not bring them back; this shallow creature was not the instrument of their torture . . . this trap in which Jasinski the physician finds himself. He *likes* Roxanne, he feels for her grandparents, he pities this weak Noni. So he remains silent, denying his ghosts their voices.

'Are you off your trolley, doctor? *Discover her own dietary needs*? This is the Olympics, not a poker game in your Aunt Fanny's front parlour. Years of struggle, mostly mine, ride on Roxi's blades! *You* know what she eats?' Noni demanded. 'You check on her? Me, I'm not allowed near the Village, but you, you've got the badge, we all know what a skating expert *you* are!'

'Roxanne's an adult, Mrs Kramer. A doctor does not "check on" healthy adults. Why plant the idea she is sick when she is not?'

'Then how come she's not making her triples? How come she can't get through the Long Free? You're so smart, Dr Butinski, so how come?'

Grant edged between them. 'Lower your voice, Noni. We've been through this before. I can still get you barred and I wouldn't hesitate to go to the press with it.'

She stepped close, the smell of cigarettes on her breath so strongly brown and thick he could have sliced it and served it. 'But you won't. That would really fix Roxi's wagon, huh? And yours.' But she hissed it through twitching ferrety lips, which meant she was safely on hold. For now.

'What about it?' he said to Jasinski when she'd flounced up the steps to her daughter and her parents, slapping the yellow pad at every empty seat she passed. 'They're only vitamins, they couldn't hurt, right?'

'She needs food and rest. Vitamins are stop-gaps, they won't help.'

'But they can't hurt, right? Get Noni off Roxanne's case, give us all a shot at serious training. We're awful close to the wire.'

Jasinski sighed and dragged himself to the dispensary to

draw useless but harmless doses of calcium and niacin, then climbed the endless stairs to where the Brauns sat, Roxanne close beside her grandfather, with whom she held hands. Jasinski dropped two small vials in her skate-bag. 'I don't know that they'll help, but they can't hurt. One of each a day, no more.' He patted her shoulder and left.

Almost before he'd turned away Noni's electric blue fingernails were rummaging nimbly through towels, skate-guards and mittens, scanning labels, her face a changing weather-map of hope, fury, and disgust.

'Is he kidding? Niacin, 25 milligrams? He might as well give her jellybeans!'

Roxanne deftly reclaimed both vials and zipped them into her purse. 'I'll keep 'em Mom, thanks. They're fine. Jasinski knows what I need.'

'What you need,' Noni said, biting off every word like a nylon thread, 'is coaching like *that*!' She nodded down at the competitor's door, which Maureen Sterling had just entered with the satyr. 'With *him* on the rail people naturally expect her to be good!'

'She is good, Mom,' Roxanne said quietly. 'Don't sell everybody short.'

Grant, on his way to the bleachers to watch Maureen, whose sessions he could not seem to pass up, paused by Jeff, heads together with the rock star, both of them blatantly close to Lloyd. That stupid young pup!

'Skates on, Jeff. Warm up for practice.'

Jeff slouched off and Grant planted himself squarely in front of the star. 'Hey, you're blocking my view, man,' drawled the star. 'D'you mind?'

'Yes I mind. Leave my skaters alone. They're not here to party.'

'Your skaters? *Yours*?' Eyebrows shot up above the black shades.

'Carlsen and Dunsmuir. The world's full of the kind of talent you're hunting. Hands off my students.'

'Ooo! Are we jealous? No, I guess not. Do you know who I am?'

'I don't care if you're queen of the fairies. Stay away from my skaters or you'll have more than a broken tooth on your mind — such as it is.'

Walking quickly, furiously away, he heard footsteps behind him and hoped, God, how he hoped they were the star's. In the corridor, away from the cameras, he could finish what Dag had started, crack the other porcelain caps, drive this steadily building frustration into the guy's face. But no, it was foolish old Lloyd, panting to keep up.

'You were magnificent, Grant! Simply splendid, my dear chap!'

'Not at all.' Strains of 'Impossible Dream' seeped into the arena, and Grant ached, now, to watch. 'I wasn't your "dear chap" even way back when, but you won't remember that far. Why don't you leave the little boys alone and encourage your daughter? You just might find she's magnificent.'

Leaving Lloyd open-mouthed, Grant took the stairs two at a time to the very last row and reached for his opera glasses. In his first pan across the rink floor he found Emma with Beejay, looking unusually disconsolate, slumped deep in her chair. Odd, she'd skated well — but Emma could handle Beejay. Even from up here they formed one supportive unit, a family.

'You look like you lost a dollar and found a dime,' Emma was saying. 'I saw most of your progrmme — you did fine.'

'I guess. I didn't miss anything.'

'So why the face?'

'You should have been here, heard the row. Ben and Dag, jeez . . .'

'Bad?'

'The worst. That Ben is such a . . . worm! And you know what? You're dead right about language. Ben's, oh, Mom — Jesus, it was filthy!'

'Most folks aren't too taken with Jesus as a cuss word either, Beej.'

'Yeah, well, anyway . . . while I was skating I listened to myself think. I sound like I've been dipped in cuss words.'

'Just wait till a guy says, "Boy, I sure hate to hear a woman swear" and you'll grow out of it fast. Sorry I'm late, had to wait for the Russian Pairs. Are they ever good! Dag and Lise messed up some. What's with his hand?'

'Chipped knuckle. That's what the row was about.'

'No wonder Ben swore. Dag's lucky he didn't horsewhip him.'

'He might have, but Dag made him back off.'

'Good for Dag. He's learning.' Emma laughed and Beejay joined in.

Watching, Grant sighed with relief and panned up to the Braun Kramers grimly discussing with Roxanne how she'd skated — but he saw no tears. Good. Close by, Willi Vanilla, his son, and albino grandson — another family. The Carlsens, fractured as they were, formed a family of sorts. Nakashima and her mother, who's hair was severly bunned but for a glossy inverted comma on each cheek, were a family. Even Jasinski had his boys — not that Grant ever saw them. He focused on the ice, on Maureen, who maybe didn't have much of a father but who had Deirdre. Was it only Grant Rivers who looked and never found, who had nobody? Mum had been all there was; life being no fairy-tale, Papa Rivera would not crawl out of the woodwork some fine day, and if he did Grant would in any case kick him right back in. Rivera had just sowed the seed. Since when did a breeze scattering seed have any bearing on the crop? Mum, she had a bearing, he was hers and no one else's, just as Roxanne was — had been — Noni's. Only when she began to pull away did Roxanne begin to be his. Maybe one day she would be; Roxanne was a very possible dream . . . if the other would go away.

Again Deirdre did not show, again there was only Maureen, a girl who nevertheless drew his eye as a magnet drew steel. And not just his, apparently. Through his glasses he saw the eyes of many men, old and young, touch this girl with admiration; the yum-num man and his Boston bean; Emma's friend Nils; Finsky; Finsky's coach; even Jasinski — and every male judge in sight. He fought an irrational desire to stand up, cup his hands, and bull-horn them all to back off, warn them to entertain no dreams, to leave perfection alone. If he had a daughter like that he'd lock her in a tower, check out every man she met, name, rank, and reputation. But what else was skating but a cold, safe tower? By accident or design, Maureen, like the other competitors, lived on and for the ice. Clever Deirdre.

But how could Deirdre bear to miss the vital first week, and half of the second? And how had she and Lloyd (slimy Lloyd!) produced this miracle of a girl? Afraid to examine his motives, he made a definite plan to pass up a nap before driving Roxanne into Barcelona for midnight ice; instead he'd visit Jeff in the Brit compound after practice, casually drop in on Maureen, quiz her about Deirdre. She didn't look the kind of girl you plopped down next to and struck up a chat, but theirs was a small world. She seemed friendly enough with Finsky, even the Boston bean.

He found her reading on a couch in the Competitor's Lounge from a heavy, scholarly-looking tome. Around her a dozen languages babbled at full volume. Maureen Sterling sat alone. Grant eased down next to her where he could watch her in the floor-to-ceiling mirror. She did not glance up but she covered the page headings with long, deft fingers.

'Your programme was great this morning,' he began.

Now she looked up, the blue of her eyes again startling him. Beautiful, but the colour was wrong, all wrong . . .

'Thank you. Jeff has improved with you, Mr Rivers.' Her voice was low, clear, controlled. Hard to imagine this girl flying into a temper or a bout of tears.

'Your father seems pleased,' he said. 'I suppose he told you.'

Her expression was all in her eyes now, hard blue sparks. He'd struck a nerve. 'My father and I have little time for each other.' Pointedly, she turned back to her book, which he saw now was a medical text.

'But surely,' he persisted, 'he's an *aficionado*, he must appreciate —'

'Mr Rivers,' she said evenly, not above shocking him. 'My mother and I live in England and Spain. My father, as you have no doubt noticed, lives mostly in Babylon — wherever he finds it.'

So did mine, he wanted to say. How many miles to Babylon? And weren't we all there once? Four thousand, five, six — or maybe Babylonian miles counted in years. Grant sixteen, Deirdre thirty-two — in those days seducing him would have sent her straight to Babylon. Grant innocent, lonely, brimming with a talent that could lead nowhere because even then he'd known, deep down in old nightmares where he dared not look, that Mum had a hole in her lung and a snake lived in it that would one day eat her alive — and then his other love appeared, vibrantly alive, adored, who came to him in dreams forever after, dreams in which he still burned for her. It hadn't seemed like Babylon. More like heaven, until hell crashed through and swept her away. Deirdre. Whose blue eyes stared at him now from Maureen's face, a face he knew from somewhere, not the cover of a skating magazine but 'up close and personal', as they said on American TV.

'My father came from Spain,' he confided suddenly. Why? He'd never told *anyone* that, hadn't Mum always said — 'You like it there?'

'Yes . . . the climate . . . my mother feels better there.'

He held his breath. 'I knew her once.' Intimately, oh, *intimately*. 'I haven't seen her in years. I was competing in England when I knew her. . .'

She shrugged. 'Skating's insular. We all meet everyone sometime.'

'Will she be at the Games?'

'Certainly.' Definite, almost defiant. Bells rang, alarm bells.

'You should do very well,' he said, out of his depth in this conversation with a girl who talked like a sophisticated young woman.

'I shall win,' she said quietly. No bravado. Just the facts.

He laughed, startled by her certainty. 'A few others think they can win too,' he said.

'*I know I can. I must.* Goodnight, Mr Rivers.'

They drove through the Montegreco night in silence, Roxanne asleep in the back, Grant glorying in solitude and the powerful engine sailing easily up and down the precipitous mountain roads. The car was built for this terrain; with luck they'd reach Barcelona with time for coffee from the vacuum flask, for Roxanne to gather herself together, stretch-out, warm-up, spend the whole ice-hour actually working instead of putting up a front for the judges. They *must* get some triples back, must — even Compulsories had them in these days. No longer were triples eye-openers, unless you had a show-stopper like Nakashima's axel. One move of that calibre counted as extra insurance. The only unusual thing Roxanne had was the old Braun spin. Be fair,

the way Roxanne did it was incredibly graceful but . . . easy.
A crowd-pleaser. Judges would shrug. No insurance there,
just a sop for Granny's pride. But incredible grace she still
had, grace she would surely need. If she were just not so
eager to please all of them: Grant, Mom will be so happy
with that . . . Grossmutti will love that . . . d'you think
Grandpa minds having to use the service elevator in the
rink?

And Grant too. If tonight he said, 'Roxanne, do a
triple-lutz over there,' she'd turn pale but she'd try. She
wouldn't remind him that she'd even lost her timing on the
double, never mind a triple. She'd try till she was
black-and-blue or fainting, whichever came first.

The brightly lit rink seemed to rush at them out of the
mountain dark, its car park empty but for a sleek black
Jaguar and a white-painted van that reminded him of an
ambulance, interior lights on, curtains drawn, and yes,
Grant could see the shadow of a nurse's cap bobbing
rhythmically as its wearer pulled wool over the flash of
knitting needles.

'We there already, Grant?' Roxanne yawned and
stretched in back. 'Gee, I could sleep for a week. Do we
have time for coffee?'

'Sweet, and laced with cream. Seems like somebody has
ice before us. Want to watch or wait here? It's an old rink,
can't be very warm.'

At this hour of the night they never were, even the best of
them, and this one was small, mounded under inches of
snow, its lights like yellow squares of fire in the night. At one
of the squares, the head and shoulders of a man in a designer
cap. The satyr. Sterling then. He might have known. And
the white van? *My mother feels better here.* No . . . just a
van . . .

'Who was at the window?' Roxanne said, rubbing her
eyes.

'The night man, I expect,' he sad. 'Snuggle down in that
fur wrap and keep your muscles warm, okay. Work your
calves.'

'I shouldn't warm up inside?'

'It's too small to have a ballet room.' He didn't want
anyone knowing they were here, and he especially didn't

want Roxanne watching Maureen. Her confidence needed building, not tearing to shreds. He drove around to the back, where the front exit and the two vehicles could be seen, but only from the driver's seat, and waited.

In less than five minutes the rink swung open for two men and two women. Maureen first, then the satyr and the coach. Between the two men, arm-in-arm with them, a slender figure in a full-length fur cape with a wide hood, the kind heroines wore in romantic movies. Her face concealed in fur, Grant still recognized her, that inviolable air of being wrapped in, trapped in, wealth — cosseted by it, safe from the cold, from importunate young lovers who didn't know when to take 'no' for an answer.

At last. Deirdre Sterling.

About to open his car door, he stopped, not wanting her to see him in the car's light, not wanting her to know what he'd seen, that she was not in fact arm-in-arm with the two men.

They supported her, literally, on both sides. Her fur boots never touched the ground. The van door flew open. They passed her, like a fragile package, to a man and a woman in uniform, and she disappeared.

The Jaguar carrying Maureen, her coach and the satyr, sped off towards Montegreco. The van pulled out in the other direction, towards the Costa Brava. It rounded the first bend so carefully it could have been carrying a cargo of finest spun glass.

Perhaps because Grant was too stunned to offer criticism of any kind, perhaps because he was the only audience, within thirty minutes of taking the ice Roxanne's body rediscovered the timing on the triple-loop, salchow and toe-loop. Her superb double-lutz came back. Suddenly superstitious, he refused to let her try to triple it. No hat-tricks tonight. In the next half-hour she astounded them both with a perfect Short Original programme. He asked her to repeat it. She did. Perfectly.

'Thank you, God,' she whispered, unlacing her boots. 'Thank you, Grant.' Eyes shut, did she even know who she prayed to anymore?

'Wow, promotion! Look love, we both know you can do it. You just have to believe you can.' She gazed at him with such pure adoration only a stone could have remained unmoved. '*Roxanne, you did it! You!*'

She nodded, radiant. 'When it's just you and me, nobody to bother us, there's nothing I can't do.'

Except put Deirdre out of my mind. Get out, he wanted to shout to the hooded figure. In his mind, deeply engraved, he saw the scene clearly, his senses filled again with the room's fragrance, cream roses, pink-and-ivory freesias, pale carpets underfoot, lace at an open window, a spring afternoon, a woman's adored flesh all his — then abruptly denied him without reason. How could he smooth away this scene, open his mind to Roxanne while Deirdre still lived in the secret places of him that no one had ever seen? If their affair had run its course, if one of them had cooled . . . but they had not, *she* had not, he knew it, so how could it ever end?

'Grant? I did okay tonight, didn't I?' Roxanne, begging reassurance.

'A World Champion, which you are. Twice over. Want to try for three?'

CHAPTER TWENTY-NINE

'I *couldn't* tell you last night at the rink, Mother. There were people around, you know how gossip flies, but Grant Rivers was quizzing me, I know it.' Maureen's voice from the Village's bank of international phones was strong, convinced, perhaps even angry.

Alarmed, yet dizzy with anticipation, Deirdre waved the nurse and her hypodermic away and told her to shut the door behind her; she felt fine, just fine! Except her mouth was a desert and her tongue clung to the roof of it. She'd known Maureen would see him of course. 'But darling, he was a nice boy, not at all the type to pry. You must be mistaken.'

'No, I was in the Skater's Lounge reading so it wasn't a coincidence that he just happened to park himself next to me and start a conversation.'

'What did you tell him?'

'Nothing Mother, of course — except what he must already know.'

Calm, Deirdre, calm. 'And that is?'

'Well, he must have noticed Lloyd drooling all over Jeff, and now Jeff's got a new flame, young and famous, and silly old Lloyd is just stricken —'

Saliva rushed suddenly to Deirdre's mouth, almost choking her. All her insides hay-wire now, systems drowsing in paralysis one minute, the next tuning up again like an orchestra, an adrenalin rush and a head-band of sweat and that ominous fluttering in her stomach. Just chemotherapy, they said, but they knew no more than she, now. When all systems go berserk, which to blame? And where had Maureen found out about Lloyd, and when had she stopped calling him 'Daddy'? Deirdre had *never* discussed Lloyd's private life with her. Hadn't she tried to keep Maureen innocent of everything?

'*Flame*?' she said lightly, spinning out time like a fishing-line. 'But darling, what *do* you mean and what an *ancient* word! Flame indeed!'

'It's back now, all the rage. And I do know about . . . alternate life-styles. Dancers and skaters talk, you know. I've known about Lloyd since I was six, and stumbled across all kinds of slimy little doings over the years.'

'He hasn't tried to —'

'Of course not. You took care of that. But now relax! I can take care of him myself. I already have, in fact. Several times.'

Several times . . . since she was six . . . so she remembered that covert hand under the sprigged little-girl nightgown and had never once mentioned it. Nor other memories either, but she almost surely had many. The night Lloyd appeared from Athens, awake and jumpy on a combination of benzedrine and vodka, and blazing anger over a business deal gone sour. His breath was sour too as he leered down at Deirdre in her nightie, then at the open door to Maureen's room. Swiftly Deirdre scrambled up, putting herself between Lloyd and Maureen's door.

'What a surprise!' Quietly she closed the adjoining door, turning the key, letting it fall silently to the carpet, toeing it deftly under the dresser as her lips and her eyes sought to distract Lloyd. 'Care for a drink?'

'No!' he said harshly, making to shoulder her out of the way.

'She's asleep. I don't think we should wake her.'

'I want to talk to her,' he said, belligerent with drink.

'I'm here. You could . . . talk to me instead.' A shoulder strap had slipped in the scuffle. Perhaps because he was exhausted, the sight of one breast was enough. He accepted the rare invitation and Maureen slept on in safety.

Deirdre shivered. Saving people from Lloyd — first Grant, then Maureen — had been habit by then. Like so many habits, it had turned out to be life-threatening. The luck of the draw. Marriage to Lloyd was a gamble she had lost but in the long run Maureen had won, so maybe they were even, she and Lloyd. All these years shielding her from vices she knew about, lies and half-truths, sheer fabrications. Daddy had business in Hong Kong, that's why he couldn't be home for Christmas . . . for Maureen's birthday . . . or Deirdre's. How much did this innocent girl guess or know? How much did Lloyd know?

'Mother, Grant Rivers wanted to know if we liked Spain, what Lloyd had said about Jeff and about me, as contenders. He was fishing!'

Deirdre tried to keep that imploring tone out of her voice, but she heard it herself, plain as the hum of the air filter, the gurgle of fluids in the IV bottle, the feeble pump of her heart under ribs which looked like bleached bones washed up on the shore. 'Did he mention me, where I was —'

'If you'd be at the Games. I said yes. He really wanted me to tell him why you hadn't appeared yet, but I kept it vague.'

Deirdre felt weak and floating, perhaps she was in heaven. 'You said?'

'That you hadn't been well — but not what's wrong.'

'Darling, we don't *know* what's wrong, even the doctors are at a loss —' Perhaps by now she should be ready for the bomb she knew to be coming, welcome it as a relief. She was not and did not. Pride stood in the way.

'It's too late to play silly beggars, Mother, really it is.' Behind its tender edges her daughter's voice rang with steel. 'We all know what's wrong.'

'All?' Don't say the word. If we don't say it, it's not real, not happening.

'Denial gets us nowhere,' her daughter's implacable, inescapable voice went on. 'The doctors know, you know, I know, Lloyd must know — which also tells me where you got it, for which I'll *never* forgive him, never.'

'The doctor's shouldn't have told you.'

'They didn't. Aids is an international scourge. I read. I know the causes, the symptoms, the progression, the treatments and the prognosis.'

So Maureen knew just about everything — even how close she'd come to being one of the sexually abused children society had discovered lately, as if they too were victims of a rare new disease. When had it started, hanging a 'disease' label on every adult weakness? Drink, gambling, perversion, drugs, child molestation — if these were sicknesses, so was everything, including greed; and if so, she'd been sick to marry Lloyd in the first place. The vicar's daughter couldn't face poverty. If they'd run out of *real* illnesses why not study her *now*, cure her *now*! Hysteria bubbled up in her throat, another phenomenon. She swallowed it back. Maureen had worried enough without her mother going spare, round the bend, off her rocker, up the twist — or whatever the latest street jargon for insanity was. But insanity *sounds* so bad, you know. Padded cells, strait-jackets, the man with the net. One could laugh about 'going spare' — until of course, one went.

Presumably Maureen also knew she'd soon be an orphan — one could not, one *refused*, to count Lloyd a parent — so perhaps her no-nonsense daughter had considered the future, what she would do with it. Hardly a question to ask by phone and she was so very tired, but —

'You will remember to see *my* solicitors, in London and Rome, darling? Yes? But what will you do with yourself after . . . you know . . . the Games?'

'Medicine, I think. I've looked into the requirements. I have Latin, you saw to that. You're not to worry. You've given me everything I need and more. . .' Maureen's voice faded off, and Deirdre, seldom angry with her daughter, her *raison d'être* since the day the child was born, could not bear her young composure, her plans for a future Deirdre would not see. She was too immature, too young to know it all, how *dare* she know everything?

Then through her fatigue Deirdre remembered: 'There are one or two things. . . You didn't know, for instance, that once I —' She whispered, but the confession came through clearly, no possibility for error. Maureen's gasp seemed to draw Deirdre through the peaks and limitless gorges of the Pyrenees straight into the Olympic Village itself.

'An affair? Mother, you're not yourself. It's the medicine. I've seen him, he had to be far too young.' Then as the truth sank in, 'Did Lloyd know?'

'I've never been sure . . . Goodnight darling. One of my team's here, knitting needles at the ready. Click-click-click.' One more click as Deirdre hung up.

At Olympic Village, Maureen Sterling counted the little

round holes in the dead receiver. When she got through she counted them again and again until they all swirled together, trickling into streams which swelled to rampaging rivers she'd never suspected were there. Through the surging rush of their waters she dimly heard a familiar voice speaking rapid, incomprehensible Russian in the next booth.

'Galina, don't panic. Slow down. Naturally your father's worried, the move to The Park, the problems —' And such an obedient *apparatchik* . . .

'Not worried, Alexei. *Frantic*! Papa goes crazy! He thinks it's something he has done, that they are punishing him again.'

Alexei almost said, 'When I come home', but checked himself. How could he say it when he wasn't sure? 'He'll get used to The Park. He'll accept it.'

'Alexei listen, you must not interrupt, then you go to the Director, beg him to help. You still have power. We have none!' Her voice shook but she recovered. 'So jumpy is Papa, yesterday he is waiting at Lenin's tomb to prove he's still loyal, a tourist yells that her purse is gone, she shouts for the police. Alexei, you know Papa, what happens to him when uniforms are close? This time they come very close, fast, straight at the queue; like a fool he screams and runs. They chase him, catch him. He does not have the purse, if he were starving he wouldn't steal a crumb from a sparrow, but they say maybe he has an accomplice or why would he run? Last night and today they hold him for questions, won't let him out, but if they are listening now they must know he is innocent!'

Of course they were damned well listening now, probably from the next-door flat, she surely knew *that*. That was the purpose of this whole charade! A planted tourist, a purse which didn't exist, police conveniently in place — but in Moscow weren't they always in place?

'They won't harm him.' No, they'll just hold him until I bring back the Gold. Not because he matters to them but because he matters to Galina, and Galina matters to me. One knot at a time, thus the net is woven.

'Alexei, you will talk to the Director, yes?'

'Yes. I'll call you tomorrow.'

'After you talk to the Director?'

And much good that would do. But like the puppet they'd made him, he called the Director for a chat. A bad time. Was there a good time? The Director lingered at the hotel over smoked salmon, thinly sliced lamb, a fantastic plum sauce, sharp but delicious, he said, a rice pilaf Alexei would not believe — 'Come over, Alexei! I'll arrange a pass, send my car for you.'

'I've eaten. Could you come here? A personal problem . . .'

The Director sighed and Alexei pictured him dabbing lamb fat off his lips with a beige Olympic napkin, swilling champagne over his plate to clean it, flicking out shreds of lamb with a little silver pick. But *of course* he would come now, this instant. Anything for his prize competitor.

The instant took two hours to cover a distance he could easily have spat. 'My boy, my boy, what can I do for you? Anything, just ask.'

With no hope whatever Alexei told the tale of the purse, of Galina's father, to a man who already knew. 'Her father is honest, you know that, incapable of stealing, but his nerves . . . his adolescence in a work camp . . .'

The Director nodded. First thing tomorrow he'd call, clear it up.

'Perhaps now?' Alexei insisted. 'You have authority. Like you, our leaders are compassionate?'

The word almost choked him but he loaded a question mark on the end of it, a subtle hint that if they were not compassionate the Director's prize flea may not jump high enough to reach for Olympic Gold. It misfired.

The Director checked his watch, today a Patek Phillipe, and frowned. 'I'm late for a policy meeting . . . after, it will be past midnight in Moscow. It is not smart, disturbing officials at their rest — or whatever they are doing.'

'What are you doing?' Hiro Nakashima thundered from one of his many offices. 'It is not enough she makes a peep show of herself for the world, now you too encourage it! I sent you there to stamp out the fires but what do you do? You add kindling!'

Trying to rest on the Western bed, too soft, not Japanese, Mieko's mother shivered in the hotel room. 'Father, she trains every day, the rink is a public place, she behaves well, no holding hands, no —'

'And restaurants, both of you together with the blond one? Like a family? Except for my own papers, the spectacle made every front page in Japan! This is training? Discretion? As usual, you disappoint.'

'But it was only a coffee-bar in the rink!'

'Coffee-bar, restaurant, the same! I shall fax.' He hung up with a crash.

Too absorbed to go downstairs for *sushi* as she had planned, she lay quiet. A week ago his anger would have terrified her. Now she pondered pathways round it. The longer she was away, living in this new wardrobe, this new persona, mother of an important skater, the bolder she grew. No longer powerless, she wondered how best to use what she had while she had it. Back in Tokyo all would disappear, a season in mist and memory only. Here the people offered friendship; she accepted all her meagre English would permit — but she learned more each day, and each day won more friends. Perhaps one of them would know how to use the temporary fame to her daughter's advantage. Best of all was the golden one, who she already trusted — but Father would explode at such an ally. The Kramer girl, sweet but vulnerable, guarded by that suspicious lynx of a mother. The old Braun man in the wheelchair showed wisdom but no promise; did not Mieko threaten his own granddaughter's ambition? There was the coach Rivers, distant, pleasant, he obviously admired Mieko's work, as did the Boston Bean's coach. Coaches all watched Mieko. English Maureen was kind but preoccupied, it seemed, with weightier matters than the Games. Mrs Crisp had a look of quiet wisdom seldom seen in Occidentals, but how did one approach a judge?

Behind concealing sunglasses Emma poked moodily at a chef's salad and wished that Willi Vanilla would go away. He would not. There he sat, his big vanilla-coloured teeth beaming brightly as he applied himself to *linguini périgordine* with single-minded dedication. His paunch told her he would not raise the matter until he'd cleaned his plate.

Then, stomach full, he could exploit this bonanza of power landed so opportunely in his lap. Emma must judge Willi's grandson before Willi judged Emma's daughter. If she marked the grandson low, Willi would retaliate on Beejay. If she claimed conflict of interest, bowed out altogether, she might never be invited back. To judge the Games was an honour not lightly offered and seldom refused. The dilemma almost choked her, but she'd be damned if she'd let him push her out! Skating was clean — but for how long, if everyone gave in to the likes of Willi?

By extension, he could even hurt Roxanne and Emma herself if he yapped loud enough about Dave and Noni, throwing a shadow over the whole US team — never mind what he could, and almost certainly would, do to Beejay. But as Nils said, one vindictive judge couldn't kill you and everyone knew how Willi operated except this was the big time, wouldn't come around again for four more years. Too late for Roxanne — and the team needed that Gold. Their skiers as usual were courageous but erratic, which spelled injuries galore. There'd already been some. Their hockey team shone, but so did the Canadians, the USSR up there as usual, with the Poles nipping like terriers at their heels.

Willi heaved a satisfied sigh, sopped up the last dab of truffle sauce with a buttery roll and grinned at her. Wedged between two of his vanilla choppers a small sprig of parsley looked all set to take root. Should she tell him? Hell, no. She looked at her watch. 'Willi, I don't have all day. Something on your mind?'

He washed the last bit of roll down with lager, coughed, and fitted a black cigarette into a nicotine-stained ivory holder. 'Emma, I merely want to compliment you on your daughter, so young, so full of promise, like my grandson, who is also a Willi.'

'Is this a replay of LA or what? If so, nothing's changed.' Oh no? In LA he had not shown his hand. Here he would. Two aces. One of them Beejay.

'Emma, my dear, dear lady! I merely wanted to ask if you'd seen the judging roster — and the order of events?'

'Cut the gaff. I'm not your "dear lady" and of course I've seen the order of events, what d'you think I am?' She took a breath, slowed down. 'Willi, look at me real close. Do I look like a moron to you?'

He laughed, the parsley a virulent green against the plastic teeth. 'If you did, I'd hardly be wasting my time on you.'

'*Gracias*, I'm sure.'

'So. If I may make a suggestion, Emma —'

Emma held up her hand. 'If you're about to offer a deal I should warn you, the answer's no, but I'd report it anyway. *I don't deal.*'

His watery blue eyes seemed to freeze over. 'How many years has Beejay put into the ice, Emma? You're passing up the chance of a lifetime.'

'One judge? You? If you're smart, you'll pass up the chance too. You can clobber Beejay to get even with me, sure, but if your marks are too far out of line you won't be asked to judge another Games — and we just might lodge a protest. Why not think positive, Willi. Your grandson might skate a crackerjack programme. I hope he does. In any case, I judge what I see. I expect you to do the same.' She told a hovering waiter to put her lunch on her own room tab and paused, waiting for the clincher.

'Emma, I am seventy-four. The next Olympiad is hardly my top priority. My grandson, however, is. Are you aware how many people suspect that when your husband died he was not, dare I say it, alone?'

'Are *you* aware that a certain whopping great fridge is the inside joke of the Games? If a bedroom fandango of a judge now dead is a crime, how about attempted bribery by a judge who's still alive? More or less.'

She marched away knowing that right then, all she really cared about was how Beejay would feel if somebody whispered in her ear about her father and Noni in a motel room. That was *her* top priority.

Two days away from Ladies and Mens Originals, one day from Pairs, the ice lay empty, not a blemish on its surface or its reputation. Skaters lounged around it, unable to tear themselves away from the scene of their future triumph or their final defeat. It was as if a morbid death-wish drew them early to the scene of their execution. Even their parents hung around, judges, coaches, camp-followers by the thousands now.

Trying and failing to remain inconspicuous, talent scouts from the shows haunted the aisles, making discreet notes on the skaters, many of whom considered their Olympic performance an audition for a show contract, knowing they could expect nothing in the way of medals, now or ever. Contracts, should they be offered, would not be lucrative, but they'd be a living, a way to get back what their parents had socked in. Not least, a way to travel the world and be paid for it. The travel, exposure to cultures other than one's own, more than compensated for the loss of college; no cast was more international than that of even the smallest ice show.

Winners' contracts were already drawn up, needing only skaters' names and signatures — and no potential medalist was proof against curiosity. Certainly not Alexei Finsky, whom the scouts eyed endlessly now, by far the best show prospect because he was best trained and most consistent. Finsky never missed, always put on a show. Until his music started he was Mr Insignificant, shuffling round, staring at the ice, working his blades in to cool them, prepare them. Hair medium-brown, face pleasant, healthy, unremarkable, he could have been any college kid out to kill time.

Then his music started and — whoom! Drama! His arms lifted, his head, even his neck, became an instrument of expression; every feature sang the story of the music. Fire burned in his eyes. He didn't just jump and spin: Finsky acted, projecting from the front rows all the way to the highest, cheapest seats. A reporter once wrote that when Finsky skated, a tornado would whip the roof off and nobody would notice. He considered skating an art, to be studied and refined. Three years choreography at the Bolshoi didn't hurt. Three more studying acting. Alexei Finsky would be a singular asset to a show — and nobody knew it better than he.

But in dollars or sterling, how valuable an asset? He wondered now, his brain cells clicking the counters of a mental abacus. With World and European titles but no

Olympic Gold, he figured maybe two million a year. With Olympic Gold, a movie contract tacked on, endorsements, a shot at a major production — maybe six, seven million a year. But only in the West. At home, a fancy *dacha* at Sochi on the Baltic, a *Lada* for Galina, maybe a *Chaika* for him — more horsepower than even the Director merited, luxury in plenty.

But what the government gave it could take away; unpredictable as the situation now was, as the future of the man with the wine-stain now was, where was the security? He could follow the Director's lead, stash accounts here there and everywhere, but he didn't want to live like that, didn't want to lie to his children, Galina's children.

If only Lise Carlsen could have lied to herself as readily as she did to everyone else! If talking stopped her thinking about the damned overheads and jumps coming up tomorrow in front of TV and judges and everybody! She tried, she really did try. Though she'd never in her life read a book from first page to last, and her writing experience comprised little more than notes passed to boys in class, she was no stranger to fiction; her face inspired such adoration that men gazed entranced as she described the family's fabulously successful business in California, their estate (the Carlsens had *never* lived in a house), and now her mother's cruel — oh cruel! — desertion. How could a woman be so heartless, she piteously begged the Japanese favourite of the 70-metre hill? He flashed his brilliant smile; he understood hardly a word of English but could sniff out an engaging liar when he heard one; his fiancée was far away in Yokohama, this pseudo-Swede was a willing stand-in, and his exploits in the Japanese press would not upset his uncle Hiro Nakashima in the least. He hoped. A man was expected to avail himself of such delights as presented themselves. Across the rink he frowned at his cousin Mieko and her mother, sitting with Lise's brother. Fools. They knew better. Such leeway as he assumed by natural right in no way extended to the female line. Did they not see the Tokyo photographer's telephoto lens aiming at them from high in the arena?

Mieko, staring glumly at the latest fax, saw nothing but the paper.

'We were only sitting there,' Dag said. 'Quit worrying. It's *your* life.'

She shook her head. 'You do not understand. He is my grandfather, how can we disobey? We love him.' She spoke simply, in deep distress.

Dag looked from mother to daughter and back again to the mother. 'The question is,' he said, '*does he love both of you*?'

Blank amazement stared back at him, widened their dark-brown eyes. He felt that somehow he'd blasphemed the illustrious Hiro Nakashima by even suggesting that he might lower himself to love this lovable girl and her mother, who lived only to obey. He thought of Lise, that maybe a year in Japan would improve her disposition, maybe even her skating.

Noni Braun broke off a square of chocolate and passed it across her mother to Roxanne. 'You skated well today. All the triples back except the combo. When Grant takes you to Perpignan tonight you will get that too, a snap. Just what I said. You need vitamims. Bigger doses would have been better, but. . .' She shrugged.

Roxanne nibbled a corner of the chocolate and surreptitiously dropped the rest into a tissue in her purse. Did Noni really think she couldn't taste the difference between chocolate and a laxative? Humour her. 'The niacin stuff helped, Mom, you were right,' she said.

Brigitta took out her mirror and patted her re-styled wig.

Noni smiled at Roxanne over it. 'I always am. You got plenty left for the Original, day after tomorrow? Double up! Twenty-five milligram's a drop in the bucket.'

'I couldn't if I wanted to,' Roxanne said, patting her purse. 'I've only two left. Jasinski's careful.'

'Careful! Careful can lose you Gold, but what do I know, huh?'

Frau Braun frowned at the mirror. 'You're *sure* this has dignity, Noni?'

'It's great. Styled like Farah Fawcett's, only grey.' Noni

rummaged in her pocket and passed Roxanne a wad of folded money. 'Run down to the cafeteria and get four coffees baby, huh?'

Roxanne got up. 'It's okay, I've got change in my purse.'

'Which you can't carry with four coffees, right?'

Roxanne headed downstars, her purse temptingly open by Noni's foot. Brigitta fretted at her wig, unconvinced that the windswept look was *her*. 'What do *you* think, Otto?' But Otto had closed his eyes, waiting for coffee.

CHAPTER THIRTY

'Thing is, Doc —' Ben Carlsen's fist shook around the first drink of the day, vodka-tonic in lieu of breakfast. 'About Dag's fist. A shot in the knuckle before they skate will hold up fine, no sweat. Pain-killer, nar-mean?'

Jasinski frowned as he dissected a square of toast into four precise triangles. Doctors prescribed to athletes reluctantly these days. 'Ben, aside from the rules prohibiting so many drugs, the injury's at the end of a long hairline crack. It could widen. Pain is the body's signal to take care, ease up.'

'Ease up. *Ease up*? After I work a lifetime? Look, I forget your name —'

'Jasinski. "J" like "Y". "S" like "ssh" .' Jasinski bit into his toast with a subdued snap. 'With pressure the crack can split, causing permanent damage.'

Ben's linen napkin swiped the table's edge; crockery rattled; a fork impaled itself in a slab of icy butter and stood quivering between them. 'Damage to a piddley knuckle? BFD to that! I'll get the *team* doctors on it!'

'I *am* a team doctor. We consulted the hotel orthopaedist. We agree that pain medication may exacerbate the injury.' Jasinski swept toast crumbs into a tissue for the sparrows on the hotel lawn. 'Ben, explain please. What is BFD?'

Ben's vague attempt at diplomacy in ruins, he swayed over the table. In spite of central heating, set at some bracing European concept of comfort, runnels of sweat glistened in the hollows of his cheeks. 'You, a doctor, you don't know from BFD? Big Fucking Deal's what *that* means, buster!' As he breathed quinine and vodka over Jasinski, his own knuckles shone white as they gripped the edge of the table. 'Tell you what, Doc Jasinski-as-in-Y, I'll bet the Commie Pairs get what *they* need to win.' He lurched to the

321

door. Jasinski let him go.

As he'd told Dag earlier, they could go with Novocaine to numb it — Ben was wrong about other teams and drugs. The stakes were too high to risk being caught with stronger drugs in the body.

'Scary,' Dag agreed. 'Dad keeps on at me, but if my fist is numb, how do I know if I've got a grip on Lise in the lifts? She's wearing silky stuff, you see. It slips like crazy. I told her when she picked it, but you know Lise —'

Jasinski had chosen not to, but he'd watched her skate. Even with little grounding in psychology he recognized sheer terror when he saw it.

At the Village, Alexei again sought out Maureen for an English breakfast at the GBR buffet. 'The best breakfast around,' he said, helping himself to ham and eggs, establishing a purpose for the visit. At a corner table they lowered their voices to casual murmurs. 'Your mother arrives when?'

'Today. A medical suite at the hotel. She hopes you'll visit this evening. She's looking forward to everything, you know, seeing us all skate, private party at the hotel after Finals, a few close friends.' Maureen lowered her head and muttered, 'Consular people, Madrid, Paris, London and Washington, of course. You *are* allowed to leave the Village then?'

'We're free to go where we wish. Until departure.'

'She has addresses . . . solicitor, branch offices.' She finished her coffee and stood. 'Mother will see you this evening then — alone, I'm afraid. She tires easily. Good luck at Originals tomorrow. Such a white-knuckler, isn't it!'

'Yes.' He nodded goodbye, a hint of the Russian wolf peering out at her from his open, honest grin. She laughed. This was more fun than the Games.

As the world press endlessly repeated, Originals were *not* Finals, *not* main events, more the opening skirmishes of pitched battles to come at the end. Those closest to the action, particularly the circle round Roxanne Braun

Kramer, knew Originals to be vital. Only one placement would do. First.

The day before, Noni Kramer smoked sixty long brown cigarettes and changed the colour of her fingernails five times, from cherry-red to mustard to purple to olive-green before settling on a pale lavender more fitting for the mother of the soon-to-be Olympic Champion. Classy — and she must not out-shine Roxanne, who refused to paint her nails at all.

Emma Crisp, busy weighing last-minute shifts in temperament and nerve in the Mens Division, planned to mark the eve of Beejay's Olympic début over a lunch with Nils and a dinner with Grant. No way would she hang around Beejay, the urge to issue last minute hints by now almost too powerful to resist. She chased away false hopes as fast as they appeared, and vowed to tend to her own devices and leave Beejay to hers. With Nils she was as comfortable as half a pair of old slippers; he knew her past as she knew his, no topics off limits. With Grant she dare not mention Roxanne or Beejay because in eighteen hours they'd be head-to-head. Roxanne, Grant's lover. Beejay, her daughter. Emma found the prospect anything but comfortable. For the rest, she locked all thoughts of Willi Vanilla back in their fright-box and resolved to judge Mens with no bias either way. After that, she'd stick around, watch Beejay compete, wave the Stars and Stripes like crazy, and not even *care* what marks Willi gave her! But she nourished one hope — heck, she was only human — that Willi's grandson skated half-way decent so that she could mark him accordingly.

Each time the TV set beat the drum for Ladies Originals, Brigitta Braun's heart danced its familiar rat-a-tat and she took a nitro, which calmed it for an hour. When it next rattled her rib-cage she took two nitros and lay down. Then it shut up for rather longer. Otto, watching her colour change from pink to tallow and back again, dare not leave her alone except when she disappeared into the toilet. He then stationed his wheelchair at the door and listened to little plastic caps being screwed off-on-off — then on again.

When she emerged, powdered and rouged and lipsticked, lizardy-green glitter over her eyes and that hideous wig on her head, his pulse juddered like a jack-hammer and he figured that maybe even he needed one of those pills he knew Noni to pop every hour. 'Tranks', she called them, as if they were sweets. Last week they'd been different, 'uppers', he thought, but by now maybe she was as high as she could get. Whatever, he gave up on Noni and treated Brigitta with kid-gloves until his own nerves finally sharpened to poisoned little arrows, and he ordered, yes ordered, Brigitta to wash the jungle off her face and take the wig to the shop, make them put it back as it had been. Corrugated. He told her that at her age the frazzled grey mop looked less than casually windswept, more a casualty pulled off the *autobahn*. She'd been rehearsing, she explained, for when they returned home in triumph to re-open the rink. Then she wept. He gave her schnapps from their own little fridge in the room, and if he'd had a respectable lap he'd have pulled her on to it. Instead, he patted her hand. She cried harder.

Ben Carlsen's nemesis, the Pair Original, loomed closer this evening. He spent the day seeking and not finding Lise, who passed up her last chance at practice to stand huddled in the team jackets of four ski-jumpers, watching Mieko's second cousin compete in the first round of the 70-metre hill. At noon Ben staggered up to his room to hunt her down inside a bottle of 'Wild Turkey'. She wasn't there, but he found his house with a 'For Sale' sign in front and wondered what it would fetch. He recalled the mortgage and panicked, but just in time his life-raft appeared, the bubble at the bottom of the bottle, an optical illusion convincing him there was more left than he'd thought, reminding him of a stewardess in Miami, dim but good, boy was she good! — and he nodded off with a smile, Lise safe and warm in the most inviolate corner of his mind.

After practice Mieko and her mother also spent time on the hill, paying less attention to the bird-men than to the future, considering, discarding, setting this on a back-burner, reserving that as a last resort. The discovery that they possessed power, which mother had confided to daughter, opened up dazzling horizons blinding to their dark, insular eyes. Access to a media clamouring insatiably for interviews bolstered and broadened this power, but it was an unfamiliar tool, their touch uncertain. How to wield it without alienating Hiro Nakashima for ever? Mieko's mother hugged one idea to herself; to share it could bury Mieko in shame and her mother in everlasting guilt. At Hiro Nakashima's social strata, virginity far outweighed wealth and breeding as a prime bargaining chip to a traditional marriage. Perhaps Mieko would find the courage — but self-discipline, as Oka-chan had found to her cost, could be a burden heavier than no discipline at all. If Mieko did what her mother hoped, it must be of her own will, her love; if she gave herself at her mother's suggestion, then Oka-chan had coerced. A Nakashima mother must protect Nakashima honour. Even now, with freedom riding her wrist like a hooded falcon, Mieko's future at stake, she could not bring herself to do otherwise. Mieko, younger, more flexible than she, might find the courage; if she did not, then a faceless young man from Hokkaido would claim the most precious prize of this Olympics.

Grant celebrated Roxanne's two perfect practice sessions, one in the early, early hours in Perpignon, today's in the Olympic arena itself, by giving her lunch in the hotel's best French restaurant, *très exclusif, très élégant*, and, as she reminded him when the waiter swished deftly away to place their order, *très* pricey. In soft peach wool, grey suede encasing her celebrated feet, happiness on her equally celebrated face, she looked a radiant twenty. This was how she used to be, should always be.

Too often lately she'd worn the frozen smile of the success who didn't quite believe it, but this new-old Roxanne turned every head in the room, even those obvious few who lived outside the skating world, recognizable by careful dress, manners, and an indefinable air of leisure foreign to anyone in sports, especially at an Olympic Games. These few looked about them. They *observed, conversed*. When Deirdre arrived, she would be like them, Grant thought, not like us. All skaters ever concentrated on were people and events to the exclusion of everything. Assassinations, elections, revolutions, floods, earthquakes and pestilence, all flew by like snowflakes, gone before they'd registered their presence. Roxanne was no exception — but then, neither was he. It came with the territory.

'Oh Grant, I'm just so relieved! I've had nightmares like you wouldn't believe, especially in the Village — skiers *shout* so! — I dreamed once that I'd finished last and shamed everybody, nobody would talk to me, even you, and it was in all the papers, big black headlines: OLYMPIC FAVOURITE BOMBS! Now you've finally got my form back for me.'

'No, *you* did, but do go on. I'll take all the flattery I can get. Really, you'll be fine.' He almost said 'knock wood' but stopped in time. No negatives. He took her wrist, too fragile still, each vein clear as a river on a map, no flesh to buttress them. 'I'm proud of you, you know that.'

She couldn't seem to stop smiling as her lunch, *très* pricey, cooled untouched on her plate. 'I knew you would be. I skated great today, huh?'

'Yes, but that's not all I'm proud of.' When, when would she realize she was more than a pair of unwilling feet doing what they'd been harassed, badgered, and threatened into doing for most of her life? 'You've grown five years in as many weeks. I'm proud of Jasinski too. He helped. I hindered.'

Her smile melted, softened. 'Oh, no. Whatever I've done I've done for us, Grant.' She picked up her fork and began to eat, but delicately, selectively. No fats. Just proteins, vegetables, and a minimum of starch. Now, she thought. Say something now. Like marriage, like babies, like a home of our own. Don't make me ask. God, don't *let* me ask! He couldn't think she'd turn him down, he couldn't, not after —

'I've told you before, you worry too much about pleasing everybody.'

'Grant, I've told *you*. I want this medal for you, your career.'

His face darkened and she knew he'd withdrawn to that other place where she could never follow.

His career. He thought now, cushioned and cosseted in

luxury, about a dark place, cold, damp, people coughing their lungs into enamel bowls, about wanting to give a woman Gold and failing, then wanting her out of it all but not like that, God not like that, then another woman loving him so much he wanted to give *her* Gold, a ring, but she left, too. A valuable lesson. When you want something too much, you lose it. He should tell Roxanne. She wanted Gold. He should tell Maureen. So did she. He was the only one who knew the secret but he didn't know what he wanted so the knowledge was useless.

The waiter, hearing his accent, asked if he was from England or America. He wanted to say limbo, but Roxanne was staring at him, anxious again. In his confusion he signed the credit slip 'Grant Rivera'. He did that often lately, but he wrote like a doctor. Nobody noticed and wouldn't care if they did.

Before the dinner hour that evening Deirdre Sterling arrived with two nurses and much equipment at the Palacia d'Estrella via a side entry leading directly to a service lift. No one saw her.

Minutes later a diffident, fresh-faced young man gave his name to reception — who knew it anyway — and he was admitted to the penthouse floor for perhaps half an hour. From there, he entered the Soviet compound for a drink before hurrying over to the arena to catch the Pairs Original.

The Director joined him immediately, speaking fast as he too must leave shortly for the arena. 'Have one, my boy!' The Director waved hot-buttered rum at him and snapped a cigar from its gold case. 'God, a heavenly drink! Out of this world and maybe the next,' acclaimed this avowed atheist.

'Thanks no,' Alexei said. 'But I do have some questions.'

The Director gave his most expansive smile and busied himself lighting the cigar, satisfied only when smoke billowed and eddied about them. 'Ask away. That's my job. I try to do a good one.'

'Again, I cannot reach Moscow by phone,' Alexei said steadily. 'Have you called them about Galina's father yet? Is he free?'

'Oh, you know the phones, some days perfect, some days

not. No luck with the father yet, it's going through channels, but I got the housing people. Galina's mother had lodged a complaint: insufficient space. They checked the regulations and guess what, she was right, so I can ease your mind on that. They flew the aunt back to Leningrad, an old ladies' home, cosy and warm, a — *a what? What did you say?'* Sheer disbelief fumbled through the smoke as the Director flapped a plump-fingered hand.

'The aunt's pigeon,' Alexei repeated, calm as Lenin's tomb.

'*A pet pigeon*? My boy, I have an Olympic team in my care. You expect me to track the fate of one old woman's skinny pigeon?' Magician fashion, he snapped his cuffs to prove they were empty, no birds up his sleeve.

Alexei's stare did not waver. 'Where is it?'

A fresh gust of smoke clouded the air. 'A terrible winter . . . food is scarce . . . who knows? But you must learn, my boy, we are men of responsibilities, we cannot worry for everyone. This is your big year!' Slowly, subtly, he drew Alexei further away from the crowd as he spoke. 'I hear a disturbing report this morning Alexei, of course I know that it's untrue but I must ask —'

'Ask anything you want.' Prudence had always governed Alexei's tongue, but since his talk with Deirdre Sterling a new recklessness seemed to be at the controls.

'I have a report that two talent scouts spoke with you this morning. Western scouts, Alexei. American, I believe.'

'So? This, as you said, is my big year. My last in competition. Naturally I must look to my future. A life of endless shortage is poor incentive. If we are now driven to nourish ourselves on skinny pigeons. . .'

'*But not you! Finsky will win! Everyone knows it!*'

'Perhaps,' Alexei conceded. 'The question I must ask myself, Igor — I may call you Igor? — is: in the Soviet Union, what *guarantees* have I for any kind of prosperity? I'm sure you know what a Gold medal is worth in the West.'

The Director paled and forgot to draw on the cigar. Unattended, it went out. 'So! Having exploited us for your training, you now — how do they say in the West, you would know better than I — you now look to make a killing?'

'But isn't that what you yourself expect to make from me? I

am the jewel in your Directorial crown. You look to angle for a promotion. Or why trouble to engineer the humiliations for Galina?'

'Oh, we all know she whines to you. They all do. That's women for you!'

'There is no time for the accusation waltz, Igor. I may make a deal with you — but in writing, *before I compete*, and the document lodged with my solicitors. They have offices in Paris, Rome, the Hague — and Tel Aviv.'

Blood suffused the Director's face. It seemed a long time before he could find his tongue. '*A deal*? But you compete tomorrow — no time to arrange, to bargain! And where would *you* get solicitors?'

'I have friends. You claim that you have influence. Use it.'

The Director slumped onto the nearest bench. 'What do you want?'

Alexei leaned in over him. 'Reinstatement of full rights and privileges for me and my family in perpetuity.'

Relief spread over the fleshy face. 'But if you return with us, that is always understood, it always was! We all knew that, including you.'

'— and guarantees, documents lodged at the Hague and the UN; to travel at will; to contract our services anywhere in the world for three months of every year for as many years as we wish to do so. The right to own property abroad. To perform or coach abroad tax-free, all foreign earnings ours to keep — wherever we wish to keep them.'

'And if we can't agree?' Igor was finding his feet. 'What of Galina?'

Not for nothing had Alexei studied drama. He shrugged, spread his hands as though he too were now letting the birds fly free. Birds like Galina, her parents, her aunt. 'As you reminded me, I cannot worry for everyone . . .'

'We could suspend you from your own team now, this very day.'

'What, and lose your own personal Gold medal? Your promotion, your perks?' Alexei took the Director's hand in his, tenderly solicitous. 'What's the time?' He consulted the Rolex glowing amid the curling wrist hairs of the Director, and adjusted his own watch.

'What *are* you doing? If you want a Rolex you have only to speak!'

329

'If I get into status symbols I'll buy my own, thanks. I'm synchronizing, as they say in American movies — but you wouldn't know that expression either, I expect. I'll look for you in the hotel lobby tomorrow at midday. We must be prompt. You'll remember I skate the Original two hours later? My solicitors will be ready for you, documents drawn up, all ready to sign.'

'But if we cannot agree?' the Director said again, his voice hoarse.

Alexei shrugged. 'No problem. Consuls from five countries want to take me home with them. All the world loves a winner.'

The Director stretched himself to full height. He was short. 'You have not yet won.'

Alexei felt the roof of his mouth shrink. 'But you said it yourself. Your very own words, Igor. "*Finsky will win. Everyone knows it.*" '

He turned his back on the Director and sent his thoughts forward, a plea to the God of his mother to watch over Alexei Finsky aka Feinstein, make him not eat his words, not choke upon them. No, forget that word. Other skaters choked under pressure. Alexei Finsky, never.

But never before had he faced this kind of pressure.

Grant hammered on Ben Carlsen's door an hour before Lise and Dag were due to compete. Otherwise Ben would have missed the event which had ruined his marriage, his business, and very nearly his children. As it was, he should have stood in bed — as they said in the country of his choice.

The top Russians, first out, to no one's surprise skated brilliantly. The youngest American couple, to everyone's surprise, did likewise. A team from Toronto equalled their performance and marks exactly, and an unknown German team brought the house to its feet — which Grant, watching from the Coaches' Bench, figured took care of the top four. Ben, breathing on to the back of his neck, had turned a bilious green, and Grant spent anxious moments wishing he'd not worn his new cashmere sports jacket.

The Carlsens took the ice for warm-up. They wore their expensive blue costumes which had set Ben back four thou.

So often had he heard the price tag, Grant felt it to be embroidered on to the garments.

Ben thumped him between the shoulder-blades. 'They're in the blue! At that money they were for Finals. The red for Originals!'

'Yes. Last minute flap. Lise slopped chocolate milk over the red while they got dressed backstage. I had to run and kiss the hotel manager's ass to get these out of storage. I promised a fat tip from you when we get back.'

'Christ . . . but . . . but what was she doing guzzling chocolate milk before coming out to skate . . . what will they wear for Finals . . . what —'

As it turned out, the problem didn't arise.

Ben was saying: 'Maybe a good idea, best costumes first. Make folks sit up and take notice. Remember 'em. Give 'em a boost for the big finish.'

Grant went rink-side to supervise the warm-up.

As usual, Lise's teeth chattered like castanets. She'd pulled inside her fear like a snail inside its shell. Grant caught her arm, freezing to the touch, and proceeded to coax her out. 'Relax. Dag's steady as a rock, you'll be back in the dressing-room and laughing before you know it. You look great, both of you, too gorgeous to be here, you should be in a show!' Lise's eyes began to brighten. He was singing her song. He poured a steady coating of flattery over her, thick as whipped cream, and finally they were doing a spin here, a jump there. Lise managed one of the crucial lifts, a table-top. Just. She wouldn't try the triple-twist on warm-up, she'd do it in the number, honest. It terrified her because the partner had to let go in mid-air for a split second, but the more she wouldn't practise, the worse it got. Grant sighed, nodded, wished them luck, and returned to his seat. He knew a dead horse when he saw one. But maybe in the programme she'd make it.

Lise and Dag Carlsen, Sweden, were announced to a few snickers from the competitors' seats — the skaters all knew they came from California — and to a great roar of approval from the general public simply because they were too beautiful to believe. In the spotlight they looked ravishing. Sky-blue silk against deeper blue ice. Speedwell blue eyes. Hair of spun gold glinting under the lights. From several rows back, Grant heard Nakashima gasp.

They started well, Dag moving like a seasoned performer. The early moves were not difficult. Dag projected perfectly, drawing the eye like a fine painting; few in the audience noticed the girl's shaky landings on the simplest jumps, a slight stumble on a step. Fewer still saw her frozen face; the competition smile still gleamed out at them, perfect teeth, a practised stretching of the lips and always the last thing to go. All saw the jump she didn't do, seemed, in fact, to forget it should have been there! The slot for the triple-twist came up empty — another element Lise left out. Grant had known she would. Spins were only a tad off synch and she seemed to pick up for a second, no doubt sensing the chequered flag, but the table-top waited for her, the last element in a programme in which she'd already ignored a jump and a lift and flubbed a step sequence. It didn't much matter now, but here came the table, a one-arm difficult for Dag because of the injury. As always, it went up laboured, pushed with sheer muscles instead of springing lively off the ice because Lise dare not spring. To spring shot you up too high and down too hard — if you missed.

She remembered to smile at the top of the table and through the first turn, but then the smile began to slip, to slide into apprehension, accelerating to terror as she felt her balance go. Her weight shifting wildly above him, Dag battled to hold on, anger and panic flickering over his face like trick masks when he felt her way too far behind him, his grip on her clenched fist a blinding pain now, no way to halt the drift. She seemed to fall incredibly slowly, landing in a heap of sky-blue, perfect timing with the clash of cymbals for their big finish. The audience held its breath.

She didn't get up. Dag leaned over her as Grant and a cluster of officials slip-slid across the ice to reach her. Stretcher-bearers followed more cautiously, arriving in time to hear Dag say, 'Why didn't you jump for it, I could have held you then! Get up, we have to get to the kiss-'n'-cry for our marks —' As he spoke, hot tears fell to the ice, freezing as they hit.

Lise opened her eyes to Grant, not her brother. 'My knee's weird, like it's on wrong.' It lay at an unnatural angle Grant didn't attempt to correct.

Under the make-up her skin was wax, more beautiful than

ever. The ambulance men bore her off and Grant couldn't help noticing how gracefully she let her arm trail over the side. He went to Ben, so still at the rail he could have been dipped in ice himself. His eyes shone like black glass and the caverns of his cheeks were the yellowish-green of old bruises. As Grant watched him, Ben's chest rose at last in a slow, ragged sob.

'I'll kill him,' he said. 'I'll kill the bastard. Where's the hospital?'

'Top floor of the hotel,' Grant said. 'I'll drive. . .'

After the second obligatory visit to the hospital on the penthouse floor Grant satisfied himself Lise was okay, and left. The room was filled with newsmen, all eager to interview the Nordic Queen propped up on pillows, surrounded by Swiss chocolates and glossy magazines and a flying wedge of male athletes waiting to autograph her cast. If Lise had one perfect element, this was it. Ben crouched in the corner, hands limp as wet laundry between his knees. Grant figured he was best left alone for a very long time. Dag had the sense to escape early, though God alone knew where he'd gone. Probably as relieved as him that the long agony was over — and just as ashamed of the thought. A dislocated knee was nothing to celebrate, but it had slipped both Grant and Dag off a very embarrassing hook.

Exhausted — drama did exhaust when the rush of adrenalin drained off — Grant stumbled through a maze of penthouse corridors, surprised by a brief glimpse of Maureen Sterling quietly closing a door before disappearing around a corner and heading for the bank of lifts.

He stood rooted to the carpet, a swarm of premonitions flapping great black wings about his head. He tried shaking them off but they wouldn't go, and he found himself backing up Maureen's trail to the extra-wide beige door she'd closed so carefully. His heart racing, he pushed and it opened slightly, like all hospital doors.

This, then, was her room. A night-light glowed in a far corner, a pink towel draped over it to soften even that small light. As his eyes adjusted he made out a nurse slumped in an easy-chair, asleep over her knitting, the dim bulb striking little sparks off metallic needles at rest. Somewhere a machine hissed faintly, oxygen perhaps, or an air-filter, and from the bed the steady breathing of the tranquillized. Beside it the scent of very fresh roses, hothouse no doubt, brought by ambulance from Barcelona with the woman they comforted.

He waited a long time before approaching the bed, looking down, relief flooding him that her face was in shadow, her hair in darkness. Some light struck her long hands, more slender even than before, and he remembered them stroking a stainless skate-blade as softly as if it had been a baby.

He forced himself, now, to bend, to peer through a kindly light into her face. Age he had prepared himself for, but from this . . . this ravaged wasteland he wanted to turn, to run, chasing it out of mind and memory. But he'd known, something in him had known. The hints were all there. Mother is not well . . . the van with a nurse in it at the Barcelona rink . . . a satyr and his helper passing her like a precious package through the van's doors . . . no Deirdre watching her daughter train in Montegreco. He leaned closer and caught the faint scent of her skin, her breath, sweet now and cloying. Searching her face, he found it gentler in age, softer than expected, not so much wrinkled as . . . empty, as if the Deirdre he remembered was melting slowly away from the inside.

He knew this look, this skin, so translucent one could almost see the skull beneath, its grottos and caverns, its secret hiding places for fears one set aside, too terrible to think except in sleep. To him, Deirdre had been inexpressibly beautiful; Mum had been plain, the goodness showing through only in her eyes, anxious to please, to do her best. But a few weeks before her death Mum's features too had melted to this spare, fleshless beauty he saw on the frilled and scented pillow.

So long resented, even hated, but always longed for, he ached now to take Deirdre up, carry her to some quiet place and rock her to sleep in his arms so she would know, know in her heart, that what remained of her cells, her skin, her bones, that all was loved, every trespass forgiven.

In this darkened room which celebrated only waste, he

turned away, saw his own face looking back at him from a dresser mirror, bones, cells, and skin all healthy, still taut with flesh and youth. He closed his eyes, opening them only when the nurse unveiled the night-light.

'You're the new doctor?' she whispered.

He nodded, looking beyond her to the mirror, seen now for what it was. A studio portrait of Maureen.

Back on the sixth floor he walked blindly by Jasinski, straight into his own room, and locked the door. In the dark — he could not look into a mirror again — he let his clothes fall off, curled himself into a foetal position on the Olympic rug to weep the night away, wrenching man-sobs, silent and dry, ripping at chest and throat until they reached, finally, his heart — the one fastness he'd protected at all cost, always, from assault. But he was exhausted now, shell-shocked, defences stripped away, the power of grief invincible after all, an easy victor over an anger which had sustained him for eighteen years.

Much later, daylight creeping up the walls and cold to his naked skin, he found himself rocking on the carpet, back and forth, back and forth, exactly the way he'd wanted to rock Deirdre and, by extension, Mum. Rest. You are loved. Unbidden, unwanted, a picture came to him so sharply it could be *now*, this moment, his old Coach from Swansea leading the chapel choir, his voice clear and sweet as a boy's. *Guardian angels watch beside you, all through the night.*

PART THREE

The Summit

CHAPTER THIRTY-ONE

The day Mens and Ladies Original Programmes were to be judged, a muffled voice phoned the Montegreco airport early in the morning and tossed a wild-card into the pot. The caller claimed to have hidden a bomb within the Olympic complex; he hung up before a panicky nightman could ask where.

Ever since the massacre at Munich years ago, crank calls at international sporting events were routine; a precocious kid looking for kicks; a lonely old man desperate for a pinch of momentary, if anonymous, fame, a report on TV to warm the winter of a lacklustre life. The investigative process was as routine, now, as the threat. The caller was probably no terrorist, but who among the organizers dare file the report under 'Crank' and forget it?

Competitors and coaches could afford to shrug nonchalantly, then within hours submerge themselves again into the Games on which they'd risked a lifetime; that was *their* pressure, no room for any other. Athletes hurtle down the side of mountains at speeds a hair short of suicidal; men without wings take to the air and launch themselves into the void, trusting to training and strong ankles to bring them safely down to hard-pack. These are not your average citizens clinging all their days to the edge of a life-raft; these players lived, and a few died, hunting down the ultimate thrill; to them, a bomb threat was of far less import than a complex fracture of the tibia. One posed a minor risk; the other, certain disaster.

As sponsors, the principality and consortium could not afford such bravado. Creating an upmarket image for a year-round resort was seventy-five per cent of the investment. As a promotional opportunity, what could be better

than invigorating footage of the luxury complex beamed
hourly around the world? Vital, then, that fond memories of
the resort linger in the public mind, beckoning holiday
makers to Montegreco's slopes far into the future. The leg of
an athlete injured in competition could be treated, and
perhaps discreetly amputated, in his own home town — but
after the Games, an integral part of the Olympic tradition.
In contrast, an explosion which bruised the thumb of just
one spectator would scream MONTEGRECO BOMB! headlines
across news sheets on every street corner, break into re-runs
of 'Eastenders' and 'Golden Girls' clear around the world.
As a Swiss banker, lips prudently pursed, remarked, the
fireball of an exploding bomb, however harmless, scarcely
enhanced the long-term aims of the consortium.

The first priority? Protect investors, spectators, and
athletes. Within seconds of the threatening call the sponsors
zoomed into overkill. Recruiting teams fanned out to scour
unemployment lines all across Western Europe. By the next
day flotillas of warm bodies in hastily fitted uniforms were
landed, bemused, at Montegreco airport. An efficient
operation, massive capital outlay, and presto! Village,
Mountain, Oval and Rink Security forces quadrupled
overnight. But in their zeal to plug every conceivable hole,
the recruiters had overlooked one vital qualification for any
job within the complex. Language. Which applicants spoke
what? Of the new influx, fully ninety-eight per cent knew
only one. German, Spanish, Italian, French, or English. For
the rest, a sprinkling of Russians, a Pole, a Czech, and a
wizened Oriental newly arrived in Paris who spoke Tibetan
and two words of French. *Oui* and *non*.

No matter. Access to each section of the compound lay in
ID photos on colour-coded badges to be worn at all times.
Each colour indicated function — on which the new guards
received a quick briefing, an explicit colour chart, and
instructions to be thorough at all costs. '*At all costs*!' the
recruiter-in-chief roared, puffed up with importance,
unaware that half the inductees understood not a word he
said. 'No cameramen backstage! No competitors in the
kitchens! No girls in the boys' showers! No unauthorized
public in the stadia! No judges in the computer rooms! No
kitchen staff in the dressing-rooms! No autograph-hounds in

the media pit! *Understand*?' The new recruits nodded, dazed by the occasion and the swift reversal of their status: yesterday, simple foot-soldiers in the army of the unemployed; today, a vital part of the Olympics! They pictured themselves, in a distant future, confiding to incredulous strangers that they, yes, *they* participated in the Montegreco Games! To prepare for the task and the telling they studied maps and colour charts endlessly, until they had committed to memory each colour-code and matched it with its venue — but mostly they admired the mountains, the Olympic motif embossed on every document, and their new uniforms, *theirs*! *To keep forever*!

Meanwhile, competitors competed. Even those unlucky few forced to withdraw found better things to do than worry about bomb threats. For Lise Carlsen, the new focus of world-wide sympathy and floral tributes worthy of a dying empress, glittering horizons opened up by the minute. Mindful of Lise's beauty, the hotel's boutiques and beauty shops tripped over themselves to provide (on consignment) anything her heart desired — so long as cameras got the prestigious brand-names correct. Hair stylists, make-up artists, and manicurists crawled over her bed and her person like blow-flies over a prime roast. When would they run across a lovelier model than Lise Carlsen to show off their designer négligées, chiffon lingerie, swan's-down bed-jackets? Expensive perfumes, labels foremost, decorated her medicine table. A life-sized satin Doberman, enviably sleek, decked out in a diamond collar, solid gold dog-tag, and wrist-to-elbow watches (all Swiss), reclined on a *chaise-longue* facing the cameras, of which there was usually one in the room. The message conveyed was that at the Montegreco resort even injuries came lapped in luxury. In their office, the executives gave quiet thanks to a God who had sent them the ideal patient on which to hang their glamorous image.

As if this were not enough, Lise set aside her eggs *gratinés* to touch up her lipstick as yet another gift arrived at the hospital wing in a wheelchair, to be housed — where else? — in the room next to hers. Mieko Nakashima's second cousin, top scorer on the 70-metre hill a day earlier, had broken an ankle at what would have been the winning distance if he could have sustained the landing. Cameramen and reporters clawed and jabbed for footage of the handsome young Japanese, his chair parked as close as possible to Lise's bed, swinging himself on to its edge in an exuberant move to compare casts. Fluffy blonde head and glossy black touched in rueful commiseration, a dynamic image beamed into every living-room in the world. Two healthy, handsome kids laughing, wiggling bare toes for their audience — Lise's toe nails an impeccable rose pink. This, the image said, was sportsmanship; laughter amid shattered hopes.

Yes, Lise radiated happiness. The truth had dawned slowly; that inside the wrenching pain in her knee lay her key to freedom. *She could quit.* No more heart-stopping seconds suspended over the ice, no more nausea as the music swept inexorably to the place where Dag hurled her from an overhead lift into a throw-jump she must land alone, no hands to steady her. *She need never skate again*! Not even a show — where she'd have to do lifts! She could act; already she'd been offered a bit part in a sit-com. A week at a fat farm and she could even model. This morning, after an agent explained the term 'contingency basis' and painted pictures of a dazzling future right outside that door, she signed him on the spot. Her dislocated knee had kicked open any door she'd ever want to go through. She would be rich, desirable. . .

She turned to Mieko's cousin and offered up her lips. As he took them a minicam whirred overhead. Beyond the ski-jumper's shoulder she wiggled playful fingers at the cameraman and the world, which included her father watching TV in a downstairs bar. He sighed, drooping with fatigue and drink and a futile desire to punish somebody, anybody, for every wasted dream.

Far away in Hokkaido the old chieftain also watched. The last of the Nakashimas indulged in neither dreams nor drink; it was not in him to waste good anger on a lost cause. He called his executive secretary and for ten minutes barked orders non-stop; he called a body-servant with instructions on which bags to pack and what to pack in them; he called his public relations chief of two decades. As far as it was possible for Hiro Nakashima to form a close relationship, this man had considered himself a friend. But today he was

an employee, Nakashima's message brief and to the point:
'Out!'

Two-and-a-half hours before he was to skate the short
Original, Alexei Finsky waited in an inconspicuous corner of
the lobby. His solicitors, summoned from Bern by Deirdre,
already conferred in a small office, awaiting whoever was
empowered to act for the athletics hierarchy of the USSR in
this highly unorthodox contract. Though quite alone,
Alexei's expression, bland as always, concealed a turmoil no
amount of self-control could conquer. Would they come? If
not, what did it mean and what to do? Suppose the Director
had been refused permission? Suppose he'd been afraid to
ask for it? If so, what avenues still lay open for Alexei
Finsky? The talent scout's glowing contract for the Gold
medal — if indeed Alexei should win it — and the scout's
contempt for anyone foolish enough to remain in Russia?
Alexei remembered his voice, his words: 'New York's got
everything you'd ever want. Hell, if you get homesick
there's 'The Russian Tearoom'. One of the best restaurants
in town, all the Russkie ex-pats hang out there.'

Alexei had nodded, strangely saddened at the prospect.
Through many visits to New York with the team he knew the
restaurant, its memorable food, it's chic American clientèle
— but it was the few lonely others who clung in his mind,
tattered-winged bats grown old waiting for courage to face
the daylight outside the cave. Many were elderly defectors
lingering for hours over a single glass of tea, gnarled fingers
squeezing a lemon slice for the last drop of juice and a
chance to speak of the past in their own language, to
postpone a return to that empty apartment, that TV
reflecting a culture they did not comprehend and to which
they felt secretly superior.

These Russians of diverse talents — dancers, writers,
poets, painters, gymnasts, skaters — all shared one
overriding need: they travelled endlessly about the world,
but always from one Russian enclave to another. Knowing it
to be forever lost to them, nonetheless they searched for
home. Softened by Western luxuries to which they had
become addicted, they shrank from a return to bread lines,

bus lines, meat lines — perhaps to no meat at all. But, surrounded by the comforts of the West, past privations of the East were recalled with nostalgic hunger: the zest of beating a cumbersome system, tracking down a plane ticket to Leningrad when they had been assured, with grim satisfaction, that the flight had sold out weeks ago; the sensuous pleasures trapped in a new winter coat for which they had queued endlessly; the oily, ovine smell of its scratchy wool; its collar and cuffs as yet unfrayed; the solid promise of its weight in the bag as they elbowed into the rush-hour Metro; the knowledge that next winter's warmth, however coarse to the touch, was assured. And food, how sharply they remembered the food when there had been so little of it! As they described the vibrant colour and pitted texture of the very last orange at the fruit-stand, they tasted afresh the triumph of a victory almost as sweet as the fruit itself; the rush of saliva as a thumbnail released its sharp citrus fragrance to those at the back of the line who were too late, only a moment too late. The mosque and minaret glamour of St Basil's domes gleaming, newly washed and splendidly incongruous through the mist of a rainy grey morning.

Moscow was all these memories and more, swirling inside endless glasses of tea, countless slices of lemon beautifully ambered after their long steepage. To Americans who said, 'Boy, I'll bet you're glad to be outta there!' they agreed because it was expected of them, but the truth lay like lead in their hearts and the lead grew heavier with every year. They had two homes, neither of which was the United States of America, hospitable as she might be. The workplace was always home — canvas is canvas, ice is ice, ballet studios were alike the world over, dust, rosin and sweat. The other home was Russia, for which they had grown too pampered.

Alexei trembled. Had his reckless demands — no, call it what it was, blackmail — shot the bolt behind him? Would exile now be forced upon him? For if the Director failed to appear, Alexei had isolated himself from all that was dear and familiar, Galina not the least of these. With solicitors waiting soberly around a table to settle his future, Alexei Finsky, alone in a luxurious hotel, the mantle of a brilliant career waiting to descend on his shoulders, acknowledged what he had not known. That he was first a Russian. Second, a Jew. Third, a skater. No Gold medal would change the order of priorities.

Let them agree, he prayed, only let them agree. Let me live three-fourths of my life — all of it if I wish — at home where I belong. I only want the *option* to come and go at will — perhaps with that in my pocket I shall not wish to go at all. He checked his watch. The Director had ten minutes left. Be prompt, yesterday's confident Alexei Finsky had ordered him, an excess of power running away with his tongue. Behind him he heard a footfall, light on the heavy carpet. It was the Pole, Jasinski, with whom he'd spoken several times, always with pleasure. Damn it, why couldn't Galina's father have been like this? Surely this quiet doctor, raised in a concentration camp, watching his family starve to death one by one to assure his survival, had suffered at least as much as the paranoiac in The Park? But no, Galina's father was now in custody again, his paranoia no doubt multiplying like bacteria in a sealed jar.

'Tell me,' Alexei asked in Polish as Jasinski murmured a polite, 'May I?' before settling into the next chair. 'Everything that happened to you in the war . . . do you . . . do you think of it very much?'

'All the time.' Jasinski spoke in Russian, but imperfectly. Alexei spoke in Polish, equally imperfect. It was a game they played, like children. Neither knew his own mistakes. 'I think of it all the time. It is my past.'

'Do you ever want to go back?'

'All the time,' he said again. 'I know I cannot. Too long in the West, one grows dependent. Luxuries become necessities with terrifying speed. When I return to Poland on vacation I am a boy again for the first three days. Then already I am tearing my hair at the roots. Why must I queue for a postage stamp to mail a card to my son? Why must my cousin stop at every gas station to gather up gasoline litre-by-small-litre as a bee gathers honey? Why must he remove and lock away his windshield wipers before I can take him to luncheon, because between the soup and the fish someone will steal them? I rage. He shrugs. But always the people hope. It is all they have.'

Alexei laughed. 'The people! We have *glasnost* and the

perestroika but also the dark suits protecting many jobs. Behind them, many uniforms.'

'The West is no different,' Jasinski said in his fractured Russian. 'What use is a four-star general in time of *peace*? The word is anathema, the end of all he has been led to believe. No. Civilians control the hope, generals control the pop. ICBM's, heat seeking this, megaton that. The world is naïve, Alexei, if it thinks they'll lie down and rust like little tin soldiers. If they die they'll die shooting and take us with them. They have power to protect and power wants only more power. As long as they make us spend more to kill each other than to protect our planet . . . but I run on . . . So rare, among skaters, to find one who thinks of something other than ice. But as you see, even at the Olympics, the leaders do not care for performance, only the medal counts. Who will win the most Golds? What — what is it?'

'The clock. It strikes midday.'

Alexei's heart hung like lead in his chest, far too heavy to beat. But then the Director, promptly as ordered, beaming, marched through the lobby flanked by two aides. His small eyes sought Alexei and nodded in triumph, almost in conspiracy as he beckoned him to join them.

'I forgot,' Jasinski was saying. 'You compete in two hours. Nervous?'

Alexei stood up and exhaled long and slow. He had not known he was holding his breath, must indeed have been holding a small reservoir for over half an hour. Against what? 'Nerves? No, doctor. I leave mine at home.'

'May I wish you luck?'

'Thank you.' But Alexei Finsky had no need of luck now. He had fired his thimbleful of power and it had detonated as intended.

Following the Director through the door to the solicitors, *his* solicitors, he felt that same power flow through his arms, his legs. Back to business again, he checked his watch. Yes, if they got a move on there would be time for a shower and a short meditation before he donned the suit of lights.

Emma Crisp dressed carefully and well ahead of schedule for her first judging stint at these Olympic Games. Dark suit and white shirt — virtually a uniform among the fraternity. Minimal make-up. Ditto jewellery, colours, finery of any kind. When the marks went up, when the TV announcers read them off and zoomed in on the offending panellist who dared go higher, or lower, than the rest, anonymity formed the one protective colouring of value.

Today she welcomed the distraction of judging — anything to stop her worrying about Beejay sweating out her final practice session before her own Original competition tonight. But who was she kidding? The other girls might be at 'rest', trembling away the afternoon praying they didn't mess up tonight. Beejay would be licking her fingers over pickled herring and for sure she'd show up to watch the men compete this afternoon. The day Beejay missed any competition any place, Emma would call in a doctor fast.

A half-hour to go before the shuttle-bus took her to the arena. From habit she skimmed the field one last time, checking track-records, consistency, the years at the top. Sometimes a newcomer dazzled like a shooting star — but more often failed miserably under pressure. What she'd watched them do all week was no indication of what they'd do today, when it counted. Finsky The Miser had not done much, but then he never did. Each move one time, no misses; he hoarded the fireworks for the programme. The Boston Bean, if he was on, could tear off the roof. If not, he moved through the music in a trance, cocky smile in place, his coach pounding an ineffectual fist into the rail. Jeffie, still in romantic mode with his flashy new conquest, might skate like a dream; too bad it couldn't be a masculine dream. . . The Czech — poor boy could be head to head with Finsky but his music and choreography killed him. A Korean on the way up, but not this time around, rough around the edges yet. And, oh God, don't forget young Willi. Her phone rang and she paused, afraid it would be old Willi, holding his stupid little gun to her head. But no. It was Nils in the lobby, waiting to escort her to the arena.

The difference between Nils and Grant Rivers! Nils determined that old Willi wouldn't get in a last threatening bolt; Grant assuming she was grown up, could take care of it herself. Two generations. No better illustrated than over meals the last two days. Yesterday lunch with Nils had Willi staring at them nonstop from across the restaurant. Grant would not have noticed; if he had it would never have crossed his mind to do anything about. For Nils, it completely ruined their meal as he muttered incessantly over a delectable cucumber cream soup, '*Gi ham én pâ kjaken!*'

'You sound like hardtack. Scratchy,' she said.

'Scratchy? If he wasn't so damned old I'd give him one on the chin!'

Emma didn't remind Nils that he was no spring chicken himself.

Willi had done the same at early lunch today, his implacable presence reminding her that the score he gave Beejay this evening would depend on the score she gave young Willi this afternoon.

Grant, making up for dinner last night, missed thanks to the Carlsen drama, had simply shrugged. 'What d'you care? He's just one judge out of nine. If she skates great and he marks low, he gets egg on his face.'

'That'll comfort Beejay, I'm sure!' Boy, was *Grant* ever in a mood!

'Relax. It's not her turn yet. By next Games, Willi will be retired or six feet under.'

'But what about Beej now, Grant? I've not asked, especially since Roxi's skating better, but where d'you think Beejay can wind up? Me, I'm too close to it to see the prospects clear, too worried about expenses —'

'Don't. After today the Committee'll grant full sponsorship. She'll be in the top eight. There's Rox, Nakashima, two Germans, that's about —'

'— that's *not* about all!' she said sharply. 'You keep forgetting Sterling.'

It seemed to her that he flushed, but just then he dropped his napkin so he'd naturally have coloured up a bit, retrieving it. He wasn't himself today at all, but maybe he was worried about the Pair, the adverse publicity. Any injury, and some idiot started a rumour about over-training — which reflected badly on the coach.

'Upset about Lise, Grant? The over-training talk . . .'

'Lise over-trained? Don't make me laugh. But I'm upset about the mess. Ben . . . his business . . . Dag, God knows what he'll do now. I don't see Lise skating much longer. I don't see me coaching another Pair, either. This time I got lucky! Only one parent to handle. Worse still when you've got two full sets battling it out. As it is, I've been juggling two egos on the ice and they don't match, never do. In the Carlsens' case they were direct opposites.'

'Looks like Dag's taken a shine to Nakashima,' she said slyly.

'Emma, no skater-talk over food, huh? Right now I've had it up to here with skaters and their romances.'

'Okay-okay, I guess you're nervous for Originals — and after last night —'

Again the look. Anger? Resentment? 'If you want to know, I was bloody tired last night and I'm bloody tired today.'

'Scared for Roxanne?'

'Among other things, yes. I don't know about you, but I've got to get ready for the Mens. You'll note I have not mentioned Jeffie, have not "put in a good word for him" or reminded you that you're judging him in two hours?'

'Thanks. Restraint appreciated. I never expected you to, anyway.'

'Thank *you*.' He'd sketched a sardonic bow, signed the tab, and left.

Yes, a whole generation of manners and concern separated Nils from Grant Rivers. That was women's-lib for you. You couldn't have it all. She headed out for the lobby and Nils, praying, as she pressed the elevator button, that young Willie would have the consideration not to mop up the ice this afternoon.

CHAPTER THIRTY-TWO

Roxanne Kramer tightened her laces. One more run-through. Mercifully, then, she could change, watch the Mens' agony, a welcome oblivion before she must drag herself back to face her own emotional Gethsemane.

Oh, to get it over! What sadist always gave Ladies the after-dinner slot, giving her nerves all day to knot up her insides? But at least after tonight she'd know where she stood. When she went to bed in her spartan cubicle at the Village, she'd know down to the last one-hundredth of one-tenth of a point if she had a chance for Gold in the Final. Lose tonight, and she'd lost, period. Win — and she still had a prayer. She breathed deeply, as she'd been trained. Except for Grant not being around much, she'd come to feel safe in the Village, the athletes jammed in together, brimming with fellowship, youth, and pride in being part of a tradition, winning or losing only slightly more momentous than the honour of participating.

Outside the Village, at rink or hotel, she looked at Grant and knew that winning still mattered. She remembered the yellowed slogan Noni pasted over her bed when she was six: *Winning may not be everything, but losing isn't anything.* Winning, now, *was* everything. To give Grant that one gift . . . he'd never be able to thank her enough. She'd be sure of him.

Beyond the walls of the Village, pressure grew. In the holy name of the media, drums beat louder for Ladies than they ever did for Men. Headlines screamed everything and meant nothing. CONFRONTATION! SPANGLES AND SPITE! OVER THE HILL AT 22? The papers pitted her against a half-dozen contenders now, locked her into blazing vendettas with skaters she'd didn't know. Old men who'd never in their lives stepped on a sheet of ice pondered, for pay and in print, whether Roxanne Braun Kramer could do it, and gravely offered up battle plans for her consideration, as if the fate of the world depended on the outcome of Ladies Figure Skating.

Half an hour to Men's Original and already banners streamed; a host of souvenir programmes waved from every direction. The arena pulsed with life. Designed like a castle, its palm trees and hot-house geraniums circled the cold, hard blue oval of ice. Above it, expensively upholstered behinds filled the high-priced seats, camp-followers armed with opera-glasses and malice. They'd applaud their favourites and let silent malice speak for the rest, tier on tier of vultures gravely waiting for falls and failure, prophecies soon to self-fulfil or self-destruct. Crammed to the arching rafters in the cheaper seats, the general public hooted and honked, a beery rabble with one talent, one intent: splinter the atmosphere with two-fingered whistles, bull-horns, anything to create a carnival mood, to shout down the reverence of the *cognoscenti*. Grant called the mob 'yobs', general public flown in from every corner of Europe at excursion rates, then shipped overland by bus as if they were potatoes and turnips, from Lyonnais. Grant said yobs whistled and shouted because voice power was all they had.

She spotted her own supporters, Stars and Stripes and something dressed up as Yankee-Doodle. But mainly she saw Noni with the old ones and felt a tender, almost overwhelming need to protect them from humiliation, from her own failure — but she *hadn't* failed yet, couldn't until tonight, when she might, God, she just might. No, she'd win the Original, they deserved that. They'd be close, down front where she could see their faces — not that it helped, their fingers knotting, strain tightening their smiles — but she knew their loyalty. No doubt at all whose side *they* were on. Hers. Overnight her resentment had turned to gratitude. It was lonely down here.

Nakashima had finished her run-through. A forest of Rising Suns rippled in support, as if competition had begun already.

'Pay no attention,' Grant said. 'Whip through your number and get off. Do everything but save plenty for

tonight, okay? Cool down in the ballet-room after. I may
have to take Jeff aside, punch his silly lights out. Look at
him strolling in like a goddamn clown! No make-up, I said,
so he's slathered it on — and a gold earring yet! Queen of
the fairies, tame rocker in tow, and judges already gathering
for the Grand March! Emma looks like thunder.'

Roxanne laughed, which perhaps he'd intended. She did a
relaxed run-through, flubbed slightly on a step, a hole in
the ice, not her fault. He nodded and she hurried off,
stopping by Noni and the old ones before rushing to the
Village to change.

'*Vas goot*!' Otto shouted, strong accent betraying his
nerves.

Noni shrugged. 'Not bad. Take your vitamins?'

'Forgot.'

'Take 'em when you go change, huh? For calm, huh?
Keep the blood pressure down, don't want that pounding,
huh? I know how it is, staring the goddamned judges down.
Your blood thumps, the crowd takes over, panic happens,
and in two seconds everything's all ape-shit. Calm, that's the
thing. Experience talkin'. I've been there. Right, Mutti?'

Otto frowned. *Ape-shit*? The coarse nature of this
middle-aged woman's vocabulary! His daughter! True,
civilized speech fled the mind in moments of frustration, as
well it might. It knew that no sedate word cut deep enough
to express profound apprehension and, inevitably, defeat.
So why not simply the *Scheisse* of the back street? Better
yet, grunt like a true ape? He glanced at Brigitta, who
frowned, then laughed, showing them an odd face, one side
briefly slack as if struck physically by Noni's vulgarity. Then
her voice dropped to a lower timbre, mixing English and
German, giggling at some private joke as Noni passed her
another pre-victory cup of champagne, courtesy of the
Parkrose Review. A paper cup. How like Noni. But
Brigitta's wig once again sat in orderly corrugations upon
her bald scalp, a style suitable for an elderly, dignified
woman. How, he wondered, had they produced this foolish
Noni? And having done it, how did they persuade
themselves to sacrifice their future on the shaky altar of her
here-today-gone-tomorrow talent? When it was no longer
worth its shrinking candle, what persuaded them, all these

decades, to shift hope like a burden from Brigitta to Noni and now to Roxanne? And if, next year, as Roxanne seemed to hope, she married her coach and produced another Olympic hopeful, must this cruel, transferable charade continue down the ages? He closed his eyes.

In the competitor section, Beejay Crisp's small, sharp teeth bit into an apple, the crimson of its peel clashing like a cymbal with her copper hair and creamy complexion. In deepest concentration, tongue-tip tracing the rim of her lips, she studied the Skating Order the way a gambler inhales a racing form. Order. A lousy word when Em told her to get her room 'in order' or else. Stick 'skating' in front of it and 'order' mattered. Who skated before you, who followed you. She knew where she'd like to be. Right after that Parisienne who turned to jelly at the word 'judge' — and right before the tallest German, sure to blow, too. Both were slower than she — hell, who wasn't? To music like 'Bugler's Holiday' she had to scoot round the ice like forked lightening just to keep up. Commentators called it 'peppy'. Nobody mentioned that if she missed a beat she'd lost her place, no way to grab the music's tail again. After her would come Nakashima and Roxi in whatever order they drew, with Sterling before or between. Another horse-race. One thing was sure: next year this time Beejay Crisp would have the triple-axel if it killed her — and Em said it might. Grant agreed she could work on it after the Games. Grant agreed. The last few days Grant Rivers had agreed to everything, spreading himself thinner than skimmed milk.

Mum would have loved this. A few years later than planned but he was here, at the Olympics, and guess what? Grant Rivers was still, for now, Grant Rivera on his own — as who wasn't? Look around. The balloon's set to go up, judges on their marks, refs at the ready, sound men checking tapes against lists, cameramen focusing on ice, judges, coaches, and rivals. The world watched and he stood right where it counted, at the rail directing a student soon to take centre-ice. Grant on his own, nobody to count on because here, in this milieu — there's a Sunday word for you, eh Mum? — here in this world-class milieu, friend turned to enemy at the edge of the ice and loneliness clung like a shroud, but we wouldn't talk about shrouds, too many rustling in the corners lately. Since she took off sixteen years ago he'd laboured on and for the ice alone, and when the time came, like now, not one real friend, not even Jasinski, who guarded his nightmares as he guarded his sons; for as long as they'd been pals Jasinski never let family cross tracks with friendship; to each relationship its compartment, to each crumb its corner. Roxi didn't count in this; lovers were not friends. Lovers demanded promises, confessions to rattle at you like old bones in the night. Most times he liked Emma Crisp as much as he liked anybody, but look at her now trying to avoid Willi Vanilla's piercing stare from the official seats, Emma in her thick coat — it's nippy judging on Olympus — friend Emma would turn temporary enemy if she marked Jeff too low because, face it, Jeff swished; Jeff, who he couldn't abide, not because he was gay but because he was sly. Jeffie made it plain he couldn't abide Grant either, but Grant qualified as friend-of-the-moment because it was lonely out there, wrapped around with the crowd, and even Jeff must feel the chill. He'd drawn first warm-up and would skate No. 4 spot, right after the Czech. Jeff's tough luck. So thank heaven Grant didn't like him because he doubted the kid had a prayer now.

Standing with Grant at the rail, the little yum-num coach chewed fingernails and antacids. No cocky talk now because in the next half-hour the Bean could hook deep into tomorrow's medal count and that, mate, was serious business. 'Who d'you fancy, then?' he pressed. 'Besides Finsky I mean?'

Grant smiled. He fancied the Czech and/or the Boston Bean but he'd be damned if he'd give this little man a sliver more confidence — inside many a small man lived a smaller man yammering to get out. He shrugged. 'It's wide open, isn't it? The Czech if he's on, then the Koreans and the Japanese. . .'

'Oh num! Num-num-num! Not the fucking Japanese, old boy.'

Grant turned away. The games drew all sorts. Even his old Swansea coach appeared at the hotel last night, thinner now and grey, his moon face a wistful oval as he shook

Grant's hand. 'I still sing for choir,' he said, '— folks at the rink often mention you and your mam. She'd be proud you did well, dai,' every lilting sentence a song in itself. Coach hadn't changed, just aged.

Deirdre's perfume hung around in his mind too, cobwebby, tainted with sickness and hospitals. She wouldn't appear until Maureen competed tonight. From the look of her, she'd have to spend herself carefully, a thimbleful at a time, and only when she cared to. But hadn't she always done that — except at first? When the opportunity came he'd talk to her. And say what, when the truth lay in the mirror? He looked over his shoulder at Lloyd, at cold grey eyes pursuing Jeff, who twisted and turned, gaudy as a parrot-fish darting to escape Lloyd's hook. He succeeded, shooting the rock star a confident, intimate smile. Lloyd, chatting to an official, cleared his throat and pitched his piercing board-room voice equidistant between the judges and Jeff himself — already on edge for a warm-up bell five minutes late in coming. But Jeff, in his flashy hot pink, his show make-up and his too-blue eyelids, would have had to be deaf to miss the silky whip of Lloyd's tongue:

'Yes, a great pity. . . Mens should, above all, be a *masculine* event. . .'

Jeff looked at his boots, slip-covered in pink lycra, his hair rigid with spray-net, but his smile faded — no lacquer in the world could nail that up. Grant eased over in his direction, murmuring to the back of the boy's neck: 'Get rid of the boot-covers and wipe the crap off your eyes, okay? You look like Miss Piggy in drag.'

Jeff, cut to the quick, gasped. 'Well! My friend's make-up artist flew in specially from London and *slaved* over this look! A professional!'

Grant did not ask what profession. Stars shone in Jeff's eyes and a boy in love, whatever his preference, wore a pathetically thin skin. 'Wash it off.'

Jeff scuttled away to re-design his 'look'. Grant saw the singer tap his wrist, and Jeff's quick turn-about. 'Sod off!' he whimpered, slapping at the celebrated hand. How old was Jeff? Twenty? Too young to fend off marauders like Lloyd and the rocker for long.

And now, ta-da! Two stars of the Ladies circuit newly

arrived from the Village, immaculate, definitely on view, Roxanne Braun Kramer and Maureen Sterling edging to their seats *together* in obvious harmony — a development typical of solitude at the top, but the innocent juxtaposition so rattled Grant that he could neither examine nor acknowledge it.

In the celebrity section, perfectly placed for candid network shots, skating's *crème de la crème* from around the globe. Nobody who was anybody missed an Olympics if he could help it. Curry. Fleming. Cousins. Hamill. Button. Hamilton, Torvill, Dean, Rodnina, Zaitsev. There was Cranston, sketch-book in hand, the Protopopovs close by, a hundred heroes who'd built their lives on the melting surface of a hazardous medium and who had prospered — and in their midst, ablaze with the fires of twin talents, skating and drama — Boitano and a stunningly beautiful Katerina Witt. They formed an international bloc, life members of an exclusive club for which the entry fee was counted in talent, guts, luck, and unbelievably hard work.

Full house. Sell out. Networks, advertisers and consortium members all patted pockets, demanding more promos, more slots, more footage and an ocean of so-so champagne to hawk in the late-night bars at three hundred per cent mark-up. At the Games, who pinched pennies? Only the money-spinners.

For Grant, the Games, so long his major goal, were more — and less — than he expected. Among all these people, many of them friends, there was still only one he knew, unequivocally, to be on his side. From the past she watched him. Years since he'd felt her presence, but it was here now. The carbolic smell of her clothes, of oatmeal at dawn, cheese butties at the rink, bacon sizzling for supper, Ovaltine for bed. Coughing into a Kleenex, she crumpled it into the pocket of her old green coat. '*I'm proud, son. Good luck.*' And who didn't need a pinch of that?

The bell rang for warm-up and five boys skated out in the first brave show of finery at the new arena. If they rewarded dazzle, Jeff's hot-pink suit trimmed in cerise bugle-beads had the Gold all wrapped up. In a burst of bravado strangely touching under Lloyd's offended, offensive gaze, Jeff sailed into a triple-lutz without preparation and far too soon. He under-rotated by a mile and carommed off the boards like a snooker ball. Blinking in disbelief he clambered to his feet, his pink backside soaked now to a blatant magenta, from the rear reminiscent of that baboon — the mandrill? — so embarrassing to parents and zoos in the mating season. Grant groaned, resolving not to laugh or send storm signals — but the judging panel must be howling.

He beckoned Jeff over. 'Trying to win the warm-up, you daft ha'porth?'

'First man with a big jump gets all the attention!' Jeff asserted.

'You got it all right. Too bad. Now relax, start with doubles. When they send you off warm-up, sit on a radiator and dry off the rump steak, okay?'

Sullen and defiant, Jeff tried to swagger off but Grant called him back. 'Jeff, your private life's your own, okay? I'm not your keeper.'

Jeff set his teeth, parrot-fish to baboon to mule in under five minutes. 'You could have fooled me.'

'I wasn't born yesterday. The leather warbler in shades is temporary, I'm sure. The ice is permanent. You're talented. Don't pin your future to a one-night-stand. You're at the Games. It's an honour to be here, so shape up.'

Chastened, Jeff made an orderly, productive warm-up.

Emma, furious in her judge's seat, wished Willi's opera glasses, trained on her from ten rows up and clear across the arena, would find a new target. Beejay and Nils, licking frozen yogurt on sticks, sat two rows below him, tracking the animosity like spectators at a tennis match. So okay folks, enough is damned well enough! We got us a wagon to fix here so stand back — and catch it first time, Willi, because I daren't risk it twice. Emma Crisp, world-ranked and dignified in her dark suit, stared hard to pin Willi's attention before giving him that universal gesture of contempt, the finger, simultaneously mouthing two words into the binoculars: '*Up yours!*'

Willi dropped his lower jaw and his glasses. Nils and Beejay scrambled to help him. When next Emma felt the focus of those round black orbs they'd turned a livid raspberry which, even as she looked, melted yogurt down the chinchilla shoulder of the woman in front. Emma beamed at Beejay, who raised a triumphant fist. First blood to the Crisps. But Willi knew the source of his indignity and tonight he'd judge it. Between them, sassy Beejay and her hot-tempered momma could sure louse up a kid's chances. Nils made them a formidable trio. But maybe Willi Jr, out on next warm-up, would skate well enough to smooth out old tempers. So concentrate, Em. Here they come, all scared witless. Good or bad, they'd worked two-thirds of their young lives for this. Watch them close. Judge them right.

By the time Jeff's turn came his costume was dry, his jumps clean, every move text-book quality. He spun to a triumphant, polished finish. Emma gave him his due. Not quite as much as the Czech, but the Czech's long programme tomorrow would be dead meat; Emma, seeing it every day, had itched to tell the Czech coach: Fix it! But judges didn't do that.

And now here came Willi Jr, wan as a lily in a cream jumpsuit, wheaten hair too thin for his years, no lashes whatever, and light watery eyes rimmed in pink, like a white mouse. All he needed was a tail. While Emma strongly disapproved of make-up for boys — she wasn't wild about it for girls — in Willi Jr's case any colour would help. Stand up, she breathed at him. Don't mop up the ice, let me give you an okay score, don't wrap your jumps, don't force me to mark you down, don't, don't — but of course he did. He opened with a disastrous fall-scramble-fall on an easy jump and went downhill from there. With little time left, totally unnerved, he ran into the wooden barrier twice, causing the TV announcer to publicly question the boy's sight. Five elements botched, unmarkable. He finished his final sit-spin sitting down — and stayed there. Emma risked a glance at the judge on her left, who lifted his shoulders a fraction, as much at a loss as she. How to mark this at Olympic level? How to leave the kid a shred of self respect? The judge on Emma's right, an elderly Russian, called the referee over. 'Is possible he is sick? Drunk? Drugged? All week I watch this boy, I see nothink like this.' The referee called another conference, after which a doctor hurried forth.

A raging fever. With that long, pale face? But yes. 104°.

'Who,' the doctor demanded, 'permitted this man to compete?'

Only his grandfather, head of his delegation, knew for sure, but Emma had an idea: *Emma, I am seventy-four. The next Olympiad is hardly my top priority. My grandson, however, is.* But only as an adjunct to the old man — for whom it was now or never. Later it would be determined the boy's blood teemed with 'flu virus compounded by an army of allergies — and he lived at close quarters with a Village full of athletes for whom it was also now or never. But they, of course, were not old Willi's priority at all.

When the referee nodded, Emma figured she'd spoken aloud. She sighed. 'We have to mark him?'

'Afraid so. He should have been withdrawn earlier but. . .'

The referee formally requested that the boy's marks be posted and that the next competitor take the ice. It was the Boston Bean, dashing out with his customary bravura, arms raised to the crowd, a wide smile displaying the genius of American orthodontia. His attitude shouted: 'Okay folks, here I am! Start the party!' Gathering speed on a corner for his big jump, he blew a mocking kiss to his coach, an inspired bit of *chutzpah* which delighted everyone but Yum-Num himself, who popped another antacid, turned his back on the camera, and sat down. A gust of applause swept the crowd. The Bean had them in his palm before he'd done a single element. When he made one minor error, a slap-dash finish to a spin he could do in his sleep, the audience groaned. Yum-Num shut his eyes and pounded a fist into the bench.

Trotting closely behind the Bean on his flower-strewn path to kiss'n'cry, Yum-Num scowled, muttering fiercely to the back of the Bean's neck: 'Other coaches get a thank-you-sir-I-owe-it-all-to-you-sir! But not me, oh no, I get ulcers! What did I tell you all week? Work the effing spins, but not you, you didn't have time. *You were too busy fucking everything on legs*! I'm surprised you haven't had a go at the trophy table!'

A second later he was smiling blandly at an announcer, who asked what went wrong in the spin. 'Slight loss of concentration?' Yum-Num suggested.

'Win some, lose some,' the Bean said airily. 'Just wait for Finals.'

The four Western judges gave him 5.9s, the rest 5.8s, which put him in first place with only Finsky, yet to skate, a serious threat. Very serious.

Alexei skated out slowly, in no rush to start. The Bean had made an error. Small, yes, but it opened the door. He only had to be perfect. Sixes were seldom given for compulsories, so he needed one more judge than the Bean to pull ahead. He ignored his Director, busy with computations any moron could do in his head. Marks seldom mattered. It was which skater took most first places. Each judge only had one first place to give. He stared gravely down the line of nine. Barring catastrophe, the four Eastern judges would give him theirs, and probably the pivot — a Swiss known to favour the most established competitors — but the Swiss could shift. Which left Crisp holding the key; her record showed her to be fair. She'd given the Bean 5.9 for technique, 5.8 for style. If she could be persuaded to give Alexei 5.9 for each, then he would temporarily have her first place. Simple. But Crisp and the Bean saluted the same flag. The great powers measured success by the same yardstick, the team medal count; ideology usually beat idealism by a hair — a tenth of a point. Match two competitors equally, you naturally gave the top mark to your own. Just, discreet, and effective — but only a Gold Medal would validate Alexei Finsky's contract, his ticket to true freedom.

Unlike the Bean, who skated with feet and personality, Alexei prepared his mind-set with optimum care. The first note of his music, a passionate Russian folk-song, appeared to flick a switch. Quiet Mr Average lit up from within, all of him, heart, head, neck, shoulders, elbows, each a vital part of a performance that only incidentally included each required element, perfectly executed. But mostly he tapped some deep emotional well that opened itself to him in competition only. In euphoric moments his trainer called it 'soul'. Heart or soul, it lifted the audience to its feet every time. This afternoon was no exception. Feet stomped. Mouths roared. Flowers rained like confetti.

Emma Crisp punched in her marks. The Bean was a

charmer and she'd known his family since Betsy Ross hemmed up the flag, but fair was fair.

Marks for Alexei Finsky, USSR: 5.9 and 5.9. Sorry, old Bean.

The winner gathered up his flowers, thrust them upon an old lady with corrugated hair in the front row who babbled her thanks in German, then he skated quietly to the kiss 'n cry booth for the inevitable post-mortem. 'Great performance, a *strong* lead!' the announcer enthused. 'Surprised?'

'Yes,' Finsky lied. 'But my English. . .'

He turned away, puzzled anew at Western thinking. Should an engineer be surprised when his motor hums at the turn of the switch?

The Japanese flunky bowed. 'Please excuse . . . my employer has private business with her nephew. If Miss Carlsen would so kind?'

'*Well*!' Lise, not kind at all, flounced off the bronze god's bed as fast as their plaster-cast embrace permitted. 'Don't you people . . . like . . . *knock* before shoving into a sick-room? And *you*,' she hissed, glaring at her brother. 'Wait till Dad sees you hanging out with *this* all the time!' Her eyes raked Mieko's face, flicked up and down her short body like twin blue lasers. She avoided the girl's more intimidating mother.

'Dad knows,' her brother said. 'And it's not his business. Mieko's mom has family stuff to talk about. Scoot — and do up your bra, why don't you?'

'Is that all you think about? *Do up my bra*?' She tucked a creamy breast back in its nest and smoothed its feathers anyway. 'What about my career you wrecked, dropping me, crippling me, the medals I could have won —' She expected Hiro Nakashima's grandnephew to take her side — this was, after all, his damned room! — but instead he waved her away. (If he'd found *his* sister in bed with a man he'd punch her eyes shut. No more than his duty.)

'Out. See you later.' Dag's palm propelled Lise towards the door, eased her and her crutch through it, and turned the key carefully behind her.

At Oka-chan's signal the obsequious servant snapped off the TV — a replay of Finsky alternating with a slalom run from earlier in the week — then Oka-chan ordered him to a chair in the corner. Drawing Mieko and Dag to her, the three stared down into the confident smile of this nephew on whom the fates had lavished so many gifts.

From his corner the servant opened his mouth but Oka-chan shut it with a gesture. It had not escaped her notice that this man her father had sent to watch over her, to help her, this spy who spoke no word of English, had managed to communicate with Lise Carlsen perfectly well and very likely reported to Tokyo daily on all of them. Especially her.

The ski-jumper considered the faces about him. Momentary power had sharpened his aunt to flint. To think Grand-uncle had given her a keeper! As well send a kitten to guard a panther. To deflect the attack he saw coming, he fixed on his cousin Mieko, the most vulnerable: 'Don't you compete today?' he said. 'Shouldn't you be resting?'

'She will rest in my room directly,' Oka-chan cut in. 'We are here to discuss your actions, not hers. You are of the family.'

'And that one? He threw a contemptuous glance at Dag, whom Oka-chan had included as buffer, should her nephew and the spy join forces and intimidate Mieko just when she needed all the confidence she could get. Dag, a foot taller than any of them, was difficult to overlook.

'He is our guest and in any case understands little Japanese as yet.'

The cousin's eyebrows lifted. 'As yet?'

Oka-chan refused to be drawn. 'Your sick-room gymnastics consume the papers at home; comic strips show contortions for lovers with porcelain legs; they sing of you in the bars; in a Ginza shop window a large screen shows your mouth in the blonde one's neck, your hand in her kimono; drunks laugh at you; reporters. . . Your link to the family is well known.'

He flushed an angry brick-red. 'And Mieko? She's in all the papers too —' he almost spat at Dag '— and she's a girl!'

'Yes, socially prominent and the friend of a round-eye! But an innocent girl. People may be surprised — but she does not drag the name Nakashima through every bar and gutter in Japan.'

The young man smiled his beautiful mocking smile and Oka-chan's fury mounted. That nature should give some so much and others so little!

'But my name is not Nakashima,' he reminded her.

'That is fortunate, or I think he would have your head.'

'You forget we live in the 20th century.'

'And you forget, nephew, that Hiro Nakashima does not!'

In the hall Oka-chan gave the minder a list of errands to which she knew he would add a call to Tokyo with details of the encounter just over. Her father would be livid. However dishonourable his behaviour, her nephew was male. If punishment was in order, Hiro Nakashima would administer it when the young man returned to Tokyo. It was not woman's business. It *had not been* woman's business. Too many things had not.

Oka-chan checked her watch. As a respite to endless hours alone in her room she daily took private lessons in English. Her father disapproved of that too, and had so informed her by fax, but by sheer numbers his imperious communications had lost their power to frighten her. With each lesson came knowledge but she lacked the confidence of the young, like Mieko, who took pleasure in using a new skill. 'I go to my professor,' she told Mieko. 'You will rest in my room, quieter than the Village, yes? Perhaps your friend will stay with you for company — after he visits his sister? Better not be too much alone before you skate, feeding your foolish fears with shadows.'

Mieko blushed, speaking rapidly to Dag, who nodded. As she left them, Oka-chan's smile had a strange quality. Mieko thought — but of course she must be wrong — that there was something of a blessing in the sweet touch of her mother's hand in farewell.

Dag tipped up her chin. He'd missed much of what Oka-chan said, but he too knew Mieko should not be alone before she skated. She had talent but no confidence; she needed love, but it came from so few directions. Her mother, a little from her coach, a lot now from himself. They were it. Mieko's team.

'I'll see Lise, smooth her down some if I can, then I'll be over, okay?'

'Okay,' she said shyly. 'I not be alone before I skate, right?'

'You got a deal.' He rubbed her cheek gently with his fist, and left.

Smooth Lise down? Who was he kidding? As he walked through her open door he collided with room service just leaving. Lise lolled against satin pillows guzzling 'Kalhua' and cream through a straw, her pretty fingers sorting petulantly through a tray of deep-fried button mushrooms stuffed with shrimp. Ben, keeping company with the satin Doberman on the chaise, trapped a bottle of scotch between his bony knees as he poured a shot unsteadily into his glass. At least he wasn't drinking from the bottle yet.

Lise was saying: 'You know, Dad, this European food sure gets old quick, it makes you feel . . . you know . . . kinda nauseated. Too rich, I guess.' She popped in another mushroom to confirm her judgement as Dag's shadow fell between her and the TV.

'Well, Mr Holier-than-thou! Like I just told Dad, you'd come around when they let you off the hook. What are you, their go-fer?'

Ben grunted. 'Did the Japanese chuck you out?'

'Not exactly.' He'd come with some vague idea of making peace and maybe finding out just what Lise expected of the skier. Too much, he had no doubt, but how much? He remembered the Rubenesque ripeness of that naked breast, ominously lush, a hot-house peach swelling with juice. 'You're developing quite a cleavage, Sis.'

'That's enough of your filthy mouth,' Ben warned.

'Cleavage didn't hurt Dolly Parton,' Lise said.

'She can sing.'

'*I* had a career too, till Brother Butterfingers couldn't hold me up.'

'A career in what? Competition? Shows? Not too many skaters leave the Olympics weighing more than when they arrived.'

Ben thumped the Doberman's snout. 'Goddamn it, you're —'

'You're drunk, Daddy, I'll handle *him*.' She turned on

Dag, every soft line of her face sharpened, like a cornered cat. 'My weight's an obsession with you, isn't it? You can't let it go, can you? You've no *idea* what I weigh!'

Dag looked her over carefully, calculated the extra curves under the satin robe. About ten pounds since they left LA — not counting the cast. 'Sis, I've had so much experience I could join a travelling show as a guess-your-weight artist and hit it within half a pound every time.'

'You may have to. I'll never let you partner *me* again and I don't know what else you're good for.'

'I can skate,' he said evenly. 'What can you do besides —'

Ben's fist flew harmlessly by his ear. 'Say it and I'll kill you!'

The arm which Dag deflected lacked the power to squash a gnat. 'I was about to warn Lise, that's all. If she's hoping to trap that guy into holy matrimony the old-fashioned way, she's wasting her time.'

Lise blanched. Bull's-eye? But she recovered fast. 'Sez who?'

'Me. His kind doesn't marry your kind.'

'What's wrong with her kind?' Ben whimpered, close to tears now, torn between defending his daughter's honour and the lurking suspicion she might actually be considering marriage to a Japanese.

Dag sighed. How to explain the cultural differences so both Ben and Lise knew how they stacked up against the Nakashimas? Knew to expect nothing. 'Right now the kid's a spoiled brat sowing his oats away from home, hoping the dust won't show.' He prayed that oats were all the Nakashima off-shoot had sown. 'His type sees Lise the way a gourmet sees a really great cheeseburger and fries, onion rings on the side. Okay for the road. Fantastic. But back home he'll stick with *sashimi* and rice and a few hundred acres of industrial Osaka. He's upper-crust.'

'What in hell d'you think *she* is?'

'It's what *he* thinks she is! The old man's not just loaded, its like . . . look, he damn near *owns* one of the richest countries in the world! Distant relatives like Lise's ski-jumper hang from every branch of the family tree. Hoping to be picked. Waiting for the call. That boy will toe the line, Dad. Sorry.'

'Sorry? You think I'd want my Lise marrying *him*?'

'Not right now, no.'

Ben blinked, the bones in his face seeming to implode, one upon another as terrible new possibilities darkened a horizon already blacker than the stuffed satin dog by his side. Would anything ever again go right for the Carlsens? He turned away from his daughter and son, wrapped his arms around the Doberman's elegant neck, and wept like a child.

'Satisfied?' Lise said to her brother.

'No. But now you both know where you stand.'

'How about you, brother dear? Where d'you stand? If, like you say, *he* won't have *me*, what makes you think *she'll* have *you*?'

In the lift heading towards Mieko's room, Dag Carlsen wondered the same thing.

CHAPTER THIRTY-THREE

Lloyd Sterling scowled over Men's Original print-outs in the arena lobby. All his plans, hopes, costume consultations, valuable time lost, for what? True, there were the finals yet, but fifth was a long way from the medal stand and what did it matter now anyhow? Didn't bear thinking about. To be out-manipulated by a pip-squeak like Dunsmuir.

Finsky. The Bean. The Czech. Some Korean called Kim Lee — weren't they all? — then Jeff, on whom he'd pinned such hopes, and who now sulked in the dressing-rooms, no doubt afraid to enter the lobby for the bus to the Village because he knew Lloyd lay in wait for a show-down. He'd never rest until he confronted the pup, shook him by the scruff of the neck and explained the meaning of gratitude, honour . . . that kind of thing. . .

He had no badge. His own fault, he should have demanded accreditation, but badges looked . . . plebeian. As he'd always maintained: if one needed a name-tag for the board meeting one shouldn't be on the board. His face was known to everybody who was anyone in skating, anyway. A supporter, confidante of officials and several Committee members. Why should a man of that stature need a badge? He'd go backstage anyway, confront the boy!

About then a bell rang far out of his hearing in the control room. A bomb, the voice said, Arena this time — all set to open in an hour for Ladies Originals. And a full house expected.

Out of nowhere walkie-talkies blatted, uniforms poured down corridors, surrounded everything that moved, including Lloyd Sterling in his camel coat. They pinned his arms, all these security forces coming at him with guns drawn. Damn it all, the idiots could shoot somebody! A guard, French by his smell, grabbed him and slammed him at the wall. What the devil —

'Who's in charge here?' he demanded. 'Get an official this instant!'

He tried French, German, Italian. Nothing. Two men held his elbows, a third stuck a gun in his back, and they marched him to Security, an office swarming with uniforms and one lone civilian. An old friend. Thank God!

'I say, old boy, what's going on, for Christ's sake. Call off your goons, won't you, they're breaking my blasted arms, I could have been shot —'

'Sorry, Lloyd. Another bomb threat, nothing I can do until we've searched everywhere . . . must open soon . . . already behind schedule, lord knows what —'

'But this is preposterous! I can't be suspected, not me —'

'We all are until we have the chap. Sure to be a hoax but rules . . . daren't risk another Munich. Be sensible, Lloyd. You surely see my position!"

'I see that you're in desperate need of organization! Not *one* of these . . . these *creatures* mauling me knows a civilized language!'

'Ninety-five per cent of the men in this room speak French.'

'Then they choose not to understand it!' Lloyd glared at the guard on his right, a face like the map of France, reeking of sweat and garlic. He'd never trusted the Frogs, now he knew why. 'If they understood me why didn't they let me go? Do I *look* like an assassin? Three bomb threats and you're still so short of suspects you pick on patrons whose favour you should be courting?'

'I'm sorry.' The official spoke politely, firmly. 'The phone people have a strong lead . . . talk of an open line, police will get him, no problem. Anyway, bomb threats are par for the course. I worry more when we *don't* have one!'

'Then why all the fuss?'

'You're not listening, Lloyd.' He kept his temper. Just. He had much to do and no time to do it in. 'We *think* we've got a lead on him, we *hope* to make an arrest. He *seems* to be some way from Montegreco so it all takes time and until we're sure, until we nab the bastard, we can't relax rules. Understand?'

*

If Lloyd failed to understand, tonight's competitors did not. Those who could be reached were told to stay away from the arena until advised otherwise. All venues would remain closed until police gave the all-clear.

In her cubicle at the Village, Roxanne Kramer sighed, part in frustration, part relief. Bomb threats came with the territory, but they sure didn't help her nerves. Organizers and cops worried about bombs; competitors worried about body-clocks. This close to the wire, nerves quivered at the slightest change in schedule. It was as if Roxanne were a bomb herself, timed to go off at 10.00 PM precisely, her probable time to compete. Earlier than that and she'd panic. Later, and her internal clock would shoot into orbit.

Her mother phoned at six. 'Is my Roxanne sleeping?'

'No, she's answering the phone, isn't she?'

'Temper! You didn't eat dinner yet?'

'Before I skate? Of course not.'

'Good. Take your vitamins?'

'Just about to.'

An impatient sigh from Noni in the hotel. 'What would you do without your mother checking on you at every turn!'

Relax maybe? 'How's Grossmutti?' Roxanne heard Noni's fingernails beating a tattoo on the phone. What colour nails today? High-tension silver?

'How *would* Mutti feel? Poppa's had enough, wants to go home. Mutti's nervous as hell, won't do a thing I tell her. Your big night, but d'you think she'll put on a dab of rouge? Lipstick? No! Over seventy and she finally remembers the word 'obey' in her marriage vows. She could at least show consideration for you, you *are* the World Champi —'

'Mom, get off her back, I don't care if she shows up in her birthday suit —'

'Oh great, just what we all want to hear after all we've done —'

Roxanne set the receiver on her pillow and tried to tune Noni's voice out. When it paused for breath she jumped back in. ' 'Bye, Mom, gotta go.'

'Go? You skate in a few hours. Where would you go?'

'Back to sleep, where else.' She hung up fast, just as the phone rang again. This was resting? But this was Grant. He'd booked them a table at the *sushi* place to eat after Originals.

'They'll tempura anything. I promise.'

'What's the occasion to be?' she asked. 'To celebrate or sympathize?'

'To eat. You're on edge. Noni been at you again?' His voice so casual he could have been asking the time. Her last competition, but no marriage proposal, no hint. Just tempura and 'Noni been at you again?'

'Just to take my vitamins.'

'A nap would do you more good, but if Jasinski gave them to you. . . I have to go, sweetheart. A visitor.' His voice dropped. 'Jeff's here,' he whispered. 'Call you later. Don't leave the Village, okay?'

'*Jeff*?' But he'd gone, brisk as ever. No time to waste. Other men said 'Love you,' when they hung up, she'd heard them, but not Grant. The word wasn't in his vocabulary. What went wrong? And when? With whom?

She snapped off her music — she literally knew it in her sleep — got a carton of skimmed milk and reached for her purse. A calcium cap and the last niacin. She paused, suddenly wary. Was this niacin the same as the other niacins? It lay in her palm, round and white, bigger than she remembered, a slash mark staring up at her, the line some pills had in case you wanted to take half. Had the others had that? Oh, what the hell, Jasinski gave it to her. It was half way to her mouth when she remembered that Noni took care of her purse every day in the bleachers while Roxanne worked out. Noni. So what was it? Speed? Aspirin? A trank? Upper? Downer? With Noni, a walking compendium of the use and abuse of every drug on and off the street, it could be anything. Remembering her promise to Grant, she called Jasinski, her fingers trembling. Keep calm. Noni wouldn't dare, not at the last minute. She'd know it could finish everything.

Jasinski came, sniffed, touched it to his tongue, and took it to the lab. He came back with brie and crackers and the news that it may take a while to analyse the pill. 'You didn't take it, so don't worry, relax. Cheese?'

'I'm supposed to be sleeping, but who could sleep with —'

'Roxanne. You're not *supposed* to do anything you don't wish to do. You are a grown woman. A pleasant conversation is far more restful than waiting for sleep to fall over you like a tent from the ceiling. Do you see a tent up there? No. When sleep is impossible, think other thoughts.'

Her laugh shook a little around the edges. 'Easy to say. The pill sure took my mind off the Games, anyway! D'you think it's anything? The taste. . .'

He spread cheese on a cracker. 'I tasted so you might think that I know something. I know nothing. I do not take pills so how can I know their taste?'

'You write prescriptions.'

He shrugged. 'Patients expect it. If I do not prescribe they feel cheated — but most of them could cure themselves if they would.'

She pictured Mom's bathroom cabinet, vials lined up like superannuated soldiers — Noni never threw an old drug away. 'What if it's a hard drug?' she said quietly. 'You know — on the banned list? Will they arrest her?'

'You did not take it so I do not know. Your blood will be tested.'

'That's just it! If she tried to give me *real* dope she's off her trolley! Sometimes she's so freaky I'm scared. What if they lock her up, what if —'

'— What if I call the lab?' He spoke briefly into the phone and turned to her, smiling. 'Niacin, a common nutrient. But not the 25 milligrams I prescribed for you. Forty times that. One thousand milligrams. Few people can tolerate so much.'

'And if they can't?'

'Itching, flushing, dizziness. Unpleasant while it lasts — one hour, perhaps two. Your mother is a medication junkie. I have many such patients. If one dose is good, forty must be magic. It does not make her wicked, merely a foolish woman over-anxious for your success.'

A foolish woman playing with dynamite. For her *success*? Roxanne clenched her fists, mentally gathering speed for the opening scratch spin. Get dizzy on that baby, hit the ice or the rail at that speed, and you could get dead! She *should* be angry, she *was* . . . but this was vintage Mom, nothing new.

'Sometimes, Doc, I'd love to walk away from Noni and keep on walking. She twists, manipulates. Look, you talked to her in LA. *Is she crazy?*'

'She is unstable. Under stress. We all are. With her, perhaps stress is a habit. My dear, if you were to take her aside, speak with her quietly, tell her you worry for her, care for her . . . Maybe she needs to hear that you love her.'

Roxanne didn't laugh. 'Would *you* love a mother who fed you "nutrients" to make you *do* better, maybe even win the Olympics for you?'

He turned away. 'My mother gave me nutrients also, even stole some, that I might win the biggest competition of all. I loved her very much.'

'I'm sorry.' Roxanne, foot-in-mouth champion. 'Can I ask you one thing?'

He nodded, his lips pale under the bright overhead lamp. 'Yes?'

'When you met me that first time, I wasn't firing on all cylinders myself. Did you think *I* was unstable? Out of my gourd? Loop-the-loop?'

He took off his glasses, polished them, put them back on. 'You were insecure.' He paused, considering. 'You remain insecure. I am sorry.'

The diagnosis rushed at her like a truck. She came back fighting. 'I've plenty to be insecure about! Noni's pulled my emotional rug out so damn many times *of course* I want to nail it down. I have to, before it slips away!' Sooner or later everything slipped away. A few months ago the Gold was hers for the taking. Now it was in doubt. For four years Grant Rivers had been hers; now that prize too seemed in doubt.

'Grant Rivers,' said this clairvoyant doctor, 'is more insecure than anyone.' He reached down and astonished them both by kissing her forehead. 'Will you do something for me, Roxanne. Try to *enjoy* the Olympic Games?'

He walked quickly down the corridor, disturbed to find his eyes blurred. These athletes, their bodies so highly trained, their minds so frighteningly erratic. What was it about the sport that bred insecurity like a virus? But then, still in the American compound, he passed a room identical to Roxanne's, heard gusts of laughter under the door, and shook his head.

Three cubicles and a million emotional miles distant, Beejay, Emma, Nils, and the Bean clustered around a Scrabble board balanced precariously on Beejay's narrow bed. Beejay had challenged the Bean's word choice.

' "Lymes"? Heck, Bean, you can do better than that!'

'With six consonants?'

'But "lymes"? Are they fruit? Or what?' said the expert on anything edible.

'Heard of Lymes disease? Catch it from deer ticks — not that you'd know. The only wildlife in LA are fleas on the dog.'

'I reckon "Lymes" is a proper name, Bean,' Emma said. 'Not allowed. What d'you say, Nils?' Attention thus diverted, Emma risked a quick glance at her watch. Three hours before Beejay skated. Lord, didn't the kid have any nerves? Emma was here to help her dress when the time came — and Nils came along for the ride, more or less chaperones, gossip being skating's insider sport. Not that Beejay and the Bean needed it. They'd bickered amiably at competitions for the last six years and likely would for the next six, but when one of them stepped on that ice, the other cheered and hollered louder than anybody. The Bean was a wildcard all right, but he was the closest Beejay would ever get to a brother. Emma trusted her with him. And considering his reputation, that said a lot. Nils brought her back to the game.

'Emma's right, Bean, but if I lend you an "I" you could make "limes".'

Beejay frowned. 'Lending's against the rules.'

'Aw come on, we're buddies!'

'Not when we're playing! Scrabble's like competition. If you don't play to win, what's the point?'

'Beejay, for God's sake let him borrow the "I"!'

'Okay-okay!' Beejay helped herself to more letters, clacking the tiles this way and that on their stand. Darting a glance at the Bean, she drew them close to her chest and gave him the poker-face. She'd picked a corker, Emma could tell. ' "Limes" it is, you heard Em. Mark it and score it.'

'You sure change your tune fast, bubble-head!'

'Sure, I can't argue all night, I've got to get gussied up soon, right?'

Emma let out a small sigh of relief. The first indication that Beejay even remembered that she competed tonight. If there'd just been the cash for a new outfit. . . The pink hung on the wardrobe door. Over and over Emma's eye returned to it, every snagged thread an accusing flag telling her she should have found the way to a new one. Grant said that under the arena lights it would look fine. So did Nils — and that other dress, safely under guard, waited for Finals. So be satisfied, Em. Beejay's here, at the Games. Most mothers would do anything if they could say that. Some, like Noni, *had* done anything! She caught Beejay smiling at her as Nils debated, with Bean's help, between 'local' and 'focal'.

'Em, quit worrying about the pink. With the music you and Grant stuck on me, I gotta move so damn fast all anybody'll notice is the colour!'

It was the Bean who finally asked the question of the evening: 'Beejay, aren't you scared *at all*? Your first really big competition?'

She thought about it. 'Nah, not the Original. What for? Everything I have to do, I've got down rock-solid. I'll just go out and do it, no sweat.'

'Your long programme's solid too, I've watched it. It's terrific.'

'I wish it had more in it. . .' For the first time ever, doubt entered Beejay's voice. Emma stepped on it fast.

'Your turn, sport. Hurry up.'

Looking around for anticipated applause, Beejay beamed. 'Thought you'd never ask.' She rubbed her palms together and clicked three tiles firmly on the board, attaching them to the 'L' on focal. ' "Lutz". How's that? Triple word score, yet! I win.' Triumph glowed in the sherry-coloured eyes. Nobody had the heart to tell her that 'Lutz', like 'Lyme', was a proper noun and not allowed.

'Don't know why I bother, playing,' the Bean groaned. 'She does it every time. Scrabble, Jacks, Monopoly.'

'You can always hope. How come you don't have a date?'

'I do. A speed-skater from Holland. We're coming to watch you. I gotta go.'

'I gotta shower. Imagine, Lutz on triple word score, though! Now that's what I call *playing* the game.'

'I call it bragging. Ta-ta for now, as Yum-Num says.'

Beejay shampooed her electric hair under hot, hot

needles, singing as she scrubbed: 'Lutz-Triple-Word-Score, Lutz-Triple-Word-Score.' Emma, busy laying out tights and bra, nevertheless noticed when the word order changed. So did Beejay, hugging herself with delight. An omen, it had to be! 'Triple-lutz-word-score, triple-lutz, triple-lutz, triple, triple, triple-lutz! Olé!'

'*Beejay!*' Emma warned. '*Don't even think about it!*'

'Mom, you know it's not one of the moves! I wouldn't even get credit if I landed it — not tonight, not in the Original.'

'So long as you know. Just remember it.'

Beejay knew, all right. She wouldn't dream of wasting it on tonight's Original. It was her long freestyle on Saturday, the Final, which needed beefing up. She'd be in that yummy dress from Mrs Cox, which had to be another good omen. Oh, lord, she could hardly wait!

Emma had other, closer worries. The marks for Willi's grandson, still quarantined, had shot him clear down to the cellar. Twenty-third — which meant he missed the cut, would not get to skate the long Free even if the doctor said okay. Worse, Emma's mark had been his lowest. At a pinch she could have upped them a tenth, max, but that would have sent old Willi a false and cringing signal: 'I'd have helped your grandson if I could, Willi, so be nice to my little girl.'

She couldn't send that signal, maybe she'd even bent over backwards to prove to him that she wasn't for sale, not even for Beejay's future. Question was, what signal would he send Beejay tonight in return? She'd talked it over by phone with Grant, who'd told her not to worry, that the Willis of the sport were on their way out. 'It's opening up,' he'd said from his room at the hotel. 'Less and less political every year. If he clobbers her, so what? Beejay's young. She can afford to hang in.'

Easy for Grant Rivers to say. He wasn't paying the bills. He was living it up at the hotel, free from worries ethical or financial.

CHAPTER THIRTY-FOUR

'Jeff, I haven't much time.' Grant said.

'The girls' Originals, yeah, I know.' Jeff sounded down.

'What can I do for you?' Grant, anxious to be rid of this handsome but oddly unappealing boy, did not ask him to sit, but he sat anyway. A bad sign.

'I just want to say thanks — for last night, I mean. You kept me on track.'

'Part of my job. I was proud of you.' The usual hackneyed words, but Jeff grinned, forgetting for an instant the subservience he'd acquired overnight and now wore like a cheap new coat.

'Hey, I did okay, huh?'

'You could even pull up a bit in Finals. Your folks here to see you?'

'I thought you knew. I was adopted.' As he spoke his accent deepened, lost its light southern topping. Lancashire sub-soil rose to the surface, too earthy for the boy's flighty manner. 'This couple took me on when I were a babbie — baby. Codgers, they were. They didn't hit me or nothin'. I can't hardly remember the chap, he snuffed it early on; she lasted until a couple of years back, put me through skating. That's when Lloyd came up trumps.'

It would be. Perhaps Lloyd was no barracuda after all, just a snouty old moray eel lurking in its cave for waifs and strays to happen by.

'Thing is, Grant — Mr Rivers, sorry — he hangs about after me, Lloyd does, and he's got muscle, know wharra I mean?'

Oh yes. Young Jeff had peered into the crystal ball, seen himself within sniffing distance of Bronze, and entertained visions of the World title next year, after Finsky turned pro. Half-smart. He figured to beat the Bean, but he couldn't;

the Bean had that irresistible extra — a winning personality. Jeff hadn't recognized it and wanted to hang in, but he'd already told Lloyd to kiss off. Too bad. Now he needed another meal-ticket and time rushed by, Jeffie with no financial backing in view.

Grant approached it head on, 'Don't depend on the rock star, Jeff.'

'Why not? I thought you could set it up for me. He sort of hinted. . .'

'Hints don't buy lessons and ice-time.'

Jeff sat down as if winded. 'He sponsored the Carlsens!'

'I'd check that with Ben Carlsen if I were you.' Poor Jeffie. His transparent face fell as he rummaged through his memory for other pigeons. You felt sorry for him even as you despised him.

'Lloyd's upset with me I know, but . . . Well, maybe if you had a word with *him*, smooth things over, like. . .'

'No. Your deal with Lloyd was private, no officials involved — or Lloyd wouldn't dare put pressure on you. *Is he*?'

Jeff nodded. 'A bit, like I'll never compete again, de-da-de-da. . .'

'Have you tried official channels?'

'That bunch of stuffed shirts? No way!'

So he had tried, and been turned down. Grant didn't blame them. Image-sensitive officials reflected the times; if one's life-style was unorthodox it did not pay to advertise it. Jeff flaunted his, a disservice to a sport demanding super-human strength and self-discipline. For too long, pot-bellied lorry-drivers had dismissed men's skating as a sport for boys too soft for football. It never had been. Finsky, the most graceful man Grant knew, spent half his life in a gym honing the ultimate skating machine — the artist-athlete. Gymnastics aside, Grant didn't know a single sport that demanded so much. Jeff didn't have enough to give. Jeff had to be driven. Finsky drove himself.

'Have you considered a show?' God, he sounded like his old Swansea coach. Join a show before the knees go, boyo, then coach, like me.

'It's too soon. I need a sponsor with money. Know any? *Anybody at all*?'

'Off-hand, no.'

'There's this woman in New York, she's after me, her brother's in real estate, they own apartments or something, accommodation'd be no problem. She says she and her brother'd back me, no sweat. I'd have to train on the East Coast, though. Yum-Num, I expect.'

'If he'd take you. He's trained the Bean from day one, remember.'

'So? You train Roxanne and Beejay. They're the same level.'

'But they're not head-to-head yet.'

Jeff blinked away possible conflict. 'We skate for different countries, the Bean and me. It'd give Yum-Num two shots at the World title.'

A calculating little sod for all his provincialism, this Jeff. 'I'll ask Yum-Num if he knows this New York family. You can't be too careful.'

'I've no time to be careful. Skating costs money.'

Grant sighed. 'Money's not your biggest problem, old lad.'

Jeff, still coiled in Grant's easy-chair, pouted. 'What d'you mean?'

'You'll take *any* sponsor? Promiscuity's never been attractive, Jeff. Now it's Russian roulette. You watch TV, read the papers. It pays to be choosy.'

Jeff rolled his eyes up. 'Oh, Mr Rivers, you're *worried* about me? That maybe I don't practise safe sex?' He hissed the esses and pursed his pretty lips. If he'd had a blush left in him he'd have dusted that off too.

'You know the odds.'

'That's nice — that you're concerned, I mean.'

He looked sincere, so why did Grant feel fangs about to clamp round his throat? 'Will that be all, Jeff? I have a lot to do. Sorry.'

Jeff sashayed to the door and Grant knew, with swift certainty, that this man-child was primed to drip venom. 'Funny you should ask,' Jeff said. 'You know Deirdre Sterling, I'll bet.'

'I didn't ask anything,' Grant said. But he knew, now, what to expect; if Grant failed to come up with a sponsor for him, Jeff might have to stoop to a smear campaign. Which would have to include Lloyd. The young fool.

'But you do know her, right?' he persisted.

'Everyone in skating knows the Sterlings.'

'Seen her lately?'

Grant tried and failed to evade the terror lying in wait behind his eyes since the moment he'd seen Deirdre asleep in the hospital wing. But he knew the truth now as he'd known it then. Jeff watched him from the open door, a young cobra stalking a bird, enjoying it, preparing to strike.

'You've seen her then. Shocking, isn't it?'

In two strides Grant had him by the neck, trapping his pretty face between the door and the frame. 'It *is* awful! And have *you* thought? *She's Lloyd's wife, you bloody idiot! How d'you think she got what she's got? Osmosis?*' He wanted to squeeze until the face broke up, until that gloating smile spilled its triumph onto the beige Olympic rings.

'Grant, d-don't smash me face in, I've got Finals day after n-next!'

The fury cleared. Jeff had stumbled on a nugget. He wanted to know its value, that's all. 'Get smart, Jeff. I'll do what I can, talk to Yum-Num. See me later at the Building.' Grant shoved, not hard, shutting the door against Jeff's outraged whimper and whatever else he might say if given the chance.

'D'you think my eyes look brighter with the darker shadow, darling? I used pale shades when I was young, but now . . .' Deirdre Sterling, propped up in bed, surrounded by creams and lotions, nodded to the mirror. 'Yes. When I get used to looking at myself I'm not *terribly* bad, am I? No one could expect me to look thirty-two forever, could they? But I wouldn't frighten little children, you think? You're frowning. Darling, am I being terribly vain?'

'Of course not.' Turning away, Maureen busied herself with her own make-up. 'You look lovely, Mother, but I wish you hadn't stopped *all* your medicine. It's rather drastic, you know. Harley Street says so.'

'Oh, doctors always flog a dead horse. Makes them feel they're earning their fee. I wasn't improving with the chemo, and already I'm heaps better without it — and I haven't stopped everything. I take painkillers galore, and don't nod off. Admit it, I do look livelier. I used to *be* lively, you know.'

Maureen thought if she had to say, 'You look lovely' once more she'd scream. Mother looked awful, worse with make-up than without. Her eyes, so deep-set now they glittered like micah chips in twin craters, cried out for dark glasses. 'They say you're not sleeping. The doctor says you need to.'

'I wish you wouldn't keep phoning him.'

'The head nurse did. She couldn't stop the chemo without his authority.'

'Busybodies! You've *slaved* for these Games and I want to see you in them, not some misty figure moving through a haze. If I'm to be drugged to the eyeballs I might as well have stayed in London and missed all the fun.'

Fun? Mother scarcely had the energy to lift her arms, her bed-bath now an exhausting chore. 'I'll do your face, darling. You know I like to dabble.'

Deirdre gave up the paint pots with a sigh and sank back into the pillows. 'When you were tiny you loved to watch Mummy dress up, remember?'

Ah, but Deirdre's room had been a boudoir then, no drip systems, no tubes, no bed-pans, no nurses to tuck her in tight, no smallest wrinkle in the starched cotton sheets a glaring affront to their efficiency.

That other Mummy, lively and fastidious, had slept between cream satin sheets, had showered twice a day, soaked in a tub of bubbles before bed, planning the next day's wardrobe as she dabbed Maureen's nose with lily-scented suds. In the morning she'd dressed for rink and ballet studio in soft tweeds for summer, furs for winter; then each afternoon the dress frocks, soft creations with skirts that 'moved' and shed her light fragrance like a nimbus all about her. In the evenings Maureen had loved watching her dress, not necessarily formal gowns, but Mother always 'dressed' and later expected her daughter to do the same. Maureen recalled Deirdre's voice then — light, with a musical laugh to soften the stings of turning a little girl into a lady. *I'd wear white gloves today, darling, since it's May. When the vicar's wife offers you her maids-of-honour, do please accept one — if you can't swallow it, excuse yourself — her terrier's always in the hall, he'll eat anything. No, baby, we only spit out at the dentist, and it's called rinsing.*

But as Deirdre weakened her voice had sharpened, planting petulant little barbs when she was tired or in pain — which seemed to be much of the time: 'You *do* plan to paste my eyelashes on eventually?' she said now. Her own had fallen out, together with most of her eyebrows. 'I haven't seen skating people for so long . . . how embarrasing if they don't recognize me.'

'Mother, they'll know you, but I'm really hopeless at false eyelashes. Suppose I got glue in your eye or something?'

'Oh, all right! I'll rest while you dress, then you can zip me up. I must look presentable — or at least not ghastly. You did say you'd become friends with Roxanne? She *isn't* still living with Grant Rivers?'

'Not at the Village, Mother. They frown on that kind of thing, I believe. And we're not *close* friends, but I like her. She's nervous, anxious, trying to please them all, and her mother's really . . . well, strange.'

Deirdre's lips, once soft and full, almost disappeared. 'Runs in the family, I expect. Jeff swears Roxanne's anorexic, Grant had a terrible time with her.'

Grant. As if she knew him well . . . but of course she did. That whispered confession from the villa, made as much to shock as to inform. The frantic, hopeless efforts to look 'pretty' again. Maureen shivered.

'He competed, did I tell you?' Deirdre said sharply, her eyes flying open, determined to stay awake, to remember. 'Before you were born.' Her knuckles whitened against the sheet. 'Sometimes, as a matter of fact, you remind me of him. Same colouring — but I expect he'll have changed now . . .'

Someone else said that lately. Jeff, was it? Blonde people must be quite colour-blind. They saw themselves as individuals but everyone else looked alike to them. 'Wait until you see little Mieko and her Swede, Mother. Talk about opposites! He's tall and golden, she's tiny and dark, and they're so sweet together. It gives one an idea of what love should be like. Utter devotion.'

'Mmm. . . Seen Alexei lately?' Deirdre's face, which had been ready to soften, sharpened again to match her voice. 'His legal affairs all in order?'

'Yes. He's looking forward to thanking you and all that, tonight.'

'You could do worse, you know. He's steady. He'd look after you —'

'*Mother! He's engaged to Galina!*'

'— or there's my solicitor's son. I do wish you were settled before, well, you know. You're quite beautiful, darling, you can have anyone you wish.'

'But I don't wish, not yet.'

Deirdre looked wistful. 'You'd better change now, dear. My dressing-room's far more comfy than a Village cubicle, I'm sure, and I do want to see you in your dress.'

'You'll be all right while I take a shower? I'll ring for Nurse to come in, in case you need anything. She's right outside.'

'Don't be silly!' Deirdre said, sharp again. 'All I need is peace and quiet!'

Maureen sighed. Since Deirdre had left the villa and her medicines behind her, her tongue cut to the bone. Sharp — but lively. In time she'd turn into a tyrant . . . but of course, there'd be no time.

She was right about the dressing-room. Oceans of space, superb lights and mirrors. She had a whole new long Freestyle to some ancient folksong. 'Impossible Dream', re-cut, was now the short Original for tonight; she'd skate in palest blue chiffon, almost white, perfect against the deeper blue of her eyes and the ice. Not lavish, like the coral she'd wear for Finals, but exquisite, something cool and calm on a still lake. Lovely, she thought, smoothing it over her hips, admiring again Deirdre's eye for line. What would she do without this woman who'd been so close, who now approached death with the same implacable gentility with which she'd lived her life, settled her affairs, spun her webs for Maureen's future with vague, well-meaning hints. Alexei. Her solicitor's son. Last month a young peer, attentive but dull. Before him a middle-aged historian they'd entertained often at Haslemere after he was widowed. All older than Maureen, with varied backgrounds, these possibles shared one quality: absolute stability. Without exception they were the kind of men a young woman could lean on.

About to enter Deirdre's room again, she paused. Voices. Drat that nurse, at her post right outside the door, she'd been told and told to let no one in!

'Maureen, there you are my dear.' The visitor was Lloyd,

looking her up and down like a coat he considered purchasing. 'How ravishing you look.' His manicured fingers touched the soft fabric of the skirt, the spangled wisps, hovering dangerously close to high-cut pant legs. 'Is this a loose thread at the hem? No . . . turn around, my dear, let me check the front —'

'*Don't even think about it*.' Deirdre's glacial voice cut across from the bed, a laser driven by a mother's protective instinct and sheer, bottomless contempt for the man who'd been her husband. Her next words, simple and clear, with no shred of restraint, shocked Lloyd, Maureen, and even Deirdre herself. Once, she wouldn't have dreamed of unwrapping this old skeleton in Maureen's presence. Now, with so little time, she must rattle it until it crumbled to dust.

'Lloyd, must you be so painfully obvious? Maureen is out of your reach and far out of your class.' Lloyd's hand leapt away from Maureen's dress as if the fabric were on fire, but Deirdre was not done. 'She's not the naïve fool I was when we married. She knows what you are. *She* has the courage to say no and mean it, I've made very sure of that. So get out!'

'Well!' Lloyd's voice shook. 'I only came to wish Maureen luck, warn her, another threat at the building, that they'll skate later than scheduled.'

'That's *all* you came for?' Deirdre heard her daughter say. 'Not to visit Mother? See if she's comfortable? Recovering? Anything you can do? No? In that case, she's quite right. Please go. And close the door behind you.'

Lloyd flushed. 'Have you forgotten that this is her room and that I am her husband?'

'Hardly. Had she married someone with a shred of decency she wouldn't be ill now with round-the-clock nurses. What will you do, Daddy, when the truth leaks out? It will, you know. There'll be even fewer doors open to you then. Even young Jeff might —'

'*That will do! I didn't come here to listen to this!*' He threw the door open and slammed it behind him.

Deirdre laughed, the echo of an old silver bell. 'Bravo, darling. You'll manage perfectly without me. What a pathetic old *roué* he is!'

*

'Soon I must to dress,' Mieko said.

'Soon you must dress.' Dag Carlsen corrected her as he agreed.

'My mother spends much time at her English class.'

'How long's it been? Two hours?'

Mieko nodded, watching his tall shadow at the window as he stared down at the street. How beautiful the back of his head against the mountains, a smoky apricot sunset burnishing his hair to bronze. 'I think,' she added quietly, 'my mother does not hurry back.'

'You're damn right. Come and look here.' Directly across the street, in a restaurant where one could linger for hours over a snack, Oka-chan sat alone, sipping from a long amber glass as she nibbled, ever so slowly, at what appeared to be a substantial meal.

Mieko blushed and said nothing.

'Sweetheart, is she up to what I think she's up to?'

'Up to?' Oh, this English, always it mixed everything up.

'Planning. Hoping to save you from a fate worse than death?'

Ah. She nodded. 'I think yes. I think she hopes we . . . you know . . .' She blushed and he nodded. 'Then I will be spoiled for marriage. Grandfather may beat me, he will beat her sure, oh yes, because she is here to watch over me — but I cannot then marry with the man from Hokkaido and shame my grandfather. He must turn instead to one of the nephews to make him a boy baby for the company. Then I shall be left alone.'

'The feudal old devil! Is that what you want, to be left alone?'

'No-no-no, I want happy, every girl wants happy, but if. . .'

He stood behind her and wrapped his arms around her, rocking her as he might rock a small child. 'Suppose you "marry with me" instead?'

A tear splashed on his wrist. 'He would not permit. I have . . . how do I say . . . I have much value to him because I am —'

'A virgin. But if we married first and told him later?'

She lowered her head and offered him the tender nape of her neck. 'I am watched. My mother is watched.'

His lips lightly touched her neck and she quivered against him. Behind her she felt his body harden against her, wanting her. She tried to turn, give him her mouth, but he held her fast. 'Look at the mountains, sweetheart.'

They rose all about her, glorious in the sunset, and forever — as this golden one behind her was glorious, forever, as his hand gently stroking her breast was forever — for how, after him, could there be another? She leaned back against him and the pressure of his body answered her, urgent yet tentative. Yes, Oka-chan. Oh yes, my mother. I read you right and you are wise, wise. . .

'Mieko,' Dag Carlsen whispered into her hair, 'I want us like those mountains. Together for a long time. You understand?'

She nodded. 'I think you want marry with me.'

'Yes.'

'Then let me turn, my Carlsen man. Let me see the face of my husband.'

They kissed slowly, tenderly, until they were not two mouths but one, until the evening turned the mountains to lavender and purple and at last to black. He closed the drapes against the night and lifted her to the bed, opening her kimono slowly, his lips following the whisper of emerald silk, adoring the ivory strength of her small body, kissing the tiny hands which touched him here and there, kissing the small hard cones of her breasts, touching his tongue to the hypnotic seduction of their dark, mysterious tips.

'You are so beautiful to my eyes,' she said, 'to my heart . . . please, please . . .' How could she wait longer? It seemed to her now she had waited her whole life for this moment, this man whose name she murmured every night like a prayer, this quivering langour as he made her pause at the gate to heaven, as his fingers parted her thighs wide in tenderness and wonder, as she received him, enclosed him, drew him into her slowly, slowly, willing him to pierce the barrier now, this moment, to penetrate her, to plunder the treasure which for so long had bound her to an archaic tradition, one he must now break forever. The breaking, when it came, opened her slowly and sweetly, the pain a joy almost too much to bear, for he was large, this gentle man who took such care, and she very, very small.

'I'm not hurting you?'

'Oh, no,' she lied. 'Now you pass the gate my world is beautiful. I happy my Carlsen with me, that he come to me in waves, like the sea. Do you hear?' She whispered into his mouth, 'When we move? Listen!

'Carl — sen—Carl — sen-Carl-sen-Carl-sen-Carl-sen-Carlsen-Carlsen-CarlsenCarlsenCarlsenCarlse-e-e-e-e-e-n!'

They reached the top of their mountain together and rested, his lips on her damp hair. 'I love you, Mieko Nakashima, little girl with a big name.'

'Not girl! I woman now, Carlsen. Now I bathe, dress, go to Building.'

He leapt up, checking his watch. 'Oh, Christ! Come on, I'll wash you, show me where your clothes are —'

She laughed and kissed the long muscles of his thigh. 'Everything is ready, we skate late, another bomb story. The phone tell me. No worry.' She blushed and covered herself. 'In Japan, all family bathe together.'

Whether, in Japan, the man eased his woman into leotards and skating dress after the bath, Dag didn't know. He washed her, kissed her, zipped her into sunshine yellow silk smothered with topaz beads. 'You're okay to skate? Lord, you just lost your virginity —'

'You will see, tonight I skate fantastic,' she said dreamily. 'I lose stranger from Hokkaido. I find a golden god in my heart. I much happy.'

'No-no, I am *very* happy,' he said.

'I also.'

Oka-chan tapped softly before she slipped into the room.

One look at Mieko's face reassured her. She smiled upon them both and kissed her daughter's warm ivory cheek, speaking rapid Japanese as she stroked her hair, touched tongue to fingertip to smooth Mieko's eyebrows, flicked rice-powder with a camel-hair brush to cover the tell-tale flush on Mieko's jaw. Such a child! Not to know that Western men grew tougher beards, left brighter traces on delicate virgin skin.

Then she took a deep, nervous breath, bowed, and spoke English in public for the first time in her life, to the man she hoped would be her son-in-law. 'Hotel bad place to leave daughter long time. You took great care for my Mieko, Mr Carlsen. *Arigato goziemashita*. I very thank — you understand?'

He blushed and nodded. '*Domo. Wakarimasu.*' Jeez! On a simple 'thank you, I understand,' he'd exhausted his entire Japanese vocabulary. He spoke to Mieko, 'Maybe later, at the building, I can ask your mother a question?'

Mieko repeated it in Japanese.

Oka-chan smiled. '*Hai!*' Yes. Unlike his weak father, this young Mr Carlsen had manners. She anticipated liking his mother very much.

CHAPTER THIRTY-FIVE

Doors to the main arena finally began to tremble, to rumble open, releasing incongruous, expectant whiffs of steam-heat, rink-ice, roses, french-fries, carnations, and fresh new paint. The crowd outside, a rampaging tide of excitement, restive and cold to the bone, surged forwards. The security chief, unnerved by the throng's size and strength, ordered the doors resealed until all off-duty guards could be summoned to the Building.

'Tell 'em to hurry! This mob's all set to stampede!'

The great mass of public packed the palatial forecourt of the Building. Shouting, roaring, they did indeed resemble a mindless, multi-coloured herd as they stomped and shoved, argued fiercely in a dozen languages, waved programmes and arms, and bashed each other on the head with national flags and one-world peace signs in their eagerness to get inside, sit down, and shout themselves hoarse again for the idols of the Ladies Original.

Above them, the dark snow-laden sky hung heavy with crowd-smells of coffee and mothballs, wet wool and pizza. Guards, intimidated, linked arms to hold back the press of bodies, to establish some order for collecting tickets, checking credentials.

At the Competitor Gates backstage conditions were no better. These steel gates accessed a maze of dressing rooms, spas and trauma rooms; below them, down miles of rabbit-warren corridors, an underground city: a switchboard room that could have housed a 747; a climate-control system to monitor sled-runs, outdoor speed-rinks, and the finer, smoother surface of figure skating rinks; evidence at every turn of engineering genius allied with sport, wired to alarm systems and complex vistas of computer terminals which controlled all facets of the complex *but* the human factor.

Backstage was the hub, nerve-centre of the Building. If a bomb existed it would be here, where it would create the most damage. The spectre of nerve-gas alone, introduced into any one of the great web of heat vents, gave the engineers nightmares. Before Munich, Olympic venues were designed with an eye to architecture, spectator comfort, the grand tradition of a forum in which athletes of the world contested their skills against their peers. After Munich, the first, the principal concern was security. At the touch of a single switch it was possible to lock every entrance and exit, and if necessary seal off each room, one from another. Search for a single bomb which may or may not exist cost thousands of man-hours and major juggling of starting times to accommodate those man-hours. Tonight the organizers were lucky. As the security chief told his lieutenants:

'We open up as soon as we pacify the mob. We just got word. There's no bomb. They caught the guy, phone in hand, a hundred miles away. A nutter, what else, the damned world's full of 'em. So we're opening up, but with maximum security. One crack-pot sets off another. They're a blasted plague. Tell your men we want extra vigilance backstage. I don't care if it's a competitor's mommy, daddy, priest, or coach. I don't care if it's God Almighty — *no badge, no entry*. Got it? Blue badges through blue doors, green through green. No exceptions, no sob-stories. If you're tempted, remember Munich. *Do I make myself clear?*'

A chorus of assent as each man checked gun, colour chart, hand-cuffs, and menacing frown, preparing to translate, as best he could, these absolutes to the rag-tag troops on the front lines.

'That's it then. These Olympic Games are again open for business.'

Ignoring Grant, Noni ushered Brigitta and Otto to the Competitors' Gate as if the Braun Kramers were visiting royalty whose fond farewells and best wishes were all that stood between disaster and their princess on her way from the Village bus to the Building.

Brigitta fussed with Roxanne's dress, a conservative little black number studded with jet beads, all discreetly covered now with a coat, but of course the family must see, family being family, and of course Brigitta professed outrage at the low-cut bodice and high-cut panties. Otto, who'd seen thighs and cleavage for seventy years, yawned, wanting the whole thing over, wishing Brigitta would lose that dangerously high flush, wishing they were home, talking some fool into buying the rink as they skimmed retirement brochures of lapping blue waters and hot white beaches. Death, he thought, must be a lot like life: purgatory today, paradise tomorrow. Maybe.

'Why,' Brigitta asked Noni plaintively, 'did you put her in black?'

'This is Compulsories, like school figures used to be — bright colours were never appropriate for figures, you know that.' Noni buffed up her nails, also varnished to a high-black gloss in a vague gesture of family unity, and tweaked a tendril of Roxanne's strawberry blonde hair to cascade, ever so casually, from its thick black net. 'And don't forget, Mutti, she *is* the favourite, the World Champion. Black *is* the power colour.'

'Where,' Otto asked, 'do you get this nonsense? Power colour indeed!'

'My publisher lets me in on all the latest fashion secrets,' she said, patting the pad, still innocent of words but now somewhat the worse for wear, cigarette burns and coffee rings liberally decorating its top sheet. 'Black also happens to be the most slenderizing colour in the spectrum.'

Otto closed his eyes. Useless to tell this shallow creature that black was not in the spectrum, remind her it was the colour for death — hardly a good omen for a competition on which so much depended.

Roxanne, silent focus of the conversation, also shut her eyes and clenched her fists. If they would just *go*, leave her with Grant so she could prepare herself! Grant saw the gesture and eased the older Brauns to the lifts, tipping the operator to be sure he wheeled Otto to his special invalid seat.

Which left Noni, who flicked nervously at her lighter and seemed prepared to hang around the Competitors' turnstile until the guards either died or lost interest. They did neither.

'Noni, you're wasting your time,' Grant said. 'You couldn't get into a backstage loo without the right colour badge — and your press pass is the wrong spectrum. Wish Roxanne luck and go, look after your parents, huh?'

She pulled on a thin brown cigarette and narrowed her eyes at both of them through the smoke. 'A champion doesn't need luck and I don't need you to patronize me. Now, Roxanne. You took your vitamins like I told you?'

Roxanne looked helplessly at Grant, who turned Noni firmly by the shoulders to a waiting lift. 'Don't push your luck, lady. We'll talk later.'

He jabbed a thumb on the up button, waiting for the door to whisper shut on Noni's smoke before he flashed his pass at the guard and steered Roxanne down the corridor to the game-room.

In a quiet corner he pulled her to him and touched his lips to her hair. 'I've got to go out front and look for Beejay, sweetheart. Now quit trembling and give me a smile. Nine judges are waiting, every one of them pulling for *you*. It's your turn. The same judges gave you the world title twice. *You*. Best in the world, right? You don't have to prove you're superwoman anymore, just Roxanne Kramer. In a couple of hours, when we go back through that turnstile, you'll have such a lead the devil himself won't be able to catch you. There's even a present waiting for you. A surprise.'

God, surprises. All she needed. 'Will I like it?'

'I hope so.'

She swallowed, unable to stay off the Olympics, the consequences. 'But Grant . . . if I blow the Original tonight, that's it for me, I'm finished, then what about *us*? That's what gets me, not the Original specially, I think I can hold the lead tonight, but the Long Free programme scares me to death, that damned triple-axel of Nakashima's, that poetry of Sterling's. If I do blow it . . . you've invested four years in me. . .'

'And you in me. But you've put in sixteen into the ice — a lot of them sheer hell. I thought you knew. Win, lose or draw, we're a team, okay?'

We're a team. Not quite 'I love you,' but if they were a team —

'I'll come in when it's time for you to skate. In the game-room, right?'

She hesitated. The consortium called it a game-room; competitors waiting for zero hour called it the executioner's room. Ping-pong and pool tables, chess sets, Monopoly boards, video games by the score, all lay quiet, neglected. Games made noise, required thought. Competitors wanted silence, their ears tuned to the applause of a rival — or lack of it. Just listening, knowing the other's music, where the jumps came, you knew what they'd landed, missed or left out. To date, Roxanne had not seen a video screen lit or a competitor playing a game in this room. Most preferred to agonize alone in the corridor leading to the ice, to walk about, keep muscles loose, to fix one's mind firmly on the first note of one's own music.

'I'll hang around here for Maureen,' she said. 'She doesn't play psych-out like the others. She'll be late, she's bringing her Mom in tonight, she said.'

His face seemed to close up, freeze, but he kissed the tip of her nose anyway. 'Whatever. Stay loose, okay?'

She watched him hurry away to Beejay, to check out her costume, give her her last minute instructions before he took his seat in the coaches' section, surrounded by that tense band of men and women all hoping to leave the Building happier, more successful, than when they arrived.

Beejay arrived in her usual slap-dash uproar; one hand clutched her skate-bag, the other a large take-out box of *paella* to stave off malnutrition until she came off and could sit down to a proper meal. She seemed to have brought her own brass band, all whooping and laughing as they tumbled out of the bus; half-a-dozen hopefuls from LA who fully expected to skate the Olympics themselves one fine day; Emma and Beejay herself; the Bean wearing a suit on his back and a blonde speed-skater around his neck, a tall Dutch girl with a wide smile and a thick plait of flaxen hair. Standing next to her, Beejay looked like an elf in a curly red cap. Quiet in the midst of happy chaos, Nils' head poked up from a mountain of parkas which he distributed like a harassed father of ten. A guard looked on with something like compassion. Emma, the Bean and Nils all had backstage badges, but Emma chose to hand Beejay over to Grant and declare them all off duty for the evening.

'She's all yours, Grant. She just beat the daylights out of us at Scrabble. Enough's enough. We need a rest. But first, Beejay old sport, a —'

'— a word in my ear!' Beejay knew the script but she nodded, fishing a garlic shrimp out of the *paella* for Emma, who took it absently — it could have been a cough-drop for all either of them would have noticed.

'Like I said, watch your language. This is the big time. If Peggy or Dick or Donna interviews you in 'Kiss'n'Cry', be a lady. You'll be in every living-room in America. If they ask serious questions, like how you feel about your chances, think. Be serious. They're professionals. This is the Olympic Games, not mud-wrestling in Atlantic City. So show respect.'

'Yes'm.' Beejay rolled her eyes up to heaven.

'And when the marks come up, pin a smile on and keep it on no matter what. No rolling your eyes like you just did. Hear me?'

Beejay sighed. 'Mom, I *know* Willi's gonna wipe the floor with me, big deal. One out of nine's not worth diddly sq —'

'That's enough. When your music starts, go for it.'

For a moment the crowd seemed to evaporate, and mother and daughter brushed fingertips on their own little island. The unspoken signals registered, to be dropped like lucky charms into the memory. Beejay: Screw Willi, Em. He's got no more clout than a bowl of tapioca. Emma: Sorry about the dress. You could have the world if I had it.

Beejay nodded, spat on her palms, played a quick patty-cake with the Bean, and soft-shoed down the hall, offering Grant a dip in the *paella*.

Nils shrugged. 'Relax, Em. It's better than if she bit her fingernails.'

Maureen arrived with coach and satyr, who took her directly to the ballet room to warm up. 'Sorry, Roxanne,' Maureen said over her shoulder, 'after barre warm-up I have to check on Mother. She's in Chaperones. I put her next to Mrs

Crisp, who looked more or less user-friendly; and Alexei's keeping an eye on her too, she likes him, but —'

'No problem,' Roxanne said, but it was — she hated waiting alone. She wondered again about the elusive Mrs Sterling. Lloyd was visible enough, God knew. Odd that Maureen and her father seldom spoke, and that Lloyd seemed so friendly with Jeff in LA. Something strange there, but neither Maureen or Grant confided and Roxanne had not asked. Enough skeletons rattled in her own family closet without rummaging through someone else's.

'Roxanne, you look lovely,' Maureen said, still talking over her shoulder, reluctant to leave her new friend, who was obviously afraid. 'My mother — she has incredible taste — says you have the best bone structure of anyone.'

'Except you, right?'

They both laughed. 'She's my mother, what do you expect?' At the last moment Maureen turned back again. 'Nakashima here yet?' she said quietly. Mieko's phenomenal leaps hung over all, but their shadows fell mostly over Roxanne, who could least afford the pressure.

Roxanne sighed. 'She will be. Bet on it.'

Initially, the arrival of Dag Carlsen with Mieko and her mother was the quietest yet. The minder, following at a discreet distance, from time to time glanced behind him through the great metal doors into the night, but no one noticed him except, of course, the guards, who tonight would have noticed a flea on the hide of an elephant — but not stars shining in the eyes of a tiny Japanese they'd admitted through this turnstile twice a day for two weeks.

To give the young couple a moment alone Oka-chan showed her badge first; the guards, unsmiling, checked her chaperone status and photo against that on their computer terminal and clicked her through. Dag, his credentials also in order, handed over Mieko's heavy skate-bag and bent low to give his new love an ounce of courage before she faced the lions.

'Sweetheart,' he whispered. 'Remember what you said. Skate fantastic.'

'Of course! I told you, Carlsen man. If I say, I mean.'

Oka-chan tapped her watch and spoke urgently in Japanese. Mieko, almost buried in the bulky Rising Sun parka and warm-ups, turned for a last longing look at Dag Carlsen as she pushed reluctantly on the turnstile bar so familiar to her palms. How could she bear to look away from him now, their future together arching like a rainbow on her horizon —

Slam! Shouts! What — what — odour swarming over her like vermin, greasy clothes, a stench of unwashed teeth, a guard towering over her, clasping her arm, shaking her, scowling, shouting in a language she did not know, plunging enormous hands into her pockets, emptying her skate-bag on to the concrete, then the shame, oh the shame, ripping open her parka, touching at her neck, the bodice of her dress — 'Pass!' he demanded, his one word of English squandered on a girl who did not yet know its many meanings.

A flash, a single exclamation in yet another language she did not know, a golden head looming taller even than the guard's, Dag's bandaged fists lifting him by the lapels of his uniform jacket, shaking him harder than the housekeeper in Atami shook the rugs, slamming him against the wall — but now a multitude appeared behind Dag, not so tall but many, many, guns drawn —

'*Iyé!*' her mother wailed '*Iyé!* — no-no! *Mieko, show badge!*'

Badge, show badge . . . the last moments in Oka-chan's room moved before her slowly, as in a nightmare, too happy she had been, thoughtless — and now the fates punished her disobedience. The badge, that priceless square of plastic the size of a packet of cigarettes bearing her name and photograph, hung always on its thick yellow cord around her neck, for without it she was not allowed backstage — but the badge lay now on Oka-chan's pillow at the hotel. Mieko's own hands had put it there when her Carlsen man opened her kimono — for what use is a square of plastic between a man and woman aching to be together, to love each other for the first time?

'Oh, Carlsen! Badge at hotel! How to warm-up? They won't let me in, the shame for my mother, Grandfather. For Japan — they send me so very far, have done me honour — I run, I run now to hotel, get badge, perhaps there is time —'

'Mieko, stop crying and listen. When I say "okay" go through the turnstile. If it's locked, duck under the rail, get behind your mother and put your skates on real quick. I'll hold things up this side as long as I have to. Stand back.'

For the rest of his life he'd bless the muscles his sister's appetite had developed as he turned, shielding Mieko between himself and the wall as he faced the armed guards, speaking to the tallest one softly, calmly, all too aware the man probably had neither English nor Swedish.

'Tell your apes to put their water-pistols away and listen. You know she's a major competitor, you've seen her every day. Get your security chief, your captain — whatever you call him — here on the double! And don't anybody *think* of laying another hand on *her, her mother*, or even *her skates* — or I'll pull your head off.' He flexed a bicep under the man's fist, and the man leapt back, intimidated. '*Okay, Mieko! Run!*'

He felt her dart to the turnstile, duck under, and run to her mother in the corridor. Perhaps it was the menace in his voice, or the word 'security', but the tall guard grunted an order into a walkie-talkie. Another kept his gun firmly on Dag. The rest clustered around Mieko but did not touch or interfere as she rapidly laced her boots, as all of them awaited the arrival of the chief from the other side of the Building.

In the tension, only Oka-chan looked into the darkness beyond the doors. She gasped, closed her eyes, and looked again. It was not possible. Only yesterday he had bullied her from the other side of the world — but no, her sight was not failing. Calmly watching the scene from the window of a black limousine at the curb sat her father. Hiro Nakashima. Like a statue he posed. She knew, without knowing why, that he had seen everything, including the tender goodbye between Mieko and her young man, and if by chance there were items he'd missed, her minder, now standing by the limousine virtually at attention, would fill him in. That was his function. Her father inclined his head, the flunky climbed in, and the car turned quietly away from the curb and purred towards the hotel.

In this warm arena, wrapped in sables and the shreds of a new-found assurance she'd thought impregnable, Hiro Nakashima's daughter shivered.

*

396

Deirdre, when Maureen checked, sat in animated conversation next to Emma Crisp. Leaving her to it, Maureen wondered what the judge would make of that exquisitely dressed woman who, under merciless arena lights, looked like a jewelled death's-head, a bundle of bones wrapped in glossy furs.

The eyes were the worst, Emma Crisp thought, trying not to stare, to watch the ice instead as the first anonymous group of five girls came out for warm-up — frightened girls from new little countries, awed by minicams, a packed arena, and the occasion itself. Even skating their best they were hopelessly out-classed, would be lucky to make the cut, and knew it. The knowledge sapped what little confidence they'd brought with them. They fell a lot and with each fall grew a little more desperate.

Emma, sorry for them, gave up and turned to Deirdre Sterling, who wasn't watching either, whose opera-glasses roamed the arena, settling at last on Grant in the Coaches' section.

'That's Grant Rivers,' Emma said. 'He trains Beejay and Roxanne and —'

'— Jeff Dunsmuir and the Swedish Pair. I know. We have been out of touch for a while but one does make an effort to keep up. . .'

And la-de-da to you, lady. Emma frowned. This woman didn't match her voice, which had that cutting clarity peculiar to the Brit upper-crust, pitched to intimidate housemaids, chauffeurs and any inferiority complex within a ten-mile radius. Physically this woman could not have intimidated a sparrow. Hardly a woman at all now, more a starving animal shrinking in its pelt, the dark-ringed eyes those of a terrified night creature trapped by the light. Sapphires sparkled in her ears with a thousand times the wattage of her eyes.

It was only when she peered deep into their crêpe-paper hollows that Emma could see the eyes at all — dull, implacable blue pools which met Emma's gaze with an anger almost tangible in that lifeless face. Startled, she moved back. What had she done? But then Deirdre Sterling shot the same flash of hatred at Mieko's mother, who wasn't even looking at them, and Emma knew, God willing, they would see their girls grow into women and perhaps into mothers. Deirdre Sterling would not.

'I saw videos of Beejay skating St Ivel, Mrs Crisp. In a couple of years she will be quite a strong little contender. A most . . . unusual name, Beejay.' Her voice faltered, betraying physical weakness under the iron will.

Emma bit her tongue. A couple of years my foot, Beejay's a strong contender right now, lady — but who could stoop to score off this poor thing? 'It's Belinda Jane really, you know.' Of course she knew. Emma smiled to soften the cut and saw an answering flicker in the woman's eyes. Everybody studied competition results — even sick parents. Rule-book listings were to ice-rinks what racing-forms were to race-tracks. Emma could bet this woman knew Beej's marks at the St Ivel down to the last hundredth of a point with every judge on the panel.

'Bald as an egg as a baby,' she said cheerfully. 'If we'd known she'd turn out a redhead *and* a tomboy we'd have picked out a name with a bit of ginger.'

Deirdre Sterling laughed softly, brittle, like breaking glass. 'I had the opposite problem,' she said. 'When my Maureen was a baby I called her Mo — but by the time she was five I knew I'd have to stop. She was nothing like a Mo at all, far too elegant even then. . .'

Emma could have played one-up-man-ship all night with zest — but not with this poor thing whose fur cuff slipped back to expose a glimpse of wrist and arm, of thin fingers weighted down with jewels, any one of which would have paid Beejay's ice fees until the cows came home. Even as she watched, the rings, no flesh to hold them, obeyed the law of gravity and slid inexorably towards the palms and out of sight, away from the light and its pitiless reflections — exactly where the woman herself would be soon. Like Dave, Emma thought, an urn of ashes that could be anybody or nobody. What good were diamonds and sapphires then?

Alexei Finsky appeared at the end of their row, excusing himself as he made his way to Deirdre Sterling, speaking to her quietly, pointing out two women over in Public dressed very nearly alike, navy coats, sensible shoes, and perky little hats that had surely originated in a uniform tailoring-shop. Deirdre gave Alexei a strained smile and briefly touched his hand. 'Sweet of you . . . but I feel wonderful, do ask them not to worry about me this evening? Just enjoy themselves?'

He left to deliver her message and resume his seat in Competitors, and Deirdre turned to Emma, 'A thoughtftul boy, Alexei,' she said, tugging at her cuffs. 'I gave tickets to a couple of the maids from my suite. Since he's the only one they know, they sent Alex to ask if I needed anything — so kind. . .'

Emma nodded. Maids? If ever she'd seen nurses in *mufti* those two were it; in what must, to them, be the alien atmosphere of an ice-rink, there was no question at all that in their capacious bags were stashed smelling salts, thermometers, and several vials of medicine; considering Deirdre's condition, it wouldn't surprise Emma if they also had walkie-talkies connecting them to a waiting ambulance, just in case.

Below, in Competitors, the Bean flashed Emma a wink as he whispered in the speed-skater's ear. Odd the way close competitors hung together even off-ice, as if subconsciously trying to dominate their nearest rivals. Alexei, the Bean, the Czech, Jeff Dunsmuir and the Korean sat all in a bunch. Behind Jeff, the rock star draped himself in a seat he shouldn't be in, but Jeff sat well forward, denying any association at all. A few rows down, with the Russian and American Pairs, Dag Carlsen rubbed his knuckles and watched the ice. Waiting. Don't we all, Emma thought. Not present were Lise Carlsen and Mieko's cousin — though God knew plaster-casts and arm-slings dotted the Competitor section like alabaster headstones on a hillside cemetery. Arms, legs, ankles, knees, necks, a few bandaged foreheads. As a group, they made a lousy ad for winter sports — but a better one than the woman beside her, who'd become quiet, sunk down into her furry collar, and again trained her binoculars on Grant Rivers.

As Emma watched, a thin trickle of tears slid off Deirdre Sterling's cheekbones to lose themselves in fur and memories that Emma Crisp, whose life — except for one unfortunate page — was an open book, could not begin to understand.

CHAPTER THIRTY-SIX

The announcement crackled over the public address system. Would the final group of Ladies — Roxanne Kramer, Maureen Sterling, Beejay Crisp, Mieko Nakashima, and the top German whose name lost itself in the rafters — please take the ice for warm-up?

Grant stiffened in his seat. An entire lifetime building to this moment, and he felt only numb, trapped between warring conflicts he could no longer avoid, a marathoner at the end of the course, the scent of victory in his nostrils, defeat snapping at his heels. Roxanne's eyes hunted him from the ice, seeking the confidence he could only give with his gift, which he'd hoped to save until they were home. The other girl, hair as black as his own, didn't look for him at all. Why should she, and why should he care? But he did.

Across the arena, among the Chaperones, the black circles of Maureen's mother's binoculars clung to him like barnacles he could not escape no matter where he turned. After all these years, how must he seem to her now, this woman who'd been his dream and was now his nightmare?

Closer in, Jeff Dunsmuir monitored him with a wary eye, watching for him to discuss the possible sponsor, but tonight Yum-Num talked fifty-to-the-dozen, at once an irritant and a cushion. Who could wander for long in the past or peer into an uncertain future while Yum-Num pelted him with verbal tennis balls outrageously off-colour in the present. Grant sat through his breezy service game, returning or letting them go as seemed required.

'Yum, oh yum, this is it, old cock, beginning of the end. . .'

You're not kidding, this Olympics is the end of a great chunk of my life and nothing about it is ending the way I expected.

But Yum-Num flowed ever onwards. 'Num, as I always say, it's not worth it, plays hell with the old tum. If they skate well they're marvels, nothing we did, oh num! But let 'em fall all over the ice and who's to blame then? Us, old lad! Yum, they can win or we can lose. We trained 'em.'

'About training,' Grant said. *Oh, stand up, Roxanne, concentrate, dammit, stop hunting for your mommy in Press, your grandparents in Public, me down here. You're out of our reach now, on your own and it's cold, I know it is. I cannot help you from here.* 'Some woman in your neck of the woods is offering to sponsor our Jeffie. Well fixed, a really sharp lady he says —'

'I think I know her, married five times, blew it every time. Got brothers, has she? And apartments?'

'How did you know?' *How do I know Maureen is my daughter? That she was no accident, just Deirdre's consolation prize to herself for a lousy marriage? That she probably shopped for sperm the way she'd shop for a coat? That I was manufacturer and delivery lad all rolled into one? A little something in a dark-haired baby, I think, a touch of Spanish blood perhaps, healthy, young, regular features, oh yes, he will do perfectly . . . Yes, that's how it would have been.* 'Is she famous?'

'Infamous. A boilin' of brothers, dole, fast food and food stamps. Albany byword, the whole family. She's the all-round expert — especially on marriage and money. Funny, people who can't manage either one know all there is to know about both. Warned me that Maxim's in Paris was a tourist trap! If she ever so much as got near Paris she's too hard-up to tip the loo attendant!'

'But the property?' Grant said. 'Jeff seemed pretty convinced.'

'She owns zip, but a kid like Jeff would never know it. Champion name-dropper, hangs on to celebrity coat-tails. First Lady of the Murmured Aside, drops 'em in like pebbles. Sings a good song, I'll give her that. . .'

'A good song?' *Good song, good year.* 'To dream the impossible dream' . . . *if he just hadn't hoped, somewhere in the back of his mind, that it was possible — but surely the point of an impossible dream is that it's always out of reach. Grab it and you kill it.* 'Jeff didn't say that she was a singer.'

Service ace to Yum-Num, who chuckled, happy to expound. 'Num! A joke, lad, wake up!' He jabbed Grant in the ribs to rouse him. 'Selling herself, she calls it, personality-wise, understand, all twinkly — woman-about-town, yum, a silver tongue and a good wardrobe, sixty-five per cent off. Manipulator, get it?'

'Uh-huh.' *Not as good as Deirdre — manipulated me into fatherhood then shoved me out the door, made me a travelling man, a show-biz man. Oh, them blades were made for skatin' — but not here, dear, is that clear, dear? Many, many songs, all sweetly sung.* Poor bright Jeffie, an apprentice puppeteer now, but he'd learn fast, he had the makings. 'No hope for Jeff then, right?'

'Num, once bitten. . . collecting protégés is part of her act, know what I mean? Tries the old scam: trust me, I'll help you. Then later, when they're making show money, she wants a per cent until kingdom come or their knees go bad, whichever comes first. On a legal contract, yet. Trouble is, she's got zip to help them *with*, know what I mean? So the coach never collects, see? Promises, promises. Class-A talker, though. Yum.'

On the ice Roxanne aimed for a triple but doubled in the last second. Damn, she couldn't get away with that! He wanted to reach across the ice, conquer her fear. *Nearly over, lover, soon it'll be your turn . . .* Yum-Num's elbow nudged his ribs. He'd forgot to return the ball.

Class-A talker. 'Kissed the blarney stone, did she?'

Yum-Num slapped his plump thighs and applauded himself, his evening a success. Grant, carefully led, had lobbed in an easy smash. 'Kissed it?' he said, laughing. 'She gave it the blow-job of its life! If she thought there was something in it for her she'd screw Idi Amin.'

'Isn't he dead?'

'See what I mean?' Yum-Num had worked hard to reach his punch-line, so game, set, and match to him. Grant wondered if he should applaud, but Yum-Num turned belatedly to the warm-up just finishing. 'Roxi looks like a pipe-cleaner in mourning, mate! Who put her in black?'

'Noni.'

Roxanne spun slim as a night wand in that dress, her shoulders narrow, like Deirdre's — but Deirdre was sick . . .

and of course he knew what it was, hadn't he as much as told Jeff Dunsmuir? *How d'you think Deirdre got it, by osmosis?* She got it from Lloyd. But who had she given it to? And when? In a few years could Roxanne look like that? Roxanne who'd lived with him and no one else for four years, and he was the first, the only, no question about it?

He shut his eyes and behind them the ice melted, disappeared. He faced the long tunnel of his future and knew finally, beyond question, that Roxanne Kramer must be in it. Compared to her health, the Games and the medal she may or may not win were no more than chaff in the wind. He'd been afraid, making his secret, tentative, almost terrified purchase this morning, that perhaps he'd simply been buying insurance. But no. It was what he wanted. But suppose it was no longer what *she* wanted? Her dependence had disturbed him and he'd welcomed, lately, the flashes of spirit that occasionally took over — but suppose that spirit flashed her right past him, driving her to more deserving, considerate arms? If she rejected him — and she had enough will to do it — what would he do with his future?

For an instant a fear so violent shook him that he thought his heart had stopped, but no, it just skipped a beat, hesitating before taking that long plunge into the labyrinth — and Grant Rivers, Coach, had no time to follow it. They called the Ladies off warm-up, and Roxanne and Maureen, black and almost-white smiling at each other, briefly came together on ice — where he'd kept all his problems all his life, solving nothing, two streams, one shadowed and hesitant, the other cool and efficient.

Out of the blue ice lake a pink neon-fish darted between them, wasting not a moment of the spotlight, soaring into a corker of a triple toe-loop, the only skater still in motion. Beejay, creature of certainty — built on what? No material floor such as supported Maureen, no emotional back-up of lover, mother, two old folks in Bonn — plus a couple of world titles to lean back on — like Roxanne. Just Emma Crisp and a pink dress beginning to show its age.

'If you hear anything, Jeff still needs a sponsor,' he pressed Yum-Num, nodding to Roxanne and Beejay that he'd follow as they disappeared backstage to wait. He stood up. 'He's not what you'd call discriminating, our Jeff.'

'Yum, I noticed, silly young bugger. But hell, who is, at that age? I'll keep my ears open.' For the first time since he'd known him, Yum-Num turned serious. 'He's got promise, that lad, but it's a jungle out there, mate. If they don't find a cure soon, nobody'll commit themselves to more than a cup of coffee in a public place — served in a sterilized cup.'

Thus spoke skating's funny man, twenty years married, father of three teenagers, and clearly, under the yo-ho-ho, worried out of his mind for them.

He was not alone.

Roxanne and Beejay waited for him in the tunnel, shaking out calves and thighs, rolling shoulders to keep loose. Beejay, who'd drawn first of the five to skate, took a few deep breaths but mostly listened to Grant — an occasion in itself. Maybe she'd finally noticed that this was the Games.

'Not the main event now, just Originals, so keep it conservative. No miracles. Jump clean, spin fast, don't get fancy. Stick to your music like glue and do nothing we haven't planned, hear me? Hear me, Beej?'

'In the Original? As if I would.'

'Okay. You know you can do it so do it. Ready?'

Representing the United States of America, Miss Belinda Jane Crisp!

Beejay blinked for a moment. Belinda Jane? 'Jeez, that's me!'

She laughed, flashed to centre-ice to wait for the clarion call of 'Bugler's Holiday'. When it came she was off, chasing that bugler as if her life depended on clinging to his coat-tails, no time for nerves, two minutes of perpetual motion, precise, efficient, completed in the triumph of a perfect programme. When her head cleared after the final scratch spin she found herself looking straight into the eyes of Willi Vanilla. She smiled at him so sweetly that Emma, watching through her own binoculars, shivered in her seat. The young madam was daring that pathetic old man! Everything clean and fast. No misses. No excuse for Willi to hit her too hard — and Willi wasn't stupid enough to try. He'd play it deftly, smoothly, mark her down some for style but so would the others, elegance not being her strong suit yet. Yep, she was right. Willi marked her lowest, but only by a tenth. No surprises right across the board. With four top prospects still to come, all with more polish and experience than Beejay, prudent judges left room at the top. As a judge herself, Emma approved; as a mother, she wished they'd seen fit to give Beejay that extra tenth for being Beejay.

The German next, as small as Beejay, feather light in the jumps but slow on the spins. Again, no misses, one wobble, no big deal. Willi marked up, the American marked down. Over all, she and Beejay came out dead even, as they should. Nobody put it just that way but Originals sorted into broad categories, from Impossible to Possible to Good to Choice, finally to Extra Choice. Among the top ten, the Long Free would separate Choice newcomers from Choice veterans — and Beejay and the German were the only real babies in Choice. The rest, older, had all seen some international action.

Nakashima up next. No big triple-axel to help now, she had to prove her mettle with marginally easier jumps they could all do — on a good day. Her landings could be a liability, but although tonight she would not be doing it, every judge on the panel had the phenomenal elevation of that jump damn near impregnated on their retinas, no way to pluck it out of their minds for the duration of Originals. It would be there waiting for them in Finals, the almond on the cake, and they knew it. A world-class show-stopper.

She skated out in yellow, a new softness in her style, a smile not just pasted on but real, dreamy, clearly offering her programme to Dag Carlsen, who couldn't take his eyes off her, didn't seem to want to, and was the only one so wrapped up in the girl that he forgot to applaud what Emma had to rate as simply fantastic. When her marks flashed on to the board every skater in the building gasped. Five-point-nine's right across for technical merit; comp and style almost as high. Emma nodded. Each judge independently, no consultations needed, had done what Emma herself would have done. Knowing that, she also knew what they'd do with Kramer and Sterling assuming they also skated well. They'd mark all three girls up so tight that any one of them could win or lose the Gold on a tenth of a point in the Final.

At rink-side, Roxanne and Grant said nothing. Maureen, with coach and the satyr, were silent too. All knew what could happen. Assuming.

Roxanne's assumptions proved correct. With the first note of music her new friend Maureen became a stranger-swan, blue-white chiffon feathers floating calmly across a still lake, no flash and dazzle, no emotion, no errors, just the perfection of an impossible dream gliding across an enchanted lake as coolly as in practice. Her take-offs lifted easily, her landings caressed the ice, prompting no bursts of second-hand triumph from her supporters, no bravura posturings from the skater herself, just the calm expectation that her body would perform as instructed. It did. She ended to silence, a vacuum, then the unanimous shuffling of feet as the crowd rose in tribute.

Emma Crisp shivered, goosebumps on her arms for what could happen to the American team in Finals. Great as Sterling had skated, her performance had been cold, calculated; if, in Finals, she were to pull out the emotional stops, then good luck Roxanne Kramer and Mieko Nakashima. Better luck next time. But would there be one? Not for Roxanne, over the hill at twenty-two. Probably not for Mieko, if the love-light in her eyes was the real thing. Marriage and competition didn't mix.

The judges gave Sterling a slight edge over Nakashima, confirming what Roxanne feared most. After a standing ovation, no margin for a single error.

'If I miss one thing,' she murmured to Grant, 'they'll wipe me out. If I skate clean they'll give me a tiny lead to keep it a horse-race. It'll look like I'm ahead but we'll be pretty well all tied, right?'

'Uh-huh. It's more or less what we expected. But you *will* skate clean and if you do the same in Free they'll give *you* the Gold. It's your turn.'

She searched his eyes, looking for that tell-tale flicker that didn't come. 'You believe that?'

He looked through her eyes into her brain, her will. 'Roxanne, you are the favourite. If you want it I believe you can have it. But don't ever forget there are millions out there who've never wanted it — they live happy lives —'

She'd tuned out. 'But Maureen, Mieko, if they want it as much —'

He shrugged. 'You're World Champion. Like Finsky. All else being equal the Champ gets the nod because the Champ's earned it, not just for one competition but for consistency through the years.'

'A "Life Achievement Award", like sick old men at Oscar night, right?'

'Since when has staying-power been a liability? If we're getting married we'll try for that life achievement award, right?'

'Married?'

He'd planned to save it, but after Sterling's performance Roxanne needed this now, a last shot of confidence before she hit the ice. 'Okay. You twisted my arm. We've got a busy night ahead. When we leave here we go to the infirmary with Jasinski for blood tests, then dinner —'

'I'm not sick, I feel fine.'

'Tests for both of us. The licence. Remember I said I had something for you? I was saving it for the trip home, but if you're going to accept, maybe you'd better wear it on the ice, cool it off. It's burning a hole in my pocket.'

They were calling her name as she opened the velvet box, but she didn't care. The traditional diamond winked up at her. How could she see anything else? 'Oh Grant, are you sure, I mean —'

'Are *you* sure?'

'They're calling my name.'

'You're World Champion. They'll wait. I won't. What d'you say?'

'Yes, of course, yes —'

He slipped it on her finger, kissed her cheek, and steered her towards the ice, a girl too happy now to be afraid of anything. But she had no idea what to be afraid of and he dare not tell her. It was Deirdre's secret, not his. But he had to know, take care of her no matter what.

And Roxanne Kramer, world champion, knew she had to win the Short Original. Must, must, must, she whispered, skating out, sneaking a last peek at the ring, watching the play of spotlights hitting the facets. This and the Games too. She'd win Originals now, couldn't lose. For one treacherous moment the thought came, crossing her mind like a shadow before happiness once again triumphed, that maybe that was why Grant gave it to her, so she'd skate well for him, for his Gold. No, he wouldn't. . .

Representing the United States of America, Miss Roxanne Braun Kramer.

A burst of applause for the World Champion, a rippling forest of American and German flags, and the audience subsided to watch. No mistakes. Get the mind off the ring and work clean. A last look at Grant, his nod of confidence, his thumbs-up, and she began to skate. As Grant River's fiancée.

Consistently, the way she'd won her previous titles, she worked from one move to the next, jump after spin after step, sharp, clean, but not *too* great — in Originals clean counted as much as great, without the risk. No bobbles, no misses — above all, no falls. Keep your head, save the fireworks for the Long Free. A lay-back spin, her best move, ended the programme. She made no mistakes — but neither had Maureen and Mieko.

'What d'you think, Grant?'

'I think you won the Original, but I'm biased. Whatever, smile when they talk to you in "Kiss'n'Cry".'

'Should I mention —' She looked down at the ring, and blushed.

'Why don't we wait. Tell your Mom and grandparents first.' Her blush deepened. He'd almost forgotten how beautiful she could be with the pressure released, even temporarily. 'Tomorrow, okay?'

The results were as Emma predicted. Roxanne Kramer won the Original by one-tenth of a point by just one judge. The three top competitors would go into the final round virtually even.

In the hotel room of his nephew, Hiro Nakashima refused to sit or to permit his nephew to sit. Lise Carlsen he ignored completely, and eventually his flunky took her firmly by the elbow, tucked her crutch under her arm, and pushed her into the hall. The door closed quietly on her outraged: 'Well!'

'Now,' Hiro Nakashima said with dignity. 'I will hear your excuses.'

The nephew looked around him, perhaps for inspiration. 'For what? So I broke my leg, couldn't finish the Games, is that my fault? — Look, I need to sit down, I do have a cast on, you know —'

Hiro Nakashima gave him a ringing back-hander across his beautiful bronze face and the nephew fell down, fortunately for him on the bed.

'For the moment you may stay there. Bed, any bed, seems to be your natural element.'

Hiro Nakashima permitted a long silence. His nephew, impatient, finally broke it. 'But I'm hurt, Nakashima-sama, I can't —'

'I did not travel so far, leave a most important conference in Hokkaido, to discuss your minor indisposition. Do you forget you are a member of this family — distant, I concede — but with a duty to protect its honour and dignity? I am this moment arrived from the arena where Mieko represents our coun —'

'— I couldn't get over there! It's too painful for me to walk, I —'

'I am not finished. I arrive to find my granddaughter — unlike you she is all Nakashima — subjected to one indignity after another by stinking guards who menace her, maul her, pull at her garments. And my grand-nephew, hero of the 70-metre hill ... where is he while this outrage is committed? He lies here in indolence and insolence.'

'*I have a broken leg.*'

'*Silence*! In addition to your other vulgarities you are a liar and a slow learner, deficiencies intolerable in a Nakashima. Your leg is not broken, your ankle is; the fracture is a simple greenstick. My ancestors marched into battle with far worse. *Marched*!'

'You just arrived, Uncle, you can't possible know —'

A long ivory hand rose like a traffic signal. The nephew's mouth closed. 'Copies of your X-rays lay on the desk of my personal physician before I permitted these Western quacks to even touch you. They were instructed to consult with him on every decision. In one respect, they failed.'

Hiro Nakashima paused to pull a long blonde hair from his nephew's shoulder and deposit it in the sink. His nephew waited, motionless, as the old man scrubbed his hands, rinsed them, dried them, and drew an orange stick fastidiously under his fingernails. He then examined his young relative with the thoughtful scrutiny he would give an unsatisfactory balance sheet.

'Tonight in the arena I saw hundreds of injured athletes. You were not among them. While Mieko Nakashima is attacked by vermin you lie here fondling a trollop. A round-eye trollop — despite her injuries and yours, which must be grave indeed to confine you both to bed for so long.'

'Great-Uncle, I —'

'Did I invite you to speak? Then remain silent. I am told that ambulatory patients will be returned to the Village to make room for new arrivals —'

'Well okay, if I have to I have to, but I'm still hurting —'

'But since your injuries give you such pain, I assume your care here to be questionable or your stamina inadequate. It remains for Mieko-chan, an untried young woman, to represent our nation and recover our family's honour before the nations of the world. You, I think, will recover faster in Tokyo. Your flight leaves tomorrow. I advise a good night's rest. Alone. Your reservation is made, a car will collect you at 7 AM.'

He snapped his fingers once, a sound remarkably like a pistol-shot, and the flunky handed the young man his marching orders in a JAL folder. Hiro Nakashima already stood at the door, his eyes hooded now, watching.

'But — but, Uncle, I can't leave yet! We have celebrations, friends on the team are throwing parties . . . and what about the closing ceremonies?'

'What about pride? You have rendered the name Nakashima a laughing-stock in every city in Japan and embarrassed me personally and deeply. Bad enough that you lack pride; you also lack shame. This we cannot accept. As your one influential relative I strongly advise you to board that plane.' The old man bowed and let himself out.

High above Montegreco the stars glittered hard as diamonds in the crisp mountain air. In his penthouse suite the oldest Nakashima sat cross-legged on a carpet decorated with nonsensical beige rings. He stared for a long time into the face of the *netsuke* carving without which he never left Japan. The monkey stared back, its sad, wizened face mourning the sorrows of the world, pondering distant griefs it could neither comprehend nor share with its illustrious owner. How long, Nakashima wondered, before his air-brained nephew and the company flunky noticed that the head of the family had deliberately referred to his granddaughter as Mieko-*chan* — a diminutive indicating a fondness not previously evidenced.

He shrugged. Let them make of it what they would.

The exodus of recovering patients had already begun. Ambulances extruded new stretcher pods into the infirmary corridors with the monotony of turtles laying eggs. Limited bed space filled rapidly with dare-devils from mountains, bob-sled runs, and the treacherous ice. The influx even included spectators; the rigours of watching were proving alarmingly hazardous to *aficionados* who became too personally involved.

They delivered one such patient immediately after the Ladies Original, an elderly German woman whose wig slipped off the gurney. Her husband, furiously following in a wheelchair, hastily clapped it back on her head before the duty nurse could blink an eye.

'Oh, Papa!' Noni shouted. 'As if the goddamn wig matters!'

'It matters to her. You were a selfish child and you're a selfish woman, Noni. Your mother is entitled to her dignity — and get those black fingernails off her face before I bite them off! They're like cockroaches!'

A doctor whisked in, clipboard in hand, a vague murmur of 'what seems to be the trouble' on his lips.

'My wife, she mixes her Englisher und Deutsch —'

Noni waved her press badge and her pad. 'Doctor, my mother's just over-excited. My parents — the Brauns here — and myself, Mrs Braun Kramer, were watching my daughter compete — Roxanne Braun Kramer, American and World Champion for the past two years? —'

Otto Braun turned purple. 'Noni, enough with the commercial! Doctor, I think my wife has a stroke. One moment she is speaking, happy, watching our granddaughter, the next she drops her purse from her shoulder and her mouth falls open and she tries to tell me something, all mixing up, that she feels itching, ants crawl on her, she wants to be sick, to lie down —'

'Dizzy,' Noni said. 'Just nerves, no need for a doctor, of course she's thrilled, my daughter just won the first part of the Gold medal, doctor —'

Otto shot his wheelchair between them so fast that both Noni and the doctor had to leap clear. 'Examine my wife!' he ordered. 'Ignore this lunatic.'

'This is my father,' Noni said. 'He knows nothing about medicine.'

'Enough to know you should not give your mother rubbish!' Otto shouted, pounding the rubber wheels of his chair in frustration.

'She took medication?' the doctor asked, smooth as a latex glove.

'Just vitamins. For high blood pressure.'

'You gave her . . .?'

'Niacin,' Noni said with some pride. 'Many doctors believe in it —'

'Prescribed by her family physician, was it?'

'No. By me. Her daughter.'

The doctor made a notation on his chart. 'Dosage?'

'A thousand milligrams,' Noni said.

'How many of them?'

'Three.'

The doctor pursed his lips and scribbled again. 'So, three thousand milligrams of niacin. I see. And she ingested them all at one time?'

'Yes. With coffee. She was tense. We all were, isn't that right, Papa?' Forgotten for the moment was Noni's irritation with Otto Braun.

The doctor motioned to a nurse and together they wheeled the gurney to an examining room, closing the door firmly behind them. Noni rapped the end of a long brown cigarette sharply on her black thumbnail.

'They're filters,' her father said through tight lips. 'No need to thrash them to death.'

'You don't smoke, what do you know?'

'I know enough not to.'

Noni turned away, black stiletto heels punishing the floor tiles up and down the waiting room. Up and down. Up and down. *Don't die, Mutti! Two more days and Roxanne will win Gold. It'll all have been worth it. Die now and she'd blow it, she'll skate like shit, all my years wasted. And yours, Mutti! We've both paid our dues, you understand, I know, only stupid Papa doesn't care. All he wants is to lie in the sun, get warm! This is our last hope, Mutti. Add up the years, go on, count! You trained for eighteen. Me, sixteen. Now Roxanne sixteen. Fifty years work invested in the ice, Mutti! Die now, and you'll flush half a century down the sewer!*

Behind her the door to the examining room swung open. That interfering bastard Jasinski, who in hell hired him, how did he get in there?

'Through the other door, Noni. The professionals' entrance. I'm sure you think that's where you belong —'

'Don't give me that! What are they doing with Mutti? There's nothing wrong with her, just excited that's all — hell, I'm excited, we all are —'

'But she may be suffering transient ischaemic attacks, you are not.'

'Tran . . . trans . . . what?

'Small strokes in a series. They come and go. Sometimes they clear up on their own, leaving only minor damage. Sometimes they're the warning of a massive stroke to come. It's too early to tell.'

'Like wait and see? If we're just going to wait and see, what do we need you guys for? I know as much as any of you, anyway.'

'If you did, you would never have given her such a dosage after she already said she felt unwell. Your intervention is delaying diagnosis.'

'That's right, blame me! It's a vitamin! You talk like I gave her poison. Why don't they pump her stomach?'

Jasinski sighed. 'She is already under stress. In the wrong circumstances, too much of anything can be poisonous. You also tried to give your daughter the same substance an hour before she competed. I am not sure, Mrs Kramer, but I think I could get you arrested for practising medicine without a licence.'

'Try it, just try it!'

Otto Kramer wheeled himself forwards. 'Did my daughter give my wife a stroke, Doctor Jasinski? If she did I'll kill her, I'll —'

'No, Otto. The side-effects of the niacin have to wear off before we know the extent of the problem. Brigitta has double vision, nausea, her speech is in and out. Who is her regular doctor in Bonn?'

Noni stepped forward. 'She doesn't need one. Whatever she's got, belly-ache, backache, she calls me, I tell her what to get from the health shop.'

Jasinski closed his eyes. This impossible, dangerous woman! After twenty-two years of her, was it surprising that her daughter had difficulty making a simple decision? Women like this should not be permitted to raise children. But she had intelligence, dripped with it — warped thinking, yes, distorted, squandered on one fragile dream that may have killed her mother and may yet kill her daughter. The snap of her lighter roused him:

'You may not smoke in here, Noni.'

She filled her mouth with smoke and blew it at him. 'A perfect example of the authority syndrome, you! Give a man a badge, in your case a degree, and he goes ape-shit. Where is the no-smoking sign? Go on, show me!'

'Behind you. In sixteen languages — at least four of which you understand. Why do you smoke, Noni? Today I counted. That is your third pack.'

'Because I'm nervous, that's why. Any wonder? After all these years, sacrifice this, that, every damned thing, Roxanne's going to blow the Gold, I can feel it, and I promised Mutti, I promised, "So okay," I told her, "I didn't ever win the Gold for you but my daughter will!" — and now Mutti's sick.'

Unbelievably, Noni Kramer's thin hard face crumpled like tissue. 'When Roxanne finds out about Mutti — she loves her grandmother — she'll blame me, she'll skate like a load of crap, and we'll lose, *we'll all lose* —'

'And you will be filled with guilt?'

She scrubbed at her eyes and rearranged her face. 'Mind your own damned business!'

She marched off in the vague direction of the rest-rooms,

missed her way, and bumped into a screen door, upon which she beat endlessly with her fists. 'Oh-my-god-oh-my-god-oh-my-god . . . Nothing ever goes right for me no matter what.'

CHAPTER THIRTY-SEVEN

Service in the hotel breakfast room the morning after Ladies Originals was slow, a clear indication of Olympic fever building and mounting. With Finals rushing upon them in all events, athletes left the isolation of the Village to frequent the hotel venues, where the media, with its need for phone banks and interview rooms, could roam freely. Even hotel guests who routinely breakfasted in their rooms — parents, coaches, deal-makers, announcers, columnists, officials — all showed up coiffed, cologned and co-ordinated, dressed to the nub for the benefit of media cameras. (Judges, for obvious reasons, were the exception; from now until the last medal was hung around the last neck, until the last tear dried and the last flag edged jerkily up its pole, judges would be ghosts prowling the corridors in the night, ducking into doorways and broom-closets at the sight of a parent or a coach.)

Noni, here on Roxanne's peremptory invitation, considered her appearance in the nature of a command performance. If Roxanne, as leader and favourite for Ladies Gold, reigned as Queen of the most glamorous event of the Games, then Noni surely had a right to sit close to the throne, to be considered, in fact, Queen Mother pro tem. To mark the occasion she wore a jade green velvet jump-suit belted in gold leather-like plastic, matching gold pumps, and iridescent green eyeshadow. Out of deference to Roxanne's image and Mutti's illness, her fingernails this morning were innocent of polish. She wondered, following the waiter, if she'd been wise. Green would have looked better than this sickly yellow, the colour of old nicotine stains. But worries aside — and did she ever have 'em, what with Roxanne *ordering* her here, what with no diagnosis on Mutti yet, what with Papa wheeling round and round the infirmary like a goddamned maniac bellowing at the nurses — despite all that she went out of her way to be gracious to the waiter, who ushered her past the hoi-poloi waiting like oxen behind the gold-tasselled rope. 'This way, madam. Miss Kramer is expecting you,' he murmured.

'I hope so,' she said, tapping him roguishly on the arm with her pad. 'I'm her mother, you know!'

'Follow me please, madam.'

Stiff-necked swine. 'How far back are you taking me? Clear to LA?'

'Your daughter requested a . . . quiet table, madam.'

Not for the first time, Noni wondered if perhaps Roxanne wasn't a tad ashamed of her mother. Grant's fault if she was. Penthouse living would do that to you every time. Roxanne was never a snob before she met Rivers.

The waiter showed her to a table so far back she might as well have gone to McDonald's for an Egg McMuffin.

'Nobody'll see us,' she said to Roxanne. 'After I spent an hour getting gussied up! Ashamed of me or something?'

'Oh, Mom, of course not, I just hate people staring when I eat, asking for autographs. Sometimes they even sit down for a chat — strangers!'

'Price of fame. Start worrying when they don't ask you. Did you order?'

'No. Have you been up to the infirmary yet to check on Grossmutti?'

Noni felt a sinking in her stomach. 'How d'you find out about her? I told that damned Jasinski not to tell you, that it would upset you before Finals —'

'It wasn't him. We couldn't find you after Originals, that's all. We never thought of the infirmary. By the time we knew what had happened you'd left. Grandpa stayed with her all night.'

'You didn't, I hope? With Finals tomorrow —'

Roxanne sighed. 'No. Grant sent me back to the Village. He stayed.'

'Noble of him. I suppose you think I should have stayed with her too.'

'Considering the pills you gave her, yes I do.'

'Where d'you get off, talking to me like that after all I've done for you?'

'What about all *she's* done for *you*, Mom? Hell, you even tried to give *me* that stuff right before I competed; you could have blown the whole thing!'

'Vitamins are nature's way.'

'From what they say, you gave her enough nature's way for six people — and it couldn't have helped anyway. Why didn't you call Jasinski to her?'

'He doesn't know his thumb from his big toe.'

'He knew enough not to let me swallow it. If he'd seen her in time he'd have given her something safe. She might not be in the infirmary now.'

'No, she might be in the morgue! High blood pressure put her where she is, young lady, not me!'

'Sssh, Mom,' Roxanne whispered. 'The waiter! The media's hot for gossip right now. Us arguing here would make a juicy little titbit for 'em.'

'Don't be so stupid! Waiters, they're faceless nobodies. I'll say any damn thing I like in front of 'em.'

'And they can sell every damn word to the press. They have. Often. And they embroider it pretty good first.'

Roxanne ordered fruit, a *croissant*, a mushroom omelette and skimmed milk.

Noni's jaw dropped but caution raised it again. She ordered black coffee.

'That's all you want?' Roxanne said when the waiter had gone.

'Course not! I'll have half yours. Better we both get half-fat than you turn into a blimp.'

'But you hate eggs! You'd eat my omelette to stop me getting fat?'

'I've done a hell of a lot more than that for you, girl. Not that I get any thanks, not me. "How's Grossmutti, Mom?" That's all you care about. How d'you think *I* felt all night, huh? Suppose she can't talk anymore? They'll blame me. Papa does, you do, the doctors. I spend my whole life trying to make it up to her, to you, you're all I've got and neither of you gives a shit!'

'Oh, God. We do, honest, Mom. But you do go overboard, always did, never letting me have friends, regular school, it was all skate Roxi, skate, skate —'

'Because you were born to skate, a natural.'

'No, you kept telling me I was. There's a difference.'

'Go ahead, blame me — but look where you are! All set for Olympic Gold. Isn't that something, doesn't it prove *I'm* good at something?'

Yes. Exploiting. Noni was an expert and didn't even know other people didn't live that way, twisting one advantage to gain another. 'Mom, you spent your life — and mine — chasing Gold, and I don't even want it that much.'

'What? You could have fooled me. See how long you get the lovey-dovey treatment when Grant Rivers hears *that*.'

Roxanne smiled, glad she wasn't wearing the ring. This was not the time.

The waiter glided forward, clattering dishes, pouring coffee, whipping the steel dome off the omelette — and giving Roxanne a chance to really look at Noni, the bags under her eyes, hands trembling as she lit a cigarette, frizzled blonde hair she'd dyed at her kitchen sink. When had she gone to a beauty shop? Never — a good haircut cost four lessons, a professional dye-job, ten. When had she sat down to a balanced meal? Most nights it was a *tostada* or a bowl of chilli at the diner on the corner. She was resourceful, why not take a regular job with a steady income? Because you couldn't work all day and supervise a skater's training full time, that's why. Harsh snow-light from the window deepened the crevasses around her eyes, the powder-filled ravines etched deep from the small, sharp nose to the tight, angry mouth. Forty-five and she looked sixty. Poor nutrition, too many cigarettes, too much make-up, skin and nails which never-never-never saw the sun.

The waiter had barely turned away when Noni halved the omelette and *croissant* and helped herself to the banana, pushing the whole around her plate with a fork, never approaching her mouth except with coffee.

'Don't worry about Grant and me, Mom. I wanted us to talk about you, get a few things straight.'

'Why not?' Noni said, tapping a cigarette on the horn-like fingernail. 'Why *not* run your mother into the ground. You never loved me, I know that.'

Roxanne reached out and took the cigarette from her mother's hand, gave her back a fork instead. 'Eat. I do love you. You're my mom. It's just that I don't like you all that much sometimes.'

'Oh great! What every mother wants to hear. Funny, my friends seem to like me. I have lots of friends, influential friends.' She touched her press badge. 'Lots of friends,' she repeated.

'Disposable friends, Mom. You go through them like a steam shovel, use them up. When they won't do any more favours you find another who will.'

'What's wrong with favours all of a sudden? What are friends for?' Noni's fingers edged towards her cigarette packet but paused, trembling.

'Maybe to enjoy? I only just met Mo Sterling but I like her, we can talk about. . . Well, you know, young women's stuff. If you hadn't always told me to watch out for Beejay, that she was a competitor, maybe I'd like her too. Friends — not that I've had many — are just . . . you know . . . *there*.'

'How about me? Wasn't I always there?'

'Sure, so you could bend me some more, push me. Love me? Not always.'

Twin red spots burned in Noni's white cheeks. 'What d'you mean?'

'In high school I won a scholarship once, remember? A two-week *cordon bleu* school in Santa Monica some place. I *liked* cooking then (God, this omelette is rubber!). You said — and I remember this, Mom, because you had my new Junior Nationals medal in your hand — "*Cordon bleu*, that's for a future *Hausfrau*. Roxanne Kramer is skating's junior champion! All that training time wasted on beating eggs, rolling pastry, gaining weight?" That's what you said, Mom. But I *liked* fixing meals, looking after a house —'

'Oh, well!' Noni said, gathering up her purse. 'You're telling me I wasted my whole life trying to roll an Olympic Gold medallist out of a gourmet chef's biscuit mix — if you'll pardon my fucking French.'

Roxanne felt herself crumbling like dough that wouldn't come up off the board — but she'd come too far to turn back. 'All so you could win your medal, Mom,' she said.

'*Not my medal*. Yours! Mutti's! I promised her, the day I ran off with your dad — she took it bad — hell, why not, she'd have won Gold herself except for Papa and the War, no Games then, killing came first. Later, she thought I could do it and I let her down too, and then you came along and —'

'And now she can't speak, think, eat. Mom, we don't know *what* she can't do anymore. Maybe we should concentrate on Grossmutti right now, huh?'

'At the Games? The Olympic Games?' Noni's head dipped to poke at the melon, swallow a wafer of flavoured water, then drank deep from her coffee cup. 'Hell, it's all a crock anyway.' She gathered up her purse and her pass and her pad. 'I'll get this.' She flicked a credit card just enough to show its colour (gold), much too fast to read the expiry date, then quick as a lizard whisked it in her purse. 'Shoot, must have left my Eurocard in the hotel, sure hate the exchange rates this far from home. They really sock it to you.'

Roxanne sighed. 'I invited you, Mom — yes, keep the receipt for the *Parkrose Review*. How about writing me up so you don't feel beholden when he starts getting the bills? Besides, your card's way out of date.'

Noni blinked. 'What d'you know, it sure fooled me.'

'Since I'm levelling here, Mom, you only fool yourself. One reason I've always felt . . . well, weird around the Crisps and the Carlsens is from way back, when we used to be friends, shop the malls together, when Emma had cash to spend, before Dave had his heart attack —'

Noni rolled up her eyes. 'Lord, spare us the morbid details!'

'I wanted a burger once and you pulled me behind a red hibiscus bush, whispered at me and gave me a food coupon to go buy it. *They all saw the coupon, Mom*! Every time I see red hibiscus I remember that.'

'Wow. So call the conductor, tune up the violins! And *do you remember*, Miss Gratitude, what Beejay Crisp skated in last night? Rags!'

'Paid for with honest money — and she looked fine.'

'Big deal. I got you to Worlds twice, didn't I? D'you hold that against me?'

'No. It's what you held against yourself. The men, just to *get* me there — and I didn't even want to go!'

'Now she tells me. What did you want, then? Cockroaches and slums?'

'No. Just somebody to care about me, not just my skating.'

Roxanne dipped into her purse and lay the velvet box between them, almost as if the ring belonged to Noni too. In a way, perhaps it did.

'I think I've found him. Let's go show Grossmutti, huh?'

At another table, equally secluded, Alexei Finsky and his Director nibbled a frugal Russian breakfast of paper-thin ham and rolls, served with quantities of tea and lemon. The Director shifted uneasily in his seat, almost offended. He'd already done so much — 'I thought it was all settled, my boy.'

'But of course it is.' Alexei Finsky said coolly, sucking the last drop of juice from the lemon. 'So there's no reason Galina can't fly in for Mens Finals tonight, right? She'd see me win your Gold medal, yes?'

The Director poured sugar in his tea directly from the bowl. '*Your* Gold, my boy.' He picked up his roll and buttered it for the second time, on top of the ham.

'Whatever. I want Galina to see me win it, naturally. I thought you'd have arranged it.' He allowed a hint of reproach to seep into his voice. 'I miss her. She's always been my focus, you understand? The morning plane leaves Moscow in two hours, you could get her on it. I would feel more secure, skate better, with more heart . . . you understand? I am sorry.'

The Director fixed him with a pale, implacable stare. 'Why do you insist? You already have cast-iron guarantees.'

Alexei looked grateful, even humble as he shredded a roll between fingers and thumb. 'You have been a wise guardian, Director. Always you tell me truths I could never discover on my own. Once you said, "Alexei, we can never have too much insurance." You were right, of course. Galina was your insurance policy but you still have her parents — and our agreement, yes? To win your Gold medal?'

'Yours,' the Director muttered, but quietly.

Alexei shrugged. 'Call it what you wish. She will be here?'

'I'll try. If they can find a seat.'

'Galina is small, I'm sure they'll find one. You will meet the plane for me? Reserve her a room at the hotel? Thank you.' He stood. 'Please excuse. I must rest for tonight's performance. It will make the world of difference, seeing Galina by your side when I skate.'

Leaving to return to the Village, a last-minute thought struck him and he ducked into the labyrinth of boutiques under the hotel, finding at last a florist who spoke some English, wore black-patent shoes, and a red dress of the perfect shade. He pointed to the shoes, the dress, and rapidly sketched the shape of a tulip on her order pad, next to Galina's name. 'In her room, if you please. This afternoon?'

The florist checked her computer terminal. 'We have no guest of that name registered, Monsieur.'

'You will have, quite soon.'

For Deirdre Sterling, the rigours of attending Ladies Original the night before had taken their toll. This morning, too tired to lift her head, much less to eat, she let the nurse put the IV needle in her arm and dozed off again, conserving strength against Maureen's Final tomorrow. Then she could let go, but not yet, not yet.

She'd hoped . . . she'd hoped so much to watch Mens tonight, see Grant again, perhaps talk to him . . . yes, of course she must talk to him, surely she'd earned that small blessing . . . but the thought of dressing . . . all simply too much. When she grew this weak a blood transfusion helped, but her time with Maureen grew short now, and she tried, oh she tried not to leave that memory with her daughter, a mother dying with a stranger's blood dripping into her veins. She wanted Maureen to remember her as she used to be, as she willed her to remember, by recalling the blissful past and ignoring the revolting present.

A shadow entered the room, she could feel it, a darkness between her and the window . . . no, it wouldn't be Death, couldn't be, there was no such figure . . . if she could will herself to reach up, open the drape, even press the bell for the nurse, but her arm . . . so heavy . . . so many times like this, then a few hours and she'd be fine again . . . must be fine for tomorrow night, that's all she wanted. Not, after all, to see Grant . . . how could she think of making herself presentable now . . . and desirable? Ah, the romance of the soul . . . but where was the body to go with it? Not this old thing! A laugh bubbled up in her throat but she couldn't allow it, she'd choke . . . had to sit up . . . was this the dementia that came towards the end of the disease? Ah, a nurse. All the cologne in this room, why did they reek of disinfectant . . . so ugly.

'Come along then, let's sit up, we don't want to choke now, do we? No, not us. Oops-a-daisy, there we go, rise and shine, Mrs S! A visitor for you, he's been here for ages, there, let me open the curtain so we can see to tell lies. Ta-ta then. Ring if you want me, the bell's here under your finger . . .'

Deirdre groaned. Mrs S! This was what she'd come to. If she had the strength she'd sack the creature. And now the light was too bright, much too bright for visitors. Lord, who was it, that damned angel here too soon? Her eyelids lifted slowly, weighted down by lead pellets that must be her lashes . . . but no, they were long gone, weren't they?

'Deirdre?'

Oh, God, this was no angel. This was Grant. But he'd been an angel once, he'd been smiling then, always smiling. Now he loomed like a thunderhead, his face set, angry, so she wanted to cringe away. So long since anyone showed her anger, they were all too kind, but not Grant. She shut her eyes to hide them, but behind her lids adrenalin rushed in suddenly, as it did these days, moment to moment —

'So okay, you're awake, good, I want some answers from you —'

He sounded . . . American! But he would, he'd lived there for so long.

'Answers?' Damn, he faded again, just when she wanted to see him —

'Yes. Nineteen years ago you got exactly what you wanted out of me. A trinket to brighten up a dying marriage.'

'Grant . . .'

He shut his eyes, trying to block her wasted arms from his mind . . . lesions, needles, if he looked at them too long he'd never go through with this, it was cruel, vicious, but he had to know.

'I gave you that trinket, Deirdre. It was a daughter, as the whole damned world will see if they look close enough. You didn't bother to tell me, no, but Dunsmuir's already seen it. I've seen it. I imagine Lloyd's not blind either. I was stupid, I must have been, I actually thought you loved me. For nineteen years I've carried this dream of the perfect woman, the one that got away, and now it's one nightmare after another, threatening everything and everybody!'

Her eyes, drooping, widened again. 'Grant, I thought I couldn't let you go but I did, and you succeeded . . . you were so young, I knew if Lloyd had got his claws in you then . . .' She shuddered, reaching up to touch his face, her fingertips like crêpe paper. 'You're still beautiful.'

'Beautiful enough back then to give you the only thing you wanted, right? A child that wasn't Lloyd's. A healthy child.'

The gargoyle smiled. He tried not to back off.

'She *is* healthy, Grant, isn't that wonderful . . .'

'Forgive me for not rejoicing yet, Deirdre. I'm still waiting for results from the infirmary on my own blood tests — and Roxanne's.'

'Tests? But you're the picture of —'

'You've got Aids, right?'

She nodded, matter-of-fact. 'I'm accustomed to the idea now. A gift from Lloyd, like my jewellery and my investments. I'm a rich woman, you see.'

'Yes,' he said, seeing nothing. He'd thought for a moment she was crying, but no, she was laughing. Hard to tell the difference now.

'Remember that day I told you I couldn't face being poor?'

Remember? He knew the room, its scent, its light, the texture of her skin, the scent of her. He'd replayed the scene a million times in hotels on the road and even, Gold help him, when he'd made love to Roxanne, robbing her to pay tribute to a woman who was nothing but a memory, faulty at that. 'Of course I remember. I never saw you again. You dropped me. I'd served my purpose.'

'Oh no . . .' She closed her eyes and for a terrible moment he thought she'd died without giving him the answer he had to have. 'It wasn't like that, you *can't* believe . . . you don't know Lloyd . . . but of course you do, he sent Jeff to you. You must know what he planned. You wanted a sponsor too, remember? And Lloyd wanted to help you, yes . . . I stopped him, I had to, couldn't let you go down that road . . . young people think they can handle the Lloyds of this world, I'm sure Jeff does . . . but Lloyd usually gets his man — or woman.' Her eyes flew open, startling, nailing him, as if he must understand something vital, vital. 'He's not just bisexual, you know. I could have accepted that. It's everything else. Drugs, perversions beyond the dreams of . . . whoever. He's the great white hunter seeking them out, no stone he'll leave unturned.'

God, he hadn't bargained for this, any of it . . . but he had to ask: 'Deirdre, I didn't know. I thought you just dropped me.'

Her face was wax now. He'd over-taxed her. 'No,' she murmured. 'I knew he'd never let me keep you. He'd have ruined you. I thought if I had your child, something from you, I could let you go . . . when I got pregnant it had to be yours because Lloyd and I had no marriage left by then, d'you see?' She nodded to herself. 'So I resumed . . . relations, I think they're called, to justify the pregnancy. Maureen was born, and I stopped. He's a beast, Grant; he likes children — I couldn't leave her alone with him for a moment, and she was too beautiful. So I put her on the ice. I remembered you told me that it took up one's entire youth. You were right. The ice saved her.'

Grant took her hand, stroked the skin that had been so dear. 'Deirdre, last night I asked Roxanne to marry me.' He felt her hand flinch, but he clasped it tight, trapped it between his. 'If you know, you must tell me. When did you get Aids?'

'It had to be after . . . after you, because when I knew I had it I had Maureen tested. She didn't know what for, thought it was glandular fever. But she was clear, Grant. So I think you must be, too. And Roxanne.'

'Does Maureen know what your illness is now?'

'She reads up on it.'

'Does she know I'm her father?'

'It's pretty obvious, isn't it? I haven't told her directly, no. If you want to, that's up to you. She's well provided for, independent — and wiser than I was, too. Lloyd doesn't have a chance with her now.'

They were quiet for a long time and Grant thought perhaps she slept, until she suddenly said: 'I don't like her, you know. Roxanne.'

'You've never met her, she's done you no harm —'

'She'll get all I ever wanted. You. Maybe the Gold. Maureen likes her, so if she plays her cards right she'll get my daughter as well.'

'Deirdre . . . I don't think Maureen's looking for a daddy, and Roxi doesn't play cards. Perhaps she'd be better off if she did.'

'Will she win the Gold?'

He shook his head to clear it. The Medal? At a time like this? 'Why?'

'Because I want it. I want it for Maureen and me. We've earned it.'

'We all think that, but there's only one Gold.'

'So bright. . .' She sighed. 'Why don't you call the lab?'

'It's too early. We had the tests last night, we won't know for seventy-two hours. We get the results right after Ladies Finals. Ironic, huh?'

'Life's ironic — and that's the *best* one can say about it.'

'Will you make it to the Mens Final tonight?'

But she was already asleep. He drew the curtains again and quietly let himself out.

CHAPTER THIRTY-EIGHT

In the hotel lobby Hiro Nakashima dismissed his interpreter for the day and, rounding a secluded corner, surprised his granddaughter and her blond man, dutifully accompanied by the woman he had sent to keep them apart. He beckoned his daughter. Obediently she followed him to the lift — but once inside did not cringe as before, like a dog awaiting its beating. She simply returned his gaze. He said he wished words in his suite. She nodded.

'*Hai, Nakashima-sama*. I too wish words with you.'

Half-respectful, half-insolent. In the penthouse suite the maid was making his bed, hoovering that idiotic rug. Intolerable. No interpreter here to tell her to leave. A robot-maid would have understood all orders!

His daughter came to his aid. 'Please come back later?' she murmured, offering the maid a discreet tip and vaguely helpless gesture. Mieko's mother was learning too much too fast for the pleasure of Hiro Nakashima.

'I send you here to guard my granddaughter from unsuitable young men. I find instead that you accompany them, encourage the association.'

She inclined her head. 'I fear it is too late to discourage it, my father. Your granddaughter is a child of the twentieth century, the *late* twentieth century! Of television, computers, instant communication — on which our fortune is built, is it not? She sees independence in her contemporaries, wants it for herself. Already she is offered lucrative show contracts — no-no, we have accepted none, but . . .' Oka-chan paused to scrutinize her father's face, to hand him his *netsuke*, that he might find a familiar comfort against the shock she was about to deliver. 'But our Mieko has accepted something else. The blond one. She wishes to marry him.'

428

He laughed. 'She may wish for the sun. I do not have to grant it.'

Oka-chan bowed. 'Forgive me, but we are not young, my father, you and I. It could be . . . not unwise, no, for you are wisdom itself — but perhaps it is premature to refuse what Mieko *may have already anticipated*?'

As she intended, it took a second to penetrate. She had rehearsed the sentence and its infinite cadences all night, discarding this word, adding that, all giving her time to reach the door, turn, watch from a safe distance. The last time he blacked her eye she had vowed it would *be* the last time. Since leaving Japan, everything she saw had strengthened that resolve.

Her father's colour faded. His long aristocratic lip curled. 'A *round-eye*? A *blond*? A *skater*? Educated in the *United States*? — where they think in slogans, no discipline, no knowledge — where they develop "inquiring" minds.'

Again she bowed. 'Pardon, please? Is that wrong, my father?'

'Lacking specific knowledge, an inquiring mind cannot find its way to the out-house,' he said coldly.

'But my father, last night you witnessed that same young man defend a Nakashima's dignity, yes? Her Carlsen man did not know the language of the guards, but he made himself understood. He accomplished.'

'With his fists.' Hiro Nakashima caressed the worn forehead of the monkey with a long, smooth thumb. 'Any man would have done the same.'

Now Oka-chan bowed very low indeed. 'Forgive me, but two Japanese men were present — three if we count your limousine driver — and none helped Mieko reach the ice, where all Japan waited to see her shine.'

'*Two men*?'

Surely she could not bow lower, but she tried. 'Yes, my father. The man you sent to help me. And yourself. I am sorry.'

'Are you saying,' he thundered, 'that I should engage in fisticuffs so my granddaughter can make an exhibition of herself before the world?'

Oka-chan fumbled in her capacious purse. 'The house-keeper faxed this morning's Tokyo and Atami papers to us

— other cities will come later. They are saying our Mieko is a national treasure.'

Our Mieko. Hiro Nakashima stared into the monkey's face for a long time. 'Has my granddaughter given her maidenhead to the Scandinavian?' he whispered, as though his enemies might even now be at the keyhole.

'How can I know? It is a delicate matter — she calls him her golden one.'

A terrible silence descended, a cloud of tradition defied, of retribution gathering. 'She must learn who rules the family. Send her to me.'

Another bow. 'It is too late, my father. She is returned to the Village — only athletes are allowed. Tomorrow she skates for our country. We would lose much face if the world saw Nakashima's granddaughter with a black eye.' She allowed no trace of triumph to enter her voice, but surely now he must hit *her*? No? She dared further: 'It would give her pleasure to receive your good wishes.' Truly, now, she felt it, a vibration as if his anger would indeed lift the ceiling, exposing Mieko and herself to naked mountains, prowling wolves.

'*Get out of my sight!*' he said, his face rigid, the *netsuke* gripped tight in his thin fingers. At the door, as she turned the handle, he added: 'You may leave the faxes.'

Just before lunch Jasinski tapped at Noni Kramer's door.

'Come in,' she called, waving her fingers to dry the final coat of silver polish. Thank God she didn't have to look at that sickly yellow again ever — Oh, God, if it wasn't the quack in his baggy grey suit. Was it all he owned? He squinted at her through his thick specs. Hadn't he even heard of contact lenses? 'Well, if it isn't the —'

'Please Noni, let us make a deal. If you try not to call me a quack I shall not call you a whore.' He rubbed his glasses, put them back on, and sighed.

'Who in hell *says* I'm a whore?'

'No one. Yet. Nor am I a quack, but you persist in calling me one. I do not care for it, either.' He sat in the corner, as far away as possible, where she would perhaps feel less threatened. 'I came from the infirmary.'

'That's nice. I was just there, thank you very much, with the World and United States Champion. There was no change in her grandmother.'

'There is now. I thought you would want to know.'

She turned away and he saw her knuckles whiten. Had she noticed the incipient liver-spots under the skin, ready to cover her hands unless she gave her health the same attention she gave her 'image', he wondered?

'Okay, spill it. What have I done wrong now?'

'Why should you imagine you have done anything but love an old lady?'

She whirled on him, an ageing vixen suspecting a trap. 'Because I've always done some damn thing wrong, haven't I? I keep my daughter out of a cooking school, two weeks, big deal, she acts like I blighted her whole messed-up life; I give her a food coupon to buy herself a meal, *that*'s wrong; I know my mom's blood pressure's going up, I look it up in the health book, give her what it says and *that*'s wrong! If I've done anything else wrong I don't want to know. *Are you listening? I don't fucking-well want to know any more!*'

'Noni, please. Your mother is recovering, you only tried to help her. You were misguided perhaps, but she did indeed experience a series of ischaemic strokes and nothing you or anyone else did could have made a difference either way. Frau Braun is an old lady. We all must die from something —'

'She's not —'

'No, of course not, she is sleeping nicely. The only residue of the strokes at present is a small loss of function in her leg, but that may pass. We must wait and see. She is a good patient.'

Relief barely had time to cross her pinched features before anger once again took the field. 'Patients! That's all you ever think about, isn't it —'

'It is why I became a doctor.'

'Yeah, tell that to your accountant — and my bank where I had to run up an overdraft to see my daughter win the Olympics! Tell me how *you* suffer!'

Jasinski took a deep breath. Who could sustain hope for a woman so limited as to find, in her daughter's medals, her only collateral for the future?

'I can only tell you that we all suffer, but that some of us suffer more than we need to. You, a good daughter, obeyed your mother's rule until nature took its course and led you to a precipitous marriage. Your father tells me that he and your mother did the same. And now your daughter Roxanne is stretched on the same rack. Can you not at some point decide that you have expiated enough, that you also deserve a life?'

He stopped, appalled that he, of all people, should voice these midnight guilts so deeply riven into his own soul. When had *he* lived for himself? Never. Every move he made had been calculated to placate the souls of those who sacrificed themselves for him. He made an excellent living but did not live excellently. Far from it. The fruits of his labours were spent repaying debts from the past. Until Montegreco, every holiday had been spent in Warsaw, where new relatives surfaced with every visit. A few years ago he'd been approached by a great-aunt-by-marriage who he'd never met; the old lady needed a wheelchair; he'd gone to great trouble and expense to send this stranger a motorized chair. When he met her he found she lived on the fifth floor of a building with no lift. The chair, unused because there was no way to get it down five flights of stairs, made a lovely conversation piece in her tiny attic room, which she in any case navigated with the aid of a cane. The chair did not help her, but stood as proof positive of the generosity and wealth of a nephew many times removed, thus reflecting well on her standing as a beloved person.

Who then was Doctor Jasinski to ridicule the endless circles of guilt which bound the unhappy Braun Kramers? At least the instruments of their misery were their parents — the misery a bi-product, an excess of love and guilt. Perhaps the projected marriage would set Noni free.

'I understand you are soon to be a mother-in-law?' He spoke carefully, uncertain how Noni had taken the news. Caution, it turned out, was in order.

'Ha! He can't even wait for them to hang the medal on her before he cashes in, can he?'

'I have the impression there is deep devotion between them, and your daughter seems to depend on —'

'Because she can't stand up for herself, never could. Hell,

when she signs that fat Gold Medal show contract *I* should manage her. *Me!* Not *him!* I could travel with her, watch her diet, see she gets her rest, but now . . .'

'Roxannes wishes to skate in a show?' That was not what she'd told him.

'Oh, she *thinks* she wants to be a housewife. So did I till I came to my senses. So did my mother! Seems like we all have to keep making the same goddamned mistake, generation after generation. She'll have a kid, Grant'll train it, and round we go again, no end to it.'

'Perhaps her children will not wish to skate?'

She looked genuinely astounded. 'Not wish? Well, my God, kids have to do something! Bankers' kids get to be bankers, accountants' kids go into Daddy's office — what are your kids? Doctors, right?'

'One is a criminal lawyer,' he said steadily.

'Same difference, he makes pots of dough. What about the other?'

'He's a gardener.'

She blinked. 'A landscape designer, like that?'

'No, just a gardener. He cuts lawns, pulls weeds, plants things.'

'Jeez, you must be *real* proud of that one!'

'As a matter of fact, I am. For a long time he disappointed me, he had not fulfilled my expectations; I assumed that my parents would also have been disappointed, had they been alive — but he is happy. He loves order, growing things, watching them thrive. My other son works all his life among people he despises, and must defend many he suspects are guilty.'

'But he's rich.'

Jasinski shrugged. 'He has all the status symbols — including the shrink.'

Again that laugh, empty, hard, desperately unhappy. 'Me, I'd sooner be the mother of a three-million a year skater than a happy *Hausfrau* any day!'

'Have you thought, Noni, what you will do when Roxanne marries? If she decided to teach, or simply be a mother, a wife. Have you thought?'

She turned her profile to him. He thought it might be possible to slice bread with her jaw-bone. 'I can't think of a fucking thing I can do — not that it's any of your business.'

He hesitated. He despised meddlers, but this family, such a history of using, manipulating. 'These strokes of your mother's. If her leg does not improve it will of course be impossible for your father to help. She may be handicapped for some time . . . perhaps forever.'

'Meaning I should go look after her, I suppose? D'you have any idea what Mutti's like to live with — and my father? They're impossible!'

'That is why you squander your life — and your daughter's — trying to please them with medals, something on which to hang their pride?'

Her palm came up and he braced himself for a slap, but then she sighed, sat down on the edge of the bed, and shut her eyes.

'If Roxanne misses the Gold,' she whispered, 'how am I gonna tell Mutti? How in hell am I going to tell her that we lost it, we lost it again?'

The gravity of the Games and his promising placement after Originals had already begun to rattle Jeff Dunsmuir before Grant opened his door to him. The boy's hands actually shook too much to latch it behind himself.

'The *Express* just asked me for an interview. Is it okay?'

'How old are you, Jeff?'

'Oh, if you're going to be sarcastic —'

'No, I mean it. I don't know. You've not been with me that long so . . .'

'Twenty-two.'

'I thought you were younger. I'm glad you're not.'

'Why?'

'Because at twenty-two I expect you to have a bit more sense than I've seen so far. Question is, what d'you usually do about interviews. You've done plenty before, right? So what's different now?'

'Everybody's asking what I'll do after the Games, see?'

'You want to know if I talked to Yum-Num about your so-called sponsor, right? I did. He said a flat-out no.'

'How come?'

'He doesn't take food stamps — and that's all she's got.'

'Bloody hell.'

'Yeah. It takes all kinds. You're not thinking of going back to Lloyd?'

'I might have to.'

'I wouldn't, Jeffie. A couple of scouts approached me about you — I'm not supposed to give you the details until after, I've got to protect your amateur status and all that, but you could do very well in a show.'

'But if I hung in for next Olympics —'

Grant shook his head. 'You're very good, Jeff — but have you seen the young stuff some of the countries are sending? Real young, like sixteen?'

'I'm better than them.'

'You are now, but in two years? Four?'

His mouth set like an angry young woman's. 'You don't want me to get a sponsor. Except for the woman from back East, you didn't try, did you?'

'No. I got to thinking. I've got this strange aversion, you see. I don't like being blackmailed.'

'Who's —'

'You were considering it. Don't.'

He smirked. 'You'll tell Maureen yourself then? And Lloyd?'

'You'd better leave while you can still stand up. You've got Finals tonight. As your coach, I'd hate to spoil your chances.'

CHAPTER THIRTY-NINE

He found Maureen in the ballet room, working out at the barre. Finsky and a couple of Russian pairs were just leaving, luminous with sweat.

Maureen, not quite finished, seemed unaware of Grant's presence as she worked her way steadily through the closing moves of the workout, body perfectly centred, isolating, stretching and cooling down muscle groups before tossing a royal blue towel around her neck and patting her streaming face. She wore a grey wool leotard, thick black tights, her black curls confined in a grey sweat-band, and black leg-warmers concertina'd round her ankles. Sweat darkened the grey leotard to a long charcoal-coloured V down the small of her back. No wonder her work on ice seemed effortless. All the effort was left here, where no one saw it but others who were engaged in the same drive to perfection.

His daughter. And he felt nothing more than the admiration he'd give any dedicated athlete who worked hard.

'So what did you come to tell me, Mr Rivers?' she said, her voice even, musical, even amused, the product of endless elocution lessons — or perhaps simply learned at her mother's knee. She gave him a look of cool appraisal. Where did an eighteen-year-old girl learn this poise? Perhaps she never met any girls, only sophisticated women. 'Something I already know?'

'Your mother wasn't sure,' he said carefully. He'd come prepared for tears, anger, anything but a fencing match.

She turned round to the mirrored wall behind her. Standing this close, her hair drawn tightly off her face, no make-up on, the resemblance was unmistakable. She had

Deirdre's eyes, that was all. 'My mother can be naïve these days, Mr Rivers. Look at us. How could I *not* notice?' She stooped to pull off the leg-warmers and hide her dismay. She'd noticed no resemblance until Mother mentioned it yesterday. What had she said? The same colouring. Yes of course, then everything had fallen into place. That mysterious un-English complexion, often admired but never explained. Now all was clear, even Lloyd's over-familiarity as a man, his aloofness as a father. Surely he must suspect — so why was she bothering to lie to Grant Rivers? Panic? What the nurse had whispered through the phone just before Maureen began her barre was not Grant Rivers' fault. She'd had to call the doctor again: 'Sorry, Miss Sterling, but she's bad with dementia again today. You know it comes and goes, but this time — well, the doctor said put her back on her medicine, see? Your mother was ever so upset, screaming at me that everybody's stealing from her — and I haven't touched a thing, honest!' Maureen had placated the nurse and calculated just how long Mother had to be kept calm, resolving not to let her attention shift from her mother and the Games for a moment. She'd come this far for Deirdre. Twelve years on ice. Nothing must get in the way, with so little time left. But now Grant Rivers arrives with this gem, just when she could not face one more crisis. How long, she wondered now, had he known before coming to her with it?

He told her without asking. 'In the hotel a picture of you caught me off guard. The room was dark and I thought at first it was a mirror.'

She nodded, determined to be cool. 'She told me about your affair, yes. When I saw you I . . . drew my own conclusions. Mr Rivers, I do hope you're not sentimental or anything. I've been without a father for so long I wouldn't know what to do with one. I'm relieved I'm not Lloyd's of course, but otherwise . . . well, you really mustn't think we owe one another a thing.'

'Our relationship means nothing to you?'

'We have none, Mr Rivers. Only biology. I've not been a daughter to you, you've not been a father to me. It's too late to start now, don't you think?'

She heard his quick intake of breath. 'You're a cool

customer, Maureen, I'll say that. I wasn't proposing to move into your life. I wanted to be sure you didn't hear it first from Dunsmuir, that's all — in case you didn't know.'

Jeff? Oh, Lord. She forced herself to laugh, knowing she sounded exactly like her mother. *Laugh lightly, darling, don't ever let strangers know you're upset*. Mother was right, that was the only way to handle the unexploded bombs life tossed one's way. 'Jeff? He must think he's found a pearl, Mr Rivers. I hope he won't do anything silly. He's quite unpredictable lately.'

'I doubt Lloyd would find it silly. I should think he'd be as mad as hell.'

'Why? Mother has served as a respectable front for all Lloyd's devious little doings from here to Timbuktu. Without her he'd never have succeeded in business — the good old boys would have tumbled him long ago. And look at the price she's paying.'

'Yes. Well, so long as you know,' he finished lamely. 'What can I say? If ever you need anything —'

'Yes, I'll be in touch, thank you.' He seemed nonplussed, this young man who happened to be her father. What kind of reception did he expect? Joy? Sorrow? She felt neither. Only numb. With the loss of a mother frighteningly imminent, of what use was a stranger father? She arranged her smile very carefully. 'Don't worry. I'm very good at managing.'

'I can see that.'

'Roxanne tells me you're engaged.'

'Yes.'

'I like Roxanne, Mr Rivers.' Now she'd shifted the talk to Roxanne the words came easily, too easily. This man had already created havoc everywhere his affections led. 'Please don't misunderstand, but I do hope you can make her happy.'

'I intend to.' Through the glass she watched a nerve beat a tattoo in his jaw. 'And don't *you* misunderstand if I tell *you* something, Miss Sterling.'

She smiled at him through the mirror, producing a deep dimple in her chin to match his own. 'I don't think I shall be devastated.'

'About the Gold. Despite our non-relationship, this

insignificant biological accident, I hope Roxanne beats the daylights out of you tomorrow.'

She hung on to her smile. 'I've said I like her, Mr Rivers, but as you know, friendship stops where the ice starts. Now if you'll excuse me . . . that will be all?' Even to herself she sounded like a duchess dismissing a butler.

'Not quite. I'm thirty-five. I need a grown-up daughter about as much as you need a father. It wasn't easy, but I came to warn you about Jeff. Instead, I feel I've engaged in a duel — and Mr Rivers doesn't fence —'

'I'm sorry, I simply must go. If you wouldn't mind. . .'

She let the shower needles sting her, chlorinated water mixing with her own hot tears, washing away sweat and shame and misdirected anger until nothing was left but the panic she started with. How could she have said all those things? Because the nurse had panicked her. She should have insisted on specifics, made her repeat everything. The dementia was back, yes, well it had been before, lots of times, but this time hadn't the doctor said everything moved as expected, to its logical conclusion — meaning Mother had no time?

She threw on a warm-up suit and ran to the hotel, Deirdre's suite, quietly placing a call to Harley Street from the sitting room.

'Maureen,' the doctor said, deliberate calm prevailing despite a waiting-room full of patients and the demands of this opinionated girl, 'I can't vouch for my exact words, no, but Deirdre must have chemo. You can't expect the nurses to take responsibility otherwise, it's not fair to them.'

'But this is not fair to *her*! She's kept herself alive for this, she's tried and tried to make it through the Games. They're over tomorrow, you *must* call off the chemo for one more day, have them give her a mild sedative. If she were well enough to refuse she'd never accept the chemo again! It makes her ill!'

'Isn't that the point? That she's not well enough?' His voice grew testy. 'You put me in an impossible position, Maureen. I consult Lloyd, and all I can get out of him is: "Do what you like!" so you see —'

'Lloyd is too busy chasing his murky little dreams. I'm not. Neither is Mother. Can you guarantee she'll live longer with the chemo than without it?'

'At her stage, of course not, at any time something will go into pneumonia, then she'll be lucky to last the next week —'

Next week, next week, next week. 'Doctor, as dreadful as chemo makes her feel, "lucky" is an unfortunate choice of word. Lloyd may tell you to do as you wish. I'm telling you to take her off it — and I have her power of attorney. Do you have a pen? This is *her* solicitor — not Lloyd's — and his phone.' She waited as he took it all down, muttering about 'irregularities' as he scribbled. 'I suggest you call him now, then get back to the head nurse right away, or I shall have to call in a local doctor to take over.'

'Could you think about this a few days, Maureen?'

'We don't have a few days, Doctor. The only thing that interests Mother is seeing my little part in the Games. I skate tomorrow.' She hung up, her palms wet. First Grant Rivers, now the doctor. Inoffensive men she had deeply offended. A bell buzzed by her chair, and the call-light from Deirdre's room flickered red on the communication panel.

'Maureen, is that you, I thought it was, guess what they want to do —'

'Don't worry. I told the doctor to cancel it. Or to neff off.'

Deirdre gave a wobbly smile. 'How coarse of you, darling.'

'Yes, I'm becoming a bitch.'

Deirdre wagged an emaciated finger as the terrible smile spread wider. 'Naughty word. We must try to be ladies,' she whispered, 'but sometimes bitches get more done.' Her hand closed around Maureen's wrist. 'They're trying to take things from me, you know. The little conch has gone, the coral one you brought up from the beach last week.'

'No, it's here in your drawer, darling, see — just slipped to the back. This competition is getting us both feather-headed — you found me that shell when I had the measles years and years ago. You put it in a pink velvet jewellery box with burgundy ribbon, remember? Lovely.'

'Did I tell you about the sea? It's very wise, you know.' The shell slipped from her finger and her wandering mind took another abrupt turn. 'They're trying to steal you, you know.'

440

'No, they're not. It's just part of the illness, I know all about it, so don't worry.'

'You're sure?' She nodded, accepting. 'Who else were you a bitch to?'

'Grant Rivers.'

'Oh, no, darling, you mustn't. None of anything was his fault. He was half my age and I needed someone. Maureen, after I'm —'

'Don't say it, Mother!'

'Why not?' She sounded like a child denied a treat. 'We know what's coming. It's better if we can talk. I told you about the sea, wastes nothing at all, a great housekeeper . . . we had one at Haslemere once.'

'She's still there, waiting for us to go home.'

'Oh. Well, after . . . you won't go and live with that girl, will you?'

'I won't live with anyone. I promise. Now sleep, then I'll take you to see Mens tonight. The last bit, at least. The top five. You'll see Jeff and the Bean and Alexei. You'll like that. I'll get us all dressed up . . .'

The phone buzzed in the sitting room. They heard the nurse pick it up, could picture her efficient little nods, no questions asked, as she said crisply, 'Yes doctor, very well doctor. I understand, doctor.'

Deirdre giggled, a little girl up to harmless mischief, and pierced Maureen with the deep blue caverns of her eyes. 'You see, darling, bitches do get more done.' Then, briefly rational again, her old self, she said: 'I wouldn't make a habit of it, though. Enemies burn all one's energy.'

Jeff Dunsmuir, also getting dolled up, this time in severe black with a white Nehru collar reminiscent of a preacher, turned petulantly to the rock star's make-up 'professional' as Grant rapped on the door. 'Oh shit.'

'Don't let him in,' hissed the artist, busily applying white foundation.

'He's my coach, dummy! I have to let him in. Scoot. Off it. Get out.'

'Well!'

'And a good thing too,' Grant said, shutting the door

behind him. 'What, no chicken entrails? Black candles? Incense? You look like the head lad at a warlock's get-together. Get that white gunk off your face and listen.'

'I've nothing to say to you.'

'Good, because I told you to listen. First: don't bother telling Maureen what she already knows. She's a godawful snob but she's got enough on her plate without you rattling her mummy's skeletons. Second: I'm going to tell you the best offer from the shows. Third: I talked to some of your officials. Ever noticed how often they're unofficial? The same the world over. Pleased you've improved but you do keep blotting your copy-book, don't you, old lad? Odds and ends you didn't mention, huh? From the few things they told me, Lloyd wasn't the first, just the most respectable so far. Working your way up the ladder of debauchery, you might say. They don't like that. Gives the sport a black eye. Lloyd muddied up the welcome mat long since, tracked in too much scandal. Under the huffing and puffing they're pretty conventional chaps. Their advice, off the record, is the same as mine. Get in a show.'

'That's cruel!'

'Before you go out to skate, let me tell you how cruel.'

'What difference would it make?'

'A lot. If you could pull to Bronze, a good American show (I can't tell you which) offers a clean-ice solo, a production number lead, a three-year contract, escalators each year your weight stays down and the jumps keep up. These are the figures.' He tossed a card over to Jeff and waited.

'That much!'

'Uh-huh. You're pretty. The other offer's nearly as good. On the other hand, if you stay amateur, and miss out on the medals next Olympics, you'll be lucky to get understudy. Know what line-pay is?'

'It can't be that bad.'

'You'd do better as a waiter. Not as glamorous — but you don't crack your knees waiting tables.' He stood up. 'So it might pay you to skate your little heart out tonight, Jeffie boy.'

'Wait! If I stay amateur, would you coach me?'

'No. Neither will Yum-Num.'

'Because I'm gay?'

'No. Because you're stupid. But you can skate. Good luck.'

As always before he competed, Alexei Finsky willed himself to sleep for two hours, then picked up the phone and called the hotel. They put him through immediately. 'Galina?'

'Who else. How did you do it?'

He sighed. 'By playing a card I don't have yet.'

She laughed. 'You'd better be sure to get it then — Papa thinks they'll send us all to Siberia if you lose.'

'Sometimes your papa is crazy.'

'Yes, but win anyway. The flowers are lovely.' Again she laughed, happy, full-throated. 'Not just the tulips, but a forest of white roses — the Director.'

'White. A peace offering.'

'Yes. They've painted your apartment, your next car is in the garage already, and my parents have a new television to watch you win.'

'Anything else?'

'The Director picked me up in a limo, said he'd call me a press conference to announce I'd withdrawn due to injury. I told him to get lost.'

'Good. Sit with the team where I can see you. I skate for us, our future.'

'You don't skate for your country?'

'You are my country.'

Emma Crisp gathered up her judging sheets, her clipboard, and her defences. She hated judging the Bean.

'How come?' Beejay said, snapping a green rubber band back and forth, back and forth at a beige-on-beige towel.

'Stop that — it's driving me nuts. Because, sport, judging's a matter of judgement, right? If you know a kid, and like him, you never know whether you're bending forwards for him, or backwards against him, see?'

'You know half the kids in skating. Why not quit judging?'

'Hush yo' mouf, honey-chile, or mama gonna hush it for you. This is Mama's game and Mama don't quit.'

'What are we waiting for?'

'Nils. He's picking us up.'

443

'*Again*?'

'Uh-huh. While we're waiting let me ask you something. If —'

'The answer's yes. It sounds great to me.'

'Beej! I haven't even asked you yet! Hell, he hasn't asked *me* yet!'

'He will. And watch your language. You're judging.'

CHAPTER FORTY

As each competitor arrived for the Mens Finals, newsmen hit them with the same old question, and each skater batted back the pious evasion. Question: Think you've a chance for Gold? Answer: It's an honour to compete. Nothing else matters. They smiled as they lied. With upwards of sixteen years apiece invested, winner-take-all, only dreamers and liberals believed anything mattered but the pot of Gold. The medal winner's name echoed down the corridors of fame, a victory clarion for all who saw him, heard of him, or read of him. Years might dim his performance and what he was famous for, but his name and the word 'winner' would be forever joined.

All the world loved a winner and all the world tried to cram itself into the complex. Officials declared the arena standing-room-only two full hours before the first man was to skate, cannily selling tickets to an adjoining hall at a picayune discount for bench seats, a mammoth TV screen, the reek of new paint, and a snack-bar hawking four kinds of soda and three of pizza at stratospheric prices. Nobody whined that they could have stayed home and watched the telly in their pyjamas. They were in *Montegreco* for the *Games*. If not exactly on the scene, they tingled to the vibrations of a mob when the arena crowd roared, they heard the bark of souvenir vendors peddling programmes and memorabilia — and when the shouting stopped they could amble over to the hotel, rubberneck around the bars, hope for a look at the winners. For sure they'd be celebrating.

In the main arena, heat rose to meet the tension, every eye hypnotized by the blue sheet of ice shining like a sapphire, still perfect, not a scratch on it.

By now the Competitor section blended seamlessly with Chaperones as parents and athletes, aloof in their world, set distance between themselves and a public sure to scream and honk, who didn't know a quad from a double, a 4.6 performance from a 5.9. The 'in' crowd knew — and felt vastly superior to those who did not. They overlooked Grant's Welsh coach, who sat in Publics but who did know, who wistfully acknowledged that he'd missed the boat, and hoped that perhaps Grant Rivers could still scramble aboard.

Lise Carlsen, enraged by the abrupt departure of her Oriental Bronze god, persuaded Ben to buy her a harem jumpsuit in pink Chinese silk. It covered her cast and reflected beautifully on her complexion. Each time a camera panned the audience she felt it linger on her, and once again she basked in its warmth. Seeing this brave young woman sign autographs, shrug ruefully at her injury, mothers around the world sighed with envy — all except her own, who watched from Sweden, who knew Lise better than Lise knew Lise, and could make a fair guess how deeply the injury had stung her husband's heart and pocket. She waited for the camera to seek out her son; it found him gazing with adoration into the eyes of the little Japanese girl with the big jumps. Mieko. Mrs Carlsen nodded. Rooms were ready to receive Mieko and her mother after the Games if the autocratic grandfather said they could visit. Dag said they'd come anyway, but what did he know of the subtle relationship between domineering men and the women they enslaved? In memory she cringed from Ben's drunken rages and punishing hands, a reflex she still must overcome. Abruptly she switched off the TV just too soon to catch a glimpse of Ben himself, more gaunt than ever and strangely pathetic now. It was unlikely a woman would ever fear Ben Carlsen again.

Beejay and Nils sat close by him, but Nils had no luck at all drawing the father of the Swedish beauty into conversation. Beejay had more. She offered him a dip into her bag of dried fishes, tiny and salted, to which Nils feared he had addicted her, and Ben Carlsen accepted two or three with a mournful smile. Encouraged, she passed the bag to Lise who, for perhaps the first and only time in her life, refused food. One glimpse of the glittering morsels produced a dainty shriek. 'They've got heads and tails and eyes!' she yelped. Beejay, not to play favourites, passed them down the line to the Braun Kramers. Noni and Roxanne declined very nicely — Beejay's mom being a judge — but Otto Braun, sitting between his daughter and granddaughter to keep the peace, scooped up a handful, washing them down with a belt of lager from a can under his seat. 'Goot!' he bellowed. 'Zalty! Mine vife would like.'

Noni shot him a scowl like a hail of bullets and chanted under her breath: 'What-am-I-gonna-do-what-am-I-gonna-do? Go back to live in the dump in LA, let Mr and Mrs Grant Rivers invite her to dinner once a month for appearance's sake, then home again to the rat-hole to do what, what, what?' She fumbled a cigarette and Roxanne leaned over her grandfather.

'Mom! No smoking — see the sign?'

'I'm Roxanne Kramer's mother. They're gonna throw me out?'

She might ask them to. 'This place is packed! After four-and-a-half minutes, the men need oxygen and there's never enough. Use your head!'

Otto Braun beamed and patted his granddaughter's shoulder, sending out a whiff of salted fish and lager. Noni turned on him.

'You're a fine one! Guzzling beer — next thing you'll have to pee and you'll have that guard carrying you to the gents, making an exhibition of us. Didn't I *tell* you to sit in the Invalid section? Yes, but you had to be down here in the swim, didn't you.'

'Big strong chap, that guard. He doesn't mind carrying me. He said so.'

'Yes,' Noni muttered, 'but it's me got to say thank-you-kindly later.'

Roxanne's head whipped around. Noni closed her mouth, snapped her purse and cigarette case shut, rapping silver fingernails on her programme.

Farther down the block Galina sat in the midst of the Russian team, her lap overflowing with red tulips, the Director glued to her side. In a corner, half hidden by palms and the media platform, Maureen offered Deirdre a carton of milk and a straw. 'Drink it, darling, you need your strength for tomorrow.'

Deirdre accepted but made no attempt to lift it to her mouth. She wore the long fur again, huge dark glasses, and once again she scanned the arena for Grant Rivers and once again found him at the rail with Yum-Num, Lloyd hovering somewhere in their vicinity.

The last five to skate would be the Czech, the Korean, the Bean, Jeff and Finsky, in that order. Yum-Num was not pleased. The skating order guaranteed that no matter how well the Bean skated the judges would leave room for Jeff, who might just pull off a zinger, and more room still for Finsky if he took the roof off.

Grant and Yum-Num bickered amiably as they waited. Grant spotted the elderly Welshman and waved, but Yum-Num's tongue reeled him back in, competition nerves feeding it more juice than his throat could swallow.

'Num, not bloody well fair,' he was saying. 'Happens every time.'

'When the Bean draws last to skate you don't say peep.'

'Beside the point, old top. Look at future potential. Finsky's at his peak and too bloody smart to hang in. He'll quit now. Which leaves the Bean, Finsky's natural heir.'

'You say he screws every girl in sight. That zaps him right there.'

'Num, just normal for his age. Started at twelve, right on schedule.' He still said 'shed-yule', part of his well-tended Brit image. 'And he screws the *opposite* sex, old lad, the way God intended.'

'So do most of the men out there — they just don't make a career of it.'

Yum-Num popped a pink antacid. 'Every competition my tum does this. No life, is it? Wife and kids want me to retire.'

'Why don't you?'

'I tried once, lived off investments, made a few more. Fine for a few weeks. But hell, I still woke up at four every morning and nodded off over dinner. Then a call from the Bean wakes me up, only nine at night but I was jiggered and I'd done nothing! The new man's okay, I sez? Well, not bad, but the Bean had lost some jumps, could I come and have a look? I nipped over to the rink, fist time I'd felt alive in weeks! That sweat and old ice smell, bloody marvellous, it was. A good thing I went in, the Bean's jumps were all to hell and gone, poor little toad. I ambled in next morning to get 'em back for him. The new man pissed his knickers and walked out. I expected the wife to do the same but num-num! She shouted Hallelujah. "Now you'll be fit to live with," she sez . . . talked to old Otto Braun this morning, thinks he wants to catch the sun in Spain, poor bugger, but num-num-num, he'll be back on the ice in three months, you wait.' He groaned as they announced the third group of men — not theirs. 'Gotta go backstage, check the Bean's got his trousers up. Our two are in the next lot. Coming? God, if they ever get stomach transplants I'm first on the list.'

Fully dressed and in his skates, the Bean lounged on a bench skimming a dog-eared *Playboy*. Yum-Num pounced. 'Mucky pictures! Lolling about playing with yourself! You should be fixing on your music, getting up for it, but not you, oh num! Num-num-num!'

The Bean clapped his hands theatrically over his crotch. 'Hell, I *am* up! *You* gave me "West Side Story"! I'm so hot to trot for Maria I could bite that bench! "Maria! Maria! I just met a girl named Mar-eee-ah".' His baritone soared through the tiled room, miles off-key but uninhibited. 'By the time I get done every woman on that panel's gonna wish her name was Maria.'

Jeff, on the next bench, rolled his eyes. 'God, he's *disgusting*.'

Yum-Num wheeled on him. 'At least he's *normally* disgusting!'

Finsky, curled in a relaxed heap, not yet laced up, laughed quietly. 'We have the new *Playboy* in our compound, Bean. If you'd asked I would have brought it. This month's centrefold is extra-fine.'

His hands sketched improbable contours. The Bean licked his chops, and Jeff pursed his lips: 'I hear they flew your girl in, Finsky. Couldn't you wait?'

No one answered. They heard the Czech's trainer grunt as he pulled off his skater's sock, unveiling an infected blister the size of a penny on the tip of the big toe. His *right* big toe.

'Oo-er,' Jeff said, 'nasty, that. Won't do his triple-lutz much good, will it?'

'He does a quad,' said the trainer, a belligerent Aussie.

'He did, you mean. You wouldn't catch me taking off from a toe like that.'

'This lad can take off barefoot and land on razor blades, mate. He's not sugar and spice.'

The Korean, with no English, nevertheless turned at the tone of voice.

Grant moved in. 'Back off, Jeff, you're out of your league.' Bad enough a last minute injury to a major entry. Worse, one's own student openly gloating. He should have chucked him to Lloyd. They deserved one another.

A wave of applause crashed through the door.

Every head swivelled, every neck braced to meet it. Roars, stomps, shouts, whistles, beating palms, all too loud to hear the music. No one said a word as the wave crested and held, sustained by far more than home-town supporters. The whole audience must be on its feet.

'Who's out there?' somebody said at last.

'A Canadian kid. Sixteen, he is.'

'Christ. Where was he after the Short?'

'Ninth?' a passing official guessed.

'Eighth — in a broken tie for seventh, very tight with sixth and fifth,' Finsky said softly, echoing what every skater and coach in the room knew. And Jeff Dunsmuir sitting fifth. The Canadian, his first time in international competition, should not have posed a threat for years, but he'd pulled off the impossible on his first crack at the big time. What would the panel do with him? Nothing so thoroughly rattled a judge's back-teeth as an unheralded comet streaking across the sport, scattering a trail of dashed hopes in its wake. Every major competition produced spoilers who skated better than they or anyone else could have expected. The Czech's blister suddenly took on new dimensions as somebody switched on the monitor for the marks. Too soon. The kid's dazzle had scrambled the board. Excruciating contortions must be performed in Accounting before the computer could spit out a verdict.

The monitor blinked, beeped, and the kid's marks sprang up, a line of invading starships, 5.7s and 5.8s straight across. With numbers like that the newest sky-walker could maybe reel in a medal if any of the top five choked — and one at least usually did.

For a millisecond the numbers stripped pretence from every face in the room, peeling nonchalant masks, exposing fear. Finsky recovered first, the Bean next. The Czech groaned — first the toe, now this. Jeff took longer. No family, no future outside the sport, he had most to lose.

A Polar Bear machine rumbled across the ice, sweeping up the Canadian's tracks, laying a pristine new surface for the last group. The best group. The Czech squirted analgesic on his toe, powdered it, spat on it, and booted up. Finsky yawned and laced his boots. The Bean serenaded Maria. Jeff combed his hair. Then as one man they faced the mirror, arching backs, twisting waists, swinging arms, rolling shoulders, touching toes, lunging, stretching, and secretly panicking. The Olympic Games. All these years preparing, suddenly they felt anything but ready. They cursed hours wasted on nothing, on 'hanging out', on watching TV, on ducking dance class to take in a movie. But again mental conditioning cut in, took over. They were the best. The best of the best.

The Czech's coach bragged too soon. Today his student could neither take off barefoot nor land on razor blades. Not even in skates, nor on the ice. No way could that sulking, angry toe catapult him high enough for a quad. A triple would have pushed it, but he tried the quad and splatted. First jump. It shot down a dull programme before it began. To his credit the Czech finished his music, refusing to limp as he shuffled to Kiss'n'Cry; once there, he did not trot out the blister as an excuse. He read his marks, shrugged, and smiled for the cameras. Two minutes later, in a corner of the locker room, he wept for himself. His last chance, and his lousy toe blew it!

The Korean, with only two triples, floundered far out of his class. What he did he did well — but it fell far short of enough. The Canadian kid had already overtaken the Czech and the Korean. How much wider would the axe of attrition swing? Only three left now, the Bean next.

Beside him, Grant felt Yum-Num tighten, watched him shut his eyes, clench his fists, heard him whisper, perhaps to himself: 'Yum, I've spent more time with this kid than I did with my own. He's like a son . . . better! *He* wouldn't even try the ice! But my little old Bean, thinks he fools everybody, but not me he doesn't, num, and not you either, God. Don't let him mess up, let him do good, never mind where he finishes. . .' Grant shook his head. He'd have sworn he knew Yum-Num, had written him off as brittle, shallow.

The crowd smiled and applauded even as the Bean erupted on to the ice with his usual dash and dazzle. Here I am! Settle back! Let's have us a time! But then everything changed. From the first note of music he yearned only towards Maria, a transformation Grant could scarcely believe.

'He's going to do it, he's finally going to do it,' Yum-Num whispered when the first triple went up smooth, came down soft, flowed easily into the next. 'Look at him, the young bugger's singing to himself! At the 'lympics!' The Bean might have taken lessons from Finsky, so soulfully did he move into the song, skating with Maria, for Maria, to Maria. Yum-num groaned. 'He'll be screwing her in a minute — if he gets an erection I'll chop it off, yum, I will! How would it look, a tent pole in them pants, what does he think he's doing?'

'He's skating his best ever. He's got the crowd. Look at their faces.'

'Num-num-num! They're not clapping, Rivers!'

'They're in a trance. He's doing a Finsky for you. Be satisfied.'

'Ah, the little love, look at that spin!' he crooned. 'Here comes the quad, if he misses it I'll kill the swine, I know damned well he screwed his brains out 'til past midnight last — *oh, beautiful, Beanie! Well done, old lad, bloody well done*!' He broke his monologue to crunch an antacid and shake his head. 'My stomach's too old for this. Rivers, if you knew how many times that kid's scared the pants off me! There should be a law. D'you know he arrived once at a big comp five minutes before he had to take the ice? Yum, *five minutes*, I was having kittens! Said he'd bust a tyre, tells a lovely lie, he does. If I didn't know him . . . he'd been having a quickie in the car park, what else. Athletes, either effing rabbits or screaming queens, no middle ground. Oh, lovely, laddie, bless his buttons, look at him, Rivers, butter wouldn't melt in his mouth. . .'

The Bean brought the house down and the marks up: 5.8s, 5.9s, and two 6.0s littered the board. On camera Yum-Num chewed furiously as they were interviewed, barely answering a question, leaving the Bean to do the honours.

And Jeff had to follow that. To stand. To wait until a troop of dewy little girls gathered up a hail of daffodil and iris.

Grant sighed. He'd been there himself, one time or another they all had. One of the worst positions in skating, waiting for somebody else's applause to fade, holding a starting pose which had once seemed dramatic. Now, frozen in the Bean's thunder, it appeared as unnatural as every other starting pose. From his expression, Jeff knew it. Again Grant felt sorry for him, wondered what portents of doom shot through his mind during this worst of all possible scenarios. Defeat? Anger? Panic?

All of those, but mostly resentment — no stranger to Jeff Dunsmuir. Why didn't they finish, what did they want, a bloody encore? Did they want him to start or not? Because he was gay and they knew it, he'd have to do better than the Bean for the same marks. He wasn't better, but with the right backing he could have been. Not fair, not bloody-well fair. He was what he was, he liked what he was. Social workers told him once that he was gay because he'd been raised by an old woman on her own, but they were miles off. Gays worked out, kept in shape, dressed well. If they were sick they had the decency to hide until they recovered or died. Homosexuality, for Jeff Dunsmuir, had more to do with aesthetics than with sex — in which his interest was, always had been, minimal.

And now, thank God, the referee at last ordered silence. In a second his music would begin. So okay, he was gay, everybody knew it and he didn't have to apologize to the audience or anybody else. Sod 'em. He didn't have to be Lloyd's plaything or the rock star's either — both turned out to be godawful bores. Another thing he'd discovered in Montegreco. Just because he wasn't straight didn't mean he had to grab at every flash-fish swimming by. He had looks. He could pick and choose. His head came up with the first note of music and he was on his way, tuning out his past and his future, everything but his programming, which had been intense.

Grant, waiting for the first jump, usually a portent of things to come, heard feet shuffle behind him. Yum-Num. Just when Grant had begun to like him, the little coach dogged his heels again, the pressure off now, a quiver full of darts ready to fly. 'He did well, my little old Bean, yum?'

'Yes.' Grant turned away. 'Now I'd like to watch Jeff.'

'Num-num old lad, after what they gave the Bean, you can write Jeff off. If there's one thing I notice about queenies, they don't hold up in the crunch. . .'

Grant ignored him. Yum-Num was not only a bigot, he was a stupid bigot. Gays were not afraid of grace; too many straights were.

Then up came the first jump, a triple-axel, best of the competition thus far, and landed like silk. Grant didn't know how long he'd been holding his breath until it came out in a whoosh. Thank God. The knowledgeable Competitor section exploded. Grant turned to Yum-Num. 'Still want to write him off?'

'Early days yet. Wait and see. He'll never hold up.'

Not just a bigot. A poor sport too. Then Grant remembered. The Bean 'like a son . . . better than a son'. Maybe if *he* had a son out there he'd be on edge too. If he had a son . . . Instead he had a daughter — and he'd told her he hoped Roxanne beat the daylights out of her. The audience roared again. Jeff hit his final difficult combination straight on, never better, and whipped easily, almost coldly, into the last series of spins at spectacular speed. Behind him Grant heard a polite throat clearing, a rubbing of palms, a sound calling up monogrammed luggage, Rolex watches, smoked salmon canapés and Concordiean hops over the Atlantic.

Lloyd, genuinely delighted, beamed. 'I say, old man —'

'Yes, he skated well, Lloyd. I'm happy for him.'

'And I! Delighted, old chap! No time at all, and you worked wonders.'

'With your help,' Grant said. He too could be generous. On occasion.

'One of the great benefits success offers the more

fortunate, like myself, is the impartial help we can offer deserving athletes like Jeff.' Lloyd delivered the line smoothly, sincerely, as if he had used it before — as no doubt he had, on speakers' platforms, at company dinners, anywhere the wealthy gathered to congratulate one another on scrambling to the top of the heap.

Grant nodded. He would not remind Lloyd that impartial help had been the farthest thing from his mind. Jeff out-smarted him, that's all. 'If you'll excuse me, Lloyd . . . the Kiss'n'Cry, Jeff's marks, you understand —'

'Of course, of course,' said Mr Suddenly Genial.

Entering the booth Grant sent a swift prayer winging to Olympus, not for a skater in black who'd just out-shone himself, but for a lady in a green cloth coat, who, if justice existed at all, would be watching. But she'd known, who better, that there was no justice, that she was dead and Deirdre dying while Lloyd puffed himself up like a blowfish with lies about impartiality, generosity and helping hands.

Jeff's marks, marginally lower than the Bean's, nevertheless knocked the Czech out of the running, tying Jeff and the young Canadian for third. Ties sent the accounting room's computer into over-drive, shot officials to panic stations. With a tie, the breaker must be taken through a dozen hoops of the rule book. Yea, verily, down past the ifs, ands, and buts even unto the ninth and tenth generations of where-as's and wherefores. The answer might not come for an hour.

Meantime Alexei Finsky sensibly waited off-ice until the uproar of Jeff's performance settled. Then he skated out, bowing to the audience, judges and, oddly, to Deirdre Sterling, before fixing his eyes steadily on Galina. The other had skated the traditional musical pattern, fast music to open up, a resting slow period in the middle, then the gallop to a fast finish.

Finsky's music sprang, as always, directly from folk roots, abrupt and constant shifts in tempo reflecting life and love, death and sorrow, jubilant rejoicing and wild, uninhibited mourning, people of the country celebrating the crops, baking the bread, indulging the young and burying the dead. Finsky acted every note, a magician revealing by turns the warmth of a country wedding, the innocence of children, the passions of the young and the griefs of the old. This, he told himself, would be their wedding song. The children would be their children, his and Galina's. He ended, not with the usual blinding spin, but a simple stop, a winding down. Like life. Then, instead of the customary bow to the panel, he approached a girl standing at the barrier, almost hidden behind a mass of scarlet tulips. His arms went out to her, crushing the flowers, scattering petals over the ice like drops of blood.

'You've won,' she whispered.

'We've won.' Briefly, over the flowers, his lips touched hers.

In unison the audience exhaled a long, soulful 'ahhh', and his coach tapped Finsky's shoulder to remind him that marks were coming up. The Director moved to enter the booth with them, but Finsky, anonymous again, weighing no more than a hundred-and-fifty pounds, average colouring, the ultimate common man, elbowed the Director aside and drew Galina into the booth to stand between Alexei and his coach.

The technical marks shot him to certain Gold. The second set lofted him to the company of skating's immortals. His style marks, 6.0s straight across. No dissent — for what man, in the history of the sport, ever had more style than Alexei Finsky?

Emma wept openly, helplessly. Not that it mattered. Nobody watched anybody but the winner as they rolled out the 1-2-3 steps, waiting for the computer to render its confirmation. Just when she'd begun to wonder if the sport was worth the scrimping, the no-time-for-Emma, the agonizing over stacks of bills in a shoe-box on the kitchen table, along came a Finsky, renewing her faith, keeping her married to this cruel, demanding discipline.

Jeff Dunsmuir, uncertain yet whether he'd won Olympic Bronze or nothing, hissed to Grant: 'Sixes! It's not fair, he did no more than I did, five triples and a quad. And that hokey country music. That peasant outfit!'

The goodwill Grant bore Jeff evaporated again, perhaps forever. 'It's not *what* he did, you twit, it's how he did it, what he wore, the music he picked. If you can't see the difference between him and the rest of you, you've wasted fifteen years. My advice is sign with that show while the offer's open.'

Jasinski, hurrying towards Grant, looked as if he'd discovered the source of the Nile. 'Now I understand,' he said. 'You have hooked an old sceptic.'

Even Otto Braun, up in the Invalid section where Noni had finally ordered him, sighed. With a student like Finsky, who needed retirement and the Med?

'He's superb,' breathed Maureen Sterling. 'He had them make a tape just for you. He and Galina will bring it to the hotel tomorrow. So thoughtful. Won't it be lovely, lying in bed, reliving that over and over again, darling?'

'Sweet of him, but it's not the same, you know. You have to *be* there. I'm glad I came,' Deirdre murmured. 'I've not missed one Olympics for twenty years. I do wish you were marrying Alexei though, he'd take care of you. . .'

'Oh, Mother!' Maureen, the steady, level foundation on which Deirdre's life rested, wanted to weep. Twenty years of Olympics, this her last. It *must* be perfect — but so much talent to defeat, first Roxanne, then the little Mieko —

'I think,' Mieko said to her Carlsen man, 'that the Russians have skated a marriage song.'

'A happy marriage,' agreed Dag Carlsen.

Even Lise Carlsen experienced a sea-change. 'God, to skate like that, not be scared . . . what d'you think it's worth, the Gold?'

'Enough to put my business on its feet,' Ben grunted.

The PA system crackled, the computer board flashed final placements: USSR — GOLD. USA — SILVER. GBR — BRONZE.

Grant Rivers congratulated Jeff, examined and praised the medal, and commiserated with the crest-fallen Canadian; to lose an Olympic medal on a tie break. . .

On his way to the Village he paused to look up at the ring of mountains, serene, uncaring in the starlight, pure, a hooked moon catching up a passing cloud, a movie-set and no camera, a reward and no one to accept it. But Roxanne would be happy, maybe even take it as a sign of glory for herself tomorrow.

'We got us one medal,' he whispered to no one at all.

Nothing answered but night wind howling off the peaks

and a crunch of snow as footsteps followed him to the village, halting him at the door. It was Maureen, shrugging out of her parka, shaking snow from her black hair.

'May I apologize for this morning, Mr Rivers? I'm not usually —'

'I wasn't exactly Sir Lochinvar myself.'

'Our situation is — well — irregular. I don't know how to speak to you.'

'Same here, so we start even.'

She frowned. 'Yes, but . . . I meant it when I said I didn't need a father.'

'Me too — I don't want to be one. But tell me something. You're young. How do you stand it, watching her die?'

She took in a long, ragged breath and for a moment she could have been middle-aged. 'Mostly I can but sometimes —' Her voice cracked and she shook her head. 'It's difficult.'

He touched her shoulder, her bones sharp and elegant under a cream silk blouse. Briefly she covered his hand with her own. 'Goodnight, Mr Rivers. Wish Roxanne good luck for tomorrow. I think you understand how I feel.'

A swirl of skirt, a lingering hint of 'Joy', and his daughter walked gracefully away from him, widening the gulf between them, eighteen years again, much too wide to bridge, now or ever. He did *not* understand how she felt about tomorrow, how could he? They were strangers.

Roxanne was not. 'What did you think?' he said, kissing her cheek.

'Ah, that Finsky's so great he makes me wonder why I bother. He goes out, opens up, risks everything. If he'd missed one jump, just one, he'd have blown that mood sky-high, but it never showed. Me, after every jump I worry I'll miss the next, or the next, always one worry ahead. He just —'

'He's one in a trillion. You're just one in a million, poor mite. Maureen Sterling sends you good luck for tomorrow.'

'Grant, I've been thinking. We've never seen her long programme. D'you suppose she can't go the distance, that she's scared to show the judges? All she's skated at the arena is "La Mancha", the short. You notice?'

Grant had. He'd hoped Roxanne had not. 'I'd say

Maureen Sterling can go any distance she sets her mind to. She's a demon in the ballet room, and she's sure to have worked on the sly in the Barcelona rink.'

'Peculiar, though, huh? You'd think she'd want to try it here. Maybe it's a surprise for her mom, a favourite song. God, she looks awful, did you see?'

'Yes.' But Deirdre's favourite song had once been 'Impossible Dream'. He rubbed his hands, suddenly cold. 'Forget Maureen's programme and go to something really earth-shaking, like when you want to be Mrs Rivers. Before we go back, or wait for LA? And the honeymoon, you name it. Any place.'

She smiled, the competition a million years away. 'Somewhere quiet, no ice. After tomorrow I don't want to see a pair of skates for . . . oh, years.'

'Yum-Num reckons the sport's an addiction. Once bitten . . .'

'Maybe that's it,' she said. 'I never got bitten. Just trapped.'

CHAPTER FORTY-ONE

Jeff Dunsmuir, preening around the hotel lobby with his Bronze hung on his neck and his contract poking out of his pocket, signed autographs and babbled endlessly about 'my producer' and 'my production number' and 'my costume designer'. Before he drove near-strangers quite mad, he wandered over to the Village to give all and sundry the benefit of his overnight expertise on the costumes of the Ladies.

He emerged from the British compound somewhat pink; Grant guessed that Maureen Sterling had invited him, with aplomb, to vacate the premises. Undaunted, he tacked himself nonchalantly in the wake of Grant, who was making last minute rounds of his skaters. Grant would have preferred, this close to count-down, and in the tight quarters assigned to competitors, to have had them to himself, but he lacked his daughter's cutting edge.

Roxanne looked exquisitely regal in sea-green chiffon, its waves breaking softly at her breasts, rhinestones like drops of surf trapped in the sun. Ash-blonde hair gleaming, her make-up a work of art, she lacked only confidence to emerge a true-beauty — but with Noni phoning in wild, last ditch directives every other minute, true confidence for Roxanne Kramer hovered in a tantalizing near distance her arms never seemed to reach. As Grant eased into the cubicle between sink and bed, he distinctly heard Noni's words crackling through the wire, no doubt calculated to instruct, but painting on coat after coat of guilt in broad inept strokes.

'— mind what I said Roxi, forget the audience, they can't give you Gold. Smile at the judges, hear me? We need the Finn, the Czech and the Russian, *especially* the Russian, thin man, white hair — hell, Emma Crisp threw her top mark away on Finsky so the Commies better come through for us now, one hand washes the other, they owe us, get it? Got your sheer tights on?'

'Mom, Finsky earned his Gold, and I'm twenty-two, I've been at this for —'

'And you know it all, sure, sure. I talked to every judge I could corner —'

'The team manager *told* you to knock that off!'

'What does he know? Don't mess up on me this time, Roxanne, it's your last chance! When it's all over *I* have to tell Mutti whether we won or lost, so we better win, but don't panic, the Gold's yours if you just don't get nerv —'

Grant, who'd been filling the small wash basin, took the receiver from Roxanne's hand and let it splash quietly in. Noni's voice gurgled on for an instant, disembodied, then with a small pop it cut out all together.

'Grant, you've fused it!'

'I'll fuse your mom if she doesn't get off your back. That colour's super on you, sweetheart. You look like a mermaid or something.'

Jeff elbowed in. 'Oo-er, Roxi, you sure do, like Grant says — but are you sure about the *green*? It's great on you, yes, but considering how tight the marks are and everything, aren't you taking a bit of a chance?'

Grant shut his eyes. He knew, oh, God he knew what was coming, should have remembered it himself — but who weighed daft old superstitions into the Olympic equation? But even if he'd remembered he'd have dismissed it as an old wives' tale. Because it was. And she looked sensational when she smiled.

'Green's my best colour, Jeff. Besides, it's almost blue, it matches my eyes. It's gorgeous, and I love it.' Roxanne's voice rose a notch. 'Why? Is Maureen Sterling in green or something? Or the Japanese?'

Jeff shook his head sadly. 'I shouldn't think so, love. You must have heard about it, God knows you've been on the circuit long enough. Green is *the* bad luck colour, kiss-of-death colour. Nobody, but absolutely nobody, competes in green unless they've got a death-wish or some —'

'*Out*!' How many more times at this Olympics would

Grant Rivers have to toss Jeff Dunsmuir through a door? As often as it took.

'But, Grant, if —' Roxanne's voice rose towards that old hysterical note he hadn't hear since her starve-and-suffer days.

'He's trying to rattle you. You know Jeff. He can't help being a bastard, he probably told Maureen that her colour's unlucky too, and I'll bet she sent him packing. Now he'll trot in and give Beejay the evil eye. The kid's a born-again swine, ignore him.'

'Okay.' She bit her lip. 'You're sure?'

'I know Jeff. Trust me.' Trust me? He recalled them now, a dozen instances drifted to the surface, self-fulfilling prophesies, no doubt. But last night the Czech wore green, the Canadian kid wore green. One got licked by a blister, the other by a heart-breaker tie. 'Roxanne, ask yourself. Noni had no complaints about the colour and she's been in the game a long time. *And* your grandmother. If anybody gave it any credence at all, they would.'

'I guess.' She regarded the dead phone floating in the basin. Gran still lay in the infirmary, speech a here-today-gone-tomorrow thing, and Noni's voice was drowned until the phone engineer stopped in. 'I'll ask Emma.'

'Fine, I have to stop in on Beejay anyhow.' He sounded more positive than he felt. Emma was a skating mom. Why should she reassure her daughter's competitor? Because Em wouldn't play games, that's why.

'Oh my God, Beej!' Roxanne's narrow hand flew to her mouth. 'You're . . . I can't believe it's you, I mean you look, well, grown up!'

'That does it,' Emma said, 'the mascara comes off, I said it was too old.'

'Oh, Mrs Crisp, she looks lovely, let her keep it on,' Roxanne said.

Grant said nothing. Couldn't she see that one look at Beejay like this and the judges wouldn't be doling out kiddy marks anymore? If she skated the way she could, if she moved fast enough, she could move into the medal class.

'You look gorgeous too, doesn't she, Beej?' Emma's voice was warm. 'The best colour I've ever seen on you, you should have worn it for Nationals.'

'I was saving it,' Roxanne said. 'Mrs Crisp, I wanted to ask you, Jeff says green's unlucky, that everybody knows it. What d'you think?'

'I think Jeff's full of it,' Emma said, so promptly that only Grant knew she spun her tale out of whole cloth, ad-libbing like crazy. 'In my day it was red, then blue, then orange, then pink. Hell, if we listened to all the old wives' tales you'd be out there in your birthday suit and goosebumps. Come to think, maybe that's what they want!' She brushed her hands together as if rinsing off garbage. 'Roxie, you're so great with hair. Can you do something with this?' She touched Beejay's copper wire, and produced a mesh elastic net the same iridescent shade as Beejay's dress. 'It's supposed to keep the hair out of her eyes, but we can't make it stay on. What d'you think?'

'I had one just like it once. Watch.' Deftly Roxanne removed a dozen wire pins, tamed the flaming hair securely into a twist, skewered the mesh over it with strong clips, then, the tip of her tongue tracing her upper lip, she drew a few strategic tendrils through the net, some on the neck, some framing the face, just enough to suggest a charming débutante. 'That'll stay on, Beejay. Just don't be raking at it, the way you do when you get mad.'

'I don't!' Beejay lied, covering her eyes against a mist of hairspray.

'You do too. And look, this is a no-no!' She set the hairpins she'd removed into an accusing row. 'They'd have flown all over the ice on the first spin. Somebody's blade hits one, and that's all she wrote!'

'I wouldn't have hit one.'

'Mieko goes after you, then Maureen, and then me. Any one of us could have hit one. I have. And it's not much fun.'

'Gee! I didn't think, sorry Roxanne. Hey, my hair's real nifty now, huh? Thanks a lot and good luck. You look like an absolute knock-out.'

As Grant, reassurance almost accomplished, ushered Roxanne out of the door, Emma said: 'Roxanne, about the green? You've seen all those pictures of Peggy on the winner's stand getting Gold? She made us all proud that day. I know. I was there. Remember the dress? A lovely apple green, it was.'

One day, Grant figured, when the dust had settled and he and Roxanne had tied the knot, he'd send Emma Crisp the biggest bunch of roses she'd ever seen. Anonymous, of course. It didn't do to kiss up a judge.

On Grant's way out the Bean staggered in, puffy-eyed and rubber-legged.

'Looks like you celebrated Silver pretty good, old Bean,' Grant said.

'Nah, I've been at the infirmary all night with Yum-Num. We popped a bottle of bubbly but it doesn't agree with his tum so he had White Russians — said the cream coats his insides — and a dozen oysters. Next thing he's on the floor, they're wheeling him up to the bone-yard with bleeding ulcers! It's a war zone up there, man! Roxanne's gran, Maureen's mom, now Yum-Num. I wish I hadn't given him a hard time about girls, most of it was just clowning around, getting him frothed up. . . I knew he had ulcers, but what's an ulcer, I thought? My Dad has 'em, my mom, everybody has 'em at competition.'

'Bean, I think Yum-Num was born with holes in his tum. A few weeks peace and quiet, milk and no booze, and he'll be fine. You did great last night. I thought Yum-Num would bust his britches with pride.'

The Bean looked glum. 'You could have fooled me. He told the doc he had Boston Bean ulcers and they'd never heal up until I quit.'

'Funny, he told me you were better than a son. Heck, he told God the same thing! How high up do you want to go? And stay humble, I mean.'

'He said that? Honest?' The Bean clutched Grant's arm and it became obvious, looking closer, that the boy's eyes were puffed up from weeping, not carousing. The Bean wandered off to change for the big Ladies night. Grant shook his head. Skating!

In the Japanese compound, Oka-Chan and Mieko faced each other across her narrow cot. In the middle of the beige Olympic spread lay a package, exquisitely wrapped in vivid red silk, bound with gold cord and sealed in wax with Hiro Nakashima's distinctive crest.

'I must not let you look inside until the moment before you skate, Mieko, no! That is what he said, that is what he means. And he will know.' Unconsciously they looked at the locked door, and Oka-chan's voice fell to a whisper. 'You understand it can be orders to go directly home after you skate? Or a framed picture of the promising young man from Hokkaido? That is how I first saw your father, in just such a picture, wrapped in just such a beautiful package.'

'He would not do that, Oka-chan, he would not —'

'You know that he would. For sure it is important. Only that one time in my life do I receive such a package with his personal seal. No one is allowed to touch it, not even his body servant.'

Mieko approached it, stroked a small ivory finger across vermilion silk. 'The quality is very fine, and it matches my dress,' she whispered.

'It means nothing. He could send a death threat in the beak of a white dove.' Oka-chan touched a hand to her daughter's troubled face. 'I may pass it to you only as you approach the ice, that is his order, and that I must do. But Mieko, child, listen! Whatever is inside, do not be afraid. On the ice you are not a Nakashima, you are Japan.'

Mieko squeezed her eyes very tight. Her mother spoke foolishly and they both knew it. For them, Hiro Nakashima was Japan. 'Oka-chan, I must tell you true. After the Games I go to Sweden, to my Carlsen's mother, no matter what he says, even if you do not come with me. I am sorry.'

Oka-chan looked at her daughter for a long time, pride and grief waging a battle in her eyes. Pride won. She smiled and bowed. 'You are Nakashima's granddaughter. You will do what you must.'

Galina helped Maureen dress, zipped up the froth of delicate coral, gave her skates one final buffing, inspected her hair through the mirror.

'Don't worry about your mother, Maureen. If Alexei says he stays with her, he stays. He will get her to the arena. A dependable man, Alexei. But your mother, she is dependable also. You know what she did for us, I think?'

Maureen nodded. 'Some of it.'

'She make possible a whole new life. We do not forget this. Soon, when you are alone — you don't mind if I speak honest? It is best to be open, to see the future — when you are alone, we will be happy if you can visit us.'

'I'd like that. I've competed in Moscow but one never sees anything but tourist stuff and, of course, the ice.'

Galina nodded. 'Always the ice. It never melts.' Their eyes locked, and this Russian girl, with troubles not so different from Maureen's, smiled. 'Are you afraid. Maureen?'

'Of the Olympics?'

'No. The future.'

Maureen looked beyond her down a long road stretching endlessly forward, no one on it but herself. 'Yes,' she said. 'I don't know life without her. Until she became ill we were never apart at all. Now, even when we're together, she's sometimes . . . not with me. You know the word "dementia"? It's part of her illness. I thought the other things were terrible, humiliating for her . . . but the mind is the worst. Later she knows she's been irrational, but she pretends, tries to cover up, you know?'

Galina nodded. 'My father is the same. Paranoids know they are paranoid, they know they build fences around their families. But we depress ourselves! You look wonderful, you will skate wonderful, and you will make Deirdre very happy. But Maureen, tell me one thing. Alexei says you do not practise your long programme in the arena. No one has seen it. Is something wrong?'

'No. It's lovely, but it's vital Mother does not see it yet. She sometimes came to the practices, you see. Every night when I was small she used to lie beside me and sing a lullaby, always the same song, until I grew old enough to sing with her. A peaceful song. Many times we both fell asleep, and when I woke up she'd be there, on my bed or on the *chaise* beside me, guarding me. She always smelled of lilies, I remember.'

'You are close to her, I know —'

'She guarded me, took care of me. I want her to know she is guarded, that she will not be alone.'

Galina wrapped her arms around Maureen Sterling and rocked her as a mother might rock a child, crooning to herself. For all her sophistication, this pampered, ravaged, girl was an immature child. How could she not know that we are all alone, always?

'Heavens, Nils, I'm not the orchid type, but it's lovely, thanks.' Uncertain if he expected to be kissed or not, Emma pinned the speckled blossom on her sensible black suit and vaguely aimed a peck at his cheek.

'Something worrying you?'

'No . . . but tonight is kinda crucial for Beejay. Look, the top three spots pretty well belong to Roxanne, Maureen and Mieko — in any order, depending how they shape up and barring a spoiler. But after this they'll all quit, right? Beejay's sixteen. Who do you see as her strongest competitor, coming up?'

'The little German. Same age, style, light, peppy, both good competitors, fierce in the crunch, neither gives an inch. Right now they're about even.'

'Yeah. So whoever finished ahead of the other tonight gets a psychological hammerlock on Ladies through every Worlds every year all the way to the next Games. By then they'll both be ready.'

'Yes. So what's the problem?'

Emma sighed. 'So I'm a skating mom after all. I used to just hope Beejay did her best. Now I hope she beats the other girl. And I *like* the other girl!'

'Emma, I'm no skating mom, but I hope for Beejay too, because I know her and I like her. It's natural. I have not met the German girl. D'you think *her* parents do not hope their little girl will beat yours? That's the sport, Emma.'

'I know — the bit I don't like.'

'You have a solution.' Nils was laughing at her. 'Withdraw Beejay.'

'As if I could. She wouldn't go!'

'Well then.' He shrugged. 'With no choice — enjoy!'

Emma muttered about understanding Yum-Num and even Noni — then again the Polar Bear padded softly out of its lair, scraping the ice, washing it, ironing out every wrinkle. The finest of the fine deserved no less.

CHAPTER FORTY-TWO

The little German girl was first out, eighty-five pounds of youth and pep and rock-solid technique. Thorough. Trust the Germans, Grant thought. He, like Emma, had discerned from precisely which direction next year's greatest threat hailed. A little girl with brown hair, saucer-eyes, the spring of an impala, and a habit of snapping her leg-elastics as she waited her turn.

She fell, not on one jump, but two, both of them triples. Sheer nerves. Grant had watched her land the same jumps in practice every day, perfect, but practice was not competition; as the standard bearer of the German team, this girl was over-young for the pressure resting on her shoulders.

'Okay, Beejay, she blew two. So you'll skate conservative, hear me?'

'Sure.'

'Know what conservative means?'

She wrinkled her brow. 'Like Em? Neither a borrower nor a lender —'

He suddenly knew the precise source of Yum-Num's ulcers. 'You know what I mean by a conservative skate, young lady!'

'Yeah, but how conservative? Waltz jumps and singles? Bunny hops? I forgot to bring my "Farmer-in-the-Dell" music, see —'

Belinda Jane Crisp, United States of America!

'Off you go, kid. You look . . . dare I say it? Romantic.'

She rolled her eyes and scooted out to wild applause from her American team members, enthusiastically led by the Bean.

'Lord, Nils, I wish I didn't have to watch this,' Emma said.

'Then go hide in the Judges' room.'

'You kidding?' They stood at the rail behind Grant, Emma conscious, for the first time in her life, of blood surging between her ears. 'Romeo and Juliet.' The perfect dress for the perfect music. Now if only her perfect daughter could rein in the tomboy for four minutes, just four, skate soft and pretty. The German girl had entered Finals in sixth, Beejay in seventh — but a strong seventh, with four-fifths tucked snugly inside it. Now if she could snag one more judge . . .

The music moved and so did Beejay, a tropical, pearlescent fish darting in blue shallows, her opening double-axel a dazzler, the triple-toe loop a mite shaky but done. Everything A-okay, but now came the slow bit, where arms and attitude showed, where she must move with balletic grace. 'And by damn, Grant, she is! More or less.'

'Emma, she's never moved like that in her life. If something goes wrong she'll be the old Beejay, cussing and whipping around like a lightning-bug.'

Nothing did go wrong, and she moved into the last quick bars with not a fall or double-foot on anything. All she had left was a double-lutz/triple-loop combination, then a closing spin. Emma began to breathe again — until she saw Beejay's face as it flashed past her, tightening up, determined, her legs and her lungs pumping like pistons around the top end, gathering speed for the long diagonal-lutz take-off. Far more speed than she needed for the double. 'Hell, she's going for the triple.'

Grant swore. 'I *told* her to keep it conservative!'

Up she went, swift as a swallow, giving it that extra thrust, a tighter pull to spin her three revolutions and bring her lightly down into the triple-loop, then the final spin in a blur, a haze, a dazzle of triumph. Delighted, remembering, only just, to bob to the judges and the audience, she gathered up her flowers, waved to her cheering supporters, and walked straight into Grant's thunder.

'What did I tell you?' he said through his teeth. '*What the hell did I say?*'

'Grant, I was on, I knew I could do it, no sweat.'

'*No sweat? If you think there's no sweat feel my palms!*' He forced his blood to stop racing. He was sounding like Yum-Num already, bleeding ulcers right around the corner.

He took a deep breath and gathered her up in a hug before she could wriggle out of it. 'Christ, but you skated, kid.'

'Sssh. Language. My mom's behind you.'

Mother and daughter smiled at one another, a million candles shining in Beejay's sherry-coloured eyes, Emma's definitely glistening.

'Well, did I do good, or what?'

'You did good.'

'Isn't this where I have to stand still to get kissed or somethin'?'

'Thought you'd never ask,' Emma said, her voice for a moment thick in her throat. Kissing Beejay was kissing quick-silver. 'You were great,' she whispered into the coppery hair.

'I know,' her daughter whispered back. 'Surprised I did the lutz?'

'Kinda.'

'You knew I was going to try it, right?'

'I figured you might.'

'And thought I'd miss it, huh?'

'Not for a second,' Emma lied. 'I knew if you went for it you'd have it.'

Abruptly, with no precedent whatever, crackling-with-energy Beejay sank down on the bench, winded. 'Holy cow, I've just skated the Olympics!'

Emma would have given a lot just then if Dave Crisp could have seen his daughter's face. But Nils saw it, patted her shoulder, and passed her a bag of salted fish. 'Now go for your marks.'

Oka-chan handed over the small-red package, a perfect match for the vermilion dress, at the very last moment.

'Your grandfather's gift, but please, do not be unhappy.'

Mieko trembled, afraid to look under the personal crest of Hiro Nakashima.

'Quickly. Soon they call your name.'

Her daughter lifted the seal, untied the golden cord, spread the red silk and lifted the lid of the small wooden box. Looking up at her, frowning absent-mindedly as if it might, given time and a little help, remember her name, was the wizened monkey-face of the *netsuke*.

Oka-chan gasped. 'He gives the Masanao? His *saru*? This I cannot believe, there is mistake . . .'

Mieko held it in her palm, smoothed her thumb over its carved wisdom, its worried, almost-human face, remembering how her grandfather had gazed upon it. 'But what does it mean? Why does he give me his treasure?'

Tears sprang into Oka-chan's sloe-eyes. 'I think . . . perhaps he tells you he loves you, gives his blessing. He is not a man for words, but my father does not waste time on the empty gesture.'

Mieko looked up at the stands, the Competitor section, her Carlsen man blew her a kiss, then they called her —

Mieko Nakashima, Japan.

Afterwards, she never remembered skating her programme, just a vague memory of thunderous applause at the spectacular triple-axel, a sea of Rising Sun banners waving in the stands, her hair whipping about her face in the final spin at centre-ice, just as she had dreamed it when Oka-chan had taken a small girl to see the rehearsal of an ice-show in Atami.

When her vision cleared she sought, and found, the big camera with the Nakashima logo, and smiled tearfully into the lens at her grandfather, bowing to him, for he might after all be watching her from Tokyo or Atami.

He was not. He stood directly under his company's camera, the flunky next to him almost buried in vermilion roses which Hiro Nakashima disdained to hurl on to the ice with the rain of offerings from the Japanese section. Instead he waited until Mieko saw him, *bowed to her*, and beckoned her to his side, gesturing the flunky to present the roses. He looked down into her face, momentarily beautiful with joy, and reached out his thin ivory hand to brush her cheek.

'Take good care of the Masanao, Mieko-chan. Of all we own, that is the piece of everlasting value. Masanao's heart is carved into it.'

Mieko-*chan*. He called her Mieko-*chan*. 'Grandfather, my Carlsen man —'

He nodded. 'We shall see. Send him to me. I have questions.'

*

471

Roxanne, who'd always refused to watch her competitors, had asked to see Maureen. Before Grant went backstage to get her he found Emma and took her with him. 'While we wait for Roxanne's turn, keep Noni well away from her, okay? That woman's mouth could sink an iceberg.'

'Yes.' The rest of her could be pretty lethal too. 'Roxanne's sure she wants to watch Sterling?'

'She says.'

'Has she seen the Japanese's marks? Or Beejay's?'

'I think not, I hope not. Corkers, weren't they?'

'Uh-huh. Even Willi came across. With all the big triples popping off out there, Roxanne's going to have to hit high gear. Think she still can?'

Grant, alone in the corridor with Emma, came to an abrupt stop. The way they were talking, in whispers, Roxanne could have been dying. 'Okay, Em, you're the only one I can level with. I think she peaked last year.'

'Agreed. If Beejay ever gets nerves like that I don't know what I'll do.'

'You're not Noni. But Beejay's in a whole new league now, too.' She'd be her country's standard-bearer next, like the little German already was. The cloak of a nation's expectations weighed damned heavy on young shoulders. 'Let's go get the World Champion, as Noni would say.'

Maureen Sterling's music had not even begun before the audience sensed that this was to be something different. The girl's first move, to absolute silence, was not a skating element at all but a deep curtsy, dark head bowed, long neck fluid as a dancer's, from which she rose with hands outstretched, palms up, less a plea than an offering of gifts for a woman in dark glasses and a fur coat in the Chaperone section. The woman removed her glasses.

The girl wore a coral chiffon dress, its floating pink sleeves black-tipped, inevitably suggesting the outstretched wing-tips of a flamingo about to lift from a lagoon, a bird of warmth and everlasting beauty, serene on blue water. For a long moment she smiled directly into the woman's eyes before her arms began their slow flutter to the first haunting notes.

The skater had chosen an ancient lullaby, its origins lost in the mists of the rugged Welsh mountains, but the air traditional, familiar to the world. Few knew the words, but from the first note every listener looked back into the past, into childhood remembered, into pleasures as simple and innocent as the melody itself.

As the girl on the ice began to move, to enter her music, she took all of them with her, the hum rising faintly at first, a nostalgic wave moving outwards from the first few rows, soon to gather in the whole swaying audience, just as audiences around the world swayed in their easy chairs.

At ice level, audible only to Grant and the woman in furs, a sweeter note took up the melody — hummed by a man who for decades had led a chapel choir in a suburb of Swansea. Hearing him, the melody's long forgotten words crept back into Grant Rivers' mind, trapping him in a flood of memory:

Sleep, my love, and peace attend thee
All through the night.
Guardian angels God will lend thee
All through the night.
Soft the drowsy hours are creeping
Hill and vale in slumber steeping
Love alone his watch is keeping
All through the night.

Not a soul in the audience could be unaware that this performance was a gift from the girl to the woman. Only those who knew the woman, who saw her up close, could know that it was also a requiem.

The audience, still gripped by the girl and the melody, followed where they led, but the woman's burning blue gaze turned to Grant at the rail, his hair as dark as the girl's:

Love's young dream alas is over
Yet my strains of love shall hover. . . .

Grant returned the gaze in the fevered eyes, which closed for a moment before returning to their true focus, the delicate bird floating above centre-ice. But the eyes burned too bright, such light could not last.

If it was against the rules for an audience to supplement a skater's music with humming sound effects of its own, not a soul would lodge an objection, least of all the one coach whose hopes of Gold lay in ruins with this performance. For years he'd pushed Welsh voices to the back of his mind but he drowned in them now, all called forth by the melody, the skater, and a chapel regular on whom Grant had not spent a thought in years — a man with no ambition, for whom Grant, therefore, had entertained little respect. All the old coach had was humility, faith, and a transparent honesty which stopped him, in the end, from winning anything else.

The skater ended her final spin, dark head tipped, a bird in sleep, arms folded to her side, wings in repose — the image a promise of rest to come.

Not until the last lingering note did Grant's memory reach back to another arena, Wembley and his professional début, his performance of 'Send in the Clowns' also a requiem. His daughter's life and his own seemed to run on parallel tracks. But perhaps Maureen's course was the steadier. She'd skated her mother's requiem while Deirdre still lived to see it.

A mass shuffling of feet as the audience stood. After that not a sound as seconds ticked by. The TV commentators, stunned to silence, committed the unforgivable sin. Dead air. An engineer's voice crackled: 'Audio?' and broke the silence. The commentator coughed, uttered a hurried 'Well!' as he riffled through stock phrases for something to say. 'Well! She certainly landed everything. Didn't she, Curt?' Curt gave a hurried: 'She sure did,' though even these experts had scarcely noticed just what she'd done, and by then it did not matter; the audience, Maureen's spell broken, sent down a deluge of applause, stamping feet, piercing whistles from a thousand pairs of lips.

The satyr, expressionless throughout the training, curved his worldly smile and nodded. Even that, in this atmosphere, a benediction for himself and his pupil. And why not? He'd created the masterpiece, designed the costume, deserved much of the credit.

Grant, staring across the arena at Deirdre's wasted face, wished for it to be over, all of it. The best performance he'd ever seen, and his daughter had skated it. Now he must send his fiancée on the ice knowing they had no hope.

Roxanne waited in the wings in her sea-green dress, her spirits falling with every second of all this endless applause for Maureen, for the flowers dropping like multi-coloured rain from every row, rink-side all the way up to the bleachers. She saw, with numbing horror, even her own supporters toss Maureen the flowers they'd brought for Roxanne herself. Don't panic. She was still ahead from Originals on the strength of her previous record.

But now Maureen was bending, slotting on skate guards for the wooden platform of the Kiss'n'Cry to get her score. Roxanne wanted to close her eyes, not to hear or see how the judges marked her friend. But she knew anyway, she could have marked it for them. It was not just that Maureen had missed nothing. She had shimmered above the crowd, above the sport, as she would soon shimmer on the Award stand.

And now she, the World champion, must follow a standing ovation — if and when the ovation ever ended. A roar as the marks went up. Roxanne tried to shut them out but the announcer's voice inexorably read them off.

To no one's surprise, the USA, its own top contender still to come, was the only hold-out. He'd left room for Roxanne. Just. The crowd booed his mark.

Roxanne shut her eyes, as did Grant, who'd appeared beside her, his smile trying to transmit confidence — but the longer Maureen's applause continued, the deeper those clapping hands dug Roxanne's pit. They'd been in the game too long, they needed no computer to tell them Roxanne had to earn perfect scores to win Gold — and that she'd never had even one. Last year, at her best, she'd gotten 5.9s straight across. Her best ever.

Even the announcer could barely be heard as the audience persisted in beating its palms in unison, each clap another nail in Roxanne's hopes.

'That's it, Grant,' Roxanne whispered.

'What is, sweetheart?' But he knew. They both did.

'We just lost Gold.'

'Does it matter that much?'

She sighed. 'To Mom, to Grossmutti, yes. And you too, right?'

'No. I thought it did. I came here with high hopes and a

sick girl — a girl I loved more than I knew. Now I've got a healthy young woman who loves me. If it turns out to have been a trade-off, I figure I still got the best of the deal. This time around, do your best but do it for you. Not Noni, the old ones, not for me. Just for Roxanne. This is your last competition. Enjoy it. When you get off we'll make honeymoon plans.'

A girl he loved more than he knew. She sighed as she took centre-ice. Everything *was* a trade off, but maybe she'd got the best of the deal anyway. Pretty soon she'd be Mrs Grant Rivers. Maureen would still be Miss Sterling, staring alone into an empty future, nothing but a medal to fill the spaces.

Even the announcer's trained enthusiasm failed to drum up that customary flourish which brought to mind heralds and gold epaulets and raised trumpets as he shouted:

Roxanne Braun Kramer, United States of America.

Roxanne's performance transmitted what her body and her heart already knew. She could not equal what she'd just seen. It was too late, a year too late, so why try and fail, why spoil the mood of the arena, Maureen's triumph and Maureen's gift? Instead she did what she had always wanted to do. A clean, safe programme under no pressure whatever. In her lovely sea-green dress, the bodice a surf of jewels, she skated a perfect programme of spins and double jumps. Not one triple. At the end she put in Grossmutti's spin and smiled into the camera, in case she was watching.

Her marks reflected what she'd known they must, but then she must wait around until the medals were awarded.

They announced Bronze first. Roxanne and Grant applauded from the side-lines, watching Beejay Crisp accept the medal — which perfectly matched her hair. Little Beejay, Olympic medallist.

Next came the Japanese girl, some small thing clasped very tight in her fist; when the Chairman tried to shake her hand she made a reluctant transfer, but there was some doubt which meant most to the girl, her medal, the golden-haired young man in the Competitor section, or the bit of wood clutched tightly in her palm. Weeping in the stands was her mother, her Oka-chan; beside her the familiar figure of a tall old Oriental gentleman who stood quite still until the Japanese flag crept up the pole. Then he bowed, and smiled upon his granddaughter.

Now it was anthem time, Golden time, the winner mounting the steps, bowing her neck to accept the heavy medal.

The orchestra leader lifted his baton, the flag ascended, fluttered, and Maureen Sterling's national anthem filled the arena.

Later, in the audience's rush for the buses, only Grant Rivers seemed to notice the girl in the coral dress deftly avoid stampeding newsmen, walk purposefully to the woman in the fur coat, stoop to kiss her as she draped the gold medal gently about the woman's throat.

EPILOGUE

The closing of the Winter Olympics was, as usual, far more relaxed than it's heavily choreographed, stunningly visual opening. The teams who had entered the great oval two weeks earlier in orderly blocks now ran exulting around the track with new-found friends, not necessarily team-mates. Most competitors had by now traded jackets with members of other national teams. Canada's promising young entry wore Finsky's USSR jacket, the Bean's Starred-and-Striped cap, and a Finn's blue-and-white mitts; from a distance boys and girls were indistinguishable; only television's zoom-lenses picked out winners, near-winners, and losers. Panoramic shots showed a rejoicing, multi-national crowd whose members had discovered that what separated them paled to insignificance by what joined them: they were human, and they aspired. For some, the quenching of the flame was anticlimax, to be passed up entirely as they concentrated on last minute deals in conference rooms, in the airport, and even in the infirmary.

Lise Carlsen was offered a contract with a model agency and another to skate in a movie with a double for the jumps — a clause she insisted on. Ben stayed sober to add his signature as witness. 'Look at it this way,' he said, 'you can live at home, save money, I'll get a housekeeper in to keep everything up.' He looked brighter than he had in months. Lise pouted prettily, reminded him of the heavy freeway traffic between house and movie studio. She'd practised saying 'movie studio' into the mirror for some time, and could now pronounce it with a curving smile and a dazzle of perfect teeth.

Grant's old coach struck the most unlikely deal of the Games. One of the talent scouts present at the Ladies Final, a woman known slightly to Grant, claimed to have wept, yes wept, darling! over Sterling's music. It would be the hit of the year, she bubbled. Was it new? Did he know its name? Grant shuffled her off on to his old coach, who mentioned the Swansea choir and said they performed 'AR HYD Y NÔS' all the time. One thing led to another and at her request he sang it later at the hotel, not in the least bashful, hadn't he been singing it all of his life, now?

'What d'ya say to a quickie single?' the scout asked. 'Next few weeks, the media's going to play the hell outta that number, yes? I caught my boyfriend whistling it right this minute, and he's tone deaf! A fast single could hit the charts.' She mentioned a figure which, while not outrageous, was more money than the Welshman had ever envisioned. His chin fell in amazement. Possibly the scout mistook it for disappointment. She doubled the figure.

'A single?' the tenor said, genuinely mystified.

'Gawd, there's one under every rock. You have a back-up group at home, yes? That number's been in your desk drawer ten years, yes? So what have you written lately?'

'Writ-*ten*?' Puzzled and excited, the coach's accent converted everything to a single query.

'Oh, Jesus, Joseph and Mary save us! Go on then, how long before you scratch out enough numbers for an album? All tear-jerkers, a heart-breaker album, right?'

It speaks for the coach's old-fashioned innocence that he thought the girl was after a photograph album. 'An album, is it? Oh, but we've only got the one, see, it belongs in the family, my mam and dad, my grandparents, my great-grandparents, even back before them, all the way to 1883, terrible yellow some of them now, faded you know — but they're family . . .'

The scout, sure now that she'd tripped over a solid gold crackpot, was ready to give up when the Welshman, ever eager to please, said: 'Will you be wait-ing a minute, then? Have a buzz with my old stu-dent? Happen he knows what you have in mind?'

Grant, summoned, knew. He explained about the album; the coach, animated now, began listing hymns — which wasn't what the scout had in mind at all. She put it this way: 'I figured something a bit more pop, Pops.'

Pops, still straddling the nineteenth and twentieth centuries, threw up his hands. With a sigh the scout harked back to a single of 'AR HYD Y NÔS', a promised hour in a recording studio in London on the way home to Wales, and enough money in the tenor's pocket to bring a smile to his face and a splendid new pipe organ to the chapel in the Swansea suburb. 'Will you be wanting the Welsh or the English, then?' he asked her.

'Oh . . . Welsh,' she said, not knowing the difference and eager to talk to a Swedish rock star who, now appearing on her horizon, directed departure operations in a coat of black floor-length leather as his backups sorted and organized the group's mountain of travel gear. From time to time the star twinkled at Lloyd Sterling. Lloyd smiled back.

Grant whispered to his ex-coach: 'You'd get a better cut if you sang in English and dickered a little. Enough for a new car for yourself maybe —'

'But why, boyo? I've everything a man needs, a good wife and family, we cannot be greedy when the Lord gives his bounty, like.'

The scout, who'd just written the advance cheque, reminded him sharply that the bounty had come down from the record company and that he should bear it firmly in mind. 'Get it, Pops?'

Secure behind the Lord's invisible shield, Pops shook her hand warmly.

In a corner of the Montegreco airport a limousine with windows of one-way glass sat idle. The ivory-coloured gentleman in its rear seat seemed uneasy, as if perhaps missing something about his austere person. From time to time he patted his pockets but always came up empty. Seldom far away, the flunky in the next seat handed him a piece of wood.

The old man glanced down, saw it was an elephant, anonymously carved, and rejected it. 'Keep it. May it bring you wisdom,' he said formally, severely, with infinite contempt.

'Yes, Nakashima-sama, I am sorry, Nakashima-sama.'

The old man checked his watch and sighed. 'How long to

wait?' He extended an empty palm as if expecting the flunky to drop an answer into it.

'Fifteen minutes, so sorry, Nakashima-sama.'

Hiro Nakashima settled back, hooded eyes closed. 'I did not speak to her Carlsen man after all,' he muttered. 'Later, later there will be time . . .' He sounded old, tired, seemed to sleep.

The flunky coughed apologetically. 'I think she leaves now, my lord,' bowing as low as is possible in the back seat of a limousine.

The SAS bird rumbled into view, its windows opaque in the morning sun. The old man, suddenly animated, climbed down to the tarmac to stare as it taxied, quivering, at the start of the runway; at last it accelerated to a whine, a scream of impatience, and began to roll. At the very last moment, as its nose lifted, Hiro Nakashima, a lonely, incongruous figure in a grey business suit, bowed deeply to the departing aircraft.

'I *knew* it was he! He knows that we leave, Mieko!' Oka-chan whispered across the aisle. 'He bows! He approves!'

Mieko, surrounded by a forest of Nordic giants, nodded. Oka-chan had been wise. Together they could take satisfaction in the small package waiting for Hiro Nakashima in his room at the hotel. At first Mieko had been reluctant. To win an Olympic medal, then give it to an old man whose pride outweighed his love for his daughter and his granddaughter, had not been easy. The Silver medal, so dear to her, could mean less to him than one of his old samurai swords. But what had compelled *him*, that unbendable old man, in the very last moment before she skated, to hand over his greatest treasure? A thread of pride, perhaps guilt for sins of omission? She touched the *netsuke* in her pocket in gratitude, but turned to the voice of her Carlsen man, who was preparing her to meet his own mother.

Beejay spat on the medal and polished it yet again on the beige-on-beige Olympic towel. 'Think the hotel'd notice if we swiped the towel, Em?'

'Yes. They *sell* souvenirs in the boutiques — for a small ransom.'

'But I'm broke! The Bean's got a towel. Yum-Num pinched it for him. He'd get one for me if I asked, he said so. Everybody's doing it.'

'You're not. Case closed.'

'*Mom-m-m!*'

'Sit. It's lecture time, sport.'

'Oh, shinola, what have I started?'

'Nothing. Get comfy. You had it coming anyway. About last night. I'm proud, real proud, and it's put you in a strong position. But. You realize that if Roxanne had done any triples, *any at all*, she'd have the Bronze?'

'But that's the ball-game. She didn't.'

'Because she had to follow Sterling, who blew her away. She blew everybody away. You were lucky you didn't have to follow her.'

'She wouldn't have blown me away.'

'You don't know. She was so damned great nobody could have followed her. It's the luck of the draw. You got lucky. Rox didn't. And you took a risk on the lutz, it paid off, you had one great day. But every day's not going to be like that, Beej. Just so you know, so you're ready to pick yourself up —'

'Dust myself off. I know, I know. And that's so corny, Em — you're lucky corn is just about my all-time favourite food.'

'Sugar lump, every food's your all-time favourite.'

'You *know* I can't stand tapioca. When are you and Nils getting hitched?'

Emma shut her eyes. 'This is what I get for raising a romantic.'

'I've been thinking. If you marry Nils he'll want you to live on a fjord or something. Then who'd train me?'

'Grant. I'm not marrying until you get through this competition lark.'

'You make it sound like it's an uphill tunnel I'm going through!'

Emma laughed. 'No — but it sure seemed like that for a long time. Now you're close to the top of the hill I can see daylight, thank God. We might even be able to get another car next year. Not new, but late model, anyway.'

'Gee, are we rich already?'

'No — but skating won't keep us so poor. The Committee'll pick up a lot of your tabs now. We'll even be able to pay Mrs Cox for the dress.'

Beejay picked thoughtfully through a tin of mixed nuts. 'You reckon that's why I got the medal? The dress made that good an impression?'

'It was great, but *you* earned the medal.'

'I'll tell you who did make an impression, Em.'

'On who?'

'Me. The German girl. I reckon Nakashima'll quit now, thank God — geez, that triple! — So there's just me and the German girl —'

'And a sleeper or two. Or three. Like Maureen Sterling this time.'

The main runway now clear, the Sterling's Lear touched lightly down, homed straight for Deirdre Sterling, her daughter, her ambulance, her small army of nurses — and Jasinski, who'd volunteered to see her and her multitude of bottles and tubes safely into the plane.

'So kind,' Deirdre fretted, 'but a fuss, really, I feel quite well now it's over. Just tired. We could have driven to the villa, it's only an hour or so.'

'But crowded,' Maureen said tightly. 'I can't see all of us, *and* Alexei and Galina, *and* everyone's luggage, crammed into the car.' She tucked blankets up to Deirdre's chin against the biting wind and tried not to replay her mother's phrase over and over in her mind. Was it her imagination or did Deirdre use it more often lately? Only an hour or so, only an hour or so — but with every day that passed it appeared less likely that Deirdre Sterling had many hours left. Reflected off the snow, a winter-white sun shot through the ambulance window to dazzle every bead of sweat until Deirdre's waxen face seemed studded with diamonds, all brighter than the solitaire she wore on her hand. Strange how good gems lost their fire when their wearer lost hers. Even Maureen's Olympic gold, clutched tightly in Deirdre's palm, looked little more than the flashy coin of a realm removed from, and inferior to, these unfeeling mountains.

She turned to their pilot. 'Can we hurry, I want to arrive at the villa before the Russians — I'm not sure they know Spanish.'

Jasinski looked at her sharply. So the girl knew. While nurses bustled about the limited cabin space, setting up Deirdre and her chair and her bottles like a piece of scenery, Jasinski drew Maureen aside. 'Miss Sterling, I have met Galina, spoken with her. It would be good to keep her with you for a few days, yes? Alexei too has great strength. It is better you are not alone in the next days. I would come myself but already I am too long from my patients in Los Angeles — and there is little I could do for your mother now.'

'I understand, doctor. Thank you. I shall manage.'

'You are strong. I cannot recommend hospitals at this point, I am sorry.'

She nodded. 'It's too late and too cruel.'

'Grant said that later you consider studying medicine?'

A shadow crossed her face, whether at the mention of Grant or the word 'later' Jasinski could not be sure. 'I plan to.'

'In that case you may wish new surroundings for a time. We have fine facilities in California — and unlike England, the weather is always good. Young people enjoy the sun.' He gave her his card and bade them a swift goodbye, watching as the graceful craft climbed like a paper dart to shoot out of sight between the peaks to northern Spain.

Jasinski sighed as he boarded the coach to the hotel. Families. He entered the lobby in time to hear Lloyd Sterling's impromptu press conference conducted in his boardroom voice, off-the-cuff but every vowel perfectly rounded, every syllable clearly enunciated.

The temperature in the lobby was a stifling 74°, but for the benefit of TV cameras Lloyd wore a grey cashmere overcoat with astrakhan collar and cuffs; the aroma of barber-shop spray clung to his silver head and matching moustache. He stood perfectly still, but more than ever resembled a sleek barracuda cruising the shallows, pale grey eyes sliding smoothly through the crowd of departing guests as his mouth answered reporters questions. Yes of course, he was immensely gratified by his daughter's victory, who would not be? A family effort, yes — in this age of rebellious youth he had determined very early that his daughter must have something toward which to direct her youth and energies. And what lay ahead? Ah yes, 'Although one remains passionately committed to amateur sport, privately supported,' he said in his dispassionate voice, 'having done everything one conceivably can for ice-skating and skiing, it may in fact be time to offer our support to other . . . areas of self-expression. On my return I hope to persuade my directors to join me in encouraging and investing in legitimate, dedicated entertainers in the musical field. Yes, young man?'

'Classical music?' the reporter asked, barely able to suppress a grin; Lloyd's exploits over the competition had gone unreported but not unnoticed.

As one in deep thought, Lloyd paused. 'Classical? . . . One thinks not. To influence today's youth one must enter their arena. One hopes to invest time and possibly business capital in a sincere attempt to encourage — may one venture to suggest — a *spiritual* aspect to the field of rock music?'

No one laughed. Lloyd's sphere of influence extended not merely to stock exchanges on both sides of the Atlantic and Pacific oceans but deep into communications round the world. His company commanded enough legal muscle to sue half the corporate world through its work-force. If any journalist noticed the increasingly limpid glances between Lloyd and the rock star, they were not about to comment on tape or in print — certainly not under their own by-line.

Marginally bolder than the rest, an elderly reporter brought the charade to a halt with an expression of casual concern. 'Your immediate plans, sir? Since your wife's health forces her to convalesce, will you join her and the new Olympic champions at the coast? Relax a little before returning to the helm?'

Lloyd checked his watch with some show of alarm, thanked the reporters, said he really must run, they understood . . . press of business, etc . . .

Jasinski watched Lloyd follow the rock star into a lift, saw their two hands fight playfully to punch in the penthouse code, saw the exchange of anticipatory smiles as the doors whispered shut. Pondering the indiscretions of elderly men, Jasinski took the next lift to the infirmary floor.

*

Noni's magenta fingernails rat-tat-tatted on the steel rail of Brigitta Braun's cot. At the other side, Otto spun his wheelchair in increasingly impatient circles. Why did they keep Brigitta so sedated? Enough to drive a man mad. All these years only one woman he could talk to, shout at, bellow for, the only one who understood him as he understood her. Now, just when they needed each other the most, they kept sending her to dreamland. He hunted a word to describe his frustration but all that came to mind was Noni's ape-shit. Ape-shit indeed! He'd rather die than say that in any language.

Noni gave him a tight, thin smile. 'Never thought *you'd* say that, Poppa.'

'Your influence,' he barked, furious that he'd spoken aloud; maybe he was getting old — but how foolish, he wouldn't be seventy-three until next month.

'If apes don't suit, try chickens.' Noni reached for a cigarette but did not light it. Nurses lurked in every corner, signs blasted from every wall. 'Chicken-shit. Used to be all the rage in the States. I like it. New World.'

'The New World is no different from the old. The same virtues apply. Respectability. Honesty. In you, these qualities missed a generation, Noni. Roxanne has them.'

'She's lived with Grant Rivers for two years! *That's respectability?*'

'Respectability and sex are completely different things. You remember the widow Streiker down the road, keeps the tavern? I'm told she gives her favours freely to clients she likes — but she does not exchange them for trips to the Olympics, for drugs, for favours from the arena guards —'

'That was for you, Papa —'

'— Yes, and it grieves me. New-World, old-world, virtue has value.'

'And it's a fucking bore. I can't be bored.'

'*Then stop with the fingernails! They are boring into my brain!*'

'Wanna know what's boring into *my* brain?'

'The health of your mother, I hope. If you had not given her that stupid, idiotic overdose of vitamins —'

'Jasinski said I didn't cause it and he's a good doctor —'

'This is the same one you told us was a fool because he tried to make Roxanne well? The doctor who succeeded?'

'Well? Is overweight healthy? Look what it cost us.'

'She eats. Sleeps. She is not now afraid of her shadow.'

'Then Jasinski must know what he's talking about. You can't have it both ways. If he's not stupid, then I didn't make Mutti sick.'

'You made Roxanne sick, almost made her anor . . . anor —'

'That's right, blame me! You can't even say it but it's all my fault. She's healthy now? She's a tub of lard! A skater with curves, 110 pounds of 'em! No wonder she lost the Games —' Magenta fingertips flew to her lips.

They both turned to the bed but Brigitta slept on, wig slightly askew, her snores blowing a lacquered grey strand rhythmically left to right, left to right like a metronome. Noni drew in a ragged breath. 'So how we gonna tell her, Poppa?' Noni whispered. 'How do we say it's all over, that we tried three times, failed three times, that we're left with a bucketful of —'

'Stop! I will not listen to your dirty mouth.'

'I was about to say a bucketful of nothing. That's what we got. Three generations. Mutti. Me. Roxanne. Bunions, blisters, toes like bunches of bananas, lousy circulation — all from the goddamn ice and the boots. That's what we got, the Braun Grand Prize. Ugly feet.'

'Noni, my dear child —'

'Three Gold medals that close. *That close!*' Her voice cracked as she held a trembling finger and thumb a fraction of an inch apart. 'It's not fair! Oh God, I tried everything I knew. Drove her across town to ballet four times a week, put up a barre in the kitchen, made her work out every night since her sixth birthday. I supervised her, timed her, planned her diet, I earned every damned cent I could, any way I could, oh Poppa, honest to God, I did try. . .'

Otto clasped her hand. 'Sssh. It's nobody's fault. We do not blame —'

'Mutti will. She'll blame me till the day she dies.'

'You cannot know that.'

Brigitta's light blue eyes opened, piercing as only old eyes can pierce. She gave them a sly smile, slightly one-sided.

'Well?' she said, the word almost clear. 'Will one of you tell, or not? Me, an invalid lying here helpless?' She smiled again, more triumphant than before. 'So. The Finals? Who gives me the results?'

For once, father and daughter were in concert. What to tell her? How much could she take? Did she know and if so, how much? It was Noni, finally, who broke the news. 'We missed the Gold. I'm sorry, Mutti.'

'But Roxanne skated beautifully, Gitta. You can be proud.'

'How many falls?'

'None.'

'Mmm. So she made all doubles. Good skater. Idiot judges.'

'But Brigitta, the others did triples, and wonderful they were.'

'Me, I like to watch girls, not kangaroos.'

'The British girl was no kangaroo, my dear.'

Frau Braun clamped her mouth shut. She had her standards.

'Nor was the Japanese, Mutti.' Noni's voice was hushed.

'Hah! So *she* got the Silver, I suppose? And who took Bronze?'

A heavy silence around the cot. Who could break the news that the Braun's had no medal at all to take home to Bonn? Then from the door a light young voice, regretful but confident.

'They gave it to Beejay, Grossmutti. She skated like a silver demon.'

Finally Frau Braun smiled wide. 'Roxanne! I tease these blind fools. They think I have no TV?' An unsteady wave excluded her husband and daughter from the conversation. 'That I come to Montegreco and miss my granddaughter in the Olympics? That tells you how stupid. Like father like daughter. You, thank God, take after me. We know what is important.'

Noni and Otto, unwilling allies, glared at one another over her head.

'Grossmutti,' Roxanne said softly, 'I didn't win a medal. Any medal.'

Brigitta Braun's smile gave a fleeting illusion of the beauty she'd once been. 'But you did my spin, you made it as good, maybe even better, than I! I wept for pride, I did! The TV man said: "In honour of her grandmother Brigitta Braun, an illustrious name! . . . the World Champion has revived the Braun spin." I have it all on tape, your nice diet doctor made it for me.'

Unseen in the doorway, Jasinski shook his dead. Diet doctor! A speciality in which he had no interest and a lingering contempt. For him, of all people, nourished on crumbs and hope and the sacrifices of his family, to be called a diet doctor! Did they not know, these guileless oldies, that in the backstreets of Los Angeles the term was synonymous with drug pusher? And that their daughter Noni played roulette with her health everytime she shovelled down amphetamines to burn off what few calories she consumed, then swallowed tranks to steady that over-manipulated pump? One day her heart would beat too fast, trip over itself, and stop. Last night after Finals he had warned her, when she asked for a trank, that pharmacology was not a roller-coaster for the heart to ride on, up and down, up and down, in whatever direction suited the whim of the moment. He'd strongly advised her to return to Bonn. Her mother needed her, and Otto Braun had compassion, however deeply buried. Noni seemed to be considering it, but with her, who could tell?

'I'll see,' she'd said. 'Poppa wants out, Mutti doesn't want to sell the rink.'

'Why don't you run it for them?'

'*Me*? *Run it*?'

'Why not — you're qualified, know the business.'

'They'd never let me.'

'Have you asked?'

'Of course I haven't.'

'Then you cannot know.'

The rink, rundown by all accounts, could be the making of Noni Kramer.

Examining the proposal, Noni tapped her small, pointed teeth. She wouldn't have to face that nerd at the *Parkrose Review*, thank him on her back for the ticket to the Games. Maybe head pro on an ice-cube in Bonn would beat being a welfare case in LA? Maybe she could even bring some business in — hell, if anybody knew about training champions it was Noni Kramer. In Bonn she'd be a Braun again — a fresh start with a respected name. Worth a try? She lit a cigarette, watched the smoke curl lazily towards the door, and abruptly stabbed it out into the ashtray. Hell, why not?

Main packing done, Roxanne nested the last shoe in the last plastic pouch, eased it into her suitcase, and started on her carry-on for the trip. Skates at the bottom as usual (Rule One: never let them out of your sight), one bulging make-up case, two magazines, a sleep mask, aspirins — damn, she'd never close the zipper on this! Then she laughed, tipped everything out and re-packed it, minus the skates.

On the stripped bunk they looked worn-out, dejected, rejected, anything but the skates of a World Champion — which, come to think of it, she still was. Not an Olympic Champion. No big medal for Grant. If she'd won a Gold she'd planned to have it framed for him, something to put in his office along with all the trophies she'd won while training with him. Now she wasn't so sure. Maybe the rewards belonged in a room she used — she'd won 'em. All these years she skated for Grossmutti, then Mom, then Grant, but the trophies and medals were *hers*! Bought with falls, bruises, shin-splints, too many diets — and her tears, way too many of those, too. No more; that chapter was over. She picked up a skate, ran a fingertip over the blade . . . a nick here and there, they'd have to be ground down, maybe one more sharpening left in this set. . . Then she laughed again. She wasn't marrying a set of steel runners. The finger wore a ring, now. If Grant truly wanted her and not her medals, she'd be Mrs Rivers pretty soon.

'Packed yet?' Grant edged into the minuscule Village cubicle and looked around, noting again her passion for neatness. Skating tights rolled in orderly little balls; plastic bags lined up like plump soldiers — panties in one, bras in another, nighties in another, all fresh and clean; no matter where she was or what the circumstances, she creamed off make-up, flossed her teeth, washed her lingerie and cleaned tomorrow's shoes before going to bed. For her, packing was merely an orderly transfer from drawer to suitcase. She never lost things or left them behind, knew exactly where in her case to locate even a needle and thread. Noni, as bad a mother as she undoubtedly was, had done lots of things right. Roxanne looked all set to zip-up and head for the plane. He saw the skates, had space for them in his own bags, but he was not about to mention them if she didn't.

'You're a neat, orderly woman, Roxanne Kramer. A miracle.'

She gave him a smile in which there was no hint of apology. He felt the first stirrings of relief, of victory. Was she through apologizing for herself? Now she was shrugging, bending over the case, her face hidden as she smoothed corners, tugged at zippers.

'No medal to pack this time,' she said, matter-of-factly.

'Nope.'

'D'you mind?'

'Only for you — it could have sweetened some of the bitterness maybe.'

'I'm not bitter,' she said, 'just glad to be out. Maureen gave hers away.'

'Yeah.' Grant's voice thickened. 'Roxanne, I just got us something better than any medal in the world.'

She looked up, perhaps expecting another sweetener, like the ring.

'The lab. I got the results. You, me, we're both in the clear.'

'Clear of what, for goodness sake?'

He sighed, hefted suitcase and carry-on into the hall as she made a last-second check of the room. 'Clear of what?' she demanded again.

'It's a long story. I'll save it for the plane. It's just —'

'Yeah?'

'I'm happy for us, relieved — but guilty as hell for feeling that way.'

Leaning across her suitcases she brushed a quick kiss on his cheek. 'We're through with guilt, Grant, both of us, I didn't have room for it, this trip.'

Outside, she took a long look at the mountains, at Olympus — which had not crowned her its goddess after all. She shivered. Whatever its virtues, Olympus was colder than hell.

With Grant, California would be warm.

The cold Montegreco sun winking on her diamond ring, she followed him to the bus, leaving her Olympic cubicle neat and tidy, a pair of skates the only evidence that Roxanne Braun Kramer had passed this way.

ALWAYS A STRANGER

Margaret P. Kirk

The tranquil Yorkshire countryside in the summer of '39 offers Lallie Wainwright, adored only child of a wealthy foundry owner, blissful happiness: as long as she has her family, dogs and Neil, her childhood friend, her life is complete.

But the war brings more than upheaval – it brings Jan Kaliski, a Polish pilot in a strange land, into Lallie's home and into her heart. Then the war, and the chaos that is war's aftermath, forces them apart. Only after heartbreak and tragedy do Lallie and Jan learn the bittersweet lesson that home is not always where the heart is . . .

'a love story in the old, grand manner – heroic and emotionally charged. She deals with big themes in the stylish and deceptively simple manner of the born storyteller. Have your handkerchiefs ready. You won't just read. You'll care.'
Sarah Harrison, author of
A FLOWER THAT'S FREE

'vivid and real . . . an irresistible read of passion and heartbreak. I couldn't put it down.'
Madge Swindells, author of
SUMMER HARVEST

'a really heartwrenching story with flashes of brilliance.'
Cynthia Harrod-Eagles, author of the *Dynasty* series

FUTURA PUBLICATIONS
FICTION
0 7088 2723 2

A LONG ROAD WINDING

Margaret P. Kirk

Michael Abramsky – born Micah the gypsy – exiled from home as a little boy, starving and badly injured, is determined no child of his shall ever want. Now a successful and wealthy businessman, he feels secure at last.

For Anna and Felix Abramsky, the Nazis destroyed all they ever held dear: they killed their only child and ruined their ballet careers. And Anna, brutally raped by a German officer, bears his child, Ellie – the very symbol of their shameful humiliation and defeat. Fleeing to England, the Abramskys adopt the destitute Micah, who soon replaces the son they have lost – the hope they have for so long been denied.

But their new-found happiness is soon threatened, as fortune plays yet another cruel trick. Ellie – now a beautiful young woman – re-enters their lives, and Anna is forced to face her long-buried past. And Michael too learns he cannot escape his past; his wealth draws his gypsy relatives and their grasping fingers like a magnet. He, and his children, must pay a heavy price for their Romani blood.

A LONG ROAD WINDING is a rich, moving, compulsively readable tribute to the unconquerable resilience of the human heart.

FUTURA PUBLICATIONS
FICTION
0 7088 3669 0

PAINTED BIRDS

Fiona Bullen

Born and raised in Singapore, Ursula Fraser is a privileged member of the British expatriate community and the darling of her father's heart. But her cosseted childhood is brutally ended with the Japanese invasion of 1941.

The only member of her immediate family to survive, Ursula is sent to live with relations in England. Desperate for love, she falls into the arms of the first man to show her any affection. But his charm masks a cruel deceit and she has many years in which to regret their hasty marriage.

When Ursula finally meets Tim Nowlton, a young ambitious Australian, she is no longer a naive and vulnerable girl. Yet Tim's offer of love after so many barren years seems irresistible . . .

'A nicely crafted first novel . . . Fiona Bullen's debut shows a knack of good descriptive writing and character portrayal'
Books

FUTURA PUBLICATIONS
FICTION
0 7088 4444 8

COAL BARON

Carol Wensby-Scott

An epic saga of a dynasty, an industry, a magnificent era.

From life he wanted everything he could seize . . .

In the mid-nineteenth century Britain ruled over half the world – and her industries were the wealthiest and most successful on earth. In the North-East coal was king, and there were fortunes to be made by those bold and tough enough to fight for them.

Among these the Joicey Family had risen in just two generations from humble pitmen working the cramped and dangerous seams of the Longbanton mine, to become the greatest coal-owners in the entire world.

This is the story of James Joicey, the man who took them there – a saga of fierce ambition fanned into lasting flame, of triumphs exploited, and disasters overcome.

It is the story of the men he befriended and the men he ruined, of the dynasty he founded – and the dynasty he destroyed.

'Fascinating, quite fascinating . . . a vivid portrayal of a North-East mining empire'
Annabel

'Finely written, always holds the interest'
Yorkshire Evening Post

'Colourful . . . compelling'
Cleveland Mail

FUTURA PUBLICATIONS
FICTION
0 7088 4064 7